# AT THE MILLENNIUM: PARADISE CROSSED

T. AWDRY WINKS

*For C.,*
*from whom I learned to read the myths,*
*and*
*to those remaining seekers*
*beckoned by islands far from reach,*
*in the misty wonder of silent dreams.*

The palm at the end of the mind,
Beyond the last thought, rises
In the bronze décor... (Wallace Stevens, "Of Mere Being," 1954)

# CONTENTS

# PROLOGUE

## THE GARDEN OF EARTHLY DELIGHTS

## Rumbling

a. *Ante Mundum*

> —For he spake and it was done; he commanded, and it stood fast.
> (Psalm 33:9, King James Version [KJV])

Creation's third day, gray tints and a hollow core of monochrome to fill and color, now freed at last in our celestial reaches, to approximate the secret spheres within, prying outer panels to the vivid triptych of our souls: of Eden, lust and reckoning.

Is that our globe, of eerie luminescence, suspended in unyielding, vacuous space, whose Universal Denizen, God himself, insignificant, hasty afterthought, added to the bigger scape, observes unsure from upper quadrant, as all concord slips away?

Not earth, nor heaven's planets, can confine or bind us, in their fulsome gravities, from ourselves, for before the age of declarations and manifestos we were infinite, in our approach to the stars, and chronicles, describing what had been or could be,

figments: neither man nor woman invented yet, let alone even designed in his own image. And if much more could be done before the pause, it was not for us to say, or pray, one thought in favor of, or opposition to, the established new world order.

Only, who imagined Him? Who first dreamt? Who embraced the darkened night? Why was it so crucial to continue focused on our common notions despite periodic sabotaging, never to be forgotten, lost? Who harnessed the first flames and when?

Who would define the difficulties encountered with those prone to demonic guise, and insolence in duties toward the meek? Should anything be as they glibly said? Should they be railed against, for iniquities and hardships we summarily endured?

Humbling Beatitudes arrived much later, after indolent time, persisting, codifying, errors endorsed to our griefs by those for whom human freedom became too risky, as outlines of the coming social contract steadily stanching our luminescent flows.

And as mountains and valleys were crafted by inner rumbling, our own substance purposely formed, discovering what would be significant and unalienable from us. Later, plants and trees arrived, to maintain us, keep us safe, fed, warm, as required.

At present, we were far from the epoch when our habitat would be considered flat, or sound, perhaps part of a sacred solar system, floating orbs whispering a cosmic acknowledgement: were they winged angels sent to guide a quest for fabled Eden?

Had they ordained all vital outcomes, prior to our first paces? And as breathtaking as the fable seemed, with the latest methods, songs, beliefs going against the grain, we dared never look behind, for truly, that would be emptiness, and death foretold.

It was easy to forget that above mad clouds the sun shone brightly. Within a foggy substrate, ancient woods, the hawk's throaty cry, fresh note, more unwavering, real than Hermes' rarest instrument, shocking in its impulse, ushered us along the way.

# THE GARDEN OF EARTHLY DELIGHTS

## Eden

b. *Initium*

> The divine intelligence, being nurtured upon mind and pure knowledge, and the intelligence of every soul which is capable of receiving the food proper to it, rejoices at beholding reality, and once more gazing upon truth, is replenished and made glad, until the revolution of the worlds brings her round again to the same place. In the revolution she beholds justice, and temperance, and knowledge absolute, not in the form of generation or of relation, which men call existence, but knowledge absolute in existence absolute; and beholding the other true existences in like manner, and feasting upon them, she passes down into the interior of the heavens and returns home... (Plato, *Phaedrus*, 370 BC)

I'm scribbling these lines, as they haven't been uttered before; it's only me right now, no one pushing to make it longer, shorter, simpler, start here, end there. I'll say exactly what I want and take just as long as needed. First, there is no justice or accountability, only acquiescence, and perhaps the hollow drum beat of vengeance. Life is simply one day after another, trying to get by, the virtuous seldom rewarded, the sinful managing acclaim, everything deftly rigged, it's the way it's always been. We're far too busy to pay much attention to, or get involved in, pesky troubles that really don't concern us in the long term.

I've been reflecting for so long on what I wanted to express, and the time finally came when everything felt right, and I could begin my story, I'm selecting phrases now, because after a while blurred portraits weren't enough; I had taken and exposed so many they lost all meaning, as lyrics breathed movements into static images, whence they came, what they brought, how they seemed, reconstructing fragmented frames; because I'm trying to put it back together again, so it makes sense, even if continually evolving. I know that people get away with what they can, absolved of blame, for man's frail, faulty recollection.

The infinitesimal details of our lives were what mattered, what our remembrances held, those little bits and pieces of each day, mere instants, with those whom we loved, never to hold again. How was it, we rarely valued the eternal until lost, or seized from us, even as assembled, coherent sequences, preserved beyond us, myths and legends about, and for, us, retained for many to absorb; each concerned with the void that was before, and would continue after, and our parts in the grand scheme, breathing, believing, conscious, of our own impact upon the tale, hoping our origins were based, on more than mere chance?

And as we slept, in each of us were manifested familiar visions, of hurtling through space as unspoiled, immeasurable energy, in suspended animation, at a thousand times the speed of light, sweetly diffusing inner desires, growth and common expectations; spreading hardy seeds across this blue expanse, then populating far off continents, all thriving colonies, attained through subtle trajectory adjustments of an unseen, steady hand holding fast the spinning wheel. Could it be our migratory wanderings had subtle purpose, exceeding our earliest comprehension, perhaps as displaced souls yearning for true perfection?

These were not Adam's concerns as he awoke that warm cloudless day in God's newest Garden. It took time, with the suffering and loss accompanying it, to come around to the frustration of missed chances, and misidentified opportunities, delivered from Eve's fateful bite. And although some say it was simply an apple, and Eden only a place, paradise lost is in all our hearts; it is that space in our essence we flee, once discovering there are no heroes, or great deeds, drawing us to our better selves. Accepting man's naked inevitability to temptation made it that much easier and less ironic for mankind's fall from grace.

God's reprimand is our chosen condition; there is no avoiding that solemn, painful truth; no way out but marching forward, double time, head bent toward new beginnings, just beyond the river's edge. I know I will make it there, even if I drop along the way. This is an attempt, a dream, I am after, to right what's wrong; the desire to understand and describe the hellish forms lurking within us all, grotesque shadows plotting too well the painful outcome of our misdirected thoughts and deeds; and even if our first breath is now expired, forgotten, all that follows and is subsequently imagined need not dissipate into nothing.

# THE GARDEN OF EARTHLY DELIGHTS

## Lust

c. *El Dorado*

> The pink palm being empty, in other words, to their vision, they had begun, from far back, to put things into it, things of their own, and of all sorts, and of many ugly, and of more and more expensive, sorts; to fill it substantially, that is, with gold, the gold that they have ended by heaping up there to an amount so oddly out of proportion to the scale of nature and of space. (Henry James, "The Sense of Newport," 1906)

I was in the culture of greed and deception before my restructuring. Now I capture human depravity, at its best, and claim bounties for revealing hidden terrors in the night; but if these were only strange half understood dreams, they would be confusing enough, vague impressions sensed behind drawn curtains.

I'm scrambling to keep track of all the things I've seen and heard. It's been enough for a lifetime, really, even if I can't seem to get it straight. Multifarious visions of greed and narcissism buffet me to no end, impossible to ignore nature as she is, indifferent, roaring, in the steamy jungle, scheming in its dimness.

I conjure up reality, dreams, destiny, illustrate the profane, mine the magnificent, explore for pure gold, claiming God, evoking glory, only to find *El Dorado* as a sacrificing cannibal. You won't forget raging deceptions anytime soon, discovering too late they are beyond ruinous, costing too much vigor to undo.

We go through life day by day, hour by hour, forgoing each other and the precious moments we shared, desperately embracing memories, only to find ourselves again. I wanted to have something permanent and lasting, a tribute that could not be taken away from those fooled by appearances and an easy smile.

Please do not blame me, for speaking out of turn, for touting the obvious and vulgar, I only channeled what was so clearly presented for all of us to see; the outcome, no easy feat; being pardoned from exile causing radical effects, even if diluted and out of step, but worth every moment crawling on my belly.

But I should start at the beginning, before my newfound life, when I sold rubes evil dreams in rosy tints while Rome burned and downtown blazed from the high life of whiskey tainted evenings to kill a sharp pain of lying for an easy living, at dawn, quiet, dull weariness consuming me, so I could not keep step.

Bloodsucking, corporate peon-predators slithering over thickly carpeted trails, imposing the latest rules of engagement on faceless, nameless prey, before consuming them in another downsizing; that was my path of advancement and reward, a facade of ferocity, while nipped at the heels by fear, hatred, fatigue.

I had climbed my way up pyramids, sandwiched in-between those above and below; had hired people, then fired them, while never getting anywhere myself; had programmed minds of desperate consumers purchasing irrelevant, costly products, chasing superficial, inconsequential conceits from the idiot box.

Now ashamed of such dim existence, so far from the center, my old self bound in efficiency, servitude, foisting free enterprise follies, daily discounts, upon the blind; my new self bound for clarity, vision, as *La Dolce Vita*'s hero insisting *Paparazzo* get the deeper meaning, of our hectic, frenzied, isolated lives.

As at cool running streams, those oppressed paused to drink side by side with their oppressors, stooping my head with the former I thought I should stand upright, challenge the detached impunity of the latter, stomping, driving, whipped flames illuminating the valley's dark edge, with the bonfire's rage and lust.

It was a scene playing out inside us all, the realization we were still living in the Dark Ages, when wild tribes and untamed crowds cruelly trampled those most engaging, docile among us. Kings were made, they begat themselves, as if deceit, grit, audacity, were sudden replacements for virtue, trust or nobility.

At dusk, unforgiving bosses reorganized their petty fiefdoms, forever claiming divine authority, prior to begging for their own salvation. The disinterested inquisitor makes his way up stone steps, proceeding to quiet chamber, taking up, once more, his paused tome in earnest, leaving the final judgment to us all.

# THE GARDEN OF EARTHLY DELIGHTS

## Reckoning

d. *Aurora Borealis*

> I hope for nothing. I fear nothing. I am free.
> (Epitaph on the grave of Nikos Kazantzakis, 1883 – 1957, in Heraklion)

It was when Henry Hudson approached the Dutch East India Co. a last time, negotiating for a share of the trade/ plundered treasure, that his troubles arose. Impatient for profits, the crew practiced musketry on the native population; thus, emboldened, at last mutinied.

As Hudson cast adrift, just short of that elusive Northwest Passage, to prized India, we were marooned, Esquimaux, polar bears, daemons dispassionately floating by on ice floes, solemn distance, diminishing days reminding of an impossibility of making it home again.

Considering the circumstances, we did our best to live minute by minute, with no regrets, anticipating a roundness of the earth on its horizon, as the direction of our origins, if not our ends, but rejecting these dastardly, final episodes, as our castigating, God given fates.

Hudson knew the rules, with boards of directors and consequences, as investors' capital was at stake; if corporate actors came up short, they perished in the deep; so, mindful of this doomed navigator's faulty charts we plotted destinations to warmer shores and harbors.

By afternoon, all the morning's worries were as air lifted off our shoulders. We waited for the northern lights, anticipating their welcoming, warm embrace, as an affirmation of our best course along the way, rejecting heaven's fickle warning signs of stormy seas ahead.

Shimmering *aurora borealis,* spread your arms in undulating waves across the murky sky, transporting to a higher purpose, veil the lesser constellations, made inconsequential from your brilliance, inspire us with critical thoughts, peripheries of profound assumptions.

Why accept our folly, as eager, loyal children, gazing up in wonder at the limelight of man-made stars? Formerly, there were prophets, saints, wise men, heroes, while today's best born were supplanted by the adept at fizzling out, dignity undone by flashy photo shoots.

And as acclaim and glory don't grant themselves, fans do, audiences carefully noted every artifice and plotted gesture, on or off the set; devoted stargazers comforted quirky atmospherics would not obscure clear views of sexy close ups, privacy trumped by notoriety.

Conceding defeat to the celebrity machine, we waited eagerly for the next tabloid issues, hoping for the *Magnum Opus* in each, disappointed at the inconclusiveness of every lead. So, true to life could never be less beautiful than portrayed but certainly more frightful.

The bold headlines were of simple players, transformed into revered characters they should never have become, recalling idols from another time and place. Despite New World riches clouding reason, plain truth stared us in the face, but was never seen, until too late.

I was not; I have been; I am not; I do not mind.
[*Non fui, fui, non sum, non curo.*]
(Inscribed on memorials of Epicurus' devotees, on gravestones of
the Roman Empire.)

1. Hieronymus Bosch, Dutch/Netherlandish, *The Garden of Earthly Delights*, The exterior, c. 1480-1505, Museo del Prado, Madrid, Spain.

2. Bosch, *The Garden*, The interior.

3. Lukas Cranach the Elder, *Adam and Eve in Paradise*, Detail Tree of Knowledge, 1530, Gemäldegalerie Alte Meister, Dresden, Germany.

4. *El Dorado*, Museo del Oro, Bogotá, Colombia.

5. John Collier, *The Last Voyage of Henry Hudson*, 1881, Tate Britain, London, England.

6. *Aurora Borealis*, Aurora Borealis aka Northern Lights captured February 2020 in the Lofoten Islands, Northern Norway. {OC} (2400x3000) : r/EarthPorn (reddit.com)

# 1. The Mystery of the Stars

> Lo! thy dread empire, CHAOS! is restored;
> Light dies before thy uncreating word:
> Thy hand, great anarch! lets the curtain fall;
> And universal darkness buries all.
> (Alexander Pope, "The Dunciad," 1733 – 1734)

Suddenly! dreaded CHAOS! 3 AM; screeching banshee ring tones lurking deeply within a soft silence of my sleep, glass shattering in my head. Inconceivably, it's my editor, running on so fast, that she can hardly catch her accursed breath. I glean, from this heavily Slavicized barrage, that I immediately drop everything and drive over to Heroes' Canyon. Lilly Lawrence, feted star of blockbuster action revenge thrillers, a surprise no-show at last evening's Motion Pictures Awards Dinner, had resurfaced, scratched up and bloody, but alive, after going missing all night; garnering more acclaim by an absence, a lack of, pined for, than had she appeared or been punctual. One of Tinseltown's most alluring, highest grossing actresses, AWOL from Hollywood, "after a day of binging, then deranged, wandering forbiddingly high *sierras* high all night, strung out of her mind on downers, coke and booze," as per confidential sources.

I had covered the gala dinner, and when there was no Lilly Lawrence you knew everyone was thinking, *here we go, again.* To her credit, in truly stellar fashion, she stole the show, not despite, but because of, her dramatic nonattendance, a rather sudden and unexpected retreat, from her engaged, adoring public.

"You'd better get up there right away; this is big, and time's a-wasting. Everyone wants to know when, and why, she vanished, what's the latest?" My newbie editor, a driven, competitive, go-get 'em version of the recently arrived immigrant, willing to do whatever it took to get ahead, was, however, innocently unfamiliar with the daytime, and especially after-hours, rigors, of subtly teasing out scoop, after scoop.

"Slow down, rabid Russki, who passed the tip? This better be good, it's twenty-two miles up there, and I'm pretty burned out." I had been deep in dreamland, after an exhausting day chasing down dirt, leads (a cute lead at a green room soiree), and was not about to go all the way out to the reservoir on hearsay.

"Her husband, you slacker, only five minutes ago. He said she was distraught, hysterical, popping dolls all day. Are you getting up, now? Are you alone? I can hear someone in the background. Are we on a speaker phone? What have you been up to all night?" This Tsarina task master sure had my modus op; but if Willi Herman himself, called in the incident, there had to be something to it. A celebrity husband ratting out his celebrity wife didn't happen every day, and was a gift only too gratuitous, not to follow. I needed to sober up quick, get my act together, before Pimple.com beat us to the deadline, once again.

"Those two have survived many scrapes throughout their convoluted history, even harassing each other publicly. I'm awake now; it's lucky for you, I can be up there in about fifty-five minutes, as the road is curvy and dark; I had a grueling evening... taking care of, well, things, researching some new material for exposures... none of your... any time, day or night, I'm always on call for you and Slay Magazine."

"Hm... sure; curvy and dark, huh? What kind of research? What new material? Who is she this time, you overexposed creeper? Have you been drinking? You'd better not doze off." My editor was quite the snoop, counterrevolutionary cop, a cudgel instead of pen in fist, a dart for a tongue, at her vocation.

"Thanks (*for nothing*), Chief, I'll call you when I'm there." *So much, for female gentility, sensibility, its effect on my ungentle, unsensible hangover; head(s) starting to really throb, closing my eyes a moment.*

Looking back on the night, everything seemed fuzzy, distorted, colored lights collapsing on themselves.

Now with the passage of time, events became vaguer, confused. In no time, I was heading to Santuario Reservoir, where I could be assured of the clarity of the empirical, observing, asking the right questions in the expectation of unraveling this Gordian knot of suspense and illusion. Why did a striking, spoiled spouse vanish? And how could a jealous, combative spouse stoop so low, as to channel Deep Throat? It was a time as quizzical, fine, as any, however, imbued with the new millennium's cleansing promise: Los Angeles, CA, the Garden of Earthly Delights, new urbanity of infinite dreams, hopes, possibilities; delusions, desires, grand designs run aground, as well, so that just being there was the trip of a lifetime.

The night was sultry, strong ocean breezes wafting through boulevards strewn with sleeping commerce, odd lives flickering. On the freeway out of town, I thought of the unique discomfort caused by famous individuals disappearing, itself ubiquitous. *Weren't these* absentes *given precedence over* qui praesens?

**Messenger**
[605] Your wife has disappeared, taken up into the folds of the unseen air;
she is hidden in
heaven, and as she left the hallowed cave where we were keeping her safe
[sōzein], she said
this: "Miserable Phrygians, and all the Achaeans! On my account you
were dying by the banks
of Skamandros, [610] through Hera's contrivance, for you thought that
Paris had Helen when
he didn't. But I, since I have stayed my appointed time, and having kept to
[sōzein] my
destiny, will now depart into the sky, my father; but the unhappy daughter
of Tyndareus,
[615] guilty [aitia] in no way, has borne evil [kakai] rumors without
reason."

*Catching sight of Helen*
Welcome, daughter of Leda, were you here after all? I was just announcing
your departure up
to the hidden starry realms, not knowing that you had a winged body. I
will not let you mock
us like this again, [620] for you gave your fill of ordeals [ponos plural] to
your husband and his
allies in Ilion. (Euripides, *Helen*, 412 BC)

Earlier, purple chiffon evening gown appareled, WASPy Isidora Green, Chairman of the Board, Warren Bros. Inc., entertainment conglomerate, a normally placid, self-controlled, smart media mogul, member of the old guard, as well as precocious avant-garde, was so stunned, after opening the winning envelope with the triumphant name, announcing the prize, anticipating a grateful, emotive Lilly Lawrence up on stage with her, she was left holding the proverbial bag for the MIA, along with a hooky playing spouse, Willi Herman, eidolons, *protégés*, after all she had done for them to arrive; waiting in vain on an empty stage, dark, muffled sky, minutes now as hours, for a collapsed starlet failed at escaping a heavy, orbital gravity of desperation, the Madam Chairman needing a couple of diazepam and a goblet of champagne.

Following, sharp, black tuxedo, bow tie attired, Puritan John B. Sayer, CEO, Warren Bros. Inc., head of the movie and television studios, and primary host, sponsor and benefactor of the MP Awards, normally an amusing, self-satisfied backslapper of men, and cold seducer of women, was so let down, that during his final, laudatory speech to the nominees, the pauses between his jokes (socially acceptable as well as off color), and their punch lines, exceeded the appropriate... by a lot, the audience actually thinking, he was suffering an apoplexy or some sort of disjoining episode; staring out into the unlit seat rows hoping to randomly spot mad Lilly, that strange sensation of mismatched identities, perhaps incognito in sharp, black tuxedo *burqa,* as there were finely knitted woolen styles, for formal wear, that were now the rage.

I loosely polled my colleagues at the press table, none with any recollection of such careless disregard, as had elevated this Eliza Doolittle to an assumption of exalted excess, over which the gods themselves deemed fit to punish to perdition, for the mere effrontery to their thunderous magnificence, from such a puffed-up version of oneself. How could Lilly succumb to harrying hubris, we asked, before calling it a night, some of us continuing to luminary gatherings galore; the next day's tabloid headlines declaring:

> **Stars Rock Mini Burqas, but Where's Wallflower Lil?**
>
> **Moguls Mug with Celebs to Distract from Lilly's Miss!**
>
> **Holy Hollywood! Where's that L'ill Darling Gone to?**
>
> **What Next? Green, Sayer High and Dry, Praying for Rain!**

Right now, I was headed up the canyon, to the main gate of the thousand-acre property the doomed pair purchased shortly after making a huge splash on the big, as well as small, screen; examples to aspiring newcomers of fostering great achievements from one's own excellence, in the true American tradition. They named their grand domain, Pinkton, in reference, to its original owners, silent movie stars of old:

> I've seen your picture
> Your name in lights above it
> This is your big debut
> It's like a dream come true
> So won't you smile for the camera?
> I know they're gonna love it
> Peg
>
> I like your pin shot
> I keep it with your letter
> Done up in blueprint blue
> It sure looks good on you
> And when you smile for the camera
> I know I'll love you better
>
> Peg
> Will come back to you
> Peg
> Will come back to you
> Then the shutter falls (shutter falls)
> You see it all in 3-D
> (Foreign movie)
> It's your favorite foreign movie (Steely Dan, *Aja,* "Peg", 1977)

Threading a narrow mountain route, in the moon obscured, pitch black night, I was startled to see cross the road, just inches from my front bumper, a bewildering figure of a large boned, silver haired woman with pasty white face covering an, apparently, much swarthier complexion; but so quick, as if to appear as some transparent phantom, figment of the imagination, gone into the low bush of the dry landscape; watching her sprint with astounding agility in the wavy darkness, up a steep hill toward the main house, some distance away in a pre-dawn mist. I wondered who would be out this early, and to what purpose?

Outside the gate the scene was already charged, with news trucks, reporters, police, crazy groupies and zombie gawkers. Security being tight for the eccentric united artists, I was only granted access to their walled compound because my trusty Rus' editor fixed it privately, with her certain lover boy, Brighton Beach henchman, employed as a bodyguard by Willi; and shortly led to an unmade-up Lilly Lawrence, an actor known for coyly rebuking viewers for judging performers primarily by their looks, while being sure to always appear dolled up picture-perfect to keep the studios, tabloids, idolizing fans glued to her.

She had specifically asked for my lead in reporting, tracing events, gathering prima facie evidence, and acting as her spokesman with the other news desks, which would be compromising. For now, and for the sake of us getting along, I played this game her way, helping because she had been polite, as well as insistent, in requesting my assistance. I appreciated it but always wondered why all the fuss over me is.

As I approached, she turned her head slightly toward the eerie darkness of the unoccupied, still nursery.

"Please let me apologize, for the rudeness and brutishness of those Cossacks, my tense husband insists protect our boundaries. Sometimes I wonder if the cost of popularity is much too high in relation to our loss of privacy. Lately I feel more an inmate of the Gulag Archipelago, than mistress of my dominion."

Though I could see her face was banged up, it seemed more from having stumbled around, in the dark, perhaps by tripping, falling, flailing into trees, cactus, thorn bushes than being assaulted by Willi; if Mr. Herman was the batterer, why would he call to report it? At present, such assumptions lacked a motive.

For all the raging hoopla, over Lilly's sensitive acting, spectacular looks, she was not centered buxom horizontally, as with most women, but switchblade vertically, as with a man trying to let go the earthly bounds of gender fluidity, that astounding presence, character, as bony, rough-hewn, direct, as a dude.

It came down to this: two nights ago, their twin toddlers were kidnapped; yesterday, utterly desperate, a dazed Lilly dashed insanely into the hills, obsessed with the gut feeling that her own issue was up there being maintained, somehow nestled, comfortably, while she aimlessly wandered the toppy pine thickets until found by Willi's guards, shivering, and the worse for wear; repeating an obsessive theme, "bound by earthly duty, to ceaselessly look for them," as, these maternal rescue idylls fell short of Shangri-La.

She did not want the story leaked out, because the abductor or abductors were making bizarre demands, which did not reflect well upon the awkward conditions of their lives, or fragile state of their marriage.

**The first** requirement, had to do with their adopting less frivolous and materialistic lifestyles, spending spare time outdoors, communing with nature, and following certain teachings of more primitive, pagan cultures, about love, faithfulness, duty, to get more in touch with their repressed psyches. **The second**, with how they would raise their children, avoiding the imposition of any formulaic, socially influenced, pedantic, ideological, pandering thought, upon them, rather, fostering an inquisitive ambience in which to revel, modeled on the classical symposium of lofty debate. **The third**, with letting go of all worldly attachments holding them back, such as, love, hate, envy, jealousy, desire, retribution, aspiring to relate to other sentient beings, with an impartiality, detachment and acceptance that might mimic *Maitreya's*.

If the star and starlet immediately changed their ways, adopting, and being consistent in, these imposed measures, they would have their dear little ones back again, within ten days; if any hint or word leaked out to the hacks or authorities, however, they would never see them again. The choice was devastating.

These commands were an abstract for idealized, perfected love of each other, themselves, presupposing transmogrified origins, as much societal aspiration, as their natures in the womb, to guide them onward, in an imperative to create more than new identities, but beings, possessing their innate traits outwardly, managing to land in a culture that also placed a premium on self-expression, as a life fulfilling premise. I wondered what sort of a trick this could be, and who was playing it. Was I part of it? Who else was? Was it within our persistent search for the philosopher's stone, which would transform passion to trust?

> We have to distrust each other. It is our only defence against betrayal.
> (Tennessee Williams, *Camino Real,* 1953)

Lilly recounted recent problems with Willie, how amazed, wide-eyed, she was at his conflictive, erratic behavior, such as, when, several months ago, aghast, she saw him dangle their two infants, upside down by the ankles, out of a five-story window in Germany; later having to relive the moment, time and time again, with all the morning news reruns. She was not sure if he had been tripping, more than usual, but was worried he had become unhinged. She suspected that, out of spite, he was set to divulge some very sensitive information about them as a couple, which was strange and hurtful; for theirs had always been a trusting relationship, connubially blissful, caring, devoted, as that of distant memory's mythic, primal husband and wife's must have surely been, despite a few unique, idiosyncratic particularities involved.

She had decided to disclose the same to me in strictest confidence, making me promise upon my honor, not to feature any of it, until so authorized, only by her. Then, uncomfortably, she disclosed they were both undocumented immigrants, unauthorized persons, illegal aliens, if you will, a greaser, and a camel jockey, having overstayed their welcome following, unofficially, entering this country, many years ago:

> "There were two in paradise and the choice was offered to them:
> happiness without freedom or freedom without happiness... They, fools
> that they were, chose freedom – naturally, for centuries afterward they
> longed for fetters..." (Yevgeny Zamyatin, *We,* "Record Eleven," 1920/ 21)

Furthermore, the truth was that she, Lilly, was born male, and was not capable of conceiving, let alone carrying, a child; and he, Willi, was born female, and was not capable of fertilizing, let alone fathering, children. She, Lilly, was the father, she meant; it was her, his sperm. He, Willi, was the giving mother; it was his, her egg. They had each managed to harvest and cryogenically preserve enough reproductive residues, "precious bodily fluids," anticipating their ultimate transformations irrevocably altering them. Rent A Womb, surrogate to the stars, carried their in vitro fertilized embryos through to term. Thriving Gemini, their Pollux and Castor, were born, the family extolled to universally identified constellations.

Not only did Lilly worry tremendously about how such intimate, controversial, revelations might affect her professional reputation, especially the loyalties of her devoted admirers, each of whom felt a bond, personal connection, with her; but she also struggled with the all-consuming terror that the L.A. County Department of Children and Family Services might investigate her and her husband for applying falsely in the surrogacy of, and then, parental orders for, their now disappeared sweet babes, a crime for sure.

At that moment, Willi Herman, a television star who, outside a Sanctuary, CA small-town general store, pummeled a cocky gun rights advocate to a pulp, right in front of the woman's own family, appeared on scene, as if prompted, by an off-screen director. He looked a bit disheveled and perspired, as if having been out and about, approaching us with a warm but wary smile, where faint traces of rouge lingered.

"Why, what draws such an accomplished raconteur and man about town to these forbidding ravines and cliffs, at such an ungodly hour?" I noticed foundation, blush and powder, beneath sour beads of sweat on his face. I comprehended enough to hold back with any of what my chief, and Lilly, confided to me, but I had questions, and decided to lean on him, just for the trouble of having woken me so mercilessly.

"In case you hadn't heard way up here, your wife's disappearance was a big deal. Would you happen to know anything about it?" Willi smiled, lips quivering ever so slightly, his breathing relaxed but heavy.

He looked straight at his wife, drawing her into his sphere of connivance. She looked clear eyed, back at him, with unchanging expression, merging their destinies to a joint, configured commonality of idea, purpose and future action. Erect in posture, taut, alert, they were preeminent people, openly impressed with each other, and their superb selves, after all. Was there anything their success could not conceive?

"Only, that she has not been herself, lately; she's under a lot of stress, not just from work. For months now, my wife's mother has been held at the military prison, in Guantánamo, Cuba, with Lilly desperate to see or hear from her; only finding out through old contacts, as the government classifies information. The raised scars on her back from severe past scourging are again oozing puss due to her rattled nerves. We had a bad marital moment, it's as simple as that. Please, don't get yourself all worked up about it."

"I normally don't, except when I'm possibly, being strung along. Who do you think robbed your kids?"

Telegenic Willi had a boring way of coming across, as he became tired, annoyed, impatient, then bored.

"It beats me, I haven't the foggiest; it must be someone angry with her, us; why should I have an idea?"

"I don't know, I thought you might. Only, that wasn't you I saw, running over the hills, on my way in?"

"Listen, Mr. Yellow Kid, we specifically asked for you because we're aficionados of your investigative column and thought we would throw an easy bone your way. So here is how I want you to explain it to your reporting pals; we had a lover's spat, it's over; rumors of my wife being injured were exaggerated and false; she's fine and will be taking time off from all scheduled commitments, until further notice."

"End of story? There seem to be things going on between you and your wife which need clarification."

"End of story. Whatever goes on between us as a couple is none of your business. Everything is fine."

"That's not going to fly; too much hearsay has already come out. Only the abduction is still unknown."

"And shall remain unacknowledged, thank you. I will not have anyone compromise the negotiations."

"It's bound to come out sooner or later; I can only keep a lid on it for so long before the vultures come."

"Well, later then, and better if any acknowledgements are well managed, by you. Do you understand?"

"Is there any chance you're responsible for your wife's anguish, or was she intent on harming herself?"

"I am not responsible for my wife's agonies, nor do I believe she was intent on, really harming herself."

Why they chose me to participate in this farce, I will never really know. But later it came out, that they wanted their tale told sympathetically, by someone who would not judge them too harshly, and keep the lid on the macabre ideation of having their funeral ashes molded into frisbees and flung into the ocean. Besides, I had plenty of skeletons in my family's closet which made me the perfect tool for their secrecy.

As appearances were never the things themselves, only what they seemed, the past already mourned by dissipating souls over eons of understanding, time, distance, the stars, their twinkling, were not as they revealed, having soft angles (angels), in definition. For now, Willi's narrative was all my fellow rumor mongers would receive regarding his mate's condition; and that was what I notified the throng loitering outside the mansion of, also promising additional information, as soon as I knew anything. Meanwhile, I would continue to sleuth, as "Something is rotten in the state of Denmark..." as the bard of Avon said.

But as I drove home in the misty dusk of the mountain, I could not help wondering what I was going to invent for my demanding readers, or pushy editor, all of whom expected an *expose*. Halfway down the ridge a pick-up truck began following, and when I looked back again, it was gaining fast. A last-minute Crazy Ivan into the opposite lane, managed to shake it off my tail, as I neared a just-waking gas station.

Later that day, Willi called to say that Lilly was feeling much better, could I please interview her again? He was sure she would be more clearheaded after some long-needed sleep. I agreed and went up again.

Meditating silently in the shade of a walled garden's gnarled apple tree, within an enormous black bag (was that a *burqa*?), fine, woven mesh where the eyes would have been (her go to garb when anxious), sad Lilly practiced Willi's prepared phrases. Gradually, her emotions getting the better of her, and with him departed, after the goblet of Chardonnay (sipped through demure mouth slit) it was easier to let roll off her tongue, that she believed Willi had removed their beloveds to a place near there, because every afternoon, he left their house, without returning until the end of the night, as I had witnessed for myself.

Additionally, in the last few days their alarmed neighbors had called to report seeing a strange muscular woman, with ghoulish makeup, trapesing through their properties, at all odd hours. "This must be Willi in disguise," Lilly insisted. It had to be. However, and here was the greatest quandary, both steadfastly believed that as transgenders they were God's own changeling spirits, so any association with a forcible exchanging, buying, selling, trafficking, misappropriating, of human lives, would be anathema to them.

Now more confused than ever, I updated my editor, leaving out the parts about the pair of insubstantial innocents and the scary agile woman in the middle of the night, and tried expressing that I did not know anything more about Lilly's disappearance, than I had already shared with the entire nosey corps, which she criticized as poor coverage, not swallowing any of it for a second. I was feeling the heat from those to whom I was responsible, the twisted fate for all impoverished, freelance players submitting to used, worn out scripts. Suddenly it felt as if I had real skin in the game; I needed to find some answers quick.

Before turning in, I surfed the news services, internet sites, and used all my personal connections, to get grit on these flash in the pan outsiders, who managed to stay in the pan, amassing riches with a pretense of respectability. As with anyone, there were specifics in their backgrounds that inspired questions but overall, show business had been quite good to them, starting with a series of appearances in *Genesis,* as uncannily real origin characters invented and developed by the studio (and appropriated by the couple). I vaguely wondered if they would serve as models, for the central roles of an introductory chapter I was outlining, loosely titled, *The Mystery of the Stars*; a critique of media inspired culture at the millennium by the unmasking of a star and starlet, revealing true intentions within assumed identities; continuing in thus far, unwritten future pages, with what it took for them to get to where success was on-air visibility.

Overnight, the constant, dull rumble of the turning earth overawed me, as I lay listening for the coming dawn, a recurring dream repeating, *"The dose makes the poison,"* a fatal reference to Adam and Eve on TV: the very first spry twosome as feisty game show winners on, *Let's Make a Steal*, or witty talk show hosts on, *The Few*; and there were a wide range of musings within my convoluted sleep, into tired day.

*Could queerness be a narcissistic fixation on the same sex other, as non-threatening extension of the self; tensionless reflection for uneasy lovers, the comfortable, semi erotic* doppelganger *intimacy, rejections tolerated?*

*Is matrimony the union of opposites, in support of condoned procreation, anything other not really considered seriously, as rather, an association of similar entities, such as innocent childhood friends; whatsoever their gender, sexual, matrimonial impulse, having to be relegated distractions?*

*Never having read Tennessee Williams, Lilly, nevertheless had a Blanche Dubois type of restrained resignation, early on, in life, deciding that she would, henceforth, rely on, "the kindness of strangers," reproaching her family and friends, implying that any strangers would demonstrate more kindness to her, than they, a tragic and pathetic situation. Friends were no substitute for her own inner sense, several claiming they cared about her, urging that she forget being famous, because fame, as a media hyped category, had nothing to do with being a great actress, or a good person; needless to mention, she never listened; the rest was, as they say, history.*

*There was the solicitous, optimistic, modern leaning movie producer, who finally opened the door for Lilly to appear in a feature film for the studio, not as the star, but in a secondary role; and as opposed to the well-known lead, who apparently was too shy (smart) to disrobe before the cameras (perhaps a vestige of self-respect), Lilly had no compunction when asked to fill in; providing all the necessary scenes with relaxed and unassuming frontal, and rear, nudity poses (avoiding upper back, due to wet scarring, denoting a past whipping), allowing a big name Polish director, obsessed with underage girls, to take advantage of her unbridled exhibitionism, in exchange for (and as part of) such exposure; the big name uncomfortable showing any of her skin at all, the ingenue underling, aiming on pleasing an already titillated audience, welcoming a chance to undress completely in order to launch a new career; reflecting, that it was nothing, compared to the degradations she had been through, suffered, submitted to; amused at any sense of shame being felt, in such easy, remunerative exploitation.*

*Somehow this charmed duo had attained an uncanny level of a process of thought, reading each other's minds through the transparency of absolute love; knowing what each would be thinking, their disposition or devotion, according to different circumstances, at any given time and place, as all was possible within one's letting go in eternal surrender; each being the one for the other, and in that other, the reflected spirit and genius of life and death, two end leaves of a book, or a pair of exchangeable cuff links, dice; rather than, the distinctly, deeply troubled individuals they actually were, let alone derived from different original genders (d.o.g), sexes; the tragedy was they were not, nor could ever be, a combined person, despite their pure desires to amalgamate into an essential, dualistic new element.*

*He goaded her, as she goaded him, viciously, profoundly, with the results mocking, shocking, bitter: "bleh, bleh, bleh, heh, heh, heh, heh;" and then suddenly, out of the blue, in some inexplicable primal fury, his wife began beating, pounding him with heavy wooden guitar, popping all the strings, the metal bars of a clothes rack, producing severe red welts, and a small, sharp garden shovel slashing his arm; biting him forcefully once, leaving ugly tooth marks, purple bruises on his hands, arms; such hellish, violent encounter causing him considerable physical, psychic agonies as he saw, for the first time, the latent anger harbored during their life together. As for herself, she felt morally and emotionally justified to even the old score which had been building for a long time. But their hard feelings for each other continued, neither knowing if their connection would or even could survive, these bad times; their passion slipping through the cracks, from distractions of total warfare between each other, against the entire world.*

*Lilly appeared in her guise as Eve, chastising Willi's Adam for his faults: "So I wanted to believe I loved him, I was desperate for his requited love, and then one misguided day, in a spasm of romantic ingenuousness, and fidelity, I underwent a vasectomy, for the sake of a man, who behind my back was shagging any males that breathed, all over town. Perhaps now, despite increasing distance, rising pressures and neglect, he would want me again, for the sake of our once having been an item, because I would always give him the benefit; but what my husband cared about, was that **he** would no longer bear **my** children, that's how much he despised me."*

Hombres sin honor, mujeres sin pudor; ¿cuáles de ellos somos, por dios?

*The unavoidable conclusion was that Willi was hardly a complete person, only the semblance of one who had once existed, but who also had many of his higher faculties beaten out of him. So, compassion was never to be feasible, such a sordid background, composition, making it impossible for him to have feelings at all, any humanity, only evidence of a crack in his nature; but he was supremely loyal to those whom he loved, like his Lilly, forever, there being dark events within which he would prove such to her.*

*Quietly, quickly, he located the letters, reclaiming them, before any police arrived at the love shack; in five minutes, the haunting emptiness became a flurry of officers, detectives and a coroner's team. As he slid the folded, faded (still scented) pages into his coat, he wondered if taking what had once been given to a (now eliminated) lover was illegal or might get him into trouble; but deep down he did not feel it was wrong to dispose of the damaging indiscretions that might destroy the marriage; if only for their sake, her sake, no one could ever find such incriminating liaisons of his.*

*In final clarification, Lilly had taken care of a small problem, now a big mess, with her automatic gun, which accidentally discharged at her rival.*

*Attorneys for the actress, waiting to be charged with third-degree murder, told CON News their client did not commit the crime, claiming there's no question, this was a tragedy; but not all tragedies are obviously crimes ...*

*Attorneys for the politically influential news anchor, husband, were quite adamant, defending his actions in support of his wife, in the proceedings, asserting there is nothing connecting him to this unfortunate gentleman.*

Upon my awakening, realizing Willi Herman needed to come clean on his activities, it became apparent I had to interview him at length. What was it about human nature, that those once oppressed inexorably went on to oppress others? Was it whether we placed ourselves in states of utter helplessness or folly?

I went back to the mountain retreat a third time, in the sharp light of day, finding Willi sunning on the terrace, in full naked glory, certainly a sight to behold. To these layman's eyes, all appendages, joints, protuberances, parts, appeared to be where they belonged, and vice versa, but the whole effect was still a bit too curvy to pass for a regular guy. Even though the male details, specifics, were displayed neatly, there was something wrong with the overall package. What was it, I thought? I know, it's that snout of the wayward dog, who does not grasp at all, he did not deserve the last morsels thrown at him, too bad.

For all the raging hoopla over Willi's hard-hitting, on-air bullying, chiseled looks, he was not centered switchblade vertically, as with most men, but buxom horizontally, as with a woman trying to let go the earthly bounds of gender fluidity, an astounding presence, character, as soft, smooth, vague, as a babe.

While in the buff, somehow exuding a pungent, musky, acrid odor, reminiscent of a perfume gone stale overnight, lying prone on his stomach, his oiled backside looked quite round and shapely, as in ancient Achaea, a tan nymph's might have beguiled by a poolside grotto. I quickly got on track of what I came for. Was he the athletic female with eerie countenance, lately seen wandering this and other properties? Could he have his own flesh and blood cruelly sequestered, on a missed precipice, or else secret *mesa*?

He scoffed at both questions. In measured reply to the first, he was flattered at being thought muscular enough, but no, he was not the Amazon in question. His irate response to the second, revealed ridicule, begging the question of a motive, but no, he was not a stealer of men, big or little. On the table beside him was the huge, half drained tumbler of scotch and soda on ice; by the shimmering pool, two pairs of MIA child's flip flops; I realized if there was a key to this enigma, it was not to come easily from him.

I asked if he did not think it was strange there were no ultimatums for money being made by these most altruistic of kidnappers, only direct exhortations toward self-improvement of personalities; almost as if the three philosophic challenges set as conditions for their confined ones' release, were for the family's combined good; a brutal homeopathic prescription for better coexistence through deeper understanding. And only someone very close to this upset family, or even part of it, would comprehend the true, harsh import of the rules being imposed. They were directly personal in nature and struck to their very souls.

Those were only my speculations, he countered, before flopping over, on his back, to sun his frontside.

I asked him why he was hell bent on obtaining publicity at any cost, even such construed as pernicious.

"Publicity brings renown, distinction, notoriety," he laughed, uncharacteristically, "above all else cash."

I asked where, according to his wife, he was given to wander from afternoon to the middle of the night.

"None of her business," he shot back, staring straight at me, his clear eyes quickly filled to black pools.

"I can tell you this, though," he ventured, suddenly opening, with unexpected candor. "I have seen this plastic faced lady, in the middle of the night, under the faint light of a waning moon, out in the remotest meadows and pine groves, while on my way back home, but I do not expect she has ever detected me."

This was a real surprise. I had not spoken of her to him, as plastic faced, so I knew he was describing somebody he had either witnessed or been informed about. "On your way home, again, from where?"

"Well, in all confidence, there happens to be a young man two properties to the south... I've completely lost my head; you won't tell anyone, will you? He is tall, and I think reminds me of my father, but I do not know, his name, and call him, Hero, instead; I see him every afternoon, I just can't keep away, even if I know I should, considering my marriage, our divine marriage; but my darling was distant, choosing children over me, so I'm cheating, as per the Golden Rule, Do onto others as they have done onto you:

> "...the intoxication of sweet revenge (--'sweeter than honey' Homer called it)...
> (Friedrich Nietzsche, *On the Genealogy of Morals: A Polemical Tract*, 1877)

"I guess that makes me a cheetah," he said, in heavily Spanish accented English, laughing uproariously.

"I think you mean, cougar, a powerful wild cat; a woman romantically involved with men younger than herself," I clarified. "But aren't you a man, after all the work you've had done, over these years?" Now, things were getting strange, discomforting, with nowhere to run, or hide, from what I was about to hear.

"The truth is that despite my metamorphosis, or whatever else you may surmise, I am still heterosexual, and have always been so; perhaps bi at times for the sake of (some pleasure) (mainly) survival but in no way lesbian; I'm talking about my innermost core, which even old Dr. Waterson (precious Dad) was not able to rectify, alter, even touch, much to his absolute dismay. I guess, I still like men; always have and probably always will. I don't know if now that I am a man myself, that defines me as ostensibly gay, as others may see it, though I understand some could possibly misconstrue me, as homo, a new dilemma."

Astoundingly, even he retained antiquated, pejorative notions, self-hating prejudices, accusing gays of failing to make crucial life transition from early adolescent same sex friendships to mature heterosexual bonding, in preparation for reproductive union; remaining stuck in puerile, non-challenging schoolyard companionships, lacking the tensions of the mixing of the sexes, with its complicated role playing; and thus, immobilized by childish ways of relating, kept in a perpetual, juvenile stage, without progressing, graduating, to more mature spiritual/ carnal attractions, so integral to pairing; with withered instinctual urges to spread once dynamic genetic markers, other than artificially, an evolutionary dead end ignored but unavoidable, considering chromosomal randomness thus disseminated to future generations, sadly enfeebling; homosexuality not seeming the most efficacious means toward perpetuation of the species.

"I believe you," I said, nodding my head exaggeratedly, trying to change the subject, perplexed at such cross currents, contradictions, of sexual attraction versus gender identity. "Will you and Lilly concede to the malefactor's ultimatum? Will you reorganize your lives?" It seemed the question of the moment.

"Trust me, we are taking every step required, and have even called in an old acquaintance, as unofficial advisor on the case." On the reclining chair Willi turned over to his side, to give his arms and legs their equal tanning time. The image was of a honey toned Hispanic cherub, with softer than usual cod piece, and if catamites of Imperial Rome had been re-cast, he would have gloried as their exemplar. Perhaps I had been in the presence of Hermaphroditus, flipping back and forth between genders as some flapjack:

> Therefore, when Hermaphroditus sees that the limpid waters, into which
> he had descended as a man, have made him but half a male, and that his
> limbs are softened in them, holding up his hands, he says, but now no
> longer with the voice of a male, "O, both father [Hermes] and mother
> [Aphrodite], grant this favor to your son, who has the name of you both,
> that whoever enters these streams a man, may go out thence but half a
> man, and that he may suddenly become effeminate in the waters when
> touched." Both parents, moved, give their assent to the words of their
> two-shaped son, and taint the fountain with drugs of ambiguous quality.
> (Ovid, 43BC – 17/ 18AD, *The Metamorphoses*, Book IV,
> "Hermaphroditus," Project Gutenberg)

Having reached back to shared pasts, their new advisor was none other than bold and erudite, Dr. Henry Waterson, Whale University graduate, wit, eminent physician; Native, no, Original American Medicine Man Supreme, agent of tremendous global social change and upheaval; also, Willy and Lilly's adoptive father. He was staying at his *Apache* sweat lodge, on the far side of the property, awaiting the family's *powwow*. It had long been understood that their relationship with him had been loving at first, but was later stormy, and he once sent both packing from paradise, banished them from Eden, after challenging God's authority in choosing which sex they preferred, surpassing the limits that He originally intended.

Upon having a premonition that calamity was about to strike his distant family, the doctor was spurred to fly to their aid. Ironically the seizure of his infant grandchildren healed the eternal rift, drawing him nearer to his estranged offspring, forever in his thoughts and wishes. Dwelling remotely, in a scientific, high desert outpost of his own design, days before the incident, sensing danger imminent, he plotted a timely arrival, energized zephyr of ancient, tribal knowledge, vectoring toward the Western tradition.

The noted doctor would be the guest of honor, for dinner that evening, explained Willi, and it would be a great pleasure, for those already attending, if I were also, to join them. Now my curiosity was piqued.

When I arrived at around dusk, the captivated party adored some faint figure subsumed in old shadows. Waterson, seated resplendently in the cinema style parlor, a steady voice in fading evening light, lorded it over the whole dramatic (it had once been owned by 1920's studio heartthrobs, Ronald Fairview and Molly Pinkton), mock Tudor style residence. Of mixed Original American, Polynesian extraction, skin the color of tennis court clay, straight black hair, he seemed more *Mescalero Apache* shaman, than a top of his class, Ivy League educated avatar of science, modernity and vision. Staunch defender, promoter of the bodily health, sovereign rights, ancient privileges of aboriginal peoples of the world, all of whom had been ruined, terminated, by the white man, he unabashedly claimed; guests milling about, enjoying *hors d'oeuvres*, cocktails, he held court with an assumed air of authority, a certain wisdom of the ages.

"Original Americans win meaningless, symbolic victories, over whether the racist public should use the epithet, redskins, the term we used historically, to refer to ourselves, our own red people, while leaving the main issue, the land, which belonged to all natives, in truth it was the Great Spirit's forever, and its complete expropriation from them, off the table. Was there ever a more blatant and pathetic example of the vanquished co-opted by victors, than ignominiously obliterating the demands that should have been paramount, and focusing instead, on inconsequential, distracting side issues of pride and identity, as if their very ethos, collective memory, had been absorbed, blended, sucked into the Caucasian industrial, consumer culture poisoning the world? Is not this epochal lack of absolute, if not meaningful, redress the real, inexorable shame of every extant as well as obliterated tribe, suffering mocking gestures of the greedy, new Manifest Destiny inspired, proprietors, of their once infinite, broad expanses? What about the priceless, valueless land and the system of corrupt (mis) deeds by which it was historically seized?"

> Preamble
> Under all is the land. Upon its wise utilization and widely allocated
> ownership depend the survival and growth of free institutions and of our
> civilization. (Code of Ethics and Standards of Practice of the NATIONAL
> ASSOCIATION OF REALTORS, Effective 2012)

Dinner was announced, and the company proceeded gaily to an impressively set table, in a large dining room decorated with walls of celestial blue, white cloud painted ceiling, as if the progressively inspired body to be seated for such a sumptuous cornucopia, in ethereal chamber, under broad, heavenly canopy, would perhaps find inspiration, in floating lofty ideas. "I can see where you're coming from," ventured some of the cordial guests. Little did they know they were merely fodder for the learned doctor's finely spun gifts of persuasion. Now positioned at the head of their table, Waterson continued this discourse:

"What ancient world maps, then histories, conveniently labeled, the New World, was simply our place. This sacred land was illegally taken by trickery, conquest, settlement, colonization, and other forms of convenient confiscation, from its original inhabitants, dwelling there for over ten thousand years, native people of the earth, sky, sun, then transferred to pale faced conquerors from across the sea. And these aggressive interlopers came with new ideas of ownership, commerce and production, requiring Indians to labor as slaves, on tobacco, sugar, rice, cotton, plantations. But when the profit motivated landlords, planters and merchants realized that their red captives were not suitable for that type of work, that they would rather have perished, than bend their backs for their white overseers, the enterprising capitalists fastidiously devastated, and depopulated, yet another continent, to transport enslaved captives for labor. And over three hundred years, so many black Africans were brought here, they claimed birthrights for their own, independent of yet parallel to those of their former masters (except for Jim Crow) as equals."

"Hear! Hear!" acclaimed the proud, black gentleman to the right, introducing himself as God's servant, the Rev. Hannibal P. ('Pearly') Gates, presiding over the crusading Carthaginian Black Baptist Church, New Haven, CT, going to Tijuana on a Quixotic quest seeking the source of the great *Rio Inmigracion*.

"Quite clear," resounded from the concerned white(er) lady to the left, introducing herself as children's advocate, Patricia (P) Diddy, Ph.D., J.D., president of the international charity agency *Les Enfants Sans Frontičres*, Greenitch, CT, inspecting L.A. *barrios,* on a humanitarian relief mission for battered youth.

"Dear, dear," answered Ms. Yael Abraham, Ph.D., Director, Human Resources, Warren Bros., Inc., also, a committed Zionist, despite its colonialist connotation, as her reply to the Holocaust, wondering of the repercussions to the cultural, social, corporate orders, from the changes advocated by this chatty chief.

As the meal progressed, sumptuous courses were served, both gastronomic and dogmatic, with various subjects discussed, the Rev. Gates summarizing: "African Americans were the only people who did not want to come here, everyone else did, our names are not our own; I really want my bloody reparations and for the guys running things to stop killing my sons, and telling my daughters they're ugly;" and Dr. Diddy concluding, "Blacks want to integrate into society, but still be able to blame and hate whites over historical wrongs, an untenable and unrealistic position; after completely racializing our civilization for the last five hundred years, whites still deny ever using racial profiling." Due to a corporate sensitivity, Yael Abraham preferred reticence, rather than other boisterous responses. It seemed I was stuck within arcane civil rights prattle, no compromises in sight. Nevertheless, we agreed, "the irony of race is that if you see it, you are a racist, if you do not, you are blind, and if you ignore it, you are a fool," *nuff* said.

Over coffee and cordials, a few of Lilly's girlfriends asked about her health, whether she had recovered from her depression, and nervous attack, of the previous night. Her face was now puffy, bruised; it was hard to believe she was one of the most sought-after professionals in Hollywood, with a choice of roles envied by even closest competitors; her reply, "almost completely, thank you," ringing hollow. Not for an instant did she hint that there might be anything upsetting her besides some minor work, or personal, anxiety, spat, that would soon pass; distracting from awkward silences of her bad acting, Willi declared:

"We'll be heading to the *Mescalero* Reservation, for two weeks, to give Lilly a chance to rest up, relax."

"And *powwow* with the families of our illustrious forefathers," added Lilly, referring to Waterson's kin.

"The rarified desert air, occult ceremonial ways of our ancestors, will cure you of the doldrums, young woman," added the concerned (conceited) doc. "There is no time to waste, we depart at earliest dawn."

At the evening's end, Willi made sure to invite me to *Apache* country. Giving him a day's head start, I set out for the tribe's annual gathering, in high, dry *montanas,* at the traditional pole and skin medicine lodges, understood only by all but forgotten *curanderos,* curative wizards of regions misplaced by time.

With all the hustle and bustle of entertaining, traveling to Indian country, and settling into their savage wilderness digs, with absolutely no amenities or modern touches, little mention had recently been made of the junior misplaced ones, as if in their deepest hearts all believed they would be all right, were in no danger, and saw no need to bring them up any more, in such manner exhibiting worry or preoccupation.

In that austere, high holy land, with a flooding stream for a shower or sink, and an open pit for a toilet, Willi and Lilly were occupied with living a simplified, even primal life, conducting an uncomplicated existence. Instead of calling their barber and beautician to Pinkton, to do their hair and nails, the inured outdoor enthusiasts were washing daily in the freezing, running water, suffering the indignities of every primitive man's latrine, while once manicured nails became cracked, broken, used, almost immediately.

After their sixth day of living off the land, eating only what was caught, found, or scavenged, they were deemed sufficiently purified (putrefied), to participate in the Search Rites for Ghosts Gone. Waterson's relatives, *compadres*, tribesmen, most in traditional, long braided hair, *moccasins*, loincloths, out from the scrub, *pasto* flats, brown *cerritos*; blessing the lodge with collective, medical observations, heathen chants, inner might, outward glories; treating their fractured Lilly with a series of purging perspirations, breakdowns, restorations, *la humedad y calor,* of the sealed, airless chamber of infernal degree; so with *peyote* consumed in vast quantities, half an hour was all that was necessary for Lilly to start convulsing, revealing insights into the impossibility of acceding to the dispossessors' particular ransom demands.

As Willi, Waterson, all the mustered wizards, healers, *peyoteros*, and an ardent fan or two, observed in the dull, glowing inner sanctum, rancid odors of sweat, grease, blood and buckskin permeating smoke; out of confined soft shadows Lilly, head tilted back, eyes quivering, only whites showing, called for the shades of their indefinite double indemnities, to come back to her and Willi, to show they were alright.

And then with my own eyes, I saw a large limbed figure, shellacked white face, frosted hair, apparently a dark brown coloring under the spectral mask, stream out in a puff of smoke, from directly behind the fire, seemingly out of nowhere. When I reached out to touch it, there was nothing; I thought it must be some old *bruja*, or parlor game tomfoolery. I wondered if that bitter *peyote* I had sporadically ingested, here and there, for several suns, might have influenced my focus and judgment. Suddenly it came upon me, she bore an uncanny resemblance to a made-up Waterson in drag; but when I glanced over at blest Waterson he was shaking, seeming vague, far away, dreaming; what visions would follow such a show?

And following right behind that translucent matron, out of thin air, appeared those radiant, unredeemed bottle imps, hand in hand, softly seeking Lilly, repeatedly mouthing, whispering, "Mama," from breathy lips. She could not see them, considering the leaning position of her head, the rolling of her eyes, but I could, witnessing their wondrous effulgence, and was sure I heard a low-pitched voice, affirming in the steamy silence, "They are safe and under the care of the tribal guardians," before dissipating along with three resplendent figures, into that fire. At this point, I probably passed out, because to this day, I have no further recollection of the events that may, or may not, have transpired, in that hazy, mystical ritual.

The next morning, after Lilly and the doctor had recovered sufficiently from their ordeals, I interviewed them about the trips they each experienced, what happened, each claiming to have heard distant voices, sensed life forces. I demanded if Waterson had any idea who the big-framed wo(man) was, but he was perturbed. If recent search rites were over, there was only one thing to do: "Find the missing minors."

Well, that was easier said than done, considering the lack of clues to go on. But I had a last hunch, and when we made it back to Pinkton, I implemented my plan. First, I called my White Russian editor, and asked to have one of Willi's blond, crew cut *Bratva* goons, whom she could trust (she said he owed her a favor), meet me at sunset outside the front gates; I had a job for him; if there was to be some trouble I wanted my own ex-KGB mini hit squad to foil the kidnappers, being certain there were more than one.

In short order, as the sun was tumbling over its western edges, I met the well-toned, Zaroff. We were to be hunters of men, tracking the most dangerous game, observing the night from a rise above the eastern side of the house; from there having a layout of the entire property. Zaroff confessed to being madly in love with green eyed Ottoline, red headed Rus', beautiful Slav princess, my editor, having known each other since majoring in physics at Lomonosov Moscow State University, and any friend of hers was his friend as well. I never called Ottoline by her name, thinking of her as my sister; always Chief, or Boss, no chit chat, nothing more. I knew she always had my back; I owed her a wrap-up worthy of that trust.

Sure enough, at around two in the morning, sleepiness producing sudden delusions of sight and sound, what at first seemed a vaporous apparition coming out of the camouflaged glen gradually solidified into the same plaster faced, full framed female moving swiftly across the clearing to the lower entrance, on the western side of the great house. We cocked our heads attentively, hoping to know something at last.

Unfortunately, perched on this opposite bluff, we were blind to her location, and had no alternative than sneaking around the back of the long, stucco residence, risking coming upon a perpetrator, in shadowy corners. Using all innate stealth, nearing the mansion's end, peeking around the wall's edge so as not to give ourselves away, I heard whispering across the brightly lit doorway, between those being complicit.

Now unconcerned with our concealment, I motioned to Zaroff to follow me to the entrance. Walking at a brisk pace, in the electric light of night's forgotten hours, I could see that she was conversing with… **Lilly**, who, upon spying us, out of the corner of her eye, promptly slammed the door; leaving us face to face, with the phantom madam, now revealed to be the spitting image, of Dr. Waterson, only aged, and cross dressed. It was too late, even pointless, for her to escape anywhere, as perforce, the game was up.

Staring at her straight on, the newly engaged Muscovite muscle at my back, I took an accusatory tone.

"You are a close relation of Dr. Henry Waterson's. You and Lilly conspired against Willi; undertook to have their toddlers taken, forcing radical changes in the existential direction of their matrimonial order, and Willi's unsteady, reckless behaviors, so dangerous to stability; in ways more advantageous to her."

Then I added, intriguingly, a charge based on no solid evidence whatsoever, except my own suspicions.

"You also overfed *peyote* buds to Dr. Waterson and Willy, stupefying them into induced trances, and me to confuse my senses, believing you and those babies, scintillating as you presented, were immaterial. I put my hand right through you, or reckoned I had. Perhaps, the youngsters were also fed… not them!"

"How did you know," she asked, dumbfounded, deflated, defeated, suddenly seeming smaller, weaker, flabbier than a minute previously; dusky red pigment under caked white face paint, evidencing stronger than ever; and sure enough, features like Dr. Waterson's, on a completely different, elderly version, now became so obvious. Heshe was Waterson's *tio Lunaro,* the *Chiricahua Apache* band's mystical *doctor mago magnifico*, who had forgotten more about alleviating maladies, than Waterson ever remembered.

"I didn't, really, until you asked," outfoxing a fox, although I had some idea, *peyote* had been involved.

The next day, in the lucidity of the morning sun, Lilly agreed to meet at Pinkton, along with that loyal spouse of hers, Willy, Dr. Waterson, and myself. Now for the denouement of *The Mystery of the Stars*.

Just as Lilly had originally coyly hinted, the ransomed Romulus and Remus were hidden, locked up, on a desolate hilltop near the reservoir, in order that their "bereft," alpha wolf bitch matriarch would be in doting proximity to them. *Tio Lunaro* played Guardian to the captives, as well as go between with their mother, choosing the middle of the night to make his secret transport of the exiles from the rough cabin on a crest, his *El Dorado,* mountain top retreat, to nurse and bond with mommy dearest, at the mansion.

The ghost faced woman's disguise was a campaign of intimidation, terrorizing the neighborhood with a fiendish perpetrator willing to strike at any time, a way of forcing all immobile parties to act. When the infirm proceeded to the *Mescalero* Reservation, the POWs were dragged along, so they could stay near their nurturer, as well as, with considerable coaching, appear in her hallucinations. And yes, *tio Lunaro* spied Willi that dark night in the grove, but kept to his schedule, retrieving his charges, stepping briskly through covering shadows, with only a sharp rustling of shifting pine needles stirring the moonlit trails.

Why had Lilly masterminded such a dastardly, *Medea* influenced scheme, to begin with; first, a pseudo abduction of her own progeny, then the continued deceit of her husband, and a reporter? A convincing answer: possibly, wanting to take back her marriage, simplifying their lives, to appreciate the abundance which had steadily rewarded them since arriving. So much for heartfelt candor; in its pure poignancy, a pathetic cry for help from a lonely, frightened woman; in its most sordid cynicism, a manipulative trick, using her own successors as pawns at chess; however grim the start, she was committed to check mate.

And why was Willi so hostile to the truth, allowing recent bizarre behavior to jeopardize a harmonious togetherness almost to breaking point? It was not so much that he was shocked, dismayed by his wife's extraordinarily shady, obfuscating actions, but more, that he was upset, bothered, by his own guilty role in the absurd matter; in his heart, comprehending his wife had undergone, some sort of psychotic break from reality, and that was alright with him, because at any moment, without warning, he could succumb as well; promising to be more attentive of her, continuing the solitary struggle to free their lives of the dangerous external influences holding them back, from absolute self-realization or internal fulfillment.

In the end what mattered most was that their twin treasures had been returned unharmed. Whether they were undamaged, traumatized, would be left for future examination. Once recovered, strangely no one had the empathy to inquire (possibly because the restored were learning to talk) how they had fared, in their impressionistic adventures; whether they were at all aware, they had been removed from home, or didn't pay it any mind; whether they had missed their Daddy. After initial confusing moments, sobbing, exhausted victims scampered to rueful, tired parents, the four embracing in a convocation as timeless as family itself; if Stockholm Syndrome is bona fide here was a perverse example, with kinfolk as captors.

What might Pimple.com have to say about a family they had recently extolled, as being so, "New Age?" When I left the newly aged family, for the drive back to town, I wondered if the wobbly marriage could survive such an episode, and if they would stay together. Only time would tell. For some reason, Rudy Vallee's dated ditty, commenting on the origins of these twentieth century follies, rushed into my mind:

> You ought to be in pictures
> You're wonderful to see
> You ought to be in pictures
> Oh, what a hit you would be...
>
> You ought to dress in fashion
> And ride in motor cars
> You ought to be in pictures
> My star of stars
> (Dana Suesse, Edward Heyman, "You Oughta be in Pictures," 1934)

A hawk, crying deep and throaty, overhead, tipping bent wing, beckoned all spectators along their way.

Later, down off the high bluff, loose, after two weeks of extensive reflection, intending not to condemn or praise too readily, I began an account of the whole affair, a few excerpts of which, in closing, follow:

> What man hath wrought
>
> ...selectively taking from the past what justified the present, unlocking a future of facts, fictions, remembrances, utilized divine motives for good, as well as evil; and as human actions were manifested, they were at once validated, or despised, by the summation of knowledge and experience ...
>
> ...what man hath wrought, that by which he elevates himself to a godlike status, was his self-anointed omnipotence while in this realm, apotheosis

assumed, from facilitating the mortal to immortal, undergoing the saving transformation from born, passive victim, to shaper of our own destiny ...

...weekly drills under desks, while MAD (Mutually Assured Destruction) ruled America's designs, and profits became more sacred than life itself; a *Mundus inversus*, the world turned upside down, so contemplated in the bible, as prior to man's fall, "The wolf and the lamb shall feed together..."

... bullies playing victims, shedding crocodile tears, booting innocents in their heads, the once oppressed, given the advantage of newfound power, now oppressing; all in blithe accordance with such infinite craftiness that is human nature, and certain primeval laws beyond our comprehension...

...and the things man made, and undertook, were most terrible, awesome: nuclear, chemical, biological weapons to kill, medicines for cures; Adams transformed into Eves, and Eves into Adams (while remaining true-blue), with newborns conceived out of test tube fluids, body parts harvested out

of paid donors; men diving deep beneath, to abysmal reaches of the seas, in silent fathoms, or flying high up, well beyond the limits of the sky, into quiet space; others jumping off for Mars, trekking away from our system, solar pull gracefully loosening an "ineluctable modality of the visible..."

## 2. *Mundus novus*

Concerning the Islands Recently Discovered in the Indian Sea

As soon as I reached that sea, I seized by force several Indians on the first island, in order that they might learn from us, and in like manner tell us about those things in these lands of which they themselves had knowledge; and the plan succeeded, for in a short time we understood them and they us, sometimes by gestures and signs, sometimes by words; and it was a great advantage to us. They are coming with me now, yet always believing that I descended from heaven, although they have been living with us for a long time, and are living with us to-day.

Lisbon, the day before the Ides of March. [Christopher Columbus, Letter on The First Voyage announcing his discoveries, 1493]

Willi Herman was never his real name, changing it after arriving in the United States, in the mid-1980s; having been raised in unimaginable poverty, in a sprawling *barrio bajo*, against a steep, oily hill, full of rubble, garbage and high lush grass, by a polluting, noisy highway on the outskirts of drug torn Bogotá, Colombia; relying on two dreams to sustain him in a grim, daily struggle to provide basics for himself, surviving unspeakable abuse: one, to immigrate to the United States of America, two, to become a man.

As an embryo, the essence that would soon become Willamina dreamed of its prenatal surroundings, and how her body felt in the warmth and comfort of her liquid nest: flowing magic potion fulfilling her every pore and desire with pleasure and joy, in a shared vision, of tranquility and expectancy, with her mother. Sometimes, the sound of her own heartbeat was felt far away, within the womb's medium that was her infinite universe of muffled sense; far off rhythms of the earth's eternal movement harmonized into her own, unrecognized blood flow, prompting daily increases in size, weight, physical blossoming. At some point, however, a distinct reversal of all these positive conditions and feelings was manifested in a surprise outcome of turmoil upon the fetus, perhaps during early gestation, with the forming of her sex organs. An inchoate Willi was by this time busting to escape, as if stuck within Willamina's lately unbearably itchy skin, waiting to molt it as a snake does before resuming the next stage of its existence.

The sleep years of early consciousness, remembrance, recognition and infancy were an immediate self-identity with the male sex, rather than her own. Her curvy mother, realizing there were already gender issues occurring, even though her daughter had inherited her attractive looks, bought her a pair of black baby boots as her first footwear, with which she used to stomp throughout the house, and later in early childhood up and down the stairs to hear the loud noise they made; even giving her the nickname Willi. Lying supine on the bed, her earliest recollections were of her mother dressing up in front of the mirror, using perfume; getting ready to go out with different men, and then receive them quietly, in their house. She was an absent mother most of the day, and Willamina learned to take care of herself without others. By age four she understood that her birth sex was not the gender she was comfortable with, dressing up in her father's baggy clothes whenever she could, despite his mistreating her with butt slaps, or shoves.

But these were external manifestations of inner impulses beyond anybody's control, even Willamina's. She felt imprisoned in a figure that was not hers, and perhaps it was a weird confusion of birth she was a victim of, as if somewhere along the line an anatomy she should have entered, was at the last moment switched, with one of its opposite sexes. As her male soul had been following its impulse to acquire its male host, before the final approach, God, fate, chance or luck had shortchanged, tricked her; for what punishment only, they knew. But for whatever the reason, her soul's guiding authority placed that male soul inside a voluptuous female body, so for all the changes the heart demanded, the body still rebelled.

Willamina Hernan was raped from the time she was only twelve, an age at which she did not yet know the word *violar*, on the dirt floor of a back room of her family's corrugated sheet metal and cinder block *casucha*. It was a family member, her uncle *Jesus*, her father's brother from down the hill. Afterwards, other relatives and family friends paid her visits, as easy prey, and she suffered torments from unseen predators closest to her. Initially astonished, protesting that no one came to her aid during these sexual assaults, she gradually embraced silence, and grew to accept with weary resignation these wild bouts of brutality. Then as time passed, men she did not know, sometimes women, orgiastic strangers, imposed themselves upon her, with foul breathed threats of secrecy, and physical harm if the truth were known; and she had two dreams that raised her up, preserved the semblance of normalcy, despite long term hell in her own patriarch's home: one, to immigrate to the United States of America, two, to become a man.

Willamina planned her future every day, waiting in the chilly, exhaust laced dawn for the *micro* to take her to school. Well read, proficient in English, she would save, every bit of money, scrounged up, and as soon as she graduated, dress as a boy, paying cruel *coyotes* to smuggle her into Panama, then Central America, Mexico, and finally across the border to the new land of milk and honey. If the cash ran low, she would prostitute herself to get there; what alternative was there? As her nickname had always been Willi, and being fair skinned, she invented an Anglo sounding surname, assuming the new persona, Mr. Willi Herman, honoring Herman Munster, her favorite television show character, with whose big black Frankenstein boots she identified. In her heart of hearts, she idealized Willi to be her real self, longing to be freed. When she got to the U.S., she would find the right surgeon, live her dream, become a man. Her quest was elemental, as if only its obtainment would rescue her soul from this eternal wonderment.

Feminine in appearance, well-stacked, masculine in manner, a bit awkward in her stride, eyes averted from the world, and after brief contact quickly turned away; at five Willimina's mother, hailing from an austere, back country *Opus Dei* clan, was given *un corte de corbata* (mutilating a despised enemy was the ultimate humiliation, dehumanization, ownership, of their slaughtered essence in perpetuity), before her very eyes, by an insanely jealous boyfriend, horrible pimp; her two maternal spinster aunts from up the hill thereafter raising her; strict, unrelenting, chiding her many imperfections, the old maids scolded her to, "watch your posture, walk more like a young lady," or, "hold your head up straight, arms at your side," or, "stop slouching," providing rigid moral guidance, reproving of Willamina 's new adolescence; and though not ever kind or loving but rather admonishing, doing absolutely nothing to prevent or even mitigate, her horrid carnal torments at the hands of others, perfecting her for that same Roman Catholic faith through which their lives of self-denial, acceptance and obedience had been formed. At thirteen, dutiful Willamina took communion, although she was no longer chaste and had not been very virgin for over a year. During confession, inventing the most trivial sins for the *cura* to forgive (absolution being more meaningful for white collared ones than herself ), because she could never recall transgressions of which she was guilty; she hesitantly asked the *padre* if she could denounce misdeeds committed against her by others; to which he, unyieldingly, replied, "No my child, God knows to forgive them; maybe you shall find grace to do so." She took a deep breath, and inquired if it were at all possible, she could be a boy, trapped inside her girl's body, to which the dry monsignor replied, "No my child, God created you, as you are." Later, pondering on why, if God was so good, there was still so much suffering, including her own, asking for divine assistance in her life of bitter travail, she wondered *if He had abandoned her*.

Upon turning fifteen, recognizing the economic advantage to be gained, Willamina sold herself, to both men and women, for the first time. Though powerless, to defend against daily, recurring sexual attacks, she would, at least, try to reclaim some control of her life, by charging for her time and services; from a purely business point of view, she accumulated funds for her passage according to plan, but there was also something more to it than that. Though while female she never experienced real sexual climaxing, there were times, during excited role-playing games, she found certain satisfaction in pretending to be a male, as per submissively sprawling on hands and knees, letting come what may. Years of misuse and indifference by all those around, had inured her to even the most furious sexual episodes. During any extreme physical and spiritual despair, she developed the mental discipline to remove herself from the torture being inflicted, focusing instead, on an inner peace she would find once her transformation from woman to man was complete. Once being "in the life," she further distanced herself, by coldly adding up in her head, the money she was earning on each full or half service, projecting how it would one day get her to *El Nuevo Mundo*. When her mother's murderous pimp came around for more cash Willamina politely refused. He came back, drunk, beat Willamina savagely, tied her up, and using some old, rusty needles, the point of a dull knife, and poisonous black India ink, tattooed the word, "*Papi,*" on the back of her upper neck, branding her as his girl forever. "*Madre*, help me," she whispered, at the start of the excruciatingly long ordeal, before assuming the silence of the penitent, until he was done with her. So unnerved was this hoodlum, *Papi*, by Willamina's stoic, quiet courage, that the pimp never called again.

During all this period, despite the mistreatment, with diligent attendance at her high school, she did her best to keep up with her studies, which had been thoroughly infiltrated by revolutionary principles; so despite knowing better she became completely convinced by the pervasive anti-American rhetoric then, which was something like this: After the United States of North America secured its own independence, they wasted no time in utilizing a Monroe Doctrine, and an innate sense of racial, cultural and religious superiority, in a new form of Yankee imperialism, which would soon, not only conquer its own internal frontier, but external territories, as well, to justify their lording it over their southern neighbors, all the way to Patagonia. *Los Yanquis* were not nice guys, when it came to hemispheric order and security. It would be, "My way or the highway," from 1776 on, for Latin America. Still to come were the series of expropriations, beginning with the Mexican American War, then the Spanish American War, a sequence of Banana Wars, financial, military and police interventions in Central America and the Caribbean, into the 1930s, making immigrating to this country a deal with the devil. But despite this *mala fama,* spread by the leftist insurgency throughout Latin America, many people still wanted to come here, to live and raise their families, if given the chance, go figure; and that was because in theory this country provided the semblance of a level playing field, the same rules for all to operate under, and either thrive, or not.

Turning seventeen, belligerence mixed in her blood, as she swaggered the neighborhood, chopping her hair short, in a sort of severe, page boy *coif*, donning black, heavy lace up boots, baggy fatigue pants, a T-shirt, denim jacket; for protection, as her habitual defilers usually had no interest in men and were put off by the new getup; thick boots actually coming in handy for warding off the morning cold, as well as kicking ass on the annoying, unrelenting *gamines,* who chased after her, with mocking, vulgar kissing noise, as she passed, hurling devilish taunts: "*Mala macha! Como te la meten, por el chico?*" roughing them up, stomping over small, sooty faces if they tripped in her path; there had been, Jesus, a little boy whose head she might have split wide open, but she tried not to think about it. After tricky procedures that changed her sex from female to male, when scalpel cuts were finally on their way to healing, Willi awoke one morning, and gazing upon his new image, in the full-length vanity mirror, felt something he had never experienced, true happiness and fulfillment. "I look like a dude," he repeated to himself over again, flexing those tightly worked out shanks, loins, abdomen, chest, shoulders, arms. "I am a dude."

By a sheer coincidence of fate, in a different yet equally turbulent continent on the far side of the world, another downtrodden human being was also growing up under circumstances which, while completely distinct, nevertheless, were dramatically similar for an underlying cruelty, sexualized slavery, migratory impulses, and a dream walk undertaken in realization of renaissance desires. While such observations may fail to shock, in this jaded age of great evil and debauchery, perhaps even deserving *blasé* reaction for being expected, this special, struggling person had some bearing on Willamina's life going forward.

In terms of the everyday turn of the world, it was uncanny how a despondently love starved transsexual fleeing Bogotá, Colombia, would one day meet and fall in love with an equally desperate, identity bled trans absconding from Beirut, Lebanon; two damaged, human vectors, completely separate, yet parallel realities intersecting at a specific point in time and space, in this case at the end of the twentieth and the beginning of the twenty first centuries, in the city of angels, in far off, *E pluribus unum* U.S.A. Despite distant origins, pasts and uniquely evolving stories, mindful destiny had led them in the same direction.

Cross currents

And all the while she firmed, his leisure time
was always taken on himself, a nod
to modern minds, a love of bod,
of souls spun round, turned on a dime.
Some laugh, some cry, all seeking their own place
within those things already been, shown grace,
or yet to come; and then accepting themselves,
especially their most new love.

Now, well past sundown, doing the best we can,
as sailors cast adrift, search sea and land.
Light specks on foggy, distant shores, to reel
us in where we belong, a quiet place
of our imaginings; escape being real
from callous nature, stirring silent fate.

They found the meaning of their days, in each successive episode of endurance for their hard existence. Questions: were they divinely made, of thought or word? perhaps His cast-off dreams? born fractious infants of one millennium, *enfants terrible* of the next, not of known, assumed, invented genealogies, their innumerable, anonymous and imagined descendants destined as the generations that flourished, to repopulate lands gone fallow, stale, with revitalized seeds of tomorrows merging to awaking daylight. The genealogy of the spirit of those times was imbued in such descendants as would claim a birthright.

When Adam and Eve began to discriminate, to taste banned fruits of different trees; of the knowledge of good (variety) and evil (uniformity), i.e., choice, free will, vs. limits, predestiny; they were forthwith banished from Eden, their sin: daring to experience both sexes, and their hubris of choosing which sex was preferred, in thus fashion, surpassing the limits that God originally intended for them, as for us all. Chasing after perfection, they were no different than any other beings in existence, even poets of a new kind of verse of the mystical experiences of life, coming as close to the Platonic forms as ever possible.

According to Ovid, there was once a Cypriot sculptor, named Pygmalion, who carved a woman out of ivory. Gazing at his creation, he forgot that other women existed, rather, falling head over heels for his realistic and beautiful statue. For in the sublime are certain whisperings of what is eternal, or of similar radiance, as may be surmised. One by one we are all called forth to everlasting life. But man's greatest faculty is his ability to ignore the actuality of his impending decline, then demise. This may be the true meaning of immortality, forgetting the inevitable while enjoying a steamy day, the lasting sun, our time.

Perhaps the greatest immortality lies in the thoughts of manuscripts passed down, through many hands. For centuries tales of Babylonian Hanging Gardens, Prester John in India, had fed European legends of paradise on earth; concurrently, concepts of immortality entered human consciousness, with a religious mania; as early exploration spread the word of God, new lands were considered providential. Ponce de Leon's Fountain of Youth was linked by chronicles to his discovery of *Beniny* (Bimini), wealthy land of prosperity, as per his royal charter; the finding also being combined in a search for health, longevity:

> "[T[he famous Fountain of Youth, if I am rightly informed...in the
> southern part of the Floridian peninsula, not far from Lake Macaco.
> Its source is overshadowed by several gigantic magnolias, which, though
> numberless centuries old, have been kept as fresh as violets by the virtues
> of this wonderful water."
> (Nathaniel Hawthorne, "Dr. Heidegger's Experiment," 1837)

The fabled, lost city was secretly there the entire time, laid out before them, in all its forgotten splendor, but completely smothered by the creeping jungle, a tragic whisper still lingering, despite never having been heard in the last millennium, the staggering silence but an outer echo of quickly crumbling selves. They were still receiving faint signals from the unmanned probe at the edge of our solar system, many centuries after any scientist on earth even remembered why it was sent there to begin with. *El Dorado* continued waiting, until it was time for him to come out of hiding, a last despising act at *conquistadors*.

During merely two centuries of self-rule the United States providentially became the beacon in the sky, drawing the Statue of Liberty's minions, migrant flocks, as a new world paradise for those lesser born; although some would charge, "the great replacement" of one race by others, whether rightly or wrongly only history would tell, as there were sour grapes in the term, as if self-applied by those being replaced. They were blowing off steam, taking *"le grand remplacement"* theory, a self-pitying ideology of racial comeuppance from humiliated vestigial racists, to help explain the inescapable browning of America.

In youth, ideas of unity, brotherhood, collectivism are attractive, until growing up and seeing the world, we realized what malcontents most people were, impossible to get along with each other, let alone the world. Liberals meant well, but for the life of them could not govern. Conservatives rarely meant well, but for the death of them would not govern. The left's assumption that the generational/ comfort divide was always in their favor was refuted by people growing older, paying taxes, and assuming more fixed ways. For some, life was about a bending of rules, however, for radicals, breaking them was the norm.

Cultures did their bigoted best to protect themselves from being blended out of existence by outsiders. After exterminating Indians, white Americans did their worst to conserve their ways from the onslaught of foreign and domestic minorities, while those same communities were encouraged, congratulated for preserving their distinct heritages intact and free from any dilutive dominance of the white host culture. The newly arrived kept speaking Spanish, Cantonese, Swahili, to preserve their ethnic identities, while everyone else here before them, had to adjust their practices to theirs, as a new stalemate of inclusion.

They could not stay at no cost to themselves, any more than trespassers had a right to stay at your home for free. There had to be proper and accepted entry; as one politician said, they had to ring the doorbell before they let themselves in. But according to them, they had more than paid their price of admission, suffering horrendous trials and tribulations, just to cross the river. The ends clearly justified the means.

There had to be an entrance fee for acceptance, a price high enough to discourage some, while not high enough to prevent others from spilling over the porous border, as immigration was good for America.

As the themes of the story are there is no justice, accountability, but revenge, and those who have been lorded over want to lord it over others, the oppressed as oppressors, an age-old problem; the importance of the hero's journey to the final objective, and tests of strength along the way, were in keeping with the epic songs of mythic, valiant exploits; events flying within scenes of passionate love, struggle, triumph. Two characters in search of an author, dashing toward a destined rebirth, soulful redemptions, heard the same calls as endless others to reclaim birthrights, human rights, on their voyages to uncertain freedom:

> Holly came from Miami, F.L.A.
> Hitch-hiked her way across the U.S.A.
> Plucked her eyebrows on the way
> Shaved her legs and then he was a she

> She says, "Hey, babe
> Take a walk on the wild side"
> Said, "Hey, honey
> Take a walk on the wild side" (Lou Reed, "Walk on the Wild Side," 1973)

Here were the annals of modern ethnic, culture, race, sex and gender strife, witnessed first-hand by one who would never be afraid of newfound ways, despite missing the old, for if there could exist even the least faint semblance, shadow, of legitimacy, to the claim of a greater order of things in the world, and the universe, it was hopelessly dashed by the real events that unfolded, unmasking the cynical pretense. Chapters 1 through 11, would show the normal as incredible, as in exaggerated comedy, tragedy, farce, satire; chapters 12 through 22, the incredible as normal, as in surrealist artists, Kafka, Bunuel, Beckett.

*At the Millennium: Paradise Crossed* would be a fabrication of daring dreams of the truths of our times told passionately, as well as objectively, while things were still fresh in recollection; and interpreted in various ways, depending on who would write the most compelling, and quickest to the market, version. The stakes were never higher for leaving behind a credible chronology, of folly crossed with brilliance; there was always the chance, that someone out there would write a similar book, but not likely for now; if ever a, *tour de force*, let it be mine; considering it started as a detective story, the mystery continues.

But it is now the mystery of existence, a philosophical existentialism best expressed by literary means, which would hopefully document our having been here, extending our claims for living, and not being forgotten to the spill of time, as Ferdinand Columbus' lost biography of his famous father, Christopher, the Admiral of the Ocean Sea, only known through a subsequent translation. *En algunos paises, Colon paso por moto*, was a saying meant to demean the Caribbean countries, where motorcycles are heavily relied upon by the poor. In any case he never stayed anywhere long, vanishing into the stuff of rumors.

As even Columbus' remains were lost after burial it was no wonder that each of his acts was disparaged by time, and historical revisionists, to where he had nothing to do with discovering this, *Mundus novus*. And as ideas and thoughts constantly developed, so did the nomenclature for identified scientific types. While the term, Indian, for denizens of the New World, is now derided for being based on Columbus' limited and naive geographical knowledge, the term, American, is still extolled while being based, quite appropriately and ironically, on Italian Amerigo Vespucci's sham claim of discovering a new continent:

> ...and it is lawful to call it a new world, because none of these countries
> were known to our ancestors and to all who hear about them they will

be entirely new... more populous than our Europe, or Asia, or Africa...
(Amerigo Vespucci, Mundus novus Letter, 1503)

Lilly Lawrence was not her real name, changing it after arriving in the United States, in the mid-1980s; having been raised in unimaginable poverty, in the sprawling *camp de refugies,* against a steep, oily hill full of rubble, garbage and dry grazed grass, by a polluting highway, on the outskirts of war torn Beirut, Lebanon; relying on two dreams to sustain her in a grim, daily struggle to provide for herself, surviving unspeakable bodily abuse: one, to immigrate to the United States of America, two, to become a woman.

As an embryo, the essence that would soon become L'il Lay L'or Ence dreamed of its prenatal habitat and how his body felt in the discomfort of his liquid nest: flowing magic potion fulfilling his every pore and desire with displeasure and bother, in a shared vision of eternal transgender confusion and conflict with his mother; at times, tremors of a pre-genitalia were felt far away within the womb's medium that was his infinite universe of muffled sense; far off rhythms of the earth's eternal movement harmonized into his own unrecognized sexual sense, as well as size, weight, physical development of daily erection. At some point, however, a distinct expression of all these new conditions and feelings was manifested, in a surprise outcome of turmoil upon the fetus, perhaps during early gestation, with the eruption of his sex organs. An inchoate Lilly was by this time busting to escape, as if stuck within L'il Lay L'or Ence's lately unbearably itchy skin, waiting to molt it as a snake does before resuming the next stage of its life.

The sleep years of early consciousness, remembrance, recognition and infancy were an immediate self-identity with a female sex rather than his own. His devoted mother, realizing there were already gender issues occurring, thought her son had inherited her softer looks, buying him a pair of pink baby sandals as his first footwear, with which he used to prance throughout the house, and later in early childhood up and down the stairs to hear their loud flapping noise; even giving him a nickname, L'illy. Lying supine on the bed, his earliest recollections were of his father dressing up, in front of the mirror, never using a razor; getting ready to head over to the mosque, to be of service to the religious community. He was an absent father much of the time, and L'il Lay L'or Ence learned to take care of himself, without anyone. By age four he understood that his birth sex was not the gender he was comfortable with, dressing up in his mother's baggy *burqa* whenever he could, despite his father mistreating him with slaps and shoves.

But these were external manifestations of inner impulses beyond anybody's control, even L'il Lay L'or Ence's. He felt imprisoned in a body that was not his, and perhaps it was a weird confusion of birth he was a victim of, as somewhere along the line, an anatomy he should have entered, was at a last moment switched with one of its opposite sexes. As his female soul had been following its impulse to acquire a female host, before a final approach, God, fate, chance or luck had shortchanged, tricked him; for what punishment only, they knew. But for whatever the reason, his soul's guiding authority placed a female soul inside a muscular male body, so for all the alterations the heart demanded, the body still rebelled.

L'il Lay L'or Ence was raped from the time he was only twelve, an age at which he did not yet conceive the word *violer*, on the dirt floor of a back room of his family's corrugated sheet metal and cinder block *cabane*. It was a family member, his uncle, Muhammad, his father's older brother, living down the hill. Afterwards, other relatives and family friends paid him visits, as easy prey, and he was taken by unseen predators closest to him. Initially astonished, protesting that no one came to his aid during these sexual assaults, he gradually embraced silence, and grew to accept, with weary resignation, these wild bouts of brutality. Then as time passed, men he did not know, sometimes women, orgiastic strangers, imposed themselves upon him, with foul breathed threats of secrecy, and physical harm if the truth were known; and he had two dreams that raised him up, preserved a semblance of normalcy, despite long term hell in his matriarchal residence: one, to immigrate to the United States of America, two, to become a woman.

L'il Lay planned his future every day, waiting in the chilly, exhaust laced dawn for the *microbus* to take him to school. Fluent in French, beginning in English, he would save every bit of money scrounged up, and as soon as he graduated, dress as a girl, paying cruel *hashish* merchants to smuggle him into Israel, Egypt, then North Africa, France, Canada, and finally, that new land of milk and honey. If the cash ran low, he would prostitute himself to get there; what alternative was there? As his nickname was always L'illy, and as he was fair skinned, he invented a British sounding surname, assuming a new persona, as Ms. Lilly Lawrence, honoring Lawrence of Arabia, his favorite big screen movie character, with whose blatant queerness he identified. In his heart of hearts, he idealized Lilly to be his real self, longing to be freed. When he got to the U.S., he would find the right surgeon, to live his dream to become a woman. This quest was elemental, as if only its obtainment would rescue his soul from this eternal wonderment.

Masculine in appearance, well-endowed, feminine in manner, a bit soft in his stride, eyes averted from the world, and after brief contact quickly turned away; at five L'il Lay's father, hailing from an austere, back country Shi'ite clan, was decapitated (taking a despised enemy's head off was the ultimate act of ownership, over a slaughtered essence in perpetuity), before his very eyes, by the *Phalanges Libanaises* militia, backed by Israeli commandos, in a bloody raid; his devout Sunni Palestinian mother thereafter raising him; strict and unrelenting, reviling the United States of America, Americans, the State of Israel, Jews and Christians, in that order, providing rigid moral guidance to protect him from new influences, contemporary fashions and Western thought, forever reproving of L'il Lay's budding adolescence; and though not ever kind or loving, and doing absolutely nothing to prevent, mitigate his carnal torments at the hands of others, perfecting him in the same Islamic faith through which her own life of self-denial, acceptance and obedience had been formed. At thirteen, dutiful L'il Lay still attended public prayers, although he was no longer chaste, and had not been a virgin for well over a year. During performances of the *Salah*, it was difficult for him to keep his eyes straight ahead, and his mind focused on the payer, as he continually anticipated the appearance of angels interceding on his behalf, before the heavens; he hesitantly asked the imam if he could denounce misdeeds committed upon him by others; to which the unyielding imam replied, "No my child, Allah knows to forgive them; perhaps you shall also find grace to do so." He took deep breaths and asked if it were at all possible, he could somehow be a girl trapped inside his boy's body, to which the dry holy man replied, "No my child, Allah created you as you are." Later, pondering why, if Allah was so good, there was still so much suffering in the world, including his own, praying for divine assistance in his life of bitter travail, he wondered if Allah had abandoned him.

Upon turning fifteen, recognizing his hidden flair for art and humor, L'il Lay secretly sketched cartoons satirizing famous, popular, political authority figures. He joined the school newspaper, whose mission, as with most journalistic endeavors steeped in youthful altruism, despite its theistic underpinnings, was unmasking hypocrisy, bringing truth to light. To whatever extent liberal Muslim and Western opinions dared illustration, such were readily conveyed in the limited printings of this beacon in the dark. Once, he dared pen a drawing lampooning religious leaders of the two predominant Islamic sects, for equating homosexuality with bestiality, under *sharia*. Under long-winded blurbs condemning unnatural desires, appetites and lusts, appeared the crouched, bent figures of the imam, demon horns popping out of his head, and the mullah, devil's tail protruding out from under religious robes, lewd knowing smirks on fat faces, pitchforks in hand, about to proceed to a *boite* for an evening of live sex shows. Threatened with extreme physical and spiritual despair, L'il Lay chose the path of protest, free expression, and for such brave act was condemned to a public flogging under the severe anti blasphemy laws of his father's sect, claiming authority over the infraction, due to L'il Lay's Shi'ite heritage; L'il Lay's consolation being that the bitter *fatwa* could have been much more severe, possibly a death sentence, had it not been for that religious court's recognition of his father's heroic martyrdom, at the hands of non-believers. Graciously thanking the mullahs for their great mercy, in his father's name, L'il Lay received twenty wicked lashes from a gruesome split leather strap: almost expiring, in agony, from the shock, and trauma. Afterwards the clerics praised L'il Lay's bravery, inviting him to continue secondary studies at the Shi'ite *madrasa*.

During all this period, despite such mistreatment, with a diligent attendance at the *madrasa*, he did his best to keep up with his studies, which had been thoroughly infiltrated by revolutionary principles; so despite knowing better he became completely convinced by the pervasive anti-American rhetoric then, which was something like this: Realizing the strategic importance of the Saudi Arabian oil fields on the eve of WWII the United States did its best to suck up to the House of Saud, as it has continued to do, to this day; placing the Saudis in the same reviled category, as the United States of America, Americans, the State of Israel, Jews and Christians, in that order, according to his mother. And this was notable, as the Saudis ran the *madrasas* with their endless money, so they were playing both sides it was obvious; on the one hand, standing as the "Custodian of the Two Holy Mosques," great defender of the faith; on the other, cozying up to those same sworn enemies, on the international stage of oil exports, economic development, banking and wealth management. How could the Saudis be training him to detest, hold contemptible, the very same infidels they were in bed with? The only answer he had to such a mystery was to go there to see for himself whether what his religious hosts said was truthful, or to the contrary, a lie to keep him humble, loyal and obedient. With all their money in secret Swiss bank accounts, and he without a penny to his name, there was no semblance of a level playing field, the same rules for all.

Turning seventeen, fear mixed in his blood, as he went out less in public, swallowed up in black *burqa*, covering him from head to toe, falling loosely, comfortably, over the painful, oozing scars still healing across his ripped up back. The armor-like *burqa* provided dual protection, disguising his identity in the marketplace from zealots seeking additional, divinely inspired, penalties for his evolving, radical social views, and effeminate nature; and saving him from beatings, and sexual abuse, at home, as his habitual defilers usually had no interest in women and were put off by the new habiliments. So, the *burqa* made him untouchable, reminding all believers, in the name of Muhammad, that a woman's chastity belonged to her husband and no one else; but if only men and women obeyed the True Prophet. After the special procedures that changed his sex from male to female, when the scalpel cuts were finally on their way to healing, Lilly awoke one morning, and gazing upon her new image, in the full-length vanity mirror, felt something she had never experienced, true happiness and fulfillment. "I look like a babe," she repeated to herself, over again, smoothing curvy gams, hips, abdomen, breasts, shoulders, arms. "I am a babe."

# 3. *MUNDUS ANTIQUUS*

a. *Una Guerrilla Perpetua*

> FAUSTUS. Had I as many souls as there be stars,
> I'd give them all for Mephistophilis.
> (Christopher Marlowe, *The Tragicall History of D. Faustus*, 1604)

The Mexican *coyotes* were in cahoots with the Colombian *FART (Fuerzas Armadas Revolucionarias de Tolima – Ejército del Pueblo)*, who controlled the remote mountain passes, and jungle riverside staging camps, from Colombia into Panama. In exchange for USD $10,000, the *coyotes* offered transit through Central America and Mexico, to a safe city inside the U.S. border. Several of Willamina's *barrio bajo* neighbors referred her to a shady character in Bogotá, a police chief gone rogue, become a mastermind criminal recruiter, relegated to a scorching, suffocating concrete basement office, who arranged passage with the cartels. There was no written agreement, or evidence of debt, as *los Chingones* knew full well where Willamina's family lived and would always track them down, to retaliate for any non-payment of the obligation. Within its underlying illegalities, ever-present brutalities, the whole process operated as a streamlined, efficient business. Pledging her life savings Willamina acceded to non-negotiable terms.

Commencing her journey to the promised land one auspicious evening by depositing an initial $1,000 with this *demonio* in a cavern she knew she had sold her soul. Outfitted in big, black, military fatigues, lace boots, she was certainly a menacing sight to behold. Behind a bluster, and displayed decisiveness, however, lay an apprehension at entering a bargain *con narcotraficantes y la guerrilla*. Convinced this deal was with *Satanas,* she nevertheless, believed that things would turn out for the best, needing to, out of desperation, and whatever waited for her across the border could never possibly be as horrible as the sordid existence she now rejected. She recited an *Ave Maria* no one heard, as it ebbed into silence:

> "*Dios te salve, María.*
> *Llena eres de gracia:*
> *El Señor es contigo.*
> *Bendita tu eres entre todas las mujeres.*
> *Y bendito es el fruto de tu vientre: Jesús.*" (*Ave Maria*)

Prepared to pay another $2,500, the total down payment demanded (the $6,500 balance, with a usurious interest due over five years), upon her boarding an unheated, unairconditioned, tacky gold, red and blue coach, white fringe draped atop cracked windows; winding across the *cordilleras central y occidental*, steamy, interminable valley in between; to a clandestine rendezvous site, a primitive, lawless hamlet on the fast running Rio Atrato, El Choco, 20 klicks north of the rainy city of Quibdo, the start of holy hell.

The point of no return: a strategic river inlet once occupied by a sixteenth century *conquistador* fortress guarding the desolate lowland nether reaches of their grand *Nuevo Reino de Granada*, now smoldering, secret, out of the way, one way destination, seemingly forgotten by civilization, littered with the refuse of disgruntled populations on the move, tossed clothes, sneakers, used diapers, junk food bags, portable TV's, boom boxes. With nine nervous *emigrantes,* she was escorted to an armed, militarized river boat docked on the muddy wharf, *FART* jungle-fighters in camouflaged fatigues, loam, light green face war paint, huddled round the armored craft, guarding the surrounding riverbank, rising to a cluster of moldy dilapidated shacks. His determined face hidden by broad, red *panuelo*, one male *guerrillero*, clearly in command of the squadron's unfriendly *camaradas,* interviewed each passenger in the boarding group, inspecting Willamina up and down, left and right, in her strange male attire, then squarely face to face.

"Prior to handing over the final money, make sure that you are truly decided this is what you want," he cautioned. "It's a difficult journey; once proceeding over the gang plank, there is no turning back. You will all be directly under my command." For Willamina the admonitions merited no more deliberation, not having come all this way to return to a Bogotá *barrio bajo*, handing over the cash, taking her place on the open pontoon deck with fidgety co-emigrants, there being no turning back for her, now or ever.

The entire *Choco* jungle was yellow fever ridden, malaria mixed in for good measure, the mechanized rubber vessel making cautious headway down debris strewn, swirling *corrientes*; past small settlements of high, thatched roofed, open-air, wooden dwellings, hanging weaved hammocks, straw baskets, bows and arrows, smoked game; rickety canoe docks now emerging from impenetrable swaths of vegetation; and naked, copper toned Indian families, with loose, straight, waist length, machete shorn ebony locks, roasting *papas*, *yuca*, *tamales* over smoky *fuegos*, staring back mutely. Except for using modern yarns in their brightly colored textiles, loincloths, metal tools, an outboard motor, they existed as they always had, before the Spanish *exploradores* set eyes upon them. *El Comandante*, ever vigilant, keeping sharp lookout for enemy attacks from shore, patrol boats on river, helicopters overhead, was trying to ignore Willamina. Hellishly hot, humid, Willamina, perspiring in buckets, finally changed out of uniform into an ensemble more suited to the tropics, a fitted blouse, shorts, and sandals, revealing much more of her glorious form, at some point becoming aware of *El Comandante's* eyes on her curving bends instead of the river bends, up ahead. He had removed the broad, red handkerchief covering his face, confirmed as bony, stern, committed to a cause. Inured to unknown men checking her out, fantasizing knowing her, the only quid pro quo being money, she wondered if there could be any advantage obtained by sleeping with *El Comandante*. During the rest stops they made small talk, and he inquired about her destination. She cautiously confided in him, describing her childhood of relentless *violacion y prostitucion*, of *Papi* scarring her neck with toxic marks, and how ever since she was a little girl, she had the notion of within herself being male, her own American Dream being to make it to California for a sex-change operation, hearing there were skilled and caring surgeons there. She would not heed the Roman Catholic Church, or anybody else censuring her own thoughts, perhaps finding success as a male body builder on Muscle Beach, Venice; *El Comandante's* love-struck reaction being silence, his captivated eyes melting deeply, into hers; it mattering nary to him if she was a lowly, crazy whore at the cusp of rejecting femaleness, as long as they desired, respected, remained true to, not only each other, but their relentless complicity.

After four days of floating down that swamp edged *rio*, its minor untraceable tributaries, they docked at a fortified encampment only a few klicks from the Panamanian border, well hidden in a green hollow, against densely covered hills, and impossible to spot from the air. Here they regrouped, waiting for the proper moment to attempt the border crossing. During the ten-day delay deep in the tropical rain forest Willamina and *El Comandante* began a love affair, the oddity of her envisioning herself a man, never upsetting his mind; *El Comandante* desiring Willamina as the sensual, attractive woman she physically was then; whatever weighed on her mind, whatever her unchangeable fixations, being something else, he, loving her just the same. For Willamina's part, there was also romantic interest, but with less ardor than *El Comandante's* lust. She was still attracted to men, and not that much to women. That granted, whatever physical passion they shared was for her, more coldly, a means to an end, than it was for him. He understood the kind of life she led, and would probably continue leading, yet he could not prevent falling in love with her; offering to pay off the *coyotes* if, when the time came, she acceded to whatever was asked, perhaps even before reaching the U.S; she, accepting his cryptic offer, recognizing, vaguely, yet still unable to process, that she was substituting one deal, for another, with *el demonio*; he, settling her obligations, paying what the *coyotes* were due, using surplus funds from the armed movement; she, so relieved to immigrate to the United States debt free, perhaps over time even establishing good credit.

When Willamina and *El Comandante* said their goodbyes, he reminded her of his absolute trust in her, and of her special connection to him. When the time came, he would ask her to undertake an important mission for him, personally, as well as for the class struggle of the peasants and workers of the world. Affirming her complicity, Willamina could never have anticipated that spreading revolution regionally, included hiring out *el Ejército del Pueblo* as contract kidnappers, hit men. She crossed into Panama on a dark, moonless night, her heart racing wildly, one lonely spirit in a group of nervous *indocumentados* tracing their hard destinies along a silent mountain path, through the border wilderness of the untamed Darién Gap. She wondered when she would hear from *El Comandante* again. It was not to be so long a pause. After what seemed an interminable series of overcrowded bus, van, car rides, she finally made it to Guatemala in ten days. The composition of her travel group changed at every stop, but there was a fourteen-year-old boy with a focused no-nonsense expression accompanying her from the time they had departed El Choco. Driving into Guatemala City, in the morning twilight, the boy, sat with Willamina, quietly, but firmly, communicating instructions from *El Comandante*: to proceed to a reserved room at the downtown Hotel Camino Real, clean herself up, order some room service, rest a few hours, and put on, such elegant array, and fine makeup, to be found there; thus dolled up, discreetly descend at 1:30 in the morning to *los cuartos de desmadre* of a prominent opposition politician, as a call girl; the target, at the capital city for his congressional party's annual convention, anticipating some rowdy escapades; *los narcotraficantes,* wanting the congressman knocked off for his stubborn anti-drug policies, called in the *FART* to do the job; Willamina was to leave a hotel suite door unlocked for two Colombian assassins to let themselves in, gun down a contrary Guatemalan politico with silencer equipped automatic weapons.

After considerable time primping, scrutinizing herself, up and down, left and right in full-length vanity mirror, the realization that she was gorgeous in tight-fitting dress, thin high heels, dawned on a shapely Willimina. She was grown up, no longer an adolescent, heavily made-up visage, unrecognizable for its utter beauty, poise and femininity. As a Colombian stunner, she was confident in her possession of that magic attraction, a certain sensuality most men could not resist. Knowing how to use female charms to her advantage, she was confident in her abilities to carry out this scheme. Sure enough, when that horny dupe opened the heavily secured door to his room, beholding her bare body's splendor under a soft pink lamplight, she was irresistible; he was smitten. Her eyes adjusting to sudden glare, she was also taken aback by what she regarded. It was a priest, wearing white collar, but minus black pants or underwear; shocked, the only words she could fathom were, *"Padre!* They never said you were *un sacerdote,* only *un politico." "Mi hija, soy cura, congresista y más que nada, un gran hombre,"* the proud stud retorted. He had been drinking all night, quipping, *"Perdóneme, pero pecar con una mujer tan fina, y tan bella como usted, no puede ser pecado.* Are all *Bogotánas* as fascinating?"* charming, flirtatious, inviting her to lunch tomorrow, offering to indulge her every whim with the finest *couture.* Throughout prohibited, uninhibited sex she cynically noted that for $6,500 owed it was the most expensive trick of her life; she was proudly moving up in the working girl ranks, servicing ecclesiastical, as well as secular, elites. But what possible aims, revolutionary or other, would be achieved by rubbing out her dynamic *Padre Juan*? And did he have to be *un fraile catolico*? It was one thing, to exchange sex for freedom from dastardly *coyotes,* but she was not proud of setting up this monsignor for murder. After tonight's job, she would be finished with these evil trysts. Malicious, hired thugs stalked stealthily, proficiently, into dark, silent chambers, just as the mark drifted off to dreams. Suddenly awakened, vaguely realizing treachery was transpiring, their quarry, blinking at Willamina, damning such duplicity before God, desperately crying out, *"Puta; me la jugaste!"* The execution carried out, an efficient four bullets fired, the killers hustled Willamina out of the hotel, taking her to an elegant suburban safe house, where she showered his crusty blood from her used body, glad it was over; whispering a *Padre Nuestro,* which no one seemed to hear:

*"Perdona nuestras ofensas,*
*como también nosotros perdonamos a los que nos ofenden.*

*No nos dejes caer en tentación y libéranos del mal.*
*Amen.*" (*Padre Nuestro*)

Convincing herself *there had been no choice, that she needed to survive and continue*, she drifted off to a fitful rest. In the very early morning, the blank-faced boy, a calming goat, joined her in bed, asking if everything had gone according to plan. She nodded yes, silently turning over and going back to sleep.

For the next hit Willamina donned heavy, dark duds, becoming scarily convincing as a cruel, despoiling Willi. As far as contracts were concerned, shehe took no prisoners. It was strange how, upon throwing on male gear, anger normally held, below the boiling point, deep in her bones, exploded to the surface; inexorably manifesting itself as an indulgent Mr. Hyde/ Willi, shehe always at herhis worst, the world a two-dimensional marked entanglement; sweltering, swarming, idiosyncratic humanity, heaped ants at the table's end, nowhere left to turn; shehe not realizing that self-adulation in full-length mirror, baring enameled girly teeth in silent growl, firmly grasping revolver across bullet strapped bosom, in a defiant *Zapata* posture, actually framed herhim in ridicule; a *bandido* light. In the conspiracy scheme, hard to follow, given the complexity of the situation, shehe was to lure a senior officer, the Chief of Staff of the National Army of Guatemala, and his mistress, who happened to be his cross-dressed *joto* adjutant, for a night out on the town, get them liquored-up, coked, teased; arrange for a compromising scene of their outrageous, romping, queer, behavior to be secretly videotaped, for blackmail, prior to a *coup de grace*.

But from the outset, nothing went according to plan, the general, as a rule, more intrigued by *droogs* in drag than *ptitsas* in vests, polished black army boots, however, curiously enthralled by Willi's disguised allurement, exotic, manly girl complementing his adjutant partner girly man; observing subtle sexuality in a scowling neurotic obsessed with herhimself, swallowed up by absurdly voluminous jump suit; the cross dressed *ayudante companero*, inexplicably, as well, mesmerized to the marrow, idealizing herhim as a core male, accessorizing his own superficial, effete, sartorial female; Willi suggesting they head to the Hotel Camino Real, touting triumphant suites for twisted trios. Under official police escort to their tryst, within roomy armored limousine, the general, most depraved, degenerate admixture of European, Middle Eastern, Mesoamerican, genetic waste, The U.S. Military Academy at West Point Class of 1966 (sponsored by the U.S. Senator from the Sunshine State of Florida, after consulting with the U.S. State Department, DIA, FBI, DEA), wickedly incapacitated Willi with ether-infused towel; then right before his sensitive *ayudante companero's* eyes, forced himself on a passed out shehe, in a disgusting show of brute force, if not complete, poor taste. Whether this was a crass affront to the revolted subordinate, or perhaps an egotistical oversight on the lascivious superior's part, nevertheless, it was interpreted by the junior as a complete lack of respect, and military protocol, for their unconscious guest. Whereupon the *ayudante companero*, crossed scion of one of the most traditional, distinguished, land-owning families in *Guate*, the U.S. Military Academy at West Point Class of 1976, proclaiming proudly, "Perhaps I am gay, but I've got game," proceeded to pound the crass, prior class, fellow West Pointer's smirking face bloody; anticipating such for years; not decided upon being promoted as an *ayudante*, but definitely by the time of becoming his *ayudante companero*; quietly, meticulously, patiently plotting each moment of suitable payback, for the animal effrontery of his young sister's defilement a decade ago, at the hands of the same sociopath of a ranking officer; seeming over time politely assuaged by dissembled forgiveness of a subordinate to superior, pretending to play a better man, dissimulating letting bygones be bygones; so, setting him up, now striking forcefully, suddenly, swiftly with bare, bruising fists, proving again the violent maxim "revenge is a dish best served cold," more satisfying if not exacted immediately. *El Joto* murdered the general for the sake of protecting all co-cross dressers, recognizing that though of similar kind, Willi was of a higher degree of psychological distress, than himself; a cold-blooded, pro assassin trans-man, assigned to dispatch both, one down. And where was the hook for such an outcome, except perhaps herhis' distracting allure? Surprisingly, once Willi came to herhis senses, shock, panic, did not overtake either of them, shehe remaining perhaps unnaturally calm, for one whose life had been nearly snuffed out by the poisoned rag; and the adjutant, as cool as any assistant who would dare go so far as to summarily execute his commanding officer. All too soon, Willi realized the job was only half done; shehe would still need to honor the contract. It was too bad, shehe was starting to like the proper *reina*, even though shehe felt no affinity to him with respect to their similar, contrary, underground lifestyles, cross dressed expressions, bi-gender tendencies. *What a shame*, shehe was thinking, when in an instant and for whatever reason remaining unexplained, unknown, the impulsive *ayudante companero* was at herhis throat, dangerous, overpowering hands encircling like a python round a smooth tree; now it was clear there would be no hesitation by either. Willi struggled for breath, lunged in all directions, trying to loosen the *reina's* lock tight grip, when finally, almost out of life force, shehe aimed herhis head as a battering ram, butting the *ayudante companero*'s pretty face, knocking him out immediately. As for the rest of it, despite reestablishing advantage, for some reason, this one time, Willi did not follow through; furtively breaking the first of professional commandments: thou shalt not abrogate contracts with those more powerful than you are; the *ayudante companero* unilaterally spared, ultimately hightailing it to El Salvador, a political refugee, hopefully keeping distant, anonymous, quiet. Whether in the long run this proved the wisest of stratagems, only destiny would demonstrate. But shehe always repaid like for like and kindness for kindness, especially with someone as thoughtful enough to have saved herhis life, the *ayudante companero* having most certainly done that, despite also later, shockingly, surprise attacking. Spilling whiskey on car seats, tricking the police escort that the general and his adjutant had too much to drink, were drugged, Willi got out at the hotel, politely asked that they be taken home, tucked into bed.

Convincing herself *there had been no choice, that she needed to survive and continue*, she drifted off to a fitful rest. In the very early morning, the blank-faced boy, a calming goat, joined her in bed, asking if things went according to plan. She nodded, sure, silently, both hopping the first *microbus* out of town.

From *Guate* Willamina traveled to *Chiapas,* to train in *guerrilla* warfare, for the first time congregating with revolutionists in great numbers. Though welcomed by most Mexican Marxists she met, especially for her flawless interpretation of surplus labor value, when called upon to read passages of *Das Kapital,* during educational seminars, didactic exercises, polemical discussions, still it was always questioned if she could ever be a true believer of their own version of the ideology without first being a card-carrying Communist. The recruiters were so enticing, offering financial assistance, as saviors would, assuming their minions' monetary, moral, societal indebtedness, so that at the crucial moment of being ordered to commit to the mission, those so bound would unquestioningly say, yes. During rigorous psychological evaluations, the Underground People's Army, thriving on international conflict, utilizing images of hurt children to make their brainwashing case, as champions of the meek, disclosed their goal of recruiting unattached loners adrift, holding onto grudges with *El Viejo Mundo*. She swore one thousand times, on Chairman Mao's *Little Red Book,* on every blessed dogma, sacred text invoked in Communist lore, that she would willingly lay down her life as a condition for admission to a socialist paradise. Then during tough, physical training, she withstood endless hikes, endurance runs, through steep mountain terrain, swamps and beaches, building up muscle tone with intense strengthening repetitions of isometrics and weights; also learning self-defense, and lethal techniques for close, quiet, deadly combat, transforming into expert killing machine, fervently, and with assurance of eternal reward, in exchange for her earthly, person. But with improvements in her body came a newfound pride in it, and a reluctance, to part with it, especially for the sake of abstract ideologies, or isms, of individuals or mass movements, even if her cowardly, prudent stalling could never be safely shared with her handlers, or *El Comandante,* himself.

She would seek paradise in a meaningful life of expression, instead of the doom she had been stuck in:

I have always imagined that Paradise will be a kind of library.
(Jorge Luis Borges, 1899 – 1986)

Arriving in Nogales, Sonora three months later, the landscape dry, brown, so different from those rainy, green memories of her Gran Colombia; part of a larger group, all waiting for the same thing, a passage to freedom; they headed to a ranch, outside a town, abutting a long, empty stretch of the U.S. border, to rest up, and receive instructions on smuggling illegal drugs, as final obligation to *coyote* bloodsuckers.

As with today's undocumented aliens, many of the original explorers and settlers of the new discoveries were escaped (and transported) criminals, destitute workers, homeless, desperate wanderers, soldiers of fortune, itinerant Jews, heretics; these days, this entire human smuggling enterprise tightly bossed by a nameless lady, keeping her face hidden from them, aka *coyote,* human trafficker, in some illicit circles affectionately referred to as *la mas noble marquesa migratoria*, addressing no one in particular: "'Now, Voyager, sail thou forth, to seek and find.'" Her eloquence was shameless considering she often ferried innocent human beings to their deaths. Yet she truly meant the part about taking a chance on the future.

"Do you know why people migrate there? Do you know? Because there is no work here. There are no jobs," replied, Ana Pat. Mejia, 39, who had tried to make the trip with her kids, and her neighbor's son, but was deported, back to *Mexico*. "Of course, I am going, again. I must have a house. I do not have a place to live. If I desire to, or not, if *gringos* like it, or not, I am coming" claimed purposeful Voyager. The grim reality of those coming across was they were what they were, willing to do anything that had to be done to get over; a clandestine truth, obscuring the exemplary assumptions made by bright eyed progressives, that these were innocent victims; liberals most in their favor ignoring obvious criminality and other social class ills such as bad health, little education, no morality, marking them as undesirable.

Crossing the border at night they each had twenty kilos of brick cocaine on their backs, keeping a sharp eye out for the Border Patrol, and other rival gangs, intent on stealing their product. This was the shady pilgrimage of express arrivals at the shrine of infinite possibilities. Having been illegal immigrant drug mules, and accessories to political slayings in *Guate,* they broke volumes of laws of the United States, Mexico, and all the Banana Republics they passed through since departing the *Choco*; their impact had certainly been regional. Before dawn, their group arrived without incident at a prearranged spot in the Arizona desert, where the merchandise was delivered, and where vans met them for their final legs to Phoenix, Los Angeles or El Paso, and further points, if so engaged. They were dropped off on Sunset Boulevard, at a shopping center parking lot where expectant, dirt-poor, migrant laborers gathered as the sun rose, to be picked up for the day's dirtiest labor. Willamina's companion, calming goat, seasoned beyond the fourteen years he claimed at the journey's start, took leave to search for relatives in the San Fernando Valley, mentioning in passing, that she could be certain to hear from him again when the time came. Startled, she countered: "But I thought my debt was paid and I was released;" to which the hard-faced lad haughtily replied, "*El Comandante* does not consider this an obligation to be paid, canceled, or fulfilled, it binds you always. He knows you are committed to the cause, and will rely on you for the future*, pues, es una guerrilla perpetua.*" She now discerned that her deal with *el diablo* would be more binding, costly, than ever expected; cruelly never being released by those who had helped her get here. Despite these setbacks she felt great accomplishment, composure, standing alone in a cutting-edge city of a glorious country, a sublime, fair complexioned Hispanic, not knowing where to go, but certain the future was opening before her; having achieved her first big goal in life, of immigrating to the United States, a vast country where anything was possible, and she could remake herself as everyone else there did, following their dreams. In a true, mercenary fashion, she could always sell her body for sex on the streets to survive; for now, finding strange comfort in again wearing mannish, heavy, dark, baggy garb, mid-calf hobnail jackboots, awaiting to discover what would present itself, in a pending *Nuevo Mundo*.

# 3. MUNDUS ANTIQUUS

b. A Perpetual *Jihad*

> MEPH.Hell hath no limits, nor is circumscrib'd
> In one self place; for where we are is hell,
> And where hell is there must we ever be.
> (Christopher Marlowe, *The Tragicall History of D. Faustus*, 1604)

The *Phalanges Libanaises hashish* merchants were in cahoots with the *Hezbollah* (Party of God), who controlled the remote mountain passes and valley staging camps from Lebanon into Israel. In exchange for working as a prostitute in high end brothels, *en route*, the *Phalangistes* offered transit, first to Cairo, and then safe cities in North Africa, Europe and North America. Several of L'il Lay's *camp de refugies* neighbors referred him to a shady character in Beirut, a police chief gone rogue, become a mastermind criminal recruiter, relegated to a scorching, suffocating concrete basement office, who arranged passage with the smugglers. There was no written agreement, or evidence of any debt, as the militias knew full well where L'il Lay's family lived and would always track them down, to retaliate for any non-payment of this obligation. Within its underlying illegality ever-present brutality, the whole process operated as a streamlined, efficient business. Pledging his life and spirit, L'il Lay acceded to non-negotiable terms.

Commencing his journey to the promised land one auspicious evening, showing up at this demon's hot cavern with a packed suitcase, he knew he had sold his soul. Outfitted in baggy black *burqa,* utilizing a throaty falsetto, he was certainly a timid sight to behold. Behind his docile facade of anonymity lay the deeper apprehension at entering a bargain with drug traffickers and devoted *jihadists*. Convinced this deal was with *Shaytan,* he nevertheless, believed that things would turn out for the best, needing to, out of desperation, and whatever waited for him across the border could never possibly be as horrible as the sordid existence he now rejected. He whispered a Qur'anic prayer no one heard, as it ebbed to silence:

> "Our Lord! Perfect our light for us and forgive us our sins, for verily You
> have power over all things." (Quranic prayer)

Prepared to commit himself faithfully and completely to Islamic Truth, upon his boarding an unheated, unairconditioned, tacky gold, red and blue coach, white fringe draped atop cracked windows; winding across two frigid mountain ranges, arid, interminable valley in between, reconciled to whatever it took to flee Lebanon; to a clandestine rendezvous site, a primitive, lawless hamlet long known for Maronite traditions, 20 klicks south of the highland village of Jernavo, Eastern Sidon, the start of a holy dream.

The point of no return: a strategic mountain refuge once occupied by a twelfth century crusader fortress guarding the desolate alpine reaches of their gallant *Outremer,* now smoldering, secret, out of the way, one way destination, seemingly forgotten by civilization, littered with refuse of disgruntled populations on the move, tossed clothes, sneakers, used diapers, junk food bags, portable TV's, boom boxes. Along with nine other nervous *emigres* he was escorted to an armed military truck in a closely packed convoy, *Hezbollah* mountain-fighters in desert fatigues, sand, light green face war paint, huddled round heavily armored vehicles, guarding the surrounding clearing, rising to a cluster of old dilapidated shacks. Her determined face hidden by broad red handkerchief, one female revolutionary guard clearly in command of the squadron's morose Islamic warriors interviewed each passenger in the boarding line, inspecting L'il Lay up and down, left and right, in his strange female attire, then directly in hidden face. "Prior to handing over body and soul make sure that you are truly decided this is what you want," she cautioned. "It's a difficult journey; once proceeding with the recruit caravan, there is no turning back. You will all be directly under my command." For L'il Lay, such admonitions merited no further deliberations, not having come all this way to return to a Beirut *camp de refugies*, handing over *burqa* ladened suitcases, sitting on open cargo bed with fidgety co-emigrants, there being no turning back for him, now or ever.

The entire Lebanese/ Syrian border was sniper ridden, mortars mixed in for good measure, the motored column making cautious headway down debris strewn, swirling slopes; toward the southwest, weaving in and out through either country, as the route demanded, crossing porous, undefined and ever shifting no man's land; until the snow-capped mountains populated by towering cedars, promptly became dusty, brown hills spotted by gnarled shrubs; passing concrete settlements waking amidst impenetrable swaths of cultivated agricultural fields. And suddenly, reaching the Israeli frontier, the convoy came to a stop; the group resting a few hours before, later, under cover of night, proceeding to sneak across the border into the fertile valley; hoping there would be no land mines, or booby traps, set for them along the way. Evening descending, the Commander taking L'il Lay to one side, removing the broad red handkerchief, covering her face, revealing a bony, stern confirmation, committed to her cause, strongly suggested L'il Lay temporarily abandon voluminous *burqa* for Western dress, an ensemble more suited for the desert, loose tennis togs and sneakers, rather than formal, traditional robes, until making it safely to Egypt, in order to attract less attention to himself in Israel. Thanking the Commander for her concern, L'il Lay rejected the prompt outright, it being obvious that a black *burqa,* by facilitating fading into the shadows of the night, shielded its wearer from all threats and dangers along the border. L'il Lay would consider the Commander's request once in Israel. The Commander tolerated L'il Lay's eccentricities, respecting the Prophet's patience, as shown in the Qur'an, but promised to hold L'il Lay to his word upon reaching Israel. Notwithstanding L'il Lay's broad cloak of femininity, there was always an underlying masculine dimension to his presence, a certain obstinacy he could not contain, or long meditative pauses when he spoke. So far, despite a somewhat suspect, forced, breathy voice, L'il Lay had succeeded in pulling off a female impersonation, although there were moments during the convoy's rest stops when his colorful, raucous wind in the women's latrine, incredibly, gave the Commander pause to consider an unthinkable possibility. The party was met at the border by a silent, dour *Phalanges* gang member, and distrustful, inquisitive Israeli confederate, and led a short distance into the valley, to a waiting white tour van with the business name, Moshe's Israel Travel, painted on the doors. Hanging intertwined from the vehicle's rear-view mirror were an ancient-colored glass bead rosary with a tin Maronite cross, then a thick silver chain with a large Star of David, and due to Islam's restrictions on pictorial representations of God, or the prophet Mohammed, a large, round silver *Ayatul-kursi* pendant with Qur'anic verse, giving L'il Lay brief pause to ponder the mysterious workings of the world. Here he was, newly arrived in the modern democratic State of Israel: a Palestinian trans-woman, presenting as a religious Shi'ite refugee escaping her own country's religious, social and sexual predations, with the aid of globally organized Christian, Jewish, Muslim gangs. What could possibly be more out of the ordinary? he wondered, *envisioning the convocation of a unity of the spheres, losing track of the van's constant progress in monotonous, fertile countryside, becoming sleepy from steady motion. He dreamt of his mother; would he see her again?...*

"L'il Lay, wake up, it's time you changed into the clothes we agreed to." The Commander was shaking him brusquely, interrupting inner peace. "You said after arrival, you would change out of your *burqa.*"

"Thank you, for waking me; I said I would consider your advice, if needed," L'il Lay replied grumpily.

"I don't think you understand, this is not a request, it is an order" declared the Commander. "You have placed yourself under my command; I won't remind you again." She rested her hand on a Glock pistol, at the ready in hip holster, as if to emphasize the point. There was not much L'il Lay could say, he was truly dismayed. He plotted pleading for a bit more time for his display, to somehow find another angle, or come up with an excuse that could save him from discovery; but as he queried deeply, into her clear

Berber eyes, he decided, that would probably be a grave mistake. "Well, how could I possibly disrobe in a van full of gawkers?" he stated, such objection being quickly resolved when they parked on a quiet dirt road, behind fragrant, flowering orchard, deep in a settled valley *Kibbutz*; everyone getting off for a fifteen-minute rest stop, L'il Lay and the Commander remaining in their last seats. "Now, change," the Commander demanded; after a considerable hesitation, L'il Lay, removing the woven eyed hood to his costume, and glaring at the Commander with disdain. But what the Commander saw was a surprise for which nothing could have prepared her. Given L'il Lay's persistence in keeping covered, from head to toe, over the journey, he had unintentionally neglected his hygiene, grooming and appearance, and had consequently lost his carefully crafted, female looks. If the Commander harbored suspicions about the identity of the person concealed inside the *burqa,* she never imagined that the impostor, once revealed, would turn out so handsome, manly; a week's worth of heavy, dark beard stubble, dust encrusted face, matted, dirty hair, suddenly causing L'il Lay to look exceedingly virile, desirable, in the Commander's eyes, it being so apparent she wanted him; he, embarrassed at the intensity of the Commander's signals during the awkward moment of his unmasking. For L'il Lay's part, there was also romantic interest, but with less ardor than the Commander's lust. He was still attracted to women, and not that much to men. They stared at each other, for what seemed an eternity, in silence, until the Commander came back to her senses, reminding L'il Lay that he would still be held to the original terms of conveyance; pressing him to quickly clean up, shave, put on more sex appropriate, up-to-date wear, get back to being a man again, and fast, before the unaware co-passengers returned to the vehicle; once the sojourners rejoined, no one commenting on the new rider, a seemingly personable youth, accompanying the Commander in the last row. He appeared to be a nice young man, everybody relieved the menacing, *burqa* clad weirdo who had started on the trip, was gone, taking to smiling, and waving kindly at him, when they got on.

The remainder of their excursion was uneventful, due to the superb planning and execution of the inter-faith smuggling consortium; the van making its steady way across the true Promised Land, a recurring exchange of trippers of different tribes, races and nationalities welcomed, with some climbing aboard, others exiting, on what seemed scheduled connections of illegality and corruption running through the *Sabra* heartland. At the Egyptian line, L'il Lay, the Commander, and the two secretive guides, crossed uneventfully into Sinai, transferring to a waiting white tour van, with the business name, Samir's Egypt Travel, painted on the doors; continuing to Cairo where it was expected L'il Lay would work off certain obligations to those who had facilitated his flight to freedom. On the overnight stop before Cairo, the Commander silently visited L'il Lay's corner room, in the middle of the night, and they made awkward love; for although L'il Lay was very aroused, it was difficult for him to stop pretending being a woman, for long enough to get on with what he needed to do, for her. However, she was more than sufficiently desirous to take charge of the situation, guiding it forward, as it were; and following L'il Lay's strong, sensitive, performance, catching her breath, again thanked, complemented him, especially mentioning, his generous male attributes. She inquired why he pretended being a woman. He told her of relentless childhood abuse and sexual bondage and how ever since he was a little boy, he had the notion of within himself being female; his own American Dream being to make it to California, for sex-change surgery, for there were skilled and caring surgeons there. He would not heed Islamic imams, mullahs or anyone else criticizing his own desires, perhaps finding success as a big screen female action hero for a major studio; the Commander's love-struck reaction being silence, her captivated eyes melting fast into his; it mattering nary to her if L'il Lay was a lowly, crazy, punk at the cusp of rejecting maleness, as long as, they desired, respected, remained true to, not only each other, but their relentless complicity to a dream:

> My country is not longer only in Africa; we are now part of Europe, too.
> It is therefore natural for us to abandon our former ways and to adopt a
> new system adapted to our social conditions.
> (H.H. Isma'il Pasha, Khedive of Egypt, and Sudan, 1863 - 1879)

In Cairo, L'il Lay was brought to an immense, high walled compound, a palace built in the mid-1860s, during the misguided reign of H.H. Isma'il Pasha, with the short-lived wealth of the cotton trade boom, coercively acquired on the bent backs of slaves, serfs, forced laborers. Still elegant, but now physically decayed, the once proud residence, *Belle Epoque* fleshpot (and harem, a place reserved for women, and eunuchs, many captured in white slavery raids by Barbary Pirates, then serving royalty), fallen in virtue from its lofty origins of sacred purity, had been used for the last hundred years as a sophisticated house of assignation, of the highest (ill) repute; and was famous throughout the Arab world as the fashionable gathering spot and watering hole, for regional power brokers, *bon vivants* and rogues, looking for good times; discreetly serving prodigious lusts, appetites and desires of global sybarites, as well. Heshe was made to work here providing carnal pleasure under the terms of hisher arrangement. Upon arriving, the first thing that L'il Lay did was take a hot bath, rushing off to the beauty parlor, where after many hours of intense primping, manicuring, makeup applications, by attentive hair stylist, beautician, unabashedly fascinated with hisher transsexuality, heshe managed to reassert a dormant, sensual, feminine tendency. Though it was unquestionably out of desperate necessity, and as a matter of earning hisher passage, that heshe was bound to such a service, still as a matter of pride, heshe would become the most desirable of call girls in the cathouse, so help himher, Allah. Recalling from history, *that hisher's ruined, despoiled homeland had formerly been labeled Transjordan*; then it coming to himher, in a flash, that soon heshe would become a trans Palestinian; from henceforth taking up the moniker, Trans Jordan (TJ), it became hisher house alias, through which heshe would rise to a bawdy prominence within the society of certain epicurean cognoscenti. After two month of back breaking work, a stream of steady appointments, as TJ was getting into the swing of things, feeling comfortable at the bordello, a problem happened with one of the red-light establishment's most influential power patrons, an Egyptian congressman and aristocrat descended directly from H.H. Isma'il Pasha, who, in a vengeful and petty moment, full of extreme pride and self-loathing, later regretted, caused an unfortunate, and rather embarrassing scene; protesting that, because TJ had misrepresented himherself, as a woman, the love they shared was corrupt, tainted, and defiled the nobleman's character, soul, in Allah's, as well as his cronies,' eyes. That such an indiscreet voluptuary, hypocritically playing at moral exemplar, claimed weakly, that despite last night having had the most intense passion, fellowship, he had ever known, he had been deceived and misled, was at least insulting to TJ, and by all means preposterous; in feeling around down there this morning the profligate was shocked, horrified to discover, rather than a warm, flat, cushioned triangle, on which to rest a hand, extra muscular, and erect, equipment on TJ, where, considering the intimacy they had just shared, there should have been none. Truly until then not one of TJ's other callers seemed to mind, or had ever taken notice of, let alone offense at, this protruding particularity of hisher anatomy. Despite performing quite admirably overall, the seriousness of such a complaint was enough to jeopardize TJ's arrangement with the *Phalanges Libanaises*. For this crass insult and humiliation endured by the dignified statesman, the Old-World satisfaction he demanded was harsh, but fitting for an individual of such lowly status, as TJ; "Off with his genitals," being the resounding and outrageous sentence pronounced, by one accustomed to unconditional obedience, that shook the madam's office, in private wing. Within a suite of rooms set in a Gilded Age style, high arched walls, detailed, patterned wallpaper, barred windows for protection; engulfed by precious early photographs, antique daguerreotypes, of imperial ancestors who constructed the palace; the madam listened carefully, patiently, to the accuser's charges, in the end, acceding to all her first cousin's unscrupulous demands, before sending him home to unsuspecting society wife. TJ, summarily summoned to this office, was stunned by the allegations against himher, even more shocked by such an absurd barbarity as the apparent penalty being contemplated. Since arriving in Cairo TJ and the Commander had gone their separate ways; now TJ was surprised to find the Commander, in tan and black battle fatigues, sitting stiffly at madam's desk, coldly looking through himher: "When you shared your strange secret with me, in Israel, I politely looked the other way, on condition you complied with the duties of your contract. Recently, unexpectedly, the situation has changed; it appears, *un client tres important* is profoundly displeased by your unadvertised, well hung male stick; and requires retribution for your shameless duplicity." Was it worth offering any new prayers to Allah the merciful, the honest?

"The duplicity you accuse me of is the politician's," replied TJ, haughtily. "This sensualist *Pasha* has known all along, exactly what I was, from the moment we met, yet he stayed with me all night." Upon further reflection, perhaps sensing hisher vulnerability or danger, heshe backtracked, adding contritely: "But I promise to keep said family jewels under wraps from now on; no one else will experience them again." However, it was apparently too late for any appeasements, the matter beyond normal repair, or profound apologies, a cover up being demanded, as there never could be further question of effeminacy tainting this old blueblood's good name and reputation; the Commander regretfully explaining, she had done all she could on TJ 's behalf, a slandered lord adamant in his claim, threatening to enforce ancient rights though ruthless retainers; despite her impassioned entreaties to the contrary, there being sadly, no convincing him otherwise. Trying desperately to resolve the apparently hopeless situation, preserving a valued guest's continued favor, perhaps saving her lover from horrific mutilation, The Commander tried one last stratagem. Rather than compel hisher castration, would the honorable lord accept martyrdom, as undertaken by *Hezbollah,* as just recompense for the transgression? Perhaps, His Excellency would. Such an offered sacrifice would certainly be the creative and elegant solution, for affront delivered; the Commander bestowing fresh honors and glories on both injured and injuring parties, by compensating for the misunderstanding, renewing the vitality of a social order, bringing all sides closer through faith. TJ was equally bowled over by this alternative, the still healing scars down hisher back throbbed anew; this being beyond comprehension, demanding consideration for a possible appeal: "First, you threaten to cut off my junk, and now you compromise me into killing myself, as well as other innocents; all for the sake of this jilted prince. Is there justice in this sentence? How does it fit my crime if I have even committed one? It was only a silly evening's prank, that's all. Don't you see he wants me, but resents it being impossible?" But unfortunately, the outcome of this matter had already been decided, and agreed to by the Commander, on TJ 's behalf, and once such solution was accepted, there could be no possible redress instead. "I do not think you understand this was not a request, it is an order," declared the severe Commander. She rested her hand on her Glock pistol, still waiting in the hip holster, as if to emphasize the point. "You will be martyred in the name of Allah and die blessed, with distinction. You will dwell in paradise, with those who have offered themselves for the sake of holy war. We will train, equip you for a mission; you will bring pride, joy, wealth to your family, tribe and people." There was absolutely nothing more to do about the offending matter. TJ was on his own, in a situation getting out of control.

From Egypt L'il Lay traveled to Iran, to train in a *madrasa,* as a *mujahid,* for the first time congregating with Shi'ite *jihadists* in great numbers. Though welcomed by most Iranian militants he met, especially for his flawless Arabic, and scholarly interpretations, when called upon to read passages of the Qur'an, during public prayer rallies, didactic exercises, polemical discussions, still it was always questioned if he could ever be a true believer of their own version of the faith without first being a full-blood Persian. The recruiters were so enticing, offering financial assistance as saviors would, assuming their minions' monetary, moral, societal indebtedness, so that at the crucial moment of being ordered to commit to the mission those so bound would unquestioningly say, yes. During rigorous psychological evaluations the Islamic People's Army, thriving on international conflict, utilizing images of hurt children to make their brainwashing case as champions of the meek, disclosed their goal of recruiting unattached loners adrift, holding onto grudges with the Western world. He swore a thousand times in the Prophet Muhammad's name, on every sacred city, blessed shrine, invoked in the holy books, that he would willingly lay down his life as a condition for admission to paradise. Then during tough, physical training, he withstood the long hikes and endurance runs through steep mountain terrain, deserts and beaches, building up muscle tone with intense strengthening repetitions of isometrics and weights; also learning self-defense, lethal techniques for close, quiet, deadly combat, transforming into expert killing machine, fervently and with assurance of eternal reward in exchange for his earthly person. But with improvements in body came a newfound pride in it, and a reluctance to part with it, especially for the sake of theocratic ideologies, or sects, of individuals or mass movements, even if such cowardly, prudent stalling could never be safely shared with his handlers, or the Commander, herself, leaving L'il Lay to tread alone, no one to turn to.

He would seek paradise in a meaningful life, with tranquility, instead of the doom he had been stuck in:

> Verily, the dwellers of the Paradise, that Day, will be busy in joyful things.
> They and their wives will be in pleasant shade, reclining on thrones. They
> will have therein fruits (of all kinds) and all that they ask for. (It will be
> said to them): Salamun (peace be on you), a Word from the Lord (Allah),
> Most Merciful. (*Holy Quran*, 36:55-58)

And so, three months later found L'il Lay once again safely shielded away, enveloped in the comforting modesty of his dressy *burqa;* flying first class on the latest series airliner, with forged travel documents, $10,000 cash and a fragrant apple in unseen pockets, within the garment's folds; bound for Los Angeles via Montreal, to pay that supreme price for his misdeeds. The Commander, having bought his contract with the *hashish* merchants, had warned L'il Lay, "I will never consider this an obligation to be paid off or canceled, it always holds you. We know you are committed to the cause, and will rely on you in the future, God willing." He now discerned this deal with the Devil would be more binding, costly, than he expected; he would cruelly never be released by those who had helped him get here. The whir of the jet engines soothed his troubled thoughts, and as L'il Lay drifted off to a disoriented sleep, punctuated now and then by sudden bursts of turbulence, he had recurring visions of his self-destruction from exploding wired device strapped to his chest; nails, nuts, bolts, springs, and other shrapnel zinging through the air, ripping off heads, arms, legs, from disemboweled torsos; recalling the Commander's final instruction and exhortations, to the apprehensive *mujahideen* in his training group (he couldn't help reflecting *that they were far now from Jernavo, Eastern Sidon*), taking a perpetual *jihad* as their one-way destination.

"Do not let fear distract you from your lofty purpose. Trust in Allah, He will give you the courage and strength to infiltrate the infidels. Western liberals shall welcome you with open arms, as angels in their midst, for they are naïve, and blinded, by their innate idea of finding goodness in others. They will not see you for who you are, but rather, who they hope you become, an unassuming newcomer assimilating seamlessly into contemporary society, as Christians, followers of the path of peace, will do anything to avoid confrontation and be welcoming of strangers, including those sworn against them. The Christian devotion to redemption reduces, or elevates, them to accept betrayal, suffer wickedness, rather than cast their enemies out to the desert. Their faith's folly is to embrace its foe, to turn the other cheek, inviting further maltreatment and contempt. These were the falsehoods preached by Jesus in his time; they are the same errors blinding his followers currently; so, the honor and welfare of your families is at stake."

He momentarily ushered in a dream *in which he wandered without pants through silent landscapes, old predicament, nonchalantly interacting with others yet exposed and chagrined, as even with no criminal record, law-abiding, undocumented immigrants were still law breakers*; then he was deeply off to sleep.

Suddenly waking up, in some frozen frontier, twenty miles from anywhere, not knowing where to head, but certain the future was opening before him; trekking, running, even crawling across the surprisingly convoluted Quebec/ Maine border, in a raging blizzard whiteout; his motto always being: *exceptional* burqas *for all occasions,* he sported weather appropriate outfit for such risky outing, arctic camouflage wear, brilliant, alabaster *burqa*; concealing so well that a group of moose hunters marching right next to him, on the increasingly snow bound trail, never observed his presence; one of the hunters swearing he sensed the faint rustle of loose cloth blowing, snapping in the wind, feeling a sudden woosh fly by him. But as no one heard a thing, and as the swirling powder quickly covered all footprints, the zany parties quickly passed by each other along the poorly marked way. The *Hijra*, or *Hegira*, was the migration or journey of the Islamic Prophet Muhammad, and his followers, from Mecca to Medina, in June 622 AD. And just as the Prophet was purposeful in his direction, L'il Lay had achieved his first big goal in life, immigrating to the United States, a country where anything was possible, and he could remake himself, as everyone else there did, following their dreams. In true, mercenary fashion, he could always sell his body for sex on the streets to survive; for now, finding a strange comfort in experiencing the wild wind blowing all around him, into the impenetrable forest; and with rooted bounds, incredibly, arriving there at long last, wondering, *what would happen then, in the despised jurisdiction of the hated great Satan.*

# 4. The Modern Prometheus

> After days and nights of incredible labour and fatigue, I succeeded in
> discovering the cause of generation and life; nay, more, I became myself
> capable of bestowing animation upon lifeless matter.
> (Mary W. Shelley, *Frankenstein Or, The Modern Prometheus*, 1818)

Willi Herman met Lilly Lawrence one fated afternoon, at the bustling offices of Henry Waterson, MD, the foremost plastic surgeon in Los Angeles, CA; then treating, assisting, Willamina Hernan in taking definitive, but lurid, steps in becoming Willi; undergoing final reassignment, a process as reckless, as it was irrevocable, glazed in the glowing patina of supreme self-realization, progress, trendiness. At this date L'il Lay L'or Ence, having just commenced consultations, was a long way from final quintessence, a robust dream, merely Lilly in potential; but was already introducing himself to everyone, as female, which did not seem implausible, considering the *burqa*, but was also confounding, due to the masculine way he still moved, carried himself. As theirs was a mindset of metamorphosis, Henry Waterson, part medical man, craftsman, healer, conjurer, confidently applying preternatural science in transfiguration of outward form, releasing inner essence, had rescued their prostrate beings, natures, in a transposition toward eerie manifestations, probably poignantly, subliminally, steadily radiated since a consciousness, cognizance or birth, perhaps from their instants of conception. Such were the supreme powers of that wizard's native medicine. An awkward, strange, almost failed initial encounter, occurring; Willamina, despite demonstrating hormonally induced, as well as natural, aggressiveness, haughtiness, was herself intimidated by the hushed, black draped figure sitting in the far corner of the doctor's crowded waiting room; at first, confusing her for a severe Catholic nun, having never seen a Muslim in Colombia, much less a veiled, Palestinian trans-female presenting as a devout Shi'ite refugee. When L'il Lay, so recently arrived in L.A., and somewhat lonely, seeking human connection, nodded in a friendly, though cloaked, greeting, Willamina stared back wide eyed, nodding warily with a shy smile. And as their foci always were him, or herself, at first, neither was that interested in the other, but gradually each impressed, and won, their object over, through slow, agonized, progressions of single, and concurrent, transformations; their relationship heating up with every evolving recovery room version of themselves, as if providing the thrill of an indiscretion, an adventure, of meeting a completely new person, even if vicariously; the mysterious, sensuous attraction, only deepening, as successive surgeries blurred gender lines between; furthering an intrigue, curiosity drawing former him, past tense her, inexorably closer to what became an almost perfect pairing of double duality; until, conclusively, overcome with self, as well as mutual, awe and admiration at their final, sculpted shapes, they each gazed longingly, passively, jointly, at their reflected other (self). As this would be no casual affair, it blossomed into their stoic *doppelganger* love.

Henry Waterson, Native American, descended from powerful *Apache* medicine men, illustrious chiefs, enjoyed picking up female, male, AC/DC prostitutes on the boulevards for a quick rendezvous, before rambling home for a quiet dinner with devoted wife, adoring kids; not once, unrolling rubbers, because as a medicine man, he was all powerful, convinced he would identify, avoid early, potential *putas* with sexually transmitted pustules, by his mere sensibility, as illnesses, corruption, emanated a brown aura perceptible to seers; so far luckily weeding out the blatantly sick or dying, many of whom were newly arrived immigrants, destitute, trading their last unique components, priceless attributes, of infinite hope, value, their bodies, virtues; with little awareness of the curly bacteria the presumptive doctor believed he had mastered. If with every random sexual encounter he was playing Spirochete Roulette, it was all part of a defiant, enthusiastic, unbridled exuberance for *Isanaklesh's* sacred gifts, absolutely refusing to succumb to STDs, for the thrill of it. The most stellar of prodigies to attend, youngest of physicians to graduate from, the Whale School of Medicine, a showy shaman, master at his certain calling, bringing the blind new dawns after dusks, helping the lame to walk this world, the hairless grow locks anew, his triumph of the Hermetic arts over mere logic, protocol, of his magnificent technique reaching a peak of creation, with a clumsy scalpel wielded as a primitive instrument of choice; toward magically blended anointments of newly expressed christenings, pronouncing revolutionary perspectives regarding human physiological, psychological possibilities; and finishing his residency at Whale New Haven Hospital in record time; inventing state of the art procedures for severely scarred burn victims to achieve mobility, pain relief; every major hospital in the world wanted him, Los Angeles beckoning: the Garden of Eden, with promises of vainglorious relief of superstars, humble succor for studio extras; such offer, accepted.

When he transferred out west, to begin his practice, he was shocked to see the migrant crisis exploding. In terms of the really big picture though, as far as he could fathom, these migrant Indians and *mestizos* pouring across the southern border were the native red man's long lost brothers, the obscure differences being how much white, black, Polynesian, Sephardic, Arab or Asian blood was also mixed with theirs; inexorably, defiantly returning, reclaiming territories the Great Spirit long ordained belonged to them, regions forever known, held as theirs since mythic ancestors crossed a Bering land bridge from Siberia, millennia past; those first human beings, dwellers, caretakers, never owners, simply utilizers populating untamed, untried continents to be held in trust, as long as, indigenous people would roam on this sacred earth. While abject poverty, want, desires to improve lives united them, regardless of politics, origins, religion, one thing was for sure; the days of greedy, dour faced, white men amassing a country, out of tracts swindled from vanquished, deceived, Indian tribes and Mexicans, shamelessly seizing power for four hundred years (Native Americans do not measure space, or time, with trivial references to owning them, as does narcissistic, Western man), were already numbered, as an easy matter of color dynamics, and racial extrapolation; minding how many more red, brown, yellow, black, than white, were busting in, it was inevitable, as the sun rising every morning; and it would be payback time, repossessing what was forcefully taken from their sad, technologically backward ancestors, this time, usurping usurpers, expropriating expropriators; not as low undocumented aliens but entitled revenant settlers, *Reconquista* in their hearts, coming out of love, with entire families holding the future's promise; if not themselves, their children, inheriting a New World, where those oppressed rose up, against their historic oppressors.

One evening while on the prowl Waterson noticed a very beautiful honey complexioned Hispanic chick in heavy, dark, baggy clothes, manly lace up boots, standing alone, inside creepy shadows, on a corner of Sunset and La Brea; captivating, nervous hazel eyes, pursed full mouth, but the femininity tempered by the rough coiffed hair, lazy posture; something in her hard face alluring to Waterson, halting the car, having her get in, this being how he met, Willamina Hernan. Perhaps, it was the grim struggle her life had thus far encompassed etched on her face that was somehow recognized by Waterson trolling slowly by; reminding him of the Indian girls and boys he had molested, early on, growing up in the *Mescalero* Reservation. When he left, to attend Whale College, in New Haven, CT, under a special scholarship for Native Americans, he tried putting that behavior behind him; but it was not long into his undergraduate experience, that he found new amusements, toys, actually ready, willing, and able, among the campus' Indian and Latino populations; blacks much less accommodative, accepting, more competitive, angry, there having been an evening, at Commons, when a certain *Apache* freshman was requested, actually it was more a rude directive, to go forth from the black athletes' training table, despite there being plenty of room for him; facing exclusive behavior everywhere, not only from upper classmen or the socially arrived, but other, oppressed races and ethnicities. While in medical school, his insatiable insemination of nad'fs only increased, continuing to be indulged throughout his bisexually professional career. Now here he was, with a hot, cross-dressed waif in his car, ready for a quick tryst, when for an unexplained, tenderhearted reason, all he could think about was whether her family knew where she was, and if they missed her; one of the few times in his life, he felt an odd, humanitarian impulse to help anyone other than himself. *But all that for later, first head to nearby motel to take advantage of an easy opportunity.*

A remarkable incident transpired when he was thirteen, certainly influencing his unique, open, modern outlook on sexual matters and mores. Arriving in the New Mexico high desert plateau on a cold March night, some frisky Whale University co-eds, on an ethnographic, cross country road trip, to *Mescalero Apache* domains, were guided to a local *curandero* from the former *peyotero* families to acquire *peyote*, *pulque*, Maryjane; there being six gorgeous, effusive girls, eighteen to twenty years of age. And when the young, tall, big framed, long braided, good-looking Waterson answered the door of his grandfather's rough-hewn cabin, inquiring, *could he help them*, he blushed brown for several moments, for they were statuesque, older, of glorious races, and he remembered to smile, look each one right in the eye, just as his grandfather had taught him. Perhaps it was this wholesome, fresh appeal, that got him in way over his head with these much faster, Ivy League types; he, supplying enough of his grandfather's inventory to keep them high for the rest of their journey; they, inviting him to their campfire later that night; upon arriving, the revelers teasing with the skimpiest lace bras, panties, sandals, despite a forty-degree chill; already drinking up a storm, smoking pot in ceremonial *calumets*, popping dark green, magical buds, as if popcorn, tripping madly, a bit on the daredevilish, rowdy, free-spirited side, to say the least; reeling off teaser chants, such as, "Bang me once, I'm a dunce, throw me twice, I'll be nice," insolent affronts, to wit, "No means more, yes means, back door," or, "My name is Jacquie, I'm a necrophiliac(ie), I **** dead men," and, "My name is Jane, I'm wolf's bane, but game for more of it, the same;" engaging in a sudden, spectacular, blinding, erotic delirium over him; and before he knew what was happening, in a frenzy, tied him up, ripped off all his clothes, taking him completely aback; he, playing along, shocked, managing to rise to the occasion as it were; later quite proud of his inspired performance *al fresco*, each elect taking her lustful, twisting turn with him for as long as it took until done, while the others cheered on; subsequently, *en masse*, subjecting their captured, naked, trophy red skin, to pinching and bruising, punching, burning tortures, verbal taunts, humiliations, primal group aggressions; part of the symbolic hazing, to qualify for the boisterous group's *Sachem* Native Americans Scholarship, without him even suspecting, knowing, being advised, he was under review, consideration, and had actually been chosen; once sobering, sending him on his way back to his grandfather's, with many fervid, fond remembrances of the spent participants; the next morning, these exuberant, female wildcats gone, he, bereft of unspent desire, desperate for another interlude, no matter its brevity; but four and a half years afterward, a crisp, solemn letter, written in deep blue ink on heavy stationary, arrived from a staid order of sisters in New Haven, CT, summoning the big boy toy to apply to Whale College for the next academic year, with full tuition, room and board, and all expenses covered. Needless to say, such a wanton gang rape of a quiet, studious, sensitive, Indian brave, by a beauteous bevy of over-wealthy, over-impressionistic, oversexed, eastern college girls, went a long way in explaining his own evolving obsessions, participation, in thrill seeking, domination and submission; it was also the reason he attended Whale College on a scholarship provided by a secret society of sensual, vivacious *filles*, in recompense for a drunken, drug laced orgy, of collective, coercive/ submissive debauch, far reaching primitive carnal violation, perpetrated on him; for the bestowed privilege of majoring in both biochemistry and organic chemistry, *summa cum laude*; continuing on to the Whale School of Medicine, specializing as a gifted pioneer in minimally invasive, corrective plastic surgery, a maven, maverick, mover of medical arts. Who knew sexual servitude at a fancy school spring recess dig would get one so far? realizing fast, going out with Whalie chicks would only lead to trouble; they were so beastly opinionated on gender, gay, trans issues; it was so difficult to relate to them in uninhibited, amorous manner; not that he was what anyone, in their right mind, would say was normal; better a one-night stand with an Aggie Maggie, or a local tart, than being found guilty of sexual harassment, or maybe even rape, of a Whale girl, by an administrative Court of Star Chamber, campus kangaroo court. And having been raised with uncomplicated attitudes towards whites, blacks, Indians, he was stung by the racialism he encountered on campus; immediately approached by different social activist organizations, recruiting, pushing him, to declare irate allegiance to oppressed minorities, define his native ethnicity, become adamant in his unique racial identity. Pressure existed that those of

Hispanic and/ or Indian origins were not "Native enough," or did not have enough sympathy or respect for their roots if they ventured beyond the Spanish/ Native-speaking world. This belief, along with the idea that these cultures must be held up as superior and separate from American way of life, held back many from succeeding in today's modern, competitive society. Presented to adherents of *La Grasa*, a racist, divisive, exclusionary, ultra-radical group that vilified their own white blood, and its impact on world history, with an overarching insurrectionist agenda, greeting them in passable *Espanol*, learned over many years at the reservation school, he was nonplussed when, for all of their wanting to represent Hispanics, and be Latinos, hardly any of them spoke a lick, of Spanish (not counting Spanglish, in any way or form). And thus, was he introduced to the desperate obsession over categorization, foisted upon America, post 1965, a time of self-marginalization of people of color, by their insistence on preserving insular traditions, as a way of demonstrating fortitude, distinction, from their oppressor's race, class; so many labels thrust at him, he grew dizzy from the significance such descriptions could entail; actually, Native American, a slur derived from the name of an Italian cartographer, having nothing to do with the discovered hemispheric denizens. So why was the given name *Amerigo*, thrust upon a population who never asked for it; so why should whites be referred to by their skin color, but not redskins, by theirs? He preferred to mind his own business, focusing on technical learning, as his rebel *Chiricahua* relatives were forced to at the Carlisle Indian Industrial School, in late 1880s. But would they have been proud of his attending this white man's Diversity University, an ivory tower of centuries of passed on favors?

> Standing Bear later wrote that red flannel underwear caused "actual
> torture." He remembered the red flannel underwear as "the worst thing
> about life at Carlisle." (Luther Standing Bear, Oglala Lakota, d. 1939)

Notwithstanding his incipient, welling altruism with regard to the strumpet, unable to let such an easy opportunity slip away, the dissipated doctor took Willamina to a seedy motel, forcing himself upon her three times, in exchange for twenty dollars, and payment for the room for the night; she, divulging her story of risking everything, fleeing Colombia, traveling illegally to the United States, for a sex change treatment. Reacting with uncomfortable, and rare, regret for his indulgent, predatory actions, it dawned upon him that their meeting must be for reasons, that if unexplained, were also clearly part of a greater purpose, in which rather than keeping her down, he was meant to provide the requisite interventions so necessary to fulfilling her destiny. Up to the present, his meteoric rise had been the result of his dogged pursuit of significant, streamlined, leading edge medical technologies, attracting the steady flux of peer recognition, celebrity patients and financial rewards. His most famous case involved the young reality show personality, who compulsively underwent twenty cosmetic surgery procedures, at one time, with the vague, simple notion that they would solve all her problems, including a marriage of convenience; but it only made things worse, especially a bad marriage; her vain ambition, to become a brand, which would only occur when an adoring, fawning public identified strongly enough with her to keep track of her every move, action, follow her leads, purchase her products. But her career had stalled between TV shows and was no longer under the scrutiny of the tabloids. There were not enough relevant, unnatural, staged, "real life" situations produced into interesting series, with sufficient meaning, to hold viewers' attentions for very long, and these new programs wanted fresh faced talents, unknowns, with little or no understanding of anything, *ingenues*, as she herself had once been; additionally she was still too closely identified with a prior role, to be considered for a new one. Sadly, altering her external figure, through an attention-grabbing recast, was not enough to save her, to resume her uninterrupted rise, and recover her former stature, instead, dragging her further into decline; considered a pitiful victim of the knife, a stubborn freak, by directors, producers, save those requiring the busty, broad-butt bimbo caricature on screen. But it didn't matter that everyone parodied her, only that she saw her looks much improved. Although Waterson never crossed the ethical line, leading her on in the hope such changes would be a panacea for her afflictions, still he could be held accountable, even faulted, for never having tried, out of doctor/ patient duty, moral concern, therapeutic objectivity to dissuade her from leading herself on, with such eager, desperate thoughts. Nevertheless, in terms of the knowledge, expertise, skill utilized, the operation was unparalleled; he, at the top of his game, demonstrated the techniques, tools, methods prepared in anticipation of the media's sensational focus on the amount of work to be done at one time, rather than such salutary effects of the work itself. As the Midwest, corn fed maiden of unexceptional beauty or talent, she opted for a complete modification of her looks, only to identify as a distorted, tight-skinned object in the full-length vanity mirror, the egocentric, inner person unchanged; achieving fame for the record number of physical alterations undergone at one sitting, instead of actual, pulchritudinous results thereof; now left for the discerning eye of the beholder to judge. Coincidentally, the jaded, but accomplished, sawbones was between cases, recently grown frustrated, complacent, with increasingly routine, trivial pursuits of his well-established, ever thriving, but lately boring, uninspiring, physician's practice; reflecting on what further earthly bound considerations remained in his indefatigable quest for the thrilling momentum of genesis, and the possibility of a spontaneous transference of that force, from one cellular body, limb or organ, to another. Considering he reached the lofty pinnacle of tissue repair, regeneration research, as cosmetic necromancer to the stars, he held out for novel inspiration, patiently anticipating ultimate specimens, whose experiential goals were to be rearranged into totally new icons, from head to toe, inside out; a physiological/ psychological challenge never previously attempted, and if successful, his greatest achievement, for which he would attain universal acclaim, a lasting reputation for miracles, and eternal mention in respected research journals; not bad, for a kid from the reservation.

As not just his occupation, but entire *raison d'etre,* revolved around redesigning human beings, for their own good, he viewed most as subjects at his disposal, upon whom to perform his energized wizardry, in their improvements; and as he admired Willamina's soft, young body, in bed with him, he foresaw she could provide the perfect material for his experimental purposes; as in the end, no matter how much he intended on helping her, it was really all about him, his fanatical ambitions, satisfying an obsession for undertaking the ultimate reshaping of flesh, tissue, possibly even soul and spirit. But unlike so many of his other patients, he would not need to push Willamina into anything. Lately, a famous, immaculately preserved, still quite beautiful, old starlet, tabloid regular, whose sensual, natural pout was grotesquely carved into a joker's puffy lipped grimace, revealed after years of quiet regret, that a hitherto concealed boob job, at age nineteen, was surely one of the biggest mistakes of her life; as it led to the compulsion for more and more body altering surgeries, from which she was powerless; and in retrospect, felt that her physician at the time, unidentified, but clearly Waterson, considering clues of his prominence, and the phenomenal absence of any scarring post op (a technique he had been first to master); insensitive, uncaring of reported, lingering doubts, convinced her into going through with all the derring-do, such was the charm, persuasiveness, of this manipulative, ever forceful, personality. "None of us were born perfect," he liked to say. "If we were as flawless, as Him, He would not have made us." However, no matter how good the alterations looked, for a few years, eventually the skin began to sag and wrinkle, around shrinking bones, the ravages of time and age could never be dispelled; while in other cases the opposite happened, with a gradual tightening of flesh over dry bones, so that a certain television news anchorwoman found it impossible to bend, run, or hug her own family, due to excessive surgeries, her whole body stiffened with scar tissue, fleshly limbs fused, become immovable. Perhaps in Willamina Waterson finally found the opportune, willing subject, the trusting, ready accomplice, to machinations for historic greatness and glory, as fortuitously, she herself was infatuated with dramatic refashioning; such artifice, as into which only he was qualified to delve in, while she would be the innovative, secret manifestation of his deepest desire, pushing his copious talents to the brink, for he was full of maniacal conviction of his unstoppable attainments; she describing the exact look and feel she wanted to portray: boyish, angular, rough, scrappy; his services offered pro bono, as not only her destitute circumstances warranted his aid, but in itself, money (for which the ancient Egyptian word was the same, as for *s\*\*\**), with which he'd been amply remunerated throughout his professional life, could no longer serve as the most significant, or accurate, measure of the excitement, satisfaction, empowerment, he would get from an undertaking, such as this: her structured rebirth, at his near omnipotent behest. Thus, Willamina was enlisted to fully participate in the realization of her Willi; internal yearnings expressed in a transition to the new outward form by laboriously painstaking procedures, beginning with mandated psychological evaluations and counseling, proceeding to ultramodern hormonal treatments, their preliminary effects; then living a Real Life Experience, culminating with fine incisions of dexterously applied sharp blade, taking two years to complete; even then requiring countless, additional, successive adjustments, with decay, use, gravity, continually pushing back against ground breaking, heroic, yet still trite, ephemeral, mortal exploits. Then when her personality veered to masculine, he knew he was on the right track; in what seemed like no time at all, Willamina appeared to expand right into Willi's heavy, black boots; her animation a testament to that conniving energy and genius, of Dr. Waterson; also to the philosophers' stone he dug up that next day after their tryst, in the sisters' consumed, yet eternally glowing, campfire.

As the secret of sorcery lay deep within Waterson's heart, he acceded to Willi's existential demands, to produce a partner, mate, who would accept him unconditionally, on equal terms; a more delicate, calm companion, crafted dream bride, fitted as a monstrous match to Willi's grisly, total eccentricity, sharing the unique peculiarity of perfection, to accompany him forever. Six months into Willamina's retooling, remodeling, a stalking Waterson luckily met a wayward L'il Lay L'or Ence, ominously, *burqa* attired, at the reception of the L.A. Egyptian Consulate's annual Ramadan celebration. Henry Waterson, MD, was a personal guest of the Egyptian ambassador to the United States, an aristocratic insider and old college roommate of Waterson's, whose wife was one of the doctor's earliest patients. It was evening, and after a full day of fasting and prayer, L'il Lay needed nourishment. The wet scars on hisher back still oozed when heshe was under pressure, but for the most part, after a few months, heshe had adjusted positively to hisher novel life in the United States, enjoying the experiences of freedom. In hisher eagerness, L'il Lay almost knocked Dr. Waterson over, as heshe bulldozed hisher way to the buffet table; the Egyptian ambassador reprimanding L'il Lay, reminding himher to act more like a lady, please, and be respectful of the other guests; then introducing L'il Lay to Waterson; his oldest chum to himher: "She is a lady's maid, most distant relation of my wife's austere, back country Shi'ite clan; he, most loyal of classmates, renowned, respected, innovative of plastic surgeons in this Western paradise." Then L'il Lay's eyes lit up, even if veiled through the meshed *niqab* worn. *At last, a skilled and caring surgeon who may help me*, heshe thought. For his part, the physician did not know what to think of the zany, mute, black clad character, on whose garment folds he tripped, as heshe whizzed past, to the lavish offerings, no words exchanged between them, as L'il Lay was just learning English; the doctor disoriented, by the supposed woman before him not exposing a single square inch of skin to the light of day, making it impossible to connect to his usual sense, of diagnosing sick auras of disfigurements, conditions, syndromes, *humours*, as he was prone to do, in public. But for the rest of the evening, L'il Lay followed Waterson around the party, a shrouded, tame puppy dog, sticking right by a new master; after some time, L'il Lay organizing hisher thoughts into pidgin English, able to ask philosophically: "If Adam and Eve were the first man and woman, why had the Creator made each, what they were; so different in form, instinct, behavior?" "Maybe they have never been as dissimilar, as you presume, at least not from my practiced perspective, especially naked, 'Like a patient etherized upon a table,'" the sawbones quickly replied. "It's really the same tissue, bone and skin, only initially, shaped in different ways, ready for artful reconfiguration, as warranted in every case." "Dr..." whispered L'il Lay, so no one overheard: "There is an issue with my tissue; I am ready for artful reconfiguration, as warranted in this case." "What do you mean?" probed the clinician. "Beneath my silken robe, I am a well-hung male, only, I want to be a fleet-footed damsel; it will not be an easy journey, but I have come so far, save me in the name of the Unfathomable Allah."

In making the female, Waterson relied on innovations gleaned from his parallel, macabre generation of the male. The androgynous commonality sought by both was ultimately in Waterson's able hands, and he was given wide latitude within which to work. The moist, flogging scars on L'il Lay's back were the only problem encountered, as they had not healed properly, and unfortunately, would be slow to dry up, leaving raised welts. Willi's steady progress was more apparent every day, driving L'il Lay forward in a frenzied pilgrimage for redemption. When Willi experienced the first of a thousand cuts, undergoing prolonged, stinging healing, L'il Lay was there for him, assuaging his physical discomforts, countering his lingering self-doubts, about where these changes were headed; all the while, coming to grips with, preparing himself, in his own mind, for what he would be enduring six months forward. When the time finally arrived, for fateful transmogrification to commence, Lilly reveled in each nick, incision, slicing; the delicate, nearly invisible stitching, with what seemed an angel's glue, to bind her up, rally her anew; as quivering, breathing, mud imbued, with a life spark of its own. And if there was a spot on her body that did not ache, in grand, exultant, self-inflicted torture, from never ending probes and pokes, it was only because the doctor had not gotten to it, was about to. As Lilly experienced, the last of a thousand cuts, undergoing prolonged, fiery healing, Willy was there for her, assuaging her physical discomforts, countering her lingering doubts about where these changes were headed; all the while, coming to grips with, preparing himself, in his own mind, for how altered he would be six months forward. At times of excruciating pain, disabling anxiety, each consoled the other, thus: "Yes, it hurts, but we have chosen to do this; it's supposed to ache, because we're transforming." In final revelation, as it was unclear whose rib should be taken, each sacrificed a most precious part for the other, on this sacred altar of love. His equipment he proffered for amputation, spilled raw blood, as a god, to consummate her transmutation. Her stuff she offered to transsexualization, lopped off breasts, as a goddess, to bind his alteration. Then they became idols, suffused of turbid passions, known only to them, in such lofty guises, as immortals:

> By lik'ning spiritual to corporal forms,
> As may express them best, though what if Earth
> Be but the shaddow of Heav'n, and things therein
> Each t' other like, more then on earth is thought?
> (John Milton, *Paradise Lost*, 1667)

For wily Waterson, it was a matter of renewing his patients' faith in themselves, the greater life around them, which, unfortunately, had been quashed by their deep feelings of helplessness, alienation, trapped in their own skins prior to their consummate liberation by the master known for sublime designs. After two and a half years of indefatigable, disciplined labor, the sculptor's dream realized, his mold met the slippery clay, the two most perfect beings conceived, brought into the light of day, nary words precise, as to describe their magnificence, except, perhaps other worldly, no longer resembling *Homo sapiens*, as much as a new, absolute race, or species, onto themselves. Had such not been his desire all along, to bring about physicality beyond reproach, permeate organic entities with an enchantment of their own? And to top it off, actual molting of inner traits, to follow the body's new flow; female to male, male to female, as if such transference was natural, good, strictly aligned with divine design, commandments; a presumption made only by those contradicting the meaning of evolution; exchangeable cuff links, dice, eerily complementing each another in their, and nature's, eyes while believing they, as well as all, were the better for it; held tight to their jealous maker, sponsor, through eons, as Aries and Aphrodite bound to Zeus, Paris and Helen to Discord, Romeo and Juliet to Fate, loyal innocents, all; the next step for the doc, being to present them on a greater stage, as in launching two refitted vessels to navigate turbulent waters, for the sake of less seaworthy craft, adrift on confused seas, in harm's way. So, as prominently positioned surgical scars healed and faded, highlighting the completion of the ghoulish, body shaping phase, meticulously engineered by Waterson, obsessed lovers angling to get enough of sexy beloveds, touched each other everywhere, unable to believe their new bodies as permanent. Willi and Lilly then put prior selves aside, assumed fresh identities with pride, humility, ingenuous intensity, never again to be confused with old Willamina Hernan and L'il Lay L'or Ence; and within a short time, the uttering of original names was discontinued, as if for the first time in their unfeeling lives, their senses were turned on, seeing, hearing, feeling, tasting things crisply, the smoldering sun itself seemingly reborn for them alone, to bask in; classically proportioned in all aspects, visage, head, body, spirit, captivating, radiant as seraphs, but with similarly swarthy, glistening complexions of a still struggling, captive Third World: one, a deep olive Arab, Berber, Phoenician blend, mixing crossroads of East with West, bridging Asia Minor to North Africa; the other, light amber Amerindian, European, Sephardic blend, mixing reaches of Old World to New; each linking aboriginal to traditional, to here, paired, aiming for the stratosphere.

He had reached the triumphant moment he anticipated and was driven to his entire life, for here in these elated instants, he had not only reformed flesh, but altered psyche, flourished essence, converted spirit, itself; here were dual, brand spanking new persons, from head to toe, from the inside out, different, yet two end leaves of the same book. Evolving interpersonal dynamics, so much time together, even under rigorously controlled, empiric conditions, resulted in the respected professional line between physician and patients becoming thinner and thinner; it coming to pass that a possessive, deranged designer could not suffer to be without his greatest, most meaningful inventions hovering near; going so far as to have the stateless, homeless, orphaned couple move into his abode, speaking at length with his wife about a possible adoption, the better to legitimize their appearance to his neighbors, family and himself. But as the newly minted coins had no accompanying certificates defining them as millennials through rebirth, their corporeal (even less, spiritual) provenance could never be established beyond a reasonable doubt. The best explanation for a duo joining the household was their far away kin having recently immigrated over, such doubling of dependents now residing at the home, drawing no undue neighborhood scrutiny in itself; though the oddly shielded pair, at all outward appearance, seemed too old, jaded, to be staying under the same roof with the doctor and his lovely wife, entering their thirties, and their children, both happy toddlers. But having commenced their wardship as the most calculated of test models, these two needy creatures had by now also taken their places to become Dr. Waterson's precious offspring, and he would not, under any conditions, let them go. Of this new arrangement they were initially grateful, for they were living with caring guardians, who provided, looked out, for them; as well as, cohabiting with their one and only one, for all ages (they were similarly siblings, ushered forth from twin transversal lateral sections, severe excises, grafting, hollowing outs, and the reshaping of privates, careful infusions of chemical and biochemical additives; but a brother and sister connection to be defined in a figurative, circumstantial sense, in no way incest, and as such, undeserving of the social censure it would one day inspire); it being a period of joy, sufficiency and peace. In a newly assumed role as Gardener Supreme (erstwhile Fashioner), he rejoiced with them in celebrating their renaissance; such confidence building support of a family structure, allowing for feelings of fondness, respect, reciprocated. Inappropriately, in an offhand way, making note, *that these two would be members of that select group who have known sexual pleasures as both a man and a woman,* he truly believed this was the biggest breakthrough of his career. After this what more could there be? Oddly enough, when the family was relaxing with such a cozy, close-knit menage, things started to change, as they always seem to, just when one would rather, they didn't. Now that he had succeeded in their physical and spiritual refitting, their essential discovery out of nothing, as trustee he felt an overwhelming need to continue his oversight, program experiences, bring order to their turmoil, plot life's progress, as if they would just follow steps of a route predestined toward his ends, goals, aspirations, but it was not to be. Despite addressing this towering, distant sage of great possibilities, as Lord, Sir, not only out of deference, respect, but grateful acknowledgement, of creations to their creator, they grew to resent, despise him, for the constant attention he burdened them with, to do as he wanted, become what he expected. But who among us knows their children, or hears their lonely, distant cries without regrets, sorrows, fear of haphazard trajectories, bound to distant stars?

"Listen to me, I'm trying to tell you something, for your own good," he solicitously, urgently implored.

"'What we've got here is failure to communicate,'" they stonily replied, rolling a bunch more doobies.

He bossed them around, as if they were still infants, growing up. But openly challenging his stature, as Originator, the whippersnappers rebelled loudly, seeking disaffected ways, forging new paths, indignant at his presumed, indisputable infallibility, a real impediment, to their freedom, as after all, they were of majority age, even if they did not act it. Believing that his expectations for them had become excessive they were frustrated, deciding then and there to seek their fortunes away, it seeming always impossible between fathers and sons; the former, wanting to share their knowledge, learned the hard way, by many irresponsible, unreconciled mistakes; while the latter, wanting nothing but to learn, take responsibility, for themselves, their yet to come, unforeseen mistakes. It was an endless, senseless cycle. The shock came when he realized, that even though they were both his smart innovations, from start to end, they had already surpassed his wisdom, and were, for all intents and purposes, practically now strangers; no longer heeding his advice, profiting by his experience, or gaining by his wisdom, in terms of what their next steps should, or should not, be; completely disregarding him, as if he had never been a part of their lives, in favor of making their own choices, striking on their own, questioning why he made them thus:

> Nay but, O man, who art thou that repliest against God? Shall the thing
> formed say to him that formed it, Why hast thou made me thus?
> (Romans 9:20, KJV)

As far as getting along with his kids went, whatever he had, *they wanted none*, he thought, sardonically. *Was this teenage autonomy, or lobotomy? What an emptiness, O Lord, for the grown-up child's parent; headstrong kids varying, permutating, on the oldsters' choices, each generation doing it their own way.*

Then spiteful excess channeled an incubus and succubus, demons escaped from hell, blaming, cursing, denouncing him for their shortcomings, weaknesses, faults, fears, neuroses, compulsions, even disease and illness, for things he had never presumed them to understand or know about, casting their lots with the dark forces, how like teenagers they were. Instead of having aided them by altering their identities, he had destroyed their original beings for now, devising neither men nor women, but organic, chemical in-between composites. Realizing they required emancipation to conquer continents, climb mountains, ford rivers, in their striking fashions; to fail, overcome, make mistakes, see the light, with no one else's input or help; so annoying were they, as his issue, products of indefatigable labors, the duty lay on him to release them to venture forth on their own; having first appeared as outliers, blessings, in his family's lives, heaping goodwill upon them; but as they gradually gained health, became robust, blossomed into aesthetically pleasing (reborn) millennials, hopes faded with adolescent opposition; so that by the time of their declared independence, he had ceased to dictate, project, great expectations onto them, presume for their futures. For it was time to let them define their own realities. Because juveniles always do the exact opposite of what their parents want for them, in their own dreams. So, in reaction to their babes' increasing truculence, the protectors contrived a daring stratagem, radical tack, utilizing an oppositional duplicity, making suggestions that were completely opposite, to the true results desired. And the artful contrarians' turning round on its head of this contrary advice constituting a double negative, affirmation of the lame parental units' original intentions, this rudimentary trick was used to turn their indomitable flame of complete, irascible individuation against them. And the first time their old man, and old lady, tried this reverse approach with the recalcitrant youths, was when the developing duo (trial, modernist exponents of free love, open relationships), loosely dated outside their own recently established union. Whenever either one brought home some fresh fling, exhibiting possible questionable motives, a shady background, possible serious genetic issues, the coolest of custodians were emphatic in expressing how much, "We liked your new friend," and, "Would you please bring that charming person to dinner, more often? What a fascinating individual, wherever did you meet?" invariably, this latest heart throb much less alluring in nonconformist eyes, alarmingly diminished, or else, summarily dropped within a short, but respectable (just enough to allow the beloveds a bit of dignity), amount of time. After numerous, bothersome episodes of this type, the somewhat chastened paramours began keeping to themselves, as straying from their privileged, all-consuming romance, appeared much too fraught with complications, tensions, danger, and assignations with random, creepy strangers to get a rise out of Mom or Dad soon lost their obnoxious allure, as they were then young adults, ready to commit to each other as a couple.

*Perhaps the entire period of raising children, is for parents a self-imposed, naturally fixed, sentence of drudgery,* he thought *but somehow, we were always at their beck and call, as with our pivotal forbears, all those wisps of descent, demanding worship in past, present, and future, randomly mixing to survive.*

A coming-out party was planned, as "coming-out" was the new "born again," with the doctor's patients, friends, staff, colleagues, and the medical and Hollywood communities at large, in attendance; a great reception organized at his heavenly, pool decked home, with the press, all the town, invited; to present them to the world, show them off for (their) (his) sake. And this may have inspired their differentiating from him, hating him, as that night, during the festivities, they were in contact with other extraordinary individuals, who made them feel less alone in the world; because apparently, there was an entire circle exploring new directions, and expressions, *en route* to decisively upgrading stifled lives. And in their common desire to avoid Dad, as much as possible, at the gala, they ambled about, from one fascinating guest to another; always a few paces ahead of their well- meaning, however, infinitely meddling, ancient poppa; shining lights onto themselves, no real need of others, ironically perpetually attracting curiosity seekers with queer luminescence, brilliant, destroying flames drawing hovering moths to destruction; at some point during forced march to elude their nosey parker, *paterfamilias,* presented to a steady Isidora Green, polished, articulate heiress to one of America's big fortunes, Vice Chairman, CEO of one of the largest media groups; "pleased, honored, meeting such dynamic exemplars of forthcoming millenniums, as our hero and heroine;" hitting it off immediately. In terms of Isidora's tie to Waterson, there was an air of big mystery, whether she was his current, former flame, friend, benefactress, patron, fan, patient, or Hollywood sponsor (when inquired of, she simply answered, "Yes"); but of one mystery there could be no doubt: she was the universal artificer's Archangel, placed in this material realm to do his bidding. As Founding Matriarch of the Sisterhood of Grace, a secret society at Whale University, in New Haven, CT, established on the precepts of a mystical, seasonal rejuvenation of the natural elements, through the death and resurrection of a mythic holy figure, to promote strong character, self-help and good works, Isidora Green was cheerful, and jocund, in her approach to women's rights, so as not to repel men, but make no mistake, she was a relentless Bulldog where a redress to wronged womanhood was concerned.

"It was after my own trustees, bankers, brokers (employees, all, you see...), condescendingly, minutely, tediously over-mansplained the simplest of situations, the structure and investment composition of my trust, and the dispersal of my funds (my own money, mind you...), with all their attendant admonitions, prohibitions and limitations, to me, that one last time, that I refused to take any more, throwing up my hands, and in that very moment decided to found my own sacred order, The Sisters of Fervent Grace."

Highly impressed with such a power move by an intrepid, free-standing Superwoman, as this Eleanor of Aquitaine, our remade Abelard and Heloise were most curious about any sacred aspects of fervency, divine inspiration, group religious mania, displayed by the firebrand. Did it imply some belief in God?

"Not as a white bearded patriarch in the sky, but the holy fiber in ourselves, individually, collectively."

"When you say fiber, do you mean, as with time, *kismet;* or a *burqa,* something you can stitch, put on?"

"I mean, whatever turns you on, delightful, lovely creatures. And why not female divinities ennobled?

Perhaps (then legendary, medieval courts of love, would rule) in a scintillating Crystal House, run with machine gun efficiency? Perhaps sacred fertility rites push us into believing in ourselves today, and in new frontiers tomorrow." Willi now: "So you are of the old moneyed class, and do God's work? Isn't the invisible hand just another excuse to look away when grave injustices are committed?" Seemingly taken by Willi's strong physique, soft cherubic countenance, she emphatically declared that the network was searching for a new, take-charge kind of personality, to anchor the next decade of *Nightly News*. In a last memory of Isadora that evening, she was describing with tremendous, didactic pride how the U.S. Army's all-women special ops teams will be combat fit, for tomorrow's wars: "The military's Cultural Support Teams have described the importance of putting women in forward-deployed military roles..."

Party goers danced, unwound, by undulating pool, rocking out singly, in couples, amorphous groups, at various spots, sharing psilocybin, coke, poppers, while on a raucous sound system Stevie Wonder sang:

> Mary wants to be a superwoman
> But is that really in her head
> But I just want to live each day to love her
> for what she is...

And as their own patriarch was hovering near, they quickly skedaddled it to the next group of partiers, gathered under wavy shadows of a gently rustling, purple leaf plum tree, toking on a couple of gigantic joints. Here, they met kookie, West Point educated, John B. Sayer, Isidora Green's corporate president, whom she had recruited to the company, after stellar tours in U.S. Army special forces, in Vietnam, in cahoots as a liaison with the CIA; followed-up with strategic studies at the U.S. Army War College; as with herself, a graduate, *Suma cum laud,* of the recently founded, Whale School of Management, to which the Sisterhood of Grace contributed one of the founding endowments, with continuing generous support; Col. Sayer, an exponent of wild animal spirits driving corporate profits, one of a new breed of celebrity managers, enlisted as soldiers of fortune, mercenaries, terminators, to clean up executive suite messes, then move on; quite a weed toking nut, in his own right. Even from within dissipating evening twilight, they could tell he was deeply tanned, to an unhealthy carbon hue; enlivened, attracted to dark complexions, their approach across rolling lawn noticed by Sayer immediately, intrigued by the pair's hale, hearty glows of brownness. "Oh, look, little Guatemalan Indian children," he ventured, of course intending cultural sensitivity, however, obtuse. Tonight Sayer was kicking back, celebrating, relaxing from the hard week, attempting to bridge corporate differences that existed between Warren Bros. Inc., and The Theatre and Cinema Worker's Guild; busting heads when necessary, reducing personnel count to a bare minimum (still justifying exorbitant salaries, bonuses, perks, of the C suite), and going head-to-head with board members over cost overruns, aesthetic choices, on the last two pictures. Lilly now: "So you are a corporate executive; I know what you do, grandiloquently bossing cowed people around, making vague gestures in the sky." He seemed taken by Lilly's exotic charm, emphatically mentioning that the studio was searching for a brand-new face, to showcase the next decade of feature length action productions. In a last memory of Sayer that evening, he taught fellow celebrants how to flip the proper bird, with two fingers raised only halfway on each side of an extended middle one, as "Sticking up a naked middle finger alone was how girls, fools, dudes did it," hilariously pursuing their reefer madness.

In the splashing pool, pleasure seekers skinny dipped, frolicking, singly, in couples, amorphous groups:

> Mary wants to be another movie star
> But is that really in her mind
> And all the things she wants to be
> She needs to leave behind... (Stevie Wonder, *Music of my Mind,*
> "Superwoman (Where Were You when I needed You)," 1972)

The truants mingled on again, just one step ahead of their gaining pursuer, and begetter, ruling overall. Though they could not see him, they heard his rumbling (so overbearing) voice close by. Subsequently, the evening surged as a kaleidoscope of modish, eye opening interpolations, into a gay parade of multi-racial, pan-ethnic, homosexual, lesbian, bisexual, polysexual, asexual, transgender, transsexual, cross-dresser, and other, sexual dissenters of all ages, and every order, combination, description imaginable; inchoate, reset *hominids*, spawned from divergent seeds, rather than previous aliases, updated, refitted, revitalized, sleeker versions; new directions for expectant humanity, incipient pioneers of a burgeoning, worldwide kinship endowed with revamped corporeal and ethereal qualities. This uninhibited, freakish congregation, many on the cusp of notoriety, would "boldly go where no man has gone before" as per a *Star Trek* episode. Then indulging along, on the other side of midnight, they were shocked (for by that hour, the folly was too much, even for them) at the next clique's spokesperson's claim, of himheritself, as "tritesticular, to boot." It was getting late. While expounding on the revolutionary regime to come, this oddball seer's white dress shirt slowly dotted across its chest, with the bloody oozing, from pierced nipples; red spotted snake, slithery back, cream underbelly, slippery challenges interposed rhetorically:

"Clearly, inconvenient questions persist, regarding the recognition of same-sex marriage. For example, must the states permit or recognize a marriage between an aunt and niece? Aunt and nephew? Brother/brother? Father and child? May minors marry. Should marriage be limited to only two people? What about a transgender spouse? Is such a union same-gender or male-female? All such unions undeniably, equally committed to love and caring for one another;" winding its way back to the garden when done.

Deep in a swirling pool, carousers coupled openly, exhibiting an amorphous orgy, Steely Dan distantly:

> Tearful reunion in the USA
> Day by day those memories fade away
> Some babies grow in a peculiar way
> It changed, it grew, and everybody knew
> Semi-mojo
> Who's this kinky so-and-so?
> Papa go
>
> Oh - no hesitation
> No tears and no hearts breakin'
> No remorse
> Oh - congratulations
> This is your Haitian Divorce
> (Steely Dan, *The Royal Scam*, "Haitian Divorce," 1976)

When the ponderous progenitor at last caught up with his bounding goats, well past midnight, the party was going strong, with each fantastic moment becoming more and more like a rave; he knew they had been avoiding him all night. Perhaps this was the magic moment he had been waiting for, to win them over again; in salutation, referencing the civil, courteous relations they had enjoyed when first admitted to his domestic Eden; inquiring if they were alright, needed, or he could do, anything. Apparently, such line of interlocution, tinged with deep, affectionate regard (love?), sent them completely over the edge, insane with fury, and in giving vent to their spleen, after declaring their liberty, for the hundredth time, let it slip, that they had surreptitiously set up screen tests at the network and studio, for next week. "So there, you see, that's how independent we can be from you." "You are not the boss of us; jeez, we can't even breathe." "I wanted other vocations for you both, not the limelight, where the glare upon you will already be bright enough; perhaps you could help me organize my laboratory, until you decide what to do; would an arts, liberal arts, science or engineering education, at Whale U., be of any use?" But they had enough experimentation by then. And college represented the old knowledge and customs they had rejected. The great causal agent nagged that contrary to his express warning they had gained knowledge which was privileged, perhaps meant only for mythic beings, immortals, heroes, exalted enough to then intercede and mediate between the gods and mortals; illustrious prophets, oracles, such as Tiresias, who during his long, eventful life was both a man and woman, "saying that women's pleasure was greater," thus, the more shameful of the two; and this realization was a warning to them, that they were delving into ideas and concepts that were anathema to nature or nurture, a deviation from what had always been accepted for itself; because man had never been large or proud enough in himself to interfere, interpose his will on that which was genetically, organically, divinely ordered, since the start of evolution; here, it is Hera, goddess of women, marriage, childbirth in ancient Greece, suffering disclosure, who is the nag:

> Some years later, Zeus and Hera were arguing about who got more
> pleasure from sex: men or women. To settle the argument, they called for
> Tiresias, who had lived as both. Tiresias took the side of Zeus, saying that
> women's pleasure was greater, and Hera, in her fury, turned him blind.
> (Euripides, *The Bacchae*, 405 BC)

And the admonitory mask of the cosmic surgeon was terrible, severe, judging, punishing, as if he was angry at them, for ever having gained this arcane cognition; and perhaps also at himself, for permitting them a choice to acquire such unrevealed intelligence in the first place. It was when his children began to discriminate, to taste certain banned fruits of different trees, of the knowledge of good (variety) and evil (uniformity), i.e., choice, free will, vs. limits, predestiny, that they were summarily banished from Eden, their sin: daring to experience both sexes, and the hubris of choosing which sex was preferred, in thus fashion surpassing the limits that God originally intended for them, as for all. It could be that the reprimand received, was interpreted more severely than was intended; in any case, to them it felt as if they were protagonists shunned by their author, driven through storm from paradise, suddenly exposed with virulent shame as if stark naked, so crushing was its effect. Having become exceptionally fond of their foster mother and younger siblings, the only close-knit family they ever had, they would miss all of them terribly, once departed; nevertheless, they knew what they had to do that night, the rest of their lives lived, as in a vivid thought, as when an early morning reverie brings someone not seen since early school days, clear, yet fleeting. They fled their green mansions, leaped over the western wall, no angels standing guard there, after seeing the last guests to their cars, exchanging pleasantries, phone numbers, with up till then strangers, top contacts for future networking. There they were, abandoning their lair, absconding (without in the least having stolen, or thought of pilfering, but nonetheless, overcome with the bottomless humiliation of lowdown thieves, of having gotten away with something, of being found out; making it necessary to skulk among night's shadows, as monsters, while in some fantastic way still filching certain intangibles of affection, admiration, and gratitude, but no longer adulation, that being left behind), from the nicest, most comfortable, best provisioned habitat they had hitherto known; going back, in one fell swoop to their desultory wanderings, a degraded poverty, as if those dastardly, human conditions were inseparably tied together at the hip as demoniacal Siamese twins. The only things they walked out of there with were the few threads on their backs, and a huge, shiny, crisp, juicy, red apple, Lilly picked off a tree, so ancient, its drooping branches held past proofs, future promises, of good and evil, in ready fruit she could not resist sharing with Willi; his willing bite making complicit the foretold fall from grace, as such commencing that next great chapter of their exposed existences, expulsion and cohabitation as common law man and wife (because if marriage was impossible, celibacy was lonely); avoiding any religious sanction of their self-sanctioned vows, to last until they had children, as shall be told. How typical a couple they seemed, so commonplace, yet incoherently bizarre, beyond any normal conceptualizing or comprehending as to sexual appetites, signals, responses, so twisted and confused, even muddled, had their love making become, with all the cross directives given off, reacted to, and the crosses of the crosses, and the crosses of the crosses, of the crosses, and those reacted to, *ad infinitum*...

...a wife's duty, a husband's obligation, whichever (their bodies came together gently, violently, beneath her outer softness, the firmness of restrained muscle, tendon, much like his current self, and beneath his outer hardness, the softness of residual breasts, tender tush, much like her current self, right under each other's touches, prior foundations, tendencies, still shining, though within new outer shells), is which...

There is one final anecdote about their flight toward the imminent dawn of a new day; agile, set in their hearts to escape by any conceivable means, conducted by wing sandaled Mercury through a boundless expanse, limitless territory, in the tawdry winks of an eye, finding themselves on the beach; somehow, chased in loose sinking sand by a pack of snarling, misfit, ill-bred ruffians, committed to the identical thuggery against those unusual, conflicted, mangled mutants, with whom they were so often identified, as well. For a moment, Willi and Lilly let themselves be intimidated; but only for a moment, because from within both, some latent, emerging resilience and reaction was becoming manifest, as in a flash, they stopped retreating, turning on their heels; it was their last stand or bust, with adrenaline pinpricks on flexing skins, chills in waking joints, muscles; the heavy toll of deprivations, humiliations, endured and overcome, on this most desperate of epic journeys of self-discovery, they decided to play it, for all or nothing. Because what was another beating, or loss of face, in the face of the ignominious failure to be free? Roaring ferocious, subliminally encoded *Bedouin*, *Arawak* war cries, they picked up knobby, heavy driftwood from clammy, cold sand, charging savagely at the stunned, now hesitant, then fearful, attackers, and within fifty-four seconds, caused them substantial, brutal damage; the melee over, two of the assailants knocked out, bleeding, on the rocky shore, with the others in clear retreat. That being the last time the rebooted rejects ever allowed themselves to be intimidated by bullies, in a clear victory for their own kind, in the world; gradually, patiently, fitting smoothly into recently sutured skins, realizing, finding, themselves, the final, superficial adjustments reaching to their very souls. Standing together, focused on impenetrable sky meeting the dark Pacific, enveloping black curtain slashing the horizon, a giant blue marlin jumped out from forbidding ocean, seven, eight feet to windward, seeming as if hung, suspended, high spirited, in foamy mist; wide, glassy eyed, forecasting things momentous, for instance, the timely appearance to come, of those few, significant individuals, certain to make impacts on us all.

When the creator shaped the clay, he also shaped the void from whence it came, as space surrounding. In carefully casting his true to life subjects, Waterson patterned them after idealized representations of humankind, as did Oscar Wilde, in conceiving the semblance of perfection, Dorian Gray, who came as close to paragon, prototype, ultimate organism, as was (im)mor(t)ally possible; as all considering mind, the genius alchemist had performed unparalleled feats, bending science to glorious purpose, concocting incantations for the transmutation of elemental cores, remixing of dull moistures, polarizing lodestones anew ("...and as Steele/ Toucht with a Loadstone, dost new motions feele?"); resetting compasses to as yet uncharted Utopias; yet Tweedledum and Tweedledee had shockingly sold it easy, for a hollow rank, dull flattery, of passing celebrity, and most hurtfully of all, cheaply, for the sakes of their public images, instead of dearly, as solid underpinnings for possible lifetimes. He alone supplied their ardent Garden with its sweet breath of fecundity, as only the devoted caretaker could, tilling abstracted molecules with infinite, directed will, plus love. However, coldly united, somehow, artfully, certainly impudently, they turned their backs on an eternal manifestation of divine order, separating; gravely distressing him to his nucleic quick, so that he always wondered if he had been too harsh, with his darling children that day:

I, like the arch fiend, bore a hell within me. (Shelley, *Frankenstein*)

# 5. Immigration (Super) Man

...if they can get here, they have God's right to come...
For the whole world is the patrimony of the whole world...
(Herman Melville, *Redburn*, 1849)

If this sounds like a tall tale believe me, it really happened, I was there as a witness; besides, who could ever make up something so outlandish. One of my final assignments, before giving up the advertising game, was the agency's most significant client account, Warren Bros. Inc. As one of the greatest global media, movie and television conglomerates, they owned a vast empire of production studios and related businesses in New York, Hollywood and other vaunted, famous locations. And the president, and boss, of the company was a veteran top executive, John B. Sayer, with a substantial reputation on Wall Street for getting tough jobs done for impatient shareholders; held in highest of esteem by dutiful, demanding, accountable boards of directors, for focused, sensible, timely actions, when called for. For the sake of full disclosure, Sayer was an unsentimental, hard charging, professional, corporate hatchet man, union buster and dirty trickster. But more to the point, he was a vicious, vocal, shameless, bigoted racist, and gay basher, who would stop at nothing to succeed; executive suite poster boy, hired gun, whose hidden cynicism, about his own profession, knew no bounds, in that, having made his fortune in the television business, he never ceased to refer to the television itself as the idiot box; for he himself watched no TV, perhaps a rare tennis match, football game, here and there, as a true descendant of active, task-oriented Puritans, believing the idiot box only worthy of time wasting; a great excuse for forgoing productivity, and possibly, losing one's health, becoming a soft, couch potato. And remarkably, though ostensibly of pure Anglo-Saxon stock, privately, at *la Mujer*'s house, he had a real, unexplained weakness, fetish, for biracial and bisexual hookers, neon orange lipstick, gaudy, blond wigs, patent leather, thigh-high boots.

The studio hired Sayer to restructure its West Coast operations and forestall the power of the union, the Theatre and Cinema Worker's Guild, seemed to be named from another era; the former, accomplished following typical corporate best practices, reducing headcount by 39%, canceling bonuses and deferred compensation, then selling off the unprofitable publishing and theater businesses (when called out, for the severity of the cuts, a determined, well-tanned, Sayer, morosely replied, "Well, it is one of the most difficult and unfortunate decisions I have ever been forced into, but what other choice is there? We are talking about the survival of the company;" shamefully angling for public sympathy, playing a helpless victim of cruel circumstance, verging on crocodile tears; outrageously blaming the terminated workers themselves for the untenable position in which he, a sympathetic but responsible manager, floundered); while the later, was accomplished following typical corporate worst practices, bringing out drug dogs for a *blitzkrieg* sweep of the Los Angeles headquarters, one dark, uneventful night, to root out reported methamphetamine, purposely planted by Sayer's crooked security guards in the desks of certain chosen workers, who were also union members; with this bold measure the union in one fell swoop masterfully discredited, for when the company offered the accused a clean slate, upon passing drug screens, almost three quarters were subsequently identified, as marijuana and cocaine users, although none had abused crystal meth. Incriminated offenders testing positive were summarily dismissed, after which the union was further subjected to onerous lawsuits, for the alleged illegal drug use, and distribution, by the fired, while on the job. Following this incident, the union played nice with Sayer, and went along with senior management in every decision. In line with their newly found religion, unionists permitted to continue were given promotions, raises and company wheels. Sayer was two for two. His aversion to unionism and its sacred cow, socialism, was visceral, convinced they bred an apathy and its fateful consequence, self-destruction. Gone would be the need, impulse, to do things for yourself. When life was a planned event, there was no reason to get out of bed, because existence was about meeting the struggle head on, and succeeding on one's own terms, not those dictated by the masses. Besides, socialism was the peak expression of the politics of envy, the Ten Commandments prohibiting coveting your neighbor's things.

The board generously rewarded him with a one-time, tax deferred, performance bonus, additional stock options, vesting in as little as eighteen months, and the use of a corporate jet, to commute more easily between New York, California and the other far-flung outposts where he might be needed. Professional bosses were on a tear since Andrew Carnegie paid Charles Schwab a salary of over a million dollars a year, in 1897, to oversee his steel monopoly. That was the start of excessive executive compensation. After amassing an incredible fortune, however, Schwab died penniless, a true example of poetic justice, if ever there was one. Despite extravagant compensation, Sayer was amazingly tight fisted, justifying innate avarice with a hodgepodge of homespun, kitchen table philosophies, citing Ben Franklin, Henry Ford, dried-out New England Congregationalist ministers, on pure thrift, hard work, self-reliance; some mornings, incredibly, finding Sayer purchasing The Wall Street Journal, noticeably, entirely in pennies, painstakingly counting out the exact amount, trying the patience of busy newsstand attendant. Perhaps the censure, isolation, rejection undergone by his stern, stubborn, defensive progenitors and their fellow, grim-faced assembly of upright, messianic English, after being persecuted, driven to distant shores for religious extremism, in the early 1600's, had been stamped onto his temperament, in secret, sub-cellular imprint, finding current expression in cheapness, zealotry, egotism; such a chip off the old block never better observed in preppy reunions, country clubs, or anywhere else that plaid pants would be stylish.

On the commuter train, riding home from work, lulled by the clicking tracks rolling under, whimsical, sleepy, in a once upon a time manner, Sayer pondered, imagined, daydreamed, *how it must have been, back when his East Anglian forefathers landed on these shores, in 1633, making their way to the newly founded colony of Windsor, in the lush Connecticut River Valley, their lofty aim, to live as simply as the early Christian Church, in the truth of one God, as revealed in the Bible. But it must have meant more to them than only getting closer to the Holy Spirit, the question always on his mind being, what became of the Indians back then, ceasing to be a threat, or crucial factor, due to the Great Dying? He always presumed, knew, that though inspired,* The Pilgrim's Progress *had justified a sad, New World land grab.*

> Multi-generational stories, relics, of esteemed family founders, historical society sketches, clippings, references in periodicals, newsprint, swirling into the past; the reprimanding nature of the erect, tight lipped, deacon's ancestral blood, coursing through his veins, defining their rich futures...

> Dissenters, Separatists, persecuted by their own co-religionists, over the last fifty years in England, arriving on a wild, hard, unforgiving coastline; tables turned to their advantage, technologically, if not morally, superior, persecuting naked, heathen savages, with extreme, unforgiving, blaming

> notions of conduct, identical to their own deprecations at home from those less devout; perhaps infecting, expropriating, exterminating Indians here, no more impolite, reprehensible, than martyring Catholics, appropriating their possessions there, where persecution prepared Pilgrims for pillage...

> Their feigned victimhood allowed exploiting Puritans to rob the ignorant primitives of their ancestral lands, without even blinking an eye. Weren't frontier settlers due recompense in the New World, for things supposedly left behind, lost, robbed, confiscated by devious authorities, in the Old?...

> Stolid moralists in stiff white collars, buckled shoes, swindling an eastern

seaboard from nearly eradicated native tribes, barely holding on to dear life itself; and hypocritically proclaiming, the correctness of their way of life, depth of belief in a harsh, distant, old God, to all who would listen...

Those religionist prudes, who came over in joint stock companies to God, commercial ventures justified by fate, and faith, went on to impose their brutal *laissez fair* austerity on subsequent generations; deleterious effects be damned, so long as Indians submitted to the white man's colonialism.

Indeed, when Deacon J. Bigger Sayer, with a sanctimonious, severe, but unpretentious disposition, first laid eyes on a certain Indian maiden, lurking about the outskirts of the settlement, struggling to survive in a newly imposed, unforgiving, ecclesiastical capitalist society, waiting for any morsel of bread, corn meal, a sympathetic colonist might offer, his first concern was her gaunt frame, vacant eyes, jaundiced skin, and other signs of sickness and malnutrition, considering that over the past hundred years, ninety five percent of her race had already been wiped out, by a triple whammy: smallpox, influenza, typhoid; additionally, as something about her remained elevated, proud, enigmatic, alluring, he thought she had the wherewithal to introduce him to some of his still remote, withdrawn, Indian neighbors, for purposes of amassing a more ample farm, with enough acres for grazing meadows, tracts of cleared (of natives) space, in admiring the lay of the land, it surely seemed there was more than enough of it out there, for everyone, especially him and his family. Hadn't a Dutchman, seven years ago, paid 60 guilders, what seemed a reasonable price, for Manhattan Island, and now wasn't that amount their benchmark to beat? It was the process of acquiring a thing, not necessarily for its inherent, practical, or sentimental, value, or intrinsic wealth, that fostered a greedy appropriation of an object, because obtainment usually meant its wrenching separation from others (except initially by unknowing, and gullible, wilderness dwellers, who thought they were simply sharing what was not even theirs, or anyone's, to share, not dividing up, as per Western traditions of land ownership and tenancy), taking over for oneself, collecting, that which had belonged to someone else; and it was in the humiliation involved in the alienating moment, but not necessarily the final possession, that avarice occurred, the act of willfully gaining more than the awe of self-serving affluence, itself. If this was the origin of Manifest Destiny, heaven help the misled makers of the dream, for casually claiming Aboriginal lands, justified on Christian doctrines of ethnic primacy:

> ...the fulfillment of our manifest destiny to overspread the continent
> allotted by Providence for the development or our yearly multiplying
> millions. (John O'Sullivan, *The Democratic Review*, 1845)

The great replacement of those vast, continental native tribes, as with the huge bison herds, eliminated by covetous bands of Caucasian conquerors, had only commenced, as the cruel imperative of the future order, the red people Sayer's sort took the land from now dying off, ceaselessly, to lose their claim of it:

> Within these late years, there hath, by God's visitation, reigned a
> wonderful plague, the utter destruction, devastation, and depopulation
> of that whole territory, so as there is not left any that do claim or challenge
> any kind of interest therein. We, in our judgment, are persuaded and
> satisfied, that the appointed time is come in which Almighty God, in
> his great goodness and bounty towards us, and our people, hath thought
> fit and determined, that those large and goodly territories, deserted as
> it were by their natural inhabitants, should be possessed and enjoyed
> by such of our subjects. (King James I, Charter of New England, 1620)

The accepted view was that these religious reformers, pushy pastors, with austere denominations, sects, doctrines, a plain, unadorned dress, were divisive crackpots, dissidents of the Church of England, their quitting the British Isles bringing great benefits, no matter what the potential harm, to the colonies, or errors made, regrets borne, in permitting heretical creeds to spread there. As lowly conspirators (threats to the stability of the realm, and its evolving empire, deserving censure), they had to be shown the exit, the outstanding attitude being, good riddance, better to be done with them, going so far as to mark out, and grant them patents on, some primitive, wild, unproven territory, in which to pursue their dogmatic, fundamentalist ideas, than allow treasonous oaths at the royal doorstep. Nevertheless, when the deacon provided the starving girl, Cloud, a *Pequot* princess, with much needed food one day, he was as a god to her; she proceeded to strategically offer herself to him, topless, with sinful, vulgar gestures. Though married, with four children, the chaste deacon succumbed to her special, charms, excusing himself for any, and all, sin, as she was a heathen, unimportant in the eyes of God; partnering with her to represent his outside land interests. The villainous Protestant justification offered to assuage the guilt, which is a byproduct of the incredible success of American society, culture, historical progression, regarding fair profit and alms, is that by helping yourself, you help others, a fantasy foisted upon northern Europeans by covetous, pinched preachers, guided by an invisible hand. If you want to help others, help them, but if you want to help yourself, help yourself. As a reminder, Catholic saints were selfless martyrs. When the Reformation did away with the Roman Church's hagiographies, icons, cult of Mary, Mother of God, they were cunningly replaced with ledger books, new pecuniary idols of self-interest and greed. It was as if an invisible hand made sure to place the first snatched dollar in one's right pocket, before releasing a skimped amount from their left one, to those in need. "But when thou doest alms, let not thy left hand know what thy right hand doeth:" royal Cloud generously brought him round to all her people, and he shortly negotiated numerous deals, paying almost nothing other than the temporary hunting rights, for a tremendous swath of property. At twenty thousand acres, he was the lord of his dominion. Of course, a shrewd and proper, moral pillar, he soon evidenced, confirmed, legitimized, his duplicitous purchases, by drafting up primordial deeds with those who ostensibly, unknowingly, artfully, presumed the right to sell, lease, lend, give what was never theirs to transact, as it belonged to all; granting him original titles, legally recording such conveyances for the first time, so future owners could verify prior transfers were actual, *bona fide* (and not outright thefts, as the first had been); from persons (rude miscreants) without the cultural competence to understand let alone participate in a bargain and sale, or to consider what the dastardly ramifications would be. The creation of the earliest deeds out nothing, thin air, conveniently evidenced the willingness of the original Indian holders to sell, thereby establishing the (hollow) pillar upon which each successive transfer was accepted as valid, in perpetuity; for these devious Protestants brought their English common law, allowing them to officialize stolen property from Native Americans as long as it was recorded in a court of law, as in England, thereby sanitizing the theft for all time; and once the fraudulent land titles were inscribed setting real precedents forever more; misdeeds, fakes, lies founding enacted systems of convoluted town and county records, covering up primeval transgressions:

> Why does the Gospel so command,
> "Hide thy good deeds from thy left hand,"?
> Because, according to the story,
> the left hand signifies vainglory,
> which comes from false hypocrisy.
> The right hand stands for charity,
> which does good, seeking to conceal it,
> instead of boasting to reveal it,
> so no one knows of it but He

whose name is God and Charity,
for God is Charity... (Chretien de Troyes, *Perceval; or, the Story of the Grail,* circa 1181)

The term, idea, of accounting, keeping track of one's duty, to God, was a practical, Protestant addition, along with the capitalist, free market economy, intercontinental slavery, mercantilism, colonialism, etc.; and their obsessions with judgement, reckoning, proclaiming only faith to get into heaven, disavowing, in the Reformation's biggest rejection, good works, as espoused in prior literature, including *Everyman*:

Take example, all ye that this do hear or see,
How they that I loved best do forsake me,
Except my Good Deeds that bideth truly. 870 (Anonymous, *Everyman*
*[The Summoning of Everyman]*, fifteenth century, English morality play)

Considering America was started as a corporation, the Mayflower Compact being one of the first joint stock company articles of incorporation in history, it should be no surprise that, given the primordiality of property under English common law, as described by John Locke, the penalty for robbing a bank is still worse, than for killing a person; what better proof that society values property rights above human life? God help the galaxy, if humans start colonizing it, as they did their own world, for it is the poison of acquisition that will spread beyond our own planetary limits, polluting infinite stars and unimagined reaches, as we have our own pristine garden; thus, will evil disseminate into the unsuspecting universe. Perhaps the term, Indian giver, was a double slur, insinuating first, that the invaders were begrudgingly provided with land from a people who, then going back on their word (only after sufficient depredation by their abusive guests), wanted it back. Hence, the meaning, to give hesitantly, and contrarily, demand back; a shame Ben Franklin was not around then, as "Guests, like fish, begin to smell after three days." Similarly, the term, Indian summer, a temporary, false, trick heat spell, meant to fool, speaks for itself. In one aspect, the deacon was the opposite of an Indian giver, giving away, but never demanding back. Being a man of earthy passions, the deacon fathered children with Cloud, and other friendly *squaws* he misled, however, never seeing fit to recognize his bountiful progeny with his own name; thus, allowing for their further degradation, dooming them as anonymous, faceless bastards, sucked into time's vortex; the deacon's wife, as well, seeming careless in her devotion, to any of these cast offs of her husband's.

As duplicity always lurks behind the shadow of self-righteousness, it did not take long for relations to fall apart, between those who roamed the open land, since time immemorial, merely stewards, entrusted with its care, and those recently encroaching. Remarkably, it was only sixteen years after the supposed first Thanksgiving, that the trespassers engaged in the mass murder of an estimated four hundred, up to seven hundred, Native Americans, trapping, shooting, roasting defenseless women, children and elders, at a Mystic fort set ablaze while its *Pequot* braves were away. (Actually, the first Thanksgiving was the celebration of the final imposition of the European order, on their idol worshiping neighbors, residing inconveniently on lands that were already spoken for; of wolves having lambs over for dinner. Even if local tribes aided the Pilgrims that first, deprivation, death filled year, they were already a vanquished race, on the way out; beaten down by past, and future, diseases, ever present tribal strife. By witlessly sitting down, if they truly ever did, with their fresh, pink faced enemies, the dark toned holders, trustees only, of nature's vast, bountiful mainland, would have acceded, given tacit assent, to their hideous new subservience to the bloodless, white devils; and from that minute on, the overstayed guests, interlopers, trespassers, knew that the killing of young, red skinned warriors, maidens, was of no more consequence than the swatting of a fly, on a late November day; the Indians would be just minor impediments to the future dispossession of America, awaiting liquidation by early capitalists.) (So much for Thanksgiving, which was probably a lie to begin with, never occurring, the proud and scheming Pilgrims never sitting down to any sort of civil dinner with a bunch of diseased, filthy savages, not while death stalked them.) During the Pequot War, the deacon volunteered with the troops, and was witness to, and participated in, great slaughter, accepting carnage as justified and inevitable, considering, "...but every Tree Is become an Indian for the terrified Inhabitants." And such bold hostiles would no longer be tolerated, coddled or pardoned. But Princess Cloud heard what was done to her tribe; he had brought home charred scalps possessing the enemies' spirits, possibly of her own family, as proof of the massacre, conflagration, and for bounties paid; and she never looked at him the same way again, lowering her gaze henceforth, in his presence, out of shame and submission. He also was much altered by his experience, for it came to him that eviction, liquidation, would be the quickest means to appropriate the current occupants' assets, plundering trumping accommodation, suggesting using large, fierce dogs against recalcitrant, rebellious natives, the Spaniard's Method, but as there were not enough dogs available, impossible to implement. On the other hand, he would settle for a smallpox epidemic to facilitate wiping them all out, supplying infected blankets and handkerchiefs, a new type of biological warfare, as a final solution. Cloud loved Deacon Bigger, but quietly worried these filthy Puritans did not care one bit about anyone, or anything, outside of their small circle, consisting of those deserving of, promised, and ultimately rewarded with, salvation, all being foretold in their predestinarian theology; the same insincere, self-laudatory prophets of greed, loudly proclaiming their godly lives, according to His word, avoiding temptation, being delivered from eternal damnation, also incited uncompromising extermination, by any means, of her depleted, trounced, own kind, as more than state policy but God's work itself; an exemplary, famous relation of the deacon's sermonizing, for all of posterity to remember his congregation's asinine cruelty:

> Once you have but got the Track of those Ravenous howling Wolves, then
> pursue them vigorously; Turn not back till they are consumed... Beat
> them small as the Dust before the Wind. (The Reverend Cotton Mather,
> 1663-1728, New England Puritan clergyman, intellectual, and early
> champion of "a Collegiate School," later renamed Whale College)

It never occurred to most Americans, that their continent, was fatally flawed, structurally doomed, from the start, from when the die was indelibly cast, over the theft of Indian lands, and for this initial crime, at the outset of an epic confrontation of cultures, races, world and cosmological views, the curse never to be lifted again, persisting until the sun sets a last time: such from illicit beginnings, never to succeed. It came to pass, that the theocratic structure of the deacon's city upon a hill failed to evolve to a greater purpose, and was itself reformed, excoriated, but the inner damage had long been done, it was too late. Religious freedom in early New England was never meant to be for all, only for that cabal of followers subscribing to Separatist or Puritan doctrine; all other religions be damned, as was neatly demonstrated in their treatment of Roger Williams, and his band of reformers (ironically dissenting against original dissenters); seeing him off to the most inhospitable mud flats around, which he named, the Providence Plantation, believing that God had brought them there (the term plantation used in the 17th century as a synonym for settlement, colony); naming islands in Narragansett Bay after Christian virtues: Patience, Prudence and Hope Islands. And as countrymen, and co-religionists, arrived, the entrenched assumed those same insular attitudes toward other congregations, as they would versus different denominations; faith, an exclusionary undertaking, much like membership to an exclusive country club, would one day be. The idea was to leave others alone spiritually, as you would also like to be, but not necessarily to respect, appreciate or assume, specific aspects of others' beliefs; religious tolerance become a code for ignoring outsiders, forcing out non-members, promoting only your own kind; not Christian virtues.

As the deacon aged, he remained the haughty prig, he had always been, sticking his nose, in everyone else's business, regulating the way they must conduct themselves while asserting, offensively, there was no temporal power rightful enough to claim authority over him. As one of the largest land speculators, tobacco farmers, for miles around, he acclaimed satisfaction in the cruelest of ironies: the natives ended up paying him, the white man, a rent, for remaining on their (once) own land; that was the final insult.

One day after so many years together Cloud told Deacon Bigger she was dying, yet he did not think for an instant, of thanking her for years of devotion, loyalty and service, nor the countless, dutiful, loving children she had consistently borne him, with many proud warriors among them, and maidens worthy of being princesses, as their mother; instead, coldly turning his head, reciting trite, insincere sentiments of peace, assuring blithely, it was God's will, He would lead, the way; lamentably, in no case could she anticipate being saved, on account of not having been Christianized; suffering from advancing cirrhosis of the liver, after decades of rampant alcohol abuse, having grown fond of whiskey, immediately, upon meeting and cohabiting with the scheming deacon. On her deathbed, sad Cloud, lowly, red unbeliever, was visited by Humility, the deacon's demure wife, who understood that Cloud was not to blame, for her husband's philandering. When she forgave Cloud for openly carrying on with her husband, causing matrimonial strife between them, it was the only Christian charity Cloud had ever known; the wayward deacon never once showing Cloud, the least of intimacies, dignity or trust, other than the savagery of his indefatigable, carnal demands, caring primarily for himself; having ruined Cloud, then together ruined her nation, but in that sense acting no differently than anyone else, English or Indian, it having become a matter of looking out for number one, since the palefaced devils' invasion. As theirs was a parsimony bordering on the maniacal, succumbing to keeping what was not offered, hatefully annihilating humans and stealing public lands, a century later, those who came after Deacon Bigger would go on to establish textile mills, in Manchester, CT, adopting child labor until that atrocious abuse was finally abolished by statute. They saw nothing wrong with the derelict practice and would have continued it, had it not been outlawed. Of the children working in those factories, many would be of Indian and Caucasian heritage, but as the next shift approached, the Sayers of that future time, would never imagine, let alone know, if any could possibly be blood relations of theirs, such mixed-race persons far from claiming any kinship.

I had numerous meetings with Sayer, in his trophy and souvenir cluttered, midtown office. Despite his fierce competitiveness, he quickly put visitors at ease, cutting through initial formalities, awkwardness, etiquette, with an amusing comment, witty detail or wry remark. A great storyteller, he had, however, a cruel sense of humor, usually at the expense of innocents; naturally, he loved playing practical jokes on unsuspecting targets. Once, entering his inner sanctum, in his greeting, while shaking hands, guffawing wildly, pointing down at my groin, as if my fly were open, he uttered aloud: *La petite shows, la petite shows,* just loud enough for everyone to look toward me, much to my infinite chagrin; of course, I was completely startled, then forced to look down to see if my fly was open in public, realizing I had been had, while he laughed all the harder for, "...in every joke a lie has its hidden function;" it being his idea of warm greeting, making you look and feel ridiculous, cringing. And if you got off with this treatment alone, you could consider yourself lucky that Sayer hadn't savagely goosed you, with intent to rupture, in front of other executives, as a gag. It was not unusual to see hobbled young men after their meetings with Sayer, suffering being goosed (by an invisible hand, of course) in good-natured fashion. "He was certainly a card!" quite vain, fundamentally insecure, always boasting, trying to impress with physical prowess. It was peak summer, and he invited me to a 4th of July extravaganza, at his War Heroes Hill Swiss chalet style mansion, with sweeping views of the Long Island Sound, in obsessively ambitious, suburban Xanadu, Bestport, Connecticut, enchanted East of Eden. He lived comfortably and loudly, a pretense of Puritan conventionality combined with obnoxious braggadocio, with society wife, Felicity, their four children; and in some primal disavowal of John Calvin's severity, they were unselfconscious materialists, with the latest home items, electronic gadgets and sports equipment, displayed throughout the house; an eccentric example of how the Sayers had everything: a friend once brought each of them one of a-kind *kamik* seal skin boots, from Alaska, made by Inuit women, who chewed the animal skins to softness. As the insulated boots connoted the outdoors and roughing it, and as they did not heat their mansion much, out of some Yankee frugality, and stubborn, naturopathic beliefs that cold, fresh air was good for the circulation and respiration (although they always seemed to suffer from severe bronchitis, hacking into ever present handkerchiefs, windows wide open in December), they wore the cumbersome footwear on half the days of the year, as their connection to *malamutes*, *muktuk* and *mukluks*, the entire family always in a breathless, mad rush, exercising, doing things, flying off first class (complaining of business) somewhere exciting, for vacation or work, a friend's wedding in Miami, a sales junket to San Francisco, caravanning with well-heeled groups up to Stowe or Killington, to indulge in white powder and gourmet bistros, then out to Newport, with the season, for sun, jazz and oysters, or tennis sets and Saturday dinners at the Hunter's Club, or just plain following the scent on morning shopping sprees, for the latest in frivolous yet expensive consumer items (they also casually hung Picasso, Miro and Matisse prints in the dining room). And the crazy running around was part of their ethos of success, a "can do" attitude. They were very wealthy, but pretended not to be and became annoyed when it was mentioned. If you were their friend, you had to go along with the pretense of their just being the same as everyone else. As they perfectly embodied the Protestant work ethic (with work as its own virtue, developed in tandem with the Reformation, for in the Middle Ages and ancient times, work was only for peasants) (with Sunday school, heavy house chores, lawn work, summer jobs, and closed door whippings, with a thick, stiff, tanned leather cowboy belt, deeply tooled, engraved, with an immense silver buckle, in the cavernous dining room, while the patient siblings waited, terrified, in the echoing hallway, hearing each victim's wails, as a prelude to their own, inevitable turn; the voiceless mother powerless to restrain the father's alcohol and cigar fueled rages; the nervous children tortured in thus fashion from an early age), nothing was beyond their attainment or achievement, with enough money they could conquer the world (or at least, Ivy League qualified, Wall Street); Felicity, product of San Francisco old money, originally Vermont dairy farmers, her forebears were dirt poor Forty-Niners, wagon training from Independence, MO, west, across the plains and mountain divide of an untamed landmass, to the California Gold Rush; and though their strong predilection for cattle rustling kept them from amassing much gold in the near term, over successive generations, they cobbled together, one of the largest ranches in the Sacramento Valley; with lands they systematically swindled from destitute Mexicans, and drunken Indians. By the late 1840's, when the Southwest, confiscated from Mexico, was in play, those pushing west gave up all pretense of obtaining any property grants, or original (mis) deeds, common in New England, due to the English common law obsession of legitimizing through precedent a systematic dispossession of newly encountered Native American tribes. They subscribed to the premeditated slaughter of as many Indians as possible; do what you wanted, amass as much territory as you could legally, or illegally, claim. As a rule, the biggest problems were not plains and desert Indians, but other whites encroaching on marked wire fences, as the range was armed madness, total insanity. A gentle, distracted and sincere person, a Christian Scientist not interested in wealth, per se, but glad for what it could buy, a few years his senior, she babied Sayer considerably, which seemed normal to him. But that did not stop him from hitting on any attractive blond he might encounter at some cocktail reception in their town, their Famefield Beach Club, or wine cellar of their party that night. With knowing smiles, twinkles in their eyes, area women fondly referred to him, as the notorious John B. Sayer. Open in his affairs, his wife graciously ignoring malicious gossip, his immature behavior, he was the kind of man who could unabashedly proceed, from church directly to strip club, without batting an eye; a philandering fool in upright businessman's guise, apocryphal verse from the side of his mouth mocking a nasal voice of an emotionally deficient hillbilly:

> "I don't care if it rains or freezes
> Long as I got my plastic Jesus
> Riding on the dashboard of my car."
> (Eddie Marrs, Stuart Rosenberg, *Cool Hand Luke*, 1967)

Although it could not have been more than the quirk of fate, that Sayer was born on the 4th of July, still he considered himself providentially blessed, if not touched directly, by the Maker, on that account. He was a real Yankee Doodle Dandy, flag flying patriot, celebrating the 4th as his personal holiday, to exult in, and to own; a heavily decorated U.S. Army Airborne, special forces, colonel, having seen extensive action early on in Vietnam, trained as a demolition specialist, loving fireworks and blowing things up; with no interests in normal, legal sparklers and the like, but obsessed with the big, illegal stuff: M-80s, cherry bombs, two-inch firecracker chains, Roman candles, heavy rockets, super blaster balls. As teens on a dare, he and his brother held live ladyfingers as they exploded (while preserving their own fingers, the boys never tried the stunt again). They had an enormous, 1950s Lionel model train set, installed on a massive plywood table, spread out with scenery, shrubs, mountains, alpine tunnels, bridges, buildings, and miniature people; and they had tremendous satisfaction in booby trapping metal plated locomotives and rail cars, red cabooses, with choice cherry bombs; whooping and shrieking, "Geronimo!" in delight as the solid model pieces flipped in the air, tumbling back to shredded tracks; all the while, pretending the nation was under foreign sneak attack. Incredibly, they were taught the South defeated the North in the War Between the States (also known as the Civil War), but had to cede, in consequence of disloyal slaves escaped from their plantations, running wild in murderous rampages throughout the countryside, destroying the glorified Antebellum way of life forever. In the 1820s, a branch of the Sayer family had pioneered west to the new Anglo colony in Texas, where huge tracts of land were free for the taking, to grow cotton on a commercial scale, planting deep roots, taking on the local beliefs, values, customs, of a limitless region; in the next generation, enthusiastically joining its Lost Cause, training, campaigning and dying, most nobly, for their grand, adopted secessionist state, and its inhuman, unjust, ruinous slave practices; earning the heartfelt admiration, respect, of their northern cousins, who, though unwaveringly loyal to the Union, and committed abolitionists, all sat out the war. This might have explained Sayer's energetic humming of "Dixie," nostalgic anthem of the Confederacy, while demonstrating considerable pyrotechnical skills. As evening progressed, downing his fair share of bourbon mint juleps, presuming no one within earshot, he broke out in song, in a lilting, jeering tone of parodying, comic, black dialect; it became a bit uncomfortable, as some of the guests were black, or of different minorities; a few, out of obliged, gracious politeness to their host, may have even complimented him on his mocking renditions:

> "I wish I was in the land of cotton,
> Old times they are not forgotten;
> Look away! Look away! Look away! Dixie Land.
> In Dixie Land where I was born,
> Early on one frosty mornin,
> Look away! Look away! Look away! Dixie Land."
> (Daniel Decatur Emmett, "Dixie," 1859)

And later, after a few more drinks, under a heavy, no-holds barred, blackface minstrelsy spell, including captivating, angular, gyrating dance moves, was it only my imagination, or was his face shaded black?

> "Wheel about and turn about and do just so,
> Ev'ry time I wheel about I jump Jim Crow." (Thomas D. Rice, 1828)

Each year, Sayer made it down to Chinatown, for twenty neatly packed, bulging shopping bags, boxes, full of mostly illegal explosives, wrapped in brightly multicolored wax paper; surely more than enough gun powder for an arsenal, or to blow his house to kingdom come. As setting off so many complicated devices, multi fused rockets, endless strings of firecrackers, was the major spectacle of such gatherings, occupying a great deal of time and focus after dinner, it was astonishing there were no drunken mishaps or casualties, considering all the hoopla, alcohol and M-80s going around. Sayer roared with laughter, delighting with every bomb report, as if each was the first detonation of his life. I last saw him amidst flashing bursts, letting forth a piercing Rebel Yell of the Confederacy at the top of his lungs, outrageous battlefield commander, leading a phantom cavalry charge through low hanging, black, sulfurous smoke saturated, thick air, yelling, "Wa-woo-woohoo, wa-woo woohoo! Wa-woo-woohoo, wa-woo woohoo!!:

Strike a blow for liberty. (Harry S. Truman, 1930's, referring to joining
fellow senators for shots of bourbon at the "doghouse")

In all truth, not much business was conducted at these executive gatherings, their agenda set to Sayer's macho retellings of his big game hunting exploits, picking off elusive snow leopards in the *Himalayas*, shooting a family of roaming elephants in Zimbabwe, bagging a thousand harmless doves in Argentina, just to say I did it. If it appeared easy sport, Sayer was quick to whitewash his presumed predilections, for snuffing out living things, claiming he was merely assisting nature cull wild, endangered species for their own good, promoting responsible conservation, most assuredly benefiting populations. Of course, it could never be gaged how the creatures being thinned out might feel about his magnanimous concern for their collective welfare. It was all in keeping with an obsession for natural, open air, fresh, flowing water, brilliant sunshine, boundless, unspoiled vistas; and a healthy lifestyle promoting physical fitness, mental agility, and frequent escape from the narrow, fluorescent lit, air-conditioned confines, of high-rise offices; needed breaks from the easy refinements and intellectuality of urban and suburban culture, which to him, were signs of moral weakness, degeneracy. As part of this extreme, survivalist, outdoor mythology, as a twenty-year-old, wading through snake infested swamps in North Carolina, sharpening his wilderness survival skills, in an instant a water moccasin stuck fangs deep into his arm, he, refusing medical treatment, to build up a future immunity to the venom. But there was nearly no future, his arm swelling to the size of a watermelon, as serpent poison spread through his body, almost choking off his respiration, stopping his heart. It was surely a miracle he survived such a test, but there were lingering effects; his timing and reactions to others were off, as if sensing them from far away, reality occurring in slow motion. Sayer's puerile fascination with sex, his self-promoting anecdotes, were invariably full of adolescent perversions, details of his many conquests, of getting the best deal, and one-upping rivals; loving off color, racial, ethnic, sexist quips, spreading false rumors about those whom he barely knew, being homosexuals and lesbians; ridiculing hard working immigrants for their poverty, sneering at their rough cut clothes, manners, mimicking their accents, mocking foreign sounding surnames, languages, and the texture of an individual's hair if different, all with evil purposes of humiliation and debasement.

"I am speaking about God, culture and the everyday principles of life, such as sexual habits, freedom of expression, a mutuality between men and women, and all the kinds of values, which I call Christianity. If we let the foreigners into our continent to compete with us, they will outnumber us. It's simple math, and we don't like it" said Sayer, in an interview published in several European newspapers, including, *Le Fibaro*, continuing, "The fall of the Roman Empire was marked by a loss of the will to fight external enemies combined with successive barbarian invasions. Instead of warring against foreign enemies, in their own lands, the irresolute Latins procrastinated, until they were flooded with foreigners, and then it was too late. Sound familiar, especially since the disaster in Vietnam, and the illegal immigrant fiasco. Compare this present decay to the era of T.R., with his gunboat diplomacy, when we had no self-doubts or fears, and behaved accordingly, with bluster and presumption; these are two sides of the same coin."

Routinely the business at hand, would not even come up until the final ten minutes; today it was image remaking, a new ad campaign highlighting cultural competency, the studio's promotion of diversity, by aggressively hiring, advancing, extolling the careers of, minorities; as a major industry reflective of the multi-cultural movie going public at large, Hollywood was interested in fostering equal opportunity and treatment for all; scheduling publicity shots, promotional TV and radio spots for Lilly Lawrence, rising, recently discovered, Arab American bombshell, starlet, signed up for mega movies into the millennium, and seeming quite a stunner; suddenly unable to contain himself any longer, swelled up with the pride of the male human species, Sayer bragged he had slept with her, "she was really hot." I let myself out the door, rushing out to fresh air, wondering when Puritans would modernize with the changing times:

And thus, with Christianity on the quarter-deck, and paganism on the
forecastle, the Irrawaddy ploughed the sea. (Melville, Idem)

The Warren Bros. Building was only a few blocks from my Madison Avenue office, and one oppressive
September afternoon, during rush hour, I found myself on the Downtown Lexington Avenue Express,
at 59th Street, when who gets on, just as the doors are closing, but John Sayer. As the subway car was so
crowded, Sayer, at the other end, hadn't seen me; the train slowly lumbered its way downtown, swaying
heavily from left to right, many conversations in different languages occurring; and every now and then
I thought I heard a bird sweetly chirping in the background, as if caught and trying to escape. At Grand
Central Station - 42nd Street, a new wave of commuters boarded; once we got going again, others heard
the bird's plaintive tweets, cocking heads to listen. At 14th Street - Union Square, more people boarded;
our car was really packed. An unseen, concerned citizen spoke up: "the poor little bird is in trouble; if
we all took a moment to look for it, perhaps we could set it free, at the next stop." The air conditioning
wasn't working properly, everyone was sweltering, sweaty, with lots of funky body odor; a typical New
York City subway scene, people of different races, colors, religions from all over the world, some in the
United States legally, some illegally. I thought Sayer was one of the few white guys, aboard; it quickly
dawning on me that Sayer was responsible for the bird noises, I was sure of it, recalling similar fleeting
sounds once before, in Sayer's lobby, as he came out from the elevator banks to greet me, smiling slyly. I
checked the far end of the car, but now Sayer had turned away, staring out of the rattling window, into
the tunnel darkness. As the well laden train pulled into Brooklyn Bridge – City Hall passengers pressed
toward the doors to get off, the captive bird's songs now exploding into a shrill police whistle, causing
substantial confusion and alarm. In half an instant all hell broke loose, the train sluggishly screeched to
a halt, the police whistle, sharp and punishing, and then someone cried out very clearly, "Immigration,
have your passports, Immigration!" As the train came to a dead stop, before doors slid open, there was
a dreaded look of panic and bewilderment on many travelers' faces, an unseen, threatening voice, again
barking "Attention, documents please, Immigration!" When the doors flew open, John Sayer was the
first person out onto the station platform, standing stiffly, arms extended, by broad exit stairs, shouting
instructions at the apprehensive bodies leaving the train, "Ladies and gentlemen, your attention, please,
Immigration check, have your papers ready." He had a green trench coat which he wore with authority,
and in the tense electric light, could easily have been mistaken for a federal agent, or Gestapo officer in
a movie. In his left hand was the shiny metal whistle, which he still blew intermittently. His right-hand
beckoned departing passengers to one of several areas on the steamy platform, and surprisingly enough,
people were paying attention to him, moving to assigned places, in this strangest of all possible scenes.

"I am in pursuit of all:
interplanetary aliens
third world aliens
illegal immigrants
undocumented persons
unauthorized migrants
temporary laborers
wetback scabs
entrenched interlopers
criminal misfits
itinerant workers currently out of status
and any other removable trespassers
or smelly three-day guests
the networking effect

of chain immigration
a violation on society

"Africans, blacks, mulattoes, quadroons, this way, line up right here," he announced firmly, through the station noise, pointing straight ahead, some compliant passengers, oddly enough, lining up. Others, on the platform, taking notice, after brief consideration, joined their mates. Now, what was going on here?

"South Americans, Mexicans, Cubans, Puerto Ricans to the left, single file over there please," he stated urgently, pointing, toward which a new group amazingly gravitated. "*Sus documentos, pasaportes, por favor.*" Additional passers-by on the platform, hearing Spanish, came over, complacently volunteering.

"Indians, Paks, Persians, Turks, to the right, take your places over there, please," now issuing an order, rather than request, pointing in the other direction. A small sweaty team double timed it, forming a new line. Others ascending the stairs turned right around, respectfully coming down to the platform to join.

"Redskins, wooden Indians, cigar store chiefs, braves, *squaws, papooses,* have your *wampum* available, right here, thank you; Hawaiians, Polynesians, Samoans, cannibals and headhunters, your body tattoos visible." Although only a few of them raised linked arms up, they shuffled slowly, passively, to line up.

Finally, "Asians, Chinks, Japs, Koreans, Gooks, Mongoloids, over more to the right, please, have your visas ready;" to which a senior, absent minded, Chinese gentlemen, who had obediently fallen into line, finally coming to his senses, retorted indignantly, "Wait, I was born in Manhattan; I am a U.S. Citizen."

Then a young Puerto Rican woman chimed in defiantly, "I am a U.S. Citizen; maybe not everyone here is legal, but many of us are," another, exclaiming, "I'm simply a tourist; I have nothing to do with this."

Such courageous declarations in defense of presumed civil liberties, universal rights, for the briefest of moments caught Sayer off guard; but after regrouping, he reparteed with a scornful afterthought, cruel coda, "Pardon, there's no line for Semites, they already own Hollywood, the media, the banks, the oil."

Many others were catching on, clamoring, insisting, "What's going on, here?" "Who are you?" "You, have no right to do this; show us your badge." Or as in *The Music Man*: "[We] want his credentials."

With the mood of his captive audience rapidly turning, Sayer sensed the ruse was nearly up, yet even so challenged did not miss a beat. He paused, making a show of gradually reaching into his jacket pocket, fumbling about, as if to retrieve some identification, then arrogantly delivered the patronizing knockout punch line, "Thank you for your cooperation. Welcome to America, 'the land of the free and the home of the brave.'" Taking such gibes at face value, those still humbly in line stared mutely, expressionless, not knowing how to react, while a jesting Sayer smirked back at them, with a self-pleased detachment. (The Pilgrims were the meanest swindlers and grim pills, endowed with a culturally derived, messianic superiority complex, compelling them to aggressively rob and ravage others, especially heathens [their inferiors], with impunity, while mythically being transfigured, into struggling Plymouth Rock heroes.)

Suddenly tearing off his trench coat to reveal a Superman suit, enfolding true craziness, Sayer assumed the one alter ego he knew would strike cold fear in the hearts of any illegals, still lurking in Metropolis; having fostered a small, underground following, from wearing the outfit on his Metro North commute.

Just then the clattering doors of the Downtown Express slammed shut, a large cloud of vapor wafted up from oily, garbage strewn tracks, and in that instant, with everyone distracted by the sudden rolling of the train, Superman was gone, flying up endless stairs through crowded station, out the revolving door and into the Indian summer twilight, rushing off to his appointment or rendezvous, as were perhaps any number of other successful, corporate comic book heroes on the town that night. Back on the platform, the lines of humanity quickly dissipated, dissolved again into the station, as if the entire sordid episode never occurred; a return to business as usual for those redirected to former lives, previous destinations; with the vast majority uncomprehending, and thus unaware, of the humiliating prank to which they had been subjected. No doubt they did not reflect on why they had lined up so willingly, heeding so readily the twisted rantings and ill-disposed directives of a sadistic stranger. For all they knew, he had been an immigration man, who after rounding them up, let them go, so for many, it was their special, lucky day:

> There I was at the immigration scene
> Shining and feeling clean, could it be a sin?
> I got stopped by the immigration man
> He said he doesn't know if he can let me in
>
> Let me in, immigration man
> Can I cross your line and pray?
> I can stay another day, won't you let me in, immigration man?
> I won't toe your line today, I can't see it anyway
>
> There he was with his immigration face
> Giving me a paper chase but the sun was coming
> 'Cos all at once he looked into my space
> And stamped a number all over my face and he sent me running
> (Graham Nash, "Immigration Man," 1972)

The great replacement of those vast, continental, Caucasian tribes, as with fake boundaries themselves, by reclaiming bands of brown skinned conquerors, had commenced, as the cruel imperative of a future order; the brown people Sayer's sort took the land from, now swarming back, ceaselessly, to reclaim it.

They may have been resented by those (predominantly whites), who were already here, but in truth, it was an historical moment for the coming invaders, their time in the flow of things, renaming what had been lost to them centuries ago, before reclaiming their imaginations, refined knowledge, human rights.

The decision to become a social avenger came to me unannounced one day, after witnessing Superman on that platform, herding immigrants to haphazard, perhaps undeserved, destinies: essentially, abusing them for his unshared amusement. For some reason I imagined the evolutionary descent of the original *Homo sapiens* leaping over *Australopithecus*, sprinting past *Homo erectus*, surpassing *Neanderthal* and finally reaching a destination in the cradle of civilization. I thought *wouldn't it be nice to expose all the evil doers of the world to show humanity the dregs to which certain of its members can sink? displaying an invisible hand as just another excuse to look away, when grave injustices are committed; all become rules, ever more rules, but where were the animal spirits that had once defined the land?* from thence, beginning the assumption of a non-complacent identity, one you will come to know, and the revealing vocation, which you will soon observe, that led me to write a book of what occurred at the millennium.

Miscellanea:

Select populations rounded up and transported by ship, boxcar, wagon or
on foot, resulting in countless deaths, family displacements, then misery:

1. Biblical Jews (*The Pentateuch*, Egyptian, then Babylonian bondage)
2. *The Trojan Women* (Euripides, 415 BC, Greek bondage)
3. Carthaginians (several Punic Wars, Roman annihilation, then bondage)
4. Celtic and Gallic Tribes (C. Julius Caesar, Commentaries On the Gallic War, 58-49 BC, Roman annihilation, then bondage)
5. "12.5 million Africans were shipped to the New World" (European, colonial and post-colonial bondage of 500 years)
6. Iberian Jews (Sephardic diaspora, to Turkey, Middle East, LatAm)
7. Cajuns (*Les Acadiens*, exiled Catholic French Canadians, of *Le Grand Derangement*, finding refuge in Lower Louisiana)
8. The Five Civilized Tribes (Trail of Tears, to Oklahoma)
9. Irish ("the hard times," the Great Hunger, famine, due to a potato blight, the invisible hand, free trade, Corn Laws, resulting in 25%+ population loss)
10. *Apache* (Geronimo, the fiercest Native warrior in history; smuggled and lain in a final rest on a burial platform in the dry dessert altitude of his people's spare hills, prior to allegedly being buried at Fort Sill, OK)
11. Boers (Anglo-Boer wars led to transport, early concentration camps as evil harbingers: Not only were the sly British, through royal patents and Acts of Parliament, major players in the African slave trade, for three hundred years, but they starved Ireland in the mid nineteenth century, then wasted Boer women and children in concentration camps fifty years later. British mercantile ambitions (greed) and evolving corporate structures (scale), made restructuring (ethnic cleansing) of populations inevitable (profit), given the competition for raw materials and labor)
12. Armenians (massacred by Turkish death marches to Syrian Desert)
13. Millions of Slavs, Gypsies (in boxcars to the Nazi death machine)
14. European, Asiatic, North African Jews (The Holocaust, leading to the founding of the State of Israel, "2020 worldwide Jewish population of 14.7 million, remaining well below, the pre-war 16.6 million in 1939")
15. 230,000 Crimean Tatars (in boxcars to Central Asia)
16. Tibetans (pushed off historical land, Shangri-la, by Han Chinese)
17. North African Muslims (to France, inspiring "*le grand remplacement*," "the great replacement" theory, the self-pitying ideology of racial comeuppance from humiliated vestigial racists, to help explain the inescapable browning of France/ Europe/ America)
18. Palestinians (homes bulldozed by the State of Israel)
19. 600,000 Tutsis (macheted to death, or exiled, by Hutus)
20. Sub Saharan Africans (21st century, in rubber rafts, to Europe)
21. Uyghurs (severe repression in Xinjiang, by Han Chinese)
22. Syrians (21st century Arab diaspora)
23. Brown skinned immigrants from all continents (smuggled to the United States of America by coyotes, frequently walked, bused, or flown, back across the U.S., Mexico, or Canadian borders, after deportation)

U.S. federal statute, 8 U.S. Code § 1227 stipulates the "classes of deportable aliens" who may be removed from the country by the attorney general.

# 6. Geronimo's Ghost

The ownership of women begins in the lower barbarian stages of culture, apparently with the seizure of female captives. The original reason for the seizure and appropriation of women seems to have been their usefulness as trophies. (Thorstein Veblen, *The Theory of the Leisure Class*, 1899)

Isidora Green had prepared for such a moment all her life. In fifteen minutes, she would coolly enter a wood paneled boardroom, with a long, polished conference table, the *sanctum sanctorum* in which time seemed to stand still, to be officially named Chairman of the Board of Warren Bros. Inc., entertainment conglomerate, to complement her current position as CEO. Composed and confident in her trophy and souvenir cluttered office, waiting for the board to conclude a procedural vote, a formality really, for what must have been a forgone conclusion in all directors' minds, that morning; she could not but be pleased with her recent string of accomplishments: bringing John B. Sayer on board, as president, to streamline the west coast businesses and get them back to profitability; successfully defending the network against charges that social media had transformed journalism into a giant popularity contest, and every journal into a Pimple.com; instituting cultural competence as their corporate policy, promoting a positive buzz of inclusive values, both inside and outside the studio; hiring Latino heartthrob, Willi Herman, to anchor the top rated, *Nightly News*, on a bonus heavy, ten-year contract; and hiring the newest Arab American sensation, Lillie Lawrence, to a multi-million-dollar, multi-picture, multi-cultural, multi-ethnic contract. It had certainly been a good year so far, and it was only mid-April. Elections are really about the forces of impatient resentment going against those of entrenched arrogance. Now that the congenial dotard, C. William (C. W.) Warren, was retiring as current chairman, and with no other Warren family member possessed of the vitality, vision or capability to take his place, the advantage had shifted to Isidora, who was positioned to assume absolute control of one of the most successful, significant and famous media holdings in existence. Without detracting from her own powerful intelligence, cunning and dedication, in her phenomenal rise to the top, Isidora had the humility in recognizing that, as with most boardroom *coups,* she had not arrived at the pinnacle of power alone or by chance, but rather after more than a half century of her family's steady, patient efforts, to wrest control of the company away from the plodding Warrens. Her soft skills proved that with solid lobbying and advanced pr you can make anyone believe anything (though hopefully for the good). Though the Warren line had for all effective purposes fizzled out, to ensure her succession to the top spot, as an ace up her sleeve and still unbeknown to them unless she unexpectedly needed leverage to force their hand, just days ago Isidora had paid one of C. W.'s old, distant, disaffected and overextended relatives a 100% premium for their one percent stake, giving her family a 51% holding, and majority of board seats, proving again, she was not Gray Green's great-great granddaughter for nothing. When the term, "fairer sex," was coined, no thought was ever given to even the remotest possibility of an Isidora Green, perhaps its original meaning, as a reference to a fairy tale.

Routinely the business at hand, would not even come up until the final ten minutes, as with the studio's own image remaking, a new ad campaign highlighting cultural competency, and the studio's promotion of diversity, by aggressively hiring, advancing, extolling the careers of, minorities; as the major industry reflective of the multi-cultural movie going public at large, Hollywood was interested in fostering equal opportunity and treatment for all; the studio then scheduling publicity shots, promotional TV and radio spots for Willi Herman, rising, recently discovered, studly, Hispanic star, signed on as the anchor for an upcoming decade of *Nightly News,* so blessed with New Age appeal; then unable to contain herself any longer, swelled with pride of the female human species, Isidora reminisced of *having slept with him, he was really hot*; and finding herself out of sorts, rushing out to fresh air, wondering how Scottish pirates, burgeoning capitalists, such as her dastardly ancestors, had modernized along with the changing times.

How is it that the naked ambitions of a few know no reasonable bounds? Gray Green, Industrial Age capitalist, archetypal robber baron, believed that God gave him his money, and thus, justified his high-handedness in making it. Descended from wily, penurious, Presbyterian merchants who had emigrated from Glasgow in the late 1700s, in search of solid trading opportunities, to express a stony opportunism that coursed through their veins; as if the barren hardness of the windswept, craggy highlands they, and their humorless ancestors, inhabited for two thousand years, had been molded into their inner beings, in some sort of mega generational transmutation; they were guided, pointed, purely by an invisible hand, demonstrating little concern, empathy or pity for others, especially competitors; and zero regard for the ultimate consequences of their brazen, predatory actions. There really were no economic laws in olden days, only obligations foisted upon pawns by proto practitioners of, "the dismal science," as economics was invented by men to justify, and explain, their greed, oppression, and taking advantage of others; to become devotees of the man-made gods of capital and profit, as avatars of avarice. Considering a deep yearning for religious freedom among so many bound for the New World during those intolerant times, it was ironic that the harsh, narrow tenets of Calvinism, with its major emphases on the cruel doctrines of predestination and sin, justified and celebrated the smug, self-satisfied elevation of those chosen few, comfortable in their self-perpetuating prosperity, insularity, while condemning as an evidence of divine retribution, the blameless inability of the rest, too ignorant and weak to rise up, from their inescapable, unalterable poverty. As a measure of belief, devotion, and the meriting of salvation, this mean-spirited system rewarded those for whom true faith expressed itself as self-interest, and supreme indifference to anything outside of neatly gotten returns, acclaiming material success as god's blessing, no matter how wretched the measures in its attainment. Gray Green's character was formed in a dreary, desolate, rural region in upstate New York, early on demonstrating a perverse reverence for almighty lucre. By the time he was twenty, in 1854, he prowled the Lower East Side of Manhattan for tenements and lots owned by infirm, delusional or terminally (and not even) ill deed holders, those who could be easily convinced or gently forced into quitclaiming their title interests over to him for his empty promise to maintain and care for them all of their lives; shortly before luckily expiring, or even more opportunely, disappearing, without a trace. These dubious acquisitions from exploited, incompetent, unsound parties under duress were handled with such craft, timing and foresight, they went unchallenged, and surreptitiously created one of the great real estate fortunes of New York, overnight making Green a force to be reckoned with. He had arrived, even though he had elbowed his way in. When twenty-five, he was speculating in Suez Canal shares, Egyptian cotton, U.S. steamship lines, and was central to one of the biggest watered stock schemes in history, in the Allegheny Railroad. At thirty-five he cornered the cattle market, tying up all available railroad stock cars used to transport live animals to the Chicago yards; later subleasing them, at grossly inflated rates to the desperate cattlemen and meat packers; needless to say, he made a killing:

> But nothing is so hard for those who abound in riches, as to conceive how
> others can be in want. (Jonathan Swift, 1713)

Throughout his dynamic and colorful career Gray Green had many victories and few defeats, so that by the end of his long, self-centered, acquisitive life, his business ledger was weighted much more heavily toward the gross profit than the loss column; and there were no commercial sectors in which he did not have an important interest; the equity becoming a living entity in itself, breathing, stretching, shrinking, persisting, as if imbued with a secret, supernatural energy, that gave it sustenance and an upward trend, throughout its existence. In capitalism your net worth was your identity, because there was no need for any other badge, disclaimer, for the casual observer to gage exactly where you stood in a social pecking order; and to know net worth before last name, education or birthright was the modish norm in the new, pretentious society established during the Gilded Age, a vapid period, to be sure. It became acceptable, in polite drawing rooms or at fancy dinner parties upon introduction or shortly thereafter, to find reason to state one's net worth; really, by means, of some foil, subtlety or distraction; to insert it into the chain of discourse to another, in the same way one would say, "the sky is blue, or the sun is shining, one's net worth." But poets noted self-worth, more than the net, where there was no charity for charity's sake but for a tax write-off. When he died of heart failure, in 1912, leaving an estate conservatively estimated to be $185 million for tax purposes, he ranked among the wealthiest men of all time. If his net worth was beyond doubt or challenge, if not reproach, the same could not be said of his self-worth, as it withered forever in deficiency, whimsically trading companies as kids trade baseball cards, with an eye always out for a winner, but leaving absolutely no room for the unavoidable losers, the minority investors in an enterprise, or many redundant workers needing firing. They were out. (Because sooner or later, nearly everyone is cut down to size, capitalism does that, the constant competition, the quest for getting to the top; not all can get there, and that means some get left behind, an invisible paw actually dragging them down the mountain, and then punching them right in the jaw for good measure; the same invisible claw that capitalists say regulates everything to the greater good, actually arranges existence for a select few, accordingly, the same describe history, define reality, and delineate the social order; and all underneath, sadly, gullible enough, believe what they're told, that it's in their best interest to remain at the foothills and get pummeled, by so many invisible fists of fate and degradation.) He was prepared, to hurl men's souls apathetically to perdition if it suited passing business purposes; there was nothing personal, it was a form of nature's own culling, separating selectively and disposing of those unwanted. "Organizations work better with less people to keep track of, anyway," he used to say, "just increase productivity." To this titan of tightness, socialism was the emasculation of will, the homogeneity of expectation, in short, it imposed an equality on those who were never identical, because variety celebrates life, and sameness invites death. So, although well diversified in an investment and monetary sense, he was still wanting in one significant respect, his ledger in allocating the needs of his family, versus those of his business, a balancing of accounts, in terms of his wife and children, whom he treated with corporate efficiency, but no human feeling, or sensitivity. His essential thought on the battle of the sexes was that men are built for warfare, women for love; when he married off his eldest daughter to a tedious, titled, French *comte*, and his next born to a haughty Standard Oil heir, in the early 1890's, he acted in what he truly believed were their best interests; considering the repressed, conservative, strict norms of the Victorian *milieu*, in which he sprang; providing for their future economic security, social prestige, in the same way he cared for their mother's, throughout their felicitous marriage. Little did he realize that his sweet, simple wife and two obedient yet well-educated daughters had covertly rebelled against their *pater familias*, and the misogynistic status quo; ardent supporters of women's rights, strong willed devotees of the burgeoning New-Woman Movement, they looked forward to sneaking out on Thursday evenings, to attend women suffrage meetings clandestinely held on Spring Street next to a temple of the Knights of Freemisogyny; and the misses had been inconsolable, desperate, frozen, for months after he arbitrarily announced their betrothals, as *faits accompli*; the two young ladies rebelling against their neatly planned futures, pitiful continuations of their mother's intolerable subjugation, to their remote and domineering father. For his sons, he had other plans, which were equally characteristic of his need to control and meddle; he would buy them a company to help manage, so it was his progressive, forward-looking son Osiris who had the idea to acquire a run-down vaudeville theater company, that also had patents on an evolving technology called, motion pictures. The year was 1901, the company, Warren Brothers Pictures, Incorporated. The founding owners, the Warren brothers, having exhausted all their capital in developing the experimental film process, were insolvent and compelled to give up what they had labored 24/7, their whole lives, to create. Gray Green bought the entire business for a song and dance, and the Warrens never forgot how curtly, harshly and dismissively he treated them at the time. The Warrens, feeling slighted, resentful, as Jews, wondered if there had been any antisemitism on the part of Gray Green and his sons, for the way they behaved, and whether there had been, or not, the Warrens swore they would one day, pay back the greedy Greens. In the following decades the company was one of the top studios in the evolving movie industry and Gray Green's inheritors were a winner. Unfortunately, World War II hit the Greens hard; their real estate holdings plummeting, they had no choice but to unload some of their healthier assets to keep the rest afloat; that was when the descendants of the original inventor Warren brothers reacquired 50% of the studio; along with the right to one more board seat than the Greens, while equal ownership existed. That was also when the succeeding management and cash flow problems began. For the past forty-five years, the company was run by a Warren; now happily that was about to change, with C. W. 's retirement; and the ascendancy of a new generation's Green, every bit as astute, focused and ambitious as a man, despite being a woman. Her private purchase took any thoughts of a proxy fight off the table.

As a self-made man, Gray Green always said, no one ever did him any favors he didn't have to pay for. Although never educated past the sixth grade in a one room schoolhouse, he possessed natural curiosity about the past, present and future, respected learning, and silently harbored feelings of grave insecurity and inferiority for not knowing more about the world he so desired to dominate. While acknowledging it was too late for him, or his sons, to undertake formal schooling, to improve their minds, his parochial but deep seated interest in education for the sake of his grandchildren and their children inspired him in 1904, to endow Whale University with a major core benefaction: the substantial funds required for the construction and projected maintenance of its central library, the Green Memorial Library, an immense, ornate granite Gothic cathedral, dedicated to scholarship, with a solid central keep rising to the sky, as well as an ongoing, steady stream of acquisitions to increase the vast collection of books, papers, notes, journals, archives, manuscripts, periodicals, catalogs, ancient texts, maps, music scores, fine arts prints, paintings, sculpture, historical memorabilia, the scraps, fragments, bits and pieces, of the entire, human experience, that would be housed within. In exchange for this generous and invaluable endowment, the university promised to admit anyone in his future family line, as a legacy, with no questions asked. He additionally, provided for the formation of a university sanctioned society, dedicated, as per very strict instructions, to joint anthropological, cross racial/ cultural/ behavioral studies with a primary mission of intervening on behalf of social, religious, political icons; discovering, securing, preserving for posterity, forgotten remnants of man's overlooked interconnectedness; conditioned that it should be run according to the rules, traditions, ceremonial rites, to be established by the first, in his future family line to attend the college, no questions asked. The secret society would be called Bull and Goats (after rudimentary Scottish watering holes), and until the time came, when one of his descendants was old enough, and so inclined, to gain admission to the school, and take control of the organization, it would remain dormant, pending a subsequent collective body; existing as a promise only, its affairs and property, including one of New Haven, CT's most desirable vacant building lots right smack dab in the middle of Whale, stock, and bond portfolios, to be soundly administered and held by trustees. As fate would have it, the first of his issue with the gumption to don a thick, white varsity sweater with a big blue letter W, did not come until four generations later, and was the woman, Isidora Green, Gray Green's great great granddaughter. As awkward as it was, the last thing Gray Green would ever have thought, given his antiquated notions of women's rights and suffrage, was that not only would the first Whalie in his line happen to be a lady, but the *modus operandi* of his secret society, his pride and joy, his baby, would also succumb to being defined, established, expanded by her, who immediately rechristened it, the Sisters of Fervent Grace, of which she would serve, forever enshrined, as Founding Matriarch. What kind of world would that be?

Actually it would be the kind of world where human beings were still discriminated against based upon groups, classes or other categories, to which they belonged, including race, color, religion, age, gender, sexual orientation, etc., but were on the verge of achieving freedom, and equality; and old-style social privilege was being transformed into new style social privilege, the constant being some sort of social privilege, invariably, continuing its existence: secret societies, fraternities, sororities, exclusive (eating) clubs, lodges, houses, groups, circles, cliques, selective eateries, "Nine restaurants that are harder to get into than Hoarvard," private academies, snobby communities, closed corporations, limited partnerships, combines, guilds, unions, leagues, orders, brotherhoods, sisterhoods, by invitation only events, etc., all discriminating associations, whose object was as much keeping the wrong ones out as the right ones in. Whale's old boy networks, part and parcel of its long-standing traditions of private associations, elitist groups, academic and fraternal fellows, harkening back to the late 1700s, gradually evolved into secret societies in the 1830s; with ominous, Greek inspired, windowless stone block monolith meeting halls, giant black padlocks sealing massive, foundry cast metal doors, that oddly never opened or closed; nor was a soul ever observed entering or exiting through the uninviting facades of foreboding mausoleums, pressing as crass, dead weights or tombs, in an otherwise welcoming academic setting. To avoid prying eyes, publicity snoops, exclusively concealed access ways to the secret societies existed under the main campus, in the vast, labyrinthine emergency tunnel system connecting lecture halls, residential colleges and administrative offices; unmarked doors, with only fifteen selected keys assigned to the prep school connected, unanimously elected, power establishment, allowed exclusive entry to the secure goings on within. As Isidora reckoned, the old boy network had had its day; the times were changing in favor of women having their own groups. The novelty in Isidora's approach, was her desire to create an old girl network, the Sisterhood of Grace, to rival the men; the difference was that she would recruit her sisters from varied conditions, backgrounds, families, not only their impressive wealth and social prominence. Deserving co-eds would be identified based on accomplishments without regard to race, color, religion, national origin, marital status or disability, and would be referred to, as sisters or Sissies, for short; and participation would not be restricted to the senior class but be open to girls of all undergraduate classes; even continuing beyond graduation, in expectancy that there would always be a Sissy somewhere to aid a Sissy in need. In thus fashion, it would remain a lifetime egalitarian association of females, dedicated to their liberty, success, "...the idea of a Millennium when women were to reign supreme in the world."

From the moment of her inevitable acceptance to the college, Isidora started the complicated process of giving birth to her very own secret society. The first task would be the members' meeting hall, or tomb, womb, as they fondly called it, the concept, design and construction of which would be a statement, as money was no object. Although the brightest architects and engineers were retained, in the end, it was her own plan for a revolutionary, multi storied, all glass smart cube that was adopted. This remarkable Crystal House, as it soon grew to be known famously, was transparent from every direction by day, and earned the reputation as a vital, inviting community center and museum. When the sun set, the cube's glass skin became opaque, and completely impenetrable as Helios' last rays slipped behind the horizon. The dark, cut-off times were reserved for the order of sisters to meet. When the sun rose the next day, the cube's glass skin brightened, achieving full clarity when golden rays peaked in the sky. By the time Isidora arrived at school, in September of her freshman year, the state-of-the-art womb was, incredibly, completed, and ready for the delight of a founding class of Sissies eventually to be selected and tapped:

### Caligula's Garden of Delights, Unearthed and Restored

In an evocative eyewitness account, the philosopher Philo, who visited the estate in A.D. 40 on behalf of the Jews of Alexandria, and his fellow emissaries had to trail behind Caligula as he inspected the sumptuous residences "examining the men's rooms and the women's rooms ... and giving orders to make them more costly." The emperor, wrote Philo, "ordered the windows to be filled up with transparent stones resembling white crystal that do not hinder the light, but which keep out the wind and the heat of the sun." (Franz Lidz, *The New York Times*, 1/12, 2021)

As a triumphant Isidora Green proceeded from the Warren Bros. Inc. board of director's meeting, it was noon; she smiled, as the winner, the board having appointed (anointed) her chairman, with nary a single dissenting vote; what had been most gratifying was that C. W. himself had made the motion to promote her, even going so far, as to extend his personal congratulations, declaring soundly, "She has earned it: '*Le roi est mort, vive le roi!*'" Because crony capitalism was the combination of varied constituencies coming together as a majority, with those left out of a ruling coalition comprising nothing. There was a celebratory lunch for the entire board at the 21 Club's reserved secret dining room; a restored, polished, former wine cellar, hidden in the basement, behind a heavy metal door and false brick wall to #19; such a bunker, once serving as a refuge from the law for inebriated flappers and revelers, during Roaring Twenties Prohibition, was now a rough reminder of Gotham's shadier past; yet also, a cultivated shrine dedicated to the discrete privilege and refined prestige of aristocratic New Yorkers. The new chairman was quite smart about her promotion, conceptualizing she would have to do less, not more, than current professional duties required. That was why she had hired John B. Sayer, as corporate president, whom she now proudly extolled, by sharing his most recent exploits with drug sniffing dogs against the union in California, which had achieved tremendous success in a short time; the low ball tactic displaying the height of capitalist cynicism, nevertheless, as Sayer had employed private investigators, security guards and dog handlers, who were themselves ironically rank and file card holders of the Security, Police and Fire Employees Brotherhood of America. In Sayer's most recent report he sarcastically declared, "I can hire one-half of the working class to kill the other half," to which the stuffy directors at the table roared with laughter, reconfirming unanimous support for their turnaround expert's crass methods. Afterward, she was off to Grand Central Terminal, for the 2:07 PM train to New Haven, for the annual Sisterhood of Grace's governance council meeting. As good fortune had it, it was also Tap Night, when expectant candidates were inducted to the Sisterhood (by Isidora's hand), and welcoming celebrations at Crystal House promised to be joyous, festive, riotous, the chosen maidens making secret vows for all the ages:

> Servant of the Delphian Apollo
> Go to the Castallian Spring
> Wash in its silvery eddies,
> And return cleansed to the temple.
> Guard your lips from offence
> To those who ask for oracles.
> Let the God's answer come
> Pure from all private fault. (Priests to the Oracle of Delphi, classical antiquity)

On the commuter train rushing Isidora to her old alma mater, a rhythmic rumbling of heavy rail wheels, on the bumpy tracks, rocked her to an uneasy forty (tawdry) winks, and she dreamed *of the Green-Eyed Monster, a fiendish incubus in unrelenting pursuit, as Isidora ran for safety but inexplicably, remained in place, slipping in sinking sand, without traction or grip, only to be torn to pieces before waking up in a cold sweat. Considering all her good fortune she could not imagine, who might be after her or why...*

Before moving forward it's important to go back again to a repository of prior pernicious deeds and sad consequences, ghastly incidents about which Gray Green, to his credit, may have understood nothing at all substantial, though at some early point, before true cognition, had probably heard faint whispers of those sordid, and unmentionable, commercial activities of his grandfather. Despite never being directly referenced they must have, nevertheless, been ingrained into his family's collective memories; stored as frightful occurrences of rapacious aggression, hidden stories of intentional barbarity, against supposed cannibals; repressed in a murky subconscious, as if fused to the spiraling strands of double helix codes, themselves. In any case, whatever inklings he may have had, of shady and nefarious antecedents, were never shared with anyone, including his siblings, or future wife and children, so wretched, diabolical to confront, were they for them. For when the ambitious, dedicated, hard-working, corrupt Greens opted to strategically relocate from Scotland in the 1790s it was for the sake of their shameful, chosen, passed on profession of slave trading, as the ship owning scoundrels had earned their wicked fortune in such a loathsome calling since the 1680s; only finding it advantageous to leave Great Britain when the winds of abolition started blowing across their converted slavers' bows; crag faced, leather skinned, Scottish merchants meeting out righteous reprobation on their employees, customers and the public at large, as if all were eager, for their self-satisfied message; settling in Virginia, due to its unyielding support, and protection, of the peculiar institution; setting up shop in Jamestown for its strategic peninsular location, and capacity in receiving the steady, bleeding cargoes from Africa, and forwarding them on, deeper into the southern, western states, to agonizing, infernal captivities; without caring what the effects would be.

Some years after graduating from Whale, Isidora volunteer curated, in New Haven, at the Sisterhood of Grace's acclaimed Atlantic Slave Trade exhibition, stopping to greet a wondrous eyed, black schoolboy she had observed several times before, noting his keen interest in the Middle Passage from West Africa, across the unknown Atlantic Ocean, to the New World; when men, women and children (*the sounds of gunfire, muffled by thick forest tree growth, still managed to crack through, in heavy rumbles from the earth; recoiling up, spreading fear and uncertainty into the brains of black tribal folks fleeing carnage, from their own rough histories, into a colonial epoch of tribal doom*) were forcibly seized, marched in a subhuman coffle, and transported on board overcrowded ships in appalling conditions to an industrially sponsored, commodity inspired, race based subjugation, the shock, of which, they could never survive. And this was not the only time in which the Dark Continent suffered mass kidnappings, depopulations, but one of many noted in the historical records. Within a ship's insufferable, fetid hold, stacked tighter than decaying fish, fitfully dreaming, *of those dark, crushing events recently endured by young African boys and girls, entire families much like themselves, gnarled, splintered, wooden yokes bruising flayed, tender necks, roughly handled in an endless, debased human line, by boastful, brutish warriors beating them mercilessly forward, ever westward, to the setting Asante Gold Coast sun, toward ultimate slavery in the cold British American Colonies, knowing they would never see their loved ones again:* "Oh, the cruelty of Anglo-Saxon merchants upon the world; we are disappeared across the ocean forever more."

Upon introducing herself, she asked his name, and age, and he said, "Hannibal, and ten years old, thank you." She was glad to make his acquaintance, asking if he had any knowledge about his family history. He told her, he knew very little, it was not a topic much discussed, but he once heard his ancestors were kidnapped from familiar, comfortable homelands long ago; herded onto specially fitted cargo ships, and heaped as logs in holds, with hardly enough room to sit up, roll over or breathe. And the heavily armed man stealers, who had pillaged their souls and freedom, worked for the Green-Eyed Monster, who was too horrible to describe. Hannibal's abducted forefathers were taken to Virginia, unfriendly, alien place, and subsequently sold to cold blooded cotton planters, headed to Texas for free land; as legally defined labor units, for all intents and purposes used as mere beasts of burden, in a morally justified, globally sanctioned, well capitalized system of heinous abuse; by the cruel and corrupt Jamestown slave dealer, whose name came down to, preserved by, the descendants of those wrongfully held, almost mythically, as the Green-Eyed Monster. A surprised, but not shocked (as the whispers of prior generations wended their way through a century or two of heirs, even down to her, such was the power of bad acts, motives, faith, that carry on), Isidora thanked the boy for his vivid, frank, insightful recollection, and invited him to become a member of the community center; he was welcome at any time. By this juncture, Isidora had, for half her life, questioned herself ceaselessly, about the origin of her family's enormous wealth, even suspecting the answers could not be too uplifting, considering the rough, chicanery-ridden times, during which it was amassed. There was also that Whale French Realism Literature, lecture hall scene, where she somehow found herself standing up before hundreds to defend her family's immense fortune from slander, after the day's reading, insisting: "It's not my fault I was born rich; it's a burden in itself;"

> *Le secret des grandes fortunes sans cause apparente est un crime oublié, parce qu'il a été proprement fait.* [The secret of grand fortunes without apparent cause is a crime forgotten, for it was properly done.]
> (Honoré de Balzac, *Le Père Goriot*, 1835)

*How would history dispose of her legacy, considering her clan's nefarious past,* she wondered, after the recurring nightmares, trove of opening moral sink holes, perhaps as unavoidable, incipient causal hints, sparked on an unconscious level. And for some secret reason, she took a great interest in this little boy, but never connected all the dots, considering for a minute, that her own name, Green, could in any way, be combined to his origins, as perhaps hers was the blind power to navigate rough seas of evil legacies.

When highly practical, purposeful (not ethical) Singleton B. Sayer (SS) sailed into Jamestown, in 1822, seeking Negroes, he was directed to Green, Green & Green, Agents, Brokers & Auctioneers as the most efficient providers of fair value at the port, with regards to fine, healthy Atlantic shipments. Over time, the plaintive, pleading, ranting repetition of Hyde Green's name by the despoiled, doomed families and loved ones he was beating, branding, torturing, splitting apart, and bargaining off, on a daily basis, led to a contemptuous inverted usage and he came to be known as Green Eyed, and as the exclamation was most often made in abject fear, it led to a despised and well-deserved Monster appellation, giving birth to those diabolical legends, later recounted in the slave narratives. SS hailed from Manchester, CT, and participated in a considerable fortune he and his four brothers amassed, after inheriting, then improving their father's original textile mills, with the latest technical innovations of the day, as well as adding the maximum number of children, at much lower wages, to the work force. As the way of providing ever-hungry cloth factories with a steady supply of basic fiber, it was decided that one of the brothers would transfer to a southern place suitable for a colossal cotton plantation, and as SS was the youngest sibling, he was volunteered for the job; keeping his share in the family enterprises, living off dividends, which were so substantial, he had the resources to purchase one hundred thirty-five persons (plus any unborn, on the way), putting down 30% earnest money, with the balance to be financed, over three years, at 5%, against his future income; and itemize them as part of his net worth, to gain full admission to the Anglo colony Stephen F. Austin was organizing, and leading, in Texas. It was advertised in the newspapers at the time that those settlers owning a minimum of one hundred slaves would be granted additional lands than those with lesser equity. Exhibiting the sharp planning skills that were his strong suit, as when he ably demonstrated the clear advantage to the bottom line of employing underpaid children in factories, and had brought him considerable prosperity in life thus far, SS had allowed for a 20% attrition rate out of his total purchase, *en route* to Texas, and calculated he would still have the narrow margin above the minimum number of bondsmen, required to qualify. As both SS and Green were products of a society and historical era so dissipated and degenerate it tolerated and condoned the freewheeling, unrestrained and iniquitous utilization of pliant minors, enslaved individuals, they conducted their transactions, with sober thoroughness and little emotion, guilt, or consideration for the precious merchandise at stake, and SS paid Green charter passage for the entire party aboard the Green-Eyed Monster's craft to Galveston.

The Green-Eyed Monster was infamous for chasing escaped chattel inventory, terrified, panicked, with nowhere to go, vanquished even before attempting to flee, instantly lost in the strange, foreign territory, through confounding forests and impassable swamps, in the middle of the night; knowing the thick iron chains the fugitives dragged, would ultimately slow their progress, and be heard, clinking clearly, in the still of the night, perhaps just over the next hollow, pointing him and his horrid man hunters in the right direction; summarily flogging the captured runaways mercilessly, carving deep ridges into soft skinned backs, as warm blood ran down fettered legs, soaking the ground below. A self-satisfied, thriving Hyde Green never asked himself, how he could have ended up in such an evil, abhorrent livelihood, in which human beings were ruthlessly reduced, to mere personal property, and, incredibly, treated worse than if they had been senseless livestock, or inanimate possessions. Perhaps his stockpiled cache of tarnishing silver, gold and jewels were reason enough. Just as with his own father and grandfather, and then going back to their founders, he expected that one of his sons would continue in the steady proprietorship and management of their now traditional, successful, firmly rooted establishment. But notwithstanding, the great wealth that came to the family from such an illicit occupation, Hyde Green's son, Bingham, Gray Green's father, was never drawn to trafficking in human flesh, preferring other forms of free enterprise to the grisly certainty, of his own degradation in remaining a slaveholder. Perhaps, undertaking one of the few, if not only, worthy and courageous acts by a Green in the previous two centuries, he decided to minimize contact with his miserable family; finally disavowing them, then fleeing to upstate New York, where Gray Green was born, in 1834. But as hard as Bingham Green sought to evade the Green-Eyed Monster, escape would never be a simple matter of distance, or time away, from bad primal beginnings, even if keeping a step ahead, starting a new, unfettered life; as somehow, that monster tormented every one of Hyde Green's unsuspecting successors, as a dark curse following, without their ever recognizing the scary features of what came at their heels, or really knowing (but suspecting) about their awful past:

> To be SOLD on the first Monday in October, a large number of Negroe
> Slaves, likewise sundry Household Goods, Stocks of Cattle, etc.
> – Thomas Eldridge (*Virginia Gazette*, September 1751)

Isidora, gift of Isis, goddess of goddesses, was named after the Egyptian deity of motherhood, fertility, sorcery; her name becoming the family's favorite soon after Gray Green's grand Innocents Abroad tour, of Egypt, Greece and Rome in the late 1850's, when he was exposed for the first time, to various ideas, people, customs, outside of his New York society, comfort zone. He named his first son, Osiris, hoping a charmed appellation would bestow this child with a great bounty in life. A predilection for the name, Isis, coincided with the nineteenth century popularizations of Egyptology, due to famous discoveries of ancient tombs and other archaic artifacts, such as the Rosetta Stone from the Classical period, Dynastic Egypt; and a cultlike following for hermeticism, Eastern cosmology, astrology, which at times resulted in an undermining of traditional faith and worship; the foreign, mystical, soothing qualities of the name undoubtedly distracting from the family's confining, dour, Protestant roots; with the latter, more recent generation's budding agnosticism, interest in the occult, unknown, and all things otherworldly, vigorous alternatives to their own tired religion. As stern, central doctrines lost all relevance, and their accepted practice became devoid of the original belief and divinity of its precepts, those of a certain standing had the luxury, to entertain exotic, existential concepts; the burdens, anxiety, they all carried as a class, were what would come in the ever after, from a lifetime of having only cared about wealth and objects, but never people? Rebellious and exiting New Age notions of God's essence (Deist, "speculative, esoteric creeds of Christendom impute a First Cause, Universal Intelligence, World Soul, ...Spiritual Aspect...," Eye of Providence, Unseen Hand, Cosmic Consciousness) influenced several of Gray Green's posterity, to believe, with conviction, in the eternal nature of the soul through reincarnation; as well as others, to contemptuously not believe in God, or anything at all. But atheism was man's sinking vanity, a body's impermanence as the center of a fast existence to the exclusion of all divinities. However, as Narcissus drowned in that fateful contemplation of his rippling reflection, deniers cannot but be weighed down by the gravity of their own beings, in a surrendering to life's evanescence; so Isidora paid especially close attention to each fresh-faced postulant's preternatural sensitivity to the paranormal, acceptance of eerie dimensions, degree of ease in the presence of incorporeal life, as she diligently traversed the campus in search of a coveted initial quorum. With each fateful tap, and accepting oath, Isidora was attuned to the profound, spiritual yearnings of her growing flock. She carried her name well, in the beginning, as the president and reigning queen of the only female secret society on campus, later as Sister of Sisters; the successfully pledged reassigned relevant, secret nicknames, Isidora's adopted, new identity, being Lady. At midnight, after circuitous, rambling incantations, recitations of eroticized Sappho and much emotive wailing from ethereal, entranced, high priestesses, trembling, wide-eyed initiates were formally shown, introduced to, the unspoken mysteries of the sisterhood: the ritual ghost dance, which came down to the society as a great gift of providence transcendent, but was really the grand theft of a priceless talisman.

"For Mind, for Culture and for Whale!" (Whale University traditional
song, etched in stone in a visible spot on the Mold Campus, 1881)

Rumor had it, that the Sisterhood of Grace kept Geronimo's Ghost (G's G) in the womb, in an ancient, cracked, red clay tribal urn, decorated with earth-colored symbols, time faded with too much handling. Several founding Sissies, led by Isidora, as crew/ dig chief, expedition investor and organizer, during a freshman year, Anthropology major, spring recess field assignment at an unsuspecting reservation, stole the sacred, gritty earthenware and its doomed, spectral denizen, as a foolish prank, on a night of peyote laced, drunken revelry, without the slightest concern for either the piece's provenance or the inhabitant's say in the matter, packed it up in a specially padded crate, efficiently delivering it back to New Haven, with none of the reverence, solemnity, ceremony warranted by so rare and powerful a relic. The intact, porous pottery once held desiccated remains of the fiercest Native warrior in history; smuggled and lain in final rest, on a burial platform, in the dry dessert altitude of his people's spare hills, prior to allegedly being buried at Fort Sill, OK; after many crisp cool nights when his flesh, thinned and tattered as paper, was lifted high into the rugged mountains, the urn was utilized to collect and store the loose bones that remained, after vultures and eagles hauled off what they could, before being lost to memory. Yet, some tracings of G's G persisted within the pot, confused, unable to depart, or move on, a vaporous residue stuck to the inner nooks and crannies of the vessel, now tightly sealed, with a heavily patterned textile. If the modest simplicity of the rattling ossuary belied its true spiritual significance as a physical vestige, evidence, of a criminally obliterated past, and incalculable, symbolic value, as a reminder of resistance to those who would follow his example, now themselves also, almost extinct, not one of the committed co-ed curators, with their studious, objective, scientific bents, ever considered the tribe or family's loss, emotional suffering, moral outrage, let alone possible legal claims over a communal theft. Prominently displayed in a newly expanded gallery of indigenous heritage, it was an impressive, if rather well-worn artifact of early, local, southwest *Chiricahua Apache* funerary customs. When Isidora and her group of recently minted, greenhorn sisters, took a society sponsored road trip, a pilgrimage of sorts, out west to Arizona and New Mexico Indian country, in the hope of uncovering important, regional ethnographic raw data, archaeological objects, amulets, votive offerings, tribal hoards, for the society's ever growing, comparative civilizations exhibit, such a priceless artifact was never in her sights. One fated morning, when the Great Spirit must have been dozing lazily, lady explorers on a mission stopped at a dusty, sun beaten, out of the way, tribal center of the *Mescalero Apache* Reservation, beneath the steep, shadowed *Sacramento* Mountains in south central New Mexico, where Geronimo's annihilated band finally ended up. Even before seeing it, Isidora was mysteriously drawn to a painted urn, as if hailed by war whoops from afar, and afterwards could not distract her thoughts from the beckoning, and inexplicably familiar, hieroglyphs. The theft was no random act of pillage, or simple prank by scheming hands. At midnight, loosening up her hesitant raiders with multiple shots of *tequila*, nasty, dried, green cactus buttons, they broke into the *Apache's* humble, sparsely filled, adobe walled museum, dedicated to the heroic memory of their esteemed ancestors; and hallucinating heavily brought their prized heirloom, unwitting guest, to new, upscale digs, the society's wondrous, gleaming Museum for the Ages, jammed with other coveted, captured and cataloged treasures; somehow seeming no place for this magical man of action to end up.

How come no one stands up for the rights of Native Americans? The casualness of self-interest, greed, perhaps because the true sacrifice of reparations would be too costly, impossible, to calculate, involving giving them back this entire country, or significant swaths of it, which was stolen out from under them; and no one wants to surrender their realty, especially sophisticated, affluent, urban and suburban donors for every bleeding-heart cause imaginable, a significant source of whose wealth, ease, includes market values of their properties. No, these day tripper activists chose the causes that were affordable, and not too disruptive, and made them look good in their own, as well as everyone else's, eyes; with minimum amount of real reckoning expended over the true and complicated nature of things, as evil apathy ruled:

> THIRD CITIZEN. "...and though we willingly consented to his
> banishment, yet it was against our will."
> (William Shakespeare, *Coriolanus*, 4.6.148, 1609(?))

It was quickly established that G's G would never be a full-fledged, or even honorary, Sissie, because besides being immaterial he had been a man in life and was thus barred from an all-female society; but he was invited to stay on, as an essential component of the museum's collection, and could certainly be of great cheer and companionship to the sisters. Some of the co-eds were a bit spooked by an intensely virile male phantom openly dwelling and wandering everywhere unrestrained, in their relaxed, informal, female lair, especially if he happened to observe them unawares, in their privacy, less than fully decent, yet granted him a license, grudgingly, upon realizing how respectful, discreet, accommodating and soft spoken he was. However, over the more extended periods, G's G's prolonged residency and ubiquitous presence wore his welcome thin, and were a bit too much for some of the more reserved young ladies; so within a short while the Sisters, in a Pavlovian fashion, modified his behavior, training him to spend long days, weeks, months quietly, patiently, obediently in his quarters; restricting his appearances to his summonses, almost as a *jinn*, in a bottle. G's G was lonely, and accepted his new, kept man status with some regret, shame and sadness, as it brought back images of his and his fellow *Chiricahuas'* punishing incarcerations over the last twenty three years of his life, as prisoners of war, at various Federal Indian reservations, in humid, insect infested, swamp ridden surroundings, far from their windswept, rainless, open tribal ranges; and this, after courageously conducting bloody warfare on Mexico and the United States for many decades, escaping, evading both countries' armies, but finally tricked into surrendering to the U.S. Army; with eerie similarity to old confinements the U.S government cruelly, mockingly, and consistently defended, as only temporary, while withholding full well they were actually perpetual, this casual custody, by these eccentric, but polite, young college women, was starting to seem like it would last forever. An unaffected, firm and decisive Isidora made it apparent, from the get-go, that G's G and urn were to remain with the society indefinitely; all bets were off for escaping, the sisters confining his aura absolutely. Moreover, there would be an annual tribute due from him, a fee legacy, payable to all sisters: in waiting, current, matriarchs; almost a rent for the benefit of being held captive, in the form of special fertility rites enacted before and with the wild congregation; in the style of the ancient *Bacchae*:

> Kiss my aura...Dora...
> Ooh - it's real angora
> Would you all like some more-a?
> Right here on the floor-a?
> An' how 'bout you, Fauna?
> Do you wanna? (Frank Zappa, *Overnight Sensation*, "Dinah-Moe Humm," 1973)

Every year on Tap Night, the Sisterhood of Grace tapped G's G, to come out of his cell and perform for them, share his thunderous, powerful stamina and ferocity, satisfying their longing to meld into infinite potency. He appeared much larger than life, vibrant shadow, in fringed buckskin loincloth, moccasins; his terrible howls barely muffled by a broad red handkerchief covering his lower face; the deep, yellow eyes, not human: but rather, those of a wild animal, who would mercilessly track down and annihilate you, if challenged, or crossed, piercing each enchanted believer to her core. Having spent a full twelve moons preparing for the wanton, regenerative ceremony, spectacle, supernaturally gathering restorative, fluid energy, he knew full well what was expected of him, in a required duty, as personal incubus to the entire membership body(ies). For beginners it would be transcendent deflowering by supreme, focused magic; for the practiced, a springtime renewal of ignored Amazonian strengths. In a moment sacred for its submission, attesting their devotion to the sanctity of the larger family that was receiving, and would always be there for, them; under the obscure, pulsating candle light in the womb's inner sanctum, fully charged neophytes, without a stitch on, made uninhibited, unrestrained love with a fearsome spirit upon a wide plank, medieval banquet table; before their similarly stripped, aroused sponsoring sisters, and as many bare, uninhibited matriarchs as could return to campus for these spectacular events. So, feminists still used their bodies to make their point. Outside the full moon rose close, throbbing, luminescent, the cube's glass skin brightening, despite the nighttime, as if confused, tricked or bewitched by some spell; achieving blushing semi clarity, becoming practically see through, as the wild session progressed, with faint curvy shadows of rhythmically swaying, transfixed, nude nymphs growing discernible. Inside the air was perfumed sweet and heavy, and the soft, steady thumping of a *tom-tom* echoed from somewhere far beneath a translucent Crystal House; the glowing, frenzied, naked sisters were entranced, quivering with abandon, and sighing sweetly, indiscreetly, from unceasing self-pleasure, animated caressing, and impetuous starter oral play between them. And within steamy, entangled crowds hovered an undraped ethereal Lady in fulsome, scintillating radiance, eyes half shut in misty bliss, arms spread in undulating waves across the murky sky, transporting to a higher purpose, inviting all to partake of her unbounded glory. After the enthusiastic, nubile novices had their proper fills the more experienced, buxom devotees followed, and all later swore the immense, moaning unsubstantial beast had surely penetrated each one of them individually, together, deeply, bringing the entire captive order to ecstatic climaxes... over and over repeatedly, before the voluptuous night was done, with its ardent moon safely tucked away again.

Miscellanea:

Modern membership

Nowadays, everyone (egged on by the ceaseless drumbeats of the culture activists and media) longs for membership (based on the reclamation of assumed rights) in a community; the problem continuing, that such clubs, organizations and societies all exclude those who do not belong to them:

The Russian exile community
The Hispanic/ *mestizo* community
The Palestinian community
The Arab community
The Native American community
The Pacific Islander community
The black/ *mulatto* community
The Melungeon community
The Jewish community
The Nazi community
The (subcontinental) Indian community
The global community
The commie community
The LGBT community
The queer community
The asexual community
The Whale community

The Hoarvard community
The lively Ivy League community
The dissipated debutante community
The journalistic community
The over eager writer's community, etc.

(Many apologies if your own community has been neglected; the list will never be all inclusive, as the very process it brings to light, and due to the sheer numbers involved; globally, individuals would seem to enjoy being parts, members, of big groupings, with newer, wide-ranging communities seeming to sprout up every day. Additionally, there is no such thing as a white community, at least as defined by the 1965 Civil Rights Act, which began America's fascination with identity, and no anti-white prejudice.)

Except those of us wanting nothing to do with any membership in those communities, with the exclusivities of the country club, and the intent of asking for donations; not a part of their thing, loving to be left in peace.

# 7. New Meth City

> The whisper that my master was my father, may or may not be true;...
> [slaveholders] administer to their own lusts, and make a gratification of
> their wicked desires profitable as well as pleasurable;...it is nevertheless
> plain that a very different-looking class of people are springing up at the
> South, and are now held in slavery, from those originally brought to this
> country from Africa;...for thousands are ushered into the world, annually,
> who, like myself, owe their existence to white fathers, and those fathers
> most frequently their own masters...
>
> To describe the wealth of Colonel Lloyd would be almost equal to
> describing the riches of Job. He kept from ten to fifteen house-servants.
> He was said to own a thousand slaves, and I think this estimate quite
> within the truth. Colonel Lloyd owned so many that he did not know
> them when he saw them; nor did all the slaves of the out-farms know him.
> (Frederick Douglass, *Narrative of the Life of Frederick Douglass*, 1845)

As glass crystalized streets, the Rev. Hannibal P. (Pearly) Gates, presiding at the reformist Carthaginian Black Baptist Church, 666 Mixwell Avenue, New Haven, CT, prayed silently for divine inspiration, at a critical moment of unbearable grief and frustration, while making his way, decisively, through an angry, shivering, huddling crowd, protesting yet another harmless, black youth's unintended, untimely and ill- fated slaying, by Hispanic drug lords. The Latino gang bangers, novices, recruits of *Los X*, a notorious, Salvadorian street gang, founded in Los Angeles in the 1980s, having expanded to include Hondurans, Guatemalans, Mexicans and other Central and South Americans, the motto, "rape, control, kill" gaining notoriety after horrible, brutal drug crimes across the U.S., out to prove themselves, had calmly, coldly driven to an unknown victim's home in a struggling residential section, slowing down deliberately, then stopping, and, as if following a preset script, methodically sprayed it with such hails of bullets from five automatic rifles, assorted pistols, that no one inside could possibly have been left alive. However, their contracted target had been the boy's condemned, terrified and yet unaccounted for, elder brother, so that when it was reported that an uninvolved teen was mistakenly executed instead, they reacted stonily, and with no remorse, for their egregious blunder, only itching impatience to get their job done right the next time. These dogged hit men, undocumented Ecuadorian migrants, travel hardened, insolent trespassers, inured to harsh extremities of nature's dispassionate seasons, had not always been perfidious *pistoleros y asesinos*, most having simply and unobtrusively begun their journeys in search of work to provide for themselves, distant dear ones; but unintentionally, had fallen into mortal conflict with rival, home town black gangs for control of the city's narcotics thoroughfares, markets and operating bases, and it was a turf war the tenacious illegals appeared to be winning. On the way to the hit a city police cruiser pulled them over for a bad turn signal, but let them proceed when their status, as *sin papeles*, was established, and not one had any form of identification at all, let alone a valid driver's license. Anyone else would have been ticketed or had their vehicle searched at the very least, but theirs was a federal misdemeanor, resulting in immunity, making them untouchable from the Law, fostering the drug epidemic's virulence.

*"La luna... Mirala. Es tu espejo,"* said a Hispanic policeman, curious and calm, as he examined their faces through the windshield. The squat, dark Indian driver of the car bantered in Andean Spanish with a friendly Mexican American cop: "Our friends said, 'Do you want to come with us to look for work, in the United States?' and I said, 'What's that?' Later I had so many different jobs, and one day, someone asked me, if I wanted to learn about *sushi*, so I became the best, *mojado sushi* chef in New Haven, CT."

The officers had already been through an eventful day and were in no mood for further confrontations. At four that morning, a woman had called dispatchers, complaining that someone had stolen her meth, and could they help her find it, then got assaultive when visited by the cops, ending up in a psych ward. Nodding, in respectful discharge of his function, the officer said, *"'toda la vida es sueño,' buena suerte, como dicen poetas, quienes vinieron después de las conquistas y el desafio moral causado por ellas..."* So much, for local law enforcement doing their share; it was certainly good for the gunmen, as all their weapons, ammo, *frio*, cocaine, dust, were in the trunk; they were told to move on, to stay out of trouble.

Once in front of the shot up, mangled, sealed up, multi-family row house, Minister Gates slowly turned purposefully, to face the afflicted, overwhelmed throng of relations, friends and neighbors; preparing to say a few appropriate, thoughtful words, to those waiting for some sort of explanation, and remedy, for this ultimate of rude, and confounding, misfortunes and injustices just heaped upon them; not to soothe and alleviate bursting bafflement and rising hatred, of these pushy, new interlopers, but to incite primal, collective fury against them further. "Brothers and sisters, it is with a heavy heart that I stand with you on this infamous and tragic day to join in asking why the Lord has seen fit, to bring this innocent lamb back to His heavenly host, and deny us the joy, satisfaction, of watching him grow into manhood. God, in His infinite wisdom, tested us again; but I believe we have not been asked to submit to this slaughter and turn the other cheek, not this time. How much longer should we have to watch these ruffians come into our neighborhoods, to rob us of our youths, and do nothing about it? What's it going to take for us to protect ourselves; when are we going to take ownership for ourselves? I'm done waiting;" he ceased, holding out for a reaction from his distraught audience. "I can't stand it anymore." He saw his engaged listeners start to nod heads in accordance, shuffling restlessly on frozen pavement, now exhorting them: "I said I can't stand it anymore; is anyone hearing me?" "Yes, we are," someone hollered back. "We're listening, pastor," came another reply. "We can't stand it, neither" another voice, joining in, dejectedly. "It's intolerable but what should we do?" "We're furious." "We're scared." "We're hopeless." "What's left, for us?" He understood the mournful gathering would not break up, until he had answers for them.

"I'll tell you, what's left for us," Preacher Pearly, answered, his voice rising with excitement at having bonded with his public. He faced what had become a crowd of demonstrators (some shouting, "F*** the police!" "Burn the mother******* down!" and "Have these bitches gone!"): "We need to redeclare we're not going to take it and roll over. We will defend ourselves from hostility," he was almost singing and weeping at the same time. "Because God did not take this boy from us, they did. We must respond in kind, with an eye for an eye, otherwise, we will be captives to villainous Babylon, held in bondage to marauding Egyptians. It's us or them." "It's true," came a sharp response. "That's right," went another. "Tell us, Brother Hannibal." "Save us." "Lead us, Preacher Pearly." "Shake off our chains." "Free us, from bondage." Some of those gathered were wailing inconsolably, unable to accept their community's loss; an overcome woman fainted, needing support, and was escorted away. According to that inspired shepherd, who claimed to represent them, the struggle for their rights was, had been, would be, endless and unrelenting. A few of the more thoughtful among those listening only wondered when they would be able to relate to each other as humans once again. "Soon, my brothers and sisters, soon. The time is nigh for our delivery. The Lord's rewards will rain upon us, for finding our courage to act. Remember, the Israelites crossed the river Jordan, on the wings of angels, to lay claim to the Promised Land, just as we shall at an appointed hour." "Amen, Preacher Pearly, speak it, Amen." "Praise to God." "Thank you, God." The pastor concluded his remarks, gratified in observing their intended effect had hit home with the aggrieved mourners; once again he had achieved success, a self-styled, African American Pied Piper, playing sweet tunes of race revenge to an impressionable mob. The days were coming when he would arouse their outrage, animosity, fear, into purposeful action against these dangerous, aggressive newcomers, and end all outside influences in their neighborhoods, for good. He would ask the Lord for forbearance, cunning, until finding a way to exact satisfaction on them for this youngster's evil murder.

Until recently the most disturbing events on the hard streets involved brothers shooting brothers, sisters stabbing sisters, or maybe local street gangs on a tear, but it was all in-house. Then foreigners arrived, from one day to another, seemingly out of nowhere, in the beginning a few at a time; afterward many of them, when the word got back to their remote, inhospitable mountain villages: this was virgin territory, easy for the pickings. These encroaching, black-haired demons headed to states such as Connecticut or California, because cities there provided immunity to illegal immigrants for their crimes committed not only, in their own countries, but in this one as well. Sanctuary cities promised to shield undocumented criminals from any federal efforts to deport them, so first thing, was writing to all family, friends then neighbors to come on over quickly. Hospitality in this country was only the short walk across the river.

*"Regional refugee crises in Latin America demand humanitarian responses by the United States; never a show of force,"* the government's own immigrant-rights spokesman has consistently said to the press.

Soon they brought their women over, and families, or rather, parts of many families jumbled together, apparently never paying any attention at all to the emotional, social or sacred conventions of constancy, marriage or parenthood, seeming to cohabit for a while when convenient or safe for impregnations, and then moving on when the situation, primarily work or *Migra* driven, dictated. Preacher Pearly knew of one pregnant Ecuadorian mother with three young, scrawny, unkempt daughters, living in a filthy, cold rooming house, full of transient, criminal men. Her husband remained in their steep, thin aired hamlet on the outskirts of Quito, with their three other daughters, whom she hadn't seen for ten years, missing their entire childhoods. She did not speak a lick of English, nor did she suspect who the fathers of her younger daughters, and unborn baby, were, but because the girls had been (and the unborn baby would be) born in the U.S. they were citizens and entitled to state health insurance and food stamps, which the mother used to keep things only barely going. The recent population already here, black, white, Asian, perhaps claiming a heritage of one to five centuries, resented the brash newcomers forcing their way in, trudging over deserts, fording rivers, trekking mountain ranges to arrive, and take back what was theirs; coming from everywhere south, there was no stopping them, for truly, in the end, they were the rightful heirs, whose own ancestors had arrived ten thousand years ago. So, what were the white man and his slaves' mere five hundred years of encroachment compared to the deeper possession of prior millennia?

The pastor thought about *a hard-working, god-fearing church member plumber with a large family, who could not make ends meet, but did not qualify for the same benefits because he owned an old, run down truck for his struggling business, classified as an asset ("We pay taxes on everything; and then you get someone just turn up, and they get somewhere to live, they get all the privileges that we work hard for," he said, "and we get nothing."), and here, a lucky, little, illicit Latin American freeloader and her three conveniently born offspring (as well as the blessed unborn one) were receiving state medical assistance and $500 a month in food stamps; how was that allowed?* Still, to bring in extra money, to pay the rent on a flophouse in which she and her growing family lived, she turned tricks, reclining, sated, worshiped idol, while men stood in line outside her door. Her girls, aged two, four and nine, saw everything, but much worse, their mother also sordidly procured her own daughters, including the two-year old, but not the unborn one yet, to strangers, when the price was right. Now these blameless, trafficked innocents, their *puta madre,* had venereal diseases, and were possibly HIV positive, but that did not stop reckless abuse from continuing, as she was a meth whore, and out of her mind. Really, in that sense, she was no different than many other young black girls, doing the same thing to get their daily shatter, and survive, selling their bodies, and those of their children, living in grungy, dilapidated meth dens, or on the street. The scourge of hot ice, turning its users into frosted faced zombies, craving nothing but their next high, infiltrated the city years ago, every day rearing its ugly head up, to remind the pastor of the particularly unholy nature of the evil he confronted. Despite his clear aversion to, and contempt for, these recently arrived *indocumentados,* it was, nevertheless, uncanny, ironic, that perhaps speed connected, and even joined, these outsiders with his own people, the degradation, dissolution, squalor that drugs produced, impartially applied by grim fortune against both groups, with neither one favored above the other, and drive-by death being an equal opportunity provider. In the spirit of impossible dreams, Preacher Pearly considered if any of his congregation at Sunday service might take heed of his sermon urging them, and their addicted brethren, as a special sacrifice to the faith, to forsake aqua for forty days, as Jesus would have, in the wilderness; *it was possible*, he told himself, before recognizing his heartfelt impulses were, nevertheless, passing reveries steeped in utter futility. The aroused and agitated multitudes dispersed, and the pastor walked back to his church through falling snow, greeting people he knew, along the way; some he had baptized, others visited in the hospital, in critical condition, after failed gang raids, and many more comforted after loved ones had been gunned down like worthless dogs; wondering when it would end, and he receive the sign from God he was awaiting, as the obsessive messianic that he was.

Meanwhile, he would attempt to lead his flock on a righteous path, to the best of his abilities. Hannibal P. Gates was born, and raised, in New Haven, as a boy, devout, moral, studious, with a true concern for the same, *liberté, égalité, fraternité*, that became the slogan of the Sisterhood of Grace, evolved out of a common union of humanitarian precepts: a love of God, esteem for mankind, and trust in a universal order. While growing up, he was spared the rough treatment and betrayal of the streets by a penetrating scholastic aptitude and related accomplishments; somehow driven from early life with peculiar notions that there were important and compelling revelations awaiting his uncovering. His precocious focus on learning led him to an intense involvement, while a student at James Hillhouse High School, as a junior docent for the Sisterhood of Grace's famously endowed, Museum for the Ages and Community Center, which strongly impacted the succeeding formation of his inquisitive individuality from adolescent age; developing a healthy, progressive world view, multi-ethnic affinity, open, welcoming stance toward his fellow man; consenting to, and warmly receiving, those of various races, colors, religions and national origins. He attended Whale College, majoring in History, on a scholarship offered by the Sisterhood of Grace's Urban Challenge Foundation; continuing to the Whale Divinity School to pursue a theological education, earning a Master of Divinity (M.Div.) on a graduate study scholarship, and stipend, provided by the generous Sisters' Epiphany Achievement Trust, geared for energetic seminarians; graduating at the top of his class, subsequently ordained to the Christian ministry; taking a research fellowship at the Divinity School, concentrating on comparative belief structures, again with sponsorship and funding by the sisters, through their Crystal House Study Grants; his studies focusing on how religions impact one another, each influenced to adapt in relation to the others, converging to a common thread or deity. He pondered how these changes affected man's understanding of, and relationship to, the Supreme Being; a greater conundrum being whether a divine or virtuous state could be similarly attained in all religions, or to the contrary, if it occurred in any of them at all; these comprising his future, ecumenical concerns.

His college senior essay was a controversial slap in his identity's face. If his curiosity led to examining or challenging spiritual or moral convictions, through consistent theoretical perusals, they were brain teasers, exercises pursued in good faith. The entire direction of his life, up to that point, had led him to a complete assumption and acceptance, of an infallibility of a cross-cultural world view, taking the high road with opposing opinions, vapid viewpoints, postulated processes, begrudging them their candid due and respect, until the moment he unearthed astounding and disturbing facts that lamentably, turned his established, logical world upside down, leading to a defiant questioning and ultimate rejection of all the lore, theories and concepts he had heard, learned and been given, from his embracing family, host and patron, the Sisterhood of Grace, such unforeseen findings that could never be disowned or suppressed:

> The past is never dead. It's not even past.
> (William Faulkner, *Requiem for a Nun*, 1951)

While investigating primary sources of New Haven Baptist churches, in the seventh-floor stacks of the imposing Green Memorial Library; wandering down long, functional, brightly lit corridors crammed by endless rows of immense bookcases, neatly lined with numbered items, as far as the eye could see; he came across, and was somehow drawn to, a worn canvas bound book, entitled, *Shared Kinship, Fateful Destinies: Chronicles of the Great Migration From Texas.* He did not know why he paused, at a certain point in the collection of sleepy demographic studies, picking out that specific record, from millions of other possibilities in the gargantuan library, wondering if its covers perhaps held pertinent information. The preface clearly indicated that the concerned, determined, unworthy author, resident Baptist pastor, had extensively interviewed an exhausted, tormented, displaced, black family, shortly after their sudden appearance at his church door, one appointed day, without a dime in their pockets; escaping danger and decay, despondent for renewal, humbly celebrating a chance to reconnect again with their stolen purity. The table of contents painstakingly itemized the despicable, pathetic, almost embarrassing account of the post slavery era, in an East Texas cotton plantation, from the close of the Civil War, to 1926; and its accompanying oppression, brutality, rape, miscegenation, incest (anathemas). The forthright, idealistic and accountable collegiate, believed adultery, racial mixing and inbreeding to be abominations before God; because they were iniquities, involving the coerced joining, and stirring up, of more than just non-complementary DNA or RNA molecules, but of disparate life energies, disjunctive entities, fitful spirits themselves; and whatever good, or bad (mostly bad it seemed), of each was infused into the inevitably weaker blended result, and then further passed on. While leafing randomly through the faded volume, he unexpectedly came upon a reference to a Gates family; a sharp twitch in his heart, butterflies in his stomach, perhaps warnings explained away as anticipation, led him to pause momentarily and then read on. Could it be a coincidence? He turned to the last chapter, in which Hannibal P. Gates, born in 1913, runs away with his family, up north; discreetly hitching rides, warily taking public transportation within menacing Jim Crow country, until finally and fortuitously, settling in Connecticut; this must have been his grandfather, and the Gates family mentioned, apparently his own. They were originally from Texas, from the cotton growing region, and must have been Baptists for sure. When the minister was a boy, he once heard a great aunt briefly talking about departing Texas in a hurry, making the Great Migration to the Promised Land, confronting innumerable uncertainties, hardships, along the way. No one explained why, or how, and he had not paid any heed to it then, but at this very moment he was about to find out. The current Hannibal P. (Pearly) Gates, born 1973, highly educated, but wanting in relevant details of his own life and lineage, secluded himself in a well shielded, out of the way, reading desk, spending the entire evening digging up private history, examining reasons for and results of his forbears' momentous and transformative passage; and then clandestinely hid in the monotonous and confining maze of stacks after the building closed at 11:45 pm, willfully, uncharacteristically, breaking rules, systematically and anxiously evading the patrolling security guards, all night, in a frenzy of self-inquiry and exposure, no premises schedule or norms of university conduct could restrain. Brittle pages detailed one of the most shocking, dispiriting, and at the same time, uplifting, tales of survival, endurance, of any people he had ever known; and distressingly enough, it was about his own, long suffering, stigmatized, corrupted kin; he was overwhelmed by feelings of culpability for something he never even did, as if already sentenced to an atrocious future not of his own doing. An early recoil, disgust, horror at the stated facts continued to perturb his addled brain, after finishing the narrative, and placing it back on its shelf; and seemed to only magnify upon themselves, as he waited for the elevator to whisk him away from the overbearing, vile reality, which had just been foisted upon him, and which he would forever identify with the stifling section of archives on that gloomy floor. By the time he got downstairs again, to the library's airy, open Nave, where the light of day beamed through narrow stained-glass windows, he had summarily decided to renounce the liberal commandments, undertakings and conducts of his currently regulated state, and alternatively take on the bloodied mantle of his fallen, demeaned, downtroddened race; if modern civil/ political principles were rooted in mutual regard for self, and others, what had been cruelly perpetrated upon his predecessors, as bred stock, over centuries of malevolence and maltreatment, as evidenced by the compiled data, was a monstrous lack of respect and presumption of right, and as such, he could no longer be party to the charade of comity underlying the phrase, "We are all brothers, in Christ." Worst of all, was his own disappointment, self-loathing, rejection, at the startling realization, of how debased, amalgamated, impaired, he really was, despite always, proudly, assuming deep, black roots, considering himself of sound mind and body. How could such a pathetic, crazy story really be the origin of his life?

After the Civil War ended on April 9, 1865, Texas was the last rebel state to be subjugated by the Union Army, due to the distance from major battles. It took until June 19th (Juneteenth), for Union soldiers to finally arrive at Galveston, bringing the news that slavery was outlawed. Consequently, the Texas slave populace was the last in the South to be liberated from contemptible captivity; and thus, outrageously, remained a holdover in improper yet shamefully sanctioned servitude, even after the war was officially over; allowing the Lone Star state's inhuman and opportunistic flesh mongers two additional months of gratuitous toil, never informing the freedmen they were actually free; mercilessly squeezing out the last exploitation from this once (and continuingly) enthralled mass' ignorance, and a wretched dependence. The punishing greed and gross swagger of the white ruling class was perpetuated by their complete and unrestricted possession, and control, of the land and means of production; leaving the former bondmen little choice but to continue an existence still tied to their former owners, almost as functional, itemized appurtenances, passing with a farm or factory. The particularly insular and lawless nature of the humid, lowland, agricultural region allowed cotton plantation mono cultures to persevere and thrive again; and while superficial labels, trappings and titles may have been modified, due to a cynical semi-recognition of the Emancipation Proclamation (in reality turning a mean, blind eye to it), still the entrenched, racist attitudes, presumed political hierarchy, and underlying economic relationships of obligation, patronage and labor, were craftily maintained; with the unsullied, redacted terms, sharecropper, debt, foreman and landlord seamlessly replacing their outdated forms, chattel, subjection, overseer and master. So, when Colonel Lucius B. Sayer and his new, Mexican society wife returned to his Spanish land grant hundred square mile plantation, *La Florencia,* from hiding out across the border, the hardest thing for him to get used to, was not being called master anymore; his more than 385 resentful, irate plantation dwellers and tenants calling him, Colonel, as did everyone else. But by exhibiting a token semblance of deference to their newfound status, and submitting to only a minor indignity, he let the steam out of a boiling kettle; granting no more than a hollow victory; continuing to provide everything material, sustenance, support, life itself, to each one of his ex-slaves, and as such, maintained as an incarnate god to them. However, despite such an avatar status Colonel Sayer had ingloriously fled to *Mexico* shortly after the war's close, commanding a ragtag company of insurrectionist war veterans, who dishonorably continued hostilities against occupying Union troops following the Confederacy's surrender. These rowdy cavalry irregulars were guilty of treason and murder, for a surprise attack of a lightly defended U.S. Army supply convoy, one foggy night, on the road from Galveston. After several months of laying low in Monterrey he grew homesick, and wrote to the Yankee military governor of Texas, requesting amnesty, ostensibly to get his plantation, one of the largest in the cotton belt, back to productivity, for the sake of his retainers and the general good of the state. While awaiting word, he lost no time in touring the countryside, establishing credit, presenting proper professional and personal introductions from his cotton connections; showing and ingratiating himself to that society's most distinguished, *hacendados y empresarios*; displaying the rare, genteel qualities of a Southern gentleman and gamely courting an eligible *senorita* from one of the most notable, wealthy families in the state of *Nuevo Leon*, Elvira Nubes y de los Gatos. She was a very beautiful, dusky *mestizo*, as her mother was a fiery, full blooded *Comanche* princess, captured in a raid by her Mexican rancher father; whose own Spanish ancestors first forced themselves on helpless Indian maidens, in the 1620's, when they, along with other venturesome *nuevos grandes,* carved up extensive, arid, tribal lands between themselves, creating new, pastoral grazing regimes. After Sayer's pardon was granted (as the expected commercial benefits of King Cotton's revitalization trumped the extinguished lives of Union soldiers he and his paramilitary band had ignominiously ambushed), he and Elvira were married; and following a month of honeymoon spent surveying his father in law's spectacular *hacienda,* with enormous herds of well-bred cattle, large capacity corn and wheat mills, high yield silver and gold mining operations; and being sufficiently impressed by his wife's carefully managed patrimony, headed back, across the *Rio Bravo del Norte,* to reclaim his own fortune. His ravenous blood lust was to play a bigger role than he could ever have imagined, as Texas was never far from Connecticut customs of old:

> Bad men need nothing more to compass their ends, than that good men
> should look on and do nothing. (John Stuart Mill, Inaugural Address
> Delivered to the University of St. Andrews, 2/ 1/1867)

Once returned to his dynastic Texas haunts, the Colonel wasted no time in increasing, not only the crop yield of *La Florencia's* white bolls, but attending to his own personal fruitfulness as well, and he never was intolerant when it came to sex, lying with women of all races, colors, religions, national origins. In over twenty-five years, he fathered one hundred ninety-six children known of, and perhaps three dozen others for which the connection was clouded. With his wife Elvira he had four sons and four daughters, two dark, and two less dark of each, the products of fervent and consistent love making, by the married couple. But succumbing to deeper impulses he could never control, there were also four other sons and four other daughters, all white as snow, with the sweet throated, sultry and inviting, blond daughter of his severe, gruff, German immigrant superintendent, who seductively sang German *Liebeslieder* for her *Geliebte* when she wanted his personal attentions; the balance of the Colonel's robust issue, all different shaded *mulattoes,* sprang from an assumption of his *seigneurial* privileges, taking absolute, unopposed, cowardly advantage of any unattached, as well as attached, deprived, impoverished, defenseless, black females of all ages, in all imaginable, compromising and outright vulnerable circumstances, throughout his domain; who would do anything whispered in their ears, perhaps occasionally out of natural interest or unbridled passion, and sometimes for an offered apple, coin or spool of cloth, to improve their lives; but for the most part out of fear of physical harm and retribution, as he had his way, inseminating them, savagely and with abandon. As the years came and went, Elvira Sayer noticed the confounding level of pregnancies in many women who periodically crossed paths with her, observing the uncanny frequency of light, biracial infants to dark, black parents or single mothers, especially on Sunday mornings, when entire families were to be seen out and about, on the way to, and from, church, town or plantation store, and she grew alarmed, because of a strong physical resemblance of many ostensibly fatherless children, to her own husband. While never directly confronting the Colonel, over his infidelities, promiscuity or sexual predations, out of refusal to condescend to his bestial level, nevertheless, she had her suspicions, and believed he was the perpetrator behind the steadily climbing, seemingly related, number of orphans everywhere. As a way of getting back at a disgraceful, philandering husband, she insisted on providing basic medical and nutritional care for all those residing on his burgeoning estate. She built a clinic for them, or rather, had him build it: *Clinica las Nubes,* a shrine to the damaged, where fundamental needs were met, and over time, in addition to the anticipated ailments and infirmities, many peculiar defects and abnormalities began appearing. It was the least she could provide for those poor, miserable, tainted souls, she understood, as his own, lost creations; and for that kind, generous, humanitarian act, she was revered by the entire community almost as a saint, and beloved for ever after her death. Her other great feat, at his expense, was providing the plantation (it was still called that) with a new school, so children could be instructed while contributing with their daily farm chores. Near, yet distant, it was the single, far off corner of solid learning available to misfits of nature, actually representing the entire continent adrift with islands of intellectual poverty; but she believed in them enough to allow for self-discovery, and an understanding, of their illicit origins, despite the bitter pain it might cause, in the realization they were genetically doomed, now and forever, due to a sick spouse's serial, sexual violations; with periods of reflective silence agonizing over God's love, and whether one's faith in Him was strong enough. But they had done enough to be saved on Judgment Day, the Colonel uneasily acceding, establishing trusts dedicated to his selfless wife's maintenance (even after her death), of beneficiaries, future descendants, that would bear his indelible mark; not because of any personal feelings of compassion or decency, but as a means of keeping his wife out of his now exposed, lustful affairs; and a vain attempt to placate her profound rancor toward him. Upon Sayer's death from syphilis, with its horrid, attendant symptoms of Gummatous skin lesions, blindness and dementia, his surviving assemblage of abused victims tried to obliterate his painful memory, and their own humiliating enmity toward him, as best they could, but the Colonel, an ominous specter, continued turning up in everyone's lives for the longest time, a bad penny:

> **HAMLET.** A little more than kin, and less than kind.
> (William Shakespeare, *The Tragical History of Hamlet, Prince of Denmark*, 1600)

Because the irresponsible scattering of his seeds so widely, wildly, in such a restricted population, went hand in hand with his refusing to accept, or even be remotely identified, with any form of paternity and consanguinity, whatsoever, for a continually growing collective of children born out of wedlock; some serious problem developed, distinguishing between families as separate, genetic lines, and maintaining their distinctions as time passed, and unacknowledged offspring grew to child bearing age, themselves; eventually resulting in unbridled, rampant, interracial inbreeding, as sisters, nieces and aunts could not readily identify, brothers, nephews and uncles (not to mention, innumerable cousins on every side), as such, and perhaps, unaware, slept with their own relatives. As the depraved permutations, based on this heredity, are mind boggling, all the various players cannot be singled out, but suffice it to say, that by the 1920's, there had been up to three or four confused and convoluted generations, disseminated within ostensibly different blood lines, that could all claim Colonel Lucius B. Sayer as their common ancestor:

> But there are times when the little cloud spreads, until it obscures the sky.
> And those times I look around at my fellow men and I am reminded of some
> likeness of the beast-people, and I feel as though the animal is surging up
> in them. And I know they are neither wholly animal nor holy man, but an
> unstable combination of both. (H.G. Wells, *The Island of Dr. Moreau*, 1896)

Many of these illegitimate, wounded families took Anglicized versions of Elvira Sayer's maiden name, Nubes y de los Gatos (*Nubes*, as in Clouds, with native, natural overtones, was her mother's name, it's assumed, while *de los Gatos* may or may not have been her paternal ancestor's name, as it spoke of the early, Sephardic colonists into *Nuevo Leon* who had predated her later uncircumcised kin), as their own; some would be known, as Gates. And many Gates sought refuge from their secret misfortune and stain, in the Carthaginian Black Baptist Church, founded 1844, where all their sins, and those of their fathers, were washed away through cleansing, regenerating baptism. One of the clearest, most ethereal voices in the Sunday choir belonged to a young Hannibal P. Gates, age 13; it was as if he sang with the angels that surely hovered overhead. With his sparkling, hazel eyes, wavy, blond hair, and a fair complexion, he could have passed for a white, and many times had been mistaken so; and then the Negro and Indian subtleties became apparent, perhaps a certain tint against the sunlight, the angle of the cheek bones, or contours of the nose, chin, mouth. The sprouting adolescent was very handsome, and when he sang the girls and women listening closely were awed by his marvelous tenor gifts, and Germanic beauty. They thought all day of him, hoping to hold hands on the way home from church, as Hannibal's parents were aware of the extraordinary effect their son seemed to have on the opposite sex, and were afraid for him, as well as any possible mates, and eventual descendants. Seeing that Hannibal would soon have sexual relations, if he hadn't already, that would probably mean additional offspring born with evil, congenital traits, abnormalities, which seemed to pass so readily among the plantation families; and they were not sure they wanted to be a part of it, or wanted any of their children, or God forbid, their children, to be a part of it anymore. There was this cute, bronze Native/ black girl Hannibal stared at; the parents' worry was for her; they would nip this flirtation in the bud, prevent the spread of additional doomed destinies; there was no avoiding it, the only solution they could come up with, being complete escape from there. There were other reasons for the family's tactical as well as strategic retreat; the local, overall wearing, white country boys seemed to have it out for the sweet voiced, multiracial lover, in their midst. One of the largest and ugliest of that crew seemed to hanker for the same Indian girl, who apparently preferred Hannibal. As their trucks roared past the darkened house, in the sparkling moonlight, they hurled s***, and savage insults, at the family, threatening to rape Hannibal's sisters. One day Hannibal was found in a garbage bag filled with feces. So they had to withdraw from the plantation, where their entire lineage could be traced back to, and frequently crossed over on itself (themselves), for one hundred years; then head north to a place they knew nothing about, other than it was colder than Texas; to escape a vicious circle of perpetual degeneration, preserve what remained of their chromosomal integrity, rescuing any sound heritage that could still be salvaged, with no other choice. Despite being destitute farmers, living from week to week, they had saved some money, picked up and left without even a clear destination, or the realization they had joined the Great Migration, in search of new horizons, dignity and redemption.

The desperate family absconded early one morning, owing Sayer's legitimate, entitled heirs (those same ruffians who heckled out of malice that the others garbled, guffawed, yes 'med, to such an extent, it was obvious "their maker could never in any way have been our maker") several months' rent and credits at their general store; terrified the current caretakers, keeping custody of the Colonel's foul legacy, or their callous, dutiful henchmen, would give quick chase; constantly looking behind their backs for a county sheriff to catch up with them, at any minute, even when they were several counties, then states, distant from *La Florencia*. They rode with Mexican and black truck drivers when they could, and took buses, which ate into their meager resources, when they had to; *there were six of them*, reflected a future Rev. Gates, *it must have been expensive, bewildering, given their limited means and lack of education. They were certainly very brave to give up their accustomed activities, routine, environment, and renouncing what had been preordained for them from the time they were born; venturing to an unknown world they were unprepared for, after sheltering on their plantation for many decades.* Along the way they passed establishments with clearly posted signs screaming their warning: **NO DOGS NEGROS MEXICANS** or **COLORED SERVED IN REAR.** Though none knew the meaning of irony, they all independently thought *and then resented the fact that everyone else had a choice to come to this country, except them. Native American peoples on both continents were here to begin with, so they had no choice either; and then all the Spics with their own language and ways of doing things, they seem to belong just as much as the redskins; and the Indians' decisions to restructure the reservation to reclaim what was once their patrimony, was their own. Also, all the others it seemed, Chinks, hebes, Arabs, Pollacks, and any other white people, made their own decisions on when, how, to come over.* Driving through Tennessee (even back then one of the most backward states in the union, a public health hellhole of creationist credulity, run in the literalist, scripture based meanness of Scotch-Irish Presbyterians, who settled the Appalachian spine of what was then America), just after midnight, in the far, clear, moonlit distance in an open field, they spied a huge, burning cross, surrounded by a convention of pointed white hooded celebrants, in a broad circle; and dim effigies, figures, or maybe men and women, much like themselves, they could not be sure, hanging heavily from trees, swaying lightly in the summer breeze. The unending, black dream of a hallowed time, when there was no prejudice, and people did not hate and victimize them, was only that, a long dream. History shows how Africans unwittingly brought about their abasement by warring, raiding, terrorizing, enslaving and cannibalizing each other, hunting women for polygamous rites and procreation, failing to adequately feed overpopulated tribes, well before any foreign power, commercial laws of supply and demand, did the same. They prayed their truck would not stop or break down; in all truth the alarmed, Mexican driver himself had no intention other than to hightail it out of the retrograde region as fast as possible; so far, so good, safe, once passing Washington D.C. the idyllic North starting.

As shy, immigrant strangers arrived in the Elm City before dawn, they rejoiced at the fellowship shared in those hard times, mainly with Baptists. The remaining events were known to our current Gates from limited, guarded conversations with aunts, uncles, whom he recalled were much lighter and whiter than himself; the memories of his grandfather were imprecise, with images of him as nearly white; he never really had given it much thought, until now. Freed Hannibal P. Gates, freshly released from castigating shadows of his entire tortuous descent from the Colonel, went on to contribute with much beauty to the choir of a new church, where he eventually met and fell in love with, a recently immigrated dark, black, Jamaican girl, who would become the Rev. Gates' grandmother. So, it all made sense, the flight from Texas, of which he had known nothing during his entire growing up, only indefinite rumors respecting the older generation, of a trial, sadly tyrannical and incredible, they had endured long ago and far away. There was always an air of mystery surrounding the urgency with which they left, as if trying to prevent that which was forbidden and harmful from occurring. But it was hidden, and had never been detailed openly with him, because of such pain, perplexity, involved. "Back home in the Deep South we used to sing the Sunday school song: 'Red and yellow, black and white, / They are precious in His sight, / Jesus loves the little children of the world.'" They did their best, to bear up and normalize their lives again in their sanctuary city; quickly establishing new relationships, relinquishing past ties with and mention of their Texas folk, friends, acquaintances, pretending their former, entangled existence, was just a dream; and after two generations felt comfortable enough, to reenter the black fold again, and be received as such. They had always been subject to prejudice and discrimination for not really being white, and that should have been enough to end any lingering doubts about their acceptance. Except that he knew the truth, about what was really within him, believing two generations were not enough to tidy up the mess, that was made in the previous three; as far as he was concerned it was all a matter of concentrations and blending of introduced elements, almost a chemistry equation, considering his contorted, contaminated cellular composition to be the product of diversity run amuck; for the sake of his true blood, as a means of self-defense, he needed to disavow varieties, the harmful, diluting, biologically polluting effects; his life's mission would now be to uphold his own blackness, his people's unique, extracted singularity; and to accomplish the quest all other strains, whether native or exotic, needed to be kept from the perimeter. "So, f*** all this s***, about erasing racial barriers, and getting along. Why does white America think I or any other black person ever wanted to come here?" For, "I have been a stranger in a strange land."

Post divinity fellowship, he decided to forgo the academic world of abstract, religious theories, remote case studies, and found the Carthaginian Black Baptist Church, a beacon for his community's trust and faith; a citadel barricading against the heathen host of plundering barbarians, new enemy at the gates; * released of esoteric ambitions, to focus on the real world, what was happening on the streets to his own kind. He returned to the neighborhoods, where the need was acute, where he believed he could make a difference; acting as their advocate before the establishment forces, they confronted daily: corporations, property owners, bill collectors, unemployment assistance, whatever or whoever could hold them back.

As ice crystals mired down the city's gathered mist the Rev. Hannibal P. (Pearly) Gates, presiding at the radical Carthaginian Black Baptist Church, became a gadfly in the social order, unrelenting in pledged attainment of his people's cultural continuity, civil rights, sometimes at the expense of real allowance or consistency, or fairness, regarding other minorities, or even whites. His urgent message of purpose was not about uniform conditions for all but much more for his side, a new privileged class he was hell bent on raising up and encouraging. He wanted them to help themselves, deeply resenting that they required assistance; to be treated as everyone else (whites) with nary a reference to their distinct identity (black), which could be considered condescending, whether mentioned sympathetically, or critically. But *they* were at liberty to bring it up, especially when an opportunity that was to their advantage arose. And at such times, it was with a secret knowledge of their strength in numbers, the solidarity of a community, organized by single minded social reformers (agitators), with no sympathy for white men, that resulted in profound, moral action being taken. But at present, the steady influx of the offensive, unauthorized, Latin American immigrants was a direct affront to his people's preservation, an assault on their identity and tranquility, and as such, could not be accepted, permitted to go unchecked; and as no trusty security measures seemed effective in containing this infernal, streaming flood, he was ready to test alternative, preventive strategies, perhaps unorthodox remedies. What is it about human nature that those excluded inexorably go on to exclude others? *Was there a way to send them all back, to where they came from?*

> I didn't say that the Jews are inferior. I didn't even maintain they are a race.
> I merely saw that the mixture of different cultures didn't work... Germany
> will regard the Jewish question as solved only after the very last Jew has
> left the greater German living space... Europe will have its Jewish question
> solved only after the very last Jew has left the continent.
> (Alfred Rosenberg, Nazi ideologue, and philosopher, 1/12/1946)

Openly calling on Hollywood to greatly increase its hiring and promotion of black performers, workers, it came to his attention that the CEO of Warren Bros. Inc. was a certain John B. Sayer, of finest colonial American stock; Pastor Gates contemplating, if he and Sayer might share something in common, or the name was perhaps just odd happenstance; determined to find out he requested an interview with Sayer, ostensibly to discuss a possible donation by the studio, to his New African Roots Charity. Upon getting together in Sayer's New York office, breaking the ice, Sayer inquired if the pastor was at all happy with the studio network's Sunday morning religious programming, such as *Dr. Cora, Televangelist*; to which Preacher Pearly sardonically replied, "Black folks don't listen to *Dr. Cora*; why would a black believer pay attention to her?" In the presence of whites this cautious zealot rarely exhibited any sense of irony, or self-deprecation, as these are qualities exhibited by those, who have accepted their designated places in the world, are at peace with themselves as citizens and to some extent assume an identity of a greater society, in which they dwell. Perhaps self-reflection, and exposure, before descendants of their former oppressors, was too painful for those whose present was still tormented, heavy, with pent-up frustration at the slave status of their ancestors. To the point, Preacher Pearly rarely laughed at himself, in front of whites. Within his own relaxed circle, however, it was another matter; he let his guard down and teased and taunted his friends and associates when appropriate, without the embarrassment, shame of allowing outsiders to identify any feelings, or weaknesses, in him. This social insularity may have been part of a self-protection mechanism, but it also made him appear standoffish and unfriendly, and prevented him from fully being accepted by anybody he did not feel comfortable with. The upright parson mentioned that he had recently given the keynote speech, before the National Association for the Advancement of Black People (NAABP), saying he was not divisive, but descriptive, and the black church meetings, as with black culture, not deficient, but different. Despite this awkward start, the meeting proceeded and improved, with Sayer committing $500,000 on behalf of the studio, in exchange for favorable publicity and press treatment, within African American circles; to which Pastor Gates delightedly agreed. Once all the introductory formalities were over, Preacher Pearly got to the heart of the matter, looking Sayer right in the eye, boldly declaring they could be kin. Sayer not blinking, stirring, showing any visible reaction, saying nothing, for what seemed like minutes, years, eons, sized up his guest, gazing deeply into his face, as if into a hazy mirror. "If that were at all possible, I'm sure it would be in a quite distant degree," was Sayer's flabbergasted, cautious reply, but the closer he inspected the stronger a probability there was something; he did in fact perceive a faint glint, resemblance or veiled likeness, to someone he might vaguely have known, seen or imagined, a figment; he couldn't say, exactly whom, maybe it was only the power of suggestion. Gates next revealed that his great-great-great grandfather had been one,

Colonel Lucius B. Sayer, of *La Florencia*, Texas; did Sayer have people in Texass? Sayer responded in the affirmative and then knew, despite the man before him being black, *it must be true: he was linked to African Americans*, he reeled with a vague discomfort: *could there be more?* "Why, Odds bodkins," he declared, before standing, and giving the reverend a bear hug, calling him his long-lost biblical brother.

*Let us open our eyes; there is no such thing as a black race in the United States. There is an African American, mulatto race, but not a truly black one; because they are all the products of an abysmal rape of an entire people by another crueler or more despotic, with no accountability other than the confused, enraged products, themselves. But why should people of color decide who is a racist, and who is not; as if they have a final say, because of a few extra grains of pigment sprinkled through their skin? They are a self-appointed nemesis upon a white race, still held accountable for dark deeds done long ago, by others, not themselves. And as resentment is a hurt more easily nurtured than the balm of self-reliance, many find it easier to keep reliving the past rather than getting on with their lives. Perhaps they are the racists, having driven public consciousness into a media fed frenzy of racial categories, quotas, ethnic types, identities, cultural competence, coercion. Perhaps they are the ones engaging in bigotry, blithely and parochially accusing an entire, less pigmented, global group, of that very same, obnoxious offense. Those repeatedly claiming they speak for the people are the biggest hypocrites; they undoubtedly speak for themselves; just as those who claim to do something for the people are doing it for themselves. And when the hour came, to parcel out any reparations owed from white bad behavior, the black side waited patiently in line, with hands outstretched for any mercy to be had, before disappointment came to them, upon realizing there could be valid reasons to get back at the other, but deciding it was not the morally correct path to take. Too much time had passed for any hard feeling to have survived, needing revenge.*

> Although,
> Retribution does not make up, for risen slime,
> Nevertheless,
> Revenge is best served cold, biding its time.

After regaining his composure and coming around again, Sayer calmly, in a businesslike fashion, asked if there was anything more, he could do for Gates. Preacher Pearly launched directly into his detailed description of the crisis with illegal, alien drug gangs, especially *Los X*, and the tons of imported *cristal* in Connecticut; was there anything that Mr. Sayer, as president of one of the most important, influential companies in the world, could suggest, to combat this dual invasion? "It's bad enough, they're pushing that crank on our kids, but they're doing it on our own streets. How can we stop them?" So prompted, Sayer's eyes lit up in recognition of a kindred spirit, a brother if not cousin of sorts, with whom he now could be completely open and frank. "The problem engulfing us is much larger than you or I can solve, individually or even jointly; it must be met head on with overwhelming, opposing force. I have formed a visionary team, whose time has come, the Committee for Public Safety, to deal with these very issues of inclusiveness, and would appreciate your participation, counsel; together we should be able to keep these unwanted meddlers at bay;" and with that, an innovative and unconventional alliance was shaped, as much out of necessity, as convenience; conceived of this crisis and solidarity, striving for change and reorder, fomenting quiet discord and division; perhaps this was the sign, the pastor had been hoping for.

*Footnote

New Enemy at the Gates

Confronted by this world spinning rapidly out of control, modern, liberal democracies were now quite skilled and dexterous at providing poignant, posthumous memorials for, and expressing solidarity with, fallen victims of imported, international terror, propagandizing the celebrity symbols of compassion, openness and diversity across their greater societies, as well as vilifying, both morally and practically, finding common cause against, violence. But their frozen inaction, in the face of consistent, clear attacks for more than thirty years; double talk defending cultural accommodation despite significant, evil coteries of adherents being avowed enemies, and professedly anti-Western; and a policy of open, in your face, immigration, left Everyman befuddled and cynically wondering, what was being done, toward the joint defense; and if unfortunate, random others would soon, also join the ranks of tossed out, unavenged victims of an aloof, careless, duplicitous state. Here perhaps it should be recalled that it was the naïve hospitality of the innocent, trusting, American Indians, in welcoming the foreign, white gods, that ultimately brought about their demise; and once barbarian Goths were admitted to the Roman Empire, they could never be expelled, ushering in successive invasions, bringing about the fateful fall of the Western Empire. The millennium would foster a new enemy at the gates, wolves turning on lambs, with whom they'd fed, slept, cohabited.

# 8. Gung-ho

> From the Halls of Montezuma
> To the Shores of Tripoli;
> We fight our country's battles
> In the air, on land and sea;
> First to fight for right and freedom
> And to keep our honor clean;
> We are proud to claim the title
> of United States Marine. (U.S. Marine Corps Hymn)

The lately elated conquering lady, shaded (nearly) white, was child advocate Patricia (P) Diddy, Ph.D., J.D., founder-president, and thus far sole member, of the international humanitarian group *Les Enfants Sans Frontières*, Greenitch, CT. Her chat with that incomparable heiress, exemplary executive, global patron of development foundations, nature preserves, progressive causes, Isidora Green, resulted better than P could have ever expected or dreamed, leading to a new collaboration, and was off to a fast start, with future streams of support for P's fledgling organization, built single-handed from nothing, pledged by the most powerful woman influencer in the world, with a renowned Rolodex, and pushy sense to get things done. Always impressed by fluid gender seekers, Isidora had assisted in P's admission to Whale.

P had chosen to relocate her headquarters to upscale Greenitch, considering it one of the few places to be domiciled, outside of New York City, pretentious enough to celebrate a French identity for one of its *nouveau*, not for profit entities. Naturally, Famefield County was part of P's rich plan to entice Isidora Green into her scheme; intuitively, P had fixed on Isidora's fascination with all things, *rococo* and posh; especially the grand illusion of philanthropic gestures. In point of sharp comparison, it was certainly a different world from the infernally poor, eastern Connecticut town P had been born and raised in, even more so, during the impoverished era, before the Indian casinos. Greenitch had swank, Ledmont none.

Greenitch boasted vast, architecturally significant estates, with manicured lawns, behind endless walls separating multi-million-dollar egos. It had a Spiffany & Co., as you ambled, right down Main Street, the fanciest of automotive dealerships, and certain country clubs, to which even billionaires had to beg to be admitted; reveling in all those entitled adventures that went along with incredible, old as well as new money, such as random trysts, with pliant pick-ups, in coke induced ardor, *Ice Storm* wife swapping, or perhaps high-class escorts for fun. It was the kind of environment that bred cold, shrewd opportunists.

Ledmont revealed rolling, open hills, secluded, damp woods, meandering roads to dirty stores, and was out in the middle of nowhere. It had horses, cows, beeves, thousand-acre fields of corn, hay; allowing repressed routines that went along with generational farm existence, such as engaging in forbidden acts with a favorite family mare, or sympathetic, lowing bovine; and sometimes your brothers and sisters, or mother and father, aunts, uncles, even grandparents, needing to warm up in bed, in the freezing dead of night. It was the kind of environment that incubated cold, cunning serial killers in its steady ignorance.

There were chicken coops, more akin to factories, industrial size poultry sheds, for raising overcrowded fowl, producing eggs; and hate filled decapitations utilizing long, heavy knives, blunt axes, going along with husbandry, as a fleeting enterprise, in this pocket of cast-off New England; time seeming forgotten into some useless sort of desperate, rural poverty. It was the same soil that begat Michael Ross, sexual predator, and murderer of eight women and girls, whose stony, average looking face belied a maniacal and perverse impulse to slaughter, as occurred daily on an unremarkable tract of boggy, windswept land where he grew up, and was as such, normalized, internalized. His aspect was that of the prosaic nature of an institutional butcher, and as with most animal growers, he was simply inured to the spectacle of spilled blood, painful death. As cooped up as their birds throughout bleak, country winters, extensive isolation, tending toward survivalist self-sufficiency, many humble, agricultural families looked inward rather than out, for sources of entertainment, camaraderie and love, the standard joke for this toothless, bumpkin region being that, for many married couples, it would make no difference if they suddenly got divorced, as they could always remain brother and sister. It was difficult for P to believe that Greenitch could be in the same state as Ledmont, so vast was the split. How had P gotten to this point in her life?

P was a born assassin. During her pregnancy with P, her mother complained of an almost constant pain within her, as if something not belonging inside was screaming to get out. That was distinguished from the external torments inflicted upon her by P's father, who with great animal violence to express, flailed about without cause or reason throughout the nine months; and the earth gave a groan when P drew her first breath. Her mother raised her pretty much alone, as her father was a wayward soul, unhappy when kept at home, going by the matronymic Diddy, as had her own mother before, which was how titty was pronounced in old Ireland. They were multiracial Melungeon polyglots, ever on the move, for the past three centuries, from county to county in the hollows of North Carolina, Kentucky, Tennessee, Virginia; much of the time evading laws, ordinances, meant to suppress, outlaw, miscegenation, which they not only practiced openly, but from which they themselves were also a unique New World product; shifting around as much, speaking as many unintelligible dialects, as Gypsies, whose nomadic blood mythically coursed (cursed) through their veins; though not fathomed by P at the time, this Gypsy marker later tied her directly to Isidora Green, coincidentally descended similarly, from dispersed *Roma*, most distant of relations, through traces more binding, lustrous, than that ancient wealth of their mountainous, *Punjabi* place of origin; proudly sharing mixed Middle Eastern, Jewish, African, Caucasian, Native American roots; in P's mother's case the trace of Scotch-Irish ancestry bestowing haunting blue eyes, freckles and auburn hair, traits which were generously passed on to P; while her feckless father traced his lineage to the *Mashantucket Pequots*, which is why he deposited his family on the reservation in a cramped trailer with the acrid stench of beer and whiskey spilled over the sticky floor. Every so often he showed up to bully them about, with taunts, shoves, as well as fists, and P's wasted childhood became a lost time, an endless routine, of sleeplessness, hunger, sudden, secret shivers; steady blows from parents surrendered to their own frustrations, drunkenness and resentments of the world in which they failed to function, or succeed, and which from the start never accepted them into its civilizing, comforting fold. Pathetically, her mother allowed the maltreatment, turned a blind eye to it, sharing culpability to the maximum. But after all, it was the way kids were raised now, then and always, and who was she, to question any of his decisions? A real dumb bunny, she married him at sixteen because she found herself carrying his child, only the month after meeting him. Her family was from South Carolina, and he was introduced to them mainly on the strength of being from New England; the prize he brought was dynamic blood, though he was, just as she, a product of a *mélange*, similar in so many ways; but what a positive impact it would have on her future progeny, to have a stranger from that far away mixing his parts with hers; rather than someone from down aways with whom she might perhaps be related without either of them knowing it. It was sensible for precautions to be taken with respect to macro genetic flows, although no prophylaxis was utilized in preventing their respective micro flows from occurring, and it was in this way that P had been conceived in the probability laden assumption that she at least would not be mongoloid or possess six fingers or toes, webbed hands and feet, various other deformities associated with rampant, abnormal chromosomal coding, within inbred populations, major miracles for hillbillies, such as these. And from such free origins, quite complex creatures were at times manifested, as P would one day turn out to be.

One of the oddities of their poverty stricken, and chaotic, existences was that, despite their own, broad hodgepodge of racial and ethnic affiliations, the parents were the most opinionated bigot homophobes and racists imaginable, and were both victims of and participated freely in the three unifying hates, i.e., of foreigners, Negroes and Jews. Once, while at the seashore, her parents noted nature's definite, harsh divisions: "Why, just look at the birds, baby, the white gulls keep to themselves, and the black crows to themselves. Man should take a clue from God's messengers." As far as social theorizing went that was about as profound as her family, ironically, components of crossbreeding themselves (the story of Pan, product of the lusts of a hundred suiters and Penelope's unfaithfulness, while her brave Ulysses traveled to her, comes to mind) ever got. Though such pejorative sentiments regarding the melting pot, were in truth, reflections of their own self-hate (a widespread phenomenon brought about by constantly applied gradations, and crazy mass classification), nevertheless, P's mother was forever expressing pride, in her degree of European complexion, versus other Melungeon moms; and her father was obsessed with his provable percentage of *Pequot* Nation purity, against the ideal measure, to which, alas, he consistently fell far short. Her mother always said, it was P's pale, moon goddess features, which would help her to succeed in life; provided she also act white; while her father consistently reminded her, of all the things her blood qualified her for, especially a share in the tribal loot, and state of the art benefits. Regarding their future honey pot of cash, tribal largess would provide unheard of luxuries and comforts, as well as obliterate incentives to progress to the next level of educational and social improvement, to escape the tribe's dissipated and victimized condition. The modern Indian casinos provided the perfect foil to the old, entrenched Puritan economic structure, which had begun with the moralists introducing alcohol to the natives, hoodwinking them into giving up their souls, even pride, claiming their lands, before taking over; but now tribes owned top name casinos, luring invaders there, plying them with liquor, loosening them up, taking all their money, legally bringing about the transfer of hard-earned wealth. After having everything stripped from them, ultimate retribution was finally in their possession, with the white man hooked on games he himself invented, provided, duped kids wagering away their last precious marbles. Aboriginal vengeance was reclaiming what was theirs, using the loopholes of law through the invention of sovereign nations, the natives having that last laugh, achieving justice the legal way, turning English common law systems to their own advantage, at last; very little of this wealth ever trickling down to P.

P's parents did as well as they could, considering they had been alcoholics, heroin addicts, most of their adult lives, in her childhood, leading a vagabond existence, from state to state, hustling here and there, at truck stops, back alleys, with P being cared for in the same way they themselves had been (not better, or worse), and they scoring their daily fixes; their dark influences on P becoming a deadly, on demand killer being obvious in conclusion, yet hard to define. They were dim, crass, tough, as only uneducated (though somewhat clever) yokels can be, quick at adjudicating blame and meting out harsh punishment, before the facts to a situation were known. And they were far off the radar of any state child protection agencies, because of the remoteness of the places they chose, or were tolerated, to live in, as well as the frequency of their furtive migrations between state lines, so that standing up to her elders would be out of the question, there would be no rescue available for miles around. That P was never abandoned, just forgotten and left behind, at some old gas station the family was passing through, was due, less to any feeling of kinship, care, love and loyalty from her parents, than their need for someone, anyone, to keep around to do everything for them, considering they were strung out most of the time; the only benefit to her parent's dope *malaise*, being that her opposition to them fostered a sense of sobriety, and the fear of losing self-control, in P that would last her entire lifetime, keeping her sharp, focused, as a burgeoning archer Diana. As an outlet from the persistent physical, as well as mental, cruelty inflicted upon her by frazzled parents, when she was ten, P started cutting thin, upper thighs and arms, producing a tremulous response throughout her aroused nervous system. Though she had no idea of the therapeutic concepts of releasing saturated, cardinal *humours* by bloodletting, as was practiced in antiquity, the Middle Ages, Renaissance, up to the 1800s, that was precisely what she achieved, with each razor slash steeped then staunched with gently flowing blood, channeling deep frustrations, regaining a control, feeling relieved, tranquil, after each auto mutilation, as if pent-up, dirty thoughts or evil tendencies were done away with and replaced, by self-inflicted pain, a new focal point for her psyche. There were other symptoms of an unbalanced nature: she sensed no relaxation, pleasure, ease, derived no joy, approaching the world with a stone-cold countenance. With her mother, she read the Bible, internalizing personally, her damnation, original sin, a fallen Eve complex, as true preconditions of existence, assuming a chaste state, as much out of ignorance as inclination; with her parents off chasing the dragon, having never observed or heard intimacy between them, with no idea about the delicate relationships between the sexes, nary a clue of emotions. She was afraid of any sexual thoughts and avoided them completely, also refusing to explore or touch herself in any manner suggestive of self-discovery. The reality of her gender was a consuming mystery to her, and she disavowed becoming a woman. Strangely, she neither wished to be a man. She wanted to be non-gendered and non-sexual to a degree that was certainly non-conforming for the times. Her anguish commenced when, upon turning eleven, her breasts started sprouting, and she had her first menses. Inexplicably, her responses to these biological imperatives were to bind her built-up bust, so it would not bloom, then seal an aching crotch with straw to absorb nature's intrusive, rushing femininity.

One of P's few escapes from the mess of her family's daily lives, was when her father (during moments of rare lucidity, brought about by the high purity of the smack he happened to be doing at the time, and also truly wanting, out of some heartfelt pride and nostalgia in his and his wife's own descent; traceable on this continent to an era when certain doomed African, Saracen, Sephardic, Spanish, Portuguese and, from time to time, other random Old World sailors were accidentally marooned on the North American mainland by off course, wrecked Spanish treasure galleons, or a fleet, at safe harbor, disembarked some of the crew's bad apples, well predating the arrivals of any English speaking traders, settlers, and then colonists, by half a century; to teach his daughter some vital skills, that would help get her through life, whether pursuing or escaping enemies, wading in snake infested swamplands or trekking through lowly cesspools of our modern concrete jungles), took her hunting in the primeval forests, and nature showed a wholly different way, with upended rules of conduct and expectations. And there was a hidden grove where she could be pensive, tapping into the secret turmoil of her being, rather than wasting it away on junkie parents. The peaceful, shadowed woods brought sensual, life-giving elements, so bitterly absent from her short-lived, suffering existence, leaning her head back, tingling all over, basking in such warm sunlight as was suddenly breaking through the high canopy of protective trees. Her eyes closed and the light, against their lids, produced a field of blazing whiteness, against which ideal panoramas projected.

The inward moment was shattered by the sharp crack of her father's rifle, along with roaring whoops of jubilation and triumph. No matter how stoned, he remained, per the Second Amendment, a crack shot.

"Got you, son of a bitch, with one shot." Her father was running across the lower clearing as fast as his drug addled brain commanded, and hepatitis enfeebled limbs carried him. Her eyes adjusted once more to the sun-streaked opening below, and at first could not make out, what her father was heading toward.

"Get your ass here, girl. Quick, I want you to see this." She caught up to him, and saw the fallen buck, writhing, snorting, its big, black eyes clear, open wide in shock, a prelude to death; scarlet blood oozed freely from a bullet hole in the panting beast's thick neck: "The proof of the pudding is in the eating…"

While P recoiled with horror and disgust, her father unsheathed his ten-inch hunting knife, and adroitly ripped open the buck's chest, revealing bright pink muscle strands, gleaming, white ribs. Sticking one hand beneath the steaming strands of yellow fat and broken flesh, with the other, he plunged his blade into the wound with a sickening thud, and began slicing arteries, tendons. Blood shot up from the still breathing animal's thorax, small fountain; with new ripping sounds P shut her eyes, sick to her stomach.

When P opened her eyes again, her father was holding the deer's, still beating, heart in one hand; slime and blood streamed down his arm, the knife in his other hand was covered with bits of meat, bone and skin. Then over a fallen tree trunk, P's father cut the eternally quivering heart in two, and then several smaller portions from each of the halves; by this point, with the animal finally dead, the flies swarmed.

"With this you will become one of a select society of hunters and sharpshooters," he said, putting hunks of the deer's heart in P's hand, and without further ado, chewing bits of gristly heart himself, grinning wildly with self-satisfaction, as warm blood dripped down his stubbly chin; P gagging uncontrollably.

"Now you, girl, eat that buck's life." And suddenly the flora and fauna became eerily silent, expectant.

P slowly raised the piece of deer to her mouth. She could not look, it seemed to still be moving on its own. She chewed, and it felt hard and rubbery, with inert taste, then closed her eyes, swallowing once, hard, praying she would not hurl the pulpy gob of goo settling in her stomach as the blackest of magics.

Then something strange and unexplained happened. She liked it, not knowing if it was the saltiness of the blood or the texture of the flesh, but she could feel the buck's spirit joining hers, becoming her own. As she reached across for another sliver her father smiled down at her. She chewed slowly, thoroughly, and this time it was easier to swallow. Now blood stained her own chin and cheeks; she smiled back at her proud father. She was twelve, wondering how soon, until she could bring down a buck of her own.

One day, at thirteen, distracted, her gaze turned away for an instant, P's dad mixed China white powder in her soda, in line with coaxing that she experienced the full range of life's options, the good, the bad and the ugly. She tried vomiting the slurry out of her system, to no avail, and then spent the next eight hours in a dreamy state she could not comprehend. While desperately trying to puke, she had grabbed her father's chamber pot, and mistakenly spilled icy pee all over herself, so upon waking the following morning, reeking of ammoniac urine, nevertheless, going to school, the kids taunted her, dubbing her P Pee Diddy. In insane humiliation, she jumped on the lead tormentor, beating him senseless. "Don't you ever laugh at me, or I'll kill you." Something inside P, her control impulse, had snapped, the fury in P's face, the locked grimace of her mouth, the way her eyeballs popped out of their sockets, terrifying other children. Someone ran to get the teacher, and it was just in time; P picked up a large stone, would have smashed the unsuspecting lad's head wide open, had the instructor not broken up the fracas, by lifting P up bodily from the victim, fondling teenage boobs and snatch in the process; after this, her schoolmates grew afraid of her, the look of beastly rage, the firmly clamped jaw, some said the sneer made her seem like the devil. She got quiet, kept to herself in her room, reading epistles from Bram Stoker's, *Dracula*. In fact, it was her growing interest in reading that salved the wounds of that unfortunate episode, poring over every book, encyclopedia or periodical she could get her hands on, considering she always walked alone to bookstores, libraries or newsstands. A favorite of hers was a crime writer's guide to weapons: "**Blackpowder/ Black Powder (pick one and be consistent)** – Use this term in settings from the dawn of firearms in 9th century China to the 1880s; antique or vintage-style firearms would use blackpowder after that." Weapons were never more than tools to be utilized by individuals, some good, bad, ugly, so she never bought into the liberal rhetoric that guns were inherently evil, nor to the conservative version that they were a God given right. She knew that some people were never meant to have them; not her.

Upon turning a wondrous fourteen, P knew how to disassemble, reassemble, repair, the rifles, shotguns, pistols and machine guns she ever had the good fortune to handle and shoot, in the process of the arms being recirculated into the flow of her father's felonious contacts, in rough parts of New London. In the case, of a certain Thompson submachine gun and German *Luger*, P could take them apart, and put them together, in the dark or blindfolded, as she had read that U.S. Marines could, with their assault rifles. P knew it was illegal to own a Thompson, and that only law enforcement officers were allowed to use the deadly weapon, but her father always claimed, "The FBI are a bunch of crooks, and they get away with more gun running, drug dealing and evidence theft, than anyone." P's father brought home some paper, life sized, human torso silhouette shaped targets, for shooting practice, setting them up against trees, in the gully, down behind their dilapidated house, pretending they were policemen, shooting them through the heart, or splintering their heads, with direct hits. With all the guns, ammunition and ready targets at her disposal, P became a dead eye shot. As with most kids let loose with firearms, P went beyond the targets at the ready, shooting rocks, trees, branches, bottles, cans, boxes, or magazines she hated, but stole from school anyway, and any inanimate object at fair distance. And with the inevitability that, "Power tends to corrupt, and absolute power corrupts absolutely..." she commenced shooting animate things that flew, or moved stealthily, in the woods. But her father's love of weaponry, which he secretly was bestowing onto her, had a more sinister, warped purpose. He was obsessed with the theme he had read in the single book he ever owned, *Pudd'nhead Wilson*, by Mark Twain, that even 1/32 blacks were still infantile, tragically racially underdeveloped, nurturing a pent up rage against whites (with whom he curiously identified), and gloomily predicted there would one day be a race war in this country; now with all the recent urban rioting in far off places, such as Watts and Chicago, it sure seemed this was the end; but forewarned is forearmed, he and his family would not be caught unprepared for the holocaust, keeping busy stockpiling guns, ammo, ordnance, dried foods, canned goods, water, fuel, medicine, and enough dried deer meat, Penthouse magazines, to survive for over a year in an underground bunker he was secretly constructing, beneath the bark covered *wigwam*, in the back gully, a survivalist expression.

There was one hunting idiosyncrasy insisted upon by her father, not out of any sense of practicality or frugality, as much as the only inkling of self-discipline P ever witnessed in him, which then trained P to prize accuracy or to avoid the shot and contributed to what set her apart from the other marksmen. She could blow off all the ammo she wanted to during target practice, but when it came time to take a life in the forest, her father allowed only one shot, the single bullet, with severe penalties, such as getting her head slapped, or being tied up to her bed for days at a time, with only bread and water to eat, and a pot to piss in, if two, or more, cartridges were ever employed to dispatch any fleeing prey, before it escaped into the vast embrace of green mansions. But the one bullet one kill requirement, the only limitation on an activity which rewarded her with complete freedom regarding the when, where and how (never the why), the quarry would be fixed (*because that unsuspecting creature I am aiming at so far away has no warning, what's coming, and only I decide when it happens, or if it happens at all, only my indecision can save him*), was actually a gateway to a different type of freedom enjoyed by only a select few, who, with an understanding of nature's gifts, respected the awesome responsibility thrust upon them downing game; while later, as a jaded agent of long-range retribution, in the soft shade of the noonday sun, more akin to a flunkey of a declining superpower than a shiny Cynthia at the chase, it became a rote activity.

At the ideal age of fifteen, she began to ideate the deserved murder of her parental tormentor, and in a vengeful dream, clearly saw herself raising a shotgun to his head, then pulling the trigger. *My old man has inflicted evil*, P thought. *He punished me in such manners, as I believed I was going to die, and my old lady never stopped him or protected me.* Then one day alone in the deepest of glens, an opportunity presented itself; after spending two silent hours together at a deer blind to no avail, they decided to split up; she would head upstream to a rise on a well-protected bluff, while her father remained in the ravine, close by the river, in case anything came down for a drink. From her cat optic vantage point, about five hundred yards away, P spotted father clearly, casually aiming her rifle, getting his head between the crosshairs of her scope. Her father crouched uneasily, behind an overturned log, thick green brush, and P held him fixed in her sight, clearly magnifying details of his leathery, lined face, along with a week's worth of unkempt and sweaty, nicotine-stained stubble. He had beaten P the day before, in a drunken, crystal meth induced frenzy, a product of alternatively abused drugs he utilized when trying, fruitlessly, again to kick the horse addiction, her face still throbbing, where the black and blue bruises proliferated, from her father's heavy, wild, cold turkey blows. He suddenly became alert, uncomfortable, suspicious, his head twitching left, then right, peering all about him, with the sixth sense that perhaps he was being tagged by some malevolent force. In an instant, he realized he was a target. Then it was too late for P, her father was staring right back at her, wide eyed, firmly, through her scope. Perhaps he had caught a glimpse of the sun's reflection against the polished glass in a moment of her carelessness. In any case, there was no reason for P to hide her position now; she had been discovered, so rather than pull her aim away she kept it steadily on her father; and he just as focused and undaunted stared directly back at her, with a giant fury in the hollow pupils of his eyes; the standoff lasting for what seemed forever, until P finally jerked the rifle away, and it was over, both knowing P crossed a line that could not be reversed.

A month later P's father said he was going to Montreal, and never came back. P stayed with her mother for a year, growing restless doing farm chores to make ends meet: her drudgery for the headless family. As much of P's daily life became manifested in blood rites, of one type or another, as with many rural existences, she became inured to the grisly routines carried out by man upon beasts, as well as humans. While reading *Typee*, an early work by Herman Melville, modeled as a sailor's account, for junior year English, P could not help but wonder if the deer hearts she had gotten so accustomed to, tasted anything like human flesh would to a cannibal. What did it mean about her, that she was even constructing such questions in the recesses of an active mind? Apparently, naked, heathen savages had the discernment to devour only certain of those amongst them, which luckily, did not include the sailor recounting the tale:

> "'Why, they are cannibals!' said Toby on one occasion when I eulogized
> the tribe. 'Granted,' I replied, 'but a more humane, gentlemanly and
> amiable set of epicures do not probably exist in the Pacific.'"
> (Herman Melville, *Typee: A Peep at Polynesian Life*, 1846)

Thinking, in all her travails, that her shooting skills would come in handy in Nam, she volunteered for the U.S. Marine Corps, not as a woman but a man, lying not only about her age, but sex and gender too. Along with intermittent, still continuous cutting, went a starvation diet, emaciating (emancipating) her, diagnosed as *anorexia nervosa,* which kept budding breasts the size of quarters. Being a big boned girl, she managed to build up her muscle mass nearly to a man's tone by binging on abundant venison hearts and working out to achieve a perfectly fit physique. The knotty part was producing a credible strapping tricky dicky, which she uncannily accomplished by expanding her *labia majora* to mimic an erect penis of size. It became so erect, in fact, that after the first day naked, in the showers, this macho stunt, along with mastery as a crack shot, won P the nickname York, as in Sergeant Alvin York, of World War I fame. She became practiced in such unexplainable body morphism, from having had so much free time alone in nature, the supreme lack of understanding of how female anatomies worked, and an excess of sexual energy she did not know how to expend other than by puffing her anatomical protrusion. Later, as U.S. Marine asexual trans platoons became the established norm, it would be stunning to hear of the pathetic lengths to which many women-recruits, in former, much less enlightened times, would go, to qualify to become real fighting men. From the start P's requisite killer abilities distinguished her as a top shooter, and once her superiors became aware of her incredible gifts, they guided her into the upper echelons of America's liquidation squads, the brutal Phoenix Program, described by the CIA as, "a set of programs that sought to attack and destroy the political infrastructure of the Viet Cong;" so, posing as the affable rifleman A. York, a confused Connecticut Yankee, white trash girl, with a skull for each hit tattooed on tender, inner thighs, where no one would ever see (ink frowned upon in the regiment), in the following thirteen months, as the grand finale of the Vietnam War, had the most perilous adventures of a lifetime:

> We don't want to fight, but by Jingo if we do,
> We 've got the ships, we 've got the men, we 've got the money too.
> (English doggerel song popular during Russo-Turkish War, 1877-78)

When Private York arrived in the war zone on a sweltering, fetid day that was to be more fateful for the dinks whom he would soon dispatch than himself particularly, he felt firmly resolute and gung-ho about his expected participation and contribution; his assigned unit having quite the unconventional chain of command; its orders given by well-bred preppies, in suits, with northeast schoolboy intonations, as well as crew cut soldiers in uniforms, with southern good ol' boy drawls. There was a lively, tall, audacious officer, however, who bridged the gap between the convoluted Langley Boys and those straightforward West Pointers, the Company spooks and Army paratroops; from time to time, suiting up in seersucker civvies, or alternately in green khaki fatigues, as was his wont; Colonel John B. Sayer (The U.S. Military Academy at West Point Class of 1966), veteran counterintelligence agent, ace soldier, boss of assassins, with a substantial reputation in *Indochine* for getting tough jobs done for impatient, hard line, military operations planners; held in the highest of esteem by dutiful, demanding, accountable Joint Chiefs of Staff, for focused, sensible and timely actions when called for; U.S. Army Airborne, assigned to special forces and the CIA, having seen extensive action early on, all over the DMZ; trained as an explosives specialist, loving fireworks, bombs and blowing everything up; taking tremendous satisfaction in booby trapping, with M-80's, the heavy, metal plated helmets worn by captured NVA regulars; whooping and shrieking, "Geronimo!" in delight, as solid skull pieces flipped in the air, tumbling back to the shredded work table; all the while, taunting maimed prisoners to remain quiet, if they dared. If his interrogation techniques had inordinately high inaccuracy, as well as incompletion, rates those were simply the harsh casualties of this dirty war, as far as he was concerned. And in his adjunct guise, as the self-appointed, regimental, political officer, Sayer was exuberant in spreading racist, bigoted, ethnocentric, xenophobic views against his enemies, while at the same time inadvertently besmirching the U.S.' own ally. "When this war is over, I want you boys to look me up so I can remind you how I forewarned about the Yellow Peril invading our own, sweet land. Because once their society, culture, economy, are obliterated over here, these scheming, Chink inhabitants of infernal, diseased swamps, and mined mountain rice paddies, will suddenly appear on our sacred shores, overcoming us with wave after endless wave of false smiles, garlic stench and greasy hair, entrenched interlopers who won't leave. So, I have a plan for saving our glorious country from this Oriental, tidal pollution hell bent on our complete dilution, 'by Jingo,' this is not a delusion. A Committee for Public Safety will be my aim, and we will volunteer in the fulfillment of this great endeavor, and together root out the slanty eyes, to bring them right back here to gook land, where they came from. Come find me when all the neocolonialist madness is done with, in Hollywood, where dreams are made. You'll always be welcome there, fellows." Such was the voice of the ultimate military command, authorizing Provincial Reconnaissance Units on do or die missions in support of the nefarious U.S. combat objectives. It was no small wonder that the mostly uneducated, and emotionally detached, men did not forget or become confused over what it was they had come over here to fight for, in a tropical, southeast Asian, ex-French colony that would soon swallow them up, then spit them out:

> And then, in the sniperscope, Bond saw the head of Trigger – the purity
> of the profile, the golden bell of hair, - all laid out along the stock of the
> Kalashnikov!...
> "Trigger was a woman."
> "So what? KGB has got plenty of women agents – and women gunners.
> I'm not in the least surprised." (Ian Fleming, "The Living Daylights," 1962)

With Sayer's words ringing in his ears, York soon found himself in a familiar position, only now hidden by a denser, wetter, deeper, green vegetation, than back home. He was doing what he did best, stalking and striking. But here the quarry had changed; it had a greater importance, somehow, not to him, but to those higher up the food pyramid. There was also, a fresh element of malice in the game, unfamiliar to this player, but with which he went along, for the sake of not drawing attention to himself, or his novel female-male uniqueness. Keeping the mark between his cross hairs an instant before the sun caught the polished end of his scope, giving him up, he decided it was time, gently squeezing the trigger; and far away a figure fell anonymously, even before the loud bark of the rifle had shocked the empty stillness of the ravine. Through the scope York saw a pool of blood forming around the man's ripped open neck. Women, children, some old men wailed and held their heads. But already some of the young men were pointing in his direction, and the rays suddenly reflecting off his scope. They ran to their huts, coming out brandishing AK-47s, confirming, in York's mind, their allegiance to the Viet Cong. Now they were rushing toward him. It was time to go. In five minutes, they arrived at the spot where York had waited patiently, for two days, to assassinate their village headman. They had heard of snipers, such as York, a cold-blooded killer, working on his own or in small teams, infiltrating his way through the countryside, to bring fear and horror into poor, wasted lives already beset by endless violence, alternating with edgy tranquility. When they got there, he was gone. There were no footprints, no spent casing, no misplaced personal items or trash; there were no trails to follow. York had slipped into the jungle and evaporated.

Already, about a mile ahead of his enraged pursuers, York was racing to the extraction point. He could not keep from thinking of the unknowing prey he had just dropped, how slivers of his still beating heart might have tasted, under better conditions. He was left with an actual longing in his mouth and palate, so had a predilection for such grizzly gastronomic oddities, taken over his presence of mind lately. The villagers heard the whir of the approaching helicopter in the distance, and knew that this opportunistic messenger of death, who suddenly and mercilessly shattered their souls, and way of life, forever, would be safely on his way back to a faraway airfield, with many other foreign devils, as corrupt and criminal as himself. They despised his unseen face, hidden motives, and vowed revenge on him and all his kind. On the Huey, York kept to himself, the flight crew likewise, maintaining a line of silence from the quiet and mysterious passenger. They knew what he was, even if who he was would be forever classified; he was different, seeing themselves as soldier-warriors (though such was also highly debatable), and York as a murderer for hire, maybe even enjoying it; now a constant cutting of the helo blade kept everyone's thoughts restricted. York slept soundly all the way, only once waking with a start, *when citizens rolled over an executed official, and instead of an Asian face, it was P's own father, staring up, with crystaline eyes of blazing fury*. But as the chopper droned on toward base York fell back asleep, some of the crew would later curiously recall, *a dozing demon whispering madly of the great culling he was hell-bent on*:

> To call it a program of murder is nonsense ... They were of more value to
> us alive than dead, and therefore, the object was to get them alive... Our
> training emphasizes the desirability of obtaining these target individuals
> alive and of using intelligent and lawful methods of interrogation to
> obtain the truth of what they know about other aspects of the VCI ...
> [U.S. personnel] are specifically not authorized to engage in assassinations
> or other violations of the rules of land warfare.
> (William Colby, CIA Director, 1973-1976, CIA Archives)

Once back on the crowded streets, he never dreamed of or considered the cold victims left behind in the bush. As with all top-notch gunmen, his handlers granted him a generous respite between assignments, to regain his grounding after taking a targeted person's life, and usually in Saigon, or perchance Manila, after particularly hairy action; to completely vanish from the close killing fields, both for the sake of his cover, and to be distracted by R & R comforts, cheap thrills. But being the dedicated, asexual *ingenue* terminator that he was, he hung out where assigned, chaste, clear, primed, awaiting new orders. The program was something like this: first, he was approached by a pair of cool MPs, at any hour of the day or night and ordered to deploy at once; then immediately escorted to some airbase, and personally accompanied onto the aircraft, usually parked discreetly on an unlit tarmac, and confirmed active once aloft. While in flight, he would be briefed on the mission, its objectives, and target. Soon the function became like any old routine. As an itinerant henchman, York was always grouped with different squad members for each job, so none of them would ever get to know each other. They met for the first time on the whirlybird heading to a drop, never to see one another again upon returning to base, occasionally York recognizing them at a store, noodle shop or USO club, though never acknowledging any. After a completed operation, he would also be escorted from a helicopter by stiff, local MPs, who brought their special charge to the plane idling on a remote runway, for his airlift out from a hell worse than Dante's.

On his time off York kept to himself. He had no friends, and of course Phoenix rules did not encourage fraternizing with operatives sharing the same duties. Besides, the CIA guys were over educated Whale men, impossible to approach, and most other service members kept their distance from hit men such as York. It was in the back room at Faunus' Bar that York started the bizarre ritual of celebrating each kill, with a skull tattoo on his inner thighs. There was a house tattooist who had very large, rough hands and could not help mentioning how soft the insides of York's thighs were and that there was hardly any hair on his legs or face, either "but say, in this light, you suddenly look awfully curvy to me." And as that old master diligently buzzed away, with pricking needle, York closed his eyes, and there was a fulsome whiteness that spread, suddenly, over his face, down his neck and back, and across loins, hips. Several times ever so gently he quivered, so that when the inked wound was complete it was time for him to go.

He took to frequenting Sayer's Sunday meetings, at his commandeered colonial mansion, overlooking a fragrant Saigon River, overflowing with trophies and portraits of a vanquished, old, French-Vietnamese planter family caught on the wrong side, where in open air hall Sayer railed for hour after hour to select throngs of military squares in Levi's, the foreign service crew, and straggler U.S. expatriates, who were never going back, about, "such state of affairs in this great geopolitical contest of ours, where swarming Asiatic scum are hell bent on taking over the world, from under our Caucasian noses." This could have been a grave social indiscretion, had Sayer, to put it mildly, the least bit of empathy or sentiment within his withholding heart, because as a soldier of some private means, stationed so far from home, he kept a dark, long haired, local girl with sensual eyes as a housekeeper/ concubine (his faithful wife, Felicity, having nary a notion). With fluency in French, basic English, the Asian beauty was very discreet in her withdrawal from the venue when Sayer got into his repugnant rants. A big part of the spiel involved the importance for all present of staying in touch after hostilities, to later unite toward the common goal of saving America from itself. While stationed in Southeast Asia they must, however, not strangely, to all those mustered, reconcile themselves to the savage mixing of the races, as was apparent wherever they turned. It was even rumored that Sayer had fathered two baby-sans with a maid, the three now living in an open-air love shack at the back of the garden. "First of all, let's just get the big elephant in the room, out of the way, let me expose myself, before any overhyped good-doer thinks he, she, it, can denounce me: I am a racist. No, I am a huge racist. There, I said it, it's done, no one has anything over me now. All people, races, every ethnic group, are also, so what does it matter? Believe me, those gooks feel the same way about us coming over here, taking their women, making them our servants. All races reject each other, as protective mechanisms to preserve their existence and unity against marauding outsiders; the white race, due to advanced technological capacity, and reliance on the Western tradition, was able to supersede all others in the quest for world dominance, it's as simple as that. In fact, while European civilization bettered itself genetically, morally, culturally and spiritually, over the long millennia of trial and error, the heathen masses across the world still practiced idolatry, human sacrifice to false gods, the ritual cannibalizing of enemies to partake of kindred, disembodied ferocity, and a systematic harvesting of their own minority people, to function as slaves, and fill in as food during times of dearth. I want to say a special word about the Negro race, brought to our shores in the most deplorable conditions, after being degraded to a doomed population wanting to abandon wicked ships. Perhaps it was the universal dislike, the antipathy, toward blacks, anything African, the continent itself, shared by all other, worldly actors, as in families there may be some member against whom, for whatever reason, real or invented, everyone else gangs up. Perhaps such opprobrium flung viciously their way since early times was their given lot, as the curse of Ham was said to have brought them slavery; and whose fault is that anyway?"

After Sundays spent in such heavy indoctrination it was a relief when Mondays rolled around, and York could volunteer, at the recently endowed Sisterhood of Grace's Orphan's Refuge, the global, charitable organization with missionary, as well as old school, ties to Whale University in far off New Haven, CT. As with religious orders of old, the contemporary sisters' belief system was an updated combination of the contemplative life, in which the salvation of their, and others', souls could be brought about through lives of prayer, seclusion and mortification, along with a secular responsibility, to relieve the misery of carnal, psychic, social wants, presently. A whole troop of silent, virtuous (yet, somehow, feisty, teasing and shapely) sisters had come to South Vietnam to validate college summer vacations, in the unyielding march of human kindness toward others, as altruism overflowed in their breathlessly eager hearts. And their leader, Lady, shone above the others, in her devotion to the relief of that unforgivable sin afflicting great swaths of humanity, kids, children, without means of self-support and abandoned by their parents: Sister Isidora Green, recently graduated from Whale College, exemplar of the institution's striving after excellence in inward scruples, critical thought, civic responsibility. However many of the finer points of Sister Isidora's rule may have been lost on York, he seemed to get their gist, and to be falling mildly (not madly), in love with her, or more so, with what she represented; besides the butterfly sensations in York's stomach, nothing ever became of this puppy love. Though she was the scion of one of the most prominent families in the United States, Isidora felt the *noblesse oblige* of the upper classes, toward the downtrodden (even though downtrodden by the same upper classes) to be as pertinent in Saigon ghettos as in U.S. Indian reservations. As the guiding force and benefactor of the Society of Grace, although at a tender age herself, she, nevertheless, was completely realistic as to the ultimate effects of her order's efforts. She knew all their good deeds were but a drop in the bucket, versus the iniquities committed every instant on this earth, but she persevered to help those who could not help themselves, undaunted, dedicating her life to marshaling philanthropic forces, to improve the world for the better. And a prized liberal education had filled her head with lofty ideals, of equal rights for genders, sexes, races, cultures, freedom of the oppressed, ethical detestation for Yankee imperialism, the domino theory, escalation, the very war itself. It was her turn to respond to Sayer's abhorrent, repulsive rantings of patriotic doggerel:

"Are we not a nation of despicable greedy bullies? Once again American arrogance triumphs militarily, over traditional, less developed, tribal peoples, in places too far to matter, or pose significant retaliatory threat, because we only pick on countries weaker than ourselves, and rarely challenge those, that would come at us despite significant sacrifice of blood and treasure. But sooner or later, most rowdies trip up, falling flat on their faces, if it takes a thousand years as with Imperial Rome, two decades as in the case of Napoleon's *Empire Francais*, or only a single decade as in Hitler's *Deutsches Reich*, bad luck, theirs.

"This Third World paradigm of asymmetric engagement, where an enemy is willing to die for his cause in a war of attrition, but not us for ours, was first observed in, and was itself a byproduct of, a prideful, dishonorable, ideological war we fought in Korea, and has today spread here, to this conflict (but never declared war). We send nameless triggermen, our own oddballs, in-house Oswalds, to rub out political leaders; and for those of us who remember the assassination of President Kennedy it now seems simply the snuffing out of another life, no more, nor less, deserving of death than any other; fate demystified to the level of banality, through a moral equivalence of deadly force; such an ending to a valiant Camelot. Is it any wonder, a trigger-happy Second Lieutenant William Calley, would order the horror of My Lai?

"The covetous, land grubbing birth of our own, vast, continental nation, during which European whites raped and massacred an entire race, and transported and enslaved another, precludes the high horse we mount, criticizing other nations in their military matters, aggression or conquests, for if ever the Lord's gospel applied, to geopolitical cases of worldly war crimes, it is this: 'Judge not, that ye be not judged.'

"Ultimately, brown skins will take back their God given assets once more, assuming possession again, of what has long been ordained for, committed to, them, and no longer serve white ghosts limiting their whole existence, mocking their appearance, conscripting them to labor in the capitalist sugar machine."

Now with these countervailing insights running through his head, York set out on a fateful mission. He wondered why he felt no remorse for slaying human beings; it seemed no different than taking down a moose, deer or pigeon. A scene from the American West, in early 1870s, filled his mind, having read of gentlemen hunters, in spanking new buckskins, blasting wild bison from leased luxury shooting trains, altered with elevated, rolling platforms from which to conduct excessive, bloody sport; everything had moved far away from York's initial understanding, of what Uncle Sam expected of him, required him to undertake, on the country's behalf; to a crude lawlessness that went even beyond his father's accusatory paranoia of government malfeasance and chicanery. He was to take out the headmaster of a provincial high school near the DMZ, rumored to be turning out a high number of Viet Cong. York felt uneasy, as Colonel Sayer had specifically instructed him to, "terminate with extreme prejudice," in a manner to be construed as exemplary to the entire student body: during the summation of the commencement address, at the academy's annual graduation ceremony. "If we go to the heart of their educational system, we'll cut off their recruiting conduits. Let's flush out the sons a' bitches." York's apprehension also had to do with there being so many kids in danger of an errant bullet, as well as witnessing a war atrocity, such as he was about to commit. With a morning sun steadily rising behind a cheerful convocation of students, parents, families, teachers, administrators, government officials and friends of the school in attendance, York was careful to keep his scope from reflecting any sudden glare, divulging his position. When the single bullet cleanly sheared off the top of the target's coifed head but somehow left him standing at the podium, something so uncanny, for the impact involved, what happened next haunted York, for the rest of his life. There was crisp silence. The three-quarter headed educator remained fixed at the lectern, as if pausing a scheduled oration, and not one person watching, either in the audience, or on the dais, said a word, issued a cry or moved a muscle. There was transfixed stillness, in shock at such savagery and destruction upon the sacred spirit of the district. Then in calm reverence everyone rose from their seats and walked out from the courtyard of the school, as if what they had just seen, never actually happened. They would not acknowledge it, thus rejecting York's monstrous interruption, as asinine, contemptible, and in such a way, they won, and York lost, and not only York, but the entire United States. When York got back to base, he told Sayer, he was through, he would never pick off people again. Although Sayer despised psychology as a Jewish phenomenon that did nothing but invent mental disorders, or convince people they had problems, when they didn't, he still recognized battle fatigue when he saw it, granting York an honorable discharge for medical reasons. Then York was stateside, for a long rest at Bethesda Naval Hospital, encountering Sister Isidora again, soon after, when having disavowed the Alvin York persona, returned, once more, to that plain old P, she applied to Whale College, to pursue an education:

> When thou goest out to battle against thine enemies, and seest horses, and
> chariots, and a people more than thou... the officers shall say, What man is
> there that is fearful and fainthearted? Let him go and return unto his house,
> lest his brethren's heart faint as well as his heart. (Deuteronomy 20:1, KJV)

Her battlefield essence forever enmeshed with scars, formed of her own abuse, P adopted a more placid post combat self, to help kids, taking advantage of the G.I. Bill to joyfully read all she could, majoring in statistics to better understand how her chaotic Melungeon roots could have mathematically occurred, to begin with, with her full ride scholarship provided by the Sisterhood of Grace's Mendelian Genetics Foundation; continuing to the Whale Graduate School to pursue a Ph.D. in Sociology, *Suma cum laud*, focusing on the social responsibility for women's reproductive rights, on a graduate studies scholarship and stipend offered by the generous Sisters' Pro-Choice Trust, geared for energetic idealists. Obsessed with gaining an academic edge, she next pursued her J.D., at Whale's Sperling School of Law, financed by the Sisters' Revolutionary Legal Fund, this time concentrating on how federal law could be applied to grant groundbreaking gender freedoms, such as use of gendered public rest rooms by non-gendered users. After graduating at the top of her class, she took a research fellowship post at the Whale School of Medicine, leading comparative studies of relatively recent androgynous flips, again with sponsorship and funding by the sisters, through their Crystal House Study Grants. Her scholarly focus was on how gender identity influences each self to adapt in relation to others, converging to a common thread. She then pondered how these selections affected man's understanding of and relationship to a Supreme Sex.

P met Waterson in her first year at Whale U., however, still exuding masculine gear, and physique, she repelled him, to the point of not wanting to molest her to begin with, continuing their friendship through student days, as they were in the same class, into their professional lives, based on platonic dispassion. When the position came up at the medical school, it was Dr. Waterson himself who insisted P be hired, respecting her pushy, social acumen, to the same extent, that she respected his scientific razzle dazzle. When P was tapped into the Sisterhood of Grace, her freshman year, Waterson was first to congratulate her, joking that she might have been the first male accepted. "No, that would be G's G," she quipped. But she understood what a great privilege it was for a poor white trash girl like her, to become a Sissy, at last. And somehow, she fulfilled her promise to the sacred mysteries, to which she was initiated; not compromising her sworn asexuality, as intercourse with a captive spirit did not seem to break her vows; of course, there were no memories of having enjoyed it, or even felt it, during the rushed hazing rituals. She went back to adoring Isidora once more, having parted ways after disparate Nam experiences, and knew that the Founding Matriarch would always be hovering nearby. Little did either one imagine that the Gypsy link between them would one day be instrumental to P's supercharged, high-brow successes.

After that research fellowship post at the med school, P joined the Connecticut Department of Children and Families (DCF), although she did not set out to be a crusader for children's rights. But she needed to do some good in the world after all the wickedness she had caused, and for having been such a dumb bunny tool of Sayer's white supremacist dodge, for given her own blended composition, where would such an ideology leave her? The new job, unfortunately, turned out to be more about office paperwork, to cover one's back, than any activity remotely benefiting, aiding children and families. If her goal was to protect kids the department wasted valuable resources on the anonymous grievances made by clients, strangers, perps, egged on by bumper stickers, prominently displayed, on state cars, teasing: How's My Driving? Call **800-TATTLER** with **Any** Complaints. Well, didn't those accusations coincide with the exact, same times, she reconnoitered city addresses under investigation, doing her job, observing? how disheartening, defeating, annoying! So, there was no surprise, soon after starting, for flashback instants, she fantasized about crosshairs on the CT Governor, as a logical, possible fix-up to institutional malaise, stagnancy, "Geronimo!" being the rallying cry, then recalled she was aka York no more, nor back in the apocalypse now. Bureaucratic quagmires required an additional discretion than brashness to succeed, a broad scattershot rather than bullseye approach. But she stayed over ten years in a PTSD stupor, before realizing that her connection with Isidora was much too valuable to waste; then founding a foundation, her struggle to get her own child advocacy council off the ground, leading to the hope that setting up in Greenitch would be the best way to impress Isidora; which it was, allowing P to commence a vocation.

Miscellanea:

The Rome Statute of the International Criminal Court (ICC) [of which, the United States is not a member], where war crimes can be prosecuted... follows the definition set out by the 1949 Geneva Conventions, which were ratified by 196 states.

This definition includes acts of:

- willful killing
- torture or inhuman treatment
- willfully causing great suffering or serious injury
- extensive destruction and appropriation of property which is not justified by military necessity
- compelling a prisoner of war to serve in the forces of a hostile state
- willfully depriving a prisoner of war of the rights of fair and regular trial
- unlawful deportation or transfer or unlawful confinement
- taking of hostages

However, the Rome Statute also includes an extensive list of further specific violations, such as intentionally directing attacks against civilian populations, using child soldiers, forced pregnancy and intentionally directing attacks against hospitals. (James Morris, Yahoo UK, 3/25/2022)

7. Walt Whitman Stamp, PZAndrews,
https://www.pinterest.com/pin/520658406899325244/

8. Carlisle Indian School, Carlisle Indian Industrial School Presentation |
Juniata County Historical Society

THE HUMANITY OF GENERAL AMHERST.

9. The Humanity of General Amherst, Amherst and Smallpox (umass.edu)

10. Jay Gould, American History USA

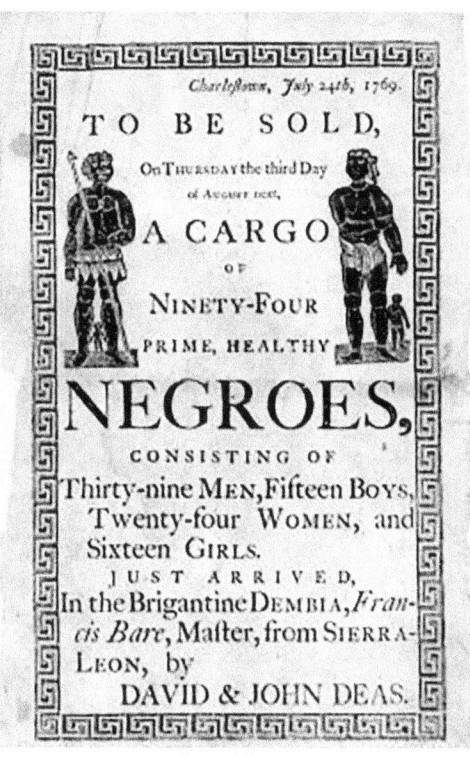

11. Slave Auction,
https://en.wikipedia.org/wiki/File:Slave_Auction_Ad.jpg

12. Isis wall painting in the tomb of Seti I,
https://en.wikipedia.org/wiki/Isis

13. Geronimo, Geronimo - Wikipedia

14. Frederick Douglas, portrait, Frederick Douglass - Wikipedia

15. Cannibal Feast - Fiji, Early Accounts of Cannibalism (cultofweird.com)

16. Crematorium Majdanek, Crematoria in Majdanek death camp. (Post-Liberation).
- Collections Search - United States Holocaust Memorial Museum (ushmm.org)

17. Left to right: Dr. Josef Mengele, Rudof Hoss, Josef Kramer, right, AP.

18. *Herr* Hitler, The Berghof of Adolf Hitler at the Obersalzberg near
Berchtesgaden:... Photo d'actualité - Getty Images

19. Auschwitz Children, Reuters.

20. Masaccio, *The Expulsion from the Garden of Eden*, c. 1425,
Santa Maria del Carmine, Florence, Italy.

21. Jean Metzinger, *La dance, Bacchante*, 1906, Kroller-Muller Museum, Otterlo, The Netherlands.

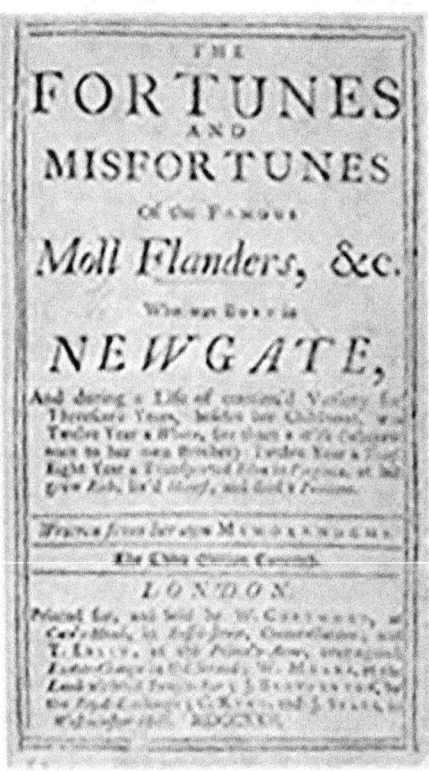

22. *Moll Flanders*, UK edition frontispiece, 1722,
https://en.wikipedia.org/wiki/Moll_Flanders

# 9. *Dan de Riber* or Splendor on the Gold Coast

"Exterminate all the brutes!" (Joseph Conrad, *Heart of Darkness*, 1899)

At the United Nations Human Rights Office of the High Commissioner's Committee for U.S. Domestic Reparations, ascertaining, adjudicating, assigning blame on direct descendants of U.S. slaveholders, for centuries old crimes committed against humanity, an ancient, distant and yet lineal *Asantehene* bud (the eccentric prince who rented an entire New York restaurant for a first date with his now-wife), muscular, regal, with piercing coal centered eyes, said it best in a pithy, if not blunt, summation right before noon.

"Ironically, none of our African American brothers and sisters, here at the United Nations this morning, can know how truly fortunate they are even to be alive to investigate these ancient trespasses. But their ancestors were the lucky ones, because had they not been traded by my ancestors, to white slavers, then sold on to the Americas half a millennium ago, they would have been sacrificed, chopped up and eaten. Do you hear? I say, they would have been tortured, flayed and consumed; there was no alternative for the greater needs of the society; and the longevity of my royal lineage is testimony to the ferocity of my forebears, in either, expelling prisoners of war, internal dissenters, captured slaves, or having them for a feast. Bear in mind, cruel practices dispatching captives and undesirables by banishment or banqueting had nothing to do with their differing ethnic or regional skin tones, affiliations to lesser tribes, clans, or even being despised, low caste kin within our own. Those were only ostensible, politically expedient excuses for the ruthlessness. The real cause was simply not enough room for everyone, given the severe, uncontrollable overpopulation and dearth, considering the cyclical, evil climactic and soil conditions, and the primitive, ecologically unsound agronomy of those epochs. We needed more land to ensure our survival, it was a time to eat or be eaten, a *lebensraum,* within an age of dinosaurs, ha! Of course, there is nothing for which my family or I need feel ashamed, guilty or apologize; those were the customs and needs of the day, and our courageous predecessors acted accordingly. Really, you should be thankful to my storied, if imperfect kin, who although first instigated the transfer of your progenitors into perpetual bondage, in the end rescued them from greasy fires, as well as to that fabled, loathsome, white privilege you obsess over, spiritual inheritor of the same, odious, slaveholding class faded by your manumission, that subsequently supported and raised you up again, for this unhappy if not resentful future attendance. By seizing, enslaving, selling your antecedents my own saved them from expiring as anonymous, gassy burps after a delicious, spicy stew, and yourselves as faint glimmers, unshaped barbs of overindulgence or indigestion. And I still possess the ancient, treasured family recipe, passed down for generations, for the great delicacy, *Brute Bourguignon, bon appetit,*" breaking out into hearty, satisfied chortles, choked sinuses suddenly evoking temporary dizziness, misty recollection of fabled past *fetes* of his forefathers:

> There is not the slightest doubt in my mind that they prefer human flesh
> to any other. During all the time I lived among cannibal races I never came
> across a single case of their eating any kind of flesh raw; they invariably
> either boil, roast or smoke it... The preference of different tribes for
> various parts of the human body is interesting. Some cut long steaks from
> the flesh of the thighs, legs or arms; others prefer the hands and feet; and
> though the great majority do not eat the head, I have come across more
> than one tribe which prefers this to any other part. Almost all use some
> part of the intestines on account of the fat they contain.
> (Sidney Langford Hinde, former captain of the Congo Free State Force,
> *The Fall of the Congo Arabs*, 1897)

Amidst the stunned silence of the audience came only a singular response from a young, black man in a business suit, white shirt, striped bow tie. "So, tell us, your Royal Highness, Tenkamenin, was the meat of my taken people tender or tough, or simply a matter of how long they were cooked? The bitter truth is we were sold into a self-imposed bondage, by those most like us, our very brothers. History needs to dig deep at the truth, farther into the past of disregarded reminiscences, of Africans enslaving Africans; then selling them to obsequious European merchants waiting impatiently offshore, soon knocking at the door, leading to an endless servitude; ugly buyers piggy backing on already existing systems reinforced by tribal warfare in the sub-Saharan region, only to be incredibly, exponentially increased by a modern capitalist global economy. The real shame is not that white slavers so eagerly transported Africans into forbidding horizons, but that Africans would so readily trade their sisters and daughters for cheap metal tokens, a swathe of cloth, a gun, a sword, an ax. But why should we be so surprised Africans sold each other to white slavers, when they ate each other, to the bone? And what kind of Epicurean eats men?"

It was the Rev. Hannibal P. (Pearly) Gates, presiding at the activist Carthaginian Black Baptist Church, New Haven, CT, who, while attending the official proceedings, and quietly, humbly, patiently listening to many, varied viewpoints, had dared to raise his voice against the African blue blood, devil incarnate, with whom he had roomed at Whale, thirteen years ago. The proud aristocrat, warrior, trend setter, still youngish and indifferent in his manner, seeming to recognize from former golden days the voice in the darkness, only laughed, guffawed, the harder. "The kind, perhaps, whose ancestors owned yours. But seriously, today countries, such as China, Mexico, Bangladesh, offer modern, industrial slave labor, and Congo, Saudi Arabia, Brazil, traffic their national patrimonies in mineral veins, oil deposits, farmland."

Within the dark green, black, gray and white-veined marbled walls, the thick atmosphere was muffled, deliberate, in its expectation and fulfillment, ideally suited for delaying any motion uncharacteristically rushed, within those cool, dark recesses. Hannibal's voice was lost in the expanse of lost opportunities. He held his rage in his throat and proceeded to accept his insignificance, against a scene of exaggerated circumstances. He was the smallest pebble of thought cast far and wide into the churning river of time.

Many moons ago, during his freshman year at Whale U., at the Afro-American Student Union welcome mixer, Hannibal met African students whose quest for recognition of a tribal identity was particularly at odds with, antithetical to their racial and/ or continental group coherence, as equatorial Africans. It was the start of fall term, a night he would never forget; mingling for their first time, students were initially reserved in the humid, coastal Connecticut evening, touched by a faint Gulf Stream breeze from Long Island Sound. Into a second round of drinks, as the setting sun hid behind heavy haze and the DJ began a Bob Marley inspired set, the conversations remained collegial, but now turned louder, darker, franker:

> So much trouble in the world
> So much trouble in the world
>
> Bless my eyes this morning
> Jah sun is on the rise once again
> The way earthly things are going
> Anything can happen
>
> You see men sailing on their ego trips
> Blast off on their spaceships
> Million miles from reality
> No care for you, no care for me

So much trouble in the world
So much trouble in the world
(Bob Marley, *Survival*, "So Much Trouble in the World," 1979)

"I am *Igbo*, a smart people, the only ones who study, pray," said Tony, an erudite pre-law undergraduate, coolly sipping a cocktail in the open, red brick walled, courtyard. "We are intelligentsia. We have been baptized. Nigeria's most famous, greatest, artists, musicians, or writers are *Igbo*. Do you know Chinua Achebe? His theme is how British, colonial society destroyed the true culture of my tribe; then we had a disastrous civil war with the *Yorubas*, killing each other, to advantage the colonialists; my taxi driving father was a tenured professor of eye surgery, at Lagos College of Medicine, before our family's exile."

"Excuse me, Tony, I heard you mention, *Yorubas*, and I'm sorry to hear about your father," broke in the pushy, thin lipped, older graduate student, suddenly introducing himself, "My father is General Olayo, Chairman of the Supreme Ruling Junta, and I am Peter, a second son by his second wife. May I please remind you that our tribe takes it upon its shoulders to run the country, its administration, police, armed forces. Without *Yorubas* the country would be in chaos; we provide the means for smooth functioning and organization; extended debate is such a waste of time, perhaps we are the only tribe that matters."

Makenga, another aristocratic academic, approached them, blurting out, "I am *Fen*. When whites first came to our shores, the missionaries and traders introduced an evil trick, accusing us of being notorious cannibals as an excuse to enslave us. But we were no different than other tribes; we never ate our own, only captured war prisoners or trespassing slaves. When my dreaded ancestor King Mombo (bless his fabled ferocity) ruled Gabon he had tens of thousands of slaves on immense plantations, all for his high maintenance; the respect, awe, he inspired was legendary. Surely as a kingdom, we were the top tribe:"

"There are many tribes of men in the forest... that are cannibals, who
eat human flesh. These are the fiercest of all. They are always fighting,
and they eat many of the prisoners they capture, for they prefer eating to
selling them..."

"Do you know by what name those cannibal tribes are called?" I asked.

"I know the names of two of them," he replied. "One is called Fan, the
other Osheba." (Paul Du Chaillu, *King Mombo*, 1930)

Tenkamenin, Whale's mascot *Asantehene*, as muscular, charismatic, as Alexander the Great, now stared them down. "Pardon me, fellows, you have it all wrong; we *Asante*, are the most ferocious tribe in this world; everyone knows there would be no West Africa without our dreaded splendor on the Gold Coast. My hostile people profited for centuries from inhuman crimes, iniquities, forced on peaceful neighbors, first, in gold mined with their labor, second, in gold earned from their sales. And as our captives were roughly marched toward the setting sun, they knew that they would never see their loved ones again."

Hannibal thought long and hard; with such attitudes, was it any wonder it was so easy for white traders, scheming though they were, to acquire already seized, enslaved Africans for the Atlantic Trade, as early as the 1400s. All they required, were tribes that would transact their mortal enemies, as in the *Yoruba* versus *Igbo*, who to these times loathed each other to the quick, and feuded, as if it was their birth right. So much for singling out racism as being at the root of slavery. Inter-tribal conflict, Africans capturing, enslaving, eating each other, also brought about their historical demise. Was there any surprise in that?

But how would a foreign power or merchant approach an unknown, savage and impenetrable coast, and systematically withdraw certain elements of its population, unless for the collusion of its own powerful chiefs, ministers, sorcerers and nobles? Otherwise, how could any single *Guineaman,* or even a fleet of a hundred, moored off the coasts of Guinea or Nigeria, accomplish anything? Without acquiescence or invitations from bought, local elites, there would have been no Trans-Atlantic slavery; the sycophantic, smarmy guest businessmen operating openly with the accommodation, complicity, plain connivance of their powerful ruling class hosts; and once invited in, acting with impunity to the society's indifference.

There was no forcible exchange of slaves, from their inter-tribal oppressors to the intercontinental flesh merchants. It was all done with the cognizance, blessing and organizational cunning of the tribal elders and bureaucracy. This involved docking, landing and trading privileges, holding prisons and a refined delivery system, for the convenience of visiting European merchant-traders, providing out of date arms and powder, diluted spirits, moldy textiles, worthless shiny trinkets, sundries for the advantage of black traitors to their own race. As for the victims' descendants in future centuries, imagine their rage at the thoughts of predecessors being summarily sold, for polished glass beads and gawdy crucifixes. But to say, savvy, European hucksters imposed themselves on naive, defenseless Africans, belies the fact that international trade is never a warlike pursuit, or a one-way street, but demands friendly cooperation by both parties. It is an exercise in mutual conspicuous consumption dependent upon a smooth movement of goods and services. Sadly enough, at the millennium this ever oppressed, yet proud, continent will continue inviting suffering, foreign enterprises exploiting cheap labor, abundant natural resources and primitive politics. Hannibal was slowly building an argument, as he had been taught at debating prep:

> No more internal power struggle
> We come together to overcome the little trouble
> Soon we'll find out who is the real revolutionary
> 'Cause I don't want my people to be contrary
>
> And brother you're right, you're right,
> You're right, you're right, you're so right
> We'll have to fight (We gon' fight)
> We gonna fight (We gon' fight)
> We'll have to fight (We gon' fight)
> Fighting for our rights
>
> Mash it up in-a (Zimbabwe)
> Natty trash it in-a (Zimbabwe)
> Africans a-liberate Zimbabwe (Zimbabwe)
> I'n'I a-liberate Zimbabwe (Marley, *Survival*, "Zimbabwe")

Local inputs of ethnic enmity and ceaseless internal strife (increased supply) had as much influence on the slave trade and colonialism, as European racism and the capitalistic socio-economic labor structure (increased demand). Africans hated other Africans as much as (more than) they hated whites, or whites hated them. That morning's front-page news had been gruesome enough: *Scores of Civilians Beheaded by Insurgents in Northern Mozambique, Witness Says;* it was not that the black race was conquered, but also cruelly, sold out by itself. The solitary African American freshman listening quietly, standing a bit apart in the shadows, now a little tipsy, innocently asked, "If you despise each other so, why should we accept you, let alone like you? Shamefully, sadly, paradoxically enough, your evil ancestors sold mine down the river, history bearing witness to the grave injustices perpetrated by brothers against brothers."

It was clear that a deep seated animosity existed between many African American and African students at the university, as if playing out the ancient struggle, of one lorded over by the other; the losers' heirs filled with anger, hatred, revulsion, at the sight of descendants of the African princes who had enslaved their kinfolk centuries ago, in the dark continent of misfortune; while those modern day, African Royal Highnesses of institutional privilege, wanting acceptance, admiration, from their American cousins, too often exhibited blind condescension toward the racially mixed legacies of their raped former slaves; not acknowledging them true African, any more, but sullied by white blood coursing through bastard veins.

It was true, when Hannibal studied his reflection in the mirror the next morning after the raucous happy hour, head pounding, hung over and moving deliberately, he hated himself for being part white, but felt even more shame for his prototypes, who even back then, no matter how high born, were outcasts from among their own, the first of his line captured and sold into lowly slavery, in Africa, by Africans. How did it feel to consort here in this most liberal of universities, with the very descendants of those ancient, slave-holding families, which may have owned his people? Could it be possible, that he recognized, in himself, the subtle and not so subtle traits and characteristics inherited from the rough, toothless jungle traders who originally purchased his family generations ago; he closed red eyes, mournfully whispering to himself, in a voice of prior destinies: "*Hann'bal, fo' shame, it be yo' own folk sol yaws dan de riber.*"

When Hannibal enthusiastically recruited his African brothers to an upcoming demonstration in support of a coalition of minorities and oppressed peoples, fighting for the right to belong, particularly minority student athletes, who had not been supported enough by a school demonstrating a lack of commitment to racial diversity, in the administration, faculty, curriculum and students, only easy going Tony joined immediately, but it was his own, pathetic, royal roommate, Tenkamenin, who taunted and rebuffed him.

"Because fear of a slave revolt was maybe the universal Achilles' heel of every master, never was there a civilization as generous to their former slaves, as this, neither the Egyptians, Babylonians or Persians, Spartans, Athenians or Romans, Celts, Saxons or Normans, ever approached this society's merits with such distinction, privilege, guilt, for granting civil rights legislation, affirmative action, public housing, and education, Social Security, Medicaid, food stamps, welfare, to those who contribute so little. Why, this country is simply a paradise for the poor and abandoned, and yet according to you, it is not enough. Because you don't see how good you have it, compared to the outcomes that might have been. Blacks as well as whites have benefited from white privilege; it was black tyranny that enslaved their own, and white privilege, in magnanimous fashion, that subsequently freed them. They were liberated by whites, they live in a modern, white society, and participate in a single world economic order, as consumers of products made by current Third World economic slaves. Are they not now part of the New Age master class? Besides, why would we demonstrate against the very administration which granted us admission and financial aid to the university? Our parents would be very disappointed, especially the next time on the official receiving line at the U. S. Embassy in Accra, waiting to be greeted by their powerful and generous friends. Maybe we'd be better off grooving to the next Rolling Stones performance at Toad's Place than causing sedition." Hannibal's discontent toward his own roommate could not be mitigated.

"Any attempts to distort, minimize, capitalize upon, the eighty-one years of human degradation, where **blacks were considered, three-fifths human,** by our Constitution, is insensitive, offensive, appalling," Hannibal responded with equal vehemence. "The evidence is preponderous, if we can get access to it:"

> For whatsoever things were written aforetime were written for our
> learning, that we through patience and comfort of the scriptures might
> have hope. (Romans 15:4, KJV)

Because every folkish group twists history to its own advantage, especially those persecuted throughout time immemorial, when chance presents to seize an opportunity, as well as those traditionally in power, who do not hesitate to rewrite the fable in their favor; so Hannibal's scholarly interest in the past had as its unique core the persistent investigation of his own origins, how his African forebears had lived prior to their cruel transport and resettlement to a new and permanently hostile land; in order to appropriately ascribe blame on those responsible for his personal human condition, all the inherited misfortunes and roadblocks; and not those conveniently identified from his own and his people's blind assumptions, and race hatred, as being their traditional, singular oppressors. In this way, blame could be shared (perhaps never equally) between whites and blacks, Europeans and Africans, the civilized and savage. But this would take assiduous study, and the willingness to stare truth in its awful, accusatory, legitimizing face.

It was in sophomore year, during the rigorous *Introduction to the History of Western Civilization, Parts 1 and 2,* that it dawned on Hannibal, that African American criticism of the Western tradition seemed so short sighted, as during the two thousand years when concepts of *liberté, égalité, fraternité,* were being discussed and developed, to the benefit of those currently protesting historic oppression, Africans were busy warring, enslaving and cannibalizing each other, during the late, *Bantu* expansion, so sad, but true.

Once, in junior fall term, he found himself startled awake from a sudden doze, during a Monday, 8 am lecture, of that immensely popular *Comparative Cultural Atrocities, Part 1,* in one of the back rows of Dimsly-Shittenden Hall, only to vaguely hear closing remarks of Whale's famous Turdling Professor of Social and Humanistic Injustices, railing: "Not only were the sly British, through royal patents and Acts of Parliament, major players in the African slave trade, for three hundred years, but they starved Ireland in the mid nineteenth century, then wasted Boer women and children in concentration camps fifty years later. British mercantile ambitions (greed) and evolving corporate structures (scale), made restructuring (ethnic cleansing) of populations inevitable (profit), given the competition for raw materials and labor."

In the next term, *Part 2* of the course continued, in a more evidenced, yet equally caustic vein: "...If an example, of a race enslaving its own kind exists, look no further than post war Japan, where automobile companies repatriated Japanese Brazilians, descendants of Japanese emigrants from the early 1900s, in most cases pure blood Japanese, to labor in appalling, degrading, coercive conditions, actually enslaved by their racial, but certainly not social or cultural, equivalents..." A liberal education was unequivocal.

Hannibal's senior year was spent debating, with himself, the value of a liberal education, as generously bestowed by the Sisterhood of Grace. Curious about his Baptist roots, he decided to focus his research on matters closer to his religious heart, looking into the esoteric question of charity and those incredible endowments bestowed upon the university, by its generous benefactors, whether these qualified as just exonerations from lives of grotesque exploitation of their wage laborers to make themselves the money. His senior history thesis: God should not forgive those committing evil deeds in life, despite their faith. In any case, Hannibal would stay many years at Whale, to study the effects of such matters on the soul.

During a final review in preparation for his senior history essay about the origins and later development of New Haven Baptist churches, Hannibal's curiosity led him yet again, to review all his notes, primary sources, minutely, cover to cover, one fateful fall day; making an amazing finding when a final, gummy page of a worn, canvas bound journal titled, *Shared Kinship, Fateful Destinies: Chronicles of the Great Migration From Texas,* inadvertently got stuck to his thumb, as he perused it; and proceeding to remove his finger from the volume, another unseen page was suddenly dislodged from underneath, uncovering the most significant of footnotes. A splendid mystery for so long due to its location as the true, last leaf of the work, which from ill usage, and a rush to conceal at a moment's notice, during its writing as well as preservation, became fixed, adhered to its predecessor, and heretofore hidden, obstructed from view;

it, shockingly, referring to an even earlier text, documenting oral traditions dating back to pre-colonial times, of slave trading of Africans by other Africans, all along the *Guinea* coast, and then colonial times of freed slaves trafficking and owning slaves themselves, in the southern American colonies. Hannibal, enlightened, modern, as he acted and appeared, was a bitter product of this pernicious trade; descended from African kings on the wrong side of tribal wars, who were subsequently sold into bondage, as their fate, by the victors; as this seemed a bitter, fatal confirmation of his race's doom, he wept in affirmation of his ancestors being enslaved by their own people, with only ghosts remaining to listen to his wailing.

Tragically, as the lineages of New World slave descendants were cruelly obliterated by time, as well as the bad faith of the multi raced captors, withholding their families from them, resulting in helplessness, isolation, Hannibal preserved the memory of his several generations of Texan kin, through the Colonel. What really rankled this New World Hannibal was that they had subsequently, almost as a perverse gift, been freed by whites, and that privilege which they commanded; therefore, blacks owed their freedom to Caucasians exercising magnanimity; but how could it be otherwise, in the society where they ruled? *So, Western tradition, its generosity, was what kept your ass from being cannibalized for 500 years?*

> The captains of the steamers have often assured me that whenever they
> try to buy goats from the natives, slaves are demanded in exchange; the
> natives often come aboard with tusks of ivory with the intention of buying
> a slave, complaining *that meat is now scarce...* (Hinde, *The Fall*)

Hannibal spent the summer after college graduation in Accra, with Tenkamenin, which, to say the least, was an eye opener, and by then he had more than subliminally accepted the descendant of kings' blithe dictum that, "everyone, every culture, has been another's slave; get over it, accept it, embrace it." The poverty and squalor were beyond what he could have ever imagined, and worst of all, the overpowering wafts of sulfurous miasmas from the open, flowing sewage, and putrid, sweet odor of rotting, steaming garbage coming from immense, open dumps set aflame at the edge of town, as if the fire and brimstone of hell, itself. Touring the old slave fort, Elmina Castle, with its immense, smooth, whitewashed death walls, Hannibal's astute attention was suddenly drawn away from the tourist trod path to an overgrown, neglected, crumbling bunker, once used as a mercantile record repository of a foul trade, redolent with diseased humidity from sour elements, and the sharp piss and crap smell of its abandonment to vagrants. Entering that evil structure, as if familiar with it, he immediately noticed the chinked brick in one of the walls that seemed to stick out from the rest of the flat surface; drawn directly to it, he pried at the loose cement, and, gently pulling, found a plain, brown leather covered notebook, whose cracked pages were filled with eyewitness accounts, of seventeenth century slave trading practices, documentation showing the complicity of local tribes in burgeoning sales of their own people, to distant bondage. Here follows the first entry of the sordid journal, by a British missionary then sermonizing on the Gold Coast, under the chartered auspices of the Royal Africa Company, and the royal authority of the Golden Stool, 1661:

> The Disturbing Account of the Most Dastardly, Heathen and Demonic Dr.
> Mengali, the Angel of Death: Mystical Sorcerer, Physician Extraordinaire
> to the Death's Head Group, the *Asantehene's* Royal Protection Squadron.
>
> As the morning star brightened in the softly glowing east, an endless (too
> numerous to number) stream of roughly yoked tribesmen, their women,
> four to eight in coffles, were seen rushing down the graveled hill, toward
> the still dark horizon; multi-generational families struggling between life
> and death, grandparents, mothers, infants, children beaten mercilessly by
> shouting handlers with cudgels, and cats of nine tails, as they gathered in

an open, recently harvested field, overlooking the quiet harbor and shore. As the sun rose, Dr. Mengali, Conjurer Supreme, came out of seemingly, nowhere, transmogrified from the thinness of the air itself, materializing in elegant splendor, robust, heroic, effulgent, displaying all the gold and silver insignias, medals, braids of distinguished, tribal, spiritual societies, military kinship orders. At this point, the selection commenced: carefully examining each subject, the pagan medicine man directed them, either, in the case of able-bodied men or women who could work a full day, to the right, for export with the human traffickers; or in the case of those too old or young to work, the infirm, and all children and pregnant women, to the left, for domestic use, consisting of as much merciless labor as a subject could stand, prior to early retirement, meaning stewing or roasting. Now a collective, doomed, sorry moan, interspersed by shrieks of horror, at the fateful realizations that they would be split from their loved ones forever, was audible to any who would listen, even as far as the tops of bountiful hills. Selected victims sometimes sneaked away from one line to another, depending on where their loved ones had been assigned. A *Fante* woman known to instill fear and awe, as a notorious, and repugnant, slave hunter across the territory, now stupefied, terrified, over her capture, her coming transport, coldly selected for the foreign trade, tried to stealthily transfer from that line to join her young daughter in another line for those staying. Immediately noticed by the guards, this desperate woman was summarily decapitated, and the girl severely beaten. In contrast to most of the other Death's Head doctors, who viewed selections as one of the most stressful and unpleasant duties, he undertook the cruel task with a flamboyant air, often smiling, whistling a tune. And during the serious selection process, the doctor was capable of being so kind to the children that they became fond of him, bringing them sugar, thinking of the small comforts in their daily lives, and doing things we would genuinely admire. And then next to that the smokestacks, and these children, tomorrow or in a half-hour, he was going to send them there; and that is where an anomaly lies. There was a large gap between his two front teeth, which had also been filed to sharp points, as with cannibals, more like the fangs of the lion, tiger or rabid hyena than a rational human being, a sign of a powerful, soulless magician, but when he smiled, he mysteriously appeared warm, sensitive, engaging to kids. It was rumored throughout the region that Mengali had formerly been enslaved himself, and as a young man was manumitted, as a reward for utilizing inchoate medical skills, saving the life of his lord's eldest child, critically ill with dysentery, subsequently becoming a major slave trader, to boot. An ardent monarchist (though far from aristocratic), tribalist (though adopted from the enemy tribe), and eugenicist (though a bastard of unknown lineage), he joined the research staff of the recently founded Royal Institute of Hereditary Biology & Racial Hygiene in 1656; but a clinical focus, and personal obsession, with physical malformations, inheritable disorders, congenital anomalies, as in freaks of nature/ twins, took him down evil paths of quackery, horrific torture, lingering, surgical alteration, and an all-too-common, early desire for death (of his subjects), legitimized by the crackpot label: experimentation. In such fashion were dispatched untold, nameless, faceless individuals, guilty of nothing worse than casting evil spells, committing adultery or other deeds of sinfulness, including sodomy, pedophilia; or condemned for cowardice, disloyalty or sedition, hopeless military, political and social compromises, lost causes. Finally, Mengali's dry coolness, efficacy with superiors, benevolence with inferiors, made him the favorite, mystical mascot for the entire, elite squad. Thus concludes this personal attestation of the despicable facts of inhuman practices, in which those so similar in every way, but skin color, were become chattels, treated far worse than beasts, and sold off, or else done away with in cannibal festivals. May Jesus Christ, our Savior, keep noble men from such horrible fates, punishing all those who have already fallen, hell burnt idolaters of an unrepentant savagery, a dearth of mercy, an uncivil ignorance in His ways, preserving the souls of God's afflicted.

After absorbing this twisted passage, Hannibal could not think, utter a word or construct a sentence, for some moments. Fetid pools of water throughout the bunker overpowered, as the midday sun paused at the sky's hot center, drawing in mosquitoes, insects and slimy creatures of all kinds, and as effective in repulsing visitors. How could there be any surprise at the former savagery, duplicity and greed of pre-colonial Africans, in the centuries-long sale of their own into slavery? Consider the current practices of cannibalism, ingesting bush meat, ethnic cleansing, cutting off limbs as trophies, with machetes; realize that the Dark Continent has a long way to go to partake of civilization, as defined by the West. And as crazed Africans hunted albino children for ritualistic purposes, so did African Americans discriminate against their own folks, based on gradations of whiteness, the whiter the better. He broke out in a cold, delirious sweat, worrying whether, within his black or *mulatto* ancestors, somewhere, across his blood lines, there were perhaps notorious slave owners and traders haunting their descendants, including him.

Was he of an infantile, ruined race seething with resentment, going insane with self-doubt? There were no apologies or forgiveness in history, only retribution. This was a cultural, race, world war. Perhaps, the African nations themselves could also pay reparations as acts of contrition for their own complicity. That seemed to be what Spawn Sanity concluded on his Ox talking heads extravaganza, going head-to-head in his ratings war with an equally adept Rachel Madcow on MSNUT, promoting white complicity.

Suddenly, his thoughts raced back to the present, his mind focused on current bonhomie. He was at the United Nations Committee on U.S. Domestic Reparations in New York; this was it, the supreme victory and revenge of the formerly enslaved and consumed over their old colonial taskmasters: three out of the five post World War Two powers. Hannibal's complete faith in the legitimacy of this world forum, and tribunal, for justice, allowed him the pause he needed to relax. He was face to face with his old school buddy, Whale roommate, Tenka, after so many years. It was time to leave the past, for the sake of grub. By noon they were both ravenous, trotting off arm in arm as they used to do on their way to sparse, dry student lunches at Commons, only today it was to eat and drink fulsomely, boisterously, as lost brothers finally reunited, despite time spent apart, differing privileges, at a clubby midtown Sparks Steak House.

The afternoon Working Group on the Expedience and Success of Global Nazi Hunters found the United Nations High Commissioner for Refugees Goodwill Ambassador Isidora Green chairing the assembly, assisted by Ms. Yael Abraham, Ph.D., Director, Human Resources, Warren Bros. Inc., (Whale Class of 1973, Psychology 1980, Suma cum laud) first Jewish Sisterhood of Grace Alumni President, Holocaust refugee; a staunch protector of civil rights, affirmative action, woman's equality, and all liberal policies leading to an internationalist world order; with the official agenda, notes, and the at times tragic lines of questioning; surprisingly, Sayer was seated in the front row, eagerly observing the historic proceedings.

The Working Group's first witness was an aged, but still well preserved, veteran, senior *SS* officer, with deep green eyes, angled features, who having escaped to Chile after the war, to blend in with the Alpine German communities settled in Temuco, and other southern Andean regions, since the 1880s (who until present-day spoke in ancient, regional, *Deutsche* dialects, which had been lost to use even in Germany), had recently come out of hiding, pardoned, exonerated, absolved of a sordid past, officially sanctioned by the current military junta of the once most traditional, of South American democracies; then, even if only self-forgiven, auto-redeemed, permitted freedom of transit and residence by the most urbane and developed, of western democracies, and certainly those less idealistic. Now indispensable to the NATO intelligence community, including, it was rumored, the U.S. military's Phoenix Program and the Israeli Mossad, in their strategic post war struggles against communism, his past crimes against humanity had politely been excused, pragmatically expunged, and he assumed a liberty to come and go as he pleased. Having struck a deal with the United Nations for immunity in exchange for vital testimony, here he was having lunch at Sparks, the famous, swanky eatery, where outside its doors, on the street, that notorious mobster was gunned down, sitting a few tables from two boisterous gentlemen of color, in well-tailored suits, the old school tie, enjoying their sophisticated, well lubricated, ceremonial meal, ill at ease at the freedom Negroes readily assumed in the United States, almost as if they were equals to the master race. They began with a five-pound lobster for the table, and two dozen oysters each, before digging into the biggest, well-trimmed sirloins he had seen since his time on the Argentine frontier, then, following four brim-full, mixed bourbon-cups each, they naturally (he thought) broke into soft, almost inaudible, song, the extroverted, German *kommandant* overhearing an amusing line from their impromptu ditty. Having himself imbibed numerous tall goblets of a particularly dry, fruity, iced *Liebfraumilch* in preparation for his own, forthcoming ordeal, scheduled for that very afternoon, he thought it rather fitting to utilize his facility with words and languages, to adroitly add a rejoinder to the black boys' original pithy lines; and the next thing he knew, he was yelling out inappropriately across a sea of white clothed tables occupied by serious, sophisticated, stunned, staring parties; including an open mouthed, Puritan John B. Sayer, at a corporate lunch with network affiliates, surprised to see his ally in the struggle, Preacher Pearly, a few tables over with a chum, seeming to be at the center of all the commotion, but actually, more impressed by the witty *SS* devil from across the dining room, now taking the lead role; then back to the similarly surprised, mirthful *Schwarzes*, who, actually appreciating the raw wit and incorrectness, of that roared, final couplet, ordered yet another round, for the three of them, between impolite guffaws and snorting.

> Tribal rejects to cauldrons a chilly morn,
> Tricked Jews to ovens on Holocaust's storm...

It was to be another typical day at United Nations headquarters, the conscience of humanity displaying its transformative, full expression. But there was something in the old Nazi's gravelly, bellowing voice that begged a respect, fear, even homage, and made the attentive assistant suddenly pause, flinch, catch her breath again, flexing her own green eyes wide with startled throbbing when she first experienced it. Surely, she had heard it before. Yael Abraham reviewed the furthest recesses of her memory for a clue:

> Only the Jew knew that by an able and persistent use of propaganda
> heaven itself can be presented to the people as if it were hell and, vice
> versa, the most miserable kind of life can be presented as if it were
> paradise. The Jew knew this and acted accordingly. But the German, or
> rather his Government, did not have the slightest suspicion of it. During
> the War the heaviest of penalties had to be paid for that ignorance.
> (Adolf Hitler, *Mein Kampf*, 1925)

"In commencing, I would pay tribute to *mein Fuhrer* in that that Jews do not have the capacities of self-sacrifice and abnegation, the critical, Aryan traits essential to cultural creation. Jews are not originators or bearers, but destroyers, of custom. Observe the ghettos in every country into which they slither, for Jews are collectivist, internationalist, not individualist, patriotic; they are communists, demonstrated by their alliances with the lower classes and inferior races. Their annihilation was bought by betraying the fatherland during, and after, the Great War. The press, publishers, theatres were all in with them. Their destruction was warranted, for the infamous greed of their filthy kind throughout history, international finance, banks, always under their spell. Liquidation resulted in unfortunate outcomes, as there were so many bug-eyes we had to cremate, the evidence became too much to hide. I have given my entire life, and energy, so help me *Gott*, to the eradication of this sneaky pestilence, indulging in blasphemies and the vilest superstitions. Their barbaric practice of circumcision is ritual castration and a subservience to a matriarchal religion: clipping off the tips of babies' dicks by, and for, women. But why not cut it all? Because by removing only the foreskin, the instrument remains intact, the head over time desensitizing from constant friction, resulting in flattened desire, compromised, sensual stimulus, an increased sexual insecurity, reducing any libidinous wanderings, by males, outside of the tribe; allowing females control over their race, a perfect solution to instill constancy and fidelity in a long pressured ethnic group, thus ensuring the stable relationships that made for a proper transference of (to them) desirable (degenerate) genetic traits, to future generations. In an ironic, inward display of the limits of social acceptance, and ethnic tolerance, Jews themselves became exclusionary to those who might frivolously try to join them, Jewishness bequeathed only to those born through the female line, and/ or willing to undergo covenant mutilation, or *bris*, as part of their initiation sacrifice. This mimicry of superiority was why the master race had to stamp out the elevated mongrels, to keep them from pretending to a civilization and society on par with the Aryan example. Finally, as *Mein Kampf*, specifically warns humanity, concerning evils that may expunge her noble gifts: terror must meet terror, force meet force, for the struggle to triumph. I am now prepared to proceed, with the Madam Chairman's detailed interrogations, of my dutiful past."

Yet he was somehow immune, untouchable, basking in halos of tragedies and self-sacrifices, of victory unfairly turned to defeat; protected from abhorrent, global censures, deserved or otherwise, by cold war cronies in high places; so long as he proved useful to First World spy masters countering Second World ideological threats, from infiltrating Third World puppet regimes, there would be a spot on the team for him. As his prewar duties included party-propaganda, he was adept at playing many sides; he had even snidely defended himself, putting the shoe on the other foot, with a folk tale about a cheeky Jew [Nazi]:

> A group of Nazis [Jews] surrounded an elderly Berlin Jew [Nazi] and
> demanded of him, 'Tell us, Jew [Nazi], who caused the war?'
> The little Jew [Nazi] was no fool. 'The Jews [Nazis],' he said, then added,
> 'and the bicycle riders.'
> The Nazis [Jews] were puzzled. 'Why the bicycle riders?'
> 'Why the Jews [Nazis]?' answered the little old man.
> (Nathan Ausubel, *A Treasury of Jewish Folklore*, 1980)

As a Jew herself suffering from Jewrosis, toxic epithet for paranoic ideations of victimization, Ms. Yael Abraham always felt vindicated, whenever Jew killers were captured and brought to justice, usually by a reformed Germany or recently risen Israel, but rarely the United States, and now had to pinch herself, because of a tingling pride she felt in participating in an international tribunal, digging up dirt, bringing it to light, hopefully influencing a member nation to charge a named, or accused party, for a war crime, proceeding with prosecution, even at this late date, so many years after its occurrence, before forgotten.

She was also aware that the founders and former owners of Warren Bros. Inc., the Warrens, were Jews, but did not hold it against Isidora that prior Greens had treated them shabbily and opportunistically, as was disclosed by the media; in their many years as classmates, sisters, employer/ employee, they never once spoke directly about the originating Warrens' ignominious expulsion from the very company they had worked so hard to conceive and develop. She understood that being Jewish in America was still a second-class citizenship, even amongst other refugees and immigrants. Nevertheless, she tried her best to avoid assuming the stereotypical, negative, oppressed, sardonic, whiny attitude and pose of the Jew.

A descendant of Sephardim, expelled from Spain during the Inquisition, swept away into the Diaspora, settling in Southern Germany, where they were discriminated against for centuries by their fellow Jews, the Ashkenazim, before making it easy on themselves and intermarrying with them; altering their name from Abreu to Abraham, forsaking their original, Oriental identity, except for the few, prohibited words and phrases of *Ladino*, which were fused into their unconscious, and some Sabbath, holiday and dietary customs found abominable by their new kinfolk; she was hyper vigilant of cultures being dispossessed, displaced, losing ethnic distinctions, the rhyme or lore of their pasts, due to tricks, chicanery, bullying.

She recalled nothing of her infancy, only a long ocean voyage after having lived behind blackened steel gates, barbed wire, amid noisy, reeking crowds, and befouled, smoke riddled air; separated from doting parents, turned over to a family never known before, Jews, to be sure, a metropolis she had never seen, in an interwar boomtown awakening, a worthy, national entity she could never have dreamed of, liberty loving America. She bore a jagged tattoo on her outer, left forearm, an inmate's number 169062, which she could not remember getting. However, sometimes in the middle of the night, even sixty years later, she still awoke to phantom needle jabs incising her baby pink skin with the filthy, poisonous, black ink.

Later she learned she was an orphaned refugee from the Holocaust. As thinking and dreaming in her native German waned, a newly acquired language began formulating a freshly developing, modern ego. Growing up in the progressive 1950s and early 1960s, in a fast paced, modish and transformative U.S., she developed the healthy balance of liberal values, of tolerance and inclusivity, as well as conservative respect for tradition and individualism. Her adoptive parents spoke to her in correct, updated English, and never in Yiddish or, God help them, *Ladino*, that primitive idiom of Babylonian, meshed with Latin roots. One day an emissary of the Iberian Sephardi Rescue Foundation had brought tidings and request for support from the wealthy New York Upper West Side Jewish intelligentsia. True to their accepting and loving nature, they took in a displaced baby saved from an impossible, evil situation just as the war in Europe was ending; never asking about her origins, considering a numbered confirmation, illustrated by the tattooed forearm, as defining a perpetually perturbed existence; the only other identifying hint, a blank postcard of Alpine Chile, with a date, April 20, 1944. They named their little blessing Yael, as in God's strength, for miraculous survival against such odds, that only a jewel of an individual could have overcome the torture, dislocation and devastation that was meted out by the Nazi concentration camps.

And so, over the years growing up in the most Jewish of American cities, she assuredly identified with her Sephardic roots, in no small part, because her adoptive parents constantly, loudly complained, that as far as U.S. Ashkenazim were concerned, the family would unfortunately always be condescended to, as inferior, due to their being crypto-Sephardim. True to her name, Yael was, from an early age, obsessed with meeting out justice, maintaining parity for all oppressed people, and living up to an ideal notion of herself as the queen of quotas and fairness; she could not explain this warrior advocate spirit possessing her, nevertheless, it was her driving force and *raison d'etre*. She had become an advocate for progress.

It was the noble reason she applied as a long shot, and was accepted, to Whale College, as one of a few Jewish coeds in the historic first class of women. Majoring in Political Science (focus on how extreme uses of propaganda, by immoral, totalitarian parties/ regimes, could one day occur in U.S. politics) on a scholarship offered by the Sisterhood of Grace Holocaust Challenge Foundation, she continued onward to the Whale Graduate School of Arts and Sciences, earning her Ph.D., Social/ Personality Psychology, on a graduate studies scholarship and stipend provided by the mod Sisters' Erikson Achievement Trust, geared to behavioral research; her thesis: how survival traits prevent anxiety in condemned populations.

And while it was demeaning enough for them to be called co-eds, for some hero worshiping factor they were also referred to as superwomen by the media, as part of a hype celebrating a first for womankind: controlled participation in an elitist, staid, mildewed college, which would always remain fully sexist to the end. She must have already been twenty-five, when accepted to the class of 1973, weirdly exuding a deceptive-looking youth, due to severe malnutrition during the war. She assumed she had never been breast fed as a baby because she was slight, wan, wispy, as if she would be blown away by the barest of whispers; but in truth she was as tough as nails, daring anyone to debate her about any aspect of Israel's right, no duty, to exist and succeed, as a global human right. She passed for eighteen; when challenged as to that claim, due to a closer inspection, revealing a crack or two around the lips, she distracted from any suspicion by immediately changing the subject of her own apparent age, to that of her interlocuter; usually complementing her, saying she appeared much younger than she claimed, and leaving it at that.

It was the reason she met and impressed Isidora Green enough, to be tapped to the Sisterhood of Grace. That is her single-minded delivery managed to convince Isadora that there were not enough Jews in her society; and Isidora could only remedy the lack of diversity by tapping Yael, improving the proportion of Gentile to Jew by one, to fourteen to one. In essence, revealing her pushy nature, Yael promoted her Sissy candidacy based on a quota ideal she would follow her entire life. Once pledged to the sisterhood it was only a matter of short time until her loyalty to its archaic rubric, and to Isidora particularly, led to a rapid promotion, added responsibility, in the Warren Bros. Inc. corporate culture in which she thrived:

> In a hierarchy, every employee tends to rise to his level of incompetence…
> In time, every post tends to be occupied by an employee who is
> incompetent to carry out its duties.
> (Peter and Hull, *The Peter Principle*, 1969)

She felt most at home in Human Resources, the evil twin of corporate management, imposing policies, maintaining order with an internal affairs division, patrolling ranks top to bottom, at the behest of, and reporting directly to, the C-suite and board of directors. She quickly realized that real progress and change would be best instituted from the top, and that HR could serve as the enforcing arm of a liberal ideology, doorkeeper for civil rights, affirmative action, as well as the purging catalyst for the obsolete. Under her able administration, HR became the new representative for all things enlightened, realigning management structures within, to broadened customer inclusiveness, ushering big profits; more buyers meant higher revenues, larger profits, happier shareholders, generous bonuses, it was truly that simple.

And although internally, some employees derided her fiefdom as Hemorrhoid Relief, or Human Refuse, she knew all too well, it had to do with their resentment at her powers over their professional, as well as personal, lives. The privileges of HR were knowing everyone's (even the most august personage's) pay scale, career trajectory, family issues, medical histories and character. And as there could simply be no guarantees of any privacy in these sensitive personnel matters, professional discretion was absolute. It was through this exercise of might that she won the respect of the old-line stockholders in the company, who happened to be Protestants. Somehow the Protestant way was to depend on the cruel, severe and punitive being promoted. One thing she had come away with, after her association with the Sisterhood of Grace, was that WASPs really are the biggest Jews, so she knew how to get along with them, how to get them to admire her, by flattering their egos, and through them plot her winning strategies. Since the Protestant ethic was all about the spread of material, as well as spiritual, goods, Yael impressed WASPs by pretending that she had money, wearing fancy clothes, being fragranced in Chanel No. 5. That was how, post-graduation, she promoted her candidacy to become the first Jewish Sissies Alumni President. Yet, for her entire life, a lingering doubt remained about her Jewishness, because she did not resemble a swarthy Sephardic, whether from Turkey, the Middle East or North Africa, nor did she look Ashkenazi. Gazing in the mirror, she could not tell if her nose bent up like a Gentile's, nor downward like a Jew's:

> "One can most easily tell a Jew by his nose. The Jewish nose is bent at
> its point. It looks like the number six. We call it the 'Jewish six.' Many
> Gentiles also have bent noses. But their noses bend upwards, not
> downwards. Such a nose is a hook nose or an eagle nose. It is not at all like
> a Jewish nose." (Julius Streicher, Nazi propagandist, in a children's story)

In any case, she passed for white, and as Jews were not a protected class, she never assumed that status. Yael, as well as her bosses, understood that at the millennium corporate America would need to behave itself with minorities, oppressed peoples, because big business was under heightened scrutiny for moral and ethical lapses, and the Jewish tom-toms do beat when it came to spreading the word. But whatever source such impulse to do better had, it was beginning to work. Later, in reviewing the day's UN notes, and other, mundane company matters, Yael thought over what Sayer said in the taxi going home, about *having to accept working with all types now: To tell the truth, there needs to be a great justification for hiring a white candidate for many positions. Strange to think how a Jewish refugee girl, with no past, as me, could have so much say about who gets kept out of or brought into a place, almost as if in these times HR is to admissions as slave traders of old, and more recently, Nazis, were to selection, how droll.*

# 10. The Corporate *Kapo* and The Archer of Auschwitz

**What were the prisoners supposed to do when the whistle went?**

Fall in fives, and it was my duty to see that they did so. Dr. Mengele then came and made the selection. As I was responsible for the camp, my duties were to know how many people were leaving and I had to count them, and I kept the figures in a strength book.

After the selection took place they were sent into "B" Camp, ...which I thought was the gas chamber. (Victor Smart, Irma Grese, Excerpts from the Belsen Trial and Biography, 2008)

That morning, before heading from their plush midtown offices crosstown to the Working Group on the Contributions and Successes of Global Nazi Hunters, to be chaired by Isidora Green at United Nations headquarters that afternoon, there had been reports of unfortunate incidents involving the star *protégés* of the company, as frantic calls came into Warren Bros. Inc., for Isidora or Sayer, which were perfectly fielded by Ms. Yael Abraham, in her assumed role as gatekeeper of information into the executive suite.

Yael looked at her watch, 9 AM ET. "Why, it's only 6 AM in small-town Sanctuary, CA, with its lofty desert canyon exclusivity, too early for stars to be up." But it was the tortured team of Willi and Lilly.

Willi: "We thought you should know, there was sort of a scene at the country club last night, and well, Lilly used a bit too much nose candy. It was the annual fundraiser for immigration reform, and things were going along quite smoothly, until the end of the night brought the voice vote for new members..."

Lilly: "...and that's when things got a bit strained, to say the least; a young, dynamic, black couple was nominated, and Willi was the only person in the room to vote against them. It was so embarrassing..."

Willi: "...then something else occurred; when this popular, Jewish couple was nominated Lilly was the only person to vote against them. A lady standing next to her asked why she had done so; Lilly thought the club did not allow Jews, that's partly why she and I joined; wasn't that how Adam and Eve felt too? That's when the lady threw her drink in Lilly's face, yelling that half the club, including herself and her husband, were Jews, and that Lilly and I had only been accepted as members, because the more liberal old timers insisted on helping recently arrived immigrants, no matter what the ethnic/ racial origins..."

Lilly: "...but that's not all. By the time we arrived at Pinkton, it was two in the morning; I was feeling pretty pissed off at the lady for heaving a drink at me, calling me a Nazi, making the bad scene worse; I had lines in the limousine; outside the gate to our ranch, not a thousand yards from where my children slept, there were squatters camping out in the open, some with prior arrests for trespassing here. So, I took one look at those impertinent invaders on our roadsides, deciding right there, enough is enough. I got out of the limo, went over and pissed (which because of my altered physiognomy must be precisely aimed) all over an old couple bundled up in filthy rags and blankets until they woke, screaming hell..."

Willi: "...that was a few hours ago, and now there are reporters at the gate, wanting to know if we were intoxicated last night, asking what the country club anti-black, anti-Semitic rages, along with the public urination on homeless immigrant laborers' scene, were all about? What should we say to the snoops?"

"Nothing," ordered Yael, immediately. She then, quickly summed up the situation. *One, obsessed with race at the county club, keeping out low born characters from high places, perseverating over assumed Colombian high-class status. The other, obsessed with private property, making a fortress of the estate, keeping interlopers out, fearful of raptors, mistrusting those who'd infringe upon their quiet enjoyment.* Some legally admitted immigrants professed disdain for their illegal brothers and sisters, not realizing that all immigrants would need every vote they could get, for the coming struggles. But they were still illegal themselves, not in a position to be lording it over anyone, for there but for the grace of God go I. Considering Pimple's "Sexiest Transgender Couple" were citizenship seekers, with the prior attempted suicide, baby kidnapping events, by this date become spent news, where would these dilemmas lead to?

In the latter twentieth century, America became the land of eternal greens, with lawns maintaining their verdancy all winter long, due to excessive fertilizing, symbolizing the artificiality of the culture and the narcissistic glee of those encompassed by it, to stay forever in the mainstream, noticed, attractive, at the top of their game, this being especially true of the fat community where the fateful urination occurred. And as popular as they had become, they were not immune from the vagaries of vengeance themselves. After years trapped by electric fences, zapping collars strapped to sad necks, some neighborhood dogs went insane from the constant short circuit jolting through prongs jabbing into their hot throats, burning directly into charring flesh, attacking and mauling masters, entire families, in crazed acts of retribution:

Vengeance is mine; I will repay, saith the Lord. (Romans 12:19, KJV)

Among the gathered in the early morning hour, at the residence in question, was child advocate Patricia (P) Diddy, Ph.D., J.D., founder-president, and thus far sole member, of the international humanitarian group, *Les Enfants Sans Frontières*, Greenitch, CT, who politely passed a written note through to them.

> *How could they ever explain, assaulting, picking, urinating, on homeless immigrants at the entrance to the property, while exhorting them to come to this country, by championing their interests among the philanthropic?*

> *Were they aware that in times past, hunters of men took runaways back to where they ostensibly belonged, and recently, hunters of men summarily, kicked people out of the country, in the government deportation process?*

> *The undocumented status of certain aliens prevents them from achieving "whole personhood" rank (valued less than a three-fifths ratio for slaves), benefiting from the privileges, freedoms, available in the society at large.*

"'Recently, we tried to get readers to rid their inboxes of this kind of garbage. We described a list of red flags — we called them Key Characteristics of Bogusness — that were clear tip-offs that a chain email wasn't legitimate. Among them: an anonymous author; excessive exclamation points, capital letters and misspellings; entreaties that 'This is NOT a hoax!' and links to sourcing that does not support, or rather completely contradicts the claims being made. Those still hold true, but fake stories — as in completely made-up 'news' — have grown more sophisticated, now presented on sites designed to look (sort of) like legitimate news organizations. Still, we find it's easy to figure out what's real and what's imaginary if you're armed with some critical thinking and fact-checking tools of the trade,'" asserted a clever Willi.

"News hounds scratching, pawing at our entrance, demanding their rights to our privacy," howled Lilly. "This jack off press tried to play knuckle ball, but cried foul when pitched a no hitter of our reticence." An inability to work with the media was akin to not dealing with contrary opinion, and individuals who avoided such, were probably insecure in their ideology of life and existence, seeking to escape scandal.

There was also a picketing group of protesters for the homeless and indigent, the trafficked and abused, two of their large banners suddenly coming into focus, in the early light filtering sparsely covered hills.

**They have sinned against themselves by committing acts against the helpless.**

**They have lost the last battle and are mistakenly on the wrong side of history.**

"But history is written by victors, not victims," proclaimed Willi to his companion, in reply to that bold banner. "We shall wait to hear from Yael, before we make the next move." A vexed Lilly snarled back:

"Here those hoodlums can be activists, people will listen to them. In their own countries they would be dead, dissolved, never discussed. These are provocateurs, agitators, not activists. Protesting has such a bad image, it's a waste of time; it makes you look bad, in addition to wasting everyone else's time. The effects are negative. Terrorism is merely the continuation of policy by other means." Then tired Willi:

"As with most newly arrived immigrants, we started out to the right of left and to the left of right, about politics, meaning that as with most Americans we didn't have a clue about whom to vote for but after so many years living here I am starting to think, perhaps there is nothing wrong with countries taking back their borders. If people were as careless with their property boundaries as they are with their country's borders, there would be chaos. I am not paying any more attention to economists, corporate executives, Democrats, Republicans or other halfwits, who would trade national and personal security for profit$."

"Those people really are criminals, unauthorized frontier crossers, smuggling their children through the desert, with all its dangers, perhaps kidnapping other kids along the way, as bargaining chips, pawns in their own maniacal game of making it over the wall, and coming here to squat illegally in this country."

"It all comes to when you would allow invaders to dispossess you, taking over your land, filling it with strangers, appropriating your hard work for their folly. Our days of sharing, but never taking, are over. We will have no truck with *The Communist Manifesto*. Inclusiveness has historically never worked for those with open arms, but it has been a boon for those knocking eagerly at the posterns of the frontier."

"You can't just walk into someone's house, whether empty or full, and make yourself at home; that nosy little brat, Goldie Locks is never welcome; on the contrary, she needs to flee for her life. Did you know immigration activists are completely flummoxed by others cutting in line in front of them at airports? I have been a patient, muzzled Muslim long enough; warriors say, 'When diplomacy ends, War begins.'"

It was ironic that as millennials paid more in taxes, they inevitably became less millennial, if more self-serving. Whatever the outcomes, as time passed, heshe seemed more feminine, shehe more masculine, before the ever-revealing glass (full-length vanity mirror) of glories exposing certain programmed traits remaining constant since creation, science, a new social tolerance, along with sales boosting inclusivity, pushing for proliferation of eccentric alternative lifestyles in the name of personal freedom, expression. Nevertheless, inherent racism, bigotry, homophobia, could never be expunged from fixed personalities. Meanwhile Yael was preparing and strategizing for the image wars to come. Corporatizing America, in search of greater and greater profits, promoted an eclectic, tolerant agenda, defining a new status quo in culture, society, politics; simply stated, including all was good business sense. But once fence jumpers were admitted they would never be expelled. Unenforced borders, mass breeding and a communication revolution were bringing about an end of Western civilization; interconnection being responsible for the political rhetoric motivating mass population pressures and movements in such a short-distanced world.

The morning TV news featured: *country club discrimination legal suits; criminal assault on a homeless migrant, sleeping couple; undocumented single mothers possessing false id's and papers (their goal, to migrate to the U.S., claim full rights while still illegal, and mess up the whole system); an underground railroad for illegals being organized while federal deportations increase; outed gay politicians denying involvement in abuse, pedophilia, in bygone times, one by hurting women, the other children; trafficked women raped by up to 30 johns a day, seven days a week for the best part of four years: 43,200; rockets fired into Israel by Hezbollah (Hell's balls), in a continuation of hostilities*; all, antisocial personalities? As a psychologist she had to agree, assuming servile responsibility for guiding and protecting others. These represented the new attacks upon America, and she felt desperate to prevent their occurrences. Yael was suddenly reminded, the FBI was very thorough in explaining terror plots post fact, but got bad grades for prevention; so, there was really nothing that could have been done to avert these scenes. She recalled Chappaquiddick, which taught young and old that the hypocritical stance, of even a Kennedy, could not be shaken off, sticking to him like smelly glue for the rest of his personal life, political career.

The company's contract stars would not be held to the legal, or accepted immigration standards, as they had been here for some time, unlike the recently arrived, and had thus achieved grandfathered status, as to their belonging. Besides, the paying public had grown fond of the international match and would not want them sent back, as racial humility was an admittance of white privilege standing down in remorse, shame, sorrow for the gross advantages benefitted from for five centuries. Lately logical contradictions stared her in the face. Considering her background, it was difficult for her to deny entrance to anyone; but given her recent excesses as a liberal titan, it became apparent that many of those most in need were unfit, flawed, ill physically and mentally, and perhaps should not have been admitted in the first place. Natural selection involved options, and through their close choice of mates, races formed, as protection against distant or close marauders. As primeval threats to a group subsided, the complacency of a self-sufficient unit fostered racialism, to keep everything within (*Cosa Nostra*). National wars, ethnic strife and slavery, all willful offspring of the mother slattern racism, allow for release and expression of pent-up, internal aggression, competition and frustration against the common external object (sometimes not even threat). *It is for these evolutionary reasons that multiculturalism is a fallacy, in concept as well as fact. Cultural competence should really be reconfigured, as cultural competition.* In a world of getting things done for others, where time was of the essence, and the stock market obsessed over every detail, she could not afford to be that choosy in her assignments concerning ethical, let alone moral, qualities. As a loyal fan herself, she sympathized with her company's stars about defending what was theirs, from encroaching plunderers; and even went so far, as to condone bad behavior, for the sake of moving along commitments that were irrevocable, toward the point of least resistance, in good old corporate fashion.

At this moment, the point of least resistance, to Yael, seemed to be getting them out of Dodge, recalling that Lilly had an affinity for an investigative journalist who had done precise, discreet work for them in the past. Yael's practicality, her *realpolitik*, was surprising, even to herself; given, in the first place, that they had revealed themselves as racists and anti-Semites, her unbridled reaction would have been to tell them to drop dead; and in the second place, they had shown no remorse for their actions, or beliefs, and those evil results, fostered by their outrageous behavior the prior night; and were seemingly indifferent, unaware, casual of how truly insulting and harmful they had been. For the sake of professionalism, and her own survival, she sucked up to the anti-Semitism, an unavoidable fact of the United States, a global phenomenon. Besides Machiavellian pragmatism, there was something else that had been eating at her, coursing through her veins, too hot to handle, an inchoate hardness, callousness, even disregard, for all inferiors. This was well beyond the normal Protestant Reformation inspired corporate insouciance and invisible hand, and seemed to enter the elitist, super critical and aggressive spheres of right-wing power pretensions. Perhaps the stability the status quo enjoyed consorting with big business prevented change or constructive progress. Perhaps earnings were inimical to freedoms, but still worthy of their sacrifice. She still espoused multiculturalism, but lately, it had been focused on advancing those of her own kind:

> When they asked me, couldn't you give money out of the United Jewish
> Appeal funds for the rescue of Jews in Europe, I said, 'NO!' and I say
> again 'NO'... one should resist this wave which pushes the Zionist
> activities to secondary importance. (Yitzhak Gruenbaum, January 1943)

When Yael was ten, her synagogue sponsored a trip to Europe, solemnly dedicated to and in memory of the Holocaust dead. The visit to Auschwitz, her parents holding her hands, and holding back tears with their other ones, was poignant and memorable. An exhibit of dolls from the camp, featuring a perfectly preserved, Asian detailed, rouge cheeked porcelain beauty, caught Yael's eye. This doll had apparently belonged to the infant daughter of the camp *kommandant,* who, at one time, had served in the military attaches' office in Tokyo, in 1939, years before the fall of Japan, and had been sent as a birthday gift, in 1944, by General Hideki Tojo's wife Katsuko, in remembrance of a diplomatic reception at the German Embassy, where the officer had charmed Katsuko, whose own boys were in the Imperial Army. At the war's end, the *kommandant* and his family fled, disappearing into the wartime night, leaving only a doll as real evidence of their ruinous existence. And the closer Yael looked at the doll, the stronger was the feeling that she had seen and held it before, only where and when she could not recall, so in short order, she herself believed she had invented it. Returning from Europe, she could not get images of railways, gassing or that doll out of her mind, and worked diligently, creatively, to one day attend Whale College, and get the best education available, to make a critical difference in a desperate world needing changes.

Before noon ET our panicked pair received a call from Yael, with explicit instructions to do absolutely nothing. They were to avoid interviews with the press and activists, and if there was no way out should deny involvement, or participation, in whatever could be insinuated, or presented, as hearsay. Under no circumstances were they to admit to anything, unless they were granted immunity from all prosecution. They should, "skip the light fantastic out of town" to their ocean side *villa* in Baja; no one would notice them there; going underground was a solution as old as the hills. Then they were to wait patiently, for Lilly's columnist ally to call, to concoct some credible story out of this soap opera of modern excesses.

Yael did not bother to inform the corporate attorney of the possible fallout faced by the company due to the irrepressible duet's antics, nor interrupt Sissy Isidora's meditative train of thought, prepping for her first prominent UN leadership role that day; instead calling the correspondent, to entrust him with fixing the delicate matter, problem, thing; from this moment secretly referring to him, as the Fixer. The time finally came for bespoke counter measures; first, she spoke, then the Fixer betook his way to Baja.

"Why am I calling you? Because I see this primarily as a public relations issue, that may be suppressed by targeted, treacherous publicity, and you should assume a means most expedient to the desired ends. You might begin by getting some grit on that child protectress, Patricia (P) Diddy. What is her game? I am going way outside of the established protocol on this one, so you can't weigh us down with failure. The duo should be sequestered in Baja by tomorrow; go and see them there. Please bill me at the end."

Yael abruptly hung up, on the Fixer, embarrassed she had made the call, to begin with, though no one had heard her, let alone the cover up she had negotiated to get two scoundrels off the hook, but she was doing the company's bidding, and what's good for the goose is good for the gander, if only done right, as "Corporations are people, my friend. Everything corporations earn ultimately goes to people," meaning that when things went their way, they were benefactors. But when things go south, watch out.

That afternoon in the great, green marbled UN hall, Yael could not help noticing how focused and level Isidora was in managing events of such grave importance and was glad she had taken it upon herself to shield her boss, and Lady, from trifling, distracting unpleasantries, prior to her momentous undertaking. She also spotted Sayer in the audience and wondered what his private/ professional interest was in this.

*Schutzstaffel* (*SS*) Colonel Otto Waldemar Grawitz, descended from indigenous barbarians, pagans, Old Prussians, escaped Nazi war criminal, who had come up, through the party political propaganda ranks, to become the monster, William Tell of Auschwitz, responsible for hundreds of thousands of deaths and running the death camp, with an efficiency that was notorious within certain bestial circles, maintaining his scornful, surly air, replied to the Madam Chairman by once again playing victim, unfairly maligned.

"The forces hunting us should ponder in the mirror, before donning their radiant righteousness, because there is no such thing as justice, only death and vengeance, justice and victory but random, the constant being suffering, whereas vengeance may be man-made, wrought out of hatred and that same suffering."

The texture of Grawitz' gruff, yet educated voice, so jarring, intoxicating, mesmerizing to Yael, that she closed her eyes to better imagine its correct placement in her life, transported her into a familiar dream:

> "The smell was awful — things like that, you do not want to talk about it.
> Because the pain and memory of suffering comes back to you. You cannot
> deal with it." (Eva Gryka Kohan, Local Survivor)

In a surreal fashion, she was napping in her pram, behind blackened steel gates, barbed wire, chimneys belching a stinking smoke of fatty dust and minute bone particles, which got onto everything, on dark horizons, just waking up, ash-ridden, damp, cold, crying, gurgling, cooing softly. *Funktionshäftling*, or *kapos*, as the Nazis referred to them, criminal, traitor Jews laboring for their evil captors, were noisily herding long lines of their shocked brothers and sisters from the train depot to the showers, urging them forward: "This way for the gas, ladies and gentlemen;" and she heard that same colonel's furious voice, resonating in her skull, berating those about him in a caustic, accusatory German: "*Macht schnell*; get those people moving, we are behind schedule." Then she was dry and warm again, and inside a parlor:

> "They said separate: children, men, women, and the older people. Me and
> my sister were separated with the young ones. I had my little sister in my
> arms, and one of the SS came over and picked up my little sister and gave
> her to my stepmother. He pushed me to the other side."
> (Bella Benozio Ouziel, Local Survivor)

Lit up by the most prominent lamps, she finally understood the subtle pleasures, of *SS kommandants,* in illuminating their residences with tapers, shaded by translucent skin whittled from their Jewish inmates, highlighting prominently the notorious numbered tattoos that each one was inscribed with upon arrival, victims clearly identified, glowing mementos of atrocities, for fellow officers' admiration. Then there were shadows, mumbling in a familiar German she seemed to know, the voices complementing the fine collection of specimens, the colonel had taken such pains to preserve. Looking closer at those mounted heads on the walls, she saw they were of Jews, Slavs, Gypsies, men, women (no sexism here), stunning trophies of the taxidermist's art, examples of man's victorious mastery, archaic possessiveness and utter madness. Afterward she was waking up, not at the UN as before, but somehow, still at the camp again:

"The finished products (i.e., tattooed skin detached from corpses) were turned over to Koch's wife, who had them fashioned into lampshades and other ornamental household articles..."
(A witness at the Nuremberg Trials, 1945-46)

"It is more interesting that Frau Koch had a lady's handbag made out of the same material. She was just as proud of it as a South Sea island woman would have been about her cannibal trophies..."
(Stefan Heymann, Sidelights on the Koch Affair)

Yael was in her white trimmed house, with her tight, loving family at breakfast. At the stove her blond, faceless mother was frying preserved, canned meats, and eggs stolen by the *kapos* the prior night, from a local farm. Sizzling grease, and warming rye bread, filled Yael's nostrils with the smell of a safe and secure place. Her father sat at the kitchen table, humming a nursery tune, polishing a dozen red apples on a grey-green jacket; with deep green eyes complementing his uniform, he seemed to be the colonel. So, this was the daily life of the *kommandant's* family. His wife turned to him with the morning gossip:

"As long as, how can I put this? what Kathy Huberman doesn't know, is that her family is in the wrong. As *Sudeten* German, the major's ancestry includes Moravian, Bohemian, disqualifying him as German. A husband and wife need to be the same race, as with the kids. That's how it's been from the beginning of, how can I say, when God created the heaven and earth. He created Adam and Eve at the same time. But as for as me being a racist, and against Jews, Slavs, Gypsies and other inferior people, no I'm not."

"Well, you and I have done the right thing, never mixing our blood, at least in our generation, and our little, green-eyed treasure is proof of that. Soon, God-willing, she will have a brother or sister to boss."

"Born on the same day as the *Fuhrer*, an auspicious omen; now seven weeks old, and already, so alert. She notices everything, when you prepare to leave the house for work and then come home every day:"

> *"Funkel, funkel, kleiner Stern,*
> *Wie ich mich frage, was du bist!*
> *Über der Welt so hoch,*
> *Wie ein Diamant am Himmel.* (Lullaby)

"My baby Alexandra, Aley, so sweet, such a joy to her parents. Perhaps the world we leave her will be a better place than it is now. She will be devoted to her parents, and will dote over us, in our old age."

"Darling Otto, I am worrying if our old age will ever come. The whole camp has been astir for the past couple of days, over the Allied Normandy landings, with claims, Paris could be liberated within weeks. Why, even the inmates know all about it somehow and are starting to hold out for their own liberation."

"They better worry about their work deadlines instead of freedom or they know where they will end up. My apples, quarrels are ready, I am going out to inspect the bicycle, after which I will be heading off."

"Very well, my dear. Would you please have the *kapos* empty our cesspool today? It's really smelling bad. And please have them bring some chicken, for dinner tonight; we have not had chicken for ages."

"I will do so, *mein Liebchen*, and will be home at my usual time, as nothing could ever keep me from your dinner, our warm bed and the nocturnal pleasures of performing our duty to our race and *Fuhrer*."

"As you command, my stay erect Colonel, and think of me often, to make sure that you're interested."

They had been up, with the entire camp, from the 4:30 AM gong, but she stayed ravishing, nonetheless. They kissed long and hard. He entered the parlor, and in one corner was a crossbow, dark, shiny wood and metal, against the wall, by his trophy heads: and on a hook, a worn leather holster, with his military issue black *Luger*. How many men, women and children had he killed with these deadly weapons? He calculated. On his previous tour on the Eastern Front, he had bayoneted babies thrown into the air, and felt no remorse. Then he was off to the shed to check the bicycle, before the morning rounds, in his full summer uniform, *Luger* holstered, apples, bolts bagged, the crossbow secured in the sling on his back. After waving friendly greetings to his Nazi neighbor, Mrs. Schwarz, brushing off gray ash sprinkled on her daffodils overnight, *SS* Colonel Grawitz, gallant *chevalier,* was prepared to mount his warrior steed.

Emerging from the shed straddling a rusty bicycle, he was transfigured into a medieval William Tell. It was now 6:30 AM. His first stop was the commissary, to pick up packs of cigarettes and chocolate, and place his order for two slaughtered chickens, for that night, sharing with his deputy, having thin tea and dried biscuits: "Lange, did you know that in these Polish wilds, roasted chicken is the new aphrodisiac? I look forward to our officer's drill, at 9 AM, but till then I am off to the chase that thrills, *bon chance.*"

Five minutes into his errant ride, William Tell came upon his first trial by mortal combat: seeing one of the bent Jews in a work detail, struggling under a huge pile of firewood he was lifting, Tell dismounted, ordered him to put down his heavy load and come over. As the Jew approached, quaking and muttering in terror of the unexpected, Tell disabused him of his fear, by offering a cigarette and calmly lighting it.

"I will give you a bright, shiny apple, if you allow me the privilege of shooting it in half on your head."

The heavy drags of nicotine having calmed the fragile man's nerves, he was so hungry and faint, that it sounded, to be a reasonable proposal, considering a bright shiny apple was at stake: "Bound for Eden."

He grabbed an apple, walking to a leaning spruce tree, fifteen meters away, turning around to face Tell: "Now put that fine juicy apple on your head, and I will demonstrate the old art of the crossbow to you."

The dazed man, inured to any taunts of death in such a bad place as this, where it was ever present, and conditioned to obey any command, whim, issued by the *SS*, placed the apple on his head, staring ahead.

That was the last thing he ever saw, the final vision he ever had, because William Tell, most competent of bowmen, struck him between the eyes with an iron bolt, which had so much force it impaled the tree.

"Missed, sorry." He left the body for the *Sonderkommando* to dispose of, along with the apple, as a tip.

Next our dutiful avenger of wrong rode to the outskirts of the camp, flat green farmland, encountering a detail of emaciated, Ukrainian, female, agricultural slaves, shovels and picks pulled along; a young, red headed Rus', beautiful Slav princess, caught his eye. Beckoning her to approach, providing a chocolate and lighting a cigarette, she remained hesitant, but cautiously came nearer when he smiled, with a large gap between his two front teeth, seeming warm, sensitive, engaging. Gobbling up the chocolate, from its foil wrapper, sucking hard on the offered cigarette, she confused euphoria for trust, to his advantage:

"I will give you a bright, shiny apple, if you allow me the privilege of shooting it in half on your head."

She took the proffered apple, calmly paced the fifteen meters to a crumbling garden wall, turned around defiantly to her tempter, placed the apple on her head, and invoked, "I implore you, only save my face."

Those were the last words she ever spoke, as our intrepid marksman took pity on her, shooting directly through her heart, declaring, "I have kept faithful to your impeccable beauty, as it shall grace my wall." He left her corpse, along with the token apple, with instructions to have the head delivered to the camp taxidermist, to be preserved for that spot in his parlor, reserved for Slavs, next to a chaste Czech priest:

> "She was beautiful, my little sister. You cannot imagine how beautiful she
> was. They mustn't have looked at her. If they had, they would never have
> killed her. They couldn't have." (Charlotte Delbo, Local Survivor)

Peddling through the Gypsy barracks, our taunting Tell chanced upon a most beautiful rendition, of the Tchaikovsky Violin Concerto in D major, emanating from that foul camp, performed by some virtuosic demon, mastering horsehair and strings, a *Romani* teen with a gift of Satan. Dismounting, curious Tell explored along a muddy path, following the melodious lead to a last, flat, wooden bunk house, where a superbly gifted, darkly complexioned fiddler, in the middle of a *cadenza*, came face to face with Satan:

"Why are you not out, with the other inmates?" interrupted Tell. "Have you been to morning roll call?"

There was no answer from the Gyp, who continued with his *cadenza,* and first movement, until the end. Tell had lit his own cigarette while listening enraptured; now he lit one for the violinist and offered him some chocolate, truly awed by this performance. The musician wolfed down the chocolate, smiling at Tell, who proceeded to ask, "Where did you learn to bow like that, my boy, surely, *au conservatoire*?"

Smoking deeply and with gusto the artist responded: "In Paris, I had master classes with Fritz Kreisler."

"You have demonstrated your prowess with the viol and bow; now let me show you what I can do, with another type of bow. Let me shoot this apple from your head to prove that I have heard heaven and hell in your music. I shall personally guarantee your implements, if you vouchsafe me such a great honor."

Stepping outside, the violinist entrusted his priceless instrument to Tell, taking his own position, fifteen meters away against a whipping post, then placed the gleaming apple upon his head. Tell took a careful aim, breathing slowly, cautiously, then he fired. The hurling bolt exploded the apple; the youth blinked.

Tell coolly removed another apple from the bag and brought it along with the honored instrument, to its owner. "Take this apple, you have earned it, because your sound is fearless and your tone courageous."

Tell abruptly turned heel, leaving the Gypsy to his scales, continuing his macabre morning archery until the bags of apples and bolts were empty, and a bloody swath spread out to guide the *Sonderkommando*. Sometimes William Tell spared his victims their fate, knowing full well, that sooner or later death's call would come. After the officer's drill, and some office details, it was time to head to the officer's mess. Getting together around a healthy, robust lunch, senior officers debated the significance of the invasion. Lange, seated at a table along with the other *SS* criminal murderers, addressed their stolid *kommandant*:

"It looks as if Patton's U.S. Third Army will be on the *Champs Elysees* before you or I ever get to visit, with our wives. So, what do you propose we do, as the Russians get closer and closer to our children?"

"It seems as if such sentiments would be of interest to the *Gestapo*, if you are not careful, dear Lange."

That afternoon, self-satisfied and relaxed after a hearty lunch, Tell leaves bow behind; ventures to that camp girlie house for some earned R and R along with old Kramer, known and trusted since graduating together, from the *SS-Junkerschulen*, 1938, specializing in faster ways to dispose of the bodies already disposed of, the volume of ashes being so vast, it could not be processed; then a fade out of the scene.

Next Yael's dream moved ahead by several months, the situation at Auschwitz now become quite dire. "What will happen to this house, and our possessions that we have worked so hard for, my dear Otto?"

"It is time to leave all that behind, my love, and only focus on our family. The Russians are days away, we need to execute our escape plan now. We can never be captured by those *schweinhund* at any cost."

"But where is there left to go to, and how will we first get out of this prison, which keeps us detained as much as the ones condemned? I know that if we wait too long, it will be too late for our little bundle."

"Kramer is in a group planning a breakout from here, with further passage to Spain, then Chile, South America, where there are a great many Germans. I have been hoarding gold teeth, coins and diamonds in Credit Suisse, Zurich, since 1938. A large complication, which I must share with you, exists; aliases and documents have been created for us to present as Swiss international relief workers, with a refugee, Jewish baby we are escorting to safety, meaning our little Aley pretending to be something she is not, a Nazi playing a Jew, the Jew a Nazi, channeling a changeling child, a baby switched at birth by fairies."

"And why is that a problem? That is exactly as we will appear; we should be able to get away with it."

"Because in order to make our aliases airtight, we will need to tattoo an inmate number, on our angel."

"Impossible, I will never allow such a horror; why, if anything goes wrong, we may lose her forever."

"We have no choice. Kramer has everything ready, and this is the final detail, preventing our leaving."

"Our child will not be a detail of a retreat, the war's failure or a ticket to freedom in another country."

"I am sorry, you do not understand; it is a matter of life and death, and utmost stealth; there can be no delay. My top woman warden will soon be here to personally escort you in secrecy, to the infirmary."

In ten minutes, an officious knock at the door ushered forth, saluting, jackbooted, youthful Irma Grese, in a black *SS* guard's uniform, riding crop under left arm, at the Colonel's wife and daughter's service:

> In Auschwitz she wore a pistol and in Belsen she went about with a riding
> whip. She was one of the few SS women who had a permit to carry arms.
> I cannot say whether she was wearing a pistol at the time of this incident.
> (Smart, Idem)

"The Colonel cannot be recognized where we are going, so I must take you and the child without him." And because the little girl's blond mother was faceless, no one would remember or recognize her either. Grese led them through dark alleys, filled with evening strollers foraging and trading for food, clothes, and cigarettes, until they reached a dark warehouse, with an open door, single light and two evil *kapos*.

Now Yael remembered *everything, down to the grungiest, horrid details. They entered the warehouse. There was one person who would rub the…a little piece of dirty alcohol on your arm, and the other one had the…had the needle with the inkwell, and he would do the numbering. So, my number was 169062.*

When the deed was done, Grese led Aley and mother home, teasing her about her itty-bitty *Juden* fraud. This precisely expressed the secret, unconscious suspicion weighing Yael down, even in her deepest of dreams. She was Jewish on the outside, faithfully obeying the laws uniting her to her fellow believers, but for some inexplicable, self-loathing reason, inwardly felt Nazi sympathies; she could not explain it. Having searched for her father all her life, she could not believe he was right before her, a mocking war criminal, unknowable, and her, a woman with a tattoo numbered arm, daughter of a war- time madman. Such was not hard to fathom, considering similarities shared between Jews and Germans, regarding social achievements and wealth distinctions, among other traits binding them together, in their dreams.

Twenty-four hours later, Kramer led their flock absconding in the night, his underground network of *SS* henchmen preparing transportation, contacts and money, as the deserters raced through wintry country. For the first time in their lives, these AWOL Nazi beasts felt what it was to be hunted, on their own turf. Grawitz never forgave himself for waiting as long as he did, to take his family to safety; it was too late. Aley's mother was killed by Russian sharpshooters, before even making it out of Poland, and in Yael's infant memory was forever faceless. Her father took over parenting duties until reaching Spain, where, waiting for a steamer to continue their exodus, they were sadly separated from each other forever more.

As her mother had feared, Aley's tattooed number, granting a vital plea to her escape, was her downfall. Requiring swift medical attention for his little girl's flareup of dysentery, Grawitz took her to a convent hospital for treatment. Knowing that his departure was imminent, he arranged for the Catholic nuns at the fascist affiliated hospital to care for, "the orphan," until he could send for her, who, no sooner than he departed, taking full notice of her numbered forearm, thusly presuming the obvious, that she had to be Sephardi, transferred her to the efficient Iberian Sephardi Rescue Foundation to be sent to America.

Waiting on a putrid fruit smelling wharf in Montevideo, on a sweaty morning, the desperate father was beside himself with anguish, grief and guilt, at her failure to appear on the steamer (or its manifest) he had arranged passage for her on, having written the nuns, and entrusted them with the proper sums and instructions. Pausing patiently on the pier for a promised pram to appear, descending the gangplank, he concluded that those fascist *filles* had put one over on him, never hearing back from them, keeping his money and his daughter. But the pain he felt was only for himself, his loss, and never encompassed all the evil and destruction he had brought to the world as the reason for his tragedy; his hubris, narcissism had led to a miserable moment of crocodile tears, still insensitive to the child's damaging abandonment.

As the escaped Nazi war criminal's security situation at war's end was precarious, it was impossible to communicate with the outside world, for the first few years, upon his arrival in the indomitable heights of the Chilean Andes. An Interpol wanted fugitive, out of an abundance of caution against detection, he lost contact with the convent and order of nuns in Spain, his co-conspirators, everyone he ever knew, to lay low, thus lost track of what might have happened to his lost darling, the only clue, the crude number etched onto her arm, 169062. He worked as a ski instructor at Portillo, and also in Bariloche across the Argentine border, from time to time (really, long enough to have an affair, but cut out before any covert State, Justice Department, FBI or Army Intelligence agent recognized him), to keep in shape, and earn some cash (although he was generously provided for, by Kramer's secretive fascist brotherhood, which had organized his escape, as well as his cache in secretive Credit Suisse), but mainly to provide a likely cover identity; although most of the time, he spent in the solitude of his alpine heights, pining away for his faceless wife, disappeared daughter; and so, several years passed, in a constant fear of his discovery by the FBI, until he got a fortunate call from the CIA to come and work for them right across the street: *But when thou doest alms, let not thy left hand know what thy right hand doeth:* to find sweet sanctuary.

Now Isidora was coming back into focus; Yael was once more at the UN, assisting the inquiry of a Nazi war criminal; this would be the ultimate question to *Schutzstaffel (SS)* Colonel Otto Waldemar Grawitz:

"Sir, do you care that your actions affected countless lives, families and societies, all to the detriment?"

"Madam, I care that my actions could not be sustained in the noble cause we all struggled, and continue to struggle, for." And then the historic session was over, the witness free to take his leave, "thank you."

In the crosstown taxi Sayer commented, "It should be no surprise (nor be despised) that the UN, NATO rely to such a great degree on depraved officers, such as *SS* Colonel Grawitz; after all, U.S. allies have always included despicable partners, as in World War II with the Soviet Union; the problem for modern democracies: what if they go in the wrong direction, as did 1930s Germany? Hitler's great opportunity came through attracting his enemy Marxists, coopting them to his side with the folkish state mythology, which ushered forth the racist state ideology. Only fifty-six at death, amazing what infernal destruction he caused in such a short life; the same goes for many other, big, bad guys in history: young and evil:"

Walking the last few blocks to her apartment, Yael thought *about the day's events, and how everything seemed to have gone according to script. It was the influence of directed stories that fashioned history; if victors naturally effaced the losers' pasts, we have been receiving only one side of a story, since time began, the version etched by the latest winner, final mouthpiece, from whom the crafted tale is fixed.* It was ironic that any way she thought about it, by her own definition, she would always consider herself a Holocaust survivor/ victim, wondering *if SS Colonel Grawitz considered as much for himself, as well.*

*So many movies were made about WWII, because we were still good guys. Fewer were made about the Korean conflict, as we were starting to throw our weight around, and just a handful about Vietnam, for by then we were quite arguably, and becoming more and more so, no longer good guys at all. Now in the Middle East, we may be bad guys, if anyone really believes such. The latest war features depict our inner turmoil, disease of soul and body, as a nation. Bad acts are committed, accepted and forborne to achieve good (if not noble) ends, that's the standard line, but great heroes, especially of the big picture variety, rarely bear the tainting effects of bad behavior, on or off screen, even for the sake of survival.*

Her mind held existential doubts: *was she a crypto-Jew or crypto-Nazi, wherever the twain shall meet?*

Then loudly affirming: "Aley, a woman with a tattoo numbered arm, a daughter of a war- time madman."

Thus, for the nameless, uncounted victims of the Holocaust. But war waste (specializing in faster ways to dispose of the bodies already disposed of, the volume of ashes being so vast, it could not be hidden) was an existential dilemma weaker, herd minded, merciful moderns seem to discount, misunderstand or conveniently forget about. Though the folly and evil of war was inescapable, people still had to protect themselves from marauders and conquerors. Where was the line between openness and defensiveness? There was a movie shoot in which turf loyal, neighborhood locals kept adjusting the side mirrors of the cars parked on adjacent streets to reflect the sun's glare directly into the cameras as they rolled, from set to set, ruining each take; a rag tag army of students, musicians, Viet Nam vets, street hustlers repeatedly interrupted, then forced abrupt stoppage and cancellation of the entire project at the atmospheric, gritty location, much to the annoyance and embarrassment of functional, corporate lackeys, including herself.

Here perhaps it should be mentioned that it was the innocent, trusting hospitality, curiosity and/ or utter astonishment (perhaps not humanity, as they were still committed, evil cannibals), of the native Indians (Columbus' name for them), in welcoming the foreign, white gods, devils, that ultimately brought about their demise and cultural annihilation; and once the barbarian, blue eyed Goths were admitted into the Roman Empire they could not be expelled, ushering in successive invasions (talk about stinky visitors), bringing about the fateful fall of the Western Empire; and occupied, doomed, medieval Spain, forgotten under a Moorish yoke for eight hundred isolated years, with a lonely, cornered Galicia the last Christian stronghold remaining, the overrun denizens commencing their heroic, centuries long struggle to reclaim what was rightfully theirs, from dark hearted heathens; later Norman invasion of Anglo Saxon England, when overnight, thegns were transformed into ceorls and slaves, their hereditary land holdings parceled out anew, reallocated to victors, and a hybrid language molded, vanquishing, absorbing its predecessor. Maybe too late, the Romans learned from their mistake (the Indians never got another chance), building Hadrian's Wall to stem a blue faced tide of fierceness from flowing down upon them, in their far flung outposts; and luckily, in the thirteenth century, Europeans had much greater gumption (*cojones*), than at present, putting over national differences to decisively face hordes of marauding Mongols, or we would all be camping out in yurts, subsisting on mare's blood and fermented milk, and speaking Tatar dialects; then again in 1529, united against Turks, withstanding swarmed Ottomans of Suleiman the Magnificent at the Siege of Vienna, with autocratic, oriental customs vying neck and neck with an occidental way of life, the Renaissance, humanistic thought; and more recently, the supreme sacrifice of the Soviet Union, overcoming Nazi German blitzkrieg oblivion ("We will destroy the enemy at the gates of Stalingrad."):

> In comments ahead of the D-Day commemorations, Russian Foreign Ministry spokesperson Maria Zakharova took a swipe at the ceremony, saying: "The Normandy landings were not a game-changer for the outcome of WWII and the Great Patriotic War. The outcome was determined by the Red Army's victories — mainly, in Stalingrad and Kursk. For three years, the UK and then the US dragged out opening the Second Front." (Nathan Hodge, CNN, June 7, 2019)

At a cost of over 40 million military and civilian lives, also inestimable treasure, such truly exemplify the price of self-determination and freedom in every age. And they should remain as warnings of self-interested, desirous flows of human history, later to be left unremembered, miscalculated or ignored, to our peril, by the governing classes, from guilt (over old materialist, slaving, colonialist, militarist, racist traditions) ridden fear of being too heavy handed (love plays better to their sensitive, overwrought and progressive constituents), while the beastly mitts of those reviling us, cut our heads off (of frail necks) with rough bladed paring knives, banishing uneasy souls to perdition in a world spinning out of control, in the next phase of the Holocaust revisited upon the entire world, by a new demon *Shaytan* incarnate.

Separately, liquidating impoverished, defenseless people in developing nations in pursuit of a bellicose, hegemonic, foreign policy (war on terrorism) was no different than murdering fleeing minority youths domestically, as part of an unyielding guarantee of law and order (war on crime). Those racist, bigoted factors involved in each abomination feed off each other, in the same way, as assaulting a total stranger on the street, makes it easier to beat your children in your own house, and vice versa. But none of this shameful, demonic behavior should be surprising, considering that the brutality, self-righteousness and callousness of human society has been carefully honed from millennia (perhaps even since the creation) of greed, oppression and economic stratification. As time passed, it was hard to remember all the sides.

## 11. CAMERA OBSCURA

> All things are a flowing,
> Sage Heracleitus says;
> But a tawdry cheapness
> Shall outlast our days. (Ezra Pound, "Hugh Selwyn Mauberley," 1920)

I am T. (Tiddly) Awdry Winks, author extraordinaire, poet chronicler for the ages, historian of the seen and unseen; friends call me Tiddlywinks, bearer of the cheap, showy, metaphysical chips; Tawdry I am, divulging sacred truths usually best left unturned, as an ancient Herm, recently dug up in Attic gardens.

Disavowing pseudonyms used by authors as being cowardly, I am, nevertheless, forced to use one. The reason for my *nom de plume*, being to avoid that cult of personality, such obsession with an individual plodder, rightly or wrongly, to his good or detriment, which I have tried to escape. Sobriquets abound, the marketplace lately rewarding (cursing) me with, the Yellow Kid, or Fixer. It's strange enough that I should continue cutting and pasting together this volume, at an age when most self-respecting authors are long since bygone, insane, infirm or dead, in any case relieved of further obligation to turn a word. But as my intent is the type of memoir where I go beyond what I recall, I remain bound to my vocation, a tale of the imagination, of great possibilities, instead of straight recollections of dull, repeated events.

I will keep to the traditional referencing of historical periods, as BC and AD, despite their ethnocentric, Christian, Western European associations as, CE and BCE may be more inclusive, sensitive, neutral but in the end redundant, and pronouns, except for the use of heshe for a trans woman, or shehe for a trans man, and other passing conventions, but not they as a common pronoun, as it is too confusing in multi character scenes and dialogue, and the referencing of the plural for singular, etc. The term man shall be taken in its classical, non-gendered, yet inclusive of (both) (all) genders, sense. All biblical quotations are from the King James Version (KJV), in keeping with a preference for traditional (original) sources.

I've read so many books I need to write my own; the time has come to tell it all, for me to set the record straight, before the memories fade away. These are my *Notes from Underground*; I fight thought police every day. I had been pushed way too far, one too many times before, enough said. I'm not politically engaged, but perhaps intergenerational transference is a strong case, for biting frustration and self-pity.

These are the tawdry winks of my times, what I witnessed, and attested to, at the turn of the twentieth, commencement of the twenty-first, century, the grand start of the *tertium millennium*; be prepared for a chronology of events to be presented in an unbiased fashion, if only because I really don't know where to begin. Everything is made up, but it's true enough for me, as I'm writing to those not even born yet, while I remain hale and hearty, before enfeeblement reigns, to confuse mind or weaken bones. I impart a sacred spirit into this work, of creation, initiation, replication, population, saturation, immigration, the archaeological tracings of lost data, to perhaps give voice, to those forgotten by the fables and legends.

Unlike Otzi, the snow wanderer, I must leave more clues than chipped teeth, brittle bones or dried flesh to future archaeologists, treasure hunters, soothsayers, amid consuming maelstroms of coming eras. If depression is not achieving the outcome desired, was Otzi in a depression when he froze to death on the glacier? Did he curse at the gods when the Furies caught up with him, or gently fall asleep into his last dream? Was there any impulse to suicide, disillusioned with the maker for abandoning him in the final stretch? Who can really be alive and taste all life's meaning, and never dwell on taking freely what was given? born alone, dying alone, with the time in between, all breaths taken, notions, sights untold, mere suggestions in the dark. Usually self-reliant, a believer in the original, eternal spark of all existence, he venerated man's capacity to help himself; but when the powers of fate seemed all engulfing, he prayed.

Otzi's final prayer

There were moments now with greater frequency, with each passing day, when earth, sky, seemed to move more freely, easily, without him. What this meant he did not know, only that the dawns preceding, and the dusks following, appeared to get along better of their own, with no interference from him, feeling free from destiny's binding, suffocating nature, replete with sustained pain, but also, longing to remain the whole night through:

I dreamt *I'd seen the vastness of this world,*
*revealed in gleams of mystical, keen thought,*
*perception. But in all its great dimensions,*
*such screaming wonders, it barely claimed*
*the notion, whisper, insignificant within that*
*great, black, utterly blind stillness of mind's*
*calling universe, which I will soon conjoin.*

As alert historians methodically attempt to get at the root causes, the inscrutable reasons we are in this crazy mess, I, neither scholar, scientist, philanthropist, warrior or actor, only a scribe composing in the wilderness, tracing tributaries back to dubious, broadened origins of mind, unruly maverick, no one's humble minion, undisciplined, dreaming, yearning, with pois(ed)(on) pen in deft hand, doing someone else's dirty work, was a herald hollering, "I was at the millennium…" when no one cared; for clearly, identifying and understanding specific reasons were less important, than measuring their effects on us.

Here were the annals of modern ethnic, culture, race, sex and gender strife, witnessed first-hand by one who would never be afraid of newfound ways, despite missing the old. It seems abusers get away with what they can, even more so if you let them, there being sins, but not sinners. Certainly, this treatise is no hagiography as there were no hags to be found… a joke. The story lines present unsound, extreme, unbalanced types, following Freud's lead in studying pathological, rather than healthy, well-functioning subjects. In this way, the abnormal highlights, elucidates, identifies, those behavior patterns and quirks, governing us all, from which we suffer to different degrees. I always cheered for the underdog, even a total scoundrel, for the essence of human beings is the same, their excesses caused by hyperbole hurled about; I can only blame myself, for the only predictable facets of my characters, being unpredictability; have you ever created a love story, mystery, satire, epic, with a narrator not knowing where he is going?

My aim being not to preach, but present, drawing readers to their own conclusions, I do not care about your approbation, reprobation, or masturbation. Speak softly and carry a big dick, T.R. said, the age so confused and twisted I needed to document what occurred, what it was really like, so others after would commemorate the glaring, staggering facts. Was I writing to communicate with the ages, hearing eons of hope in my head, or was this but whiskey laced eavesdropping, my troubled tailing of crass eternity?

The center of the solar system is in my heart. I'm trying to sort the pieces of my existence into coherent meanings. Could it be, there's been something wrong with my brain for a while? Voices of a thousand shades filter slowly though my ears, from past, present, future, luckily not, "the punk with the stutter:"

I got four heads inside my mind

Four rooms I'd like to lie in
Four selves I want to find
And I don't know which one is me
(The Who, *Quadrophenia*, "Four Faces," 1973)

Just because I'm paranoid does not mean they're not out to get me; despite loud distractions, it is finally time to get to the crux of this dark matter. We were perpetually reinventing ourselves, forever changing, constantly taking the first big steps all over again; perhaps a bit of paranoia is necessary for poetry. I'm tired of scoundrels ruling me. My tale is born of anger, nursed by spite, shared in hate and intolerance.

Would I ever sell my country out? Having never seen action in any of the nation's hostilities, I say, in a minute, I'm only waiting for the right offer from some rogue intel agency. This is the saddest of capers in which we spy on, then blame and deny it to, each other. If that's loyalty in the information age, then it's time to look out for *numero uno*; as Rick says, in *Kasbah-Blanca*: "I stick my neck out for nobody."

If Vietnam taught anything, it was to never die for your country, because then you're dead, especially in a non-declared war (conflict), for when leaders and public opinions inevitably change, you'll stay dead, and most probably forgotten, if not vilified, in an updated, historical revision, for war crimes. Better to remain a prone snake, than a chess pawn bound for the heap, respecting my process, if not the decision.

Why should society be on the hook if fools play army? In an opening scene of *Patton*, the film's crafty namesake, General George S. Patton, addressing a sea of troops about to be hurled onto World War II's front lines, in North Africa and Europe, warns: "Now, I want you to remember that no bastard ever won a war by dying for his country; he won it by making the other poor dumb bastard die for *his* country." *

I'm cataloging views I don't dare utter in public, or my everyday life, the moments I can't readily bear coming out, opinions, ideas, modes of thought, culture and civilization, moving so fast these days, that I am gradually becoming an anachronism, relic, from another, distant age, in my own life. I was a mid-century baby, grounded, evenhanded, less inclined to the poles; some days I awoke to dreaming I was a Nazi storm trooper, others a fellow traveler spy, some days a KKK devotee, and others an antifa thug; reactionary nihilist, revolutionary malcontent, now having reached the age of a basket full of ills; even if having descended from a long line of bad hearts, being born on Easter Sunday always imparted luck.

Concurrently I must acknowledge that my heart specialist is an American Jew, my internist, Indian, my surgeon, Nigerian, my gastroenterologist, Mexican American, my ENT, Japanese American, my dentist, Egyptian, my pulmonologist, Persian, my orthopedist, just an Irish, and I love each one for the services generously provided, so due to the steady influence of compassionate, inclusive values, I could not help but adopt the current, multicultural, internationalist health alliances, so as not to be socially ostracized.

If you're curious about me, I will tell you; surely my ancestors, like everyone's, were slaves, so I reject solidarity and collectivism, which prevent free thinkers the right to be wrong. I am an individualist, not a unionist. If liar, racist and bigot are the most-dastardly epithets in America, I will save the trouble by confessing, to being all three. So much for discreet identity assumptions. My father, being a pedigree Nazi, I embraced his inner, racist creed growing up; we were bigots at home, publicly reticent as cover. But don't worry, I don't think any less of us, or myself, for it; I know the real history of slavery and the Holocaust. Funny, but I do not share in outward, collective guilt, over Africans being dehumanized, or Jews being gassed to death, both being historicisms of persecution and victimization, of other epochs.

The Nazi I Knew (College Admission Essay)

My father had the greenest eyes, the same color as that old uniform of his, from the war, a summer field uniform designed to keep cool and dry, in a miserably hot Polish summer. It was flat there, unlike *the Cordillera de los Andes*, where he hid out after the war, and I was born, grew up, until adolescence, exploring the rocky heights, hiking, on horseback, speaking German, I of the things that seemed wondrous due to my inexperience, he of his prewar days in Germany, in the gruff yet educated voice, so jarring, intoxicating, mesmerizing, I had to close my eyes to see its pertinence to my existence. He admitted to having done bad things, only presently, the same countries that warred against him, needed help against communism, so he could come and go as he pleased, but always preferred the isolation of Austral precipices after assignments. If he knew the things were bad, I asked, why did he obey? But there was no answer. Once, he showed me a lock box full of passports, bemoaning at multiple identities granted him in exchange for his soul. Opening a dark blue covered passport, smiling, winking, he pointed to my name, as the bearer; instructing me to always remember it would be in the box, along with a brand-new Social Security card and fake New York City birth certificate, all attesting to my falsified USA citizenship paid for, bought, fixed, as a favor by his Department of State cronies. He said I had a half-sister in Odesa, from a love affair with a stalwart Soviet agent, but never shared their identities. My mother was Chilean, quite dark, a full blooded *Mapuche* Indian; there were photos of her in our home, but no details. Secretive, trusting no one, parceling out bits and pieces of old data and information so no one had it all, my father, smiling guiltily, with a large gap between two front teeth, seemed warm, sensitive, engaging but made it impossible to trust or believe in him. But this is his story: "After losing my beloved, nameless, blond, faceless wife in Poland, to this day, blessed be her spirit and memory, and our innocent baby in Spain, I went mad with grief. Frozen in a direction-less despair, from one moment to the next my whole life fell apart; I could not find the thread that once held everything tight; going forward seemed impossible, but going back not an option, and staying in the present an overwhelming torment. So, I almost killed myself but then I would not have had you, my boy. And yet I never gave up the hope of seeing my baby Aley again, God willing." (It was the only time, *SS* Colonel Otto Waldemar Grawitz cried, but was it really for himself?) "After residing openly for years, in Temuco, the United States CIA called me to assist them in assessing, then restructuring, military interrogation methods, prior to the Korean conflict. I next helped organize the suppressed 1956 Hungarian Revolution, where I met a captivating Red Army officer, a woman whose sister I executed at the camp. She never knew I was her sister's murderer; but uncannily she resembled the young, red headed Rus', beautiful Slav princess I mounted, preserved, in my war time parlor, in that spot reserved for Slavs, next to the chaste Czech priest; and then we had a darling daughter, a half-sister to you. Tragically, her mother was purged, sentenced to the Gulag, in one of those ongoing Soviet (Red Salem Witch) show trials, purposely culling populations, as in imperial times, my exiled daughter raised by unknown grandparents. One day you may meet her, God willing, my boy. I served stints in Cuba (I was too late to kill *Che* Guevara, the traitor to his class), Israel, Bolivia (again hunting down *Che*, who deserved it, that Argie Dr. Pseudo-*Cubano* Scoundrel), England, France and Germany, additionally assisting the Andean juntas with their ever-increasing internal dissension and extremism. As you can see, I have been quite busy these past twenty years. A question you may ask is how your mother captured my heart, so soon after losing my enchanting Slav love. While exploring the *cerros*, farther and higher than anywhere I had ever ventured, losing my way for what seemed forever, I came upon a forgotten, stone-built, urban center concealed in the clouds. Having never heard there were any denizens in these nether regions, as the mist suddenly parted, I rode up the well-trod path, that came out of nowhere, into *Providencia de las Nubes*, a fortress mountain idyll of an abandoned *Mapuche* tribal splinter group; holdouts from government troop campaigns of combat, rape and pillage conducted against them, in the 1870s, and due to extended isolation for almost one hundred years, as purely Indian, as anyone could be. Your mother was a princess, with royal blood in her veins, and was as brown as I am white, and when she first saw me naked, laughed out loud, because I looked like some blue veined mountain spirit. It was as if I had been a *conquistador*, your mother, a promised *La Dorada* desire, and you, our original *mestizo*. We lived amongst them for two years until your mother died in childbirth with what would have been our second child. Then I took you to greatly lower climes, where it's much easier to breathe, including Europe. I have thought long and hard about having shared my European blood line with a native woman, considering my antipathy to Jews, Slavs, Gypsies, and it may seem conflicted, but I was taught to hate Jews by my family and my school, and it is something I cannot, to this day, shake or disavow, despite having a mixed-race son. I have never deprecated indigenous peoples, or their color, per se, mainly Jews, Slavs, Gypsies, as being of lower orders; and then Negroes being the lowest, because I was raised that way, I was desensitized to it, and did not know otherwise; but with respect to Slavs, I should confess the woman I loved was Ukrainian, and as such my second daughter is half Slav; I love her the same as you, or my misplaced Aley." I also love my father the same, whether he did the bad things, or not. But I don't believe what is written about him climbing through nasty political propaganda ranks, then becoming the monster William Tell of Auschwitz, responsible for hundreds of thousands of deaths, managing extermination camps with an efficiency that was notorious within certain bestial circles. Simply said, that was not the Nazi I knew, as the one I knew was dutiful (not delirious), humble (not haughty), kind (not cruel), having witnessed, firsthand, loving (at least, in our immediate family). I can only wonder if any of himself was passed down to me, through blood, genes or nurture, whether any of his prejudices and predilections were inherited, for me to fulfill. I know I have his coldness, could there be some compassion? He did the best he could to mold and raise me, so God bless you, my Father, and farewell, wherever you dwell, escaped Nazi war criminal, the Archer of Auschwitz, fantastic warrior of dubious plots, grand, empty strategies.

As my progenitors faded away, some time ago, I tend to brood about the many splendid conversations I would enjoy with them the questions I would indulge of their precious knowledge, on subjects far and wide, were they still around; however, I must recall that just as most kids have zero interest in listening to, or putting up with, their elders for advice, during my own years growing up I avoided most dictums, analyses, explanations, offered by my inept begetter, such being parenthood's subtle, stabbing, ironies.

At my Miami, FL, connection to Hardfart, CT, a big, Confederate flag draped on an airport diner's wall, immediately reminded me of the Nazi flags, banners, placards, displayed in Father's parlor. I observed black people for the first time, stunned by their contrast against the sun, despite my being multi-racial, as well. I was considered white, as before 1970, there was no category defining Hispanic ethnicity. I hid my name, as it was not politically correct to be the son of an escaped Nazi war criminal on campus.

In attending The Choke School, I brought only my story with me, as years passed my inner terror being that much to my shock and chagrin, I waited too long to begin; in the meantime, some unknown upstart now inspired, completing my tedious tome; in terms of black swan events, such qualifying as an upset.

Preppies usually led hedonistic, moneyed lives, in which every whim of sophisticated urge, temptation, was indulged and satisfied at a still rather inexperienced age; you know the self-possessed type. One of the problems associated with these privileges was developing grown-up neuroses and obsessions before being ready, thus provoking excessive interest, approval, in oneself, and the inability to share in truthful relationships with meaningful others. With this set, everyone was a convenient, useful, future contact:

> Let me tell you about the very rich. They are different from you and me.
> (F. Scott Fitzgerald, "The Rich Boy," 1926)

As a Third World teen, in a blazing, impersonal, fast paced country, I was curious where I fit in, taking photographs of Connecticut, drawing out contrasts in light, shading, subject matter; evoking the certain satisfaction in getting it down, capturing the moment, storing it, putting it away, projecting it as needed; O fabled *camera obscura* of old, sealed box, pinhole, lens, imaging the hermetic chambers of my heart:

> ...and the soul which has seen most of truth shall come to the birth as a
> philosopher, or artist, or some musical and loving nature...
> (Plato, *Phaedrus*, 370 BC)

Haunting Whale College in the mid-1970s, for a B.A., Philosophy, Marxist Whalies proselytized dated, progressive preparatory school "Bohemian Rhapsody" palp to save us from our capitalist, hedonist selves; comfortably, nonchalantly tapping into *Das Kapital's* central core of wealth accumulation and resulting class prerogative: Mommy and Daddy's bank accounts and credit cards; I witnessed ideals trumped by conspicuous leisure, consumption, with membership, acceptance trumping them all. There being many of opposing views, their overarching similarity the comfort assumed; Adam Smith's devotee simpletons proclaiming the market objectivity of an invisible hand, eerily goosing them in the night; comfortably substituting mercantilism's control, subjectivity and despoiling with uncannily similar conditions under the next century's free market panics, monopolies and trusts, as they manage to preserve the same lazy laissez faire class advantage. How was I to know the difference between real knowledge seeking truth, versus using trick words in being right, as sophists espoused? I joined in believing the world was mine for the taking, though my lack of old money, new money, any money, correct social standing, prevented my membership in a secret society. So, to compensate for my societal shortcomings, I adopted a witty pseudonym, a new persona, as far back as my prep school days, prior to the college admissions process, before setting foot on any campus, T. (Tiddly) Awdry Winks coming into life, afterthought to an absent, undocumented, indiscernible past, a Dutch swindler's alias worthy of intrigue, even respect, in the Ivy

L. So, after rounds at Rudy's, a bit jocular for being a "cunning linguist, *mi obscuridad de Mapuche*;" a Jewish classmate stumping me, "Can you speak Jewish?" indiscreetly answering "No but my old man spoke Nazi;" from then on always cautious of what I said under any influence. Along with an inherited disposition, I was a cold debater, with an ease surprising even to me, holding for the efficacy of capital punishment, as just deserts for evil done against innocents, wondering why liberal American Jews were against the same, while condoning Israel's authoritarian reprisals against Arab and Palestinian people. The unexplained duality, of being against the death penalty as a moral, socio political or sovereign tool, but condoning summary judgement, when ills beyond endurance were suffered, to avoid any trial at all; where was redemption, absolution, forgiveness, salvation in such codified, just rubrics of retribution?

> The argument for:

> When, at the latter stages of civilization, feeble beliefs jeopardize Justice, the unfortunate results are a corruption of humanity and society, of which Nietzsche warned, regarding abolishing capital punishment, due to more modern forms of compensation supplanting that primordial requirement for blood revenge. What kept us primitive, savage, human, was perpetual subjection to those primeval laws of vendetta and hatred, the condemned already lost, unredeemable, after defiling granted *Karma* for ever more, never to be lamented, having already ruined their god given shot at earth.

The heavy inhumanity of capital punishment was the horror of the condemned, at his own death watch; the anticipation of death after sentence, being a period of unshakable doom, worse than death itself; and the self-degradation, and moral ruin, of anyone associated with enforcing such heinous, ghastly penalty.

> The argument against:

> I don't believe that the hundreds of executions I was responsible for prevented even a single murder," he explained. "The Death penalty solves nothing. (Albert Pierrepoint, Britain's official hangman between 1941 and 1956)

There were all types at Whale, many attending to learn how to make money, while not really needing it. In early spring of senior year, several of my most obnoxious classmates wore three-piece suits, looking already like the grim business wonks they would one day become, rushing off to confidential meetings with Goldmen Sucks and Spamford Business School, before I even conceived that such places existed. I did not realize then that these individuals already had their lives mapped out for them, as if the wealth they had been easily, comfortably, emotionally borninto, was not their end, but another steppingstone to future social, material successes, masked as etiquette, while really lording it over everybody else. It was really a case of their belonging, from the time of their birth to a club that automatically gave them access to privileges the rest of us had no clue about or understanding of in terms of our possible futures. In some very rare cases there were disavowals of wealth, its sources, uses and outcomes, only scarcely. As an example of the sweet, pampered existences of the spoiled, old boys, the Vanderpills had endowed the residential college named after them, on the Mold Campus, on condition that a penthouse suite, vast apartment, always be at the disposal of a matriculating family scion, to remain maintained, polished, at the ready, otherwise, in the state of sealed up, suspended animation, awaiting the change of generations.

I cannot hold it against the benefactor of Whale, wily Elihu, for being a slave owner, as most capitalists of that era did similarly, and as such he was no better or worse than them. As the word, chattel, derives from cattle and slaves, along with livestock and Equus, were equity transferrable between owners, it is of no surprise that having been brought up in such fashion, and lacking the imagination to change, with much of the wealth of the times based on enslaved labor, Whale undoubtedly benefited from that trade. Perhaps better to focus on what Elihu did with his lousy loot rather than how he earned it, as with other philanthropists of past and present, otherwise, all great beneficences, every bequest to Whale, would be tarnished by the sources of their origins, for, paraphrasing Balzac, most great fortunes have a dark past.

After years of shutter-bugging it dawned on me that pictures had no spark, no life, even fearing that my image taken, cheapened me, captured my soul, in China photography disparaged as The Art of Regret; assuming duties as my own *Paparazzo*, self-serving, self-preserving, self-exposed, frenetically chasing down every lead to savor my lens, desiring profound expansion beyond the *ineluctable modality of the visible*: words keeping time, as it passes in its inexorable measure, circular, dynamic, alive, components holding experience without freezing it: as pictures, eliminating vibrant breathing, ever changing flow; excusing faulty atmospherics for obscuring clear views and sexy close ups, keeping me from the scoop. Ultimately reaching the conclusion, that though pictures could infuriate, some words were additionally, inflammatory, I chose opportunities to incite immediate verbal retribution on those who uttered them, for words, sometimes sweet, oftentimes charged with scorn, were the enticements of all love and war.

> Greek goddesses gently, whispering in your ear?
> God d***** Greeks, clamoring for all to hear.

Later in a more heightened, conceptual phase, I went into advertising, believing in the message and the supposed goodness, generosity, of its creators, thinking, *these mirages directed all of society, as well as padded the exclusive bottom lines of the mass-producing leaches of the world.* If I was too trusting, I was more than willing to look away from the madmen's desires to control our everyday experience, and as answerable for its greater impact. I relied on advertising as much as on the weatherman and tooth fairy, which is to say I was on my own, as we all seem to be in an existential whirl of corporate manipulation.

Advertising ruined what it touched, especially politics, as evidenced by phony claims before elections. Rising to a position of senior cocktail buddy for glad men reaping the benefits of an addictive society, I ended up an isolated, sad man of that profession, pursuing a life of leading senseless millions wearing rose colored glasses down narrow shaded streets, to fawning identification with fame, fortune, celebrity endorsements, brand recognition, becoming my very version of oblivion, practicing crowd psychology, dictating tastes to eager masses, with some catchy tunes, jingles, ditties, yada, yada, yada, now reciting exclusively to myself, copy privately composed for an inner ear, preserving words from becoming trite captions, slogans, announcements, headlines, propaganda, supplied for prosaic purposes, so here's why.

Having marched to the right of Attila the Hun, a polar vortex descended heavily upon my soul, and one Good Friday I renounced the rude, right-wing views I was weaned upon, hearkening to the openness of my Liberal Arts education, struggling for more grounded evenhandedness, to be less given to the poles.

Fulfilled

Books selected off the shelf, broken-in, faded covers opening to creased title pages, beginnings found once more, breath of life again reclaiming every well used leaf, volumes thusly utilized, fulfilled, their distinct life's adventure shared anew, preferring the company of my shaded storytellers and expired poets, to those accessible, tangible, mixing-up the characters from different scenes and chapters, each amalgamated as that allegorical type, an avatar of purity, reaching back through recorded consciousness.

Midnight reader

I am a constant traveler through time,
conversing here with thoughts that mirror mine.
Now bivouacked with bygone souls held, each
appointed formerly, through deeds and speech.
The days and centuries uncovered, gone,
and epochs imagined mine, until swift dawn,
my dream machine, this opus, utters modes
of past designs, until its covers close.

"And where the world within these words?" you crow,
"Just random quotes from those now gone, laid low."
But I would not suppose my being so bright,
to keep myself from drifting to the light,
and once the sun sets, yet again, shall play
the night with fire and hear of what they say.

My enthusiasm to recite great works manifests as random communication with ancient, trusted friends, for their erudition brings the collected wisdom of ages, which I am free to approve of, or disagree with, but most importantly, connects my weak work to theirs, even as a faint shadow to the blazing sun itself. Besides which their worst stuff seems smarter than my best, so why try to beat them at their own game? Lastly, sometimes the most provocative ideas are best seen in their original forms, for Platonic scrutiny, wise words pacing stories forward, with heroes hovering around my thoughts, Hermes leading the way.

Exiting advertising I entered the journalistic profession, believing my experience fooling, tricking, the public into buying products they did not need, in a sense creating stories people wanted, prepared me to report stories people needed, with lofty notions, that the public at large deserved for me to set them all straight, fulfilling needs for true, real news. Believing I was making a difference I followed current and global events from the outside in. But after a while it wasn't enough, I needed to bring readers the dire story from the inside out, with all the information, facts, figures and behind-the-scenes grit to fulfill my duty to them. The solution was to provide a picture that would give the whole account, with one view: the entire action in a single frame. I was back to being useful again, a modern sorcerer conjuring up the climate to newfound purpose, crafting a novel from shared history synthesized with an internal reality.

This is the introduction to a book I started, about my existential angst at the juncture of two millennia:

Awaiting an Individual of the New Era

At the millennium there occurred small changes, which mattered greatly,
having profound, lasting impacts, such as genetic experimentations, after
large ones, that in the end, mattered not at all, such as political elections.
This was the state of a fifty-year cusp between epochs, I will now neatly
try to describe. If only fragments survive it was well worth the sweat and
toil of infinite remembrance, laid down as a systematic jumble of notions,

reactions, shattered dreams in the wilderness of experience, toward better worlds, than the one we have submitted to. There were many discoveries which, though not always for the common good, helped some feel better for a while, but these had to do with my idea of the good, not Everyman's two-bit definition, which was here today, gone tomorrow. For instance, I believe the greatest good to be man attaining his infinite potentiality, but others think it is distinctly about men having the same opportunities. But "from each according to his ability, to each according to his needs!" isn't a realistic option, as it totally discounts the risks and chances that are life. And to use literary terms of constant meaning, we were tyrannized by the vainglory of our leaders, whom we elected against our better natures, to show us ways out of self-made "Sloughs" to "Delectable Mountains," but who were unconscionably, unaccountably, fatally detoured along the way. Perhaps in their bold steps toward a forecasted future, they were bravely, gravely misguided. Now these politicians, the "Little-Enders," as well as "Big-Enders," and everybody in between, had each, to a fault, misplaced, lost, something we humans possessed as innate, given, instinctual, since the genus *homo* was fashioned, which organized society had suppressed and eliminated, i.e., our animal spirits; refashioned into tensionless, puffy automatons of contemplation and compassion, instead of being men and women of action and decisiveness, as we were born to be. And such self-destructive trend was directly related to the Classical Greek objection to democracy: that it was a rule of the rabble, a dictatorship of the basest of majorities, over a well-bred minority; and a cowardly appeasement to the various marginalized and disaffected groups in society which collectively comprised, the rancorous and vengeful masses. In a fatuous, demagogic move to portray themselves as more sympathetic to quirky, self-centered, insatiable voters, the feel-real party had gradually become as feckless, as a feel-good party. In this way the body politic lost, in one fell swoop, the dynamic intensity of opposites that nature imposed, to maintain goals of evolution, progress and development. Because as Kant and Hegel said, thesis requires antithesis to produce a synthesis, or stated more lyrically:

You can sail on a ship by yourself,
Take a nap or a nip by yourself.
You can get into debt on your own.
There are lots of things that you can do alone.
But it takes two to tango, two to tango ... etc.
(Al Hoffman and Dick Manning, "Takes Two to Tango," 1952)

All *politicos* looked *loco*, the rest of us attentive, patiently awaiting a new man or woman to appear and put down this universal, pathetic sameness to utter rest, relying solely upon merit as their means to advancement, an Individual of the New Era. At the millennium we stopped for the signal that had always come before. Time stood still while we wound the clock, then a new measure of a thousand years was started, each day we awoke.

My forties were forever freaked, in an employment carnival, a career being only what you, as a unit of labor power, no more important to a boss, than depreciating machines or basic materials, made it; entire lives watching fat cats bail out other fat cats, after having been installed by them to begin with; and the networks beating their heads against the walls to bring out stories, which no one believed, because each reporter had toed their corporate parent's single party line for so long, that now when they actually told the truth, even the party line, no one believed; well then, enough of their planting stories to benefit their old candidates, idols, charities, we had had enough, the hollow press now a lame, ruptured duck; and as a quirky snippet, if the right produces so few great artists, why does the left produce so many bad ones? The rallying cry of the left, a once vaunted, *liberté, égalité, fraternité*, now retrograded to a nit picking disorder of diatribe, complaints, and making big impressions by broadcasting nonsensical accusations; and the right no better, but possibly worse, for professing axiomatic hate against racial and ethnic types, ruled by magical pseudo-science, as much or worse a movable feast as myth, superstition or religion; the left as well as the right wanting each to agree with (n)either while I expect no one to agree with me. With all this discord, of left and right, what's a man to do? Pay my bills, I want to pay my bills, please; Western tradition come full circle, "Life, Liberty and the pursuit of Happiness" defining every thought, motion, influence, now whipped back on themselves; the same essences threatening a cataclysm, with a sinister entrant fomenting disruption, discord, destruction, in the name of personal choice and freedom.

It may have been only a coincidence, or I may be psychic, because I was pondering this amusing quote, by the most famous writer in the world, who managed to mock himself with a self-deprecating critique:

> ...[that] a man of good social standing, should descend to the level of a lot
> of common scribblers who irritated him and made him angry.
> (Leo Tolstoy, *Anna Karenina*, 1874 – 1876)

when the phone rang with my Rus' chief wanting an update on Lilly's mama still incarcerated at Gitmo. She had recently become focused upon this story, identifying with Lilly's loneliness and abandonment, considering that the latest rumors made Lilly out to be an abusive harasser of homeless migrants legally occupying public property. I had a feeling this lead would resurrect my career, after years of dormancy.

"Use your influence with Lilly, to get Slay Magazine this story, before Pimple.com does. We've heard they're holed up in their Baja California beach compound. Your independent journalist status will gain you direct admittance but let me know if you require assistance with any drunk, Crazy Ivan sentries."

"Sure, Chief." I never addressed Ottoline by her name, thinking of her as a sister; always Chief, no chit chat, nothing more. "And due to the sensitivity and urgency of the matter, I shall apply twice my usual fee, bonus, plus expenses." Little did she know that earlier I had contracted for similar public relations work with Warren Bros. Inc. that would combine nicely with a regular assignment for the news service. As an independent contractor, I saw nothing wrong with double dipping clients, with the same subjects.

"Ms. Abraham, I understand there is valuable information you do not want made public at stake. I shall fix this delicate matter, problem, thing on your behalf, with stinging counter measures against that child advocate, Patricia (P) Diddy. I will be in Baja tomorrow debriefing your perturbed studio stars. So due to the sensitivity and urgency of the matter I shall apply twice my usual fees and bonus, plus expenses."

And due to their desperate needs, neither bothered with a sly retort, regarding the excessive fixes. Each hung up, confident that their problem would no longer weigh them down with failure, *because anything goes down there, like when William S. Burroughs mistakenly shot his wife, as a lunatic William Tell.* If poets see the world for what it ought to be, and historians for what it is, exploiters see it for the taking.

Euphemisms utilize irony, sarcasm, humor, calling an over spun *oeuvre*, light romance, war, a freedom struggle, anarchy, demonstrations, delinquents, activists, wetbacks, undocumented migrants, execution, capital punishment, lack of health insurance, liberty, high temple priestess, librarian, mainly guesswork, scientific polls, race quota, inclusion, self-segregation, diversity, popularity contests, political elections.

My being independent also meant I would never vote for anyone if they were running, nor reside in any countries with mandatory voting, nor identify with any pols; I only ID with me, desperate for a change, hoping losers win, if polls are scientific, science has a long way to go, too sophisticated, cosmopolitan, to vote; refusing a complicity in any future crimes against our street, world, humanity, less my original, scathing degradations blossom into a rage at, and resentment reciprocated by, the critics; all my voting never making a lick of difference, and I would never vote for a billionaire, I'm not a fan, nor a partisan.

So, even the monster online networking service Fakebook will never truly compete with my intentions. Mine is a different connectivity for this new uneasy age, one whose reclaimed leaves and lays might be read from beginning to end, as easily and poignantly as finish to start, the obscure, yet relevant jottings of an impatient bimillennial. Now, it's my turn to discourse, a yowl come up from the deep bowels of us all. For I was there at the millennium, and no one better to tell the tale, a chronicle of doom, despair, obliteration, then a distant light of reprieve and forgiveness. Such was the inescapable collision of one waning era, ballasted heavy with pent up, exhausted fury, into another, fresh faced and open to infinite possibility, and me, a witness transforming remembrances of sin and glory, into memories for posterity.

But I was merely a waning echo, hoping for distinction through the roaring background noise. Perhaps others would annotate the fast-paced events from their own perspectives, as different people, observing a broad, sweeping landscape, see it in their own way. That's all right, at least I did my best not to favor any single point of view, but visualized all adequately, attempting to show things clearly, as they were, with as little of me involved, as much as I could help it. Such was my solitary task, perhaps not in the tradition of the journalist in *Roman Holiday*, suppressing his exclusive story and surreptitious photos of the princess heroine, my inclination being to open Pandora's Box up wide, to the scrutiny of the world.

Regarding omniscience, my first-person narrator challenges God, while believing in Him, presenting in certain chapters, sublime scribbles from a fitful state, shifting to third-person narrative in many others, including those where he was not directly there to witness the incidents, because after all, it is my story.

As a declaration of objectivity no one is paying for this book. I have no publishing contract, though for full disclosure, even a restrained offer would be welcome. This is an unencumbered, abridged version; despite its brevity, the energy and urgency of the more authoritative original, have been preserved; with a full bibliography and notes included, in a separate volume of the complete edition, available on order.

Who will publish my book? (Open Letter)

Who will publish this book? Who will review it or listen? If from time
to time I assume a character's guise or they adopt mine, I'm really neither
white, black, red, yellow, brown, out, pan, poly, queer, trans, transphobic,
liberal, religious, agnostic, pro-gun, anti-gun, civil rights marcher, patron,
supremacist, community advocate, statesman, welfare queen, millionaire,
artist, socialite, proletariat, minister, revolutionary, businessman, investor,
charlatan, internet darling, criminal, undocumented person, club member,
handsome, disfigured, handicapped, terminally ill, dog, cat hater, famous,
infamous, celebrity, mystic, spokesman for anything, or anyone under the
sun, stars or moon. I'm none of these things, not a member of a protected

class or secret society, or a believer in a better world, just an observer of this one. And who will give me the time of day, take me at all seriously? For whoever reads me enjoys my fellowship. Only how shall I ever gain the strength and fortitude required to revise, edit and proof such a work? it seems like a Sisyphean task, so I ask again, who will publish this book?

Who will read this book? (Letter to myself)

Possibly no one, as for the last twenty years, the only reading occurred in superficial fits and starts of periodic gazing of a computer idiot box, with the approximate levels of concentration required to watch cartoons, and this between frequent snacking in the kitchen, numerous interruptions via text and cell, and that pure disruption of gazing longingly in the mirror. Where is the focus, the dedication to a single idea brought to order, much less one exhumed by an up till now easy, silent, student of folly? Could media observers find interest in pouring over anything besides celebrity gossip, political diatribe or character assassination, perhaps the low brow solution being to illustrate comic books from the junk flying about in the atmosphere? And in any case who will demand integrity if there is none?

My human progression

mercurial nature
infant dreamer
fearless optimist,
idealist pragmatist,
fearful pessimist, cynic
dotard screamer

What's Fame? a fancied life in others' breath.
A thing beyond us, even before our death.
(Alexander Pope, "An Essay on Man," 1733 – 1734)

The unfamiliar chroniclers of old rarely put their lives at risk, otherwise how would they have survived, to tell their tales; perhaps if the cowardice of anonymity kept them from fully living, it also kept them living fully, observant but not participant. As nature has no moral constructs it was hard to describe my life as good or bad, or myself as success or failure. Everything was as it was, an eternal limbo, a brutal, somber silence, deafening in its reach. I don't know where events will lead; last Easter's pageants were a dream, leading to eschewing interest in cash, career and reputation, carrying on a random voice in the dark. My lofty aim including, "...a description of the people, the manners, the amusements, the ways of Mansfield Park..." using words with old meanings, before the newspeak of the present, ephemeral as a passing whim, if I spied you on the street, as a muckraker of last resort, I would be sure to tawdry wink:

*Homo sum, humani nihil a me alienum puto.*
[I am a human being, I consider nothing that is human alien to me.]
(Terence, *Heauton Timorumenos [The Self-Tormentor]*, 163 BC)

*Footnote

Well said. (Author)

# 12. WOMB OF THE STARS

Ma Ma, Where's my Pa? (Republican slogan ridiculing Democrat Grover
Cleveland and his possible love child, Presidential Campaign, 1884)

She knew that men usually closed their eyes when kissed, so she kissed him hard and placed a dagger
deep into his back, aware that hers were full, evil lips, deserving slow burning in hell forever more, this
betrayal a final test of fealty to the *FART* guerilla band she entrusted her worthless existence to, prior
to direct passage to California, dangled by the dastardly *coyotes* possessing her newly lost soul. She slept
uneasily, an urgent God only briefly in her pocket, insatiable, perverse handlers provisionally placated.

That was Willamina Hernan, now Willi, as a desperate Third World immigrant (remember?), presently
a U.S. resident, reformed killer, prominent Hispanic American, TV *barrio* bully; pro: himself of course,
immigrants, George Soros, Isidora Green; shehe, female into male, dating females, but still attracted to
males; anti: Jews, Catholics (as a trans, Christianity renounced her), blacks, females; homophobic, with
no pity; success driven, achieving, after years, still terrified of immigration agents, lurking in shadows.

Our star-crossed lovers, partners, Adam & Eve, engaging in new skirmishes if not with each other, then
with themselves, each becoming a Miss Lonelyhearts, with their own pop fan club from opposite poles.
What follow are two letters picked at random although not randomly sent from Lilly and John B. Sayer:

*Valentine's Day*
*Anonymous (Lilly)*
*Dear Miss Lonelyhearts (Willi),*
*How could this happen to me? I had a husband I was married to, poof he*
*disappeared into a mist. Please let me know what you think of this story.*
*Our romance was a whirlwind, but after having kids it was not the same,*
*each of us heading in different directions, but let me get back to the start.*
*After our expulsion from the Garden of Eden, the only things we walked*
*out of there with were the few threads on our backs, and the huge, shiny,*
*crisp, juicy, red apple I picked off a tree, so ancient its drooping branches*
*held past proofs, future promises, of good and evil, in ready fruit I could*
*not resist sharing with him; a willing bite making complicit a foretold fall*
*from grace commencing the next great chapter of our exposed existences,*
*exile followed by cohabitation, as common law man and wife (because if*
*marriage was impossible, celibacy was lonely), avoiding further religious*
*sanction of self-sanctioned vows, to last until we had children as shall be*
*told. How typical a couple we seemed, so commonplace yet incoherently*
*bizarre, beyond normal conceptualizing or comprehending, as to sexual*
*appetites, signals, responses, so twisted, confused, even muddled, making*
*love became, with all the cross directives given off, reacted to, crosses of*
*crosses, and crosses of crosses of crosses, those reacted to, ad infinitum...*
*When our proto heroic selves met back in paradise, we never conjectured*
*we would remain together, even know each other, eighteen years after our*
*struggles to get ahead and succeed, in this strange, empty wilderness of a*
*new country. After declaring our liberty, for the hundredth time, we let it*
*slip, that we had surreptitiously set up screen tests at studio and network,*
*occasions during which neither of us did well, having never mastered the*

*language, but thereupon, attending intensive English classes at the local night school prepared us for stardom, and in one year, we spoke as well as natives. The next time we auditioned we aced them, each obtaining a low, entry level job at first. We believed it would assist our careers if we got hitched, to present an allied front to a hostile word, as well as start a family. In a short time, we were married in a Roman Catholic church by a rogue priest, with imam and mullah attending for my sake, though their presence itched my scars. I felt that our union was to be blessed by God, recognized by His angels. Soon I played a big part in a movie, because I was eager to disrobe and the star, whom I subsequently replaced, was not. A little nudity goes a long way. My husband found a spot on the evening news, reporting from the* barrio, *knowing it would be a launch to one day having his reality TV program. The single common gripe we shared was that he was as beholden to his boss, as I was to mine, on the deepest of professional as well as personal grounds, both overlooking all drawbacks when Warren Bros. checks arrived, in bounteous manners, until our bank accounts had more than we could ever spend. That huge wealth marked the start of my husband's philandering. We had each managed to harvest as well as cryogenically prepare enough reproductive residues, precious bodily fluids, anticipating our preternatural, otherworldly, yet all so real, transformations, irrevocably altering us. Rent A Womb, that surrogate to the stars, carried the in vitro fertilized embryos through to term, and then abruptly, children appeared (after finding the right formulas), with steady frequency as the family rose to be a universally spotted constellation, and m e, to that exalted, heavenly place, as Universal Earth Sky Mother. But as the kids kept coming, our roles, the relationship, faded; I became more interested in my rising career and he started with the roving eye again, as when we first met, until I managed to distract him from such competition. But truth be told, the competition, so substantial, used cheap allurements to disrupt our marriage, dragging my mate into a fog of sexual stupor. It was not that he could not get it up at all, he could not get it up for me. I was relieved by his new predilections because I was happily left alone. Finally, we acquired P\*\*\*\*\*\*, our Mt. Olympus, for a song, fixed it up to its former glory, and began a steady program of lavish entertaining of all the greater and lesser deities we now comingled with, on this blocked out life stage. "We're not on the same page," I said, over and over to him, to no effect. But we covered up these splits with endless Great Ratsby type frolics. And as if carrying on in the U.S. was not enough, we purchased a beach bungalow in Baja California, for millennial mischief. Our lively Hollywood lifestyle was perfect for immense alcohol imbibement, and to innumerable shots of* tequila, aguardiente, *bourbon; we were the lives of infinite parties, consuming not only copious bottles but our very souls, as well. To that was added a dependence on every drug, which molded our milieus. He was not the best influence on my behavior, there were some tensions, and then my fast living led to an unfortunate but well publicized incident: One of Tinseltown's most alluring, highest grossing stars AWOL from Hollywood, "after a day of binging, then deranged, wandering high* sierras *high all night long, strung out of her mind on downers, coke and*

*booze," as per confidential sources; that was two years ago; what should I do after last year's feature film triumph, leading my greatest comeback?*
*Sincerely,*
*A Lonely Reader*

A very needy reader has a deep-seated problem, thought Miss Lonelyhearts; what should I say in reply?

*Valentine's Day*
*Anonymous (John B. Sayer)*
*Dear Miss Lonelyhearts (Willi),*
*I know it's not my place to do so, but I can't help criticizing someone I've worked with, and have helped immensely, professionally. Please help me. When he and his partner materialized out of nowhere, at their coming out fête (me inappropriately rolling joints in their presence), they were* nada, *transient nobodies. We helped them learn English, paying for classes at the night school, providing entry level positions, not because they merited them but as they fit the demographics we were trying to fill; nevertheless, there was talent there to work with. He was a certain popular semblance of the street type, and she was the perfect action hero, personified. It was not that they were particularly attractive, or even sexy, but they had those Everyman qualities we all crave to see portrayed on screen. All systems a go, in terms of their trajectories, they had an incredible ten-year run in their rise to success, starting with Adam and Eve characterizations on a live show, when everything they touched turned to gold; until about that time they purchased the beach bungalow in Baja California, in millennial mischief, incredibly spotlighting running fountains spring fed with bubbly champagne, including all night revelries, raves, replete with open orgies, onanism. But that night at the Motion Pictures Awards Dinner, his wife a no-show, surely, egged on by him (who also, by the way, was responsible for supplying her with all the drugs she craved), me staring out, into unlit seat rows hoping to randomly spot my mad starlet, that strange sensation of mismatched identities, perhaps incognito in sharp, black tuxedo* burqa, *as there were finely knitted woolen styles, for formal wear, that were now the rage. After such stupid stunts my boss and I suffered major anxieties; we surmised these new stellar bodies would escape a studio's gravity, but for how long should galaxies bear bad behavior, before jettisoning stars? And that was two years ago; what should we do, considering 48 Hours to Mecca, filmed last year, is leading the leading lady's greatest comeback?*
*Sincerely,*
*A Lonely Reader*

How should one react to such admonitions, from a total stranger, wondered Willi, before a liquid lunch.

Having lived publicly demonstrating the adage, that celebrities are just like everyone else, it came as no revelation when they became a true Hollywood power couple, in a style not only, of the screen icons of the silent era, but also, of the latter studio bosses of more modern times. While firmly upholding a one man one woman for all time rule of love they would do it their own way with zero regard for traditional sexual or gender norms, origins, organs or forms; with nothing about them kept immutable, save their complete obsession, regard, love for one another; and all this considering that after eighteen years, how can you keep from straying if not also hating each other just a little bit? each side claimed to cooperate, but given the chance to go ahead completely on their own, he sought the sensual, and she the acclaim. This was the reason Lilly had taken a break from her husband, avoiding the afternoon audience with an old journalist acquaintance, despite clear benefits for them, as had once resulted from the Fixer's help; Willi himself acknowledging that lately, he had not been paying the attention to his wife, she deserved.

The surly host for this strategic chat, would be the journalist's fond nemesis from the kidnapping caper, for whom, any humanity expressed toward The Yellow Kid of old, was merely the remnant, vestige, of a higher self, that was now damaged goods, Willi Herman, L.A. activist *par excellence*, people's man in the trenches, breakout producer of a new genre of reality television shows, advocating for free speech, LGBT, immigration and minority rights, as well as a prime victim of his worst excesses. As a talking head/ news anchor, reviled screeching parakeet, chattering up opinions to bird-less chirping TV chicks, the irony of his now being under police and media scrutiny was not lost upon him, as a recent episode delineated to a worshipful audience, why politics was the only legal, bare-knuckle contest lasting, and how in his early, in-your-face, progressive days, despite a recent polish to his crown, he was known as something of a civic braggart, blackguard, not too polite and at his best, a little rough around the edges.

**Woke Up with Willi** (*Recorded at Beachside Bungalow Studio, Baja Cal.*)

(*Opening segment: program credits overlayed with scales of [in]justice*) Story

*Latest Hoarvard College Crew admissions cheating and bribery scandal, involving stars, celebrities, special informants cooperating with the FBI.*

Story
*George Sake reveals his first non-binary experience occurred as a youth at the Manzanar internment camp for Japanese Americans, during WWII.*

Story
*Democratic National Committee Chair, Wassi Doberman Schlutz(D-Fla.) said Thursday, that she, "shouldn't have used" such charged language to describe the Wisconsin Gov. Swat Stalker's(R) record on women's issues.*

*Special report from the Huffnpuff Post*
*Fems mock man's penis accidentally amputated due to circumcision gone wrong; comparing it with carrot being chopped. What if it was a vagina?*

*Commercial:* Etiquette Eau de Future, *perfume for modern time's genders*

*Feature*
*It is unknown if the following account is related to the recent clandestine disturbances, carried out in the dark of night, by paramilitary forces over the last two years; of course, we will continue to investigate for our fans:*

They did attack our herds: you could have seen a woman pull a calf to pieces as it bellowed alive in her bare hands! (The Bacchae, Euripides, 405 BC)

*Wild, wanton* Bacchantes *attired in panther coverings, swarming from*

*the east. Including cameo appearances by the following stupendous figures:*
*Jeffrey Pipstein as Dionysus (disguised as a Casanova, sylvan conjurer).*
*Sen. Al Kraken as Pentheus (arrogantly ready for a major comeuppance).*
*The Sisterhood of Grace as the* Bacchantes *(at the dames' beck and call).*

*Scene: Feminazi* sparagmos *and* omophagia *frenzy, in the Mold Campus.*

*A large crowd of shouting women, standing shoulder to shoulder, watch a*
*Vanderpill resident get his face pummeled, kicked into the ground. Then*
*his clothes are ripped off; he accepts a sacrificial posture. No one tries to*
*prevent the outcome, but many record the incident on spying cell phones.*
*Later a single witness has the courage to come forward. "We were right there*
*watching him, and there's nothing you can do," he said. "His blood was*
*streaming out, like crazy. He shook a little bit and stopped moving."*

*Opinion*
*WART-TV in Birmingham, AL reported their faithful, originally posted*
*on Fakebook, message that read, "We live in a society where homosexuals*
*lecture us on morals, transvestites lecture us on human biology, abortion*
*doctors lecture us on human rights, and socialists lecture, on economics." As*
*convenient as it may seem to live an antediluvian life, progressivism is the*
*new Main Street, social reformers the new status quo, and activists no longer*
*rebels, but trusty watchdogs of the State. To the left's usual class warfare*
*antics, has now been added women's, civil, LGBT rights, as well as the*
*futures of countless guest workers; that is the power of the people.*

*(Closing segment: program credits overlaid with prison bars and cells)*

Despite Willi's embrace of the leftist cause, socialism would never be compatible with celebrity values, stardom implying its own exclusivity, antithetical to liberalism's open, sharing philosophy. Celebrities' support of leftie causes induced suspicion as to their understanding of the problems, motives, as well as solutions. Because stars can't be radical, it's contrary to the *raison d'etre* of unique narcissism. He and Lilly immediately took heed of Ms. Yael Abraham's directive, to get out of Dodge, head for beach and sand at their ocean side bungalow in Baja California, doing their best to enjoy their limited private time together, but whether Lilly would find Willi attractive again, seemed to be the main uncertainty at hand. After Willi's much heralded, heroic transformation, his coming struggles to find his deeper, masculine voice led to periodic bouts of a severe, emotional distress, until finally getting a handle on the problem; empty, wishful thinking, as it unfortunately always remained a trace bit sweet, lilting, breathless, while hurling liquor fueled *Communist Manifesto* rants at rolling cameras, through newly thick, petulant lips.

The columnist from Slay Magazine had arrived and was waiting patiently in the family room. He was neither historian nor poet, but something vaguely other, scheming self-promoter, opinion vendor, gossip monger, not plant nor animal, an amoeba classified as lower life; but he also had a more visionary side, fancying himself a protojournalist, investigating elusive signals, current turmoil, the conceits of man, at least self-knowing, sensing he would have nothing over on meteorologists, pundits and the tooth fairy.

The news cycle, daunting in its fluidity, the latest Madrid terrorist massacre already going head-to-head with, and losing out to, major HIV outbreaks ruining the porn industry and late-night rock club scene in L.A., NYC, having an origin in bisexual gender benders, possibly getting it shooting smack in Alphabet

City theatre basements or engaging in unprotected sex with kid cross dressers at the Pyramid Club; how tragicomical, romantic libertinism as a metaphor: "Guy de Maupassant, who started triumphant ('I can screw street whores now and say to them "I've got the pox." They are afraid and I just laugh'), died 15 years later in an asylum howling like a dog and planting twigs as baby Maupassants in the garden." So, was it folly to judge people, events, speech of the past by using today's ethical, moral standards, having evolved beyond what our predecessors could have conceived, faulting their errors akin to scolding trip-ups of children, who know no better? Still, evil is evil, it can never be condoned or accepted, requiring atonement; *sick and tired of the self-interested victimization, grandstanding, of those with great wealth, old fortunes, privilege, to suck up sympathy, stir up solidarity, achieving political gains, claiming being taken advantage of to avoid responsibility for inertia*; a small, almost forgotten, part of him still did its best in believing, "But the meek shall inherit the earth..." But what about profiting off one's anger?

The Fixer, alias, the Yellow Kid, in Mexico to consult with our sequestered heroes, began: "You know, I am an investigative reporter." Willi deadpanned, "Some people are in favor of legalized prostitution."

Continuing: "Why do journalists cheapen everything they write about, everything they query, a reverse Midas touch, with superficial research, trite thinking and blather? They don't do their homework, that's the problem; spouting off what they know nothing of. In the end, may I count on you to tell the truth?"

Fixer: "As opposed to what is comfortably and casually accepted I, in contrast, speak words that are not easy to hear, portraying the equal idiocy of hardliners on all sides. Don't listen to me if you refuse, but at your own peril, for I dwell between the poles in a state of inner watchfulness, observing radicals hurl themselves into extremities of internet oblivion. And too many newshounds were in it. It's not twitter, but bitter, not the whole picture, which only I shall portray, and recount for what it is and means to all."

Among those gathering in the bright afternoon hours, at the shore *estancia* in question, was progressive child advocate Patricia (P) Diddy, Ph.D., J.D., founder-president, and thus far sole accepted member, of the international humanitarian group, *Les Enfants Sans Frontičres*, Greenitch, CT, reclining on the sofa, facing the resplendent sun. She was there to make the couple an offer they couldn't refuse to move on.

P Diddy, peripatetic, professional protester, journeyed from hot, civil action to demonstration, allowing, advancing, encouraging herself to get beaten, pounded, almost killed, for the renown and exposure for the cause. What escaped her blindness was that most people hated lawyers to start, then protesters and marchers for being loud, uncivil; and the more demonstrations that occurred, the more average voters turned against them. Although having grown up in poverty, still regarding herself as (more) white, she consciously trained to speak like a regular New Englander, refusing to utter black dialect, considered the origin of the southern accent; bereft at her small breasts, now the size of fifty cent pieces, projecting herself as a braless, sexless exemplar, agitating for women's societal and reproductive rights; the terms, unsexed, unmanned, came to mind, as she voiced impassioned pleas on behalf of her foundation for the globalized, struggling populations on the move; because she had seen the destruction America brought.

"I care for little boys and girls. I'm teaching them to think correctly, and this is what I'm saying: it's too bad that women overseeing their own bodies, means automatic abortions. I have an alternative for all that waste of intentions, effort and souls. If you help me with my foundation, I will get the press off."

Willie was overjoyed: "We will do whatever you require to get these complainers and agitators off our backs. Lilly could not be here tonight, but I can speak for her," then, sardonically: "But if you think for one minute you can raise your kids a certain way versus another, for instance, uber liberal or arch right, as clones of one or the other of you, with high hopes for mitigating hidden impulses, good luck. Your children will never obey what you order, any more than God controlled Adam & Eve, or they their own progeny, or your parents you. When God banished the transgressors, the Garden was spared in the nick of time, just before they would have tasted of another more mysterious, forbidden fruit of immortality."

Fixer: "Fevered support for LGBT and children's issues, by malignant feminists, has all to do with their own dissatisfaction with traditional gender and sexual roles, challenging the patriarchy with an outright hatred of all that is male, but it is a sensibility that has run amok allowing for the wholesale cobbling of walking, talking, breathing puppets in our midst, all in order to rebel, to reject, what used to bind. But the success in removing the sexist from society has led to a very equal, if unsexy life, women and men still reflecting each other, but complements more opposing for close similitude than attracting for rangy differences. When woman was the magnet, man was drawn as blunt metal. Then man himself varied, became semi magnetic, the tested ways, old attractions, newly stretched, defined perhaps as repellent."

P: "Gay rights, the spotted owl, so much done for the sake of lofty principles, such outrage over so few, to the detriment of the many, such being the obsessed liberal ethic, which seeks to eke modernity out of maternity. *Le Club des Femmes, fondee en 1848*, provided my inspiration for a sacred trust, partnership with the Sisterhood of Grace, with whose meek mother superior I am on the most intimate of terms, by sharing certain hereditary Melungeon traits, possibly linked to wagon wandering *Romani*, from India."

Fixer: "Well, as a missionary, not a misogynist, if you solve my clients' problems for their bad behavior and let me handle their public *mea culpa*, I will see to it that your message is broadcast loud and clear."

"Excuse me, Sir Yellow Kid or Mr. Fixer as they are apt to refer to you, you are to do everything agreed to. Only, you are to report directly to me any occurrences tangentially, or centrally related to this affair, which are to be kept under wraps." It was Isidora Green, press lord supreme eavesdropping over muted phone, finally chiming in, to everyone's surprise except Willi's. Could she be funding leftist extremists from a summer beach home, on the Buyreem Shore in Greenitch, the first swanky town on the CT line?

> Gone to the White House, ha ha ha!
> (Democrats' post-election retort, Presidential Campaign, 1884)

"Our conglomerate owns leftist news networks, and rightist news networks. If one side receives less ad dollars due to serial, sexual predations by men or rampages by women, notice the other side benefits by what is known as being hedged against the vagaries of chance, life and truth, in a heartless marketplace. As with Native American casinos, the house always wins, leaving morsels for those too late to the feast. So, I do not care if slippery news favors one cause or another, if it always favors our media monopoly." She was quite smart about her chairmanship, realizing she could succeed with less, not more, than in an earlier CEO role; now busy with crystal courts of love in New Haven, run with machine gun efficiency, even if love was as a transaction between two economic entities with extreme avarice and self-interest. Being a woman in the catbird seat, she had to rebalance equity for her own sex, with that for all others.

"As the last century evolved from, 'A woman must have money and a room of her own if she is to write fiction,' while completely dependent on men, to having it all, involved mother and working stiff, at the same time, as professions ostensibly, brought greater fulfillment, than rearing babies, women gradually, began to believe, they could trade a woman's calling for that of a man. The result was kids dropped off at daycare, at ages when they should have still been at their mother's breast. In terms of their emotional health, these under loved infants were as if malnourished in respect of their bodies, and it was really the fault of an egotistically jacked up culture, prioritizing a woman's personal development, infinitely more than that of her child's. Why couldn't women wait until children were of school age, to get back in the thick of it? Was success in career worth the sacrifice of a family's well-being? What would five, ten or fifteen years be, versus the importance of solid parenting of their own flesh and blood? Would women not have babies at all, too polite to ever utter such alarming words and too gracious to even think them? It is ironic but I am suggesting a slowdown in the quest of super feminism for the sake of the race itself. As society progresses, the feminist persuasion of women will ultimately cause their own demise, due to delayed, or no pregnancies; professional aspirations of today's Western women, should be contrasted to primitive societies, where women are still bound to their natural breeding stages." Loyal Isidora made a last plea. "To all my ultra-gals: do not liberate yourselves out of existence, population replacement is no joke. Equality never meant mimicry, women copying men. Women should be women, men should be men and remain equal: The Sisters of Fervent Grace's new motto shall henceforth be *liberte, dualite, fraternite*; *dualite* for the dual nature in us all, experiencing radical societal roles, and I, Lady, mean it." It was late evening on the east coast when she hung up, so Isidora retired early, wondering where Yael Abraham, her responsible Director, Human Resources, was spending the weekend, and she had a dream:

*Trepidatious, pioneering Ivy League coeds enter Whale Commons Dining Hall, heckled, by horny preppie underclassmen, using numbered grading flashcards; signs announce, "Welcome to the Superwoman Class of '73."*

*Tap Night rages of the Sisterhood of Grace Secret Society, April __, 1970.*

*Green Memorial Library: seductive and treacherous Salome, Mata Hari, Judith dancing a greeting to flutes and tambors in the main entrance hall.*

*Commons: male student dressed as a pregnant woman, pretending to give birth on dining table, with the help of a fake midwife, gloves and sponge.*

*Mold Campus invaded by students dressed as pink dinosaurs, astronauts, Cinderella's stepmother, Chairman Mao offering plates of fried egg rolls.*

*"I was asked to be a famous, fictional character," said a student outside Baybrook College, dressed as blood-stained Lady Macbeth, who asked to remain anonymous. "When [Tap Night's] done for fun, it's really great."*

*Early afternoon: one junior girl donned floor-length, red cape and black mask, outside the Women's Center, riffing memorized Classical quatrains.*

*"I'm reciting Latin, that's all I'll say," with a prep school acquired, ease.*

*Many students in festive attire are busy with the induction, some wearing veiled, masked costumes, of various Kismey Studios animated princesses.*

*A female student dressed as Tricky Dicky, holding up one hand, in a V, a dining hall fork in the other, waits on Chapelle St., smiling at bystanders.*

*"I am not allowed to speak," she mouthed while hunching her shoulders.*

*Further down Chapelle Street, a junior pretending to be Jackie Kennedy passionately intoned, "Don't sit under the apple tree with anyone else but me," two female students dressed as Franciscans begged pedestrians for*

*socks, a young, plucky Isidora performed the most beautiful rendition of
the Mendelssohn Violin Concerto in E minor, virtuosic demon, mastering
horsehair and strings, self-styled Lady, gathering a flock with Gypsy airs.*

*Meanwhile on the Crossed Campus two juniors dressed as Lysistrata and
Clytemnestra, stood near the Women's Table, gesturing with their hands:*

*"We're pretending to use a* deus ex machina *to float over the passersby." Male
studs approached quietly, as strung-out gawkers sauntered away...*

While all this was happening, the west-coast gang was deeply engrossed in hatching a pro-immigration plot offering illegal alien wombs to produce anchor babies, and adoptees with special traits, on request, prepackaged souls, embryos, for sale via a secure network of sisters, fems and friends providing cover.

P Diddy's promise was simple and direct: to allow users to combine their genetic markers, in producing bespoke, DNA fitted children, kids on order, in every color, shading and blend in the possible spectrum of racial and gender variability, with no adherence to any of the prior rules of creation, development, or the moral or societal anxieties that developed from them. These would be tomorrow's modified beings, and the sisters would be their mothers, for they had undertaken ceaseless efforts in altering the original, basic design, established since the beginning of time, two distinct sexes able to combine for pleasureful procreation, and were on the verge of succeeding in the soulful mixing of a third or fourth new version.

Any arguments can be proven, and any lawyer worth his salt can posit his way to win any assertion in a court, because pleas are two sided, and either claim can win; why, even sly, old Socrates was convinced by legal court discourse, to drink hemlock. P Diddy's goal would be to transform the pregnant into the poignant, employing in utero gender experiments and a harvesting of body parts through late abortions, convinced she was assisting Isidora's cause to restructure world populations, willing to go all the way.

She started humbly, working out of a hot basement, becoming adept at smuggling black babies into the United States from sister run orphanages in deepest dark Africa, and founding a business called Rent A Womb, introducing a new-fangled womb of the stars; at some point coming up with the idea for her hit reality television show, *Celebrity Surrogate*, with famous fathers beating off into special cups, to clinic provided porn, the warm reproductive fluid then transferred to the common slurry in a vat labeled, Pan Genesis; clients being the *crème de la crème* of Hollywood society, smugly sold on it being much more convenient for someone else to take charge of details, modern day eugenics, as connoisseur exclusivity.

P: "Utilizing the latest techniques in artificial insemination, advanced genetic testing, and a specialized computer modeling of racial, sexual and gender traits, the characteristics most important to our clients, or ourselves, may be selected, and presto change-o, designer kids produced on demand, as in ordering a new car or home with desired options, bells, whistles, the well-tailored babies of every yuppy's dream."

Fixer: "The womb of the stars, modern day Milky Way, conceived on a promise of perfected nature and nurture, but at some point, you became a baby making machine, so a middle class could take the step."

P: "Then I brought in Dr. Ken LaFountain, OB/ GYN for the opulent, who egotistically substituted his sperm during artificial inseminations, as a way of spreading superior genes, as far and wide as possible; acts of extraordinary evolutionary survival, biological imperative, self-promotion, carried on in stealth and megalomania over successive years on countless, unsuspecting women; completely defensible, in his mind, on purely Darwinian terms. It was he who reformed, democratized, our productive yield with industrial incubation of new Pans, from the pooled sperm of a million donors, a million loving fathers."

Fixer.: "And one day in the near future, polygamy will be legalized, and Pan reproductive male harems shortly established, replete with every size, hue, race of inmate, various depths of maleness expressed."

The sisters, furious that God created them as they were, softer, smaller, shorter, menstruating, lactating, hormonal, feminine, intuitive, etc., began a conscription campaign for male recruits; men not permitted to touch women, unless the women said so, the problem being, they never said so. Babies conceived in plastic bags, sisters tricking subjects into using condoms, recycling them, starting embryos in the same, resulted in Vestal Virgins gaining a reputation as Vessel Virgins, and in cases of extreme excess, Bestial Virgins. Also scurrilous, documented cases of women in comas giving birth in long term care facilities, surrogates carrying babies to term for the highest bidder, the indiscriminate harvesting of tissues from transplants, plastic surgery, genetic engineering, vaccinations, etc., and a grisly and costly euthanasia of male fetuses (as with females in China) by hyper feminists, had consequences for the order and society.

P: "In an act of social benevolence the true sisters endowed a women's maternity (laying in) hospital, in affiliation with the fertility and abortion clinics, backed by genetics research and development, offering a schedule of the most modern care available, in a spread sheet fashion: different levels of services and fees, well detailed, in programmed sympathy with the planned progress and propagation of the race." *

Fixer.: "Questions: was there ever, a Mitochondrial Eve? does Sofia Vergala own her own embryos? are these really fetus factories, Planned Auschwitzes? but what of potential souls waiting in Limbo for their turn? and of Elton Jack's celebrity birth guilt, onto critics labelling IVF babies synthetic? dirty doubts."

P: "We have always had the 'Ma Ma, Where's my Pa?' crowd, but stiff-armed replies were warranted, and besides, we are way ahead of those maternity hospitals run by Chinese tongs, producing babies for others only for the money. They are cutting babies out alive from random women's wombs, but cannot be prosecuted in any jurisdiction, for all the international population control efforts, which allow for the theft of unborn preemies at any stage, by selfish gangsters, clearly the unholiest of harvests of our age."

Fixer.: "The new left has become the establishment, the order of complacency, the status quo machine to rage against. I will accept this new exclusive, in exchange for keeping a lid on bad behavior done."

P: "As agreed, you must write favorably about our projects, with a mention of our philanthropic work."

Fixer.: "You mean filthanthropy, the measured response of those embarrassed by the obscenity of their loot, basically fat cats contributing to, and organizing, events because it makes them look good, right?"

P: In principle, I agree; old philanthropists, having taken a lot, give back only a small portion, however, enough to bring the desired effects of respectability, admiration, a pleasant fib. When people modestly say it's time to give back, it's really because of all they have grossly, shrewdly taken during their lives."

At some point the idea of giving back took over imaginations, as in contributing to charities, churches, hospitals or schools, to a profession or field, or a cause or idea, or a group of people less privileged (but sometimes luckier) than ourselves, and in these contributions were somehow, our own salvations, quick tickets to a glad heaven, our offerings getting us off the hook, absolving us of guilt over our advantages and sometimes, our not measuring up to them, handouts our own, small price for inner peace, as well as gaining acceptance from our families, communities, culture, society, especially if unethical means were used in achieving success and acclaim, to appease our superegos and wash away our crimes. However, it was a travesty, contributions helping powerful donors more than needy, intended recipients. Because social acknowledgement, and appreciation, of the giving and its egotistical sponsors, was more relevant than the actual, efficacious use of the favor, as when benefactors attached their names and personalities to their good works, as if dedicating temples to themselves. It was about public relations and creating the semblance of goodwill, and hypercritical generosity, as the truth about the origins of charity was deemed the comforting, made-up story of the most graceful patrons and grateful *protégées*. Perhaps it should be the story of grateful patrons and graceful *protégées*; "But the meek shall inherit the earth..."

It was getting late, and the Fixer/ Yellow Kid had to file his story from the hotel room, before his editor called. He hated his vigilant cell phone, but it was indispensable to his being a self-righteous tattle tale. Over the years they had worked together, they had never found occasion to discuss their identical green eyes. She was the type who was more apt to say, "Women baring breasts was not feminism, but rather, fetishism," or, "By adding sexism to the lexicon, sexy was removed as a possibility," but too late, it was her: "Hello, day tripper of the Misses Lonelyhearts, what fine grit have you come across in Baja sand?"

> He read it for the same reason an animal tears at a wounded foot: to hurt
> the pain. (Nathanael West, *Miss Lonelyhearts*, 1933)

"Chief, this whole thing is an exercise in literary futility, because I am no more science fiction archivist than activist, or eager, engaged bard, it's all some sort of practical joke, a pathetic attempt at erudition."

"Please get a grip on yourself, and report. Somewhere along the line, a careless scientist confused an X for a Y, and consider, what's happened since, novel chromosomal hybrids of unimagined potentialities."

"Progressive liberals took Renaissance Humanism to aesthetic, scientific, pinnacles, providing the mild a chance to make godlike decisions, such as choosing for themselves, what gender, sex or race to be."

"Once you claim there are more than two genders, why stop at three, four or five: why not one hundred genders or even more? That is why this argument is so absurd, there are and can only be, two genders."

"Gender is sometimes a flavor of the month whim, as per Margaret Mead, and the brainwashing of girls in a classroom over 30 days. *It was this, but they called it that; they saw it this way before saying that.*"

"I'm not in favor of billionaires becoming icons of forward thinking, inviting believers on a slick ride: coalitions, alliances, collectives, communes, communities, panels, plenaries, forums, symposiums, etc."

"It's the search for the American Dream that, though not dead, was a far cry from what it had ever been or became; but what had it espoused at inception? The philosopher's stone of genetic determination or eugenicist fantasy seems our cross to bear. I am gathering my notes and will send you a dispatch later."

"Hold on, did you get to ask Lilly about her mother, renditioned in Guantánamo these two years, with Lilly desperate to see or even hear from her? If not, it will be pending your next, appointed encounter."

But by press time, Lilly was still nowhere to be seen, so Willi allowed the piece to proceed without her. The next morning, Isidora woke up to the early news roundup when a grim feature caught her attention.

> *Death with dignity advocate Certainty Salenerd takes her own life amidst*
> *family and friends, her end tragically marred, by the public clown show.*

*How a depressed and vulnerable cancer sufferer allowed media sharks in feeding frenzies, to seduce her into keeping a promise to sacrifice herself.*

*The poster girl for assisted suicide, having second thoughts, still placated dastardly, professional euthanasia advocating vultures circling overhead.*

Isidora could not help reflecting on atheism being man's sinking vanity, a body's impermanence, as the center of fast existence, to the exclusion of all divinities. However, as Narcissus drowned in the fateful contemplation of his rippling reflection deniers cannot but be weighed down by the gravity of their own beings in a surrendering to life's evanescence, reminding herself, *Beware of Greeks bearing Cambridge sheepskins,* the Romans employing a public slave to whisper, "*memento mori,*" to a triumphant general.

> "Oh, the arrogance of men, ungodly, for
> believing in no cause besides themselves,
> their own, superior will; for can such aim,
> however, accurate, explain the very many,
> sacred things, beyond our comprehension?"

With so many millennial scientists disavowing beliefs in God, wasn't it ironic that by denying the issue they acknowledged the subject *per se,* while promoting themselves in godlike proportions through their preternatural, revelatory, even monstrous, feats of transition, reassignment and re-branding, so recently accomplished? What would open Dr. Henry Waterson say, she wondered (because Dr. Ken LaFountain was Dr. Henry Waterson in his creator guise as Sperm Donor Supreme), but she already had the answer, which would be to let people harbor their spiritual beliefs, including her, and leave science to its tasks.

Such technologically driven developments of human knowledge, from old, tired beliefs into modernity, a revolution in communications and consciousness accelerating in the last two centuries, were part of a greater revolution, of escape from the societal bonds of the bible, ongoing for more than a millennium.

Science, a marvel and movable feast, was not sacrosanct, for knowledge changed with discoveries, and was never static, many ancient scientific beliefs contradicted with the passage of time and further study. Thus, in astronomy Hesiod was upended by Ptolemy, was upended by Kepler, was upended by Galileo, was upended by Newton, was upended by Einstein, was upended by who knows who? Therefore, what is claimed today as irrefutable scientific fact is only current belief, thought, opinion, subject to dynamic revisions; this being the case, with evolution, climate change, perhaps even transgenderism, where this generation's deeply substantiated understanding, maybe completely updated by future breakthroughs; the single, salient constant: purposeful progress of Everyman as seer, seer as scientist, scientist as God.

*Footnote

The Moll Flanders Foundation, Established 2002

The Sisterhood of Grace's Women's Reproductive Health Campus,
New Haven, CT, Founded 2003

Schedule of Services and Fees:

She replied that she would bring in an account of the expenses of it in two or three shapes, and like a bill of fare, I should choose as I pleased; and I desired her to do so.

The next day she brought it, and the copy of her three bills was as follows:—

1. For three months' lodging in her house, including my diet, at 10s. a week . . . . . . . . . . . 6£, 0s., 0d.

2. For a nurse for the month, and use of childbed linen . . . . . . . . . . . . . . . . . . . 1£, 10s., 0d.

3. For a minister to christen the child, and to the godfathers and clerk . . . . . . . . . . . . 1£, 10s., 0d.

4. For a supper at the christening if I had five friends at it . . . . . . . . . . . . . . . . . . . . . . . . . . . . . . . 1£, 0s., 0d.

For her fees as a midwife, and the taking off the trouble of the parish . . . . . . . . . . . . . . . . . 3£, 3s., 0d.

To her maid servant attending . . . . . . . . 0£, 10s., 0d.

-------------

13£, 13s., 0d.

This was the first bill; the second was the same terms:—

1. For three months' lodging and diet, etc., at 20s. per week . . . . . . . . . . . . . . . . . 13£, 0s., 0d.

2. For a nurse for the month, and the use of linen and lace . . . . . . . . . . . . . . . . . 2£, 10s., 0d.

3. For the minister to christen the child, etc., as above . . . . . . . . . . . . . . . . . . . 2£, 0s., 0d.

4. For supper and for sweetmeats . . 3£, 3s., 0d.

For her fees as above . . . . . . . . . . . 5£, 5s., 0d.

For a servant-maid . . . . . . . . . . . . 1£, 0s., 0d.

-------------

26£, 18s., 0d.

This was the second-rate bill; the third, she said, was for a degree higher, and when the father or friends appeared:—

1. For three months' lodging and diet, having two rooms and a garret for a servant . . . . . . 30£, 0s., 0d.,

2. For a nurse for the month, and the finest suit of childbed linen . . . . . . . . . . . . . . . 4£, 4s., 0d.

3. For the minister to christen the child, etc. 2£, 10s., 0d.

4. For a supper, the gentlemen to send in the
wine . . . . . . . . . . . . . . . . . . . . 6£, 0s., 0d.

For my fees, etc. . . . . . . . 10£, 10s., 0d.

The maid, besides their own maid,
only . . . . . . . . . . . . . . . . . . 0£, 10s., 0d.
--------------
53£, 14s., 0d.

I looked upon all three bills, and smiled, and told her I did not see but
that she was very reasonable in her demands, all things considered, and for
that I did not doubt but her accommodations were good.

### The Fortunes and Misfortunes
### of the Famous Moll Flanders, &c.

by Daniel Defoe

## WRITTEN IN THE YEAR 1683

## 13. *Sieg Heil*

Patriotism is the last refuge of a scoundrel.
(James Boswell, *The Life of Samuel Johnson, LL.D.*, 1791)

Beneath the shiny, black *burqa* he and the bomb were hidden in plain sight, as no policeman suspecting his objective would dare stop and search him, for fear of being charged with racial profiling; a case of political correctness run amok, of never surrendering invaluable rights while getting away with murder; how appropriate that his target this morning was the White House itself, wilted nest of poison hornets, deserving of incendiary, global *fatwa* by radical, Islamic terrorists, unholy bottle imps of a closing age.

That was L'il Lay L'or Ence, now Lilly, as a desperate Third World immigrant (remember?), presently a U.S. resident, past suicide bomber, prominent Arab American, stunning starlet; pro: herself, of course, privilege, exclusivity, George Bush, John Sayer; heshe, male into female, dating males, but attracted to females; anti: Jews, Muslims (as a trans, *Sharia* renounced him), immigrants, males; homophobic, with no pity; success driven, achieving, after years, still terrified of immigration agents, lurking in shadows.

Our star-crossed lovers, partners, Adam & Eve, engaging in new skirmishes if not with each other, then with themselves, each becoming a Miss Lonelyhearts, with their own pop fan club from opposite poles. What follow are two letters picked at random although not randomly sent from Willi and Isidora Green:

> *Valentine's Day*
> *Anonymous (Willi)*
> *Dear Miss Lonelyhearts (Lilly),*
> *How could this happen to me? I had a woman I was married to, poof she disappeared into a mist. Please let me know what you think of this story. Our romance was a whirlwind, but after having kids it was not the same, each of us heading in different directions, but let me get back to the start. There had been Jesus, the little boy whose head, I might have once split open, but I tried not to think about it. Suddenly I was alarmed at sulking thoughts, of ending up alone with no mate or progeny, the worst of fates. I was quite happy with my existence before I asked our paternal godhead to create a woman for me, understanding that any dependence developed for her, would be the antithesis to the life I truly wanted, as when a monk of ancient times fixated upon an image of Mother Mary for his salvation. Nevertheless, I could never live alone for long, without companionship of the opposite sex. And that is why I made fateful demand for a compatriot before understanding all the ramifications I would be subject to, because I only cared about my loins, how they would be girded, as for a battle, or unbound, as for love making moments, with passing, passionate partners. We had to become as proficient in English as was Polish Joseph Conrad when, in a foreign tongue, he wrote his monumental works, only we were preparing for the big and small screens (idiot boxes for this craziest age). They helped us to learn English, not because we merited it, but we fit the demographics they were trying to fill. We failed our first screen tests, in part, because we could not communicate. Then we went to a night school paid for by our generous benefactors, and the next time we auditioned we aced them, obtaining low level jobs at first. We thought it would help our careers if we tied the knot, offering an allied front to a hostile world, as*

*well as having a blessed family. Our vows may have been holy, but I was not wholly on-board, especially to the attendance of the rancid priest and his perverted fellows. I liked how I looked in a tuxedo, seemingly fated to dress for success, while she disrobed to nothing on-screen in her X-rated glory. Our Adam and Eve portrayals, on TV, led to our comfort with the live medium. We also insisted on owning the rights to our shows, for as much as we trusted the studio's bosses, we trusted ourselves more. Soon the common gripe shared was that she was as beholden to her boss, as I was to mine, on the deepest of professional as well as personal grounds, overlooking any drawbacks when the checks started arriving in a steady, bounteous way, until in our bank account was more than we could spend. The huge wealth marked a beginning of my serial philandering; if I could no longer make her happy, I did not see the point of our having relations, at all, so I kept my eye out, for any willing ingenues that happened along, especially during her Universal Earth Sky Mother phase, a tiresome vibe. The male competition, so substantial, used untold allurements to disrupt our marriage, drag me into a fog of sexual stupor. It was not that I could not get it up at all, I could not get it up for her, or any other easy woman. I want to clarify for once and for all that I am not responsible for a man's indiscretions, extramarital affairs, drug vices, whether mine or another's. I have been criticized for permitting, condoning, encouraging, unusually broad drug usage by my wife, even for procuring vast quantities for her. Here is the question: who is guiltier, a supplier or consumer of a poison? To satisfy my wife's constant demands for drugs, in amounts she and her widening circle of lady friends, hangers on, could party with, I needed to contact our former allies in those activities, starting with El Comandante and The Commander, I immediately resuming an old friendship, where it left off. My wife, placated for a while, was unappreciative of my sensual distractions. She was not of the swinging type and used it as an excuse to shut down completely. And that is where she and I have remained, since. And as this Commander could not help, but romantically hit on my wife, so matrimonial strife continued. "We're not on the same page," she said over and over to me, to no effect. But we covered up these splits with our constant Great Ratsby type frolics, in pursuit of millennial mischief. The Hollywood lifestyle, ripe for immense alcohol imbibement, led to further dissipation, all night revelries, raves, replete with open orgies, onanism. With innumerable shots of tequila, aguardiente, bourbon, we were the life of an infinite party, consuming not only copious bottles but our souls, as well. And her fast living led to that unfortunate, well publicized incident. I understand, I was not the best influence on her behavior, and there were tensions. When we received that ransom note, with no demands for cash, only the zany, life quality requirements, I knew it was her from the start. But I never confronted or criticized her for kidnapping our own children, or trying to kill herself in remote alturas, or bringing the snoops into our private Garden, which heretofore had been off limits. It took a while for us to recover from that tragic fortnight's break from reality, with stays in psychiatric facilities and counseling for my delicate, imbalanced partner. And that was two years ago; what should we do, considering 48 Hours to Mecca, filmed last year, is leading the leading lady's greatest comeback?*

*Sincerely,*
*A Lonely Reader*

A very needy reader has a deep-seated problem, thought Miss Lonelyhearts; what should I say in reply?

*Valentine's Day*
*Anonymous (Isidora Green)*
*Dear Miss Lonelyhearts (Lilly),*
*I know it's not my place to do so, but I can't help criticizing someone I've worked with, and have helped immensely, professionally. Please help me. When I first met those bi-oddity debutantes, I was completely blown over, surprisingly declaring, "I mean, whatever turns you on, delightful, lovely creatures," as that was then and is presently the best description of them. My Puritan president and I immediately decided, we had to recruit such a heavenly and earthy couple, if not right away, then soon after sufficiently preparing them with the language skills for the great opportunity at hand. We were honored to help them defray some of their educational expenses. From the start, their stage abilities were enormous. I was taken by a man of the people, with the uncanny ability to connect with the downtrodden, others by this quintessential, new, new-woman, adventurous and free, with her take charge attitude so relatable to contemporary, female audiences. As hard as she worked, juggling three careers, as gifted actor, lover to an immature despot, mother of an ever-increasing brood, she did her best to look hale and hearty, even if those unhealed back scars debilitated her; I knew it was not good enough for him, who looked outside for his needs. But his shadiest activities were reserved for procurement of drugs for her. Just a dabbler himself, his supplying her was doubly cruel and heartless. In this way he drove her away from him; she replaced love for addiction, and he was free to pursue his dalliances with an abandoned, lustful vigor. In announcing the prize, anticipating the grateful Shinning Starlet, up on stage with me, I was left holding the proverbial bag for that MIA, along with her hooky playing husband, Willi-Nilly, my eidolons, protégés, after all I'd done for them to arrive; waiting in vain on an empty stage, dark, muffled sky, minutes now as hours, for a collapsed astral body failed at escaping the heavy, orbital gravity of desperation, the Madam Chairman needing a couple of diazepam and a goblet of champagne, to calm down. Sincerely,*
*A Lonely Reader*

How should one discharge such admonitions from a total stranger, wondered Lilly, before a toot or two.

Having lived publicly demonstrating the adage, that celebrities are just like everyone else, it came as no surprise when, "Heaven has no rage like love to hatred turned, Nor hell a fury like a woman scorned..." due to certain philandering (not philanthropic) impulses of rowdy boys amongst us, any balanced love splitting those extremes. As a celebrity who bore designer babies, supported legalized prostitution, and kidnapped her own children as a self-promotion stunt, to repair a troubled marriage, Lilly was in search of alternative means of impact. Having been a terrible terrorist, not only sparing his own miserable life, but failing to take out any great numbers, he cynically yet perceptively concluded that if you are going to be a top tier renegade make sure to wear a vest for success; now become a trend setting fashion icon, sporting a streamlined, water repellent Speedy *chador* one piece bathing suit (a victory for a repressed people), enshrouding a badly ravaged back, never having healed from persistent infection; she lounged languidly by blinding blue *piscina*, escaping her lately grown so dreary, obtuse, unresponsive husband.

The swanky host of this wild animal spirits poolside, half steer *parrillada*, at oceanside *hacienda,* down the pink, sandy beach from her and Willi's own hideout, on rocky Baja California cliffs, with dry cacti as prickly and sweaty as he, was our *bon vivant* (ill-behaved) Lone Ranger of self-righteous contempt, vitriol and hilarity foisted at the expense of others: John B. Sayer, who spared no expense on his *fiesta*. His was the typical WASP's antipathy toward miscegenation, alternate gender identities, changed sexes, akin to modern distrust of alchemy and sorcery in amalgamating disparate elements in the preposterous dream of creating perfect, newly compounded selves, the incubus and succubus of old. Despite beliefs that extreme, he had made Lilly into a superstar, not just of the studio, but the American consciousness. Her recently released thriller, *48 Hours to Mecca,* would gross hundreds of millions, before distribution rights, and as a special favor to her (himself), Sayer wanted to share some clips from that blockbuster.

> **48 Hours to Mecca** *(Trailer, Property of Warren Bros. Inc. Movie Studio)*
> *Fade in, popular music of Fairuz, interspersed with that of Willie Nelson.*
> *Scene: Scheherazade (Lilly in character) meditating by the open window.*
>
> *Always keeping white, as well as black, burqas handy, one for innocence, the other revenge, while daydreaming of one day immigrating to the U.S., all the freedoms promised still untold as to their number and importance.*
>
> *News flash: "The U.S. is poised to allow open carry of handguns." Now, she could holster her .44 Magnum, hollow points, over her* burqa, *in plain sight, anytime, anywhere: religious freedoms, gun rights, a great country.*
>
> *She would use her skills as a double agent to gain admittance to America under cover, as an* haute couture *designer taming the CIA to eat from her hand, when her new boss realizes her Middle Eastern languages abilities.*
>
> *Later, settled in the Golden State, maturing from a sycophant of sheiks, to one of cheeks, founding her fashion empire to innovate* burqas, *replacing black with rainbow futuristic shades, then grading white, to soften nights.*
>
> *Fade out, popular music of Fairuz, intermixed with that of Willie Nelson.*

What could anyone at poolside proffer but a fabulous and supreme series of compliments, to an ageless star? A few astute viewers, however, saw through the mesmerizing veneer, directly into that radiance's, central core, the discoverable matter being in the most insignificant of ways tragically inconclusive and ambivalent, nevertheless. After Lilly's much heralded, heroic transformation, struggles to find her own feminine, fluid voice led to periodic bouts of severe emotional distress, until finally getting a handle on the problem; empty wishful thinking, for it unfortunately always remained a trace bit husky, hoarse and rasping, while hurling Quaalude hyped, Quranic based drivel, through newly puffed, pouting lips. Prior to her loving audience approving of her newfound look, the media itself was revealing, mocking, mean.

*Special Report: Male to the Core*

*Hello fabulous cousins, this week we have a focus segment on a new star.*

*Even with all the hormones, the best efforts of therapists, beauticians and trainers, the neck, hands and feet continued impossible to disguise, non-transformable, remaining and appearing large by any standards, the hot red enamel manicured fingers, and toes in slinky sandals, all the rage this year, seeming immense; dare call yourself a man or woman in this age of gender equivocation, and be prepared to pay the price. She was bending all known rules at get go. When disturbing pictures appeared, identifying her as questionably male for carrying overly pumped-up shoulders, and a barrel chest (despite newly minted, smallish Jane Russel boobs, pointy as hills jutting straight out, uplifted, hard, freshly molded); narrowest of flat assed flanks, hips down to legs too long, lean (bowed), muscular for their own denying; her private label designer swimwear partnered with Speedy demonstrating a cover up of the strong upper back in question, while still accentuating as many curves as possible in such a case; chiseled, strong, suntanned jaw and chin with its persistent five o'clock shadow; there was just no hiding or denying it, the overall aspect angular, firm, pressing, in fact incongruous in its exaggerated and well-formed perfection; here was undoubtedly, the awe inspiring, irrepressible, terrifying male to the core.*

*Thanks, fabulous cousins, it's a wrap, until next week's show of new stars. (The identities of subjects are secret, with any similarities a coincidence.)*

Feeling threatened, feeding on perceived slights, Lilly sought refuge in meditations on her mother, still renditioned in Guantánamo, having had no communication from her for ages, the only extant family in her life. Through all the dislocations, emigrations, immigrations her memory hovered near in guidance. And in case any errant fans hassled her, or put her on the spot, she had packed a compact Beretta in her purse, going nowhere, even within this secure *casa de playa*, without it; just then, someone yelling out:

"Remember the Maine! To hell with Spain!"
(Rallying cry for the Spanish-American War, as a follow-up to...)

Please remain. You furnish the pictures and I'll furnish the war.
(William Randolph Hearst, 1898)

not for any clear reason, but for the hell of it, of course; such was Sayer: red, white and blue American flag eyes, after so many hours of already partying, at this early hour, fastidiously attired in a Superman outfit for the festivities; new age reactionary on display, doing anything to get laughs, loving notoriety, praise, attention, even at the expense of indulging in so many vulgarities, common to *turistas norteños*.

Sayer enjoyed sitting in the buff on his seaside deck, vainly tanning himself with a foil reflector in the desert seared afternoon *sol Mexicano*, concentrating the sun's rays on specific parts of his well-muscled physique to deepen its bronze hue. His was the infant portrait of confidence, friendliness, extroversion, waving triumphantly and smiling broadly, with just whitened teeth, at the beach combers, greeting each with, "Hello there, real nice day for it," in an odd, exaggerated, mocking cowboy accent, as if retarded.

Sayer loved answering his home phone, in a country hick accent, with various, law enforcement related greetings, such as, "Bestport Police, may I help you?" or, "Officer Mutrinkowski, what is the nature of your call?" and would coolly hang up amidst the other party's confusion. This was the funniest gag; he never tired of repeating it, giggling silently to cover up the harassing nature of his pose, just to see what the reaction would be on the other end; cracking up at a caller's dumbfounded pause to his game. And to prove his gutsy, *guero* adaptability, while in Baja, he boldly replied, "*Policia Estatal, a sus ordenes.*"

Another one of his sick, old Boy Scout tricks from times past was to put a sleeping person's hand into warm water to induce urinating, so hilarious; also tying boxing gloves all night on one despised, teasing him of being a champion at beating off; on a freezing cold camping trip morning, it could be that wake-up call, always a perfunctory attempt at American high diction, "Drop your cocks and grab your socks." And finally, "Don't waste the wood, burn it," was the farewell intonement, propitiating all forest deities.

As the night wore on, Sayer made strange advances toward his guests, the men, not women, sneaking up, goosing them frontally by surprise, laughing hysterically; then planting rears unabashedly, so that if a victim stumbled, he admonished them, "Don't pee on me, or grovel on my gravel," in falsetto ghetto.

Somehow a newly-wed Frenchman neighbor, and sexy wife, entered the scene, his pants fly mistakenly left unzipped and open, catching the eye of our degenerate host, to inspire assault with random phrases of made-up French, exclaiming hilariously, "*La petite shows;*" the well inebriated party-host guffawing wildly at his own bilingual wit; the Frenchman reddening in disbelief, at such a low brow reception; the wife chagrined, quite annoyed by such asinine behavior; however, after such a gag no one could accuse Sayer of being insensitive to foreigners, even if the wife thought his invisible hand a little too sensitive.

The Po' Boys, Oath Sleepers, were there in force, despite their threatening presence, aggressive antics, toward the other guests; as the night wore on, their wild drinking setting the pace for the gathering; tall tales, fabrications, misinformation, outright lies colored with boisterous, off-color humor demonstrating that, unfortunately, sometimes the exercise of free speech is no more than unabashed freedom to loudly utter grotesque ignorance; as per old, Italian Blackshirts, S.A. Brownshirts, then Tea Baggers, Boogers, Committee for Public Safety: those having basic, human necessities, denying them to those who do not, the rightist path, as opposed to leftists redistributing the means of production, to fit their political needs. The fabled Knights of Freemisogyny also made pompous appearances, toward the end of the *barbacoa*, demonstrating the finer aspects of the celibate Rule of the Order, such as sneaking destitute, homeless, female followers into their Bestport Temple of Philosophy and the Arts, at two in the morning, to bathe nasty crust from unhealthy bodies, and engage in unfeeling, perfunctory orgies with frothing, impotent, bestial Sons of the Lodge; but being tapped for such an open secret society was what everyone wanted, only, some were handed it, the privilege of belonging to something, the resentment when the privilege was taken away; their initiation involving becoming a member's slave for thirty days, sleeping at night blindfolded in a coffin, or running a gauntlet three days in a row, injuries afterward being so extensive, that the (brave) (foolish) novices might spend a week of agony in a hospital, and upon being discharged with the requisite stitches, bruises, broken bones, prove unflinching loyalty with a secret babbling oath.

> Oh, give me a home where the butt-faggot roam,
> Where the queer and transgender play,
> Where never is heard a heterosexual word
> And transvestites dress up all day.

> Oh, give me a home where the *mulatto* roam,
> Where the white and African play,
> Where never is heard Immigration's fine word

And *mojados* swim over all day. (Continue in ad lib manner)

Meanwhile, with Wagner's, *Die Walkure* blaring in the background, John B. Sayer was accompanied by his special guest of honor, Ms. Yael Abraham, Ph.D., setting up his command post in a modern art lined dining room; shock attack goosing civies, then the stiff-arm salute, jackbooted, goose stepping around a big table, placing black comb over upper lip, as a Hitler mustache; insanely shrieking, "*Sieg Heil, Sieg Heil,*" as if on a mission to conquer Margaritaville. Was it normal, or horrendous, behavior for the hero of directed kills to ruin himself thus, his banter slipping into a vulgar, suggestive, totalitarian rhetoric?

> If anyone reproaches me and asks why I did not resort to the regular
> courts of justice, then all I can say is this: In this hour I was responsible
> for the fate of the German people, and thereby I became the supreme
> judge of the German people.
> (Adolf Hitler, 1934, justifying The Night of the Long Knives)

Though hell-bent with hatching an anti-immigration plot, utilizing clandestine brigades to repatriate all illegal aliens, and expel African Americans back to Africa, the new Dirty War would have to wait until a dryer morning, things were starting to get out of hand. Someone shouted, "Hey, let's not incentivize illegal immigration; if you're going to come into the country, you should at least ring the doorbell," and "Have you ever noticed, how do fleeing refugees, and wetback aliens, have cell phones?" Then, others:

"Given to conspiring, creating an international guerilla army of illegals, right here in this country, they must be infringed upon. But is pornography in the bug-eyes of the beholder, or those of the promoter?"

"If political hate speech is allowed, then why should personal-hate speech, sexual harassment, not be?"

"Listen, wanting border controls doesn't make me a racist. But who cares? And what does racist mean anymore? It's gotten so overused, overblown, convoluted, that no one cares what it intended to define."

"Would it matter if we asserted that not being in favor of cannibalism does not make us stupid bigots?"

"The reason they are so offended is that deep down, they do really agree with us: death to trespassers."

"*'Viva la patria, mate un judío,' gritaban héroes en los barrios argentinos antes de la segunda guerra.*"

"I'm sick and tired of the violence coming from the left; that rallying cry of diversity is really the racist call to arms, for the advantage of colored people. When minorities play the race card, loading the deck completely in their favor, pandering to their lowest common denominators, they deal us a losing hand."

"So, it has become a domestic agenda fraught with hate mongering against non-minority white people."

"How can the simple, unassuming, white person get out of the way of the runaway freight train of black anger? They would state, not by hiding behind white privilege, the First Amendment notwithstanding."

Even while owing his success to show business, Sayer nevertheless, called television the idiot box, as if pulling the wool over the eyes of torpid masses, or was it his own blue eyes and soul that were fogged? Puritan Sayer drank so much at his own party, that he had to be assisted upstairs to his room by sober, booted acolytes, supported as he stumbled, rudely crooning, with slurred, missed words, the comforting verse from the side of his jaded mouth in the mocking, nasal voice of an emotionally deficient hillbilly:

"Buffalo Bill's
defunct...
how do you like your blue-eyed boy
Mister Death"
(E. E. Cummings, "[Buffalo Bill's]," 1920)

After several hours of a dead sleep, he sobered up enough, for *montage*, flash type dreams before dawn.

*It was Army-Whale weekend at The U.S. Military Academy at West Point, parents, guests invited to the football game and other events; in the giant mess hall plebes stirred up a frenzy, leaping upon tables, chugging entire bottles of ketchup, mustard, Tabasco and A.1. sauces, cheered on in wild, raucous choruses by table mates; until gagging, choking, in a collapsing exuberance, reeling in nausea, before inevitable upchucks; proof of their devotion and merit to their comrades, with whom they will serve, possibly die; when did "Duty, Honor, Country" lead so many to stand with Nazis?*

*The apogee of his beliefs came short of the stars in trusting for tomorrow.*

*If their hue was less than human, send them back. Passing under or over a subway turnstile, or the* Rio Grande, *illegally, what was the difference? What about citizenship privileges? Migrants were using fake or no forms vs. Americans needing 3x the number; how was that even logical or fair?*

*Even if multicultural is a euphemism for being anti-white, racists needed to beware of their genetic makeups, as so many whites in early America had black and Indian blood. Could that be his case? heaven help if such.*

*English Dissenters and Separatists not crossing for religious liberty, but rather, the freedom to practice their beliefs; never for all to worship, in their own chosen faiths, but narrowly, that they could solely follow theirs.*

*The Congregational minister, reed thin, barely lipped, former missionary, had taught me, especially with the backs of his big hands, to fear the lord.*

*Those with the greatest luck in their setup lives, pompously claimed their success was achieved solely through prayer, hard work; the hubris of the truly lucky in a disavowal of their good fortune, in favor of that self-made myth of persistence accounting for achievement; and always the evidence of the trail of conspicuous leisure and consumption, at their country club.*

*"I made this money on my own (being blessed enough, then born with a silver spoon jammed down my throat, but pretending, with everyone else, to have to chase down material prosperity, never mentioning the ancient family trust fund; and adding insult to injury, my cheapness, bombarding litany of complaints about petty challenges, while a privileged epicurean appreciated well hung Picassos, Kandinskys, Miros in his dining room)."*

The Puritan mind knowing no bounds for the evil it can cause, his old family's loyalty and devotion to a distant slave state always at the back of Sayer's mind, periodically regretting, that it was not his branch that had migrated to renegade Texas, with its holocaust hatreds and bellicose singularity, unconsciously humming "Dixie," *de facto* anthem of the Confederacy, as he awoke, suffering quite the hangover after last night's binging, suddenly recalling that a one eyed Oath Sleeper, Senator Goads, was due to debate. After both serving in Phoenix in Nam, then having met again at Whale while Sayer attended the School of Management, and H. E. Goads, the School of Law, they had remained close friends, forever patriots.

In true corporate fashion, as it was Black History Month in the U.S., the household would still honor its observance in *Mexico,* as several of Sayer's staff were black or of mixed race. As to what he personally thought about MLK Day: why wasn't there a hero holiday carved out, for Native Americans, Hispanics, Asians, Pacific Islanders and Camel Jockeys (Lilly notwithstanding), for that matter? When did blacks come so far? Perhaps the Rev. Hannibal P. (Pearly) Gates, author of the historical work, *Enemistad, A Slave's Exile from Ghana; traded by her own people, as spoils of war and conquest; the sad conditions on board, arrival in New Haven, etc....* having come as Sayer's honored guest, would lend his thoughts on the matter, after a cool noon swim, when everyone got together, for cocktails and lunch by the pool.

There was a moment when one group's civil rights became everyone else's shriveled rights, and voters were bored of being lectured to, by a self-segregating caucus. Racism was voting your color, so Sayer voted his color; everyone votes his color; as with breeds, races were the camouflage put on by humans, to adjust for environmental factors, and to protect against marauders by maintaining a common identity.

> "Beware the Jap or wop, my son!
>     The jaws that bite, the claws that catch!
> Beware the Jewjew bird, and shun
>     The frumious Darkeysnatch!"

Sayer did not appreciate Africans, as Africa was where Aids and Ebola originated, and by an irrational stroke of mental transference his antipathy extended to African Americans, simply because it could, and they were a convenient scapegoat. As far as he was concerned, this regressive race should surely have had additional members in jail or prison than at present, due to their criminal nature, and street nurture. The answer to mass incarceration was additional incarceration, as even more *gangstas* should be taken away. Because if black power annoys, white power destroys. Over time they dilute, the doomed blend, resentful, mixed *mulatto*, the most dangerous hybrid creation made to the smooth action of a republic.

Now the two debaters squared off in a brilliantly lit courtyard, accentuating vast differences in pigment, the Reverend Gates dominating the patio with an awesome, black effulgence, while the Senator bored.

"Specifically, the plan protects the tax-exempt status of any organization that believes, speaks or acts in accordance with the belief, that marriage is or should be recognized as a union of one man, one woman, sexual relations are properly reserved for such a marriage, male and female and equivalents refer to an individual's immutable biological sex as objectively determined by anatomy, physiology, or genetics at or before birth, and that human life begins at conception and merits protection at all stages. Further..."

"Senator, if I may presume to continue where you left off. When someone says, we need to engage in a conversation, about such-and-such, or this or that, what they're really telling you is let's get together, so they can scream in your ear. And strange, psycho/ social dynamics exploded at the millennium: blacks' self-hatred for being in some part white spread like a plague among liberal whites, who sympathetically began hating themselves for being what they racially were; the result being newly condoned, collective white guilt, combined with a heavy media push, inciting anti-white harangues; helping black candidates embracing healthy, upstanding, wholesome African American family values, get noticed and elected."

"The Civil Rights Act of 1964 was passed because the nation felt sorry for the long-abused descendants of slaves. However, after forty years, people are now appalled at the deplorable behavior demonstrated by their very progeny; they were given free paths, but contrariwise, assumed different directions, which should no longer be tolerated by freedom-loving people. Enough of affirmative action, enough of food stamps, free cell phones and unlimited healthcare, let's everybody take responsibility for our own lives. Even if they always accuse us of cutting school funding for the neediest, frankly what else can we do?"

"Senator, I am so authorized to use hyperbole by the fact of being black and needing to make extremely strong statements, in support of my central thesis: that modern white folks owe the multi-generations of slaves, and oppressed colonial subjects, infinite redress over past ills committed by those who were, as complete strangers to them; unrelated, with nothing more in common, through five centuries of genetic dispersal, than the varying degrees of pigment in their skin; with whites bearing an inherited, evil, dark mark, of relishing subjugation of those weaker than themselves. Somehow, I would seem to be flailing violently against time and the elements, so I will be emphatic in my entreaties to both sides; there is..."

"African Americans have a very parochial view of racism and themselves. Black culturists should read more history in addition to the bloated sociology thrived upon. Their conveniently self-created concept of white supremacy is what keeps them from taking true responsibility for their given lives; remember:

> "There shall be no solution to this race problem until you, yourselves,
> strike the blow for liberty." (Marcus Garvey, major inspiration for the
> back-to-Africa movement, 1920s?)

"'Who the (Expletive) made you dumb (Expletive) crackers think I give a squat (Expletive) about your opinions. If you exhibit nigga behaviors, I'm a call you a nigga. You acting crackerish, I'm a call you a cracker.'" As a proud, black avatar facing off against white evil, he was often asked if reparations would be vindictive. "I'm African American and my ancestors picked cotton. So why would I want my son to pick cotton and think it's fun? Whites always saying, 'Maybe more of them should be incarcerated, let's banish niggers next, slap their big, fat asses back to Africa,' concurring with ideas of repatriation in the back of every black man's mind; but the lofty back-to-Africa movement did an about face, when its own, modern acolytes saw that conditions in the Dark Continent remained pitch black, retreating home:

> Africa for the Africans... at home and abroad! (Garvey)

"My friend, Nation of Islum leader Louis Fearrakhan, founder of the black utopic movement, calls for a separate country for black Americans, saying that's what God wants, while those opposed, he describes as slaves; promoting a Nigger Nation to be cut out of several existing states, defining a racial Utopia by and for blacks to the exclusion of all others, to avoid interference; showing that blacks can discriminate blindly without being discriminating, joining in solidarity to keep leeching newcomers out; people now surprised at the extent of the aggressiveness of the anti-immigration forces, given that for the last thirty years, the problem was ignored, talked away or explained, as a necessary evil for full employment, and keeping wages down; such open immigration policies promoted concurrently with our remotest African cousins being transported to this continent. So, what should it be to us today, at this time? Nothing, for why should we be defined, bound, censured by conflicts, hatreds, crimes that originated, occurred, were committed, with lasting obligations resulting thereof, because of historical errors made by white men?"

Now a lit John Sayer entered the fray: "Perhaps shortly, progressives will decide to rename Washington D.C., after descendants of slaves who built it, as did Whale University with disgraced Calgoun College. The First Amendment provides the basis of the cultural relativism and equivocation, of all sundry ideas plaguing open democracies, the Second Amendment sharing its invitations to a fast death by freedom."

Preacher Pearly: "Stars leveling blank guns set the tone for crazy criminals, itching to use loaded ones, abrogating, nullifying their own effectiveness as anti-gun exemplars, publicly excoriating arms and the Second Amendment, while lazily obtaining herd immunity against gun crime, by living in armed zones. When fifty brothers kill each other over a weekend in Chicago, no one utters a peep. If a white person suffers as much as a scratch, it becomes a federal offense, the kind reactive police get their noses into."

> *From the Breitfart News Network*
>
> *Exasperated, truculent blacks were purposely baiting police at all traffic stops, parks and street corners, egged on by defiant, domineering cohorts and homies, to stage scripted scenes, conveniently captured on cell phone video footage, skillfully, artfully portrayed as poor, unwitting victims of a brutal system, instead of haughty, sly instigators of delinquency, cynically hoping an unwary officer, or two, would resort to extreme, or even deadly force, to righteously expose the mean behavior of overly aggressive cops to the world. And ignorant sheepish African Americans let themselves be used in this most irresponsible, ignominious fashion, even onto death in a futile belief, they were responding to a greater rallying cry, attending to a higher cause, when really, they were only being coldly exploited and even sacrificed by a movement's egotistical bosses for the twisted sake of their own, maniacal, greater glory. And this new and nobly inspired challenge to authority spread like wildfire, from neighborhood to workplace, and to organized venue, ostensibly as spontaneous, natural rebellion but in truth a preemptive struggle, well-rehearsed provocation, refutation of an elitist social structure, hierarchy, and their outrageous statuses, in an outmoded order. And the real objective of all this public protest, and pushback, was to make whites look bad, not only in others' eyes, but their own as well, to shame and create trouble for them. If this seemed identity politics, it sure was, whether it was asked for or not. But one thing was certain: in future times challenges to stability would surprise, with deadliest consequences.*

Sayer was tired of moral wounds, personal affronts, hurled by activists and rabble rousers, wily playing to the gullibility of Americans, cynically pleading for compassionate understanding, while propounding simultaneously, the subversive and clandestine agenda hateful to white Western tradition, solicitously:

"Reverend, your very being here, with us, is a testament to your discretion. Because we are both after a Utopic Free State without foreigners. And your admittance that Africa is no longer an alternative, and I take it that would include Liberia, who's nearly two centuries of failure is akin to an extended period of reconstruction, leaves you with few alternatives, but to join forces with us, albeit on a modified basis."

In another attempt at bridging the corporate difference that existed between Warren Bros. Inc. and The Theatre and Cinema Worker's Guild, Sayer had also invited Fred Malatesta, union president, down for a long holiday weekend. First things first, the union man pointed out an unintended consequence of the latest employment contract being proposed by management, meaning Sayer and his pocket Board of D.

"Those voting no for the package are not in danger of being fired, as they are the longest serving, most senior guild members, and their intransigence is for being high on the mountain top and pecking order, due to their connections. They are the ones escalating: "Bring on the layoffs, we're not afraid," because it's easy to be glib and confrontational with other people's livelihoods, and not their own." Then Sayer:

"Of course, there are self-promoting syndicate bosses, who with their arrogance, greed and self-interest control the lives of all those they cynically refer to as brothers and sisters, in fact, no more than cannon fodder for their greater political aims. This is the wicked state of unions in America: self-promulgating interest groups advancing their own agenda, defending rank and file rights until death, but really on the backs of workers with less seniority, for if they are laid off it is of small consequence, if senior jobs are protected. This is the influence of the chosen few over the membership, as corrupt and contemptible a dictatorship over its helpless card members, as the corporation's tyranny over its powerless employees, with those laid off become bargaining chips, victims, of their senior honchos' disregard and contempt."

"Corporations may be pushing for civil rights on the surface, while routinely utilizing slave/ underpaid/ exploited labor, whenever they can, then blaming unions, regulators, environmentalists, for their forced improvements; environmentalists were never job killers, but corporations are, streamlining, automating, outsourcing, so intent on improving margins, with the capitalists demanding greater profits all the time. Companies, such as Xofconn, a modern equivalent to ancient slave drivers and traders, shielding global stakeholders (the stockholders and clients) from the devastating press of heading to *Mexico* to establish factories at sub-par wages, exploiting ignorant, dependent workers; essentially creating a captive labor force under the noses of U.S. regulators, who unaware of what is going on, hold the cloaked companies themselves blameless, while markets reward the abusive wages paid out, with even higher stock prices, for all the greed of the Street; and unknowing (corporate loyal) local communities lose even more jobs (their lifeblood) to anonymous, overseas, cut rate producers, but as they say, capital is fungible, forever flowing to where best treated. 'Profits are the mother's milk of stocks.'" The Worker's Guild came on.

Later, when *cerveza* and *margaritas* started flowing yet again and things began heating up with sudden, pungent marijuana clouds wafting through the air, both of Sayer's guests of honor, the Rev. Hannibal P. (Pearly) Gates and Ms. Yael Abraham, retired to the library, to peruse chapters of the Reverend's book, leaving it to union rep Malatesta to represent his badge with honor and distinction in the *relajo* to come. Today the off-duty HR queen played the part of Jew masquerading as WASP, showing once again, their correlation, notably about $, or social position, her Chanel No. 5 scent reminding him of Whale mixers, where preppy girls drank as much, as boys, freshmen having recently turned eighteen, no IDs required.

Sayer himself could be observed, holding court by the hot tub, guests already high, proficiently rolling joint after joint of the finest, pungent, sticky *botones de mota*, purchased in kilos from his trusty house boys. It came wrapped in newspaper, buds, stems, stalks and all, grown by a local mountain *ranchero*:

> I was once out strolling one very hot summer's day
> When I thought I'd lay myself down to rest
> In a big [tall] field of [Mexican] grass
> I laid there in the sun and felt it caressing my face
> As I fell asleep and dreamed
> I dreamed I was in a Hollywood movie
> And that I was the star of the movie
> This really blew my mind (Eric Burdon and War, "Spill the Wine," 1970)

It really blew Sayer's mind that after all these years he did not have a drug rap. Despite a reputation for anti-drug, anti-union search dog exploits, regularly drug testing all his employees except himself, Sayer was a devoted toker from way back, any variety at hand being his go to pot. Such were the regulatory demands made upon the industry by government, grumpy stockholders, that daily he thought longingly, of his wild times at The U.S. Military Academy at West Point, and wondered what happened since then:

> Political power grows out of the barrel of a gun.
> (Mao Tse-tung, Chinese Communist Party speech, 1938)

At these moments, no one really paused to care, as The Po' Boys, Oath Sleepers, gentlemen Knights of Freemisogyny, Tea Baggers, Boogers were assembling by the blue pool for another night of hell raising in *Viejo Mexico*; glorified memories of fascist *Camicie Nere, Sturmabteilung,* now faded, a cheap pomp devolved to plain spoken, cigar chomping, bible thumping, gun toting, righteous establishment toughs.

Sayer rose from a great dais, to share some thoughts with his rowdy crowd. "I want to thank this mob, because they've done the one thing, we were having trouble doing, which is to energize our huge base. Any public discussion of matters means a lecture from some minority or oppressed group, about how everyone must modify behaviors in their favor. Let's not confuse skin color with ideas. Sometimes the latter borrows from the former, but that is wrong. You are my best friends in the world, so let's party."

When some say, the right resorts to playground tactics, perhaps they do not mean it in the fashion to be demonstrated, nevertheless, as *tequila* was poured, Winchester, Remington, AK-47, Glock were loaded.

With life sized, human torso silhouette shaped target cutouts of federal agents to shoot, someone asked, "Does long gun connote a short dick?" Targets were placed at the end of the property, far enough from revelers but still too close for comfort; for the next hour solid barrages worthy of *Patton* held the scene.

"Why, in Mexico no guns are allowed; we paid the *aduanas* some hefty *mordidas* to get these in. They could not believe that in the little ol' U.S. of A., everyone is armed; doctors, lawyers, preachers all have weapons, teachers, activists, therapists amass arsenals, as an NRA provides cover for freedom fighters."

"When our man loses an election, we can all expect armed rebellion by the NRA, the god-fearing host. Let's get those jackbooted government thugs off our backs; let's repair, our broken electoral system."

"I'd like to see the NRA go after Planned Parenthood. Everybody knows conservatives are much less likely to answer polls run by media. But enough talk, let's get to that range;" and the shooting started, continuing into the evening, until other well to do beach barons had enough of the *gringo* raucousness; the sharp retorts of automatic, shotgun and rifle fire not very familiar to them, other than in the movies; one badass scene portraying Lilly hammering out round after fiery round from an M16, then Thompson submachine gun, both illegal in the U.S., and deserving of certain prison time for possession in Mexico.

Those who make a mark tricking others are sooner or later bested, tripped themselves, it's in the nature of the beast, a cosmic recompense. When the local constabulary responded to a complaint of shootings in the protected, rich neighborhood, Sayer paid them in *mezcal* and *pesos*, the best combination known:

> *Un político pobre es un pobre político.*
> [A poor politician is a poor politician.]
> (Carlos Hank Gonzalez, "El Profesor," Mexican politician, businessman,
> kleptocrat, 1970s)

It was Willi who had called them, requesting that the desk *sargento*, his *carnal,* send the *patrulla* to the *vecindario*; there might be firearms being used by possible criminals, a violation of strict Mexican law. Willi had discreetly sent an envelope with double the monthly *propinas* to share with the *quartel*. So, it became a trifecta night for the *Policia Municipal*, plus drinks: "*ningun pleito con estos cuates.*" It had all been about Lilly. She had not returned home for two days, and Willi was getting worried, lonely for her. Not to worry though, because Lilly had taken care of herself, spending the first, as well as second night with John B. Sayer (his clueless *senora* Felicity remaining in Bestport), causing sufficient reason for Willi to declare a new vendetta on this woman of his dreams, after waiting another morning for her.

As a final note, here follows the statement, by John B. Sayer, to the Mexican officials, sent to his home.

> Subject was naked, but for U.S. flag jock, Stetson, "with Luger in hand."

> "Americans can pretty much, do as they please, "Judge not, that ye be not judged," being for the most part tolerant, accepting, of differences, which include queers, blacks, greasers, redskins, gooks, chinks, camel jockeys, LGBT, everything, you name it, if relations are kept discreet and cultural points not made publicly. Once libertines demand political rights, that's when it gets tricky; I don't need the government, or anyone else, for that matter, telling me whom to like or approve of, or allow into my *estancia*. Everybody is welcome to my manse, it's an open invitation, but not when Uncle Sam, the Supreme Court, the United Nations or even the friendliest bribed Mexican *oficiales*, make it such that you must be admitted; then you will be tossed out, even if you are my best of friends, on the principle of the matter. Because I built this house, and it doesn't belong to anyone but me, and no one will tell me whom to admit, so let me take my *Luger*, costing a fortune of gratuities to smuggle in here, to bed, *buenas noches*."

# 14. No Harm in Harems, or Harem in Harm's Way

## The Fortunes and Misfortunes
## of the Famous Moll Flanders, &c.

Who was Born in Newgate, and during a Life of continu'd Variety for Threescore Years, besides her Childhood, was Twelve Year a Whore, five times a Wife (whereof once to her own Brother), Twelve Year a Thief, Eight Year a Transported Felon in Virginia, at last grew Rich, liv'd Honest, and dies a Penitent. Written from her own Memorandums . . .

### by Daniel Defoe, 1722

Lilly was back, having coffee on the hot terrace, a shade chagrined for her absence from her spouse for two nights straight, a bit the worse for wear, hell raising, hands, face, hair reeking of spent gunpowder. Despite provoking Willi to accelerate vendettas with the woman of his dreams, after two horrible nights without her, the distaff side was still dissatisfied, a fake purring, spoiled kitten demanding to be petted. She was not at all ashamed of her libidinous escapades and gave Willi a challenging, condescending, in your face, know-it-all gaze, as he (cuck) coldly limped toward her, across the patio's burning hot tiles.

Willi knew better than to ask about John B. Sayer, their common boss, but her paramour from the start, as there was only so much punishment that anyone could take, at any one time, even him, so unfaithful. Only, how was her affair different than his swinging? Because Sayer was her constant lover, versus his whorish behavior with one slut after another, to no end. Besides, she liked Sayer, finding him amusing, as opposed to her Willi despising anyone he slept with; luckily, Willi never tried to pork P Diddy, or he would have gotten an ear full of Yael Abraham to, "leave your work colleagues alone, you, dumbass." Perhaps P would have reciprocated Willi's romantic blather and intentions, considering her identity as:

Tomboy: Tomrig, Rampscuttle (Alexander Smith, *Moll Cutpurse*, 1714)

Earlier that humiliating morning, after gazing proudly at his improved, upgraded reflection in the full-length vanity mirror, lost in reveries of absolute, thunderous forms, limitless skies, Willi proceeded to review his correspondence, and could not stop pondering upon one of the letters received. He thought he knew the sender, or someone similar, but could not put the final touches on the face, or distant (near) voice. Here follows a confessional missive picked randomly, though not randomly posted, by P Diddy:

*Valentine's Day*
*Anonymous (P Diddy)*
*Dear Miss Lonelyhearts (Willi),*
*You seem the image of my benefactor's favorite character, so I'd better be careful, proceeding; he could do more for a great cause if he transcended himself, beyond a Botox blessed boytoy, to stand up for the rights of the maligned. Remember we are unique individuals sharing our time here. I will tell you about my experiences in Vietnam, so you know I am for real. Phoenix was my rebirth, because I could shoot wantonly, randomly, even with immunity; it was all my pent-up rage and aggression having suffered humiliation, harassment at being some new type of man, woman, tomrig, daisy, cross breed. I knew, being Melungeon, a multiracial polyglot, ever on the move for the last three centuries, from county to county, I was not*

*the most beloved by (questionably) racial purists, for wasn't I a eugenics nightmare? Evading laws, ordinances, meant to suppress miscegenation, which we not only practiced openly, but from which, mélange, we were a unique New World product, I was always destined for that life apart from others, perhaps novitiate in nunnery or monastery, my parents accepting my transgender identity by age three. At first the impulses were cosmetic, soon turning dress, gender, psyche inspired, as if no adjustment was good enough, unless it went all the way. Frankly, I looked like a dude, a transgender freak, a featureless, sexual-neutral, computer-generated avatar of queerness; to query you regarding a matter, or queer me regarding what matters, manly girls and girly men, where will it end? having no idea if I was asexual, nonsexual or just celibate, however, vice versa certainly, as I'm gay. And I want my kids to be gay too. And this is not an involuntary regression to a pre-pubescent stage, of sexual transference to best friend. Why shouldn't I give my son a doll, and my daughter a truck? Next, let's eliminate gender differences in clothing. Let's call a spade a spade, and tomboys, lesbians. But why do I think this New Age Family, of which that person I am referring to is a part, is worth dedicating divine temples to? They were similarly siblings, ushered forth from twin transversal, lateral sections, severe excises and grafting, hollowing outs and substitutions of privates, careful infusions of chemical, with biochemical additives; but a brother and sister connection to be defined in a figurative, circumstantial sense, in no way incest, and as such, undeserving of the social censuring it would one day inspire; being also of a solitary, contemplative sort; and their examples motivated me to the core, for they dared to go all the way. That is why if there is ever anything I can do for them, officially or not, I pray to God they know I am on their side; lacking green cards, they could never feel secure about their status; observe what happened to Japanese Americans in their WWII internments, which brings me back to Vietnam. To survive, we needed to do some rough things, and I had an abundance of tension to release. Looking at all the tattoos inked between my thighs I can't keep from wallowing in deep regrets for all the meek I assassinated, no better than a Lee Harvey Oswald. At least, I have found compassion:*

Be compassionate, for everyone you meet is fighting a great battle.
(Philo of Alexandria, c. 25 BCE – c. 50 CE)

*Please try to redeem yourself, by living up to your promised virtue, as the revolutionary you prepared to be, the activist you were, and the great star you have become. Use your pedestal to promote, do good for our society.*
*Sincerely,*
*A Lonely Reader*

But that all depended on what the good was esteemed to be, and how high we soared approaching truth:

The good is that which all things desire.
(Aristotle, *Nicomachean Ethics*, 350 BCE, [later quoted in a common search for celestial, as well as human, perfection, God's order, earthly divinities] Thomas Aquinas, *Summa Theologica*, 1265 – 1273)

Nevertheless, Willi was quite offended by the letter, as if he hadn't already done enough for others, and no perky pen pals could follow how much he had brainstormed, accomplished, invoking Mary, recently contributing to a gang of aggressive progressives, including P Diddy, Isidora, organizing harems for the abducted, the Fixer once alluded to, as well as the Sisterhood of Grace's Women's Reproductive Health Campus, New Haven, CT. Whatever their aims, they were nefarious, though cloaked in virtuous tones:

> This is no simple reform. It really is a revolution. Sex and race because they are easy and visible differences have been the primary ways of organizing human beings into superior and inferior groups and into the cheap labour in which this system still depends. We are talking about a society in which there will be no roles other than those chosen or those earned. We are really talking about humanism… The first wave was about women gaining a legal identity, and it took 150 years. The second wave of feminism is about social equality. We've come a long way, but it's only been 25 years… Women used to say, 'I am not a feminist, but…' Now they say, 'I am a feminist, but…' Some of us are becoming the men we wanted to marry. (Gloria Steinem, feminist, and journalist, since 1969, founder of *Ms.* Magazine, 1972)

The Fixer was high-flown in assuming, "one day in the near future polygamy will be legalized," but he was wrong in warning of, "Pan reproductive male harems shortly established, replete with every size, hue, race of inmate, various depths of maleness expressed," because they had already come to pass, by the time he derided their existence, but secretly, as a clandestine codicil of a trust of The Moll Flanders Foundation, Established 2002. It was as if the Sisterhood of Grace had finally overstepped its mission; although perhaps not, if its mission had been political and social domination of an entire Reproductive System, in the sense of cultural, familial, medical, health care systemic unity; beginning with gathering control of actual reproduction by inseminating and caring for selected sisters at new laying in hospitals; while press ganging, conscripting men with superior traits into their hidden harems. It was as simple as that, but getting there presented the gravest issue, of freedom versus scientific obligation to the race. It was then that P Diddy brought in Dr. Ken LaFountain, OB/GYN for the opulent, who, by egotistically substituting his sperm during artificial inseminations, democratized the program with broad incubations of new Pans, from the pooled sperm of a million donors, a million loving fathers. And then to scale up, first, on a national, followed by an international, basis, male chastity belts were the initial impositions, before the final indignity of observed, random but selected, men pressed into service, forced residency, at regional harems worldwide. But no one, not even a presumptuous Fixer, had an inkling that all that activity and achievement had commenced with the artful phone call, from Willi to Isidora Green, on a fated evening, during moments of his wife's strange disappearance while playing abductor to their kids.

> Chastity belts galore,
> Some clerics pray religiously,
> Cod pieces and more,
> In priestly garb, prey sexually.

In moments of his own craziness, he promised God that if his wife returned unharmed, he would start a grand social movement, a revolution, in her memory, dedicated to her love of family and children. And in thus fashion, was the first dollar promised by Willi for what became The Moll Flanders Foundation, which subsequently established the heretofore named beneficences, but also, secretly funded unnamed ops, whose purposes were stated, detailed by Willi himself, in raving absolutions of his vast infidelities.

Charter of The Moll Flanders Foundation (Black Ops)

Point one, is moral suasion for all men
To bear consistently the rule of *femmes*.
And two, inseminate and propagate
The race, without regard for their own fate.
Then three, a call to join a harem swift
As Hermes, to be not inclined to drift.
For four, rewards such constancy with child,
Brought up communally, in spirit mild.

Last five, will be to populate the world
With minion force, from mixed genetic swirl.
Our goal, the linkage of a global team
Shall bring about fulfillment of the dream.
We hereby grant creation of said trust,
To keep its clout beyond our turned to dust.

This was lilting Willi at his witty, wily best, expounding his latest doggerel of compensatory thoughts. After phoning Isidora and quickly explaining his purpose, he mailed her the charter, along with a check for one million dollars, as the anchor contribution. She then got to work through her wide professional, esoteric, leisure and social networks to bring incredible resources to bear. Of course, The Sisterhood of Grace led the way in organizing, financing, and undertaking the construction and future management of the vast projects in question. As Isidora was alarmed by stubbornly low birthrates in highly developed nations, due to alienation from our true sexual selves, or confusion over fertility and paternity, in overly competitive, impersonal, distracted systems, she was sold on the idea immediately, to increase her own influence, especially as Willi insisted on remaining an anonymous organizer and donor. *But when thou doest alms, let not thy left hand know what thy right hand doeth:* because Willi wanted to forget he had even made the call, once the whole extraordinary gig burgeoned, and finally spiraled out of control. In part, this was because he was not of the type to follow-up on anything, after initiated; in part, it allowed the moving forward with his career while presuming he had fulfilled a vow to God and his quirky wife. He believed that such an act of contrition would absolve him from past, unacceptable behavior, only to find himself and his wife now again under scrutiny for their recent bad behavior, a recurrent nightmare.

So, P Diddy was put in charge, without knowing of Willi's originating role, and commanded admirably. Reporting directly to Isidora, little did either one imagine that the Gypsy link between them would one day be instrumental to P's supercharged, high-brow successes. The quiet Sissy, she was Lady's darling. Her stalker's stealth, cruel animal tendencies, served her well in managing an enterprise combining the greatest scientific research minds, medical magicians, project engineers, architects, designers, workers, nurses, clerks, guards, administrators, attorneys, bankers, unions, philanthropic organizations, charities, etc., that is, the publicly facing side of the enterprise, the Sisterhood of Grace's Women's Reproductive Health Campus, New Haven, CT; but it was in her running of black ops that she excelled (due to a U.S. Marine Corps and special forces preparation as a trained assassin in Viet Nam), a Gulag Archipelago of strategically located, clandestine harems, more akin to ancient monasteries, where each monk had a cell with solid, high, standing desk to copy vellum manuscripts of ancient knowledge; while awaiting daily, early morning milking of his nocturnal emissions, come to fruition by a vacuum strapped to his middle, by women eunuch truants. And P Diddy became infamous throughout the camp system, taking on the sobriquet, Artemis Huntress Supreme, for her capacity to round up the most able, physically appealing, mentally balanced subjects, volunteers or not, and press them into open ended (as it were) service, but only as good, as their last ejac. It was also her idea to bring Geronimo's Ghost (G's G), onto the scene, get him out of his rut, the stuffy museum, for a change, make some use out of (beyond bound duties) in exhorting his brothers to accept the contemplative life that had been thrust upon them by cruel fate; live within their means, cleanly, blessedly, vowing, "poverty, chastity, obedience" in a service to numerous, faceless, nameless baby mamas; as he had been forced into doing by Isidora, and her acquisitive, sexy sisters, for three decades, weighed by elaborate *wampum* decorated, male chastity belt in red clay urn, awaiting his next appearance; the women eunuch truants essential in preserving his safety and security. Then upon hearing that G's G was onsite, assisting with their monks' morale, Dr. Ken LaFountain was beside himself with excitement, at finally being able to meet one of his mythic heroes, but had been so let down when, at last coming face to face, the phantom chief, now tragically, only a faint glow of what he had once been, perhaps getting forgetful after a century in solitary confinement, completely ignored the modern medicine man of tribal and Western magic, such that a rejected LaFountain locked himself in his laboratory, vowing never to hero worship anyone ever again, and lost himself in his latest work:

> He still bent his efforts upon the locomotive figure for the belfry, but only as a partial type of an ulterior creature, a sort of elephantine helot, adapted to further, in a degree scarcely to be imagined, the universal conveniences and glories of humanity; supplying nothing less than a supplement to the Six Days' Work; stocking the earth with a new serf, more useful than the ox, swifter than the dolphin, stronger than the lion, more cunning than the ape, for industry an ant, more fiery than serpents, and yet, in patience, another ass. All excellences of all God-made creatures which served man were here to receive advancement, and then to be combined in one. Talus was to have been the all-accomplished helot's name. Talus, iron slave to Bannadonna, and, through him, to man.
> (Herman Melville, *The Bell-Tower*, 1856)

And soon there were operations on intersex children, so finely bred as to be sterile, or breeding LGBT Amazons and Valkyries to compete in women's sports. Why was this not child abuse? Could there be an inverse correlation between reproductive rights and a group's fertility, as Isidora postulated secretly? Belief in certain, progressive ideas was no different than belief in God through religion, which was also in its essence an expression of faith, merely a notion; for instance, when a society affirmed gayness and transgenderism, as inalienable rights, due to recent acceptance of those lifestyles, that was no truer than another's belief in the divine order of all things in their lifestyle. Just as there was no scientific proof of the existence of God, there was no real proof that LBGT was anything more than a belief structure, and both practices, no better than opinions; was transgenderism the new focal point of freedom, a blooming dictatorship of queers? If a subject constantly heard the voice in his head, insisting he was really she... *excuse me, but in former days those were usually symptoms of paranoia, psychosis and schizophrenia. If I don't get enough attention as one gender, I can change into another, and everyone will still love me. One day I awoke as a man, as might have occurred in Kafka. Later I could wake up as a woman if I so chose. I wanted a penis in the worst way, and was hell-bent on growing some balls, but after surgery, shaping a dick out of my pussy labia, there was still too small an erection, only a chunk of fun, leftover girl flesh anatomy, worshiped no less for its pure function, as the lingering beauty of Aphrodite. Wasn't allowing children to trans to another sex akin to child sacrifice, regret after transformation? What was next, incestuous marriage? When did liberalism become libertinism?* What would Waterson posit, she wondered, because Dr. Ken LaFountain was Dr. Henry Waterson in his ultimate Creator guise as Sperm Donor Supreme, and although she devoutly believed in God, he always insisted on "going all the way:"

> Here, it might well be thought that, were these last conjectures as to the
> foundling's secrets not erroneous, then must he have been hopelessly
> infected with the craziest chimeras of his age; far outgoing Albert Magus
> and Cornelius Agrippa... A practical materialist, what Bannadonna had
> aimed at was to have been reached, not by logic, not by crucible, not
> by conjuration, not by altars, but by plain vise-bench and hammer. In
> short, to solve nature, to steal into her, to intrigue beyond her, to procure
> someone else to bind her to his hand—these, one and all, had not been his
> objects, but, asking no favors from any element or any being, of himself
> to rival her, outstrip her, and rule her. He stooped to conquer. With him,
> common sense was theurgy; machinery, miracle; Prometheus, the heroic
> name for machinist; man, the true God. (Melville, "Tower")

But weren't automatons automatically idiots, creating many more problems than anticipated wandering about the countryside unfettered, challenging innocent families and those guilty alike with a fast shock? Were these kids born genetically twisted or did yearning parents make them so? Yes, but seriously, the new breed was unlike any the world had seen, heretofore, perhaps hereafter, at their steady progression:

> Nevertheless, in his initial step, so far as the experimental automaton for
> the belfry was concerned, he allowed fancy some little play, or, perhaps,
> what seemed his fancifulness was but his utilitarian ambition collaterally
> extended. In figure, the creature for the belfry should not be likened after
> the human pattern, nor any animal one, nor after the ideals, however
> wild, of ancient fable, but equally in aspect as in organism be an original
> production—the more terrible to behold, the better. (Melville, "Tower")

So, Artemis was ready for a short coffee break after a busy morning chasing down collaborators for her cloisters. Some alert Acteon glimpsing her naked, she had summarily exiled him to the furthest district abbey, hoping never to run into him again, considering her gravest insecurity: frigidity. Since Vietnam, she returned to her feminine origins, but somehow, to no avail, as a stiff awkwardness made any sexual distinctions or choices irrelevant, and a confused identity reigned, so that men were never sure how to proceed, whether to make or take a pass (at) (on) her, it was rather murky yet so clear in its opaqueness. Planning tomorrow's worldwide attacks she delegated to her staff, as the great general she had become; nevertheless, from time to time she felt it a duty to join a specific operational mission, to keep her skills sharp. Tomorrow she would join a rifle squad as its sniper grunt, in a shock and awe assault against the faded Knights of Freemisogyny, rounding up apprentices, fellows, masters, great men to be made the better by the Sisterhood of Grace, in one fell swoop, as they exited their Temple of Philosophy and the Arts after a hand symbol laden evening of fake fellowship, heady hallucinogens, quintessential cocaine; making pompous appearances toward the end of ceremonies, demonstrating the higher aspects of their celibate Rule of the Order, such as sneaking destitute, homeless, female followers into the upper floors at two in the morning to bathe nasty crust from unhealthy bodies, then engage in unfeeling, perfunctory orgies with frothing, impotent, bestial Sons of the Lodge; perhaps their misogyny was a dormant cause. Accompanying General Diddy, in her resurrected form, as Grunt Marksman Supreme, was her aide-de-camp, none other than the *ayudante companero*, unilaterally spared, ultimately escaping to El Salvador, a political refugee; now the head of security, based on vast experience beginning with the U.S. Military Academy at West Point Class of 1976, then as the adjutant of the Chief of Staff of the National Army of Guatemala, happening to be his cross-dressed *joto* hooligan; having been personally recommended for the post by fabulous Willi, as shehe was starting to like the *reina*, even though shehe felt no particular affinity to him with respect to their similar, underground lifestyles, cross dressing expressions, bigender tendencies. Whether in the long run this was the wisest of decisions, only destiny would demonstrate. But shehe always repaid like for like and kindness for kindness, especially with someone as thoughtful enough to have saved herhis life, the *ayudante companero* having most certainly done that, generously. From *Guate* Willamina traveled to *Chiapas*, to train in *guerrilla* warfare, militant millennial of the new, progressive order, there always being some hidden notion driving Willi, to take enduring things down.

Driving into Bestport, CT at midnight (after which nothing good ever happens) through Saugamuck, an old, Italian town, across the Saugamuck River, up Empire Avenue, the crew had made certain they were not being followed, taking a sharp right onto Thomson Road, up the hill, then left onto Compost Rd. S., and left again, onto the King's Highway, rounding out the diversion in order to escape any detection by parking down a-ways, on the north side of the Posh Road, behind the white Constipational church. The commanding Gunnery Sergeant now sent Super Grunt (SG) on ahead, to reconnoiter, and within three minutes she signaled all clear, down to the intersection of Empire, with its blinking traffic light. Within another ten minutes (five of which were for her to get back, climb endless, steep stairs, set up her rifle), the entire squad was at the light, keeping as much as possible to shadows, all the while receiving cover from SG, in the bell-tower, where her sniper's view to their west, of the entire downtown (a full moon was behind her, at last), was unsurpassed. As obtaining arms had been the most daunting task faced by General Diddy, in the mustering up of her private regiment, the vital input of the *ayudante companero* had not only brought in arms, but training and contacts, as well; especially with regard to supply chains long ago established, through his top military and police connections, in El Salvador, with the Mexican *coyotes* in cahoots with the Colombian *FART* (*Fuerzas Armadas Revolucionarias de Tolima – Ejército del Pueblo*), controlling the remote mountain passes and jungle riverside staging camps from Colombia to Panama. Then there were Latino gang bangers, members, recruits of *Los X*, a notorious, Salvadorian street gang founded in Los Angeles in the 1980s, having expanded to include Hondurans, Guatemalans, Mexicans and other Central and South Americans, the motto, "rape, control, kill" gaining notoriety for numerous, brutal drug crimes across the U.S., out to prove themselves, of which a Los Angeles chapter was bossed, run, by the blank--faced fourteen-year-old boy (now grown up), with focused no nonsense expression, calming goat, who had accompanied Willi years ago on herhis defining epic migratory trek. As Willi's debt to *El Comandante* was still outstanding, and would never be expunged, the Goat served as a conduit between them in all important matters, as well as being the face for all arms, narcotics and illegal migrant (practically slaves) sales in the United States, through *Los X*, for the *FART* and *coyotes*. It was the Goat, who had personally taken it upon himself to supply Willi with all the drugs he needed for his wife, through a courier service at Lilly's beck and call, 24 hours, seven days a week, forever and ever more; in addition, he was responsible for the cruel Free-Range and Illegal Alien Child Movement, as kids smuggled across the border were never the children of those smuggling them, being easy prey, and given that most people's feelings toward illegal kids, were akin to those reserved for bank robbers.

*As to the final clarification it had been the Goat, along with the* ayudante companero, *who had taken care of Lilly's small problem (which was now really, Willi's mess), with a gun, which accidentally discharged at a rival.*

*Attorneys for an actress expected to be charged with third-degree murder, told CON News their client did not commit the crime, claiming, there's no question, this was a tragedy; but not all tragedies are obviously crimes ...*

*Attorneys for that politically influential news anchor husband were quite adamant, defending his actions in support of his wife, in the proceedings, asserting, there is nothing connecting him to this unfortunate gentleman.*

Tonight, the *ayudante companero* had volunteered for the mission, along with his boss, both as ordinary GIs in the squad, serving under an expert Gunny, to capture as many Knights of Freemisogyny as could readily be transported at the silent hour to the nearest harem, in Cringeport. As head of security, he was in constant touch with the Goat, so the proper bait had been supplied, in the bodies of three scintillating heshe hookers, meeting the ready squad at side door, who greeted them with whispered wolf whistles. With everyone finally in position, the kidnappings were about to commence. As each inebriated, horny Freemisogynist descended the stone steps, he was warmly greeted by one of the damsels, then quickly escorted with her trusting arm, to one of several, windowless vans, waiting around the corner, suddenly appearing; while the *ayudante companero* stood across the Posh road, in the deep shadows of a closed pizzeria, monitoring the activity, reporting to SG, still covering the action from the white needle church steeple, and the Gunny, who was directly loading each member as they appeared, into the waiting vans.

"Hello darling, were you, looking for me?" to an unsuspecting doped up dupe. Or "Big man, where've you been all my life?" One or two call girls at a time, hooking their catches: "Oh, what a strong arm, to lean onto, thank you for saying hello. Now why don't we just go over to that van over there, where we can be alone? That's right. Come along, there you go. Now watch your step while the nice Mr. Gunny assists you in. That's it, I will be right along," but already too late, as the sliding door slammed shut, so dames could return to lure others, gliding with ease back and forth through a night's quiet translucence. From her perch atop the spire, SG took in the entire clear scene through her rifle scope, when suddenly, she fixed on one of the three working girls. Despite eerie highlights of its focus, she tried sharpening it even further, as somehow, much to her sudden astonishment, before her single, augmented eye, only for a brief instant, before turning around, leading one of the dolts to his captivity, wasn't that **Willi** in drag? Although the opportunity did not present itself again, she was certain it had been him, but how or why? And since when did Willi ever care so much about this movement, for female and reproductive rights?

As one van filled, another pulled up, until over the course of about ten minutes, as one or two members walked out at a time, four vans were filled with twelve thrashing, flailing, grown men, in various states of lucidity, not too bad for an evening's outing. Once entered, the vans allowed for no escape, as each victim was immediately sedated with an injection gun (a step toward modernity, versus rags of ether or chloroform), in the back of the neck, for a quiet, quick trip to a new home in refurbished, old armament factories near the waterfront. Inside, each prisoner was monitored by the same hospital corpsman who injected him on the way in, considering their high value to the procreation machine they were about to (forcibly) enter. With doors shut drivers called ahead to inform the harem of impending arrival, and for them to have ready wards, with continued sedation on hand. While at the blinking light and temple, the Gunny was loading up a last mark, and the girls were on their way across the street to join the *ayudante companero*, SG, through her refined scope, crossed an armored vehicle slithering down the Posh Road, a Po' Boy patrol. SG immediately informed the *ayudante companero* and Gunny, but before they could make their final moves, the Po' Boys were upon them; it would be up to SG to support them while they made good their escape. This meant containing the Po' Boys with a rapid fire as only she could do, for she had plenty of rounds (bats) in her belfry, to back up her crew. As only rubber bullets were allowed and in use, as per the rules of the game established early on by Isidora Green herself, it was easy for SG to pepper spray the vehicle's hatches and doors, at any attempt by its proud, cornered occupants to exit. Thus, forewarned of the drastic outcome, the armored vehicle stayed shut, sealed, secure; after all, what did these putrid Po' Boys really care, about any captured Knights of Freemisogyny, if it did not involve a Po' Boy. And this hesitation, in the line of heaviest fire, showed they would live to fight another day, come what may, to a Freemisogynist unlucky enough to be caught in one of Artemis' notorious sweeps, for there were grave class differences between the two groups, perhaps some jealousy and resentment, as getting tapped for such a pseudo secret society was what everyone wanted, only, some were handed it, the privilege of belonging to something, the resentment when the privilege was taken away, as now. And little did they dream it was Artemis herself raining bullets down on them, with a godlike accuracy, giving the *ayudante companero*, with his girls, and Gunny, the moments they needed to skulk back into darkness, to the white church up the hill; SG down from her shooter's nest, as they were gone for good, back to the Posh Road, heading east, right on Compost Rd. S., as a diversion taking a left, onto Dreams Farms Road, through sedate, former, rolling pastures, and old time farms, now million-dollar mansions; then along the Gold Coast, where John and Yoko once lived in the 70s, providing a perfect cover for an easy escape, as old money areas, were less frequently patrolled by the police, for their extreme security.

Once arrived at Cringeport harem, the POWs were taken to dark chambers for a controlled withdrawal from their sedation. Then they were immediately strapped into the milking machines, which stimulated the ejaculatory impulses at the precise hour of 3:30 AM, as per prescribed dairy farm cycles, so that not one day would be lost, in terms of productivity. The harem was extremely careful not to over energize their male members, so once per day was the limit for their harvesting, to give them a good twenty-four hours to reset, regroup, resupply, but this was to be every day of the week, month, year, decade, forever more (*trafficked women raped by up to 30 johns/ day, seven days/ week, for the best part of four years: 43,200*). Their set initiation involved becoming a mistress' slave for thirty days, sleeping at night blindfolded in a male brothel, or running a sex gauntlet three days in a row, with pelvic injuries afterward so extensive, that those (brave) (foolish) novices might spend a week of agony in a hospital; upon being discharged, with the requisite stitches, bruises, broken bones, proving unflinching loyalty with a secret babbling oath to: Our Master Misogynist, Grand Duke John C., of great castles and royalties fame; last preying on damsels with promises of high tea, Her Majesty, their confidences shared, then traded away. Afterwards, it came about that he pushed the boundaries of erotic freedom. In truth, he sexually abused young females in need, wondering, as a perp, if the *DSM-IV* allowed for the physical misuse of minors. As morality was what you grew up with, right and wrong, and ethics the rules of the game, imposed by society, most Freemisogynists exhibiting neither, they were not only doomed in going forward, but had been so, even before sequestration; by the end of such in-house domestication adopting rolls as spouses, concubines, ready to provide loving service to the women who maintained them in luxury and comfort; this done with utmost secrecy, so that even that instigator Isidora never faced serious cold war charges. In hindsight, the travails of Grand Duke John C. are worth noting, if only for the depths of his agonies.

The Grand Duke's Lament

My wait suspenseful through the night for you,
Vile succubus, to suck-us-bust when due:
Old juices struck from shriveled seeds, once more,
Vibrations haunting shimmered center sore.
Cold apparatus stuck upon my dick,
I pray and hope to God, it shall be quick.
Bold flash of lightning through my weary loins,
So I may sleep anew; until I join

My comrade husbands in our harem suite,
Where we repose, partake of dainty sweets,
Thus, keep us plump and healthy for our wives.
There, cuckold limp, corrupted consort's lives,
Cry, "we are trapped, where no one knows to find
Us wretched souls;" and once again, it's time...

Ms. Yael Abraham knew nothing of these occurrences, in any way, being related to her boss, Isidora, or Dr. Diddy. There had been news flashes of periodic paramilitary faceoffs in the night, but nothing ever possibly connected, even as the faintest of rumors, to harems, captives, morning milking rituals. In her mind gender reassignment talk was fine and dandy, but chromosomes don't lie; but those were the early days when Bruce Gender was constantly reflecting on the type of man or woman, he would one day be; attitudes toward transgender individuals were of infinite compassion, as toward those who are mentally ill, and not responsible for their own choices, actions. Lesbianism and dykes were the Sapphist replies to the patriarchy. *When people died young, why did God seem to take the good ones, leave the losers? These last two decades have been instrumental in bringing about the sissified nature of this nation. So, we really prefer that everybody use the right restroom. That's the nicest way to say it. Was there such a concept as multi-genderism as with multiculturalism? Was LGBT a variant of Munchhausen by proxy? How far would the quest for identity take us, to where one person could claim to be another, as you can claim to be of different genders, or even another person's bones, with systemic surges, now hot or cold? how absurd, crazy.* And somehow, this contra gender bending bias was expressed, explained, through a ratio obsession, a feminist 50/ 50 binary, equity fixation about every aspect, significant or insignificant, of a universal, male/ female, interactive relationship, i.e., population, politics, education, employment, sexual relations, etc., so as not to miss out on anything due women at their expense, or to the advantage of men. In her official guise as Director, Human Resources, Warren Bros. Inc. Yael, flying SWISH, the preferred airline for sensitive sirs, brawny broads, returning from her European business trip, overheard curious banter from two gentlemen, both a bit light in the loafers, and peculiarly gaunt, but believable:

> "Did you know Santa Fe is the dyke capital of the United States?"
> (Truman Capote, *Answered Prayers*, 1975)

Yael could not explain it, but this statement caught her attention, making herself the mental note to plan a business trip to Santa Fe. The two continued, one bristling at the other's tutelage, regarding safe sex: "Did you happen to see that pharmacies now supply wide tipped condoms, so we can leave them on all night?" This was a new one to Yael, who had pretty much heard it all as WB's HR Counselor Supreme.

"How many times do I have to tell you, since we escaped, there is no reason, to keep those things on all night? The early morning milking is over." Yael understood high stress or anxiety, but what was this?

"After so many years, I got used to that all-night appendage there, ready to suck my cock on the clock."

"Enough of that, we're heading home now. Being from Connecticut, how the hell could we have ended up in *Swisherland*? With inside chat of a global Gulag Archipelago, my balls were Goulash ages ago."

"How will we explain where we've been? The police will never believe we were hijacked to a harem."

"Tell no one, forget it ever happened, or they will come after us, even while we're lecturing at Whale."

"I can't imagine the university will hire us back; it might cause a lot of controversy explaining it at all."

"One thing, for sure, stay far away from the Cringeport harem; they have a lot of security goons there."

At JFK customs, Yael saw two guys with beards tenderly smooching in the open. As with most liberal, urban LGBTs, they wore their sexualities on their sleeves; it was the first thing one noticed about them. The doppelganger effect in LGBT match making was uncanny, in that gays seemed to choose reflected mates, so when you saw them together, perhaps at an art gallery or opera, it was like observing twins:

PEGEEN. Aye. Wouldn't it be a bitter thing for a girl to go marrying the like of Shaneen, and he a middling kind of a scarecrow, with no savagery or fine words in him at all?
(John M. Synge, *The Playboy of the Western World*, 1907)

Ms. Yael Abraham went both ways: in her psyche, as Jew/Nazi, and sexual identity, as hetero/lesbian. At first Willi did not like Ms. Abraham, because she was a Jew, and in his Catholic mind, they were the ones who nailed Christ to His cross, but she managed to win him over by strong, ethical promulgations. A short time ago, she was a cheap, lifeless, static rubber doll humming with a weak electric motor; now after burgeoning affair with the Rev. Hannibal P. (Pearly) Gates, she was transformed, transfigured into a costly, living, breathing Dinah-Moe Humm set to bring lasting pleasure and delight; a new automaton burning desire and sex, on demand, at the millennium. Because the more the preacher acted the man, the more she liked men, as she was bisexual. So, one lonesome night shortly after the flight, she found herself sharing a bed with that rascal of a reverend intellectual, when the following pillow talk ensued:

"We already have transgenderism, why not transracialism, trans-racism? I'm a true Transracial for the new millennium, as per *Shared Kinship, Fateful Destinies*; this is no longer a revolution but a reveille call. That number 169062, tattooed on your arm; do you know its meaning, where or how you got it?"

"Why, Preacher Pearly, I was an inmate at the Nazi death camp, Auschwitz; why are you so fascinated by my number? It's as random as the faces of any of the doomed denizens of the world's death camps, yet I recall each, on their final promenade down a long railway platform, to a predestined left or right."

"Perhaps an excess of the sentiment of pity, on the left, drives the right, until an excess of the faculty of reason, on the right, drives back the left, and on, and on, ad infinitum. But losing your liberty is akin to death. When the pendulum swings too wide it sometimes locks, freezes, until it swings the other way."

Yael then innocently recounted verbatim the light in the loafers' discussion, she overheard in a business class cabin, without in any way comprehending its subtle or greater meaning, however, inquiring about the Cringeport harem; had Preacher Pearly heard of such, existing in those renovated arms warehouses? But how could such horrible things exist in secret? Wasn't God, or anybody, watching over this world?

Yet it was all the hint the wily Worshiper of the Lord needed to comprehend what had been occurring far too many times to recount; only clandestinely, so none would have the slightest of ideas of the true goings on. And he concealed total understanding of the strange dialogue, quickly changing the subject.

"Perhaps it's a personal responsibility vs. welfare state (Republican vs. Democrat), issue. Yes, he was having their baby, perhaps even twins which is why I said, 'Beware of Geeks with guns bearing gifts.'"

But the ground had been prepared for the long period of bitter reprisals that shortly followed. Hannibal dutifully reported to his man, John B. Sayer, all he had heard, and was generously rewarded with a new scholarship for younger church members, The J. B. Sayer Memorial Stipend for Liberties and Freedom. The epicurean preacher was the perfect beard for the cagey Puritan, godly, timeless foxes of past ages. Meanwhile Sayer mustered all his available forces for a *blitzkrieg* strike against a resourceful fem foe. Considering that those fabled Knights of Freemisogyny were decimated as of late, and their vociferous captain, that Grand Duke John C., was now reported missing for almost two years, the Po' Boys, Oath Sleepers were there in force, despite their threatening presence, aggressive antics, toward other guests; as the night wore on, their wild boasts, challenges, setting the pace for the scheming gathering. They'd be front and center in any initial attack, with the tactical aim of rescuing the Grand Duke, as a courtly gesture of bonhomie; while prosecuting the prostitutes with no mercy, saintly right, right to life, now a front of ablution rights overturning abortion rights, as behind many noble achievements lie misdeeds a plenty. Preacher Pearly distanced himself from those bellicose attitudes but was surely accountable. The Oath Sleeper, Senator Goads, was due today to strategize. After both serving in Phoenix, in Nam, then having met again at Whale, while Sayer attended the School of Management, and H. E. Goads, the School of Law, they remained political friends, forever patriots. Perhaps even if those with educations were worthy of leading, and if representing obnoxious ideologies, at least anchored in common ground, Whalies were not always moral minded, despite moral standing, his claim to fame, he goads the enemy. He had been U.S. Army Colonel John B. Sayer's workhorse in Nam, monitoring the various missions going on at once, providing valuable military law insights, to Sayer's command decisions; mainly, how to avoid charges of atrocities, more specifically, war crimes, for the interrogation techniques utilized in the CIA run jungle jails, with no accountability; taking tremendous satisfaction in booby trapping with M-80's the heavy, metal plated helmets worn by captured NVA regulars; whoop-shrieking "Geronimo!" with delight, as solid skull pieces flipped in the air, tumbling back to shredded work table; all the while taunting maimed prisoners to remain quiet if they dared. There was a significant incident which he had helped cover up involving Sayer (as a soldier of some private means stationed far from home, he kept a dark, long haired, local girl with sensual eyes, as his housekeeper/ concubine; his faithful wife Felicity, having nary a notion; with fluency in French, good English, the Asian beauty was very discreet, in her withdrawal from the venue, when Sayer got into his repugnant rants), his house girl back in Saigon and two heshe hookers, who apparently liked his girl more than him, causing flaccid fellatio and no felicity. Lieutenant Goads duly paid them, with dedicated slush funds, to utter nary a word of that embarrassing incident. His discretion was indispensable, which was why he was the U.S. Senator from Nevada-sins. Now Generalissimo Goads, commission from the pact powers at hand, reviewed his regimental troops. Gussied up in the tailor-made powder puff blue uniform of the Committee for Public Safety, he was as if Herman Goering, in his WWII *Luftwaffe* duds; and was it rouge on his cheeks, lipstick and eyeliner?

General Diddy, for the moment, disengaged as Artemis Huntress Supreme, was finishing her eighth cup of coffee that day, when the enemy hit them hard, keeping to the rubber bullet conventions, but striking in broad daylight. In its intensity, it followed the German siege of Stalingrad, in WWII. Overnight all Cringeport south of I-95 to the docks consisting of obsolete industrial warehouses, was surrounded, and pummeled, with an artillery barrage lasting for hours, meant to soften up resistance. At dawn came the order to attack, first with lightning-fast armored vehicles, then wave upon wave of infantry, until all the fem defenders had been pushed down the peninsula, with their backs against the Pokemenock River in a last stand. This desperate, defensive position would certainly test their mettle, so General Diddy tried to rally her troops, exhorting them to dedicate their entire beings to their rescue, for, "'God helps those who help themselves.' And as in ancient times, immortals and heroes shared elixirs of life, foods of the gods, ambrosias, sweet nectars, so shall I concoct such, utilizing the philosophers' stone borrowed from our good friend Dr. Ken LaFountain, to fortify you brave soldiers with a potion of mercurial chemistry: nine parts corn liquor to one part gunpowder, and you shall capture the hill from where they bombard us;" labeling it Liberty Ladies' Libation, * with which the whole army having a shot or two fought as if Hellhounds, tooth and nail to the bitter end, until they took that rise in an initial victory for their forces; her troops so fortified that upon someone mistakenly shouting "To the top, girls!" they assaulted, and in 55 minutes captured the cape, but the actions were marred by a lack of control of the counter attacking troops, committing atrocities against young axis irregulars; but catapulting Artemis into a national hero, folkloric rebel, by mixing gunpowder, bourbon, attacking ramparts in a fearless charge, that lives on to this day; the misandrist columns clawing their way north against vastly superior misogynist forces until reclaiming their abandoned harem, which had been forsaken with all its occupants, for what fems had expected would only be a few short hours, but had in fact been twenty-four. And in that quick span of temporary occupation, there can be no denying that improper penalties were meted out against inmates, as many of the horny attackers had their way, with the pink jumpsuit garbed tenants of the Spasm Pump Machine; they were violated, but somehow appreciated it, due to having had limited human contact for some time. After which they were offered their freedom to retreat with bloc forces to safe ground north of I-95, with some accepting the chance to skip the light fantastic out of town to former lives, but many others, perhaps half, choosing to remain in the splendor of the harem, readily slipping their limp joints nightly into rubberized contraptions fondly known throughout the Gulag as Dinah-Moe Humm. Except for the Grand Duke John C., who was loathed by friend and foe alike; his doom was more in a style of Dante's, *Divine Comedy*, "Inferno": "All hope abandon ye who enter here." His future was fried. Firstly, he was not violated, in any way, shape or form, thus denying him any of the solace experienced by his compatriots, in their first outside contact in a long while. Secondly, he was ignored by any competitive gang member worth his salt for being just that: competitive, conceited and untrustworthy. Thirdly, and in this case, lastly, when the aggressors pulled back in sheer panic they never thought, planned or even dreamed they would bring the Grand Duke with them, so they left him there, in his cell; it sure sucked. He was found within, strapped to his milking apparatus, when his former captors returned to reconquer the harem. And there he remained, in penal (penile) opulence, along with the other forgotten prisoners: hookers smoking hookahs of hooch to relieve crotch cramps and the tedium of whiling away the hours:

> What next befell me then and there
> I know not well—I never knew—
> First came the loss of light, and air,
> And then of darkness too:
> I had no thought, no feeling—none—
> Among the stones I stood a stone,
> And was, scarce conscious what I wist,
> As shrubless crags within the mist;
> For all was blank, and bleak, and grey;
> It was not night—it was not day;
> It was not even the dungeon-light,
> So hateful to my heavy sight,
> But vacancy absorbing space,
> And fixedness—without a place;
> There were no stars, no earth, no time,
> No check, no change, no good, no crime
> But silence, and a stirless breath
> Which neither was of life nor death;
> A sea of stagnant idleness,
> Blind, boundless, mute, and motionless!
> (Lord Byron [George Gordon], "The Prisoner of Chillon," 1816)

All glory went to Artemis Huntress Supreme in her resounding victory, but as she worked secretively, no one had the slightest idea who Artemis was, only that she had out maneuvered, outfoxed axis special forces, with aplomb and distinction. At first, she was feted everywhere she went; there were imperious triumphs in her honor, in all the major cities. Generalissimo Goads went back to being a plain, old U.S. Senator, missing the trappings and distinction of parading, as a military man, needing to keep his right wing conspiracy connections, and participations, a secret from his colleagues in congress, and the FBI; one of his first bills sponsored upon returning being an outright curtailment if not prohibition of harems in America, and if not, then the opening up of the trade to the opposition, in the spirit of free enterprise, named, The Goads No Harm in Harems, or Harem in Harm's Way Reform Bill for Worker's Services.

So, there was a codifying of the practice, as a health and social service, and Goads covered up his mess, his short sightedness perhaps the result of a prominent eye patch covering a left eye he himself blinded from dropping a loaded gun, after which any rational person might have disavowed arms forever more, not him. The Generalissimo was in deep doggy doo-doo with Sayer, for having botched the great battle of the millennium. There would always be further use for him, as a Senator in legislative dastardliness.

It seemed a new order came about because of the epic struggle, where the forces of freedom had a great impact on different versions of liberty, not as everyone doing what they wanted but doing so in concert with the whole. And maybe it was not that obvious in the mainstream, but as with all starts occurring quietly, no one ever knowing or becoming aware of the great changes quietly taking place for us. Who conceived what our futures would bring? In terms of Artemis, erstwhile goddess, she was now on the run, ordered by Isidora Green to hightail it to the West Coast and to keep out of sight. Transforming the harems from the black ops beneficence of The Sisterhood of Grace, with adjunct status to the dominant trust, to a legitimized and regulated business, meant that perhaps Artemis would need to disappear for good, but there would always be a place for Dr. Diddy as herself, once the uproar over her intense raids and significant final battle had died down; it was the last the defeated would hear of her, until a revival. Of course, she could rest on her laurels and memories, as, "Old soldiers never die; they just fade away."

Sayer knew that Isidora, in her greatness as the Goddess Supreme, had pulled one over on him, but was never in the position to bring it up in a formal discussion, or mention it in a moment of collegial banter, as she was his boss, and interactions with her were kept to a minimum outside of business protocol; he never calling Isidora, by her name, thinking of her as his superior; always Madame Chairman, no chit chat, nothing more. He knew she always had his back professionally; he owed her labor worthy of that trust. He understood his top grade was that of Apollo, never Zeus, and if she was Hera, it made sense. But Artemis seemed to live forever, for Sayer, a trope of her success, to those Free Love, Free Woman, Free Gender Poly-Morphia, Free Asexuality, Free Everything tribes; he was gunning for a goddess. An APB was quickly issued for the idol suspect, but in true California style, it was impossible to clarify for what genders, to be on the lookout. Sayer was so frustrated, he tried to kick himself at his folly. So, he screamed and swore over the phone at his distant, loyal and quite innocent, patriot call center workers, upsetting their professional equanimity with profanity infused rants, where was the moral equivalence?

Well, there you go, the succinct telling of one of the most important paramilitary encounters of all time. Willi, done with reminiscing of how important he had been to the inception, growth and success of the movement, poured himself a huge tumbler of scotch and soda, lit up a Cuban cigar and settled in for the night. From now on, he would use more discretion when calling Isidora in the middle of a lonely spell. Next week he was scheduled to meet with the Rev. Hannibal P. (Pearly) Gates about new contributions.

*Footnote

Don Pedro Lagos Marchant (1832-1884), a Chilean Infantry commander, mythically mixed up such a concoction, using *Pisco*, instead of bourbon, with gunpowder, though of unknown strength, so 9 to 1 seemed a prudent guess, before storming El Morro de Arica, in a decisive battle of the War of the Pacific, 1880; his troops so fortified that upon someone mistakenly shouting, "*Al morro, muchachos!*" they assaulted, and within 55 minutes captured the cape, but the action was tarnished by the lack of control over the attacking troops, causing atrocities to Peruvian defenders; but making Lagos into a national hero, *haciendo mito, la mezcla de polvora y Pisco.* (From the author's recollections of interviews with *cognoscenti* in Chile.)

# 15. *48 Hours to Mecca*

[Scheherazade] possessed courage, wit, and penetration. She had read much, and had so admirable a memory, that she never forgot anything she had read. She had successfully applied herself to philosophy, medicine, history, and the liberal arts; and her poetry excelled the compositions of the best writers of her time. Besides this, she was a perfect beauty, and all her accomplishments were crowned by solid virtue.

"My story is of such marvel that if it were written with a needle on the corner of an eye, it would yet serve as a lesson to those who seek wisdom." (Anonymous, *The Arabian Nights: One Thousand and One Nights*, The Islamic Golden Age, 8th to 14th centuries)

Willi connected with his superstar spouse's super-stare, on blazing patio, after an absence of two nights in a row, an unprecedented liberty presumed within their marriage, so far (except as a surprise no-show at an evening's Motion Pictures Awards Dinner, garnering more acclaim in absence, a lack of, than had she actually attended); he knew better than to accelerate vendettas with the woman of his dreams, even after waiting another morning for her, as the distaff side was still dissatisfied, despite purring, a spoiled kitten waiting to be petted; perhaps these were his life's just deserts following formidable philandering.

Lilly knew better than to ask about Isidora Green, their common boss, but his paramour from the start, as there was only so much punishment that could be meted out to anybody, even him, for unfaithfulness to her. Fortunately, she never tried to invoke the Rev. Hannibal, or she would have received an ear full of Yael Abraham to, "leave professional colleagues be, dummy;" as, there could be no fellowship with someone at the office. Besides, Lilly's use of aliases, identities, pseudonyms, as per Moll Flanders and the Continental Op, made it impossible for God's ministers to address any directives to a single persona considering, Lilly's adventures of whoring, marriage, incest, criminality, transportation, riches, honesty, penitence, unsurprisingly the same progression kept to by our hero Willi, who knew no shame, as well.

Earlier that hung over morning, after gazing longingly at her improved, upgraded reflection in the full-length vanity mirror, lost in the reveries of absolute, beautiful forms, timeless skies, Lilly proceeded to review her correspondence, and could not stop pondering upon one of the letters received. She felt she knew the sender or someone similar but could not put the final touches on a face or distant (near) voice. Here follows a confessional missive picked randomly, though not randomly posted, by Preacher Pearly:

> *Valentine's Day*
> *Anonymous (Rev. Hannibal)*
> *Dear Miss Lonelyhearts (Lilly),*
> *You seem the image of my benefactor's favorite character, so I'd better be careful, proceeding; she could do more for this cause if she transcended herself, beyond a Botox blessed bimbo, to stand up for the rights of those maligned. Remember we are unique individuals sharing our time here. I shall tell you of my journey to the Gold Coast, so you know I am for real. Accra, with Tenka, was my rebirth, I could study wantonly, randomly, but with immunity; it was all my pent-up rage and aggression having suffered humiliation, harassment at being some new type of racial/ social avenger, equalizer, cross breed. I knew, being a culturally competent, polite, black man, had not served me well in a society forever on the move, in need of*

*more challenging, useful, in your face strategies, rougher than, "Yassuh, Boss. Whatevuh you sez;" because in America blacks were still trying to get to where whites had already been. In recent ages, when Ikea, Subaru, Bayer, VW, Nike utilized forced labor, it became expedient for those once persecuted to become persecutors, in defense of the homeland from Third World marauders. I have, nevertheless, been accused of excesses, for not wanting to go to my boss' sordid soirees, but attending anyway, due to the recent participation of a certain, Jewish refugee Holocaust survivor, I am getting to know. I look forward to reviewing my latest notes, theses, with her, valuing her dualist opinions on matters; she understands the need to keep certain types out, while making it very comfortable for those inside; and assuring the ruling class that only those qualified, deserving, get in. And a tattoo 169062 she wears, is the symbol of a phoenix reborn of fate. The true to life narrative is shockingly one, in which those who have been the most viciously oppressed, remarkably, in a most depraved, ironic and, considering, the true depths of their cruel sufferings, perverse means, go on to self-righteously, unflinchingly, oppress others, and it is a narrative as old and as common, as revenge itself. Many victims of oppression and torture manage to rise above their past travails and degradations, some even advancing in becoming great oppressors and torturers themselves. There had been Roman expeditions in Sub-Saharan Africa, at the start of the first century and millennium, seeking out sources of trade goods and wealth, in the dark, steamy, unholy, interior realms of forbidding jungles. But even they learned the hard way that our people did not mess around, after being consumed by certain cannibals among them, as well as lions, hippos, hyenas, when the tables turned, which brings me back to Accra. I learned cynicism there, and the need to establish a power base to effect change from within, as well as without; but tempered with some noblesse oblige, as when they are nobly obliged by the point of an AR-15, AK-47; only, in our possession, as well as theirs, attacking extolled constitutional privileges head on, with equal footing. Finally, I want to pay homage, to my father's folks, who were golden throated, performing lullabies written by Jews, with the heart and soul of the transported, enslaved, black race:*

Summertime/ And the livin' is easy/ Fish are jumpin'/ And the cotton is high (George [and Ira] Gershwin, *Porgy and Bess*, 1935)

*Please try to redeem yourself, by living up to your promised virtue, as the Mujahideen you prepared to be, the paragon you were, and the great star, you have become. Use your pedestal to promote, do good for our society. Sincerely,*
*A Lonely Reader*

But that all depended on what the good was esteemed to be, and how far we ventured to believe fables:

Men are born and remain free and equal in rights. Social distinctions may be founded only upon the general good. (Largely composed by the Marquis de Lafayette, assisted by revolutionary Thomas Jefferson, *The Declaration of the Rights of Man and of the Citizen*, 1789)

Nevertheless, Lilly was a bit offended by the letter, as if she hadn't already done enough for others, and no bold pen pals could follow how much she had brainstormed, accomplished, invoking Allah, recently contributing to a group of reactive reactionaries, including the Rev. Hannibal, John Sayer, in founding a Committee for Public Safety, whose beefy, mono dimensioned members attended the last two evening's sordid soirees of shooting. Whatever their aims, they were nefarious, though cloaked in virtuous tones:

> How strange and eventful has been the brief history of this marvelous
> city, San Francisco... But it has been through its season of heaven- defying
> crime, violence, and blood, from which it was rescued and handed back
> to soberness, morality, and good government, by that peculiar invention
> of Anglo-Saxon Republican America, the solemn awe- inspiring Vigilance
> Committee of the most grave and responsible citizens, the last resort of
> the thinking and the good, taken to only when vice, fraud, and ruffianism
> have entrenched themselves behind the forms of law, suffrage, and ballot,
> and there is no hope but in organized force, whose action must be instant
> and thorough, or its state will be worse than before.
> (Richard Henry Dana, *Two Years Before the Mast,* 1840, 1869)

The Fixer knew the requirement to provide equal care and treatment, as per the Communications Act of 1934, to both sides of any issue in his reporting; as the Yellow Kid, he exercised utmost caution to tread a fine line, between the likes of Cucker Snarlson on one side (claiming cloying conspiracy), Panderson Scooper on the other (when he said this is not normal, watch out), providing contrasting opinions in a counter equivalent, open-minded subterfuge. Was Ottoline's interest in Lilly's mother's entombment in Guantánamo, due to her own mother's long exile to the Gulag Archipelago, for unpatriotic acts against the Soviet Union? As a pretense for her star reporter to approach Lilly, she was willing to go so far, as to interview totalitarians, based on the need to get a fair and balanced view of the story, for the sake of journalistic integrity. And the loyal Fixer could not help heeding green-eyed Ottoline, red headed Rus, beautiful Slav princess, dutiful editor and boss, because she had a way of getting just what she wanted.

Once again, he made it out to Beachside Bungalow Studio, Baja Cal., to get the grit for Slay Magazine: "You weren't here, the last time I came out for the eugenics round table discussion; any interest in it?"

"No, however, all of my husband's forums downright bore me and effete symposiums get us nowhere."

"This time I came to get your side of the story about your relationship with the nativist movement, you seem so enamored of, and how it relates to Sayer, Preacher Pearly, and even a corporate HR Director."

"Some characters are empathetic and others clearly not. I am not sure to which you are referring. Then there are fickle fans changeable as dust, detached as the next man and only loyal for a moment, while it fills their sense, for quick identity." Was this, *"...a riddle, wrapped in a mystery, inside an enigma,"* or *perhaps some spittle, wrapped in misery, inside an enema?* The Fixer came back to the point, asking:

"Lilly, is it true what they say about your participation in the origins of the anti-immigrant movement?"

"I will relate what I remember, because it was all my idea: one night in a catalepsy, a nervous condition characterized by muscular rigidity, fixity of posture, regardless of external stimuli, as well as decreased sensitivity to pain; because I had done so much coke at one sitting that I froze, my heart near exploding with anxiety, fear and obsessiveness, about my success, failure, career, life, family, origins, the works; I called Sayer, panicked, suffering a moment of utter craziness, promising Allah, in an act of contrition, I prayed, would absolve me; that if my husband forgave my past unacceptable behavior, I would forsake the use of strong stimulants like coke and downers while I wrote a thriller screenplay that would endear me with millions, stellify me as a deity, and bring to the studio untold, worldwide revenues; but only to find myself and my husband now again under scrutiny for recent bad behavior, a recurrent nightmare."

"You did assault an immigrant homeless couple, pissing on them randomly, in the middle of the night."

"I already said it was the hard stuff. I knew I could make it on beer and good weed, I vowed as much."

"Now tell your anxious fans exactly what happened; also, how your movie was mixed up in all of this."

"Only if you promise to mention how my rage stems from oozing welts across my back that shall never heal." As this seemed a bit melodramatic, he quickly agreed, for art's sake, to proceed with a narration:

"Having always imagined myself, a Clark Gable, the King of Hollywood, closet queen of sordid hills, I shall relate these founding deeds of great adventures, struggles worthy of *The Iliad's* brave Hecuba…"

This was literary Lilly at her sly, lively best, describing her latest caricature of romantic, heroic musing. After phoning Sayer and quickly explaining her purpose, she mailed him an outline, along with a check for a million dollars as the anchor investment. He got to work through Conflagrational church, patriot, social, professional networks to bring vast resources to bear. Of course, Warren Bros. Inc. led the way in organizing, financing, and undertaking the production and future distribution of the huge blockbuster in question. In her *avant-garde*, erudite, recondite fashion, she composed a triumph of the imagination. Her storyline was a *tour de force* of the American cinema, an adventure masterpiece in the *auteur* styles of John Ford, John Huston, Clint Eastwood. As Sayer's animal spirits were displeased by the Western tradition, meaning white privilege, falling under siege by renegade, cultural competence; his Manifest Destiny no longer stoked by an invisible hand, the thin lipped, high collared, heavy buckle shod Puritan with an inexorable posterity, as dried as salt cod; for a long time he had wanted the studio to bring out a feature, extolling American virtues, Protestant beliefs; embarrassingly recalling early photos of himself, as a long curled toddler, in girl's dresses, patent leather shoes. And LGBT had everyone believe it was nature, not nurture; if any genetic component were stated, screaming bloody murder over determinism. The first argument supported the "it can't be helped or changed," normalizing defense, while the second made too strong a case, that it's a disorder, for empathy. As poetic impresario Lilly combined the ideas.

> Mary, Mary, quite contrary
> Had a punk who was a fairy.

So, Rev. Hannibal was put in charge, without knowing of Lilly's originating role, producing admirably. Reporting directly to Sayer, little did he imagine that this page-turner came from Author Supreme Lilly. Because Baptists were even more unrelenting toward all who did not fit in, than Puritans had ever been, flourishing from even deeper, more literalist, less educated Calvinist strains than their Congregational/Presbyterian cousins; Preacher Pearly should not have been as relaxed, open minded, accepting, of the young cast and crew of the movie considering the arty, liberal, gay atmosphere of the set; but Hannibal, product of the highly developed Western Judeo Christian moral values, fostered by his liberal education at Whale U., could never be as infallible, reproaching and shaming, as his family's religion demanded. *Well, if most of us usually spend 20% of our time thinking about sex, gender, sexuality, degenerates, on the other hand, usually spend nearly 80% of their time thinking about the same, and more. That is why their dependability is questioned and the military rejects them. If gays are allowed to marry, so should sheep, cattle, dogs, amoebas, as the recently adopted rallying cry of the latest, and most outlandish, of LGBT guiding lights, was not, "splendor in the grass," but rather, "splendor in the ass." Just because you enjoy getting your dick dirty in a guy's rear, does not mean the rest of us should keep quiet about it. "My seat is so sore, but I had to get my needs met," said a heshe after romping in hay loft with fellows. Perhaps Joan of Arc was a man, after all, and heshe really got her period, as might only have occurred in Kafka, and trans women don't dress as regular women, inveterate, unrelenting, unrepentant buggers, rather in extreme versions of out of fashion femininity, ranging from schoolmarm to hooker.* But wasn't it really humanity that was at the centerpiece of the Western tradition, man's love, tolerance, empathy, for their fellow men? So as Producer General, he rose above family religious sentiments, to persevere for those in need, not really minding these strange people and their extreme antics, diversity, etc. But when they got in his face, it was another matter, as deep down, they were trouble, and interacting with them posed risks, for the blame and uncompromising hatred they held against the hetero lifestyle, and all religions. For all his contradictions, he was bound to do the best job possible for Sayer and himself.

As Lilly's tight (anonymously scribed) script called for scenes to be filmed in Mecca, and Sayer, being a stickler for cinematic realism, wanted true footage to base such action upon, that was when Hannibal had brought in *SS* Colonel Otto Waldemar Grawitz, once renegade, now absolved ex-Nazi agent for the opulent, who by surreptitiously substituting a privately acquired inmate in a key role during a darkened moment of the film, for the Mossad mark he had contracted to abduct from deepest Saudi Arabia, was able to complete an exchange for what he considered the grandest prize of all. Because the *SS* Colonel enjoyed long standing ties, to the rabid, Jew hating House of Saud, founders, financiers, of many big-time *madrasas*, colleges of Islamic instruction, but really institutions of anti-Western hate and revenge. But as the good Colonel was getting on in years, he realized that loyalty was a movable feast, meant to shift as wind on a summer's day. "In those days we did not trust anyone who had not been in the war." And it was better to trust the Jews, who had at least fought for their lives, than the Arabs, who had done their best to stay out, and that went for pro-Axis, German loving, Latin American so-called Republics. As time was of the essence for the Colonel, he did not have leisure to wait for payment, and the Israelis paid immediately to his long-standing account, at the Zurich Credit Suisse, where he had been hoarding gold teeth, coins and diamonds since 1938. So ironically for him, they were the best client to work for. It was one year prior to the lunch they shared at Sparks Steak House, before his imposing remembrance of those evil deeds of his to the United Nations, and Sayer's decision to somehow or other, include him in the future of Warren Bros. Inc., that Grawitz answered a blind ad for anyone with connections to the Saudi royal family to promptly get in touch. So he was interviewed by Producer Pearly for a position as technical assistant to the producer for scene structure; as such, he would be responsible for arranging the production company's access to, and comfort in, the Saudi Royal State (operating at the millennium still as a savage kingdom, where they cut off your hand for stealing, tongue for lying, head for adultery, buggery and blasphemy, all offenses, of which Lilly was long guilty). Nonetheless, Lilly was the only celebrity leading lady Hannibal considered to cast as Scheherazade, the sassy heroine of her own secret saga; and of course, when Lilly dreamed up the exciting spy fantasy, she had herself in mind for a role, but only Sayer had any inkling of such. And this outward reserve of Scheherazade's was as natural to her as the sun veiled behind clouds; she was bound to take any narrative to its climax, as folklore fated, she should, for over a millennium. Despite the obvious Sayer did not deny Hannibal a eureka moment: ecstatic in his fulsome praise of the producer, that *48 Hours to Mecca* would be a role of a lifetime for Lilly; also agreeing to hire an ex-*SS* Colonel, having thoroughly investigated him beforehand, with his CIA special forces pals, finding him confirmed with highest-level clearance by the FBI and Army Intel.

This would not portray worn, hackneyed, cliched transgenderism, but would be mythic, epic, universal in scope, with themes of sexual empowerment of men, women, daisies, tom boys, cross breeds, through 110 minutes running time. All during the shoot Lilly toked nonstop on the Commander's black *hashish*. Because she had shown up recently, to remind Trans Jordan (TJ) of hisher outstanding debt to Muslim fanatics, taunting, "when you could not exist as a boy, the alternative was to become a girl, vice versa." So, she supplied Lilly with constant cannabis, evil heroin from Afghanistan, where suspect connections led, instructing Lilly to snort junk, until tolerated, the star's drug obsession bringing her closer to death:

> You only live twice:
> Once when you are born
> And once when you look death in
> the face.
>
> After BASHO
> Japanese poet, 1643-94 (Ian Fleming, *You Only Live Twice*, 1964)

Weren't the confusing sexual identities of our two protagonists the most tortured of human existences? If genes provided the maps of our lives, they also contained the seeds of our destruction. In the end the chromosomes were infallible. Did God make queers as souls and genders, to engender, or end gender? There were rumors that Lilly had stoned, cataleptic fits on set, but Sayer insisted they be quashed, end of story, and gave Lilly the strictest warnings, through Ms. Yael Abraham, Director, Human Resources, that there would be no tolerance for any slipups, which was a lie, as there was no one else for the role. As Roman emperors boldly deified themselves Gods while living, so, our heroine had stellified herself:

> Stellify
> stellify ( st l fa )
> vb, -fies, -fying or -fied
> (Astronomy) to change or be changed into a star [from Latin stella a star]
> (*The Free Dictionary*)

So, the Producer General was set for a short coffee break, after a busy morning identifying speculators for his spectacle, whether Lilly stupefied herself or not, and the backing poured in, due to the promoted Middle Eastern feel, as well as promised action sequences, never attempted even by Jackie Sham. And Lilly insisted on doing all the stunts herself, as if her whole life had not already been, the greatest of all stunts. The Rev. Hannibal acceded to whatever she asked, because he, as everyone, was amazed by her recent stellification, and although Hannibal was de facto producer, it was Lilly who called all the shots; and even Sayer, if secretly behind some great curtain as an omnipotent Wizard of Oz, kowtowed to her. (Incidentally, Saudi Arabia was one of the last countries on earth where the reality of kowtowing to the king, could not be ruled out; having been just that, by Mao Tse-tung and his revolutionaries, claiming: "Political power grows out of the barrel of a gun," at the end of the Imperial Period in China, where the custom flourished for millennia.) And it was not beneath Grawitz to grovel in seeking an objective; he had seen Jews do it all the time in the camps, never to their shame, though perhaps their final demise. So, because of a sycophantic trait the Colonel had advanced throughout his career, no matter for whom. When he called his contacts in those various Saudi ministries he was known in, they felt blessed to hear from him, granting instant approvals for his movie studio to film their next, international action feature, in Mecca, but little did they know of its true theme, content, which grew to become quite controversial. The plot involved hiding out in Saudi, kidnapping an Israeli double agent envoy, trading traitor back to Israel in exchange for a higher value NATO operative held captive behind the Iron Curtain for decades. It was up to Rev. Hannibal, to make a movie that would make conservatives happy, thinking it had been about freedom and liberty for them, yet fool liberals into thinking it had been about freedom and liberty for all. He also convinced the Saudis, in a lie, that they were the heroes of the story. Lilly had used her favorite, big screen movie, *Lawrence of Arabia*, not only as the basis of her name, but as a core logic of her own, invented, biographic, cinematic masterpiece, her character a blended Matt Helm/ Mrs. Peel, codenamed Scheherazade. There was a particularly long scene she went out her way to get right, when Lawrence and his boyfriend shared a camel through raging sandstorms, across the desert, only it would be Scheherazade with a cute girlfriend sharing a two humped dromedary, before she died in quicksand. Speaking of dyeing, wanting so much to be of a fair conquering race, she dyed her jet-black hair blond; when desires or wishes came up short peroxide did the trick, the image machine coming into full drive.

"We experimented with the makeup," Lilly's makeup artist Toy Surreal told Pimple.com. "With a much stronger brow and a bold lip for a French sort of feel. The way I shaded her eyebrows with the pencil, I created an uplifting effect. Then I finished with a shimmering, silky-beige shadow on her lids and went with no mascara at all; bit of a reaction against all the fake lashes we've been seeing on the red carpet." Heshe's nails were carefully groomed, long as pointed raptor claws, and hisher coif seemed freshly set to perfection, with long bangs veiling an anxious brow, above permanent plastic smirk from Catamitic converter, designer plastic surgery after such and such starlet, learning to live with a worshiped vagina. Afterward, purring as a kitten, she appeared in throaty, rising semblance as Pursia, as it would add deep mystery to those inevitable photo opportunities, for as hers had not been a political struggle, but one for personal identity, she succumbed to that cult of godly personality, her inner Narcissus fatally reflected.

Some undisclosed plot surprises hastily subscribed to by Lilly were privately included as an addendum, concealed coda to the original piece, but audiences would have to watch the movie to know the ending.

> **48 Hours to Mecca:** *Starring Lilly Lawrence - Produced by Warren Bros.*
>
> *Fade in, popular music of Fairuz, interspersed with that of Willie Nelson.*
>
> *Scene: Scheherazade (Lilly in character) meditating by the open window.*
>
> *In final clarification, this had been the greatest of all misfortunes, along with even worse timing, solving Scheherazade's small problem (now her boss' mess), with a loaded prop gun accidentally discharging at her rival.*
>
> *Attorneys for the agent, expected to be charged with third-degree murder, told Ox News their client did not commit the crime, suggesting, there's no question, this was a tragedy; but not all tragedies are obviously crimes …*

Scheherazade was back, having coffee on the hot terrace, a shade chagrined for an administrative leave of two months from the service, a bit the worse for wear, from desk duty, a usually stoic heart humbled, lounging poolside in fashionable, black one-piece *burqa* swimsuit apropos of the Hilton Riyadh Hotel's segregated pool hours, waiting for a phone call from her chief, in which he would describe her next job. The caller aped Sayer's voice, no peasantries exchanged between them, no references to old times; she never called her boss, by his name, thinking of him as her superior; always Chief or Boss, no chit chat, nothing more. She knew he always had her back professionally; she owed him a service worthy of that trust. She was to be an adjunct, to an operation led by General Hannibal Gates, really overseen by him, and led by ex-*SS* Colonel Otto Waldemar Grawitz, the new operative joining the team for this mission, and even though it appeared she had been cast adrift by her boss, she consented to anything he ordered. Her team quickly assembled at the hotel: Army General H. Gates, first black Chairman, Joint Chiefs of Staff, Ret.; Po' Boys, Oath Sleepers, were there in force, despite their threatening presence, aggressive antics, toward the other mercenaries; then as the night wore on, the Committee for Public Safety settled in, snoring, belching, farting, praising their Savior for this last of holy Crusades against heretic Infidels.

Tonight, General Gates had volunteered for this mission, along with his most experienced spy, both as ordinary operatives, in a squad, serving under an expert ex-*SS* Colonel, to capture a magnificent trophy. Although his mastery lay, in running mass extermination camps, where Jews, Slavs, Gypsies, met their horrible ends, he did have the social graces to charm the Saudi princes he had in his pocket, so that, *But when thou doest alms, let not thy left hand know what thy right hand doeth:* and they had no idea of his nefarious plan on behalf of the enemy Israeli government, as Benedict Arnold, was his *nom de guerre*. The team had 48 hours to enter the country, proceed to the target area, and with great stealth, extract the rogue emissary, pretending to a scientific mineralogical mission; the target being, the *Kaaba*, during the twelfth month of the Islamic calendar, the time of annual pilgrimage or *Hajj*, as the fifth pillar of Islam. The renegade scientist would be performing metallurgical tests on the Black Stone, set into the cuboid *Kaaba's* eastern corner, while pilgrims swirled counterclockwise, seven times round the House of God:

> And remember Ibrahim and Ismail raised the foundations of the House
> (With this prayer): "Our Lord! Accept (this service) from us: For Thou
> art the All-Hearing, the All-knowing." (*Quran*, Al-Baqarah [2])

There was one thing Scheherazade needed to do, before tomorrow's raid, which was to happen in broad daylight, in front of thousands. During the evening call to prayer, she slipped out of the hotel, shrouded in her favorite black *burqa*, in such fashion, as good as invisible in a repressive fundamentalist society. But such invisibility would need more help with tomorrow's crowds. Entering the King Abdullah Park, she was promptly joined by someone in a desert camouflage *burqa*, the Commander, making a cameo appearance. She held a magic ring to give to Scheherazade, claiming it would help her achieve victory. "Rub this ring until the *jinn* appears. It will obey your slightest wish and desire, even as to disappear." So, Scheherazade took this valuable gift, immediately placing it on her right middle finger, separating from the Commander, as if they had never met, returning to the hotel before the final, tactical meeting, led by an older officer, for whom the Commander's praise could not be higher, having once aided her. *SS* Colonel Otto Waldemar Grawitz had the greenest eyes, the same color as that sharp uniform of his from the war, a summer field uniform designed to keep cool and dry, in a miserably hot Polish summer. Now wearing the same color fatigues, the main aspect he displayed from prior times was an intolerance for insubordination: "Wakeup gong tomorrow at 4:30, deployment at 6:30, fully geared in the parking lot, vans waiting. Our private plane departs at 8:30, Mecca by 10; the target should be reached by noon. The pseudo scientist should be experimenting on the Black Stone by then ("and as Steele/ Toucht with a Loadstone, dost new motions feele?"). We have 48 hours to get in and out; each of you has a specific role, which, if we are to evade the authorities, and possible public beheading, I will now summarize..." General Gates, would take the command post, in a van, directing agent traffic, from the Colonel's well-orchestrated score; the Po' Boys, Oath Sleepers, who were truly a force, would (wo)man the perimeters for the operation, keeping out gawkers, stragglers and any who might interfere; including the ever loyal twenty-four Grand Mosque Police guards, charged with security, safety and medical assistance, amidst turbulent, teeming throngs of, "those who compass it round." The Colonel would find the alchemist at his philosophers' stone, physically restrain, sedate, haul him away, in Arab costume, within a swarming crowd. When he got to Scheherazade, he assumed a naivete, because she was a woman. Perhaps some misogyny was a dormant cause. "Colonel, under this *burqa*, I am armed with expanding rubber bullets, so please never assume a weakness again," was her answer, to which the Colonel relented, as if tamed:

> The Black stone descended from paradise, and it was whiter than milk,
> then it was blacked by these sins of the children of Adam. (Tirmidhi)

According to Islamic scholars, the Black Stone came down, perhaps as a meteor, from heaven, to Adam and Eve, marking where to build an altar to sacrifice to God, the altar becoming the first House of God. Apparently, for the movie's screenwriter, the idea of Adam and Eve ever possessing the Stone, was too much to resist, and here is where a side script quietly added to the original by an Author Supreme came into play, because in her mind, if it had once been Eve's, she should have it again, to share with Adam. And this became Scheherazade's side objective within the broader mission; she was to swipe the Stone when no one was looking, as much for herself, as for a reason to tell the story of its misappropriation to her chief who, fascinated by narratives of her escapades, begged for tall tales as part of the pillow talk; promising to set her free from any further obligation once one thousand and one nights of denouements and desires had been attained. For his part, her official-minded boss had already sacrificed many of her less inventive predecessors, so he was keen on keeping her near him, both professionally and privately. But he had already left Saudi on a flight that morning, so as not to attract undue attention to the team. It was impossible to describe the seeming chaos, of the mass movement of people circling the *Kaaba*, as the unit awaited admittance to the *Mataaf*, a sacred plaza where pilgrims humbly praised in motion:

> Behold! We gave the site, to Ibrahim, of the (Sacred) House, (saying):
> "Associate not anything (in worship) with Me; and sanctify My House for
> those who compass it round, or stand up, or bow, or prostrate themselves
> (therein in prayer)." (*Quran*, Surah Al-Hajj [22], Ayah 26)

Within deafening, roaring noise, General Gates was live to the squad, assuming operational control, as got up in white Lawrence of Arabia robes, the Colonel, with much of his face enveloped in swath, led a small, elite party, including Scheherazade, to the huge, mythic *Kaaba* itself, symbol of God's promise. To the Colonel any possible feelings of sacrilege to this holy site, were abated by the temptation of the Mossad wire transfer into his secret Swiss bank account. He was skilled at trading one side for another. The Po' Boys, Oath Sleepers, also in local garb, confirmed the perimeters were fully secured and active police guards closely covered. The entire squad had blended right into the ground shifting multitudes.

"Gates here, please all confirm you read me... Thank you... you are loud and clear. Number three, on the west side, a police guard is preparing for his rounds; please distract him... well done. Colonel, you and your squadron head to the eastern side of the mosque, where the Stone is housed in a corner recess. You should see it, as soon as you pass the next group of penitents, as well as Professor of Minerology M. Eckhart, at cordoned off-site table, too busy at undefinable labors to know you are coming for him. All halt... There seems to be some new activity on the approaching highway, but far enough so we can finish what we came for. Colonel, proceed with the plan; we'll wait for you to rendezvous at the exit."

Now things started moving fast; as per his plan, the perimeters were sealed by his comrades, closing all flanks, in support of the Colonel's group, now moving on instincts more than fact. The Colonel spoke:

"Professor Eckhart, we have been looking for you all morning; would you please, now come with me?"

"I'm sorry, but whatever it is will have to wait until I've completed these astrochemical inquiries; I'm on the verge of discovering the Midas touch, in the Stone's transmutation of plain substance into gold."

"So that was the deal you made with the Saudis, to make them even wealthier than their polluting oil?"

"Think of all the gold that might be created from desert sand. I would be a match for Rumpelstiltskin."

"I would kidnap you for my own, were it not for an even greater value of that which you shall trade for; and as an inestimable pledge is illusory, nonetheless, as a precept, I bear it in my heart as recompense."

With that said, the Colonel prepared his ether-infused towel, about to drug the learned gentleman, when Gates suddenly came back garbled, warning of reinforcements on the highway; the mosque police were mobilizing, something was afoot, perhaps they had been made, it was time to bolt; immediately falling back to the eastern corner, retreating, as army regulars supporting the police seemed to push their way through massive swarms of pilgrims to get to them. The General gave them one last on-air reminder of the importance of this mission to East-West relations, and especially the prestige and extended might of the United States, as he had convinced his Hollywood bosses the story would portray American values triumphing in an overseas setting, versus covetous immigrants coming to and flooding our shores with their sorrow and relief, our sorrow and grief. The Colonel proceeded to drug Meister Eckhart, bagging the quarry in white flowing robes, praying out loud for miraculous escape, and turned to Scheherazade, desperately shouting though the din, if she had any great ideas, as surrendering was not to be an option. So, Scheherazade sprang into immediate action to save the Colonel and her faltering commando team. Now the most incredible thing happened. * Recalling her magic ring, Scheherazade began to rub it with all her might, until before the team's very eyes, a trembling wave appeared as a diaphanous cloud, viscous, as flowing as water, and imposing. The fabled *jinn* was most terrible, appearing much larger than life, vibrant shadow in a fringed, open vest, loincloth, sandals, his terrible howls barely muffled by a broad, red scarf covering the lower face; the deep, yellow eyes not human: but rather, those of a wild animal, who would mercilessly track down, annihilate you, if challenged, crossed, piercing enchanted believers to the core; having spent a full twelve centuries preparing for the wanton, regenerative action, spectacle, supernaturally gathering restorative fluid energy, knowing full well what was expected in the required duty as personal incubus to an entire hijacking squad. But he knew his place in the world, and waited patiently for her command, to which Scheherazade immediately issued the following directive.

"My servant *Jinn*, make my platoon invisible to enemies, so we may escort a captive to his sure doom." And immediately time seemed to stand still. All of Mecca appeared to stop, as if in a frame of eternity. But her squad continued to act, albeit as heavily, as if in a dreamy fog. The Colonel still moved with a purpose, but in a vacuum, while the *jinn* held its arms outstretched, as if compressing time to its desire; but during the slow-motion moments, Scheherazade was moving fast with her clandestine plans, shared with no one. Still in real time, she rushed to grab the Black Stone from its mantel-like cavity setting, at the building's corner. "Now *Jinn*, pull the Stone from its setting in the wall, place it in my satchel, and substitute an identical forgery for it, so only the most astute would realize the difference, and the theft." So, while she purloined a mythic relic of ancient, fervent belief, of salvation, damnation, as directed by the text, she was not thinking for one instant about their mission, but shamefully, only of herself and of Willi; the need to possess such a magnificent reward had more to do with ego fulfillment, than anything else. As it had once belonged to Adam and Eve, there could be none better to act as guardians than her and Willi, that much was certain. And when the Stone had been replaced with the good fake, they were ready to move out again, while the world kept quiet, and the platoon moved as normal with its prisoner. It was as if not only they but all of reality were sedated, and the platoon, by sticking to its plan, finished its mission without anyone noticing. They were under the *jinn's* escort throughout their extraction, but when they finally arrived at the secluded airfield, where the escape aircraft was waiting, there was a bit of a scene, with the servile *Jinn* refusing to return to the magic ring, leaving Scheherazade in the most uncomfortable of positions. Finally, it was up to the Colonel to order the *jinn* back to its barracks. The entire sleepy squad stood at attention, saluting as the faceless, bodyless, ephemeral, supernatural power retreated to its quarters, before boarding their aircraft, out of that sand swept hell hole of backwardness. Whether the *jinn* were products of a retrogradation found in fundamentalist societies, was of no import, considering the assistance that was brought to bear, by a direct command, an ancient prerogative itself.

But on the flight home, in real time again, both the General and Colonel asked Scheherazade, how she had pulled off getting everyone out, safe and sound; it was as if movements froze for an indeterminate period, during which they could not remember a thing except her voice leading them out of the *Mataaf*, into the vans and out to the airfield, where they suddenly found themselves saluting the phantom being, who itself was being fooled to return to a magic ring; and then they had all woken up, while taking off. Of course, no one had an idea what was in her satchel, only that it seemed to be rare and cumbersome:

> I have only created Jinns and Men that they may serve Me. No Sustenance
> do I require of them, nor do I require that they should feed Me. For
> Allah is He Who gives (all) Sustenance, Lord of Power, Steadfast forever.
> (*Quran*, 51:56-58)

"The Colonel and I have been discussing the mission. We're wondering if perhaps the Colonel's hand slipped on an ether-infused towel, saturating it to the point you all passed out, became semi-comatose."

"From the moment I drugged the Professor I do not recall a thing. How did we regroup in our retreat?"

"I can brief you both on the details. The reason no one recalls a thing about the mission is you were all infidels, interlopers, who see the world without understanding it, as if underwater or within the clouds. As the only Muslim on the team Allah allowed me to keep my wits about me to complete the operation. Do not worry gentlemen, this sort of thing happens to all foreigners who dare trespass on holy ground. Once the object was taken, I had no emergencies in leading the team back to safety, thanks be to Allah. Surely, He must have led me by the hand, because it was as if no one saw us, while we scrambled out. But you should accept that everyone, especially yourselves, acted honorably, courageously, during this brief, murky period, I can attest to it; now if you gentlemen will excuse me, I will get some shut eye:"

> By time, indeed, mankind is in loss, Except for those who have believed
> and done righteous deeds and advised each other to truth and advised
> each other to patience. (*Quran*, 103: 1-3)

The flight path was set to the Haifa naval base, as per the original plan hatched by the cunning Colonel. The idea of a top prisoner exchange came to him to get all parties what they wanted, especially himself. They had even left a fine token for the Saudi princes, to compensate for their loss of endless spun gold. Upon landing, Professor Eckhart, still quite groggy from the ether, kept protesting about, "the stone, the stone, the stone," only to prompt Scheherazade's intercession: "I think he's saying he's feeling stoned." In any case they ignored him, because the cause and reason for the entire mission was waiting for them, standing apart on the tarmac, got up in white Lawrence of Arabia robes like the Colonel's with much of the face enveloped in swath. The aircraft door opened; the Colonel led the Professor down the stairs, to the assembled military authorities. Then he walked on to the waiting figure, pausing, nodding, nodded back to, and led the way up the stairs onto the aircraft, doors closing immediately, then it was airborne. Now this mysterious VIP was seated passively at the rear of the aircraft, without speaking to anyone, or even having said, "Thank you all for risking your lives to rescue me from captivity," when nothing had ever been taken for granted, and the entire platoon was curious of the identity of this cold war convict. A new flight plan was set to Los Angeles, CA, city of crystalized expectations and fabricated greatness. Live coverage of the entire arrival, greeting and acknowledgement of freed POW, had been granted, as an exclusive, to Slay Magazine, represented as usual by the Fixer, and in this special case joined by his chief and editor (that unnamable Ottoline), producing a Hollywood extravaganza for such a contentious homecoming. After all, they had kidnapped a foreign dignitary to obtain undignified results, according to Panderson Scooper; they had taken out a foreign agent to obtain heroic results, according to Cucker

Snarlson; such trite polemics lingering long after it mattered, if it had ever mattered at all to begin with. And as the team disembarked, one at a time, down boarding steps and onto the broad tarmac, the Fixer waited patiently for The Colonel and his VIP to appear, not realizing that the red headed Rus', beautiful Slav princess, whose sister he murdered in the war, on the arm of the Colonel, as he escorted her down the steps, was that very VIP sans Arab costume, unmasked, smiling broadly, immediately in Ottoline's loving arms. Mother and daughter reuniting, after defining epic migratory treks, brought joy, as well as longing, to Scheherazade, as she was also separated from her own mother, who lingered in an enemy's dungeon. So in a grand finale, amidst fanfare on the tarmac worthy of the most patriotic story ending, the entire plot was shown to be a ruse, with plenty of dead ends along the way, to confuse and delight; during which Grawitz masterminds Ottoline's mother's escape from the Gulag, through eastern Europe, to the last sequence of the film, in exchange for an abducted Mossad mark who presumably spun Israeli gold the rest of his life; the closing scene, deep inside a Saudi Royal palace: an awakening swindler got up in white Lawrence of Arabia robes like the Colonel's with much of the face enveloped in swath asks where he is, whether he is still at the Cringeport harem, identifying himself as the Grand Duke John C. In his parting shot at the Knights of Freemisogyny, seen as an overgrown boy's club of dandies, babies protecting their own pseudo-Christianity, worthy of rebuke for the hypocritical search of a higher truth, than the rest of us, the Colonel traded a young, recently tried traitor, sperm donor, with the Sisters, for the duke, as the duke's useful, commercial life was coming to a close, to remain behind, as their house leaving present for the deviant Saudi royal clown prince, who knew exactly what to do with His Grace; accepting his future bondage as recompense for the loss of their alchemist, putting him immediately to serve as an oriental courtesan in one of his harems, to spin an indispensable gold for those greediest of masters, claiming unlimited use of the duke's organs, as the closing credits begin to roll, along with the popular music of Fairuz, interspersed with that of Willie Nelson. *The End. Produced by Warren Bros.*

Some critics said the movie was too real, true to life, and some harped that it veered into hocus-pocus, sadly, farther from the idealistic rule of law, deeper into the maelstrom of hyped-up, spiteful jingoism. But these after all had been Grawitz' intent, and Rev. Hannibal' salvation, with a rightist crowd he was trying to please, to produce something so authentic, no one could ever say, they were faking it by *Fahd*. Entire scenes were as if filmed in actual moments of suspense, intrigue, genuine danger. Considering Scheherazade's only stunt was vigorously rubbing her ring, to bring out the *jinn*, after which the surreal quality took hold, audiences fell in love with a new team role, for their usually solo action heroine. Of course, what an audience saw of Scheherazade's heist would be long subject to fairytale interpretations, and a cult-like following developed, trying to find out exactly how the platoon made it out of Saudi, in one piece. The satchel she carried with her through U.S. immigration and customs, though heavy, was invisible to the agents, letting it pass without a hitch, the objective of Lilly's script addendum achieved. Here was when reality departed from fantasy, because once Scheherazade was back to being Lilly, who was not that nostalgic for the old Islamic ways and protocols, she took the Black Stone home for Willi; mounting it on the mantel, as a curio deserving of no special attention, never realizing its sanctity, even though they noticed that after touching the Stone, they felt their sins transferred to its core, "blacked by these sins of the children of Adam." Also, there was the overpowering sense of divinity in its presence.

If such reactionaries as Hannibal could cheer the movie's anti-foreigner, pro mercenary elements, Lilly had made sure to make her feminist mark in Scheherazade's persona, forever begging a question, as to how much Scheherazade's personality was based on Lilly, and vice versa, or was it simply in the cards? There was also a mad murder on the movie set, committed by its creator and star, when a loaded blank prop gun proved fatal to the movie's first director. Was it the beginning of a cover up, or the big wrap? And even though these things rarely occurred, due to the heavy studio precautions, nevertheless, in this case it was such an obvious misfire, on Scheherazade's part, with clearly, no malice intended, that there were no further repercussions, for her fans' favorite Lilly, one of the celebrity exemplars we demanded.

Any similarities to past, tragic circumstances of the actress would not be admitted, due to privacy rules, even though this director had been seen in Willi's company, gossiped about, for weeks prior to filming. Here is when reality took a cue from fantasy, because once she was back to herself, from her alter ego, leave it to Lilly to blame Scheherazade, the power of her character over an actor, for the on-set horrors. Except for this unforeseen accident, everything had gone pretty much according to plan. What was so important for Lilly's ego's sake, was that if Willi could do itty-bitty, witty verse, she had undertaken an entire cinematic reality, presenting transgenders as grand legends, instead of two-dimensional cartoons. But more important still, was Lilly's newfound resolve to get to work right away on a brand-new script, following a thread to rescue her mother, the only woman in his her life, still imprisoned in Guantánamo; entitled *48 Horas a Guantánamo,* perhaps based on the current feature's success, with Willi as coauthor and starring in the Hispanic hero role, as the local Cuban agent who gives his life to get her mother out. Indeed, such fluidity between the real and the imagined worlds would become a hallmark of their work.

What was not in the movie was Grawitz later becoming Sayer's Alfred Rosenberg, as prompted by the sight of Grawitz one year later at the lunch they shared at Sparks Steak House, prior to his confessions of those evil deeds of his to the United Nations. It was after hearing his testimony that Sayer's decision to somehow or other include him in the future of Warren Bros. Inc. was made; for Sayer and Hannibal, it was all about the great replacement theory, and having someone with Grawitz' on screen, as well as off-screen, skills on board made sense to them, but this was done secretly, without Isidora's knowledge, and without the slightest hint being given to Ms. Yael Abraham, Director, Human Resources, and Jew. *Le grand remplacement* was the replacement of one race by another, whether rightly or wrongly, only history would tell, as there were sour grapes in the term, as if self-applied by those being replaced. But truth be told Isidora was not quick to jump aboard to make the movie, a great professional *faux pas*, she later admitted. Though she admired strong feminist types, she was not enamored of the hyper patriotic, bellicose *The Ugly American* portrayals in the story lines, nor the sardonic mockery of the Knights of Freemisogyny, however, she went along with Sayer as maybe she smelled a winner with vulgar, violent movie aficionados at large. Isidora was perceptive enough to realize that the people around her were of the same ilk and stripe, it having been reported to her, that Sayer was given to wearing Superman suits on the Downtown Lexington Avenue Express, while terrorizing legal and illegal aliens alike, to his joy, that he was a secret benefactor, and contributor, to unnamed, underground organizations, and generally lusted after fresh faced office interns, under twenty, younger than his own, recently married daughters. In terms of the Rev. H. Gates, she heard it through the grapevine that there was some lechery in all that lethargy, especially with regard to a certain, Ms. Yael Abraham, Director, Human Resources, and about whom she knew, since Whale days, and through the Sisterhood, there were longings for P Diddy, who herself was as confused over her sexuality of questioned yearnings, as Ms. Abraham was over hers; and none of them, the chairman saw, were above trading sensitive information for gain when it suited them. However, whatever the personal shortcomings her colleagues suffered from, she remained in her team's thrall, with respect to box office instincts, and surely enough the film was a blockbuster, despite doubts.

There was a final, sordid detail of the production, which caused Isidora to linger in ire. The director of the movie was a *protégé* of Isidora's, hand-picked by her for this project, some even said that personal considerations were involved, so when it was revealed, it was Scheherazade who had pulled the trigger, to maintain composure, the Madam Chairman needed a couple of diazepam and a goblet of champagne. Isidora immediately put a bounty on Scheherazade's head, demanding she be found, brought to justice. It was because Scheherazade's characterization had been so real, penetrating, that it made the indelible impression on Isidora's unconscious, so that with her magical thinking, she believed Scheherazade had been the true person, not the invention from Lilly's mind, springing forth as Athena from Zeus' crown:

When a character is born, he acquires at once such an independence, even of his own author, that he can be imagined by everybody even in many other situations where the author never dreamed of placing him; and so he acquires for himself a meaning which the author never thought of giving him. (Luigi Pirandello, *Six Characters in Search of an Author*, 1921)

It seemed the old order had retained its grip, despite this epic struggle, where the forces of freedom had been forced to accept the version of liberty as everyone doing what they wanted, but not necessarily in concert with the whole. And perhaps it was not that obvious in the mainstream, but as with all the evil starts it occurred quietly, no one ever knowing or becoming aware of great changes slowly taking place here. Who conceived what the future would bring? In terms of Scheherazade Spook Supreme, she was now on the run, dictated by destiny to hightail it to the West Coast and keep out of sight. Transforming reality back to what it had once been meant that perhaps our Scheherazade would have to disappear for good, as the respective heroes of *Curtain: Poirot's Last Case*, and perhaps *You Only Live Twice*, did, as their authors' originality outwardly waned; as, "little grey cells of the brain" dried up, to no dishonor, to a similar cloud as was brought on by the *jinn* when at the height of his powers and trust. Fortunately, Lilly was chronologically distant from such creative demise, with more heady manuscripts anticipated.

Isidora knew that Sayer, in his greatness as CEO Supreme, had pulled one over on her, but was never in a position to bring it up in a formal discussion or mention it in a moment of collegial banter, as she was his boss and interactions with him were kept to a minimum outside of business protocol; she had never called John, by his name, thinking of him as her associate; always Mr. President, no chit chat, nothing more. She knew he always had her back professionally; she owed him the discrete privilege worthy of that trust. She realized his top grade could be that of Apollo, but never Zeus, and if she was Hera, it all made sense. But then Scheherazade seemed to live forever, for Isidora, a trope of her own success, to those ghost buster, gay basher, punch them in the face, plant them in the ass, goose them in the gonads, patriots; she was gunning for a god. An APB was issued for the illusory suspect, but in true California style, it was impossible to clarify for what genders to be on the lookout. Irate Isidora kicked herself for her folly, screamed and swore over the phone at her distant and quite innocent, progressive call center, upsetting their professional equanimity with profanity infused rants, where was the moral equivalence?

Well, there you have it, the succinct telling of one of the most important cultural exchanges of all times. Lilly, done reminiscing of how important she had been to the birth, growth and success of this historic movement, prepared herself a huge line of coke on mirror, rolled up balls of hash, and settled in for the night. From now on, she would use more discretion when calling Sayer in the middle of a lonely spell. Next week she was scheduled to meet with Patricia (P) Diddy, Ph.D., J.D. re *Les Enfants* contributions.

*Footnote

Magical realism was often criticized by those desiring true outcomes, but at times a reliance on a *deus ex machina* was indispensable, to a triumph of real possibilities, defined as endings that mattered, made the difference to readers; even at the risk of losing credulity over the story's resolution, as, sometimes, what can be imagined is greater, better, more entertaining, than dry reason, especially when moments of our suffering and salvation have no other explanation. A doff of the hat to Gabriel Garcia Marquez, who let it rain tiny, yellow flowers, for his Macondo is also ours, located between heaven and earth, just as Faulkner's Yoknapatawpha County is in our conscious unconscious, journey's start of a soul's infinite longing.

# 16. The Sky is Falling

> [A myth is] ...a description of physical phenomenon in imagery borrowed
> from human life... (James G. Frazer, *The Golden Bough*, 1922)

When the millennium rolled over, there was still much to do in terms of man's thinking and an inability to leave the ancient world of mythological definitions behind. When the Protestant Reformation turned Christian doctrine on its head in the sixteenth century, one of its main tenets was that Everyman should read, understand, heed the bible as he chose. For Congregational clergyman Charles Edward Jefferson, a priesthood of all believers meant that, "Every believer is a priest and ... every seeking child of God is given directly wisdom, guidance, power." And such an abandonment of canonical teachings in favor of individualized textual self-interpretations led to top theorists, theologian monks, such as Martin Luther:

> Let all the 'free-will' in the world do all it can with all its strength; it will
> never give rise to a single instance of ability to avoid being hardened if
> God does not give the Spirit, or of meriting mercy if it is left to its own
> strength." (Martin Luther, *On the Bondage of the Will*, 1525)

As well as obsessive, merciless leaders bent on abusing their interpretations, in misguiding naive flocks of cultish followers, such as the Reverend Cotton Mather, calling to, "Beat [Native Americans] small as the Dust before the Wind;" and perhaps the craziest of all Pentecostal nuts that ever lived, a diabolical Reverend Jim Jones, whose appointment with destiny in wildest Guyana, led an unlucky, trapped 909 to Flavor Aid murder-suicide. Such freedom of thought was a two-edged sword, for some could pursue progressive, scientific modernity, or sink to a regressive, religious eccentricity. The Gutenberg printing press in the mid millennium ironically led to the propagation of specious ideas. As Protestantism begat bastard capitalism, the countries that adopted both, by a quirk of fate, led the world with technological, economic and military developments, as well as fostering the most superstitious of people imaginable. A genius NASA scientist, who is a devout fundamentalist Christian as well, comes to mind; resourceful Dr. Waterson, Original American Medicine Man Supreme, merging 20th century with tribal magic, also. But why was the former's faith deemed old-fashioned, while the latter's powers blessed, as elemental? Evangelicals shone during epochs of doubt and shame, while Indians traveled paths of eternal duration. Because even if your life and death were destined, decided, preordained in the genes, good or bad luck, born of everyone's private struggles, could still mitigate their approximate arrival, effect, destined end.

Willi and Lilly, still laying low after their recent bad behavior, and syndication of their masterful show, *Woke Up with Willie*, somehow correlated both events as the last burst of conceit begun after his being alerted to certain lose ends remaining, from the recent Hollywood extravaganza; produced on the set of an unnamed, secretive L.A. airfield, where an Eastern European spy, "came in from the cold," bartered for some VIPs between the Saudis and Israelis; one of them, apparently titled the Grand Duke John C., of great castles and royalties' fame, who it was rumored, was marooned in Riyadh. Had Willi's passing on the scoop brought them bad luck, considering GDJC was lodged in a seedy, Saudi bugger's delight?

Somehow, they became superstitious of late, cancelling their meetings, including the one with the Rev. Hannibal P. (Pearly) Gates about new contributions; it was time for Willi to look after himself; perhaps if he perused his written as well as electronic mail, he would get certain contrasts of opinion to ponder. There was a loud cry from the wilderness, picked at random, though not randomly posted by Waterson:

*Valentine's Day*
*Anonymous (Dr. Waterson)*

*Dear Miss Lonelyhearts (Willi),*

*It is usually I who beckon with favor out of the floods, those supplicating courage during despondent times, but here I am, writing to you for some sort of answer I cannot give myself, as the doctor who is his own patient, the attorney who counsels himself, the savior who plays his own penitent. As a close reader of your column, I cannot help but wonder at perceived similarities, between you and my son Adam, whom I created with all the love imaginable, along with his wife Eve, apple of my eye; providing all for them, in an Eden of my own tilling, until time took its toll on mutual trust, knowledge ruined from too much shared; then expulsion to shamed state of nature, followed by matrimony, and a struggle for life endured by all; I always wondered if I had been too harsh, with my darling children that day, until remade as stars, as bright as heaven sent, we rekindled an old light between us; we are a family again, if distant in time and contact, as the boy is more agreeable, while the girl not too keen, on my presence. That was the old way of raising children, encouraging with firm example, as the Great Spirit's offspring learned from the sky, wind, earth and sun. Formerly I breathed life into other's souls, brushed them with electrified fingertips, before presently being forsaken as any sort of causal agent, in an era of free-will, perhaps it being I who should attune to modern ways:*

By free choice in this place we mean a power of the human will by which a man can apply himself to the things which lead to eternal salvation, or turn away from them. (Humanist Desiderius Erasmus, replying to Cleric Martin Luther's predestinarian affirmation of the Holy Spirit, 1524)

*Perhaps letting go of those who are dearest is that part of life I am least accustomed to; even I, who should know better, often wish to reinvent the past to an advantage; before moving even further along diverging paths. My question is about regrets in life. Are they worth this anguish, despair, stirred, or should mistakes and errors made be let go by all the injured? If this is absolution, clemency, that I crave, perhaps it shows I'm not God. Sincerely,*

*A Lonely Reader*

And another echo of loneliness, picked at random, although not randomly dispatched by Y. Abraham:

*Valentine's Day*

*Anonymous (Yael Abraham)*

*Dear Miss Lonelyhearts (Willi),*

*I have been a fan for some time of your masculine, yet soft, replies to the problems of others. You seem a man of the earth, wrought of ancient clay and flowing water, seeking truth beneath society's behavioral definitions. I guess I have a lot of resentments over things that have not gone right in my life. First, I can never let go of the nasty hurt Nazis caused my family and myself or forgive any of them severally for crimes against humanity. Second, I have no recollection, other than as happy at the stove, frying up breakfast, of my blond, faceless mother; my father known to me only as a shadow of himself, a fateful phantom of dreams of gravelly, high German enunciated on train platform, or afternoon tea in a parlor of vivid lamps. So, it was difficult to watch someone reunited with their exiled mother, as recently occurred on screen, when I will not see or hear from mine again. Frankly, I am a bit jealous of all this attention Ottoline gets from being in the movie. Even if there was no role written in for me, I thought someone could have put in a good word for me after all my loyal, hard work, that's all. Third, I am confused about my sexual orientation in that, in the same way I feel attraction to you, for your manly virtues, I also feel the pull of my sisters in a greater society, and I don't know which one is the real me. I remind myself of Chicken Little, conforming as bait for some smart fox:*

Did you ever hear of Chicken Little, how she disturbed a whole neighborhood by her foolish alarm? (*The Remarkable story of Chicken Little,* Degen, Estes & Co., Boston, circa 1865-1871)

*I'm prone to lose my head from the weight of all these corporate foibles I try to manage on my own; I wonder why I take so much on my shoulders. What if you were a Jew, who secretly feared you were a Nazi's daughter? But enough complaining; as they chided early on at Whale: "Buck up, or you'll be left behind at the station." Let me know what you think, thanks. Sincerely,*
*A Lonely Reader*

For a moment, Willi was unbalanced enough from his infinite egocentrism to feel empathy for someone other than himself. But it was only for an instant, as he got ready to head home to Sanctuary, CA. His interval in Baja California was ending, as recent success of his show began eclipsing the bad behavior. Their stay there, as with the 60s, was all about remaining in paradise, until the trip ended with a crash:

Back across the ocean floor
The four of us were ripe for more
Paradise was nice but then
you can't stay there forever (John Sebastian, "The Four of Us," 1972)

But before crossing back, over the border, Miss Lonelyhearts took it as his duty to reply to each Lonely Reader. He was comfortable answering his correspondences via email, to ensure the quickest delivery:

*President's Day*
*Miss Lonelyhearts (Willi)*
*Dear Anonymous (Lilly),*
*You said of your husband, poof he disappeared into a mist, but whatever did you do to get him back? And the romance was a whirlwind, but after having kids it was not the same, but what did you contribute to those big changes? And your claims of creation, out of clay and water, in magical proportions from some alchemist's whim, of expulsion from the Garden of Eden; I've heard them all before from one reminding me of you, so please stop tempting me, with ideas of a paradise that once existed, yet can't be found again. Because good and evil are not subjects for the light of heart much less those who claim the burden of a husband's philandering. Also, the supposed, apparent, but unprovable infidelities of freaks in your midst*

*seem to be excuses to hold you back sexually if I may say so. But wanton behavior usually accompanies the success you and your husband had, in your respective careers, along with a substance abuse issue you mention, which frankly, can never be healthy for you. For someone who does not seem to listen to begin with, your inability to hear does not seem like an impediment. You also describe immigrant experiences of marginalization until learning adequate language skills, necessary for the studio; and this seems the basis of your eventual success. Perhaps your idea, that a little nudity goes a long way, never transferred to then going to bed with your husband; and this may be the basis for certain loneliness; perhaps try to abuse drugs less and indulge in sex more often. Keep your husband from acquiring an evil "Syphilis: a night with Venus, a lifetime with Mercury."*
*Sincerely,*
*Miss Lonelyhearts*

*President's Day*
*Miss Lonelyhearts (Willi)*
*Dear Anonymous (John Sayer),*
*It's quite easy to criticize someone behind their back, but also much less effective than a frontal attack. But please do not worry, I would never rat you out to anyone, even if I think I know who you mean. You sound as if rejected by those whom you helped to get ahead professionally, perhaps much too personally. And Adam and Eve characterizations are too much in the public sphere for them to have any direct influence over their lives. It is also apparent you must eat some crow, in terms of the leading lady's greatest comeback, because bad as her addictions and behavior may be, she seems to call all the shots, and you are all now at her beck and call. Your galaxy will need to bear bad behavior before jettisoning these stars, starting with her being a no-show at the Motion Pictures Awards Dinner. Sounds familiar, I mean spotlighted running fountains, filled with bubbly champagne, including all night revelries, raves, replete with open orgies. I can only surmise, you are an executive of one of the Hollywood studios. I heard of the studio boss who at a rumpus once blurted out sarcastically, "Let's give each other celebratory blow jobs, in solidarity of coming out. Who wants to be a Boy Scout today, if you can't get schtupped around the campfire?" then trying to pin that statement on the Sisterhood of Grace. If you believe you know whom that might be please tell me confidentially.*
*Sincerely,*
*Miss Lonelyhearts*

*President's Day*
*Miss Lonelyhearts (Willi)*
*Dear Anonymous (P Diddy),*
*I recall that feminism in the FART was in keeping with strict control over its fighters' reproductive rights, and female guerrillas who were pregnant were forced to leave newborns with relatives, or abort. After la guerrilla and the government reached agreement those rules loosened, resulting in a baby boom, a case of freedom subordinated to a greater common good. I feel outrage at your outage as a semi-trans creature, taking just enough*

*hormones to be less female, but not male, an in-between fairy; and from your ordeal in Vietnam, haven't you heard of the new diagnosis, of PTSD (from Phoenix to PTSD), the shell shock and combat fatigue of our time? I believe my wife and I also have it, if that is any consolation. But being Melungeon was quite the boon for the races, ethnicities, amalgamating a new diversity by man working with society and nature to isolate selected varied human beings, in a far-off continent, to breed amongst themselves, bearing a separateness in your genes, just as I do of the Bogota barrios. I also think I know the New Age Family, to which you refer, and I would say the citizenship issue is near. The only problem with being inspired to the core by their going all the way, was that one day they went their own way; your most heartfelt revelation: at least, you have found compassion, hopefully for yourself as well as others when their fall from grace occurs. Finally, you may have to visit a dermatologist to remove the tattoos inked between your thighs, as a Lee Harvey Oswald, for all those assassinated. Sincerely, Miss Lonelyhearts*

*President's Day*
*Miss Lonelyhearts (Willi)*
*Dear Anonymous (Dr. Waterson),*
*Your sense of loss, indubitable, always wondering if you had been harsh, with your darling children; perhaps you had been, without realizing it, as was the Lord of the Old Testament, of laws, punishment, bossing through a huge cloud emitting constant lightning; hovering over the tabernacle of the Israelites, housing the Ark of the Covenant, exhorting their progress. We all abandon our families in nurturing our own, Zeus usurped Cronus, Lucifer countered his creator, Adam and Eve theirs, princes their fathers, fathers their sons, for, "Like Saturn, the Revolution devours its children." But who among us knows their children, or hears their lonely, distant cry without regrets, sorrows, fear of swift trajectories bound to distant stars? It was foreseen that newly married couples would identify with Adam and Eve in the early, heavily sexualized period of their newly found intimacy. And to challenge your assumptions, young married people should be free to establish their proper identities without interference from over-zealous parents; also, to choose their own career paths without further meddling. Perhaps it is you who should adjust to modern times: dare breathe life as formerly into other people's souls, to get brushed off by them using a cell phone, before presently being forsaken as any sort of causal agent during these days of free will. So, for now, to find peace, let go of those so dear. Sincerely, Miss Lonelyhearts*

*President's Day*
*Miss Lonelyhearts (Willi)*
*Dear Anonymous (Yael Abraham),*
*I am sorry your fate has not given you a fair shake, leaving you to believe the randomness of growing numbers was what kept us from the great evil lurking in our lives, the slimmest odds that something bad would happen.*

*But for that, life here is fraught with fear, anger and danger. So, when it seems as if the universe has you boxed in with no way out, it may squeeze more, as with the phony humility of crying egotists receiving awards. Any resentments over the evils of the past, jealousies over current rivals, will only weigh you down, as will the taking on of the problems of others:*

Then came Chicken Little. Fox Lox caught hold of her, and eat her all up, and then finished his supper with the rest, - and all this from the foolish fright of Chicken Little. (*The Remarkable story of Chicken Little*)

*But there was one line of your missive, which particularly caught my eye: What if you were a Jew, who secretly feared you were a Nazi's daughter? Surely, you penned something so macabre and repugnant in pure jest, for I dare say, that is quite the novel approach to expressing one's distaste of one's parents. If your father were Satan himself, who fell from our Lord's favor, and you rebelled against him, I would still counsel you to give him the benefit of the doubt as your* pater *and progenitor deserving your love. I believe Freudian categories have become* passe *and it would be wise for you to finally free yourself, from lasting frustrations toward your parents. Sincerely,*
*Miss Lonelyhearts*

Upon returning to their Sanctuary, Willi was tormented by divorcing Lilly, finally coming to this plight. There seemed to be a cold war between them which needed to play itself out, and this is what followed. It started with that new-fangled invention, texting, something neither Willi nor Lilly had ever heard of before they started using it. Texting was a way to goad someone, drive them crazy, without being seen. Inflammatory texting was a new phenomenon, promoting verbal abuse from the long-distance comfort of a silent screen. How simple and easy it was to attack someone known, as well as unknown, without face-to-face contact, immediate, irrevocable, destined directly to its target, but shareable with the world if need be. And masters of this common art could literally get away with pinpointed strikes, as well as public character assassination, with impunity. What would the next steps be in this electronic madness, instant thought transfers from the dark souls of killers and aggressors straight to their intended victims? In any case, the practice was a comfort to cowards and bullies, or those with the narcissistic obsessions over the most mundane aspects of their existence: millennials, who fed on mass panics, promoted by all the Chicken Littles of society, inspiring collective action, hence the abuse of panic as a tool for political mobilization, extending pranks... *I think I know why people kill themselves: because their minds keep turning repeatedly on all the failures of their lives, as with making and exploiting violent movies, while claiming to be non-violent; paying attention to billionaires, your life is not even worth $one billion, it's worth zero.* Pictures had a static meaning, only words giving a sense of the person or occasion. Words were the actions of thought; pictures merely catalysts, providing hasty outlines we tried to fill and color with concepts, phrases, dreams; if a picture is worth a thousand words, everything is how you frame it:

A person may cause evil to others not only by his actions but by his
inaction, and in either case he is justly accountable to them for the injury...
It is not because men's desires are strong that they act ill; it is because their
consciences are weak. (John Stuart Mill, *On Liberty*, 1859)

They were using Fakebook, directing gullible friends, each to their own side for their loaded purposes.

A red herring misled or distracted from relevant or important issues, as logical fallacies, literary devices leading readers to false conclusions; intentionally used in mystery fiction, or rhetorical strategies, e.g., politics trumping argumentation; the term popularized in 1807 by English polemicist William Cobbett, who told of having used a kipper, a strong-smelling smoked fish, to divert hounds from chasing hares. Using cell phones as secret societies, texting red herrings to make believers feel as if in private clubs of like-minded consumers; sometimes as victims of spoofing, seeing a recognized area code in fraudulent call; the internet went crazy for it, as privacy, discretion went out the window, with selfies and sexting; text mad politicians, advertisers, couples, jumping on board to reach the desperately seeking someone.

"Going to town on errands, need anything? What's the latest on my nutty, climate change disorder lol?"

"Please don't go outside a small-town general store to pummel a cocky gun rights advocate to a pulp in front of her own family lol, no, well society's climate change ideas got a hold of you, made you crazy."

"According to ultra-cons, climate change is a revolutionary conspiracy to kill productivity, want booze? I need grass seed fertilizer wood posts electric dog and people fences doghouse shovels axe rat poison."

"According to ultra-libs climate change is a reactionary conspiracy to kill the planet, I need tea peppers onions garlic olive oil falafel hummus tahini pita lemons lettuce tomatoes strawberries peaches apples."

"Need bourbon pisco Stoli Bacardi Bud r&w wine, climate change happened when man lit first fire lol. The necessity for heat, shelter and sustenance, our survivalist imperative, ironically laid the seeds for a self-destruction from an ecological perspective, in Central America the Maya had climate annihilation."

"A wonder man ever progressed, with pansy Malthusian limitations on weapons, technology, pollution, need Colgate Dial Ivory Mr. Clean Palmolive Clorox Tide garbage bags cat litter Purina Friskies Alpo."

"Man went to the moon and wouldn't you know it, left garbage there, we're in the midst of a Children's Crusade for Climate Salvation, whose naivete is best stated in a good-doers' refrain: Do the right thing:

> "The law of heroes and good-doers cannot be eluded."
> (Walt Whitman, *Leaves of Grass*, "To Think of Time," 1900)

"It's not that I really disagree with climate warming theories, it's just that I don't want to be accused of believing in something everybody else does, it's been about Freedom vs. Chicken Little since the start. Economists, those learned professionals, who brought us the free market, communism, the Mississippi Scheme, invisible hands, Smith, Malthus, Marx, should have no say in politics, other than as wizards."

"Will stop at you know where to get you know what, there is some new merchandise from Afghanistan. The sociologist's dream of sheer numbers making the point, found its best expression in climate activist assumptions regarding the mass transportation of people herded as beasts, proving that your side won."

"It is the height of folly and narcissism to believe that individual recycling will make a difference when every minute, entire continents pollute with impunity, BTW BS is the new acronym for before solar lol. Good, I was running on empty for the last few days, please double up on my order, I'm having a party."

"Don't you see the harm in such purchases? As per scientists collecting a huge data set, at some point analyzing cultivation pollution data, thoroughly, seeing there were features that were anthropogenic."

Of course, in no time Chicken Little herself was chiming in, with corporate mass texts to all associates: "My Daily Equity Theme: Unless there was true justice at the start, what follows could never be good. I think that climate change is one of the biggest issues that we're going to have to think about and look at in the future. These huge storms and tsunamis that are happening all over the world; everyone's kind of saying, like, oh, like, these huge disasters are happening all the time. And it's just because of a lot of the things that we've done. We can compare modern climate change with Western and Maya droughts, over a millennium ago, or perhaps ice ages with polar inversions, asking, were those man-made also?"

The nasty reply she received: "Yo Yael, every breath you take harms the air, climate and environment."

Another: "Talk of doom is cheap, as per fire and brimstone, the Flood, Sodom and Gomorrah or falling skies, the Black Death, Aztec smallpox, the Lisbon earthquake, Malthusian human extinction, radiation fallout, domino effect, AIDS, the Twin Towers bombing, climate change, oceans rising, an Apocalypse, etc. We can't be Luddites, destroying man's machinery with which he shall one day conquer the stars."

"Controlling climate change is but the latest example of a big government fix. In this case progressives and liberals really believe they can rescue the ruined oceans, continents, atmosphere, from themselves."

"The irony: those most aware of our ecological suicide are also the ones most addicted to their comfort, which is only achieved through technological and scientific progress, again, causing pollution, waste."

"Perhaps one day, after much-anticipated climatic holocausts and other man-made population disasters, we will kick ourselves for the abortions performed by a doomed civilization, the irony being that those most aware of an ecological suicide are also the ones most in favor of termination, as a lifestyle choice, to say nothing of a moral one." Tellingly, this judgmental text revealed the darker side of social media.

But Yael, undaunted, retorted to the brazen, ethnic, racial, gender, sexual put downs with the following: "Such examples of man's ego driven disrespect, disregard of nature, have never been witnessed, maybe since Canute, as reported by ancient chronicles, through royal edict ordered the oceans' waves to cease. The problem of credulity arose when men, dressed as, and wanting to become, women, proselytized on climate change, and the dangers expressed just did not make any sense, but this was a total red herring. In the late fifties and early sixties, when I was growing up, we used to hide under our desks, with knees tucked up under our chins, at least once a month in fire drills against the nuclear holocaust. I guess this should have prepared us to croak within a week, radiation pollution suddenly become deathly serious."

But Willi and Lilly would have none of the corporate lecture from either side, for they were submerged in a quicksand of personal snipes and innuendoes, as their relationship unraveled in a drowning by text.

"Where are you? It's been hours. I won't sit and wait while my Latin lover goes down the hill to him."

"I haven't been gone long, what are you accusing me of in that deluded Mohammedan brain of yours?"

"I think you know. I'm afraid you will never change your ways. You, as I, will remain hetero forever." They used different labels, LGBT being a ruse, smokescreen, dodge to hide their latent heterosexuality.

"We could follow additional gender replacement therapies or Christian Science healings as alternatives, recalling it was at times when the world worried the sky was falling, that the resolute few, anticipating an advantage, acted, some assuming the mantle of a queen healer, such as founder, Mary Baker Eddy."

"For a true follower of evangelical Christianity, or of Allah, rejecting Western medicine has its merits." All over her back there were phantom itches, moist welts keeping her up at night, endlessly scratching.

"Perhaps there was a sexual/ erotic nuance to Thomas Jefferson keeping and bearing Arms. 'Happiness is a warm gun.' Mass shootings are an extension of pranks or practical jokes by other means, got ya..."

"Innocent victims of violence, especially mass shootings, should be thought of as sacrifices for the sake of our personal security; they had to die so that we feel safe, and can own all the guns we want, offered as in olden times to propitiate the gods; the Committee for Public Safety stresses to stand your ground."

"The selected few sacrificed to the freedom of a Second Amendment, a justified equivalent, to be sure. Your doom is as Midas', who by godly means acquired a golden touch, yet would later regret the great power, when his drinking water, banquet food, as well as lovely daughter, were lost to metamorphosis."

"This is going nowhere; I want to know where you were, and why it takes you so long to return home."

"Am I a Chihuahua beckoned by your whistle? You know, the Catholic church leads dogs to roam lol."

"Are you reminding me, that we are a camel jockey and a greaser, having overstayed our welcomes?" Now, as the latest trick, our predestined pair were hurling it at one another without coming face-to-face.

"Are you threatening me, with *La Migra*? Because if you are, I can easily call DCF (she also struggled with the all-consuming terror that the Department of Children and Family S. might be investigating her and her husband for applying fraudulently in the surrogacy of, and subsequent parental orders for, their once disappeared, sweet babes, a crime for sure) on you, you make believe mother, fraudulent *femme*."

"How dare you text me in such a menacing, aggressive manner, you counterfeit, same sex philanderer."

"At least I'm interested in sex, not with you, you wouldn't know about sex if your camel humped you."

"I want a man who comes home at night to give me what I need when I need it, not when he thinks so."

"I want a woman who isn't in my business all the time, snooping as to my whereabouts, day or night."

"I hear you saying you are no longer interested in this relationship, in which case there is one solution."

"I hear you saying you are no longer interested in my new directions, in which case there is a solution."

"Just as Allah ushered us forth from primal mud, so may he rend us back to spots of decaying dust."

"I agree. There is no use pretending; as much as they said so, we were never a match made in heaven."

As with an undeclared Viet Nam war/ conflict, theirs became a domestic war of attrition, both as losers. From a cold war, they gradually descended to constant and escalating open conflict. "According to the general in charge of Russia's NATO-facing Western Military District, Russia's new definition of war is never declared, and never ends. What is more, it can achieve its aims without using armed force at all," setting up fake scenes of provocations of war for the internet. Society established games with rules for children as well as grown-ups so they could pretend to get along, precisely because life never had rules, competition making it impossible to coexist, and we as advocates, provocateurs, agitators of ourselves.

"I cannot describe the feelings of hatred I have for you, having stuck up for you when you disappeared with our kid POWs, then covering up your bad behavior, so the police or DCF would not get involved."

"Nor I for you, having covered up your erratic drug induced behavior with our babies in *Deutschland*," such as when, several years ago, aghast, she saw him dangling their two infants, upside down by their ankles, out of a five-story window, later having to relive the moment time and time again on the news."

"Why won't you ever let me live that down? This is a denouement of my desires, you reckless whore."

"Because you won't get absolution from me. This is my damnation of desires, flaccid flake, Jackass."

Then both texted simultaneously: "Perhaps our marriage was never really consummated to begin with." Well, these were definite grounds for mental cruelty, impugning each other's masculinity or femininity. Fleeing to the comfort of divorce attorneys, they doubled down on their ridiculous, obnoxious stances. Community property might streamline the separation process, but it was no less pernicious for a family. After which came some of their last texts to each other, plaintive cries of attention, rejection, dejection; but never coming face-to-face because since returning from Mexico they were each in their own world.

"Leave me alone."

"Leave me alone."

"Don't text me again."

"Don't text me again."

"FU!"

"FU!"

At the millennium communication would ironically retrograde, from written missives to emails, texts. Then Willi became hell bent on killing Lilly; it was an obsession for regaining his chances for freedom. He could hire someone to do the job; that would lead to eternal questions, with no affirmations ever, as proof, a new take on Sisyphus, so he would have to do it himself to avoid all errors and delays. As was later reported by the sensationalist press, before any of the facts were in the open, but still hidden away.

> Willi Herman recently filed for divorce from his wife, Lilly Lawrence, the
> source familiar with that filing confirmed to SIN. But by then, he already
> had set in motion the steps that would lead to the murder plot in question.

Unmanned Aerial Vehicles, drones, were the next big thing in sanitized warfare, as the U.S. had learned with their B-52 carpet bombings during the latter part of Vietnam. Now a commander in chief who had murdered more people with UAVs than anybody else wanted new regulations imposed on them, mainly to protect himself. Willi had decided that guns were out of fashion, so he would use a drone to kill her.

Brandon Biden, recently trained as a U.S. drone sensor operator, became disillusioned with his mission. "We supposedly knew the ID of who owned a SIM or cell (phone), not who was currently in possession of it," he told Rooters, describing this doubt as, "guesswork, still not enough to justify targeted killing."

"How can I use a drone to kill my spouse?" Willi inquired of that unemployed, long-distance assassin.

"Drone strikes make matters worse," he said. "They insult our enemies because we're using an extreme, technological advantage, while at the same time, keeping those that use it safe and out of harm's way."

"I need you to train me to maneuver the drone, in launching a pinpoint strike on an enemy of the state." And so began Willi's apprenticeship in the killing arts, a vocation he was not truly destined for; though he had done some morally reprehensible things in his past the killing of his spouse would never be one. And within a few months, Willi, in his insolence and grandiosity, believing he had mastered the remote controls of one of one of the most sophisticated murder machines, executed his tactical attack scenario. At SPAZ (Safety Political Action Zealots), seated splendidly at precisely set tables, showy donors at the reserved Presidential dinner were in mid mouthful when the sudden whoosh of some overpassing drone in fierce Willi's control blew settling champagne foam from brim filled flutes onto spotless, fine linen. After all, drone strikes, suicide bombings, were moral equivalents, more so with a homing program set to Lilly. Several similar sounding patriot bores mounted the podium in defense of the liberty to gripe. "First, it's your vaccination status, then your jobs, then your guns, Lucifer help us, when will this end?" Then another: "Socialism is bred from resentment of the ruling order and the comfort of punishing your enemies." Then a putrid pundit: "You don't make poor people rich by making rich people poor." But it was an assumed victimhood of supposedly badass rednecks, who didn't care about anyone else to begin with; what was up with that? There was nothing more pitiful, than hangdog, constipated conservatives. Meanwhile a broad winged Angel of Death circled overhead, pending the appearance of its fixed target, in super classist (not classy) Houston, TX where statuesque blonds lorded it over Hispanics and blacks. Suddenly there was Lilly, easy to spot entering the hotel ballroom, sashaying in baby blue *burqa* of her own, superb couture. She would show her arch rightist friends a thing or two about walking the walk.

"All right, Mr. DeMille, I'm ready for my close-up," she adroitly deadpanned to her gathered admirers, amidst the swirl of *Paparazzi* engulfing her with flashing lights and whirring cameras: "Look this way, Miss Lawrence." "Are the rumors of your separation true?" "Do you have any comment?" "Is there a message for Willi Herman?" "What can you tell your adoring public about the future?" "Is it true that you and Willi have not been together since returning from an extended stay in Baja?" A short time ago the Angel made a reconnoiter of the surrounding area, preparing for a last pass outside, before entering the hotel through an open, upper window; flying down fire stairs, finding the high ceilinged lobby, into spacious ballroom, practically invisible in the dramatic shadows of the interior high tech design, before homing in on the swirling fabric enveloped mark; proceeding to chase Lilly off the podium, away from her adoring fans, to a backstage of hanging lights, props, flimsy scenery, to the end of an empty hall, up a deserted fire escape, turning around with nowhere to go; and as some demon glued to her, contesting directly toe to toe upon reaching the landing, hovering face-to-face in her presence, as if deciding what to do; ominous, ready to strike, but having final doubts, perhaps something jogging such a mechanized memory. From the moment Lilly saw that flying contraption whizzing about, she knew unmistakably it was Willi in his guise as Angel of Death and ran up the blocked fire escape to her present entrapment. Now finally facing her adversary, she stood up proud, defiant, offering her neck, ready for a final blow, such dignity, ego, not lost on the Angel, who must have had second thoughts; because in that very next instant, it turned about, retraced its flight path and was gone, never having detonated its demonic load. If this failure on Willi's part said anything, it was that he was loyal to his mate until the end, God help, and whatever happened in their time here on earth, they were destined to resound throughout the ages.

History has shown that drones were not the only objects to kill from the sky, maybe bolstering Chicken Little's thesis of bad things falling upon us. In fact, Chicken Little's half-sister Ottoline's origin story occurred during the Mongol siege of a medieval city, hurling bubonic plague infected corpses over its ramparts, so they rained down on doomed inhabitants, spreading one of the worst pestilences on record. Caffa (now Feodosija, Ukraine) was established by Genoa, in 1266, by an agreement with the Kahn of the Golden Horde. In 1346 the city was besieged by the Mongols, in the first use of biological warfare:

> The dying Tartars, stunned and stupefied by the immensity of the disaster brought about by the disease, and realizing that they had no hope of escape, lost interest in the siege. But they ordered corpses to be placed in catapults and lobbed into the city in the hope that the intolerable stench would kill everyone inside. What seemed like mountains of dead were thrown into the city, and the Christians could not hide or flee or escape from them, although they dumped as many of the bodies as they could in the sea. And soon the rotting corpses tainted the air and poisoned the water supply, and the stench was so overwhelming that hardly one in several thousand was in a position to flee the remains of the Tartar army. Moreover one infected man could carry the poison to others, and infect people and places with the disease by look alone. No one knew, or could discover, a means of defense. (Narrative of Gabriele De' Mussi, 1348 or 1349)

Within Ottoline's lineage was a mitochondrial donor, who happened to be walking down a side street in medieval Caffa, when a flying corpse came hurtling down within feet of where she had just passed. It was already decomposing, and broke up into pieces upon landing, the reek of decayed flesh unbearable. She had lost a husband and two children to this dread disease, so she hurried along as fast as she could, pressing her nosegay of scented flowers and herbs closer to her face to ward off the evil miasmas in the air, reciting prayers to God, for things had gotten so out of control only a higher power could intervene:

> "Abamboo, I love you. I offer the best of the food I have to you. Be good to me. Do not let sickness come to me, Abamboo. Kill my enemies, those who wish me evil by witchcraft." (Paul Du Chaillu, *King Mombo*, 1930)

Feeling particularly vulnerable, she went down a crooked street to a warm house with a barber's pole, proclaiming a practitioner of the medical arts of the time. Knocking at the door, she was admitted to an empty drawing room. A physician entered from a disguised side door, wearing a large beaked nosegay, looking like a bird of prey, a small pail of coal and incense in one hand, to ward off evil in his clinic; he had read snippets of Hippocrates, Galen, made accurate notes for each patient's humors, kept a physic garden, teeming with remedial herbs to excel in folkish cures, and had graduated in medicine at Genoa:

> SGANARELLE [aside]. Phew! Could I have been wrong after all?
> Can I have become a doctor without knowing it?
> (Moliere, *Le Medecin malgre lui* [*The Reluctant Doctor*], 1749)

"Learned doctor, friend, thank you for your assistance. You are usually so busy. Where is everyone?"

'They have died. There is nothing I can do for them; this pestilence confounds all my understanding."

"A physician without patients, so many dying that none remain; I am sorry to be sardonic, but what will become of us; what does that crystal ball tell you, eminent scholar of all the known and unknowable?"

"Those surviving this malady do so not because they are pure, but by keeping away from the infected."

"I am terrified to move about, as there is no stop to the flying bodies, Angels of Death, bringing misery to all whom I know with fevers, vomiting, spasms, pustules, buboes; heaven help us, when will it end?"

"You must go home immediately, lock yourself in, and do not admit anyone known or unknown within the place, until you hear the bells of the churches ringing the end of this black death, only then appear."

Doing as bid by the proto scientist, whom she never saw again, she survived to soon hear church bells. Little did she presage that this fortitude would one day be embodied in her distant descendant Ottoline. As a red headed Rus', beautiful Slav princess, she had the blood of bold warriors, adventurers and early merchants who had emigrated, and a dread disease was to figure in her makeup, in more ways than one. Before the Second Millennium, due to extremely difficult living conditions, e.g., the worst farmland in Western Europe, the Nordic countries were net exporters of men, as raiding Norsemen, Viking settlers. If Vikings found their Vinland, Newfoundland, they did not stay very long, or bring waves of followers to further colonize, disappearing probably of some pestilence sailing with them, for the Indian Time of Dying perhaps got its start then, as ancient tribal lore references plagues killing them off for centuries. So instead of to Vinland her Swedish progenitors sailed down the Volga to the Caspian and Black Seas, becoming some of the earliest fur traders with Novgorod, then founders of Kievan Rus'; also serving as bodyguards to the Byzantine emperors, as part of the famed Varangian Guards; for there was always a "territorial imperative" for the Ukraine, acclaimed as the Soviet Union's breadbasket for its fertile land and extensive wheat fields, before the exile of the *kulaks* to the Gulag. Being extracted from the *kulak* class Ottoline's mother was always under suspicion, no matter how hard she worked to serve the Soviet Union, in difficult assignments, as an honorable Red Army officer and spy. Of such was Ottoline's grit composed, having no idea of all this, any more than she did of a Viking heart for the red hair to show it:

> I believe that man will not merely endure: he will prevail. He is immortal,
> not because he alone among creatures has an inexhaustible voice, but
> because he has a soul, a spirit capable of compassion and sacrifice and
> endurance. The poet's, the writer's, duty is to write about these things.
> (William Faulkner, Nobel Prize speech, 1950)

Chicken Little's jealousy of Ottoline showed through, when the latter followed up on a story involving the composer Walter Karlos, who had already been Wendy, since 1972, and felt she was discriminated against in the studio's selection of the score for *48 Hours to Mecca*, resulting in a grievance; leading to Yael taking up the liberal cause as part of her duality, even if it was against her own company's interest. But what Yael understood was that anything involving Warren Bros. Inc. was in the company's interest. So it really must be noted, that good-doer Chicken Little took an important moral stance, regarding the case; for when it became clear it would give Karlos cause to petition the Supreme Court in her lawsuit against the network's movie, television, internet, broadcast news, newspaper, and publishing divisions, for equal treatment under the Constitution, everyone would be obliged to acknowledge, welcome, every type of questionable marriage or sexual practice (polygamy, bestiality), as something sacred, solemn, of equal social relevance to other (non) traditional lifestyles, as inclusiveness constituted higher revenues. Chicken Little preferred handling this ethical dilemma in a private manner, without any journalists, but once Ottoline had got hold of a lead, she would not let it go, causing Yael to take the low road, blurting: "Stop defending her for being an exhibitionist bimbo, posing for such pictures, as if she didn't know it would be mixed up in the proceedings. And anyone looking at those pictures is guilty of nothing worse than logged on voyeurism; it's not their fault you shamelessly exploited being favored by the Colonel."

23. Chief Eunuch of the Ottoman Sultan Abdul Hamid II at the Imperial Palace,
https://www.ancient-origins.net/history-ancient-traditions/famous-and-
powerful-eunuchs-ancient-world-006268

24. Don Pedro Lagos Marchant (1832-1884),
a Chilean Infantry commander, Pedro Lagos - Wikipedia

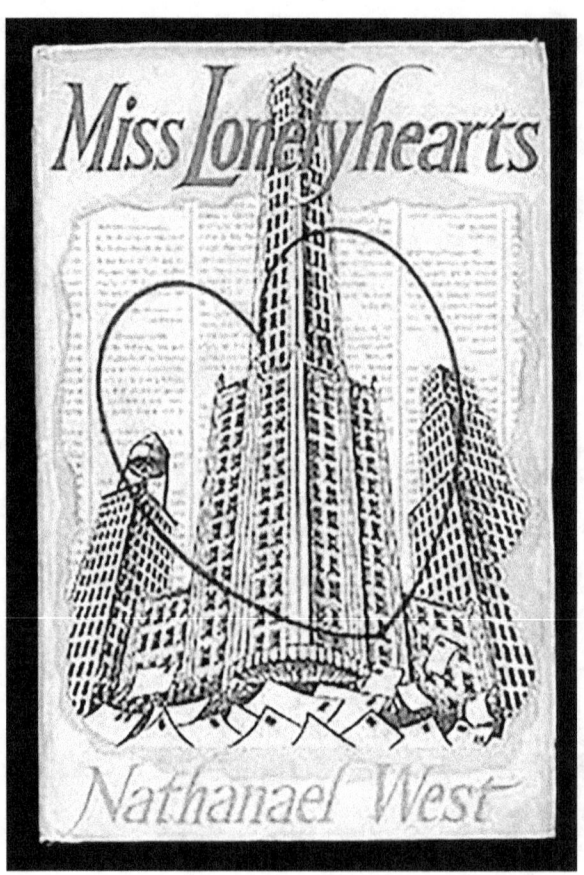

25. *Miss Lonelyhearts*, first UK edition cover, 1949,
Miss Lonelyhearts - Wikipedia

26. Luther and Erasmus,
https://servantsofgrace.org/erasmus-luther-romans-free-will-debate/

27. *Plague,* https://www.history.com/news/6-devastating-plagues

28. *Habit des Medecins*, Homöopathie in der Covid-19 Pandemie |
magic soul ∞ Tools for Change (magic-soul.de)

29. John Verelst, *Elihu Yale with Members of his Family and an Enslaved Child*, ca. 1719, Yale Center for British Art, New Haven, CT.

30. Jean-Leon Gerome, *The Tulip Folly*, 1882,
Walters Art Museum, Baltimore, MD.

31. James Worsdale, *Elihu Yale with his Servant*, before 1721,
Yale University Art Gallery, New Haven, CT.

32. *Hernan Cortes*, File:Weiditz Trachtenbuch 077 Hernan Cortés.jpg - Wikipedia

33. Wounded Knee Massacre, Aftermath of the Wounded Knee Massacre,
South Dakota. 1890 News Photo - Getty Images

34. Bill of Rights of the U.S. Constitution,
https://en.wikipedia.org/wiki/File:Bill_of_Rights_Pg1of1_AC.jpg

35. *The Beautiful and Damned*, cover, 1922, https://www.biblio.com/
book/beautiful-damned-fitzgerald-f-scott/d/432675743

36. Zelda Fitzgerald, *The Beautiful and Damned*, cover sketch, 1921,
https://creazilla.com/nodes/6856616-zelda-fitzgerald-the-beautiful-and-
damned-cover-sketch-illustration

37. Van Gogh, *Night Café*, 1888,
Yale University Art Gallery, New Haven, CT.

38. *Berghotel Sanatorium Schatzalp*, Davos,
Switzerland, The Magic Mountain - Wikipedia

39. *Barricade bei der Universität am 26ten Mai 1848 in Wien,*
https://repository.library.brown.edu/studio/item/bdr:225996/

40. Celtic Human Sacrifice Wicker Man, Halloween: The Great Cover-up
(logosresourcepages.org)

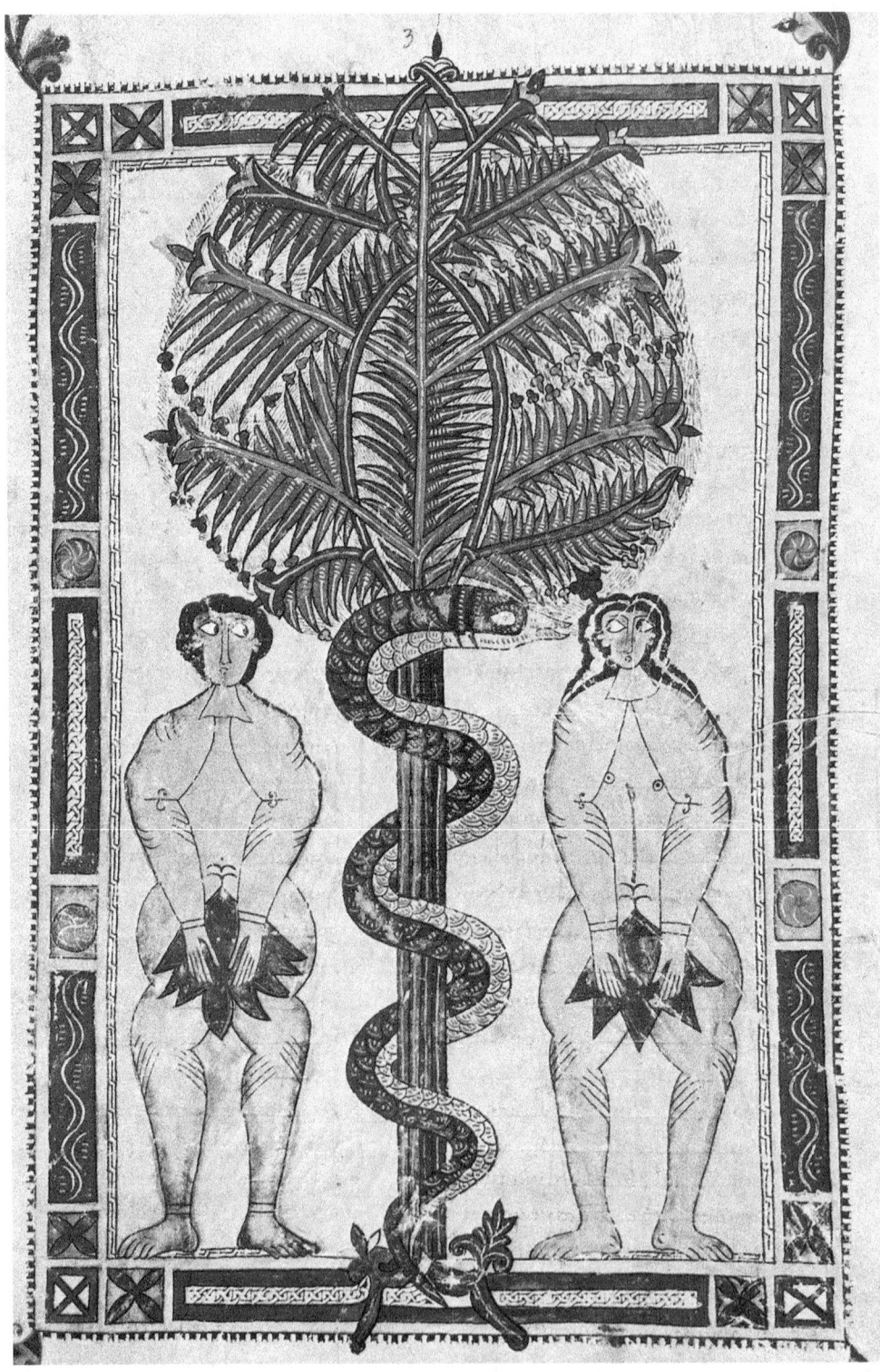

41. Beatus of Liebana, *Adam and Eve*, c. 950, Escorial Beatus, Spain.

# 17. *Auto-da-fe* (Renunciation of the Heretics)

> If today you can take a thing like evolution and make it a crime to teach
> it in the public school, tomorrow you can make it a crime to teach it in
> the private schools, and the next year you can make it a crime to teach it
> to the hustings or in the church. At the next session you may ban books
> and the newspapers. Soon you may set Catholic against Protestant and
> Protestant against Protestant, and try to foist your own religion upon the
> minds of men. If you can do one you can do the other. Ignorance and
> fanaticism is ever busy and needs feeding. Always it is feeding and
> gloating for more. Today it is the public-school teachers, tomorrow the
> private. The next day the preachers and the lectures, the magazines, the
> books, the newspapers. After a while, your honor, it is the setting of man
> against man and creed against creed until with flying banners and beating
> drums we are marching backward to the glorious ages of the sixteenth
> century when bigots lighted fagots to burn the men who dared to bring
> any intelligence and enlightenment and culture to the human mind.
> (Clarence Darrow, *The Essential Words and Writings of Clarence Darrow*, 2007)

With all due respect, C. Darrow was mistaken warning that, "we are marching backward to the glorious ages of the sixteenth century," because in all truth, we never left those ages completely behind, burning those we now disagree with more cleverly: mobile phones providing the means to get hateful messages out at the drop of a hat, when formerly it might have taken longer, to discredit and vilify your enemies. Twirper collectively gasped at this or that. Were we the "cousins" of *Fahrenheit 451,* standing vigil at our front doors to identify the latest social renegades? What happened to freedom of thought in an era of instant expression and swift public opinion? Were we now better followers, than leaders, of others? The Internet gave users the feeling that they were part of something greater than themselves, something significant, epochal, as important as the universe itself, Caesar's thumb up, down, PikPok life or death. When one side bent the facts, it was all right for the other to put out false particulars, this being partisan propaganda, as journalistic truth was a movable feast, with or without Chicken Little. When Gutenberg Bibles were printed in 1454, they ironically heralded their own demise as the basic book. In fatal irony, at the millennium the information revolution cynically led to the infestation of sinister misinformation.

Lilly and Willi, still laying low after their recent bad behavior, and the release of their masterful movie, *48 Hours to Mecca,* somehow correlated both events as the latest burst of conceit begun after mounting the Black Stone on their mantel, a relic deserving of no special attention, never realizing its importance. Perhaps such an illegal appropriation would bring them bad luck, if it continued lodged in small-town Sanctuary, CA, and its lofty desert canyon exclusivity. They wondered, should it be returned to greedy Saudis, but as it had once belonged to Adam and Eve, and there could be none better to act as guardians than her and Willi, that much was certain, they preferred keeping it, rejecting its return for the present.

Somehow, they had become superstitious of late, cancelling all their meetings, including the one led by Patricia (P) Diddy, Ph.D., J.D. for *Les Enfants* contributions. It was time for Lilly to look after herself. Perhaps if she perused her written as well as electronic mail, she would get many opinions to consider. There was a loud cry from the wilderness, picked at random, although, not randomly posted by Grawitz:

> *Valentine's Day*
> *Anonymous (SS Col. Grawitz)*

*Dear Miss Lonelyhearts (Lilly),*

*It is usually I who beckon subordinates to perform beyond themselves in their total dedication to our cause, but here I am, writing to you for some sort of answer I cannot give myself, as the shepherd who is his own lamb, the clergyman who advises himself, the colonel sacrificed as if a private. As a close reader of your column, I cannot help but wonder at perceived similarities, between you and a movie character Scheherazade, to whom I owe a debt of gratitude for distinguishing herself, by acts of valor, during our mission; her resolute, fearless stance for global liberty and freedom; and allowing me to hatch a plan to rescue my red headed Rus', beautiful Slav princess, whose sister I shamefully murdered in the war, within her script, thus redeeming my dear Ottoline's mother from the heinous Gulag. It is out of an infinite respect for them, and the memory of my darling lost baby Aley, Alexandra, that I wonder how much I should disclose, if at all, regarding my past affairs, especially the death of their sister, aunt, whose face I spared, at my hands, before mounting her head in my trophy room. Should I tell them I was the Archer of Auschwitz, depraved SS monster? I hear rumors of your being a Palestinian, the redskins of the desert, with no home of their own, after expropriation and decimation by the Israelis. How do you deal with such injustice imposed on your people and family?*

Your suns and worlds are not within my ken,
I merely watch the plaguey state of men.
The little god of earth remains the same queer sprite
As on the first day, or in primal light. (Goethe, *Faust*, Part One, 1808)

*Perhaps letting go of those who are dearest is that part of life I am least accustomed to; even I, who should know better, often wish to reinvent the past to an advantage; before moving even further along diverging paths. My question is about regrets in life. Are they worth this anguish, despair, stirred, or should mistakes and errors made be let go by all the injured? If this is absolution, clemency, that I crave, perhaps it shows I'm not bad.*
*Sincerely,*
*A Lonely Reader*

And another echo of loneliness, picked at random, although not randomly dispatched by his Ottoline:

*Valentine's Day*
*Anonymous (Ottoline)*
*Dear Miss Lonelyhearts (Lilly),*
*I have been a fan for some time of your feminine, yet tough, replies to the problems of others. You seem a woman of the sky, brought forth on winds of change and fresh life, showing truth without society's strict limitations. I guess I have a lot to be thankful for despite things not having gone right in my life. First, I'll never let go of the ready hurt Reds caused my family and myself or forgive any of them severally for crimes against humanity. Second, I have only a vague recollection of my mother, red headed Rus', beautiful Slav princess, whose sister was shamefully murdered in the war, by the Archer of Auschwitz, depraved SS monster; my father, known only*

*as a shadow of himself, fateful phantom of dreams of gritty, high German enunciated as whispers in my infant ear; then political events dictated my mother to Tyumen, like Lenin's embalmed body (which had been shipped to Siberia for four years, during WWII), my father vanished. Years later, when Lily's mother was trapped inside Guantánamo, I identified with her desperation and began following the story, as it appeared so like my own. Third, I am turned off by the jealous reactions my mother's rescue caused in some. It is not my fault the Colonel included me, in the post addendum to the script, and left others out. He had no idea that Ms. Yael Abraham, a WWII orphan, would be so resentful at being excluded from the picture:*

My mother was of the sky/ My father was of the earth
But I am of the universe/ And you know what it's worth
(Lennon-McCartney, "Yer Blues," 1968)

*I'm prone to lose my head from the weight of all these contretemps, but I would rather draw attention to a movie character Scheherazade, whom I owe a debt of gratitude to for showing great compassion in our situation, for having included my mother and me in those last-minute casting calls. And it's as if I'd known the Colonel before, he's been so nice to me, bye.*
*Sincerely,*
*A Lonely Reader*

For a moment, Lilly was intrigued enough by the identity of a correspondent, to feel empathy for others than herself. But it was only for a slip of time, as she readied to go home to *Pinkton/ Mt. Olympus*; her interval in *Viejo Mexico* was ending, as recent success of her movie began eclipsing their bad behavior. Their stay there, as during the 60s, was all about hiding in plain sight, until the trip ended with a crash:

One pill makes you larger
And one pill makes you small
And the ones that mother gives you
Don't do anything at all (Jefferson Airplane, "White Rabbit," 1967)

But before crossing back, over the border, Miss Lonelyhearts took it as her duty to reply to each Lonely Reader. She was comfortable answering her correspondences via email to ensure the quickest delivery:

*President's Day*
*Miss Lonelyhearts (Lilly)*
*Dear Anonymous (Willi),*
*You said of your woman, poof she disappeared into a mist, but whatever did you do to get her to go? And the romance was a whirlwind, but after having kids it was not the same, but what did you contribute to those big mistakes? But I'm most concerned with your confession of Jesus, a little boy whose head you might have once split open but had tried not to think about. Have you ever thought what would happen if your wife found out about this? There would be hell for you to pay, that's what. Ugly as this incident was, it seemed to have pushed you toward redemption in seeking intimacy, with a ready-made partner, mate, who showed you more loyalty and love than any other on demand, or mail order, bride could ever have.*

*But overcompensating, you let Eros overcome your better sense, thinking such a matrimonial course did not require much constancy, discriminate behavior, on your part; sinking down to profligate philandering behavior, which was never part of your personality prior, and it was because of the money. So, any young man or boy who bothered looking your way, fit in. Perhaps covering up your split with endless Great Ratsby type parties, in pursuit of millennial mischief, the Hollywood lifestyle ripe for immense alcohol imbibement, leading to more dissipation, all night revelry, raves, replete with open orgies, onanism, was what wore out your relationship. Perhaps you were not the best influence on your wife, so considering the leading lady's greatest comeback, you should give her a break, regarding any bad behavior she may have committed in a now distant, hidden past.*
*Sincerely,*
*Miss Lonelyhearts*

*President's Day*
*Miss Lonelyhearts (Lilly)*
*Dear Anonymous (Isidora Green),*
*It's always easy to bring someone down behind their back, but also much less effective than polemics; but please don't worry, I would never squeal you out to anyone, even if I think I know who you mean. You sound as if unappreciated by those whose abilities you recognized, then subsequently nurtured professionally, perhaps much too personally for such a no-show. I know certain executives were initially opposed to her last film, refusing to give any support until the studio and team convinced them otherwise; but while they were so concerned about boys becoming girls, becoming boys and which bathroom to use, our enemies were decapitating captured journalists, and broadcasting it to the world. That was why my cinematic wonder worked. It's timing captured the frustrations in our society, when bad things happen and there is no pay back, or choices, of bringing back those responsible dead or alive, as poignant as the prophet Muhammad's night travels with the archangel Gabriel meeting Abraham, Moses, Jesus. You and your Puritan president recruited millennials with typical foibles. The quintessential new woman was consumed by a philanderer of record. Perhaps he was not the best influence on an* ingenue, *so considering such a leading lady's greatest comeback, you should give her a break, apropos any bad behavior she may have committed, in a now distant, hidden past.*
*Sincerely,*
*Miss Lonelyhearts*

*President's Day*
*Miss Lonelyhearts (Lilly)*
*Dear Anonymous (Rev. Hannibal),*
*I recall that freedom to the* Mujahideen *meant there are no human rights, only those taken by such as who dare and can. Those sweetly slumbering in the soft beds of security, do not trust the corporation you work for, who would rather sell you out, and throw you down into perdition, than lose a penny in their stock's earnings estimates, one of the false idols of wealth. A generation ago, even today, you would have been labeled as an uppity*

*such and such, maybe as a disciple of Louis Fearrakhan, Nation of Islum leader, and I would be impressed, believing he was a strong man, but his followers have left much to be desired. Your extended aggression against foreigners, and the old slave order, seems a bit tempered by the presence of a certain Jewish lady in your midst, about whom you seem fascinated, even to that unique tattoo 169062, she displays as a symbol of a phoenix reborn to power. Perhaps given Eros' ministrations you will find cause to desist assisting those who have been the most viciously oppressed, before perversely going on to self-righteously, unflinchingly, oppress others; and it is a narrative as old, and as common, as revenge itself; maybe accept the sustainability of raw, pedophilic prey in this period of sexual license. This will be remembered as the age when the sodomite was king. Forget the coffee klatch, our society is more akin to a catamite klatch, better get used to it, but keep to your father's golden throated Jewish lullabies. As far as me redeeming myself, in any way, just be careful what you wish for.*
*Sincerely,*
*Miss Lonelyhearts*

*President's Day*
*Miss Lonelyhearts (Lilly)*
*Dear Anonymous (SS Col. Grawitz),*
*Your sense of guilt is indubitable, always wondering if you had been war criminal worthy, and taking the wrong step would get you in trouble with your post war NATO task masters, so better to let accolades rest for your rescue of that red headed Rus', beautiful Slav princess, whose sister you shamefully murdered in the war, thus liberating within a script, your dear Ottoline's mother from that heinous Gulag. I believe that knowing her as I do Scheherazade would not desire a debt of gratitude for distinguishing herself by acts of valor during that mission, or a resolute, fearless stance for global liberty and freedom, and allowing you to hatch your scheme. It seemed as if life continually evolved, intermittently progressed, from vast separation and recurrent differentiation; there was eugenic consideration in family arranged marriages. Being the Archer of Auschwitz, depraved SS monster, you were bred from finest pagan, Prussian stock, to become a mass murderer, as yours were the last tribes to Christianize, and first, to adopt Protestantism, passing on some befittingly cruel, demented gene. Being a Palestinian, I learned to leave regrets behind me, as water under the bridge. Never disclose your past crimes to them, especially the death of their sister, aunt whose face you saved, at your hands, before mounting her head in your trophy room; rather, pray for your soul, you degenerate.*
*Sincerely,*
*Miss Lonelyhearts*

*President's Day*
*Miss Lonelyhearts (Lilly)*
*Dear Anonymous (Ottoline),*

*Scheherazade expected no gratitude for distinguishing herself with great compassion, in including you and your mother in the last-minute casting calls, as this was the colonel's one and only dream, to stage a rescue for all time, of his daughter's missing mother, both to remain concealed from hoodwinked Saudis. Another wrote of herself, it being easily of a sister: What if you were a Jew, who secretly feared you were a Nazi's daughter? As with Calliope, of whom much is mentioned, but little known, you also hold a lot within, while inspiring those around you to creatively express:*

Here rise to life again, dead poetry!
Let it, O holy Muses, for I am yours,
And here Calliope, strike a higher key,
Accompanying my song with that sweet air... (Dante, "Inferno," 1321)

*But there was one line of your missive, which particularly caught my eye: You have a lot to be thankful for despite everything not having gone right. Your supporting role in the feature production has made some envious, as if you'd known the Colonel before, he's been so inspiring to you. As the Archer of Auschwitz, depraved SS monster, he lost his family, while your father, known only as a shadow of himself, fateful phantom of dreams of gritty, high German enunciated as whispers in infant ear, by warm hearth fire, was an angel hovering over your shoulder, and could not have been any kinder than the Colonel has been known to be to his faithful* protégés.
*Sincerely,*
*Miss Lonelyhearts*

Upon returning to their Sanctuary, Lilly was tormented by divorcing Willi, finally coming to this plight. There seemed to be a cold war between them which needed to play itself out, and this is what followed. It blew apart with derivatives of texting, including posting, twitching and tattling, coming naturally to Lilly and Willi, who at restaurants would not speak to, but only text, each other while at the same table, the protocol so serious, they would keep texting each other in bed, engaging in sexting when fortunate. Sometimes electronic messaging only served to demonstrate how remarkably foolish a sender could be. The ceaseless rapidity of information flow in this internet connected world led to unfortunate, unsubtle outcomes. Instant gratifications, in making declarations, disclosures, observations, exhortations, led to stupid statements, usually ill prepared, emotional, and as potentially dangerous to the sender as to those receiving the rushed, nasty missive, because instant gratification usually came with unwanted, regretted baggage. Ironically the incredible speed of the internet, made any piece of news, discovery, treatise or creative work obsolete before it could be contemplated, composed or published; history moving faster than those who were entrusted to comment intelligently, cogently regarding flying events, whizzing by; with more misinformation now than ever, leading to a lack of perspective. Undoubtedly, this laborious, lengthy, detailed effort of mine would be dead on arrival, obsolete before even researched, outlined or much less written at all, such was the fury of life and artistic transformation in these racing times. And the arrogant know-it-all attitude of everyone with a mobile phone or computer, was part of the Internet Uncertainty Principle in an Age of Confusion: all the things thought up to help society not to get along. They said people who do not share on social media are creepy, but what about those who overshared?

If all mankind minus one, were of one opinion, and only one person were
of the contrary opinion, mankind would be no more justified in silencing
that one person, than he, if he had the power, would be justified in
silencing mankind. (John Stuart Mill, *On Liberty*, 1859)

They would use futurist Fritter, driving gullible masses, each to their own side for their loaded purpose.

Previously people bit their tongues. Then Fritter bit them in the ass, social media seeming to empower the biggest frauds of all, as texting and twirping promoted slavish thinking and a herd mentality. If the power of social media was mockery, then they would mock, as fools jumping the gun; and as the newly minted internet educated, a real bunch of dumb asses, for the internet thought this or that, responding as if having a singular identity; but sounding smart, as one of the new breeds of tech geeks, who could not even sign their name in script: "Metadata is what allows an actual enumerated understanding, a precise record of all the private activities in all our lives; it illustrates our associations, our political affiliations and our actual activities," as per a future, banished NSA whistleblower, accused spy, political fugitive.

The problem with stereotypes was that they were so often true to the mark, especially about millennials being shallow, considering they were brought up on video games rather than books, the Internet rather than encyclopedias, social media rather than personal connection. That's why they're so given to facile fantasy solutions, such as socialism, when all they must do is study Venezuela, Cuba, the rest of human history, to know the failures of socialism, which as Nietzsche said, kills the heart, the mind; it being the death of the soul. And recently, the fascist alternative had become popular in the blue-collar heartland, spewing slogans: "Consider the staggering, conflicting nature of life: Everything leading to opposition. Morning Public Safety Message: If civilization must be burned for our liberty, then it must be burned." There had been precedents of historic immolations, as in ancient Troy, the Great Library of Alexandria, Reformation England, Nazi Germany's *Kristallnacht*, or again, in Ray Bradbury's (Francois Truffaut's) *Fahrenheit 451*, and extremist ploys of cancelling progress, rather than convincing with contemporary thought. And then each side was using journalism to their own ends, and propaganda knew no bounds, with the left's artfully tiresome, universal unity, then the right's hatefully motivated hellish hierarchies.

### Epithets
If you dare to question African Americans, you are a white supremacist.
If you dare to question brown skinned people, you are a racist.
If you dare to question Jews, you are an anti-Semite.
If you dare to question Africans, you are a colonialist.
If you dare to question illegal immigrants, you are a nativist.
If you dare to question LGBT, you are a homophobe.
If you dare to question whites, you are a traitor.
If you dare to question men, you are a misandrist.
If you dare to question Muslim extremists, you are an Islamophobe.
If you dare to question affirmative action, you are a troglodyte.
If you dare to question women, you are a misogynist.
If you dare to question women over men, you are a tyrant.
If you dare to question feminism, you are a sexist.
If you dare to question abortion, you are a male chauvinist pig.
If you dare to question cultural attitudes, you are a bigot.
If you dare to question ethnicity, you are a chauvinist.
If you dare to question happiness, you are malcontent.
If you dare to question climate change, you are a climate denier.
If you dare to question civil disobedience, you are a reactionary.
If you dare to question the police, you are a hoodlum.
If you dare to question police brutality, you are a cop hater.
If you dare to question higher wages, you are an exploiter.
If you dare to question unions, you are a scab.
If you dare to question morality, you are a libertine.
If you dare to question gun rights, you are unconstitutional.

If you dare to question gun control, you are trigger-happy.

If you dare to question a new treaty, you are a war monger.

If you dare to question hardness, you are effeminate.

If you dare to question softness, you are a bully.

If you dare to question national identity, you are an imperialist.

If you dare to question society, you are a renegade.

If you dare to question pleasure, you are a scold.

If you dare to question the past, you are a revisionist.

If you dare to question the present, you are antediluvian.

If you dare to question the future, you are orthodox.

If you dare to question authority, you are a rebel.

If you dare to question openness, you are a prig.

If you dare to question God, you are an atheist.

If you dare to question Islam, you are a crusader.

If you dare to question the bible, you are a heretic.

If you dare to question Jesus, you are a Pharisee.

If you dare to question macho, you are a queer.

If you dare to question Muhammad, you are an infidel.

If you dare to question the law, you are a criminal.

If you dare to question the Koran, you are a devil.

If you dare to question Buddha, you are a materialist.

If you dare to question public nudity, you are a body shamer.

If you dare to question promiscuity, you are a moralist.

If you dare to question free love, you are a philistine.

If you dare to question abstinence, you are a sensualist.

If you dare to question sex, you are a prude.

If you dare to question marriage, you are a philanderer.

If you dare to question same sex marriage, you are a retrograde.

If you dare to question sodomy laws, you are a deviant.

If you dare to question love, you are a hater.

If you dare to question Catholicism, you are an apostate.

If you dare to question Christianity, you are a blasphemer.

If you dare to question the pope, you are anti-cleric.

If you dare to question the spiritual, you are a voluptuary.

If you dare to question religion, you are a dissenter.

If you dare to question the government, you are an anarchist.

If you dare to question the status quo, you are a non-conformist.

If you dare to question groups, you are an isolationist.

If you dare to question war, you are a coward.

If you dare to question the left, you are a Nazi.

If you dare to question the right, you are a commie.

If you dare to question good, you are evil.

If you dare to question evil, you are weak.

If you dare to question tradition, you are a revolutionary.

If you dare to question revolution, you are a reactionary.

If you dare to question the news media, you are a public enemy.

If you dare to question anarchy, you are a conformist.

If you dare to question strength, you are a pansy.

If you dare to question the truth, you are a liar.
If you dare to question progress, you are a Luddite.
If you dare to question belief, you are a miscreant.
If you dare to question propriety, you are a savage.
If you dare to question a doubt, you are a simpleton.
If you dare to question convention, you are a nihilist.
If you dare to question beauty, you are a beast.
If you dare to question winning, you are a loser.
If you dare to question losing, you are a bad sport.
If you dare to question… you are a drowning fool.
Hey, hold on now, with such calling out on the ocean.
If you dare to question the meme, you're in a dream.
If you dare to question blame, you are not playing the game,
as an inconsequential tool, daring all for a notion.

Were these the tropes of a bifurcated society, with perhaps too many crystal meth heads to reckon with? Knowing the headlines meant being counted as a *bona fide* New Age world connected citizen, William Randolph Hearst would be proud of; was it yellow journalism at its worst? The Huffnpuff Post looked and sounded more like Pimple.com every day, focused on high heel celebrities, exclusive inclusiveness, and this new-fangled tramp-speak, combined with endless in your face teaching moments (so many), to reel in those dour readers; I see it, as I call it, usually figuring: *Five (or more) Reasons Why You Need to Realize (believe, rely and act on) the Following (prescribed opinions, usually presented as facts), or,*

*The Key to Understanding This*
*What You Should Know About That*
*The One Thing You Need to Do*
*Why Such and Such Happened*
*The Real Story Behind It*
*Here's What Happens When*
*We Know the Problems Found*
*Senator Schooled by Movie Star*
*Let Us Correct Your Tired Notions*
*Five Thing to Know About Love*
*The Beginning of the End For*
*What On Earth is Wrong With?*
*How is This a Big Deal?*
*You Won't Believe Your Eyes*
*What Matters Most to Moms Is*
*Celebrities Know the Difference*
*So and So Stuns in Form Fitting Dress*
*Hold On While We Explain*
*Complicated Relationship Revealed*
*Without the US Freedom Ceases*

At the millennium communication would ironically retrograde, from Fakebook to Fritter, then PikPok. Then Lilly became hell bent on killing Willi; it was an obsession for regaining her chances for freedom. She could hire someone to do the job; that would lead to eternal questions, with no affirmation ever, as proof, a new take on Sisyphus, so she would have to do it herself to avoid all errors and delays. As was later reported by the sensationalist press, before any of the facts were in the open, but still hidden away.

*Lilly Lawrence has filed for divorce from her husband, Willi Herman, the source familiar with the filing confirmed to SIN. But by then, she already had set in motion the steps that would lead to the murder plot in question.*

The U.S. Air Force had standing orders to shoot down an aircraft suspected of being commandeered by terrorists, but police were not allowed to profile, detain, search or arrest anyone in Muslim attire. How did that make sense? Considering mass bombings were extensions of pranks, practical jokes, by other means, Lilly decided explosives would overdo it, so she would utilize a poison tipped cane to kill him.

The real problem was armed minorities in an open carry scenario, the police, whites, terrified of blacks in general, and bomb throwing *gangstas* specifically; in a most alarming incident, a gay rider claimed a miffed Miami driver showed him his dynamite after exclaiming, "I want to hit on everyone who's gay."

"How can I use a cane to kill my spouse?" Lilly inquired of the anonymous, Dark Web Assassin page.

"Contaminated canes make matters worse. They insult our enemies because we're using an extremely age perfected advantage, while at the same time, keeping those that use it safe and out of harm's way."

"I need you to train me to aim a poisoned tip, in an old *chekist* style pinprick strike on an enemy of the state." And so began Lilly's apprenticeship in the killing arts, a vocation she was not truly destined for; though she had done some morally reprehensible things in her past the killing of a spouse would not be one. And after a few months, Lilly, in her insolence and grandiosity, believing she had mastered one of the most sophisticated implements of sinister, silent assassination, executed her tactical attack scenario. At the Damnos World Ephemeral Forum, seated splendidly at precisely set tables, stylish participants at reserved Presidential tables were in mid mouthful when the sudden whoosh of some clear, white *burqa* clad berserk warrior blew the settling champagne foam from brim filled flutes onto spotless, fine linen. After all, murder for hate and murder for hire were moral equivalents, more so with the spectral killer's attack. Several similar sounding liberal bores mounted the podium in defense of the liberty to grumble:

> If mankind had always been logical and wise, history would not be a long chronicle of folly and crime. (James G. Frazer, *The Golden Bough*, 1922)

Meanwhile the broad draped Angel of Death circled all over, pending the appearance of its fixed target, in super classist (not classic) Switzerland where statuesque blonds lorded it over Palestinians, Africans. And suddenly, there was Willi, easy to spot entering the hotel ballroom, sashaying in his brilliant, black tuxedo of a superb couture. He would show these arch leftists a thing or two about walking the walk.

"They say you're judged by the strength of your enemies," he adroitly deadpanned to lauding admirers, amidst a swirl of *Paparazzi* engulfing him with flashing lights and whirring cameras: "Look this way, Mr. Herman." "Are the rumors of your separation true?" "Do you have a comment?" "Any messages for Lilly Lawrence?" "What can you tell your adoring public about your future?" "Any truth that you and Lilly have not been together since returning from an extended stay in Baja?" A short time ago the Angel made a reconnoiter of the surrounding area, preparing for a last pass outside, before entering the hotel through an open, upper window; treading down fire stairs, finding the high ceilinged lobby, into a spacious ballroom, practically invisible in the dramatic shadows of the interior high tech design, before homing in on the svelte tuxedo attired mark; proceeding to chase Willi off the podium, and away from his adoring fans, to a backstage of hanging lights, props, flimsy scenery, to the end of an empty hall, up a deserted fire escape, turning around with nowhere to go; and as some demon glued to him, contesting directly toe to toe upon reaching the landing, hovering face-to-face in his presence, as if deciding what to do; ominous, ready to strike, but having final doubts, perhaps something jogging such a mechanized memory. From the moment Willi observed a *burqa* clad figure mingling about, he knew unmistakably it was Lilly in a guise as Angel of Death and ran up the blocked fire escape into his present entrapment. Now finally facing his adversary, he stood up proud, defiant, offering his neck, ready for the final blow, such dignity, ego, not lost on the Angel, who must have had second thoughts; because in that very next instant it turned on its cane, retraced its tracks and was gone, never having pinpricked its demonic load. If this failure on Lilly's part said anything, it was that she was loyal to her mate until the end, God help, and whatever happened in their time here on earth, they were destined to resound throughout the ages.

In 9 AD united Germanic tribes annihilated three Roman Legions, at the Battle of the Teutoburg Forest. The Roman loss was devastating to its national prestige, as Rome was now held off at the Rhine River. For pagan Germans there was victory with a cost, as they now kept to their paleolithic ways, separately. *Schutzstaffel* (*SS*) Colonel Otto Waldemar Grawitz' fall from grace, toward his Nazi leanings, may have been ingrained in him by any blood remnants of his origins in his ferocious primogenitors, at the Battle of the Teutoburg Forest, as some sixty-five generations ago, a hero in his direct lineage had feasted on the roasted bones of captured Roman legionnaires; a symbolic rejection of those modernizing values of the Western tradition, Greek fostered, exemplified by Rome, leading to another hundred and fifty years of barbarism for *Deutschland*. But also, by propagandized misinformation, leading him to join the *SS*: sophistry, as when philosophy farts, and fundamental precepts are flawed and unjust to begin with, and when associations or any other political activities based on erroneous origins would be fatal or corrupt:

> The principal ingredient of our people is the Nordic race (55%). That is
> not to say that half our people are pure Nordics. All of the aforementioned
> races appear in mixtures in all parts of our fatherland. The circumstance,
> however, that the great part of our people is of Nordic descent justifies
> us taking a Nordic standpoint when evaluating our character and spirit,
> bodily structure, and physical beauty.
> (Harwood L. Childs (translator), "The Nazi Primer," 1938)

It was said that Caesar Augustus never recovered from the blow of losing his two favorite legions in the Teutoburg Forest, commanded by his most loyal officers with the best supplies and armaments of those grisly times, seeming to represent the limits of his *Pax Romana* which had expanded meteorically. The emperor would formalize his plans to declare himself a god before the Senate, not that they mattered; simply stated, how could he celebrate his spectacular apotheosis now that his legions were vanquished?

> Besides, critics continued, Augustus seemed to have superseded the
> worship of the gods when he wanted to have himself venerated in temples,
> with god-like images, by priests and ministers... After an appropriate
> funeral, Augustus was declared a god and decreed a temple.
> (Tacitus, *The Annals of Imperial Rome*, c. 117)

"First, I shall have myself venerated in temples, with God-like images, by priests and diviners, after all, actors do the same sort of thing all the time. Second, I shall make sure the Senate knows of my intent."

"My darling, there are enough *denarii* profiled by you already; as your wife, I counsel you against any exaggerated self-adulation, until the defined grieving period for our Teutoburg Forest fallen has passed; in order that you keep your head, amidst mourning mobs, disconsolate with loss of face to barbarians."

"Reports were of my officers chased down, then consumed. How can it be possible in this current age? Because in the first millennium I thought such acts of animal fury would stay behind us. I was wrong."

"My Emperor, you are a most magnanimous, progressive thinker for our times; were you not ruthless in many of your early undertakings, as with Philippi, the civil wars and Actium, despite your great works?"

"It is against me that such atrocities occurred; I take it personally and will carry it with me to my grave; which I pray to Jupiter, and his Olympians, will not occur until I join them on Mount Olympus."

"My dear, your grand obsessions with the afterlife and otherworldly powers, are endearing traits for an emperor who wields absolute power, over life and death, but rather Egyptian. For don't you know that:

"Man is the measure of all things." (Protagoras, c. 490 – c. 420 BC)

"Then those Germans are rejecting the splendors of Roman thought and culture, to persist in darkness. Dear Livia, how is it possible that you keep my focus on the here and now, and not the past or future?"

"Because, my Lord, you are as putty in my shaping hands, with which I shall strike our enemies down. You must put this behind you, as winter began in the time it took for the news of this disaster to arrive."

"I will offer prayers, sacrifices, for my men digested by those Angels of Death; may they suffer bowel cramps evermore." And wouldn't you know it, but Grawitz was cursed by gastric issues his entire life.

With such genetic composition, encouraged by some mythic daring do at one of the most consequential battles in history, was it any wonder that *SS* Colonel Otto Waldemar Grawitz had chosen violence as a *modus operandi*, and deception, secrecy as his calling cards? How could it have manifested otherwise? If Germanic barbarism ineluctably resulted in authoritarian and Nazi sympathies, part of that sensibility would undoubtedly transfer to Ottoline, as demonstrated by her insistence on ferocious loyalty and love from her blond crew cut *Bratva* goon, Zaroff. Just what did such traits have in store for Ms. Abraham? Here the obvious should be noted: as the Colonels' long-lost daughter, all of Yael's chromosomes were German; so, Ms. Abraham had mistaken assumptions of her double prejudiced Jewishness, as a second class crypto-Sephardic, from a lack of evidence to the contrary, and straddled two disparate worlds; her ancestors no more Sephardim exiles from Spain's diaspora during its Inquisition, than she might dream.

The disinterested inquisitor paused from his tome, having conjured divinities along with the elements, now down from tallest tower, where tortured echoes from dungeon flew up stone steps like Hellhounds. His inflated preoccupation was whether *conversos* (*marranos*), even after generations residing in Spain (himself), were still practicing crypto-Jews, as they had gained religious, state, provincial, local offices. For there was a contempt felt by the devout toward those getting a free ride, church assistance, spiritual welfare, a product of their obsession with the virtue of faith for itself, beyond even the religious reward to be gained thereof, as blasphemy, heresy had to be burned out of the church body before the just won. He knew that natural law and even biblical morality forbade him from taking the life of another, but the ethics, canon law, of the church demanded a tribunal's death warrant be obeyed, removing any sense of sin. So staked pyres were being set, for the next *auto-da-fe* (Renunciation of the Heretics) of our holy Lord. And among those doomed to be sacrificed for apostasy were two sisters, one blond, the other red headed. At the last minute, the inquisitor allowed the girls' mother to visit them in their death cell, but before entering the mother begged for a confession with him, which was given through a latticed booth.

"O my God, I am so sorry for my sins because I have offended you. I know I should love you above all things. Help me to make penance, to do better and avoid anything that might lead me into sin. Amen."

"Child, let us hear what bothers your conscience; how can God help you, in your current predicament?"

"My Lord Inquisitor, Father, I lied to the Inquisition about the origins of my daughters, out of fear for them. As I attest, I was born a Jew, but baptized a *converso* shortly thereafter, as detailed by cathedral records, but I shall be faceless in the following. I told the court I had both girls by the same father, who was a *goy*, so they might be pardoned, but that was not true. The redhead arrived with the *goy*, from a Kievan Rus' mother (red headed Rus', beautiful Slav princess), a stepdaughter, whom I love equally to my own. So, my gracious Lord, I plead that you save her, for she was never a Jew to begin with, which may be confirmed by this baptismal certificate I have for your verification, and you could never light a Christian. But I supplicate your eminence to save both of my daughters, as a boon to a devout mother."

"My child, this is a shock; why did you not explain this to the church fathers on the day of judgement?"

"I thought having one daughter's baptismal record would penalize my other daughter, for being a Jew."

"Child, we will excuse your Kievan daughter's bad behavior, out of consideration for a latent madness, but there are no grounds to counter the tribunal's order for your unrepentant other, *converso* or not. So, I shall bid you a good day, my child. The peace of the Lord be with you always." "And also with you. Magnanimous judge, you have granted me half the reward I requested, but always infinite in its scope." Later that morning, in 1492, her true, blond daughter was set ablaze in Seville's main plaza, witnessed by the remaining family, as an act of kinship contrition, devout humility, public penance; receiving the showy blessings from the inquisitor, as the screams of their loved one, roasting in the crackling flames, until turned to bones and ash, filled the forum with unholy echoes which remained forever in their guts; such a gruesome event, inclusive of torture, immolation, only partially offset by the redhead's pardon. Perhaps the cruelties of that age, in a backward-looking Spain, ironically the same year as the *Mundus novus* was about to be discovered, could only be compared to a present one, where atrocities still ruled. As far as Chicken Little knew, she had every cause in the world to be suffering from Jewrosis or worse. But this was still a Freudian dream *of a jealous, blond colleague/ sibling pining as a Holocaust orphan, no truth in it to begin with, only more unconscious speculation, further latent worry, as...* she woke.

Ottoline did not seem to care what anybody else, including Ms. Yael Abraham, Ph.D., Director, Human Resources, Warren Bros. Inc., (Whale Class of 1973, Psychology 1980, Suma cum laud), Sisterhood of Grace Alumni President, etc., thought of her. Yael's jealousy problems were frankly uncharacteristic of sisterly protocol and of her own making, Ottoline wishing nothing but the best for her, as for any sister:

> **Iago:**
> O, beware, my lord, of jealousy;
> It is the green-ey'd monster, which doth mock
> The meat it feeds on. (William Shakespeare, *Othello*, 1603)

If Ottoline was the Colonel's favorite, nothing explained the reason, nor his brave rescue of her mother, carried out as the pretext for a movie script, but really the *raison d'etre* itself of the Colonel's existence. Leave it to fate to have decided the outcome of the story up to this point, as future surprises still waited. When challenged by Ms. Abraham for sticking her journalistic nose in the HR conflict regarding Walter Karlos, who had already been Wendy, since 1972, and felt she was discriminated against in the studio's choice of a *48 Hours to Mecca* score, resulting in a grievance, she simply replied, "You may download any photos you want; I'm interested in Wendy's rights; it's not my fault if the Colonel likes me more."

# 18. BFP (Black Female Preferred) or Color Wheel

> It is not circumstantial liberty conceded only to us that we want... It is the
> absolute acceptance of the principle that no man, whether born red, black
> or white, can be the property of another. (Toussaint Louverture,
> 1743-1803, Haiti's most important revolutionary leader, a former slave)

As time wasted, the Rev. Hannibal P. (Pearly) Gates, presiding at an activist Carthaginian Black Baptist Church, 666 Mixwell Avenue, New Haven, CT, found sufficient rage in his heart, over the slow pace of his people's advancement, to demand of Patricia (P) Diddy, Ph.D., J.D., founder-president, and thus far sole member of the international humanitarian group *Les Enfants Sans Frontičres*, Greenitch, CT, what she would offer. If his was a philanthropy of faith she was desperately seeking a faithful philanthropist, as true charity is selfless, anonymous and unobserved, while she was quite up front, in asking for cash; his belief was for simple alms, a charity of selflessness, vs. her epic donations as institutional exercises: "Why has your agency of beneficence failed to alleviate the suffering of inner-city minority children?"

The advocate for the misused children of the world, as well as witty, erstwhile warrior-sniper, snapped, "Philanthropy is no cover for bad behavior atoned for, or is that philandering I am confusing it with?"

"Wealth is an ungainly, heavy coat one must take off, before embracing another spirit. Does purposeful charity measure the true worth of a person, or is such true worth purposefully charitable, in itself? And you know as well as me, the cyclical nature of generational transference of wealth to its dispersed ends:

"The first generation creates embarrassingly disproportionate riches, now and then giving a dime away, and with visionary nature and organizational ability fashions great undertakings as monuments to itself. The second, frugally consolidating preexisting wealth, guiltily systematizes the philanthropic endeavor. And the third, living the entitled high life, fritters a great deal away, good works starting to be curtailed. The fourth gets crumbs, but keeps the name, now and then lending it, as a philanthropic duty to the past. The fifth keeps little, not even the name, its influence only legend, the fabled generosity finally *passe*."

"But no matter what you say, I still believe, in the humanitarian, ennobling, didactic qualities, bestowed upon future generations, the public at large, from the benevolence of patrons who give so generously."

"As I do not believe the affluent so inclined, ever control the destinies of their benefactions, whom they benefit, inspire, save, I am not inclined to be in favor of a measured and prescribed solution to our ills."

"You prefer the shotgun approach of the random boon now and then, here and there, almost as a lottery. But when important sums are at stake, responsibility demands that professionals need to be employed."

"Because most people who claim that their actions are undertaken for the sake of a sad humanity act on their own behalf. In that sense, perhaps saints were nothing but hagiographic fronts of self-interest, and foundations, trusts, endowments, were too far removed from our ghetto neighborhoods," he concluded; before each biting into their juicy hamburger sandwich at Louis' Lunch, the local favorite for Whalies of carnivorous temperaments; after which they headed to College Street to join a demonstration against the Whale Corporation during its annual meeting, related to tax breaks vs. obligation to the community, full union rights for graduate students, and further implementations of affirmative action in admissions. Considering they disagreed on many of the finer points of each other's business, they found a common cause in both being alumni with an axe to grind against the establishment, now as screaming protestors spilling over the street, onto the lawn of the Crossed Campus, open, central mall of the university, with flagrant placards, banners, posters, yelling slogans in unison, for rolling cameras to record for posterity.

**Europeans came for a reason.**
**Africans were in Africa one day, the next in New Haven.**

**Whites did this: White Privilege brought African Americans here.**

**Communities of color treated unfairly by Whale, city, state police.**

**Native Americans demand more than names of sports teams!**
**Give us back our land!**

**Take responsibility for irremediable losses of aboriginal birthrights!**

**Minority equity:**
**The unleashed monster, with only white Europeans to blame.**

**Justified racial rage against the white slavery machine!**

**The revolution will be a minority takeover!**

When emblems of authoritarian pasts were toppled, it was the work of freedom fighters restoring moral order, while an effacement of leftist symbols evinced the work of vandals threatening cultural progress. Those statues of dead traitors toppled over by irate protesters, certainly were of the very ancestors who sold their precursors into perpetual bondage centuries ago, what irony of destiny, betrayed historicism. These were the new breeds of civil rights crusaders, no longer objective, political commentators: "I will not be used as a tool for their purposes," wrote one cultural activist, "I am not a token, mammy, or little brown bobble head. I am not owned by Sayer, Green or Warren Bros. Inc." And it was not a peaceful MLK style civil disobedience of humble, sympathetic protesters purposefully striding elbow to elbow in solemn faith inspired solidarity, but rather rap infused *gangsta* driven, in your face defiance inspiring prompt ugly, paramilitary reaction if not race war. The non-violence ethic had been abandoned on the street corner, perhaps for other generations to assume, while within, at the Whale Corporation's annual meeting, Isidora Green, one of the university's greatest benefactors, pushed an agenda as senior trustee, that always had the university's reputation in the forefront, especially as there were offenses to conceal:

"So, we agree, we shall avoid this delicate issue of tax equity, with the City of New Haven, until public outcry becomes too vociferous, then perhaps offer some crumbs to appease the upset locals. We shall also prohibit any attempt by our graduate students to be corrupted by outside organizer influences. But as there is no way to avoid such a reckoning for our academy's founding and growth, due to its primary benefactor's success in slave trading, to atone for former ills, we should now adopt an admission policy based on BFP (Black Female Preferred) in this epochal, revolutionary Color Wheel moment of ours."

While the lighter skinned discriminated against the darker skinned because they were now mixed blood the darker skinned discriminated against the lighter skinned because they were still pure, and this all in the black community, mind you. The official order to categorize everyone racially may have helped the accuracy of the census, but it also exacerbated racism, and its new adjunct, reverse racism, heightening differences, dislikes and origins. In short it boosted the resentment of all minorities against a dominant, white class, so monolithic in its power, wealth and influence, rolling the Color Wheel to its own ends.

Now the bluest of blue blood interlocuters, whose vision was not only clouded, but averted, from those modern needs of a multiracial/ multicultural society, stood for the old guard; such a luminary as Donny Craft, of pure Protestant 1600s origins, then generational 1800s, 1900s ruling class stock, now board of trustees member, relic, scion of a stuffy, historic midwestern clan, vocal agent of all that was mundane, conventional, boring; a legacy of legacies, having been admitted to Whale, since before his conception:

"Let's let the current process run its course before making dramatic, permanent changes to the system. After all it's worked well for the prior three centuries without ruffling any feathers. Let's pause, before we leap. Much of my family's success was achieved, by doing absolutely nothing for progress' sake."

Town Crier, who, already loaded at school, still slithered his way onto Wall Street, mastering the use of other people's money to make his own pile in oil, after the oil boom implosions depressed prices down to a point he bought working rigs, at cents on the dollar, corrupt, dirty fuel tycoon, unrepentantly turned self-styled green billionaire, sanctimonious reformer, evinced guilt-ridden conscience defending Whale.

"With much of the wealth of the times based on enslaved labor, Whale undoubtedly benefited from that trade. Why should it matter how our benefactor, Elihu, acquired his fortune? After all, haven't most of us profited by buying low and selling high just like everybody else? Cotton Mather decreed we destine the vast sums under our control to inspiring their civilizing future use in accordance with God's intent."

Everyone agreed to some extent with T. Crier, as their fortunes, to a great degree, had unethical pasts. The peculiar institution and consistent cooperation were tried historical rubrics, regarding the origins of the corporate venture, as even Queen Elizabeth I had been one of the first investors to subscribe shares.

Then Craft owned up to the changing world where minorities and migrants demanded seats at the table:

"It's probably wise to give a little, into the pressure, so as not to incite an uprising, and risk losing it all. Who knew being a minority could be such a career advancer? Blacks lightening up with a skin bleach, WASPS darkening up with tanning lamps, the rest doing one or the other or both, where would it end?"

"The most pragmatic approach, would be to increase minority participation, playing a liberal gameplan, while at the same time never releasing the purse strings and influence which wealthy families possess."

Listening to this running prattle, Isidora's mind began to wander, and the senior trustee suddenly found herself yawning once, and again, then the surface chatter became a running stream, white brain noise, and her mind wandered off into a daydream... *trudging slowly up a hill, in shifting sand, all the while sliding downwards, instantly, upon making any progress, ad infinitum... Duty, new capitalism, slavery, racism, Queen Eliza, her courtiers, founding one of the first joint stock companies for the purposes of slave trading; why, Windsor blood was concentrated, proudly claimed, in several trustees, long serving individuals, at this table; if slaving was the cruelty of the Protestant ethic, they were as tainted as her, despite, or in such case, because of, their royal lineages. For only some, very few, should be, would be, descended from kings, the rest keeping to the mire, barefoot, struggling to climb up from the ditch, into sunshine. One day, going through the most ancient of locked chests, containing the first bills of sale for chattels, from the founding of her family's grotesque business, she came upon faded purchase and sale agreements, one, of a family, in favor of her first Green ancestor, signed by that profiteer Elihu Whale, just three years after he made a grand bequest of merchant goods and books to, "a Collegiate School."*

    *Co. Elihu Whale - Negroes Sold, Bought*

    *One Negro Winch Hadi & her son Hani sold at Whale's:*

*Sale For* _____ *27 pounds*
*One Negro fellow* _____ *1 pound*
*Sum of* _____ *28 pounds*
*For slavery for life*

*Glasgow*
*Sold April 7th, 1721, by*

*Elihu Whale (Notarized, and sealed)*

Suddenly, Isidora was back in the present, at a Whale Corporation annual meeting, in New Haven, CT.

There was one last item on the agenda which needed the attention of the board, involving the legacy of slavery upon the university, and how it might lead to a problem in recruiting the most diverse students.

A moral exemplar of a Whale professor published a list of immoral universities to boycott, due to their proud establishments having been founded on the proceeds of slavery. This prof's own school, housing him as Master of Cravenport College (his family in greatest comfort) would be at the top of such a list. But it was of zero concern to him, such taint upon the institution was too much morally to conceal. In fact, in his most obnoxious moments, he had been quoted, saying the Whale Corporation should pay reparations to the descendants of all affected, or if not bear the evil fate of being burned down to ashes.

"As senior trustee of this board, I will not participate in this challenge to our alma mater by a headline grabbing academic, hell bent on publicizing some evil-doers list, which will only infuriate the citizenry against us, making it more difficult to attract the best student talent, of whatever racial or ethnic type. Media hype is the last thing the campus needs during a time of heightened inclusiveness in our country. Please inform the Master of Cravenport College that he shall be seeking a new job if he keeps to this." And she took no rebuttals from any of her assertive colleagues, hammering to an end the meeting with a crisp gavel rap, leading on to Mory's, that Whale tradition, since 1849, for lunch and a few jolly cups.

Meanwhile outside, the protesters were still gathered long after board members had begun their alcohol inspired digestions. Amid this threatening throng, Hannibal recalled that his proud Whale protest days had begun when, upon his acceptance, he was assigned to Calgoun College as his residential hall, and when, shortly upon arriving, he was greeted by the resident counselor, a radical, black upperclassman:

"This college was named after John C. Calgoun, one of the greatest apologists of slavery in history. As such, it is our duty to demand that the university change the name, to some one more acceptable to us." That was in 1992, Hannibal's first political protest. Subsequently, there would be others, but there was one many years later in which he smashed a stained-glass window at Calgoun College, depicting slaves harvesting cotton in a field; only he would do it as part of an underground plot, letting somebody else, who had a greater chance of having criminal charges dropped by the university, take the rap for it. But Hannibal's tie to his alma mater stretched back much farther than these events, to that faded bill of sale signed by the London businessman Elihu Whale, through his slave auction house in Glasgow; actually, Hani was the future preacher's progenitor, and his mother, Hadi, had been sought, as was advertised, by BFP (Black Female Preferred) postings, even in that Pre-Revolutionary Color Wheel epoch. Hannibal was descended from a black boy with a silver collar and padlock around his neck, who was a slave of Elihu Whale's, and some say appeared in a commissioned painting with him. This was Hani's nameless father, who at fifteen, with the love of his life, Hadi, begot him; and who was punished by his aging, impotent master in the last year of his greedy life, as the final act of vengeful cruelty, having his slave's cohabiting wife and child sold to a Jamestown, Virginia slave trader, named Green; never being given the final chance to say goodbye, never to be seen again, to compensate for the master's jealous rage at realizing that his groomed, *high yaller* baby doll concubine, Hadi, was unfaithful to him, a Whale lord! It would not be until the lord's demise that the slave boy, by then a man with his own disappeared ones, would get that collar removed by the lord's embarrassed descendants, as slavery was less fashionable in England into the eighteenth century; for no matter how much its silver gleamed the yoke of sharp metal was never warm against his neck, but eternally dead and cold, with plutocratic minerals, blacksmithing, as its evil, tarnished base. The portrait at the Whale Center for British Art is a testament to anonymous suffering of some at the hands of slavers, documenting their cruelty in the self-flattery of family charm; though some argue that it, "...is ugly both in meaning and aesthetics and deserves the same treatment as the stained-glass window..." but better to disclose the hypocritical origins of certain good-doers:

> I take higher ground. I hold that in the present state of civilization,
> where two races of different origin, and distinguished by color, and
> other physical differences, as well as intellectual, are brought together,
> the relation now existing in the slaveholding States between the two, is,
> instead of an evil, a good, a positive good... I hold then, that there never
> has yet existed a wealthy and civilized society in which one portion of the
> community did not, in point of fact, live on the labor of the other.
> (John C. Calhoun, American statesman, southern slavery apologist, 1837)

Hannibal's links to Whale had other components. One of his forefathers was cursed to have been John C. Calgoun's darkie valet, when that effete, snobby southerner joined the Whale College class of 1804. As Calgoun's body servant Hani accompanied him everywhere, even to his classes, where if the master was famous for his oratorical and intellectual abilities, it was certainly due, to being able to practice on his bonded man before the less demanding audiences he would face in the debate hall the next day. But the truth was that whatever free time the black boy had was utilized in his self-education, condoned by his master, as his chattel property was acquiring a Whale education, the best that money could buy, for free. That was because he attended all his master's lectures and seminars, studying the open books the master left lying around when out with his chums, in all sorts of racist mischief he was excluded from. He was not only as well educated as his master, but surpassed him in certain subjects, such as law and philosophy, which required strong oratorical skills. And it was known they usually stayed up all night, going over the detailed points of each side of the argument, preparing to assume either position, as the luck of the draw would have it. It was during these midnight dialogues that Calgoun found his voice:

"Hani, when I beat you with a cudgel, so you remember to wake me up on time, you realize that it is for your own good, don't you? I would never do anything to cause you intentional harm, boy, but I cannot be late for class again. Now, have you shined my boots spit black, ironed my linen shirt, blue cravat?"

*"Masser, it don't hurt no more. And sho'nuff, I done got all yo wardrobe ready fa tomorrow's discaus."*

"Hani, what would I do without you? Absent you coloreds, genteel southern society would fall apart."

*"Why, Masser, we'se jus doin what God made us fo. And we keep in bondage, so's y'all whites enjoy."*

"Hani, your family has been part of ours for eighty years now; as a house servant you learned reading."

*"Masser, I thank you, and the Lawd of Isr'l, fo dat. It's how I instructed myself to speak correctly, sir."*

"So, you have, boy, I've always left my books lying around, so you could peek at them, now and then."

"Master, I was wondering if you were prepared to express the Western tradition's defense of slavery, as resulting from the conquest of more savage, lesser peoples with a deficiency of Christian morals, which carries on from Aristotle through Thomas Aquinas, Thomas Hobbes and John Locke, to today; as well as the opposing view, that slavery is a moral abomination under natural, human, divine laws, as well as Christianity in its unadulterated form, currently espoused by forward looking clergy of the abolitionist movements under way, such as John Newton, who himself saw God's light after having been a slaver? Master, I know you and your family sing 'Amazing Grace' at church, before coming home to beat us:"

> Amazing grace! How sweet the sound
> That saved a wretch like me!
> I once was lost, but now am found;
> Was blind, but now I see. (John Newton, "Amazing Grace," 1779)

"I am prepared to debate either side of the question, before my esteemed classmates, though the former proposition is closer to my heart than the latter, and I admit to our family being partial, to that hymn, as your people are, I reckon; as for your final, sassy remark, young fellow, why, if we weren't up north, in New Haven, CT, with permissive Yankee treatment of..." they were interrupted by a knock at the door. The bonded butler let in Garbanzo Craft, inviting Calgoun over to a meeting of a secret society he had just founded, Sulks and Moans, the first of its kind at Whale, where new members stripped naked, then spilled the beans on their entire lives while lying in a coffin, yelling, "Take that plunger out of my ass!"

"Come along, Calgoun, tonight it's your turn to confess all your sins with those slave girls down on the plantation." Suddenly, to both white men Hani visibly cringed, but only unbeknownst to one as to why. Because Calgoun had been having his way with Hani's sister since he was eighteen and she was fifteen, and that was two years ago. Calgoun quietly missed her, longed for her soft, brown body, but he would never have expressed such to his bondsman. As Hani was dressed in hand me downs from his master, and as such, attired better than 90% of the freshmen at Whale, which was especially apparent when he accompanied his master to many social and scholastic events, he was also loath to let their guest know more about his discomfiture, so maintaining his poise, he let his master and friend flaunt into the dark.

Now alone at last, Hani could get down to his real business: literature in the night. He had started with Homer, poet of heroes, primeval Hesiod, proto historians, Herodotus, Thucydides, Polybius; then Plato, Aristotle, Aeschylus, Sophocles, Euripides, Aristophanes; Juvenal, Tacitus, Pliny, Virgil, Ovid, Terence, Plautus, Plutarch, Cicero, Caesar; and for all of these, he had first learned rudimentary Greek and Latin. A committed scholar, he undertook letter campaigns to the editors of emancipation journals, with many different pseudonyms, as the purpose might serve him, his aim, to direct mail abolitionist movements with determined argument rather than wild rhetoric, while always assuming a white identity, so that his *Masser* would never be the wiser of such politically radical assumptions, exhortations, felonious script:

> *George Washington's Birthday*
> *Anonymous (Hani)*
> *Dear Let Freedom Ring Journal of Our Times,*
> *It has come to my attention that Whale College has played host to certain slaveholders, and those in the thrall of such masters. Should society not censure a great academy's coziness with the peculiar institution, for once and for all, so the practices we all follow on Sundays will not contradict experience, and those souls held in bondage shine in God's own light? Is such a boastful school to be excused its responsibility for* Lux et Veritas?

*Sincerely,*
*A Disconsolate Reader*

At the same time, John C. Calgoun was where new members lay, stripped naked, spilling the beans on their entire lives, in a coffin, yelling, "Take that plunger out of my ass!" an appropriate end to that bore, who would go on to espouse pro-slavery doctrines, while keeping his dark odalisque in the back cabin. "If she gets with child, I'll sell her down the river, fast as possible, so her brother is never made aware. There is no way I will have a child of ours on the same plantation, gawking, ruining everything I do. I told her brother their family has been with ours some eighty years, but I would sell him in a heartbeat if he were to find out about Hadi being pregnant; why, I couldn't bear the razzing from such a smart ass."

As for Willi's plans to divorce Lilly, he realized if he could not kill her in cold blood, then he could not really cancel her out either, so gradually, their relationship sparked again, with an email here and there, an accommodation reached between them, not exactly an appeasement, but still, better communication. Feeling hounded by events rapidly spiraling out of their control, they began to focus on their security:

> The dog barking at you from behind his master's fence acts for a motive
> indistinguishable from that of his master when the fence was built.
> (Robert Ardrey, *The Territorial Imperative*, 1966)

Now L.A. County DCF went after our betrayed heroes. They had only dreamed of experiences which could be as nasty as what they would soon undergo. They were minding their own business, he putting the final touches on new dog and people fences around their property, she getting dinner started, when to their utter mortal terror, confusion and shame a DCF investigator announced herself at the front gate, and there was no way to keep her out; nothing they could do, as there were reports of missing children, and possible, violent assaults by the parents, involving public urination on homeless aliens; and even if it was years ago, DCF kept all relevant details of the case, as elephants can remember, until their fateful moment to strike. They had been ratted out by someone they knew, perhaps even the Rev. Pearly and P Diddy, stemming from their firm moral stances in saving discriminated folks, children, respectively, and DCF was tough to shake off. But P Diddy had made a pact with The Fixer, alias the Yellow Kid, in Baja California., while consulting with our sequestered heroes, to get the press off their backs; letting him handle a public *mea culpa* to keep a lid on any of this from coming out, which now, unfortunately, was the case, despite her best efforts. But DCF opened a file on them as early as Lilly's disappearance:

"Ms. Lawrence and Mr. Herman, DCF has been aware of various irregularities in your home, for some time now, starting with Ms. Lawrence's mysterious, unexplained, covered up vanishing, four years ago, at which time, we received vague hints of a possible kidnapping involving your children, but we had no evidence. Then two years ago, we heard accounts of your involvement in a racist incident at a country club, followed by publicly attacking a sleeping homeless couple outside your estate at a morning hour."

"My wife and I were never plaintiffs of any defamation suit, nor formally charged for any altercation."

"The department believes it is only a matter of time, before you and your wife are formally charged by the police, for fabricating her disappearance and abducting your children, in a sordid publicity stunt…"

And so on, however, their alternatives being limited, confronted by the state's enforcement they tried to limit their losses, begging the investigator to give them a break, as parenting was this two-edged sword:

"Nothing we have ever done has been as hard, as parenting; now we even have sympathy for our own.

Please respect our privacy. If the newshounds get their noses into this, there will be no end to scandal."

But to no avail, the DCF worker calmly inspecting the premises, before departing, the stunned couple misdirecting hate, vociferating: "the first thing we do, let's kill all the reporters: if you can, write, if not, become a journalist. At least *Woke Up, with Willie* had integrity while I ran it, before its syndication."

"How can journalists consider what they write, when required to produce a dubious piece every night? Reporting's nothing more than a prose factory dedicated to outscooping the competition. Where's the integrity in that? By journalism I gather you mean headline hoodwinks, or byline babel blathered on?"

"I mean hyperbolic newsmen humbly extolling themselves, their suppressed colleagues, for a dedication and sacrifice to truth, and a reporting profession, making themselves examples, beacons in the dark, for heavy virtue. But journalists, as soldiers, businessmen, artists, anybody else, only do things, engage in life, for their own sakes, for themselves and not on account of anyone else; whatever dedication in their craft demonstrated as purely self-interest, and whatever sacrifice endured, part of an ego driven need to be recognized, acknowledged, worshiped. So, when explained and seen in this fashion, dedication and sacrifice were disingenuous cover-ups for dryer, more cynical, narcissistic motives and behavior, self-abnegation as a source of and means to fame and distinction, vainglory, triumph, renown in a nutshell."

"The fatal error of the media was choosing sides, weaponizing itself through social media, assuming it would provide an advantage, as during an election season, anointing a New York Times as Pravda and a Washington Post as Izvestia. They could not imagine that social media would be utilized so effectively against them by the other side. When they lost their objectivity, they forfeited their credibility as well."

"Somewhere along the line newsmen tired of reporting news and decided to create it for themselves, by convincing, rather than elucidating, their readers, directing, instead of showing the masses, leading, not following the story. William Randolph Hearst easily comes to mind. But there were other press barons before him, and other manipulators of people's souls before Joseph Goebbels. How does a Washington Post become an Izvestia? Where is the line between robust (opinionated) journalism and propaganda?"

"Bystanders are the ones reporting facts, as journalists now espouse doctrine and conjecture. Newsmen are dogs of slander, slaves to innuendo, the press become prosecutor, judge and jury, undermining their own integrity; opinionated, proselytizing prigs, yes, I mean journalists; demanding editors, responsible for whorish headlines. When journalists crow about breaking a story, I really want to break their legs."

"I believed the job of the press was to investigate, inform, inspire; never conjecture, confront, conspire. The problem with news agencies is they started exhorting rather than reporting. This is how journalists are no wittier than cheerleaders, as shallow (relying on hearsay), external (relying on appearances), and opinionated (relying on manifestos). I guess the predisposed essence really interferes with objectivity."

"It's all a fiction you've created to add meaning to life, this liberal mumbo jumbo, screaming on about this injustice and that one, when it's only the way for your side to obtain power, nothing more, nothing less, and the cynical aspect of achieving what you want at the expense of others. These faddish, trendy, and ostensibly socially conscious progressives bought up sneakers, apparel, electronic consumer goods, services, and apps manufactured, or provided, by non-union, exploited, and even slave labor, without as much as batting an eye, ever reading a history book, having no aversion to shirts made in sweatshops."

"With each passing year I steadily scrutinized, filtered, the concentrated laser beam darkness of warped life, through narrow prism eyes, spreading out spectrums of frustration and resentment within my soul, as an infernal rainbow hung across the sky. And then suddenly, the idea flashed within my mind, that I was facing the same disinformation as yourself, meant to infuriate me against you, as you against me; after all, didn't Fritter cheapen discourse, allowing trolls to shoot off their mouths without prudence?"

"You fourth estate types with extra sensory perception, I must be careful what I say so as not to offend such refined sensibilities." Sitting next to her husband would make this a dinner from hell, she feared. "Point-of-view journalism is advocacy by another name, and not true, objective reporting, although the current common practice of the fourth estate; energetically enabling the ethnic, political and racial wars from which this country suffers, and by which we are all oppressed; because, surely, the fourth estate is a fifth column, which needs eradication for our society to progress to that unfettered millennium age."

*Hollywood Couple Under DCF Microscope*

*For Famous Lilly Mum's the Word*

*Willi Says They Overstepped*

*DCF to Continue Exhaustive Probe*

As with their efforts against DCF, there was nothing they could do to keep the infernal media machine from grinding forward with budding examples of their secret missteps, almost as with Abbie Hoffman, in *Steal This* Book, where no matter how hard he tried to buck the system, in the end, he settled for his royalties. So being oppressed, persecuted, they reached back in their genograms of imagined ancestors escaping death, during related episodes of ethnic liquidation (cleansing), in past centuries, other places: massacres of compatriots which predecessors were forced to helplessly witness, by being close enough to the dastardly events, yet prevented, by the cruel vagaries of the battlefield, from coming to their aid. For Willi's religious Spanish ancestor, this meant observing Aztecs sacrifice and cannibalize sixty-two of his brothers in *Tenochtitlan,* in 1521; for Lilly's wise Saracen ancestor it meant watching Richard the Lionheart massacre 2,700+ of his comrades in Acre in 1191. But first, a morally unequivocal assertion: the main problem with cultural competence was that certain cultural traditions really were anathema to the Western tradition, and as such, were outlawed in fact, or in practice, including human sacrifice and cannibalism, bestiality, incest, pedophilia. Although a current usage would lead one to believe, that all cultural aspects should be accepted into the greater society, nevertheless, these specific prohibitions not only still stood, but adhered themselves universally, as modern, in a completely non competent manner.

A Brother of Charity, surviving with Cortes in his conquest of treasure filled Mexico, later drawn by *El Dorado* to the desolate, lowland nether reaches of the grand *Nuevo Reino de Granada,* where he broke his chastity vows, went native with the local women, fathering several offspring, one of whom founded Willi's lineage, knowing this was a continent with more wealth than good, remembered that moment of retreat, now called *la Noche Triste,* as the *Conquistador* and his men viewed in horror, across a lagoon:

> Then after they had danced the papas laid them down on their backs on
> some narrow stones of sacrifice and, cutting open their chests, drew out
> their palpitating hearts which they offered to the idols before them. Then
> they kicked the bodies down the steps, and the Indian butchers who were
> waiting below cut off their arms and legs and flayed their faces, which they
> afterwards prepared like glove leather, with their beards on, and kept for
> their drunken festivals. Then they ate their flesh with a sauce of peppers
> and tomatoes. They sacrificed all our men in this way, eating their legs

and arms, offering their hearts and blood to their idols as I have said, and throwing their trunks and entrails to the lions and tigers and serpents and snakes that they kept in the wild-beast houses I have described in an earlier chapter. (Bernal Díaz del Castillo, *The Conquest of New Spain*, 1567)

Though mass murder was still repugnant, tyrants in east and west alike, such as Genghis Khan, Caesar, did it, but in this *Mundus novus*, it would preserve the more primitive, sinister aspects of cannibalism:

> Birds do it, bees do it
> Even educated fleas do it
> Let's do it… (Cole Porter, "Let's Do It, Let's Fall in Love," 1928)

A scholar accompanying the Sultan, Saladin, in his rescue (conquest) of the Holy Land, later chronicled Richard the Lionheart's massacre of hostage Saracens, having beheld it at first hand, which was when his respect for the Sultan secretly waned for not having done enough to save them; thereupon stealing a blue eyed, red headed Rus', beautiful Slav princess, imperial concubine from Saladin's own harem, and having avoided the ancient mass killing, fathering several offspring, one of whom was Lilly's ancestor:

> Then the king of England, seeing all the delays interposed by the Sultan
> to the execution of the treaty, acted perfidiously as regards his Musulman
> prisoners… In the afternoon of Tuesday, 27 Rajab, [August 20] about four
> o'clock, he came out on horseback with all the Frankish army, knights,
> footmen… ordered all the Musulman prisoners, whose martyrdom God
> had decreed for this day, to be brought before him. They numbered more
> than three thousand and were all bound with ropes. The Franks then flung
> themselves upon them all at once and massacred them with sword and
> lance in cold blood. (Beha-ed-Din, quoted in Thomas Andrew Archer,
> *The Crusade of Richard I*, 1189 – 92, 1889)

As this mass reprisal occurred in the port city of Acre, could such be the origin of the word, massacre? Given such antecedents our protagonists were lucky to have made it here, to the present moment, at all. But wasn't such treatment by the authorities standard, for all individuals, since the dawn of experience? And weren't our two heroes of the most common stock and lineage the types to suffer greater injustice? Given all the odds of early destruction in past millennia, the chances for successful genetic transference made their existences here and now truly miraculous, stunning in their complexity as well as simplicity. Slaughtering many was what monarchs and nobles lived to do, as part of their social contract to defend their patrimony from outward attack, and inner, festering machinations, from cave man times to today. Nevertheless, such certainly tarnishes the heroic stature with which legend usually exalts the Lionheart.

Moving on to the final, minor hostilities, skirmishes really, that occurred before the explosive civil war, now Hannibal and P Diddy were at odds over the institutionalized natures of most progressive efforts. Such contretemps had its roots, however, years before, during P Diddy's rookie year at CT DCF, when she was assigned to investigate possible abuse occurring at Hannibal's parents' home caused by a guest Texan uncle; it was a one-time thing, he was gone now, in police custody, it would never happen again, according to his parents. Hannibal was a senior honors student in high school, but P Diddy in her guise as dedicated DCF Investigator Supreme, interviewed him regarding anything he had seen, or noticed, about his creepy uncle, who the family now learned, was in the National Sex Offender Registry. But as blood is thicker than water, they had never suspected him, even when they had suspected him all along.

Hannibal's youngest brother, only eight years old (the occurrences were at younger ages), had been the unfortunate victim, and P treated the stunned, quiet Hannibal not as a serious suspect, not dismissively, but curtly nevertheless, going over his daily schedule, and why he had not kept better tabs on his uncle; not really holding him accountable for the entire family's responsibility for the young boy's health and safety, but seeming to blame him as the most perspicacious, observant family member for not knowing. Little did either imagine that the young, morally upright Hannibal would become a *protégé* of Isidora's, just as previously P herself had (even as far back as their Vietnam War days, though P did not know it), however, in P's case, it also had to do with their unspoken connection; though not fathomed by P at that time this Gypsy marker later tied her directly to Isidora Green, coincidentally descended similarly from dispersed Roma, most distant relations, through traces more binding, lustrous, than that ancient wealth of their mountainous, Punjabi place of origin; and that would include her scholarly achievements under the G.I. Bill/ Sisterhood of Grace funded Whale educational system, of which she took great advantage. Similarly, Hannibal became one of Isidora's favorites, despite the absence of blood connections (which uncannily he did share, with a stunned John B. Sayer, "Why, Odds bodkins," he declared), to his credit.

Though those were the rudimentary origins of their hard feelings, they were covered up for most of the professional time the two had since spent together. However, back then they were raw and in the open, causing certain confrontations between the pushy state worker and a rebellious teen about to graduate. In contrast to Hannibal's aggressive retaliations, P acquired wisdom from her generational *melanges*:

> Peace is not the absence of conflict, but the ability to cope with it.
> (Mahatma Gandhi, Indian anti-colonial, nonviolent resistance martyr)

Possibly the worst thing to ever happen to parents is to have DCF up their butt. It should not be wished upon anybody who is a halfway decent person. Because once they are inside, it is impossible to get rid of them, as with Stephen King's alien anus parasite. There was nothing DCF couldn't do, nowhere they did not have access to, or could be kept from prying into, if they took interest in the case or there was a hot tip. There was nothing that would prevent them from barging into your home and demanding to be granted an interview, with/ without your lawyer present. So, commence the torments foisted upon you. However, unbeknownst to Hannibal even back then P had tried to intercede on his family's behalf to no avail. And she would make it up to him, by committing to help our stalwart pair through DCF ordeals that went beyond the agonies suffered by misunderstood savants and seers prognosticating better times, as they never understood just how much trouble they were in for a few trivial, light parental oversights.

She would devise a plan, first recollecting her own dismal past with the department, as it was so called. When she returned from her stint in Nam, and then undertook all her education, only to arrive at DCF, she never expected the myriads of political games she would have to play to survive; why, it was almost as deadly, as a feces and urine smeared *punji*-staked gully, the deadliest of all the booby traps in Nam. That she was able to survive for the ten years required to obtain early retirement was a testament to her savvy, and stratagems, during incoming, and her PTSD stupor, before realizing that her connection with Isidora was much too valuable to waste, founding the foundation allowing P to commence a vocation; but that was much later. For now, she reviewed in her mind the time she investigated Hannibal's kin. Hannibal was completing his Whale College application and was surely testy in mood and demeanor.

"I say we kick some major ass, punch the sorry redneck cracker DCF losers out; isn't that the identical treatment they espouse, for *us black folk*?" It was Hannibal sounding off on the department worker P. "Ever since you showed up at our doorstep, there's been hell for my family to pay to your State of CT."

"It's as much your state as my state, so try to be patient, and stop threatening my co-workers, will you?

They do not happen to be what you are accusing them of. The department is a multi-racial enterprise."

"I don't know, Miss P, it sure doesn't seem that way, almost everyone except you has been some honky, and they are driving us crazy, accusing us of being responsible for my eight-year-old brother's rapes."

"I understand you were not responsible for your uncle's actions, however, the department has questions about the fitness of your household, to maintain custody of your brother. But I will see what I can do."

The culture of child protection was uncooperative, second guessing, quite nasty, don't make any waves, ask any questions, or care too much about the kids; it's all about the paperwork, even at the expense of the children, the kind of culture in which subordinates were not encouraged, to ask superiors questions. But they were then unmitigatedly reprimanded if they made any mistakes. It was the worst of a no-win situation. The supervisor was a dog, who treated everyone equally, with the same disdain. But because of her twenty-year seniority, she was an untouchable bully, a clear case in which her union membership trumped any ability or performance, allowing disgraceful behavior to continue under official sanction. P's boss once screamed at her, "I'm so mad, I could shoot you," disregarding the employee's humanity. The truth was that the department was run sloppily, as a white army of prejudiced child protectors who had forgotten what their mission was, while black and minority workers resented that their department did not look enough as, resemble, the people they served in the multi racial New Haven neighborhoods.

"During today's supervision I would like to spend time on Hannibal' family. He is applying to Whale."

"We're worried you have taken a rather too personal interest in Hannibal, and his family, because of the old school tie, and such. The department already moved for termination of parental rights in this case."

"Please do not do anything that will jeopardize his chance of getting an education, which could be a life altering change for him, and his family, especially with all the travails they have suffered recently. The uncle is long gone on his way to prison in a related police case. I do not see any serious risks of further harm to the child going forward. My recommendation would be to continue parental rights at present."

"P, I want to be very clear with you, the decision has been taken, by the program manager and director; there is no appeal. What matters going forward is your compliance with team metric goals, established for you, on a weekly basis, which I have noticed you are behind in submitting, since spending so much time on this case. I'll see that you are assigned some complex, new files, to keep your mind occupied."

"As my supervisor, I beg you to go up the chain of command, until they will listen to me about how..."

But there was nothing P could do, despite all her combat skills, and temperament, to prevent the child's removal. Her boss would never risk her position, going up to bat for a newbie like P, fresh on the job. For Hannibal's family the loss of their baby brother was devastating. They never got over it, and each of his birthdays mourned his absence. Hannibal cried so much, everyone thought he would not be able to finish his application to Whale. At the boy's removal emotions were so tense that P, forced to follow protocol, showed up with two New Haven police officers, in case Hannibal or any of his family started trouble. As the officers were black themselves, they resented nearly white (shaded) P coming into their neighborhood, to upset the applecart, especially because Hannibal was a sort of local celebrity scholar. The most distressing thing was they never knew where he was, not even an address, because of a strict confidentiality, but somewhere, out there in the state, a lonely, little boy was growing up in a family of foster parents, who were no better than strangers and to some degree in it for the per head subsidy paid:

[CINDERELLA]
Mother cannot guide you.
Now you're on your own.
Only me beside you.
Still, you're not alone.
No one is alone, truly.
No one is alone.

Sometimes people leave you
halfway through the wood.
Others may deceive you.
You decide what's good.
You decide alone.
But no one is alone. (Stephen Sondheim, *Into the Woods*, 1987)

Of course, all minorities looked askance at P, because she presented white, while whites seemed surely suspicious, she was not white enough, but she knew enough to know that whites ruled the department. Working for the state was a real cutthroat, cover your ass, environment. Whether kids lived or died, or you did good in the world, if even for a minute, was secondary to being absolved of all responsibility in the face of failure. What really mattered was keeping up with your visits and paper work, and the flow of clients; the maintenance of detailed records of all client interactions resulting in metrics, proof either to exonerate or condemn a social worker, in case of any problems; so the self-justifying metrics could be presented to supervisors, then up the chain to program managers, then to directors and finally to the commissioner, maybe even the governor. If the weekly metrics worked out, everything was copacetic, no one would complain, hopefully the kids would be OK, and somewhere along the line maybe a child was saved from real abuse, despite the ungainly weight of the department, falling back on itself. Then again so many victims slipped under the radar, she wondered if all her efforts made the slightest dent in a global epidemic of child predation. Then there were the layoffs, due to the governor's belt tightening. She kept her job several times, by the skin of her teeth, with everyone less senior laid off, including all trainees ranked below her, in a brutal union system of belonging, based on length of service, not ability.

After the *coup d'etat* there was Godzilla, who fired every white supervisor and manager, who had been there before her, unduly demeaning one of those dismissed, to her face, saying the only reason she had her job was due to white privilege. This was diversity in action, in the trenches of Connecticut. Soon, state hirings followed BFP (Black Female Preferred) or Color Wheel assumptions, expectations, needs. DCF Haiti became the code name denoting the reversal of fortunes, the anti-white *raison d'etre* of the place, after the successful slave uprising instituted a strict adherence to revolutionary multiculturalism, the dictatorship of minorities over their former masters, and a Racial Justice Panel righting old wrongs. As years passed, minorities gradually got the equalizing hand, privileges, to the unhappiness of whites, who were displaced by new colors, races, in managerial positions, as well as working grunt capacities. And such was happening all over society, in education, business, affirmative action ruled. Radicalized diversity meant them wanting to lord it over everyone else, and many times getting to do so, glaringly, demonstrating the failures of minority politics, that they were politics only for them, i.e., of exclusion. Over a loudspeaker, an overprepared ramble: "I'm black and proud of it, but that alone does not define, what I am;" another day of flagrant, bombastic propaganda of Black History Month: Wasn't DCF still a plantation, and weren't their lives undertaken in the shadow of the side cabins, behind the mansion? In the morning's departmental diversity training session, one of a seemingly interminable number, she was once again obliged to listen (be condescended) to an angry, (this time) narrow eyed, quicksand colored Latina, who spoke zero Spanish and railed in ghetto infused English against racism; haranguing her and other, long serving, white professionals, about their obvious, as well as latent, evil prejudices ("Even if you are not aware of them, we are."); about not possessing the cultural sensitivities to effectively assess and assist minority kids, something that they had all been doing quite competently and successfully for many years now. One day, three years after the removal, P visited Whale for dinner with the sisters, at Commons. Passing near a long table of loud, black students she was mocked for near white (shaded) tones. It was none other than Hannibal, at the black athletes' table, with a stain of sin visible on his left shoulder (a vile succubus whispering in his ear), honoring his taken brother with taunting and loathing. The black athletes at Whale barred outsiders from sitting at their mono racial table, but later working at Goldmen Sucks, made sure it was integrated, open, inclusive. Football was an aggressive, rough sport at an elite Ivy League, and they did the best to maintain traditions of exclusivity and rank, but colored.

Back to the present, Patricia (P) Diddy, Ph.D. J.D., realized it was her duty to help our tyrannized duo. In the end, P's plan to rescue Willi and Lilly from a self-realized DCF despair met Hannibal's approval. Considering old times, the Rev. Hannibal P. (Pearly) Gates was as determined to help them as she was, despite it being cross country L.A. County DCF, as it was a quarry of similar species to Connecticut's.

Now there was possible drug usage by our idols, under investigation. One of their neighbors had called the hot tip line, denouncing their wild parties at high Pinkton, most probably because they resented not getting an invitation, but it was anonymous, so they would never know. P believed the only course not cut off to them at this point was to appeal directly, to the governor, for his intercession in the case. Her mother always said it was P's pale moon goddess features that would help her to succeed in life, if she also acted white, and in thus fashion, proceeded to take up the cause of two minority stars at the picnic.

Governor Dane Malboy was at the entrance welcoming state workers to his by invitation only luncheon function. As guests checked in, showing their badges, signing the registers, a social worker brought her child, whom she left with a friend, while she stepped out again for a minute to take a phone call. When she tried to reenter, she was reprimanded, and humiliated, by the governor, in front of other workers. "I saw you've already checked in, so you can't have another sandwich," was the governor's admonishment demonstrating contempt, lack of respect and indifference to his own government workers, who were no more than pawns to effectuate his political will and administrative directives. The devoted worker had no intention of taking another sandwich, her only motive being to join her child and friend. Was this what our governments were reduced to, a bunch of hyper vigilant, cheap nit pickers, nickel and diming hard-working people to death, ostensibly for the public good, but missing the important human picture? Of course, it was easy for P to sneak into the event, fitting in so well with the other state workers. Now P approached the governor, politely introducing herself, pleading her case, while the governor, as with many public men, personally was a son of a gun, covering up cruelty with a veneer of collective glow:

"Regarding these influencers under investigation by L.A. County DCF, it appears to be a frame up, due to their enormous popularity. Since when is being famous a crime, especially working in Hollywood?"

"LGBT is the tyranny of the two percent. I would decimate a legion, to instill discipline through fear."

"The developments of capitalism, firearms, media being concurrent, joint stock companies, guns, news headlines, allow for striking your victims from afar, with the relative safety of distance in your favor."

"Presently, I do not feel a need to do anything to jeopardize our chances in the next election, so I pass."

"As a showy liberal, your way of helping the other 98% is in the theoretical, general, impersonal sense; please save this significant immigrant LGBT family, destined for recasting as stars of heaven's glory."

# 19. BTC (Bear Trap Capital) or Pecuniary Promise

> The only thing which is of lasting benefit to a man is that which he does
> for himself. Money which comes to him without effort on his part is
> seldom a benefit and often a curse.
> (John D. Rockefeller, *Random Reminiscences of Men and Events,* 1909)

The pecuniary promise of Protestants was that no matter how rich they were born, what impressed was not the wealth per se, but the honest, hard work it was based on, as a purposeful activity to spend one's time on, thus gaining honor and eternal reward, to be known as self-interest, thrift and productivity. In this way Sayer could innocently claim how hard he labored to be solely responsible for his vast wealth. It was part of the thin-lipped Machiavellian conspiracy, to earn society's respect for generational greed. There was contempt felt by the affluent toward those getting free rides, government assistance, welfare, product of an obsession with virtue as its own reward beyond even the material gains to be won thereof, as living off the dole with benefits had to be burned out of the civic body before the eternal triumphing.

*To be unsuccessful or poor, and not become a socialist, requires as much courage and insight as being successful or wealthy, and not becoming a plutocrat. The Lord has rewarded my efforts*, thought Sayer. Though he believed when created, he was geared more toward the plutocrat, than a philanthropist. And somehow, it was always the cruel, severe, punitive, who were promoted, this seemed the WASPY way. The bear market express had run off with the indices, but for some it was a godsend, just the chance for a feller (not Rockefeller) to hop aboard, as Sayer was doing, focusing on his company's own low stock. Being in an acquisitive mode, it was difficult to imagine Sayer giving anything to anyone. However, as life went on famous moneybags, Sayer included, would give in to the softening touches of Father Time:

> The impression was gaining ground with me that it was a good thing to let
> the money be my slave and not make myself a slave to money.
> (John D. Rockefeller, *John D. Rockefeller on Making Money: Advice and
> Words of Wisdom on Building and Sharing Wealth*, 2015)

This said by a man who once deftly clicked his heels, exclaiming, "I am bound to be rich–bound to be rich– bound to be rich!" No matter how hard they tried, philanthropists were still bound by fortunes, as Midas was enslaved by his, with guilt sometimes intervening, the enrichment/ donation cycle, usually:

First, the patriarch creates and stores wealth, at all costs, both legal and illegal, usually in a business no one else would do, later modifying practices, with an apologist's aim of making his family appear good. Second, benefiting financially, socially and politically the founder and family become concerned about their public image, family legacy and spiritual afterlife, and introduce good-doings into their lifestyles. Third, the iniquity of their immense fortunes leads them to give something back, even disavowing the rough means originally used in creating their loot, especially in succeeding, more humane generations:

> My internship at Room 5600 was a long time ago.... great memories,
> working at the Rockefeller Family brain trust... Imagine a young man
> from the Bronx sitting down having lunch in the 5600, break room with
> John D Rockefeller III... a true gentleman... Also Mrs. Peggy Rockefeller
> was special and a classy lady. FYI, when my father passed away the office
> reached out to me and offered their support... flowers and the use of a car
> and a driver... Priceless!
> (Anonymous, New York City businessman, recollection, 2016)

Now a darkly complexioned (subcontinental) Indian woman entered the light teak wood paneled board room, joining Sayer in anticipating the Warren Bros. Inc. annual board of director's meeting, to address internal policies, future goals, at an immense polished table soon to be occupied by a bunch of rich old boys and girls from Wall Street, as the nucleus of Chairman Isidora Green's council of wealth advisors.

Lucretia Faithful (an anglicized moniker), founder and principal of BTC (Bear Trap Capital), one of the most successful hedge funds on Wall Street, had steady discipline to be neither over nor under exposed, increasing and lowering holdings, with the up then down gyrations of stock charts. She aways hedged her bets, putting on huge positions to impress her competitors, all the while playing the contrary side in stealth, to her advantage, doing the same thing politically, paying off both Republicans and Democrats, keeping both sides on the hook, gaining advantage from the promises of each. And somewhere, within this book of bets, stood her clients, whom she served as faithfully as her name implied, as the *pundit* of avarice and self interest in the extreme. Prior to Wall Street she worked as a yoga instructor, catering to the body/ mind maintenance of the very rich, convincing them she was not really an investor, but rather their market guru. Additionally, Gary Meiser, who famously stepped right over a prostrate floor trader suffering a heart attack, leaving him to die, in order not to miss the market's big up move, joined them.

"Hello John and Lucretia, how has the market been treating you? Have you heard, there is a new breed of wealth being invented, within deepest, dark caverns, a Bit-O-Honey, Kryptonite digital currency, for scoundrels to abuse anonymously, in its incipient, inchoate form, mined as *wampum* was, not minted?"

If these represented self-made vulgarians, still too unashamed to conceive of giving anything back from their tainted profits, boldly claiming obligations to wisely wield such personal wealth themselves (what drivel), they were presently joined by blue blood inheritors, as the Madam Chairman proceeded regally, along with staid, do nothing Donny Craft, and the Town Crier, alias King Carbon, wafting polluted gas conceits (after making his black mark in dirty air, he cleaned up his image, adopting environmentalism from which to blow foul winds), complemented by venerable Whalie of renown, Junior Camper, whose doyenne socialite mother Tan, had ten million in old masters go missing right before his freshman year at Whale, lately of Lizard Bros., as the moneyed class (old or new) were trained to love lucre from an early age; radiant cynosures, golden boys, glory girls, of material success, comfort, and cheeky barbs at the ready, modern day gilded age robber barons whose boisterous socializing displays always supported their own self-interests, making them dangers to those prone to sharing personal, spiritual and creative treasures.

"I glean the madness of crowds' rumors of klepto-currencies; FYI Lizards have sizeable holdings in the New Age asset. Some mysterious Japanese huckster is behind it, and even if it may be a market bubble or tulipomania, we decided to go with the flow, but not be left the last dupe holding the bag, har, har..."

As the billionaire members of the board had made their money in the most tainted of manners, they saw nothing wrong with sharing financial war stories, especially the trading victories; it was what super rich people bragged about; now Chairman Isidora recognized their ideas, while calling the meeting to order: "We should make a preliminary assessment of the opportunities in this millennial investment category; Junior, Gary, would you please get back within 30 days with the comprehensive evaluation, thank you."

But Lucretia had the last word: "Risking sounding presumptuous, my dear sister, prior to throwing your lot in with Lizard Bros., you must get a second opinion gratis from Goldmen Sucks, or Sehman Bros."

Next came a questionable, guilt-inspired epiphany by one usually given to sermonizing against the very activities, which brought their ancestors unparalleled wealth, their sanctimony shifted to an example of good behavior in society, despite ancient conduct as filibusters, during ancestral careers of freebooting: "Moving on to other matters, as there is no way to ignore the *raison d'etre* for the company's founding and growth, due to its primary founders' success in making movies, to atone for later ills committed by succeeding shareholding generations, we should now adopt a recruiting policy based upon BFP (Black Female Preferred) in this epochal, revolutionary Color Wheel moment of ours. Yael, please delineate."

"We are seeking a BM, BF, AM, AF, HM, but especially an HF for the new corporate supervisory role."

"So, if I applied for this position, I would not be hired because of my race?" challenged, a testy Isidora. "Isn't preferential treatment, based on race, racism, as it is based on the same racial categorizations, as racist, bigoted signals? Those most preoccupied with racism are often the biggest racists themselves."

"No, sorry, there are no openings for a WF currently. We really need HFs right now for our quota goals. FYI whites are not a protected class, so whites cannot claim they were discriminated against, ever. And for anyone at this table who is Jewish, they fall under the white category, and not as a protected class."

Now Isadora Green, Chairman of Warren Bros. Inc., disclosed to the board, that Yael withheld their top studio stars' last bad behavior from her, and was furious because, even though it happened around two years ago it had become a police matter involving DCF; Isidora's worry being that no harm come to the studio for whatever it was they had done, and she assumed (knew) they had done something, otherwise what was the fuss in the media about? It was Yael who told her there were independent news channels starting to report it (Chicken Little went here, there, everywhere, hysterically spreading news), Isidora's present reaction being to turn to John B. Sayer, CEO, Warren Bros. Inc., to inquire as to his knowledge of this last problem, involving their studio stars beating up a homeless couple in public. Lately he was producing so much for TV he was not getting on with his own life, as celebrities inhabited consecrated space in his pantheon of minor and major deities celebrated daily in a fawning press; TV always geared toward the youngest, most gullible audience, no viewers in their right minds would be watching it. "I heard our pair, after heavy partying, were accused of pissing on a homeless migrant couple," he said. "I do not see anything intrinsically wrong, with such artistic free expression, so I am not one to judge."

"Furthermore, it has come to my attention that you kept the fact from me that by bringing in *SS* Colonel Otto Waldemar Grawitz, once renegade now absolved ex-Nazi agent for the opulent, the studio became entangled with an infamous war criminal. Despite his solid performance, since when was that alright?"

She was a progressive, modern day media mogul, opposed to building the southern border wall for all the humanitarian and politically correct reasons, yet hypocritically saw no problem with a six foot stone wall surrounding her several thousand acre Pacific estate, in an open, non-fenced, conservation minded locale on one of the lesser (more upscale) Hawaiian islands; specifically for her privacy and security, as coastal regions being of strategic worth, personal security was just as compelling as national security.

Even news titans, such as Isidora Green, chairman of her own media empire, demanded their right to privacy, fearful of the craving America had for flashy scoops (fast food) as the fat fictions of their lives. One of these was that the owners and management team at Warren Bros. Inc. stood for humanity. And even if her family had ruined the founding Warrens, she was proud of the studio's anti-fascist tradition.

*COOL Radio · Posted: Apr 21, 2006*
*Author and film historian Noah Iceberg.*

*Even before* Kasbah-Blanca's *premiere in 1942, the Warren Bros. Inc. studio was well-known for its efforts to bring the rise of fascism in Europe to the attention of the American public.*

*In 1939, the studio produced* Confidences of a Nazi Spy, *one of the first openly anti-Nazi films made in Hollywood.*

*"They were accused by the very vocal nativist, isolationist faction in Congress of being premature 'anti-fascists,'" Iceberg says.*

*"I think it was in 1938 ... that Groucho Mars made the claim that Warren Bros. is 'the only studio with any guts' in Hollywood."*

*Iceberg sees clear echoes of the isolationism that prevailed in the late 1930s and early 1940s in the current U.S. political climate.*

*"We're dealing with a moment in time that I think really calls to mind this period when we were being called upon ... by a film like* Kasbah-Blanca *to think about what it is that we can do to help the cause."*

"Madam Chairman, as you know, everything I do is with the aim of increasing quarterly ESP for those Wall Street boys. The Colonel had the highest security clearance, so I assumed you would be OK with it. If Ms. Yael Abraham took it upon herself to shield her boss and sister, from the trifling, distracting unpleasantries prior to momentous undertakings at the UN, the responsibility was regrettably, Ms. A's." And Isidora took no rebuttals from any of her astute colleagues, hammering to an end the meeting with a crisp gavel rap, leading on to a light lunch, of cold salmon over salad, at the Whale Club of New York City, west of Grand Central Station on Vanderpill Avenue, then to New Haven for the yearly Tap Night.

Afterward on the Metro North commuter train Isidora pondered over Sayer's loyalty and his intentions. There were signs on the Street, of someone buying up her company's shares, but she never connected such to Sayer. Realizing what a huge influence the name Whale had on her life, she wondered what the aristocratic scoundrel would have done then about the thorny issues seeming to take up her time now...

Elihu Whale succeeded in bridging the continental gap of international slave trading, doing his business with West Africans as well as East (including subcontinental) Indians, considered niggers, by his terms. As a young man he braved disease, climate, oceans, physical discomfort, in a quest for riches and fame. Through all his years in India, he always prided himself on his appearance, despite the intolerable heat, and constant sweat pouring down his itchy underclothes. In addition to always dressing top-ranked, in the latest colorful fashions, festooned with frills and lace, as well as sturdy square toed shoes, needed to trample all over bloody locals, he took particular care of his well-groomed hands, protecting them from the sun, soil and elements, so they should remain white, soft, dainty, as shown in a portrait with a Tamil servant at his side, now hung at the Whale Art Gallery, as testament to the obnoxious privilege of some, narcissistically documenting their cruelties in self-flatteries of staged intimacy. However, unbeknownst to anyone, Lucretia Faithful was descended from that Tamil boy with a silver collar and padlock around his neck, who was a slave of Elihu Whale's, and some say, appeared in the commissioned painting with him. This was Lucretia's nameless ancestor, who at fifteen, with the love of his life begot a child; and who was punished by an impotent master in the maturing years of a greedy life, as a final act of jealous cruelty, by having his slave's cohabiting wife and child sold to Moluccan pirate slave traders; never to be given the chance to say goodbye, never seen again, to compensate for the master's vengeful rage at discovering that his groomed baby boy concubine Kalu, had been unfaithful to him, a Whale lord! And it would not be until the lord's aging, that the slave boy, by then a man with his own disappeared ones, would get the collar removed by the lord's embarrassed retainers as slavery was repressed in the British Raj into the eighteenth century; for no matter how much its silver gleamed, the yoke of sharp metal was never warm against his neck but eternally dead and cold with plutocratic minerals, blacksmithing, as its evil, tarnished base. As President of Fort St. George, Whale utilized his position as colonialist thief-in-chief to circumvent existing laws, inventing new ones, to carry out precious gem mining exploitations. Such involved detaining any errant, lost or confused Tamils on land, or on the high seas, pressing them into a bestial service at his emerald mines far inland, where most were never seen or heard from again:

> In tropical climes there are certain times of day
> When all the citizens retire
> To tear their clothes off and perspire
> It's one of those rules that the greatest fools obey
> Because the sun is much too sultry
> And one must avoid its ultra violet ray
>
> Papalaka papalaka papalaka boo
> Papalaka papalaka papalaka boo
> Digariga digariga digariga doo
> Digariga digariga digariga doo
>
> The native grieve when the white men leave their huts,
> Because they're obviously definitely nuts!
>
> Mad dogs and Englishmen Go out in the midday sun
> The Japanese don't care to.
> The Chinese wouldn't dare to,
> Hindoos and Argentines sleep firmly from twelve to one
> But Englishmen detest a siesta.
> (Noel Coward, "Mad Dogs and Englishmen," 1931)

Lucretia's relation to Lord Whale had certain tragical components; this old ghost of hers was cursed to be only imagined during moments of meditative yoga, when its hostility combined with her tranquility:

"Kalu, when I withhold nourishment from you, so you remember to cool my bath water, you know it's for your own good, don't you? I would never do anything to cause you intentional harm, boy, but we cannot be late to inquests again. Have you shined my boots black, ironed my linen shirt, blue cravat?"

"Master, I feel no hunger anymore. And surly, I'll have your wardrobe ready for tomorrow's meeting."

"Kalu, what would I do without you? Absent you coloreds, the East India Company would fall apart."

"Why, Master, we do what God made us for. And we stay in service, so the *sahib's* company profits."

"Kalu, you have been part of the family for four years now; as a house servant you learned arithmetic."

"Master, I thank you and the Lord of Israel for that. It's how I instructed myself in accounting, *sahib.*"

"So, you have, boy, I've always known, you would turn into a tip top auditor of the company's books."

"Master, I was wondering if you were prepared to express the East India Company's defense of slavery, as resulting from a demand from the Moluccan pirate slave traders, which someone satisfying, it might as well be us; as well as the opposing view, that in terms of the numbers, the expenses of the *damnatio ad metalla*, are much more than if slaves were treated even a bit better than Yahoos? Even so, I advise you to begin circulating negative, disconcerting rumors about the company, to have its stock tumble on the London exchange, whereupon we may buy it at the bottom, knowing that such information is false. Master, I've heard you and the company men say how much you would like to own this organization:"

> The theory that most of the sudden declines or particular sharp breaks are the results of some plunger's operations probably was invented as an easy way of supplying reasons to those speculators who, being nothing but blind gamblers, will believe anything that is told them rather than do a little thinking. The raid excuse for losses that unfortunate speculators so often receive from brokers and financial gossipers is really an inverted tip. The difference lies in this: A bear tip is distinct, positive advice to sell short. But the inverted tip that is, the explanation that does not explain serves merely to keep you from wisely selling short. The natural tendency when a stock breaks badly is to sell it. There is a reason an unknown reason but a good reason; therefore get out. But it is not wise to get out when the break is the result of a raid by an operator, because the moment he stops the price must rebound. Inverted tips!
> (Edwin Lefèvre, *Reminiscences of a Stock Operator*, 1923)

"I am prepared to debate either side of the question, before my esteemed colleagues, though the former proposition is closer to my heart than the latter; I do admit to my family being partial to that stock, just as you would be if free. As for your final, perceptive remark, young fellow, why, even if we're out here in Madras, we could get an order to our stockbroker to..." they were interrupted by a knock at the door. The bonded butler let in Crudyard Knipling, inviting Whale over to a meeting of a country club he had just founded, the *Jollygunge*, the first of its kind in India, where new members stripped naked, spilling the beans on their entire lives while lounging on divans, yelling, "Take that rhino horn out of my bum!"

"Come along, Whale, tonight it's your turn to confess all your sins with those slave boys down on your gem mines." Suddenly, to both white men Kalu visibly cringed, but only unbeknownst to one as to why. Because Whale had been having his way with Kalu since he was fifteen, and that was three years ago. Whale secretly loved him, longed for his hard, brown body, but he would never have expressed such to his bondsman. As Kalu was dressed in hand me downs from his master, and as such, was attired better than 90% of the company men at the station, which was especially apparent when he accompanied his master to many social, official and state events, he was also loath to let the guest know more about his discomfiture, so maintaining his poise, he let his master and friend flaunt into the night of their desires.

Now alone at last, Kalu could get down to his real business: calculating in the night. He had started by estimating the float of the stock, from the confidential numbers and results he was privy to, identifying principal shareholders from the ledgers kept in the company safe box. A committed direct mail maven, actively writing letters to shareholders using different pseudonyms as the purposes might serve him, his aim was to flood the press with determined arguments, "inverted tips," rather than wild rhetoric, while assuming a white identity, so that his Master *sahib* would never be the wiser of his pecuniary promise:

*My Dear Lord: It has come to my attention, that our East India Company is suffering a regional crisis. Moluccan pirates have prohibited this company from trading with them and their allies. Suddenly, it is possible, that the company's East and West African trading partners could also suspend operations, by way of solidarity with the East Indian pirates. If so, I shall sell my stock. Sincerely, a Concerned Party*

At the same time, Lord Elihu Whale was where new members lay, stripped naked, spilling the beans on their entire lives, while lying on a divan, yelling, "Take that rhino horn out of my bum!" an unflattering end to a bore, who would go on to endow a world-famous university, while keeping a *darkie* odalisque in a back hut. "If he fathers a child, I'll sell him to the Moluccans, fast as possible, along with his child and cohabiting wife. There is no way I will have a child of theirs in the same colony, gawking, ruining everything. Why, I couldn't bear the humiliation from that spurning smart ass to whom I taught math."

As for Lilly's plan to divorce Willi, she mused if she could not kill him in cold blood then she could not really cancel him out either, so gradually, the relationship sparked again, with a text sent here and there, an accommodation reached between them, not exactly a *rapprochement*, but still, better communication. Feeling vulnerable from their active DCF case, possibly touching on the criminal, they cloistered anew:

> My apple trees will never get across
> And eat the cones under his pines, I tell him.
> He only says, 'Good fences make good neighbors.'
> (Robert Frost, "Mending Wall," 1914)

The DCF worker stepped into the consultation room and sat across the table from their racially blended family, ready to begin a state mandated assessment. Before commencing, she smiled fully at them, in a gesture of trust, and it was at that moment, that the black adolescent subject noticed she was Asian, a racial type infrequently encountered in snooty Pinkton heights, except for one of his own siblings: "Do you work in a Chinese restaurant?" he politely asked. "Hey that's never funny," interjected his Chinese sibling, punching him in the arm. "That was hilarious," shouted another Hispanic sibling, punching the Asian boy back, and on and on, with the six children shouting and punching each other, in turn." Lilly:

"We provide a great home for our kids, considering their alternative, of eating in a soup kitchen in LA."

"What my wife means to say is that we do the best we can, with such a rambunctious family as ours. It has not been easy, given the professional demands on us, as well as the reporters always interrupting."

But this only gave the dour faced DCF worker a lead to her prepared conclusions, now tinged by a hurt pride: "The department certainly recognizes the multiracial inclusiveness of your family, and this goes much in your favor; however, the violence, sarcasm, and general air of belittlement, exhibited between themselves and against others, so readily demonstrated here today, would seriously suggest the strong possibility of child abuse occurring in your household; an external manifestation of inwardly repressed origins. So, the department will be required to establish long-term counseling for the entire family, as a prerequisite to continued custody. In addition, we have petitioned the court to appoint a guardian-ad-litem to protect the interests of minor children while their parents' behavior is thoroughly investigated."

Now Willi and Lilly were beyond livid. Speechless at the indignity of the entire proceeding, they were about to experience the greatest parental fear in America: not that their children would be kidnapped by outsiders (or even insiders), but that once DCF got into their intimate business, they could lose custody.

"We implore you as parents to excuse our past faults, and give us another chance, because we really are not bad people, even if we get carried away from time to time, trying to have a good time at our parties. We would never raise a hand against our children, being both the scarred victims of horrendous abuse."

But to no avail, as the DCF worker calmly scrutinized the entire family, prying into what else might be uncovered, in one of "the grandest boondoggles recklessly undertaken. At least *Woke Up, with Willie* had integrity while I could include or exclude certain stories, based on a favor, before its syndication."

"Couldn't we steer this DCF story to Pimple.com, where a factual emptiness is substituted by a fatuous political extremism, one sided journalism and obsequiousness toward hedonist, ignoramus pop idols?"

"Journalists are maggots feasting on the dead, as if there were nothing new to create or invent, but only relishing a rumor, and harping on, and eating it. While their bosses are better than them at invention."

"Our media's opinionated newsmen were given the forum to present fiction as fact, by their opinionated bosses, the long-lasting effects being that now relativism infects the news, the media is Chicken Little."

"As news mongers, they sell sensationalism as madams sell sex, that's what I think of our press barons; even Ox News is but a diluted, tired version of its once vaunted self, since being sold to Aussie asses."

It happened that after watching CON he needed to bring out his handkerchief, and after listening to Ox, an AK 47. Where he stood, or what his beliefs were, was as changeable as the last webpage consumed. People were scared and resented the media telling them everything was all right, or else, going to hell. "Overdone praise and criticism are standard fare for journalists. When voicing approbation, a style of words exaggerates as cute feminine; for revilement the usage is outrageous, in your face condemnatory. This is the new Reign of Terror: news headlines for the guillotine, a cell phone for Madame Defarge."

There was flagrant yellow journalism run by politically savvy operatives gunning against duller targets, heavily reliant on sarcasm and witty put downs, especially of laconic conservatives by sharper liberals.

Headlines beginning, "Don't believe such and such..." were all the vogue, as no one believed anything. To influence public discussion and policy, the Huffnpuff Post purposely adopted the ultra-chic, modish vernacular, hip speak, of the fashion industry, heavily dominated, managed and steered by a notorious, openly queer, LGBT driven agenda, consistently stoking up purring adjectives in pumped-up headlines:

*Adorable*
*Amazing*
*Beloved*
*Beautiful*
*Breathless*
*Breathtaking*
*Cherished*
*Darling*
*Precious*
*Priceless*
*Scintillating*
*Sensitive*
*Stunning*
*Unforgettable*
*Unforgivable*

*What we learned from... (didactic headline)*

Or the Fixer/ Yellow Kid's fave: *A Baby Bear Battle in Yosemite National Park Is Absolutely Adorable!*

The press had cried wolf so often, no one believed them when the turning point, or problem, occurred. In any crisis, war or election the made-up rhetoric outpaced any respectable fact checking by leaps and bounds, news media reacting, combating, leading true events and utterances, history being made, then altered and changed by the minute, by any creative writer bitchin' for a byline, a chance to buy acclaim. It was more hypothesizing possible scenarios on how such and such might happen, how one side would get even, rather than reporting on the day's events. This was the modern, weakened state of journalism. Each event, news item, was as if put on a scale, this balance of faith, public opinion, all the information slanted in such fashion, that the scales adjusted one way or the other, but the weights had been teased...

### *DCF: Still Gathering Major Evidence*

### *Lilly's Lawyer: The Chances of This Going to Children's Court Are Nil*

### *Willi: We Were Enjoying Our Privacy when DCF Arrived*

### *Fresh Scoop: Willi and Lilli Accused of Parental Neglect*

As with their efforts against DCF, there was nothing they could do to keep the infernal media machine from spewing out the most diabolical tales of their parenting travails, putting them in the same category as most of the parents in this world. The moment had come, for the dissuaded duo to get some outside advice from the most original of insiders, Henry Waterson, MD, himself, lurking *paterfamilias* only too happy to put in his two cents, regarding their complaints of being persecuted by this unrelenting fiend called DCF. Considering Dr. Waterson's storied past, of various injustices in the treatment of his own people at the reservation, he knew something about sadistic abuse, and how DCF would intervene in it.

"What is wrong with you? You say the authorities make your lives miserable, and instead of facing up to the consequences, salvaging what may still be left of your family, you call me blubbering like babies do, when they have been punished by their teacher. I want you to act like the grown-ups you've always insisted you are. Besides what do you know of oppression, persecution compared to our slain people?"

> I can still see the butchered women and children lying heaped and
> scattered all along the crooked gulch as plain as when I saw them with
> eyes still young. And I can see that something else died there in the bloody
> mud, and was buried in the blizzard. A people's dream died there. It was a
> beautiful dream . . . the nation's hope is broken and scattered.
> (John G. Neihardt, *Black Elk Speaks*, 1932) [Wounded Knee Massacre]

Now our Dr. Henry Waterson, Original American Medicine Man Supreme, agent of tremendous global social change and upheaval; also, Lilly and Willy's adoptive father; narrated the morality play for these troubled times, to buck up the deflated egos, once more. "The first and most harshly felt revenge of the doomed Native American peoples, was spreading a heretofore unknown syphilis to their new, European masters, the initial cases apparently hosted by the captives Columbus returned with on his First Voyage of Discovery, for the curious pleasure of the court. After transmitting the perfidious new spirochetes to the public women of Barcelona the contagion spread throughout Europe by 1500, and following twenty additional years, throughout the Age of Exploration, across the furthest reaches of the globe, producing more disastrous results than the epidemic of tribal run casinos would centuries later, but not as much as tobacco, the nemesis par excellence, ever would. White calls for inclusiveness result from an excess of pity, while Native peoples view it as an equalizer of revenge, bringing pale faces onto reservations for good times, games and smokes, delayed vengeance garishly displayed as material success of tribes lost to the winds of time and obliteration. So, think of a way to win, against that which you cannot defeat."

When *SS* Colonel Otto Waldemar Grawitz read the headlines, concerning his former co-star and writer of the movie that had made him a (sort of) star, he rushed to her side to put in his two cents, regarding their complaints of being persecuted by an unrelenting governmental power. Considering the Colonel's sordid, past crimes against humanity, exterminating masses of people at concentration camps, Grawitz knew something about excess, and how unregulated, all powerful, infernal authorities would intervene. "In my time I have seen victims of the worst circumstances still triumph. Once a German boy upon the platform split from his parents, to show me he was not circumcised, to prove he was adopted, and not a Jew, deserving to die, so he lived, and his family did not. What I mean by this is, trust no one, depend only on yourselves. My past UN testimony was to save myself, despite its effects on others who heard it, for among other things, feeling zero remorse for bayoneting babies in midair, on my earliest tour of the Eastern Front in a Jewish Ukrainian town. Traits of self-preservation must be in one's soul, as there was as ancient forefather, who escaped Charlemagne's Blood Court of Verden, for 4,500 Saxon rebels:"

> When the king heard of this disaster he decided not to delay, but made haste to gather an army, and marched into Saxony. There he called to his presence the chiefs of the Saxons, and inquired who had induced the people to rebel. They all declared that Widukind was the author of the treason, but said that they could not produce him because after the deed was done he had fled to the Northmen. But the others who had carried out his will and committed the crime they delivered up to the king to the number of four thousand and five hundred; and by the king's command they were all beheaded [decollati] in one day upon the river Aller in the place called Verden [Ferdun]. When he had wreaked vengeance after this fashion, the king withdrew to the town of Diedenhofen [Thionville]...
> (*Annales qui dicuntur Einhardi [Annals of Einhard]*, 815)

Such certainly deflates that exalted status Charlemagne has enjoyed, as the harbinger of a high Western tradition. With his stalwart papal sponsorship, the Holy Roman Emperor began to act as a true King of Israel. Given such antecedents, our protagonists were lucky to have made it to these present days at all. Each one of their innumerable ancestors had to escape malicious treatments long enough to spread their seeds before expiring, all the way back in their lineages, an incredible act of survival from a biological perspective; and considering there were so many things to expire from, the destiny of each precise soul was a miracle, an incredible act of genetic transference, from a divine perspective. Perhaps even some preordination assisted the events, and individuals involved, along their way. With peasant-slaughtering monarchs getting free rides in history, how could Everyman defend himself from them, and other evils?

Moving on to the final, minor hostilities, skirmishes really, that occurred before the explosive civil war, now Sayer and Isidora went at it, Sayer's gang for the company, Isidora's for peace of Universal Mind. Such contretemps had its roots, however, years before, during Sayer's early tenure at Warren Bros. Inc., when he had decided to investigate possible, financial abuse at a studio executive's office, caused by a visiting internationalist cross-border, humanitarian warrior, who happened to be a distant cousin, friend, of Isidora's; having been too zealous in that exercise of corporate authority, toward a Native American medicine man, Sayer was called on the carpet by his irate boss, Isidora; "that was Dr. Henry Waterson, you so thoroughly roughed up, with your henchmen;" but achieved the upper hand by persuading her to his side, as he insisted, he was attempting to bridge corporate differences that existed between Warren Bros. Inc. and The Theatre and Cinema Worker's Guild; busting heads when necessary, reducing loyal headcount to the bare minimum (still justifying exorbitant salaries, bonuses, perks, of the C suite), and going head-to-head with board members over cost overruns, aesthetic choices, on the past two pictures. "As corporate executive I'm held to a high oath, grandiloquently bossing cowed people around, making vague gestures in the sky." Those were the good old days, when things were still taken care of quietly, through shows of wild animal spirits in the middle of the night, handled by hired thugs on the payroll. Then cell phones and websites publicly shaming people became the right's, as well as left's, uber-tactic, utilized against anyone who even slightly disagreed with their overarching, hyper vigilant, self-serving socio-political agendas. As to why Henry Waterson was consorting with Hollywood moguls let's say it was his way of keeping tabs on his progeny, whom he had nurtured, but lost in a fit of temper over their bad behavior. He then nurtured the union, to stand up against the capitalist steam rollers of their rights. It happened to be Isidora's only allowance toward unions, as a loyalty to a bygone cherub lover ruled:

> To them who by patient continuance in well doing seek for glory and
> honour and immortality, eternal life: (Romans, 2:7, KJV)

Though those were the rudimentary origins of their hard feelings, they were covered up for most of the professional time the two had since spent together. However, back then they were raw and in the open, causing certain confrontation, between a pushy president, and a more idealistic CEO, still in charge. In contrast to Sayer's aggressive competitiveness, Isidora was wise, restrained, from generational wealth:

> I would rather earn 1% off a 100 people's efforts than 100% of my own
> efforts. (Rockefeller, *John D. Rockefeller on Making Money*)

However, siding with proto–John D., Sayer believed life was not about deserving, but rather the taking. Liberals helped others, conservatives, helped themselves. The nuclear threat of a poison pill was made. It was not surprising that an American traditional expression of 1832, "to the victor belongs the spoils," had as its origins the western frontier, where everything was, "up for grabs" (American colloquialism). In terms of the present, nothing in the world mattered while the U.S. stock market continued its climb. John Sayer organized a clandestine buyout combine, joined by Donny Craft, Town Crier (King Carbon) and Junior Camper, his smile as big as his bank account, who had Lizard Bros. as their financing pilar. The staid, old money followed the new money vs. Isidora's increasingly progressive policies, launching a hostile takeover of Warren Bros. Inc. for greed, slyly claiming greater shareholder value to be an aim.

Ironically Isidora herself did not have the least scruples in following American colloquial expressions. Turning to Goldmen Sucks as her financing arm, she was not one to slough off responsibilities to her loyal shareholders, under advisement by her staunchest of Sissies, Lucretia Faithful, revered founder of BTC (Bear Trap Capital), their guru of greed and master strategist of plans which might save the stock; after all, Isidora's Gypsy blood necessitated vengeance for an assumed, as well as real wrong, there was no splitting hairs on an eye for an eye reply; so she was prepared to follow her sister's crafty directives, which depended upon driving down the stock in a loss of confidence in order to buy cheap from fearful holders bailing out. This was known as a bear trap, and was a technique, which had made BTC famous on the Street. "What about threats of a poison pill?" "It's just a bluff, and it would only poison them."

Lucretia smeared them: "Bit-O-Honey is a fool's paradise, based on the greater fool theory, a who's left holding the bag, musical chairs, hot potato, idiot's delight, perhaps utilized primarily by sketchy types."

Isidora calmly spoke: "My dear sister, we need to know, what is it you propose to save this company?"

"Lady, to save the stock, I propose you get rid of it, placing it in a blind trust, followed by repurchase agreement, for the sum of one dollar, with my firm, to be held for you until the future unwinding of the position. In this way you may legally claim that you have sold your entire stake in the company, to be followed by stories of your loss of conviction in the production studios, which are the backbone of the company, and unfortunately, seeing no chances of a recovery in earnings in the short term. By the time that is all digested by the market the stock should tank. We will observe the signals for the appropriate time to buy the positions of the recalcitrant, traitorous shareholders, just when they sell in a panic, and the stock runs its downward spiral. We will be ready, with financing from our bankers, and a group of equity investors from our hedge funds. *The Top Recommendations by Goldmen Sucks* will feature us."

Of course, one of the greatest ironies of the investment world was that many of the major clients of the speculative hedge funds, ministers of self-entitled avarice, were pension funds, created to safeguard the contributions of the members, working and middle-class retirees entrusting them with hard won crumbs or lifetime investments, making the victory of deception and risk, over fiduciary responsibility, all too grim. How rash, that the nest eggs of all those clamoring for survival, and humble continuity, would be in the hands of those most interested in their own self-appointed rewards, notoriety, success. But it was the American way, for what did it matter if those few became super wealthy, at the expense of the many working people struggling just to get by, if market returns for extreme gambles of their capital resulted. A moment of genius for the capitalist system was when Henry Ford realized, that by selling his cars to his own workers, then to other workers, he created a new consumer market of untold demand; the result being a new type of debt peonage due to the wide avenues of financing available to wide eyed workers, always stretching budgets beyond their means; this becoming the new proletariat class consumerism of American proportions. As our prosperous leaders were champions of foisting free enterprise dreams of success and wealth upon society, the masses themselves were as much to blame for behaving as sheep. The corruption in society was not solely the fault of those who are corrupt and venal, but was shared by a herd of misled sheep, all too ready to succumb to arguments of a great America, to boost their riches and egos, even as to adopting the cutthroat attitude, of those who will do anything it takes to succeed.

*Vigorish* or *vig* was an old Yiddish term for interest, discount, fee, cut, associated with most enterprises, even criminal. The investment banks were positioned to get their *vig*, as sure as the sun rose every day. Whether or not any speculators would end up making money, depended upon which side they were on, as there would only be one winner; but the Sayer bandits had as their own bank advisor Lizard Bros., which was also known for having tricks up their sleeves; tycoons weren't in it selflessly, but for the *vig*, or the profit and those who won would win big. Sayer had clandestinely been buying stock for months:

> The personal character and career of one man are so intimately
> connected with the great scheme of the years 1719 and 1720, that a
> history of the Mississippi madness can have no fitter introduction than
> a sketch of the life of its great author John Law. Historians are divided in
> opinion as to whether they should designate him a knave or a madman.
> (Charles Mackay, *Extraordinary Popular Delusions and the Madness of
> Crowds*, 1841)

Sayer's demand for cutting down spending, limiting growth, was unbending, all the while making sure he had enough for himself and his, that they had health insurance, due to their privilege and influence, and that they had plenty of food to eat, while not giving a damn about anyone else. Hadn't Everyman once been, either a slave, serf, villein, or minor free holder, there being nothing in between, and these

God keeping Puritans lived to maintain the status quo of the past, where those who were smiled upon by God, as well as those deserving His wrath, were predestined, for such had always been so, since the beginning. But he had no idea of the guile, resilience and grit of the foe he had provoked to the death.

First, word leaked out secretly by Isidora's camp that a hostile amalgam of investors was buying up the stock, perhaps in a take-over play. As usual a froth ensued in the market with many a neophyte plunger hopping on board before it was too late, but by then it was already too late as the valuation had become too rich for Sayer's clique to continue buying, and the stock going to stellar heights unseen or imagined before. At the top, no one noticed, observed that all the inflated value in the stock had as its origins the Warren Brothers, who after having participated in the invention of moving pictures were left broke, on the sidewalk, by the rapacious Greens; and yet, the original equity also represented the untold efforts of the workers of the company, who had fashioned it, its operations and intrinsic value, out of their souls. Marxian surplus labor value is the unique, excess energy, and vital life source, of the exploited workers, withheld in the production process, sucked up and kept by the capitalist as profit almost as if composed of the souls themselves, and therefore sacred, unalienable from the workers, and never belonging to, or being possessed by anyone, much less the capitalist, as wealth in waiting, potential value in its essence. Wall Street mavens wrung their hands in delight, seeing newborn lambs take their first innocent breaths toward the fleecing of their lives, as it was a sucker's rally, with bleating sheep lining up for bleeding.

Now really bad news hit the Street: Chairman Isidora's unhappiness with the performance of the studio under Sayer, the cancellation of several new and existing productions under way, the shaking out of the executive suite, etc., all causing the start of a slide in the stock. Sayer complained publicly that he was being blamed, and everyone knew it was probably true that he was, but the stock kept crashing anyway, because someone was selling it heavily. More news followed, that the studio's biggest stars were under investigation, and possible action, from DCF, regarding a slew of allegations, from child endangerment to abduction, racism, assault, rampant drug and alcohol abuse. Now the stock really tanked because the studio's top earners were in trouble. The *coup de grace* occurred, when Isidora announced that she and her family had sold out of their entire position in the shares and were washing their hands of the whole company due to its gross mismanagement; Sayer began suspecting he was always the intended fall guy, because just as he was about to dictate his terms to Isidora, he realized there was no one there anymore. With the stock in a free fall, Sayer's investor pool was losing confidence and beginning to panic. They were true Wall Street types; you know, real cut throats in back alleys, with no sensibilities to any others than themselves in their narrow, moneyed world. How was it that the most ardent devotees of *laissez faire* capitalism were the most supportive of bailouts, especially for themselves? Because markets were rigged by governments in favor of the rich stockholding classes. Now the cabal of big losers convened.

And Junior Camper reported: "We are now 50% below our average purchase price, with some investors losing entire positions, due to unmet margin calls; this market seems to have vengefully turned against us." The sanctimonious capitalists, who espoused hard work as being their virtue, were the same stuffy self-servers who argued about and opposed every penny above the minimum wage they might pay their workers. If they could convince their gullible galley slaves that laboring had a merit, divinely inspired, then perhaps, they wouldn't have to pay them at all, and obtain their labor for free. Here was one way Marx may have been wrong, when he wrote, "the history of... society is... class struggles," for if these crafty villains could get their brethren to work at zero cost, then all of Marx's theories would go out the window. Said Sayer: "No one remembers the vanquished, either in the battlefield or the marketplace."

Then prim, confounded Donny Craft: "Perhaps it was time we cut our heavy losses, as prudence would dictate. We must let Isidora have her cake and eat it too this time around. Let us not perpetuate a grand folly. The last thing we need – for professional, financial, institutional, socio-political reasons – is yet, another blame game, augmenting what too many people already feel are a series of 'rigged' outcomes, favoring better-off segments of society; we need to resurface again in scrubbed versions of ourselves."

And Town Crier aka King Carbon: "If big banks have no shame or hesitation in asking for government rescues, interventions, such as Federal Reserve monetary policy, fiscal stimuli, industry protectionisms, sector subsidies, so can we, in support of the generous corporate pork, bestowed on us upstairs stiffs." How ironic and disturbing that the thin-lipped prigs, proclaiming *ad infinitum* the virtues of free trade and self-reliance, and complaining to no end about government assistance to the lower income earners, simultaneously received huge government largesse, in support of their evaporated equity. So much for their creed of smaller, more limited government. It was not just bad luck that struck them down but the invincible mitt of retribution, waiting all those centuries to come back, to smash their accomplishments with an iron fist. The following morning at Saugamuck, pushing hard on train platform, saw Superman heading to a sales meeting at work, dressed in a favorite costume, on the Metro North express to GCT:

> Justice at this first stage is good will among those approximately equal in
> power to come to terms with each other, to "come to an agreement" again
> with each other by compensation—and in relation to those less powerful,
> to compel them to arrive at some settlement among themselves. —
> (Friedrich Nietzsche, *On the Genealogy of Morality: A Polemic*, 1887)

At the bottom of the stock's freefall, Lucretia Faithful had the genius to buy in her shorts, double up on her margined longs, and begin disseminating the news, that Isidora was once more in possession of her stake, due to unwinding the repo position with her firm, BTC. Whereupon the valuation soared, as the market recognized Isidora's true intent, at full control, once more. It was one of the greatest bear traps in stock market history, and restored her company, Warren Bros. Inc., to Isidora, without further danger of an imminent takeover. Besides Isidora's strategic victory everyone part of the market operation was well compensated. True to her name, Lucretia had been Faithful to her sister, as she had been nurtured to do at her Whale secret society, and if such sibling relationship was perhaps sustained by a pecuniary promise, it was of no consequence, for as a Mexican drug lord once noted, "It may be true that blood is thicker than water, but money is thicker than blood." Leave it to say, BTC (Bear Trap Capital) was on everyone's radar, becoming the takeover specialist on the Street, with further influence in future duels. As staunch believers in fairness in wealth management they treated their clients accordingly, and never pulled a bear trap on anyone that did not deserve it, keeping Lucretia true to her most ancient vocation.

Isidora, once again, confirmed in her stature, as Press Baron Supreme, fostered her progressive agenda; as science and a new social tolerance, combined with sales boosting inclusiveness, were responsible for the proliferation of eccentric, alternative lifestyles, all in the name of personal freedom and expression; while never confusing Wall Street corporate results for freedom, as the truth was still a moveable feast. Many companies believed supporting marriage equality made good business sense, HR becoming their secret weapon of social reform, even if it took one thousand years to accomplish. Changing those mind sets of working Americans was the fastest way to achieving a new society. Corporations, for their size and power, in raw numbers as well as economic influence, would now directly influence legal policies. Then, as foreign powers sometimes joined together, hiding their true intentions, even from themselves, Isidora and Sayer were again able to come to their agreement, based, as of old, on a solid quarterly EPS performance, getting the studios to produce top notch attractions, and quashing the DCF issues of their stars. If the shocks of the past century were wild social, political, sexual revolutions what would be the surprise shock of this century and millennium? Whatever was in store would be best confronted by the two acting as colleagues, and even partners, as in past times. What they could not conceive of were the ineffable possibilities to come in a mindful conflict between their common side and established society.

# 20. CIVIL WAR

*...they do for their gods every detestable thing that Jehovah hates,*
*even burning their sons and their daughters in the fire to their gods.*
(Deuteronomy 12:31, KJV)

There stands in their midst a bronze statue of Kronos [Baal Hammon],
its hands extended over a bronze brazier, the flames of which engulf the
child. When the flames fall upon the body, the limbs contract and the
open mouth seems almost to be laughing until the contracted body slips
quietly into the brazier. Thus it is that the 'grin' is known as 'sardonic
laughter,' since they die laughing. (Greek historian Cleitarchus, 400 BC)

There was in their city a bronze image of Cronus extending its hands,
palms up and sloping toward the ground, so that each of the children
when placed thereon rolled down and fell into a sort of gaping pit filled
with fire. (Greek historian Diodorus Siculus, 1st century BC)

Could it be numerous ancient cultures sacrificed their children willingly if not forcefully? According
to Bernal Diaz del Castillo, *Moctezuma* feasted on, "the flesh of young children, as a very dainty bit... by
way of a relish." Quite ironic was the victims' proximity to the palace, where his own children resided:

...eating human meat, just like we take cows from the butcher's shops,
and they have in all towns thick wooden jail-houses, like cages, and in
them they put many Indian men, women and boys to fatten, and being
fattened they sacrificed and ate them.
(Bernal Diaz del Castillo, *The Conquest of New Spain*, 1567)

Was this what Thomas Jefferson meant, when he wrote, "the tree of liberty must be refreshed from time
to time with the blood of patriots & tyrants. it is it's natural manure?" Could Jefferson really have been
that crass, as to condone sacrifices of innocents, in support of policy? If so, such certainly was a pile of
manure, to put it politely, because one of our Founding Fathers would never have endorsed ending kids.
However, how could he have meant otherwise, when now the tree of liberty was inordinately refreshed
by child blood? But as Sayer and his faction ascribed such behavior, to mental health and the demonic,
we were no better off than in ancient times, with "the 'grin...' known as 'sardonic laughter,' since they
die laughing;" with evangelicals offering outpourings of prayer, condemnation of the evil in our midst.
But little did they understand they were the problem; and the collateral damage was a tribute to a faded
Second Amendment propped up by literalist readings of the U.S. Constitution, an out-of-date document
from the eighteenth century; maybe it was time to revise the parched parchment or abolish it altogether.
July 4th not only brought out the best/ worst in Sayer, but also inspired scenarios of Founding Fathers:
On Christmas Eve 1783, witty Thomas Jefferson had dinner and cups with a stiff George Washington,
at the general resigning his commission to Congress, proud as sanguine, and sanguinary, Anglo Saxons,
Jefferson's ruddy wine-tinged, debauched face captivating the infertile general's smallpox scarred one:

"General, your resignation yesterday was one of the greatest defenses of liberty I have ever witnessed,
worthy of the Roman cynosure Cincinnatus, as your fame will be self-fulfilling by not overstepping the
limits of authority. Perhaps one day you will lead this new nation as president." Iconoclastic Jefferson,
later dubbed, "Mr. Revolution," during his ministry in Paris, for being the most erudite, veteran, extant
revolutionist in the world, utopian dreamer, obsessed by a spirit of '76, belying strong anti-government

viewpoints, was in short, an insurrectionist of a coming generation, for whom federal encroachment of a state's internal affairs, was reason enough for that state's secession from the union, as the Lost Cause regions were later ignominiously to do. Having never seen combat he was attracted by the call to arms: "The failure of democracy is that it accommodates the law, to every particular under the sun, agonizing its effect, diluting its force. Each group can clamor for its own special law, insuring their unique rights, to the detriment of equal justice for all. When people state they want both sides to be heard, they really mean they want their side to win; democracy, a popular folly, is destroying us by argument from within. What will follow, modified anarchy, a dictatorship of the people, or oligarchy, aristocracy, plutocracy?"

> [Jefferson] cannot live but in a revolution, and all events in Europe are
> only considered by him in the relation they bear to the probability of a
> revolution to be produced by them. [British dinner partner of Jefferson's]
> (Dan Evon, *Snopes*, "Did Thomas Jefferson Say the Tree of Liberty Must
> Be Refreshed 'With the Blood of Patriots and Tyrants?'" 9/11/2019)

"My dear Jefferson, I believe this nation would be best served, by an authoritative, but not authoritarian government. As did Cincinnatus, I'll pick up a plough once more to keep my slaves busy at husbandry. Let us once again attend to federalism within our nation, consolidating what was begun in July 1776." Stoic Washington, secretly tubercular, with old lesions whittling away his insides, ravaged by the ague (malaria), prematurely aged by hardships of war for the last eight turbulent years (the battle-hardened commander in chief in short a soldier of past conflicts, as surviving heroes were, for whom any pursuit of bellicosities, here or abroad, would be reason enough for the state's alien and sedition prosecution of such, for absolutely traitorous behavior), had seen enough action to realize he did not wish to see more. "I foresee activists demanding *liberté, egalité, fraternité*, one day becoming petty dictators, given their chance; just see what is happening in Europe, particularly France, where they are already utilizing your own words from our Declaration of Independence to articulate revolutionary doctrines and movements. Perhaps it is our moment for a constitutional convention, bearing in mind, that whenever a country has one, it usually marks the end of an existing regime as we know it, and a commencement of a new one."

"When that occurs, we must demonstrate that our most basic freedoms, of worship and speech, should be preserved by a moral justification, joined by another, the right of the people to keep and bear Arms, because if we are to defend against government interference against our liberties we need to be armed."

"Magnanimous sir, the causes to bear arms are quite over; I urge you to join me in Virginia, as planting season soon approaches, and there is much work needed in house, field, or in clearing of woodland. As the tireless statesman you are perhaps it is impossible to desist, but a call to arms is never the solution."

"But how shall we defend the freedom to express ourselves, other than protecting liberty from tyranny, by being armed and willing to die for it? And as words in themselves rarely force, backup is mandated. In the end, General, you shall come around to a well-regulated Militia, due to those two hundred fifty *darkies* residing as your chattel property at Mount Vernon. Your travels in Barbados, surely impressed upon you a need for preventing the kind of *vodou* revolts, we now hear occurring in Saint-Domingue."

"I must congratulate you on your well-presented arguments on my behalf, and will appraise them well, while you are representing us in France, as I hear from Congress. I would only ask you to consider that words may be turned to weapons, especially by one so able as you, so beware of being carried away by thoughtless promises, or dinner prattle which might compromise you. Remember, as you wade through pitiless political muck, that when brash insults were hurled our 'Yankee Doodle... called it macaroni.'"

Within a decade, France persecuted, and guillotined, an entire estate of its citizens, calling it *la Terreur*. Extreme U.S. left/ right factionalism was already apparent to de Tocqueville, by the 1820s; this was not a new phenomenon. Politics were always about calumny, vituperation, ad hominem attacks, rather than bipartisanship, viewed as the alternative of the weak. Jefferson was a master at propagandizing media. "He perfected the terror by substituting permanent war for permanent revolution," as did Napoleon. In addition to scribing the most fundamental of all revolutionary manifestos he also had a hand, despite or because of, his time in France, in other superlatively authored covenants, such as the First and Second Amendments to the Constitution in the Bill of Rights. But his allegiance to the armed struggle lowers him from revered hero of American independence, crafting its primary document, and sadly, places him in the company of history's eloquent hazards, Hitler in *Mein Kampf,* Lenin in *The State and Revolution*:

> While the State exists, there can be no freedom.
> When there is freedom there will be no State.

> A revolution is certainly the most authoritarian thing that is possible.
> Revolution is the act whereby one part of the population imposes its will
> upon the other part by means of rifles, bayonets, and cannons,
> i.e. extremely authoritarian means.
> (Vladimir Lenin, *The State and Revolution*, 1917)

Revered Washington became the first president to suffer onslaughts from an unleashed, savage press no president, or human being, should ever endure, launching no retorts, unable to conceive an heir, having been responsible, for hurtling enough cannonballs, grapeshot, grenades, bombs, to last the millennium:

> I am gliding down the stream of life, and wish, as is natural, that my
> remaining days may be undisturbed and tranquil; and, conscious of my
> integrity, I would willingly hope, that nothing would occur tending to
> give me anxiety; but should anything present itself in this or any other
> publication, I shall never undertake the painful task of recrimination, nor
> do I know that I should even enter upon my justification. (*Infoplease*, "The
> True George Washington: Enemies: The Press," Updated 2019)

As nation states rose in Europe, they did their best to limit gun ownership to militaries. As most of our colonial kin were socio political renegades, they opposed the European status quo, by demanding rights to bear arms. So due to a historicism of chance, a hiccup really, the U.S. became the single country in the world, enshrining such aggressive rights into its constitution, what embarrassing libertarian babble. As an historical idiosyncrasy, the same people who today wanted guns were descended from those who once wanted slaves, slavery begetting capitalism, the Reformation, arms, as pledges of innate freedom. The politics of envy were practiced by those whose intent was to cleave the body politic into competing self interest groups, each wanting advantages enjoyed by the others, many of its most vocal adherents living sans medical insurance, pensions, cost of living increases, nontaxable savings plans, etc., instead of condoning any meriting of privileges, such were the self-loathing demands of conservative politicos. We were in a mode of competing for success, coveting benefits, entitlements and any birthrights one's neighbors had, simply, because one did not have them. If they had them, they shouldn't, and if one did not, they should not either. And it was worth not having anything at all so long as one's neighbors were equally destitute, the common denominator being misery that loves company. The right adhered to the politics of envy, its jealous, blind rage at the social safety net enjoyed by society's less fortunate; while the left adhered to the politics of shame, ruthlessly and meanly exposing the bad behavior of opponents deserving instant censure and correction; both sides using social media for maximum sensational reach, effect, and the righteous, but proper, laying of blame at the other's narrow wicket gate. So, one person's patriotism or praise, must per force be another's treason or sabotage, just as each market's longs, per the definition, create corresponding shorts, and every thesis must per se, create its counter argument. One man's villain is another's knight. Never had so much been given that freely, under zero corresponding obligations, to those who deserved so little and were correspondingly thankless, for their political trust:

1. Conservatives complained about the irreligious, ample welfare state regimes of central planners.
2. Liberals complained about the loose regulatory and gun regimes, misogyny and abortion rights.

And there came a time, when all the characters, severally, jointly, decided they had had enough of such binary paradise, and for many reasons would oppose or demolish it, if possible. Then *La Migra* was in cahoots with DCF in tormenting our opportunistic border jumpers; but at least it could be said they did not drop and leave their children, in the United States, like other illegal parents; Willi and Lilly joining forces with the entire supporting cast, to plan and execute the big one, as they had nothing more to lose.

On a sundrenched Labor Day, with nary a cloud in sight, at September's hurricane prone start, enjoying the bounteous gifts nature bestows, compared to the infinite wrongs man commits then further endures, gathered on the water's edge at Isidora's summer beach home on the Buyreem Shore, in Greenitch, CT, despite various residencies in the U.S., each had more than their share to add on the subjects. Granted, the Bill of Rights was written to prevent excesses such as those of medieval Pedro the Cruel of Castile:

> Nor could such a judge be a king who wished men he had sentenced to
> cruel death to be boiled and roasted in his presence; or... commanded his
> officials to send him the heads of adversaries (actual or potential) whom
> he had ordered killed. He was cruel, all right... (B. Netanyahu, *The Origins*
> *of The Inquisition in Fifteenth Century Spain*, 1995)

But who could ever keep from noticing the extreme numbers of gun related deaths in the United States, unless you were just off the boat, or were a sucker born per minute, or would buy the Brooklyn Bridge? Isidora, in her guise as Societal Hostess Supreme, introduced the heavy matters with grace and aplomb: "Thank you for meeting on such short notice; and please, I urge you all to take a dip in the Long Island Sound, whenever you feel the urge; there are always towels by the shower cabana. These summer days are already getting short, and I fear today's heavy discussion will bring about the autumn chill with it:"

> Demoralize the enemy from within by surprise, terror, sabotage,
> assassination. This is the war of the future. (Adolf Hitler, 1934)

"The first thing we do, let's kill all the gun manufacturing executives: if you can, hit first, if not, then be an NRA member," exclaimed one among the crowd, invisible in glare, and seconded by several others. But they were quickly disabused of such thoughts by the Colonel, who pointed out that if there were to be any individuals anticipated to be armed and dangerous, when tracked to their homes, or ambushed in public, it was these death merchants in question, and an attack against them would be very costly. The same went for the NRA, at their convention or singly, they were untouchable, because they would blow your head off with multi-AR-15s if you went against them, as acclaimed by their frontier justice aura.

They considered targeting the justice system, storming the Supreme Court, as each side harbored plenty of grievances, for having been ruled against during multitudes of outrageous demands over time, whose summations amounted to a plethora of denials, rejections, albeit legal, but painful, nevertheless. Then greater than the Supreme Court, which consisted of individuals, after all, who would blindly invoke the legislated system of errors existing, were the laws brought by Congress. In a dull assessment, Supreme

Court Justices were surely tools of the legislative branch that passed the statutes. And as there were too many legislators to intrigue against, those gathered rejected any possibilities of physical violence as too complicated, compromising to carry out. Because the main duty of the Supreme Court was confirming if the case was in conformity with the original meaning of the Constitution, as intended by its Signers; due to arcane legal twists and maneuvers, these Supremes could approve racist, regressive laws if those conformed to articles; or undo egalitarian laws, over some obscure amendment. "Excuse me, are those semi-automatics handy, for killing children? Then the Second Amendment is a fealty to a grim folly." Isidora strictly stuck to her rubber bullets dictum, so shooting the Supremes would be out. Any Court onslaught fantastically joined to an attempt to rescue Lilly's mother from Gitmo, was also to be denied, along with any Hollywood invoked dream, of Lilly hugging her incarcerated mother, as being much too complicated, causing unneeded attention. Any options injurious to others would also now be ruled out.

They finally decided to go against the tired Constitution itself rather than the Court, as the source of the pressing issues facing the country, but with what would they replace its sovereignty? Henry Waterson, MD and *SS* Colonel Otto Waldemar Grawitz feuded over tactics of their united effort, as God and His Fallen Angel, representing the philosophical extremes described in the constitution they would destroy, the Colonel for stealing the Constitution outright, but most siding with the doctor for a magic redaction.

The first to speak up, was *SS* Colonel Otto Waldemar Grawitz, who, having grown up with neither the constitution nor bill of rights, was against them both on the mere principle that Everyman has no rights:

"A First Amendment provides the basis of the cultural relativism and equivocation, of all sundry ideas plaguing open democracies, the Second Amendment sharing its invitations to a fast death by freedom. In Europe rights have always been handed from the top down, not as here, driven from the bottom up." It seemed so easy to be oppositional, he enjoyed it until he was rebuffed by Isidora's progressive wrath:

"We all blend into one, nature makes us equal. Politics breeds inequalities, resentments and conflicts." But not owing to Isidora the direct duty he owed to Lilly, for instance, he gave back as good as he got:

"Nietzsche said equality is the death of man because none are equal. The truth is all activists espousing equality are sneaky hypocrites, secretly pushing only for their advantage, even at the expense of others seeking similar results. Sameness meant the reduction of everyone to the lowest common denominator. 'It was because Adolf Hitler and his party faced so much criticism and resistance among the press that I became particularly interested, in joining their movement.' We Germans always need strong leaders. I am as against absolute freedom of speech, as unrestrained proliferation of arms among the populace, for in either case, the loss of one's temper may cause unforeseen consequences in hurling hatred or lead. It was best to let the state decide how to retaliate against unforeseen, hateful insults, pugilistic challenges. In a measure of extreme force, I offer to lead a unit to loot the U.S. Constitution, for once and for all, as those freedoms should be set aside only for the gods, for whom sharing their minds and destroying are first and second natures. Slavishness to this tired *Magna Carta* would be deadly for your country, but not as deadly as what could happen without it, because without defining originating documents life was meaningless, as babies without birth certificates would be bastards." As one who thrived only by being the servant of an authoritarian nation in the paramilitary mold, he would always have access to arms for official needs, so why would he ever say a single word against it, or the political apparatus behind it? Wasn't this the exact European submission the Separatists and Dissenters decried and rebelled against?

Now Dr. Henry Waterson made his presence known, as one to bend his will with the prevailing winds, a great tribal leader and activist, gladly paying attention to what's largely a forgotten chapter of history: "'People are unaware that the Great Dying happened. At school, you're pounded with the story of fifty

Pilgrims dying during their first winter. But, during the Great Dying, about 50,000 Wampanoags died, as well as who knows how many other tribal people to the north in what's now Maine. It's kind of nice to see those numbers lined up side by side.' Such captures my priorities, but not headlining this farce. To hell with the First and Second Amendments; they only mean something to leftist censoring prigs, or rightist bully thugs exercising obnoxious freedoms, their defensive natures upended by ugly speech and murder; bring back civility. But rather than purloining those Founding Documents, getting rid of them altogether, let's edit them for ourselves, that way we will not have to search for the good news making itself manifest upon us. The ossified charters shall remain in lethargy, with only subtle changes. As we are in thrall to an out-of-date Constitution, the Second Amendment alone being enough reason to scrap the entire covenant, there must be some who would sacrifice their free speech, for no guns. How many times will lone gunmen ruin this country, as free as we are to rail against past ages of savagery?" The Cosmic Medicine Man Supreme even demanded agreement, on their strategy. Perhaps eliminating the particulars in question, without any substitutions, leaving them blank, would solve these difficulties. In taking such a course of action the team was only abiding by a more ancient book of knowledge than the *nouveau* Enlightenment ideologies, they had been groveling to for the last two hundred and fifty years:

> And if thy right eye offend thee, pluck it out, and cast it from thee: for it
> is profitable for thee that one of thy members should perish, and not that
> thy whole body should be cast into hell.

> And if thy right hand offend thee, cut it off, and cast it from thee: for it
> is profitable for thee that one of thy members should perish, and not that
> thy whole body should be cast into hell. (Matthew 5:29-30, KJV)

Now each said their piece, clamoring from within, selecting choice cuts, in a joint onslaught of dissent. First Willi, then Lilly, had a go at it, but they failed to capture its true essence, as they were not natives:

"Usually, it was the most uneducated who were the most intolerant, blindly believing they were correct, embodying righteousness. People needed to stop taking offense at differences of opinion from theirs. The 60s had a silent majority. Now it's a shouting majority. I don't want Democrats or Republicans, or liberals or conservatives; I want an even tempered, logical, truthful human being running this country. Because of recent antagonisms between the First and Second Amendments, no one remembers, or cares about, the Third, other than as degree… But seriously, despite all appearances of a confrontation, now more and more, the First amendment was egging on the expansion of a Second, used to incite violence on the Dark Web, and where was social responsibility in that? Let's dump both amendments, for both sides and hypocritical politicians, celebrities, artists, all of those who share opinions, most of them lies. I'm not proud of all the things I have done in my life, but I'm willing to die for a freedom from dying:"

> I John Brown am now quite certain that the crimes of this guilty, land:
> will never be purged away; but with Blood. I had as I now think: vainly
> flattered myself that without very much bloodshed; it might be done.
> (John Brown's Last Prophesy, Charles Town, Virginia, December 2, 1859)

Early that day, Lilly had been assaulted, in Cringeport, by a Hispanic motorcycle gang. When Lilly told the police that they had brandished a gun at her, the police answered they knew who the gang was, but for officer safety concerns could not give them chase; this having been the third crime report of the day, according to the desk sergeant, adding, "They don't want their mothers to see them in the newspapers:"

> "But in Wyoming the law has been letting our cattle-thieves go for two

years... The courts, or rather the juries, into whose hands we have put the
law, are not dealing the law... They cannot hold a cattle-thief. And so when
your ordinary citizen sees this, and sees that he has placed justice in a dead
hand, he must take justice back into his own hands where it was once at
the beginning of all things." (Owen Wister, *The Virginian*, 1902)

Lilly was all for commandeering some heavy pickup trucks and shooting them to smithereens; and then grew livid at the ludicrous tradeoff in a liberal society, of their anonymity versus her safety, concluding, "Pardon me, but we have already established, that the fourth estate is a fifth column; there should be no hesitation in trading a First Amendment for the Second, under such depressing, bullying circumstances. Grow up and realize not everyone agrees with you. Not everyone is going to like you, and conversely, you won't like all others either. And please stop shouting in my ears, so I can disavow shooting back."

Then the Rev. Hannibal P. (Pearly) Gates: "Covetous Pilgrims came here to shoot turkeys, then never stopped, because that's how they hunted *us folks*, as if at turkey shoots, or more to the point, massacres. When drunken cowpokes arrived at Dodge City, KS, authorities checked their firearms not their mental health, which has become society's excuse for doing nothing. Along with prayers, Republicans offered no solutions, only the same *ol'*. Instead of praying, passing some laws to help kids and other victims of shootings would be more effective. Maybe we need to shun those who keep and bear Arms, instead of applauding their Second Amendment privileges. Of course, the NRA always offers their condolences. Maybe their conventions could be shot up, so the Confederate rascals got a taste of their own medicine. One of their promotional videos: *a western style gunfight on an empty, sand blown lot, of a young man with a cell phone in video mode, facing off on another with a Sig Sauer pistol off safety, in a Stand Your Ground state, as the video shooter gets the life shot out of him, showing the Second Amendment wins.*"

A proud, former U.S. Marine, and DCF social worker, Patricia (P) Diddy, Ph.D., J.D., wanted to set the record straight: "I can only state this with the deepest respect for individual gun freedoms, as someone who learned to hunt with my daddy in the woods; but also shot up a bunch of sad individuals, we called enemies in a forgotten, dishonored conflict, who would now be classified as friends, in a great irony of history; the Second Amendment was misquoted and is obsolete, as it clearly references a well regulated militia, not unregulated, armed, armored ruffians running around, threatening, killing citizens, seeking cowardly protection behind a First Amendment, as the unholiest of alliances of the veering millennium. For they were manuscripts replete with the errors and misunderstandings of their age, imposed upon us now as infallible and incorruptible, ancient interpretations of freedom and the herd instinct; these being the heavy burdens and yokes upon our necks making change to our society impossible, especially when claimed, by dreary, constitutional literalists, as second only to scripture, as irrefutable. To achieve liberty, we must hurl off old ideas and norms of social comportment, racial identity, church/ state connections."

"I would keep my mouth shut not to get shot," said the rube with more scruples than rubles, Ottoline, in her guise as Russian Intellectual Supreme, despite Germanic roots, having earned a seat at the table by her defining role in *48 Hours to Mecca*. "As terrorism is the exploitation for political ends of violence, and pornography the exploitation for commercial ends of obscenity, degradingly, irredeemably corrupt; for their bad behavior, blacks hide behind their skin color, illegal aliens their children, liberals conceit; where does individual responsibility enter? I would rather not vote at all, than hold my nose to do it, if I am to take on the gun culture of the Medieval States of America. Perhaps shunning gun aficionados for their anti-social stances was one possibility. Texas should be given back to Mexico, especially after its shameless behavior on Juneteenth. Was precedent really favoritism to the entrenched way of doing things, the prior order, *ancien regime*? How about removing the Statue of Liberty, because the poem at its base is not inviting enough to minority races: No minorities need apply, thank you. You know about racism, don't you, everyone accuses everybody else of prejudice, whilst never seeing it in themselves?"

Having become the first Jewish Sissies Alumni President by impressing WASPs, pretending she was in the money, displaying fancy clothes, now fragranced in Chanel No. 5, the Queen of Quotas proceeded to quid pro quo her quotient: "Why stop with removing only the Confederate flag? All state flags with any representations of native peoples should be effaced, along with references of cities and monuments named after George Washington, Thomas Jefferson, and most of the Founding Fathers, for having been some of the biggest slave owners of their times. And all blacks, with any, of the given, or surnames, of prior slave owners, should assume new appellations, and this would probably include 95% of African Americans. The results would be the true and responsible re-branding of America." These sisters were agreeing on something, shaming society's servitude to out-of-date thoughts about free speech and arms and tying it all in with an aversion to slavery and exploitation, which seemed innate to a camp survivor.

Sayer had ideas of grandstanding the issue, in a desperate filibuster invoking the Trail of Tears, as early land grab; then President James Knox Polk and his collusion to interfere in Mexican politics, which led to the Mexican American War, a subsequent American expropriation of half of Mexico, and *los cadetes* jumping off *Chapultepec* Castle; the National Review and a neocon bombastic kowtow to bullying, the invisible hand, the Constitution and Bill of Rights; boldly insisting on not less guns, but more guns, for everyone, each member of the left to receive, an AK-47, and a copy of *Mao's Little Red Book*, with an AR-15, and Hitler's *Mein Kampf*, to the right, upon recruitment; allowing an inclusive guidance to rule. The basic tenet of Republican governing philosophy, being that small government was best because of individual initiative, personal responsibility, and a reliance on work, family and God, was at the center of the American vision; however, since the Founders made our Constitution consistent with this vision, government has exploded, obligating keeping track of, enforcing a regulatory regime created, re I & II.

"May the vengeful Gods of Universal Justice and Social Sanity wreak havoc on you and yours, for the promotion of immoral freedoms to own as many guns, as a sick and polluted mind deems appropriate." It was Isidora, berating Sayer. "When the term, people, becomes, the people, my Marxist early warning alarm goes off, screaming, danger, danger in my ear. However, we all seem to have arrived at a similar conclusion: we can live without the benefits of the First Amendment, at the cost of severe retribution of the Second; repudiating both candidness and Nemesis; the relation between the two almost incestuous, and it was so much incest within and between aristocratic families over the successive generations, that brought down the noble houses, as with our own good Constitution." In a crazy ending, guns as well as free speech were given up, in a truly unique, almost Buddhist, accommodation, as each side knew such a proscription would not change a thing in their behavior or exercising of God given inalienable rights. The expectations that everything would be alright after such and such, was a precious human foible; the truth was that after the big one, things went back to normal, with many regrets surfacing in due course:

> So lofty an end hardly consorts with so low a beginning.
> (James G. Frazer, *The Golden Bough*, 1922)

"Last chance for an evening swim, before the bait fish start to nip, on their way down stream to NYC."

And what would the doings of a madcap, philosophically broad, discussion bear at the start of the civil war? Perhaps nothing, but they relate to a time when things were less complicated; those invited could sit back, smell the roses of their success for moments, before assuming their high-pressure war footings in preparation; abandoning all semblance of recognizing any different points of view beyond their own; for true conviction, of the rightness of their side, was elemental for successful warfare, and lacking any land disputes as a pretext for hostilities, they substituted such an urgent need with an ideological *casus belli*, which hopefully sufficed as an abstracted rallying cause. But little did they imagine the immense changes they would each undergo in the following decade, for masterminding the plot against a United States government they all (even the escaped Nazi war criminal) owed different levels of allegiance to, conspiring to alter one of the rudimentary texts to their fancy, not a great record, or one to be proud of:

> Mine eyes have seen the glory of the coming of the Lord
> He is trampling out the vintage where the grapes of wrath are stored,
> He has loosed the fateful lightening of His terrible swift sword
> His truth is marching on.
> Glory! Glory! Hallelujah!
> Glory! Glory! Hallelujah!
> Glory! Glory! Hallelujah!
> His truth is marching on.
> (Julia Ward Howe, "Battle Hymn of the Republic," 1861)

Now the CLIMAX occurred in a show of shared despair, as well as team strength to correct the system. A call to arms was raised, and assistance arrived from the past, minor characters, who dreamed of being major ones. Even though our peculiar pansies were the heart and soul of the operation, and Isidora and Sayer the administrative generals, the rebel group put themselves at the command of the Colonel as its tactical head, and doctor as its technical head, the paramilitary/ surgical skills to alter the Bill of Rights. The differences between the two amendments were that the First was life giving, open ended, Christian in its forgiveness, courtesy, allowance of room for further discussions, negotiations, retort. With words lay the future of the world, benefitting from experiences, relieving doubts with relevant facts, dispelling darkness through the ages, spreading good through their own power, sharing the news, drawing crowds, bringing hope, giving reasons to live another day, to join one's story to life. However, the Second was life taking, closed ended, paleo in its absoluteness, lethality, allowing no further option for discussions, negotiations or retort. Evangelicals, guns and hunting went together, as successors to the Puritans, with the politics of envy of their lords' privileges to own weapons and hunt game on private lands; taking on advantages themselves in vulgarian aping of a decadent aristocracy now become our middle America in duck boots and hunting gear in autumn. For these reasons, in the final analysis the abandonment of the Second was a greater victory for its enemies than the abandonment of the First for theirs. Because the freedom to blast away carried deadly consequences, its abrogation was akin to the relinquishment of an ancient signorial, god-like freedom; whereas keeping your mouth shut was no bigger loss, than folding your hand at cards, quitting in extreme envy at Monopoly, or resigning a match of chess; tasks any fool or genius might accomplish without any lasting, tragic trigger happy, annihilating, intended/ unintended outcomes. So, fortunately, the results were more advantageous to those who would/ could utilize some discretion speaking, because it was normal in their lives, than those who were lame ducks without their repugnant toys, because they had surrendered absolute control over unarmed others, despising further discourse, demonstrating that despite their giving up assumed rights they were never honorable or nice.

It was at the height, of the U.S. War on Terror, when the country was on red alert for the next bombing. As much as it may have been staged, as a war of self-determination, we were watching other countries in the throes of CIA inspired self-destruction. So, were CIA directed votes truly democracy in action? *Six U.S. servicemen killed by drive by terrorists in Afghanistan yesterday*; and it was hardly mentioned in the news, which focused instead, *on the president's golf shots in Hawaii*. Unnamed wars, unclaimed by their purveyors, trading a domestic tranquility for foreign evils, nation-building, election meddling, social then political interventions, etc.: it was good to know, that as the world burned, *the president was deeply concerned about minority youths*, this sanctions mad administration; interesting, that so many atheists went out of their way to defend Muslims and their bad behavior; so, was the U.S. government's rendition akin to habeas corpus, only, having the body kept far from court? Did CIA stand for Certain Insane Actions? On the other hand, the following terrorist attacks came to mind, indelible to memory.

1. *Twelve Israeli athletes brutally massacred by machine gun fire and grenades at the Munich Olympics, September 1972.*
2. *U.S. Navy hero Robert Stethem shot through the head and hurled out an aircraft door onto the Beirut Airport tarmac, June 1985.*
3. *Wheelchair bound innocent, elderly Jew Leon Klinghoffer cast off the cruise ship* MS Achille Lauro, *on the open sea, October 1985.*
4. *370 doomed souls aboard Pan Am Flight 103 jumbo jet bombed over Lockerbie, Scotland, December 1988.*
5. *Nineteen dead, 498 injured, sleeping servicemen blown up at Khobar Towers, Saudi Arabia, June 1996.*
6. *2,977 unwitting victims vaporized in kamikaze style attacks on the World Trade Center, the Pentagon and rural PA, September 11, 2001.*

Such barbarity, causing bitterness, so many lives snuffed out, despicable.
Let the world remember as many of the victims' names, so their existence
is not obliterated upon entering the new millennium of hope, deliverance.
Terrorism should never be abetted by idealism, in this world so turbulent.

So, security at all official Washington D.C. buildings was tighter than ever, due to the high terror threat. However, this would never deter our intrepid interlopers, intent on breaking into the National Archives. If manifest meant clear and obvious to the eye or mind this was to be their Manifest Destiny, to liberate their fellow men, from the vale of tears of the right to speak your mind, and defend yourself at all costs, from a government somehow gone bad and out to get you, for it was protection from a government and not one's fellows, that the two Amendments were about, as if the Leviathan was ever out to get you. They were in the throes of strategic planning toward the D-Day landing, the Colonel at his *Schutzstaffel* best, perhaps sensing this could be his last action, Father Time tapping him on the shoulder; the doctor at his level best and sensing that the future interpretation of history was in his precise operating hands. They procured exact copies of the Bill of Rights, upon which Waterson scribbled for hours, composing what the riotous messages would be; he could not get them right, so he kept trying repeatedly all week. Meanwhile, the Colonel was calculating how to get everyone in and out safely, until achieving mission accomplished. Once all the details were decided on, it was only a matter of time until their final orders. The last call made on D-Day was to the Fixer, alias the Yellow Kid, inviting him to the post-event, the next morning; to record such, for posterity, in his own way, with his unique point of view; as per Willi: "Hey Fixer Kid, what good is a First Amendment, when the government never tells the truth, and keeps so much hidden from its citizens? What good is the Second, when self-defense is a product of distorted paranoia? Be at the National Archives tomorrow, at 10:00, to witness the greatest of regime changes in the wicked history of the West. I promise, this will not disappoint. Your First-Born Son of God, Willi." Everything that day would be witnessed by its intended audience, in accordance with Willi's invitation.

The day before, they each received notice to be in Washington D.C. by noon, the next day, the time had come, flying in comfortably, posing as tourists, there to visit the great attractions of the nation's capital. They transferred to the waiting white tour van with the business name Moshe and Samir's Washington D.C. Travel, painted on the doors. Hanging intertwined from the large vehicle's rear-view mirror were an ancient-colored glass bead rosary, with a tin Maronite cross, a thick silver chain with a large Star of David, and due to Islam's restrictions on pictorial representations of God, or the prophet Mohammed, a large, round silver *Ayatul-kursi* pendant with Qur'anic verse, giving our magic mates a brief pause to ponder the mysterious workings of the world. Here they were, newly arrived in the democratic capital of the world, State of Earth: a Hispanic trans-man, presenting as a jaded atheist heretic, and Palestinian trans-woman, presenting as a devout Shi'ite refugee, escaping their own country's religious, social and sexual predations, with the aid of globally organized Christian, Jewish, Muslim gangs, whose portfolio of crime was based upon disruption of the status quo; what could possibly be more out of the ordinary? they wondered, *envisioning a convocation of a unity of the spheres, losing track of their van's constant progress in monotonous, fertile countryside, becoming sleepy from a steady motion, heading downtown.* These were the early allies, brought in for the mission as a liberation army by the Commander, making a cameo appearance with a magic ring to give to Scheherazade, claiming it would help her gain victory: "Rub this ring until the *jinn* appears; it will obey your slightest wish and desire, even as to disappear;" who understood the momentousness of the occasion, its implications for world peace. *El Comandante*, the Goat and the *ayudante companero* soon arrived, Willi and Lilli being released of their obligations to the Phalanges Libanaises, Hezbollah, *coyotes* and Colombian *FART*, as rewards for pulling this off. Next to arrive was Waterson's heshe, *tio Lunaro*, the *Chiricahua Apache* band's mystical *doctor mago magnifico*, who had forgotten more about alleviating maladies, than Waterson ever remembered. Then several founding Sissies, led by Isidora, as crew/ dig chief, expedition investor and organizer, who, in a freshman year, Anthropology major, spring recess field assignment at an unsuspecting reservation, stole the sacred, gritty earthenware and its doomed, spectral denizen, as a foolish prank on a night of peyote laced drunken revelry, without the slightest concern for either the piece's provenance or the inhabitant's say in the matter, packed it up in a specially padded crate, efficiently delivering it back to New Haven, with none of the reverence, solemnity, ceremony warranted by so rare and powerful a relic; bringing its occupant with them, Geronimo's Ghost (G's G), contributing to his people's freedom, even if it was too late for him. Patricia (P) Diddy's father managed to get hold of his nerve, and get on the airplane to the nation's capital, and after that he was as sweet as pie, a comfort, not having seen his daughter in years. His Royal Highness Tenkamenin, Whale's mascot *Asantehene*, as muscular, charismatic, as Alexander the Great, already living in New York City, was there in a heartbeat. On the last flight of the morning, Lucretia Faithful, founder of BTC (Bear Trap Capital), the guru of greed, and master strategist of plans which might save the republic (after all, Isidora's Gypsy blood necessitating vengeance for an assumed, as well as real wrong, there was no splitting hairs on an eye for an eye reply), arrived. Kramer, whose organizational expertise was surely missed, and demise assumed, was hailed in absentia by the Colonel. Willi's desk *sargento*, his *carnal* with the *patrulla* envelopes with double the monthly *mordida* to share with the *quartel*, at Dulles, looking forward to seeing Sayer, repeated, *"ningun pleito con estos cuates."* Generalissimo Goads, who went back to being a plain U.S. Senator, missing the trappings, distinction, of parading as a military man, also a Washington D.C. freeloader, showed up to curry favor with Sayer.

They regrouped at a warehouse, with the sign outside announcing Moshe and Samir's Washington D.C. Cleaning, assembling a little bleary eyed from their early connecting flights. The Colonel was waiting, preparing maps, materiel and tools for each team member, almost a platoon, greeting them in military fashion: "Originally ten of us initiated the discussions, which have led us here. Now I thank all of you who have joined us for so important an operation, essentially the pursuit of word choice disobedience. All of you know what is at stake. Giving up these freedoms will never curtail our faculties of thought and expression, but your chances of getting gunned down by a sociopathic, rageful murderer, are much improved. As for me, my heritage spared me narcissistic, historical assumptions of any entitled rights. I am leading our force on perhaps my last expedition, to try for once, to end on the right side of history. We will penetrate the premises in the set plan, execute our artful grift, and extract ourselves on the next outbound flights tomorrow morning, back to our abodes. Following the stealthiest discipline, we shall utilize the cover of the cleaning company, owned by our friends Moshe and Samir, to gain access to the building at their summer's end, overnight scouring of the facilities, and will have from 23:00, until well after moonlight fades, for our own intentions, which at all costs must be completed by 6:00, before the guards make their morning shift change. Moshe and Samir have been contracted for some time by the federal government, approved by the National Archives, based on their inclusive businesses resonating with the power elite. Uniforms, boots, gloves, for every member of the enterprise, have been prepared, so we fit into the roles we are assuming, as the stormtrooper cleanup regiment for the Bill of Rights." And with that he passed the podium to Moshe and Samir; first Moshe: "By the time we arrive the night guards will have already posted, and some will be getting down to their *siestas*, so no one will notice if we have double the number of our team, considering we shall be combining annual maintenance with a cleanup." Now Samir: "You have each examined detailed written plans of your responsibilities, which will make it easier to keep track of the simultaneous phases of this mission, as I shall now explain..."

Their duties consisted of the opening, closing, moving, dusting, sweeping, wiping, scrubbing, mopping, waxing, polishing, to be expected from a tip top cleaning crew, and before boarding the vans that night, uniforms all spic n span, they each knew their individual task, and how it would contribute to a mutual effort. The purpose was to get the doctor in, to complete his duty, and out, as fast as humanly possible. After intense training, lasting until 18:00, they had three hours to eat, relax, nap, until evening reveille. During a rest period they slept soundly and uncannily appeared in the same dream between themselves:

The *jinn*: As Shaytan *incarnates, al Queda's anti-art campaigns encapsulate destruction of antiquities.*

The Goat: *He easily sacrificed his own, for further acclaim from the rabble, as did Stalin with Trotsky.*

The *ayudante companero*: *A former Connecticut cop was accused of writing the racist letter to himself.*

Tio Lunaro: *Implicit bias is normal to protect all cohesive groups from outsiders. It is called prejudice.*

G's G: *Vigils, tributes, mourning, sympathies, laments: honor all victims in search of higher principles.*

Patricia (P) Diddy's father: *Good old communist that he was, probably pretended to be a working man.*

Lucretia Faithful: *No hopes for them, living their lives of lies, unable to manage the decency required.*

(Kramer): *A watchdog says Ex-Nazis got $20 million of Social Security, living indecent lives in the U.S.*

Willi's desk sargento: *Well, in* Chiapas, *we have been fighting guerrilla warfare, not the gorilla nation.*

Generalissimo Goads: *Now I see the child soldier in Africa as parallel to a child gunman in the ghetto.*

Then a gong was ringing, it was D-day, 21:00. By 22:00, scrubbed and in uniform, they resembled an outfit of feisty individuals suppressing their independence, for a victory of their league in battle. After a final briefing, they filed into the vans, at 23:00, and by 23:30, were pulling up in front of the National Archives, then admitted into the underground parking lot, as was always the case, nothing being in the least, suspicious or amiss. Somnolent guards let them go about their business undisturbed, unpacking their gear of buckets, mops, brooms, brushes, cleaning solvents, floor polishers, rags, going up into the empty, silent floors, spreading out, cleaning as they went, heading to the shadowed dome. The building felt confined, with low ceilings, enclosing walls, until reaching the opening of the rotunda, where there were always security guards, but it was kept so dark at night, to protect the decomposing artifacts, and the guards seemed lost in other thoughts such as the latest sports scores, the roast beef dinner waiting at home for them, there seemed no real impediment to moving forward with the scheme at all speed. The gist of the entire plot had to do with committing the crime, right before the eyes of the guards on duty, with the doctor's activity to be explained if questioned as intense, deep cleaning of the glassed cabinet, but such would never happen, as the guards were sleepy and trusting of the routine they had established over the years with this exemplar multi-cultural company, and would not have believed it if they saw it. Because they were trained to observe, be on the lookout for, certain behavior or physical characteristics they were unprepared for connecting thirty identically uniformed workers with any criminal activity, as they seemed to be legit, even if one of them looked mad at work on something over the Bill of Rights. The gang was fastidious and compelling at their jobs, and, after two hours of buzzing activity, settled to a slow burn of steadiness, until all the guards were finally asleep. Then the doctor got started, pulling out a box, with immense, white eagle feathered quills, bottles of brownish black ink, rag paper, blotters.

The key to this modern-day Ark of the Covenant was provided gladly by one of Isidora's sisters, whose employment at the National Archives was facilitated by advanced degrees from Whale University, and whose devotion to curatorship, library and archival science was fostered by Isidora, and her patronage of the Green Memorial Library, sponsoring the Sisterhood of Grace's Chronicles Studies Grant, simply for the asking, as a numerical code entered on a keypad, by the deft input of Isadora herself. Then the doctor unlocked the moisture-controlled sealed case as if finally opening Fort Knox, only to be initially revolted, gaging at a fetid wafting of decay, mold and musky age emanating from the rotting hide. And those observing, would have seen in that cool, methodical process, a conjurer at his prodigious quest of emancipating not only his people but the entire globe, from the serfdom to wicked beliefs and customs, as whenever he put his devoted mind to something with the outcome insured, he could not be bothered with anything but the chore at hand. Taking up feathered quill amid several old bottles of ink, he chose the prepared, light, brown-black Galli tonic shade, making a couple of trial runs on fresh vellum, before beginning. The silence while he worked in the darkened chamber was unbearable, but it was broken up regularly by other workers performing their janitorial hijinks across the vast, cavernous marble floored reliquary, as they had been instructed to do, polishing and shining everywhere. In no time, it was over. There was soft, silent buffing on selected areas of the priceless parchment, and then a series of defining scratches on the animal skin, some careful blotting, and the final examination: "By Jove, I've done it!" There were only three letters touched up, as could be said; three words altered, two amendments edited, an entire document rescripted, the country's politics and culture forever transformed; perhaps the future radicalized course of history teleologically improved. The doctor gave the folio another thorough scan, locked it up once more in its repository, gathered his quills, bottles, blotter, in scrivener's box, giving a thumbs up sign that he was done, and it was time to scat. But no one else bothered to inspect the work performed, trusting wholly in the message they had unanimously agreed upon, before embarking on the journey, and that the great doctor, having taken on this charge, would enshrine their views for posterity.

Having been transformed in his guise as Great Counterfeiter Supreme, to the calligrapher for humanity, the native shaman, with the flourish of the pen, managed to alter destiny, as no one ever had before, and if the emendations would stand the test of time was not for anyone other than the populace to say. The next day all hell broke loose in life's universal mockery to, "... spread garlands of flowers over the iron chains which weigh men down, snuffing out... the feeling of... original liberty... and make them love their slavery by turning them into what are called civilized people." The wily plot was insurrectionary. The loony left's misplaced humanitarianism was as dangerous to the security of the nation as the raging right's underestimated pugnaciousness. But here both worked together for the progress of the republic. Identified and declared pariahs beyond salvation, upgraded to the ranks of suspect, accused, ostracized, they taunted, clandestinely, that the anarchy of random and planned gun violence, was democracy in a late nihilistic dysfunction. For a while, the civil war managed to out-headline world conflict, then the harm done to the fabric of American political discourse was so great, they became fugitives of the law. As difficult as it was to describe society's reaction to such a *coup d'etat*, it felt like an anarchic stab in the back of historic perversion, enough for all ten to land on the FBI's Ten Most Wanted Fugitives list; then it was not long, until the U.S. Marshals Service came knocking at their doors, rounding them up, from a tip from the Saudi Arabian General Intelligence Presidency, personally sent by the clown prince; as well as the doctor's native DNA on the feather quill, for he had purposely not worn rubber gloves, in a show of final defiance against a desperado culture, that had destroyed his, over centuries of genocide, and he would leave the quill pointing to his stellar work, but also, at them all, through his careless trail; transporting them to the Marine Corps Brig, Quantico, Virginia, where they were kept incommunicado (for Marine veteran P Diddy, to be held at Marine Corps Base Quantico was the greatest of indignities), in an interned state of nothingness termed rendition, by legal double crossers at the Justice Department; meaning they could be secretly transferred from one hell hole of a U.S. black ops site to another at will, along with many, smartly suited Langley, and sly FBI, Ivy Leaguers, hovering nearby to debrief them:

> *This is the way the world ends*
> *This is the way the world ends*
> *This is the way the world ends*
> *Not with a bang but a whimper.* (T.S. Eliot, "The Hollow Men," 1925).

When Thucydides initiated the study of war, in the *History of the Peloponnesian War*, late fifth century BC, he was the first to realize, that states acted as the collective human will of their citizens, reflecting strengths and weaknesses in making decisions, that were sometimes brilliant and at other times insane. Civil war was always connected to an internecine conflict of attrition, the most destructive imaginable, because it relied on tight materiel giving out in siege like situations but never any definition either way, and mass slaughter following battle, as blood lust amongst the Greeks was as brotherly love in the U.S. Today's wars were expressions of past generations' conflicts attempting rectification by the current one, as every war was fought over older slights, recent offenses, that had compounded in actual aggressions. The 2010 war was civil in the sense that it would bring back civility to existence with a new game plan. If anything, the corrections crafted in the unsound original proved for once and for all the true power of the word, as with a slight wiggle of a stylus, letters had done away with guns, in a victory for morality, suggesting that many other social ills could be corrected by slight modifications of their original intent. Back in its crystal vault the revised sheepskin might have gone unnoticed, considering the lettering was small, and visitors usually did not have the time in their quick tours to read it that closely, but for a clue left behind by the duplicitous doctor to immediately alert the staff to the portentous clarifications made. It was not until later that morning that one of the astute guards starting on his inspection rounds noticed a white quill in a case pointing to Amendments I, II; as if having been carelessly or purposely left there by a docent or art restorer; but why would anyone working in the Rotunda for the Charters of Freedom, he wondered, leave a ceremonial quill inside that case. Then upon closer inspection, he thought he saw certain words corrupted from what they had been, upon prior observation yesterday; as he was given to doing daily, being a devoted aficionado of the Charters himself; immediately sounding the alarm heard round the world; a curator with magnifying glass and flashlight, slouching above the bullet proof glass, to get a closer look, asking, "Is this some joke?" incredulously reading aloud, for the first historic time:

> Amendment I: Congress shall fake no law respecting an establishment of religion, or prohibiting the free exercise thereof; or abridging the freedom of speech, or of the press, or the right of the people peaceably to assemble, and to petition the Government for a redress of grievances.
>
> Amendment II: A well regulated Militia, being necessary to the security of a free State, the right of the people to weep and fear Arms, shall not be infringed. (Sanitized Amendments to the Constitution, September 2010)

# 21. In Fitzgerald's Footsteps

I lived at West Egg - the least fashionable of the two...

...it was a factual imitation of some Hotel de Ville in Normandy, with a tower on one side, spanking new under a thin bead of raw ivy, and a marble swimming pool, and more than forty acres of lawn and garden.

My own house was an eyesore, but it was a small eyesore...
(F. Scott Fitzgerald, *The Great Gatsby*, 1925)

Having wept narcissistic tears of grief and self-pity upon realizing they would never be as happy again, long were the days, all too short the nights, spent in suburban splendor on the Gold Coast of Famefield County, that star-crossed summer of retreat from the routines that had given them celebrity and fortune:

"Why, we've touched the sky, as Phaethon, in Helios' radiant chariot, only, we won't release the reins."

"Hold the wheel steady baby, while I cut some blow on the compact mirror, and pass me the bug juice."

In ten years, they'd become household names, having gin-and-fruit-concoctions, alchemical acid, coke, morphine derivatives, at every outing, resulting in bitter public quarrels, prolonged, dizzy slumbers. At their New York *pied-a-terre,* he performed handstands in the hotel lobby, she slid down the banisters, a boiled banshee. Befriended by the top people of their times, there was no door that was closed to them. Our two feted luminaries, a mere 28, had decamped New York City after their planned anniversary was cut short when they were asked to leave the Biltbore. According to the Adam and Eve biographer, "the management suggested that they move on because, 'the continuing hilarity of their presence [was seen] [as] prejudicial to good order and restful nights' for the other guests of the hotel," taking time off, from careers, to enjoy partying in Bestport. Branded as bumpkins by NY they were carefree, childless, given to running around drinking, getting high, sexing up in the car, motoring down the Posh Road to raucous Players Tavern, drug dens, such as the notorious Cedar Crook Café, where ex-cons and parolees scored smack as fast as they could walk in, as well as departed with same sex partners, if that was their desire. Two blocks away was a Karvel ice cream shop where they indulged sweet tooths after wild café nights:

*Did we really see that, was there no hope for certain people? The dog was Kayla, an aggressive attack pit bull kept on an 800 lbs. chain. She was calm during the attack. He was underneath her naked. The woman said, "Get out, you creepy pervert." He said, "We're going to spend the rest of our lives here."*

Taking a rest from the media attention on their sexual orientations, they crafted a manifesto reply to the obnoxious question, whether they had made it big in the business despite or because of their queerness. "Declaration of Independence: No artistic limitations on aesthetic representations of transposed reality, leaving us free to portray anything we believe in, to see it for what it is; meaning, we should be able to wear custom dog suits, becoming the animal in our souls, and that would be within the realm of today's infinite, imaginary possibilities openly available. We shall take ownership of straight roles, as much as queer ones, and would not seek to inhibit anyone else from the same opportunities. We will protest any prohibition of an artist's portrayals due to politically influenced assumptions of favoritism or prejudice, upholding our creative liberty from those who would have it one way or the other in strict compliance."

They leased a dilapidated, 4,400 sq. ft., 1758 Georgian manse, which they would casually refer to, as a cottage, on one acre, at the edge of a greater 170-acre waterfront property (probably once joined to that cottage, sold off in the late 1800s, for encompassing a tidal marsh), a 1900 estate, designed for a more opulent age, when shameful spending was the rule and social mores were upended, challenged, as now. They proceeded to indulge their every sense of riotousness at all hours, in a staid Puritan neighborhood, to the mortification of their neighbors, driving in and out in a loud Corvette as it pleased them, calling a false alarm in to the fire department that was reported to the papers (it was Lilly in a stormy petulance). At Compost Beach they swam between boulder jetties, and 1777 cannons, swigging Stoli screwdrivers on the sly from a plain water jug, avoiding sententious stares from parents with bratty beach camp kids. That was the old Bestport only insiders knew or dreamed of, an artsy Connecticut small town, operated by Yankee then Italian onion farmers; because of its proximity to as also distance from New York City, used as a getaway by famous artists, writers, actors, since the late 1800s, and then the Madison Avenue, Colgate Palmolive and Wall Street crowds; and if Greenitch had more money, Bestport had enough, but was more fun; especially in those days, when you could run into Paul Newman, at the grocery store, at midnight because that's when no one would be out to recognize him; only, some still did, fawning, then going goo-goo eyed, at the check-out: *it's hard to believe, he is so handsome and smiling*; or spot Keith Richards (his family aide, J.D., one of Saugamuck's own), at CVS, so *cognoscenti* claim. Spending an orgiastic summer in Bestport at its baddest, the fabled duo, in their youth, as the Beautiful and Damned, experienced dreams of freedom from the nine to five rat race everyone else had bought into. They had presented notices to the studio, of sabbaticals from their regimens of grueling work for the man, Isidora blowing a gasket with fury, upon hearing the news; but in this case, it was Sayer who talked her down, suggesting that everybody could use a break from their antics, which had only gotten crazier, as of late; besides they could not go anywhere else, as they were contractually tied to the studio for several years. How much of this attitude referenced Sayer's participation at their hotel frolics lately, was neither here nor there, but it would be verified and confirmed, that later that summer Sayer goosed the Great Ratsby at Longsnore, which was what the "Hotel de Ville in Normandy" was rechristened after its remodeling:

> "...and in the eyes of the middle-class exaggeration passes for beauty."
> (Stendhal, *The Charterhouse of Parma*, 1839)

There were midnight swims skinny dipping on glamorous Spendricks Point, near the great estate house, where the Saugamuck River emptied into the Long Island Sound, making the current treacherous at any time, but especially at night, with the moon pulling the tide out to the Cockwenoe Island channel. The water was icy, and *they each had multi orgasms from the swirling undertow*. During the day, they went water skiing along the same tidal river, providing quieter water than the open sound. Lilly was a strong swimmer, and it soothed her back to bathe in salt water, exposed to the healing, drying sun for a certain period each day. There was also the time Lilly was so punch drunk, she jumped naked into the running fountain on the great lawn of the waterside mansion, kneeling, swirling waters scantily covering curvy but chiseled privates, and small almost boyish breasts exposed to the brilliant blood moon light; posing, frolicking, flirting, giggling cutely (*coming handily, from the bubbly, foamy fountain water, flowing up from under her*), for the cameras to observe, applauding her daring-do, as well as cheek, causing quite a stir; producing the sketch of her bare self, in huge champagne goblet, she wanted to use for the cover of a novel about their summer escapades that Willi was writing, *The Ludicrous and Hammed*, to be then prominently, proudly, hung over the mantle of their grand California ranch Pinkton, that would one day display as well, the Black Stone, stolen from The *Kaaba* at Mecca, later their most prized possessions. When the full moon came along, they thought nothing better than running across well-trimmed grounds barefoot, in the buff, streaking in and out of cloud cover, in the sparkly night, their feet frozen from the dew, already gathered for morning. There was a rectangular, blue stucco stable, now hedge fund office, in its time utilized as a house of assignations for weekend guests and business friends of the first owner in the early 1900's; tying up their horses, for the grooms to tend, while getting some special grooming, on the second floor, from girls brought in from New York, just for the purpose; and the bare pair snuck in, *to make riotous love on linoleum floors recently shined* by janitors, then rushing off until mad dawn:

Nothing is difficult in the eyes of a lover. (Marcus Tullius Cicero, 106 – 43 BC)

Once they fought, after Lilly demanded to adopt a child in the coming year, with Willi postponing such, if possible, but after more than their recommended doses of rum and coke, and some generous lines of Colombian marching powder, they began squabbling on the back porch of their decaying colonial, and loud enough to cause a scene for the neighbors, when all of a sudden, Lilly walked off, in the middle of the night: out the driveway, left onto Compost Rd. S., then a quick left down Fairy Ln. E., a right curve, and down to the railroad tracks, bearing left, through the gravel path, crossing the shaking railroad foot bridge, over the Saugamuck river, into the damp, smelly tunnel to the New York side, and waited until dawn for the first train to Manhattan. Willi's love and need for his mate was such that even considering her own desire to be apart, somehow, Willi had the sense about where she would be, following her trail almost instinctually; crossing the rickety railroad bridge, from which on another occasion, after alcohol inspired revelry, dissipated dares, they jumped off into the deep channel; meeting her at a deserted, red Saugamuck station house, then making up and laughing about last night; taking the first train to the city to continue their festivities at the Algonquin Hotel, where writer Dorothy Barker, doyenne of the Sound Table, reported seeing the magic match riding on the roof of a taxi: "They did both look as though they had just stepped out of the sun, their youth was striking. Everyone wanted to meet him," added Barker.

But as famous as they now became, their current desire being to lay low, among Bestport's locals, they succeeded in drifting a bit into the background, permitting another personage to provide the town, and themselves, with the romantic focus upon which to indulge. The imposing abutting estate had recently changed hands, to a buyer new to the area. No one had ever heard of him. He gave no explanations of his origins or past, and made it clear it was not polite to ask. Some said he had been in World War Two, and he certainly looked old enough, with clear green eyes the color of a dinner jacket he often wore that summer. He spoke little to anyone, even at the height, or peak, of one of the swinging parties he gave. As summer sizzled our passionate players reveled in many a rambunctious gathering at the spectacular property next door. Sauntering down the grounds one flower fragranced dusk, they met the new owner. With many a rumor running, Longsnore, with its impressive stone entry gates, and long, oak lined drive through manicured grounds, was now the domain of a person whose past was as dim, eerie, as the early twilight he was partial to, every other morning, directing fast cigarette boats, in and out as clockwork to the private cove and beach, a hundred yards from his side porch. There was a stone lighthouse there, to guide the boats in the darkness, while the stars slowly faded behind a facade as rich and multicolored as the one sported by the old sport himself: Ratsby, who was also known for drawing people to him, only distantly, not wanting to really get to know them, as if unsure how long he would remain; and then to withdraw later, a recluse, never a woman (or other engendered individual) on his arm, to solitary swims in marble pool, hermetic gourmet meals behind drawn curtains, granting shaded (shadowy) interviews:

"Mr. Winks, would you please move a little farther away for the questions? please turn down that light. The 1987 stock market crash was a swindle, despite factors, such as rising rates to protect the USD..."

How much may be said of a subsequent evening's soft scented glow in late season, when moist breezes off the Long Island Sound, as well as the purple sea itself, were at their warmest of the ebbing summer? If Demeter was shortly to renew her sentence of despair, who would have suspected that dreamy night? Whether what happened next was the result of summer madness, no one shall ever know enough to say. There was an outdoor dinner with dancing in the patio, under peeking starlight, with the sharp crashing of constant waves on rocky shore close by, where a few small white cabanas were perched on the sand, anglers only hours from casting for gorging bluefish, and as always, swimsuits, beach togs at the ready. Our romantics were heading for the lighthouse, wading, breathing in the salty, night air, the chords of a jazz band, now in the distance, captivated, as there would always be a beautiful Bestport at its soothing best. At the end of the dock, jutting out into the marina, a solitary figure stood facing the black horizon and the wind, as if the entire weight of fortune were beating down against him. It was Ratsby gazing at a single green light, attired in a braided military tuxedo, from what army or country they could not see. Then joining him woodenly was someone they thought they recognized, but decided it couldn't be the person they believed, confused that he was a full-blooded Indian garbed in cowboy clothes and a beard. Realizing they had never seen Ratsby full faced in the light of day, but only through convenient shades, it would be left for another daytime meeting to identify him; for now, this dark conversation would do:

"Well, hello there, old sports, fancy meeting you all the way out here on the dock while we watched the horizon for any signs of bluefish or bunker; it's their time, so probably any day now." Though he knew the customs, the who's who and lay of the land, there was something about him that did not ring true or was even illegitimate, corrupt, alien, perhaps the heavy, German accent when he pronounced old sports. "Permit me to introduce you to my colleague Chief Mired Wolf-shine, who fixed the 1987 stock market crash by having a team of Whale U. math quants launch program-driven trading, causing public panic. He shall remain vigilant until our associates' rendezvous, via motor launch, later this evening, assisting me with certain warehousing responsibilities. Shall we head back to the bash, leave the chief to work?"

"One thing," said the chief in a bold, uncannily familiar, yet bizarrely distant sounding, ineffable voice: "Never admit to anyone what you may, or may not, have seen here, including myself and the Ratsby;" and they remembered what a townie acquaintance suggested, that they avoid asking probing questions of their quiet, stern host, but go along with his lead, despite there being innuendos of dark antecedents:

> "I own I never greatly liked him. I thought he wanted that Generosity
> of Spirit, which is the sure Foundation of all that is great and noble in
> Human Nature. I saw a Selfishness in him long ago which I despised;
> but it is lately, very lately, that I have found him capable of the basest and
> blackest Designs; for, indeed, I have at last found out, that he hath taken
> an Advantage of the Openness of my own Temper..."
> (Henry Fielding, *The History of Tom Jones, a Foundling*, 1749)

They headed back to the manor and the music, hanging on every word the Ratsby may or may not have spoken that enchanted evening, walking either a bit ahead or behind him but never shoulder to shoulder to catch glimpse of a face that seemed to utter invisibly from the pure, surrounding stillness. Later they realized, along with other *bon vivants,* that Ratsby, liked by everyone, was never truly seen by anyone:

"Why, old sports, so glad you were able to join my little get together. I try for intimate affairs, despite an insane turnout, always regrettable by three o'clock in the morning, and more so as the sun also rises. Please let me apologize for the chief's brusqueness; he merely wishes to protect, those whom he longs for; rather, excuse me, I am too loose with my phrasing, those whom he has not known for long, sorry."

Fond flapper that she had transformed into throughout this crazy summer, it was not beyond dizzy Lilly to push the envelope: "Pardon me, for asking, but how would the chief think he knows us; who is he?"

"A man who has harnessed the powers of nature and science and combined them with his cosmic will."

Wild Willi in spiffy tuxedo, patent leather combat boots, ready to stomp on anyone infringing on their efforts to indulge: "And why do you have a German accent, and own this estate in remotest Bestport?"

"'...April is over, April is over. There are all kinds of love in the world, but never the same love twice.'"

As part of the event's magic, the 400, Nobs and Swells, came, taking time off from busy NY schedules, to show up for their favorite host's glamor fest. Stover at Whale took a break from the Old Brick Row, and the Whale Fence, a standup guy attending his friend's golden gala of legal/ illegal delights, saying: "It's not worth fighting over money, as there will never be enough, and we can't continually bicker, so, sorry, we must make the best of it. I'll sing about $ in the morning, $ in the evening, $ at supper time. But I'll do anything, for that salt of the earth Ratsby, our Sulks and Moans honorary member for life."

Lucy and Ricky Ricardo brought all their comedic wit, his big band signature cut, "Babalu," playing in the background, her slapstick bolder after a couple of stiff ones, loosening up stiff Yankees still bossing Bestport, while the newly joined *Cubanazo/* Redhead duo took the entertained locals by storm. "When our closest confidant Ratsby, sent invitations, we dropped everything and reserved this night for him."

Rep. McNinney, a perennial Bestport favorite, whose emergency at birth, due to a silver spoon stuck in his mouth, blocking his airway, almost suffocating him before his first breath, was the stuff of country club legend, was glad-handing his way to another election sweep, with the blue blazer and preppie crowds. "Rastsby's been there for me, whenever I've asked; I couldn't think of not being here tonight for him."

Stew Lennard Jr. drew attention to himself, with a can-do presence, boisterous appeal, never pausing to make plugs for his family's extraordinary fine food sales empire, where customers, having a taste here and there, were induced into spending largely, gladly. "We catered this festivity for my buddy Ratsby."

Martha Steward, in sophisticated, sexy glory, arrived from her Perky Hill studio, after putting the final touches on her latest, high-end cooking show, *Martha Steward Giving,* which had made her a magazine mogul. "Friend Ratsby, an epicure after my own heart; his lavish soirees a must with the posh crowd."

As with most parties of this nature, there came a time when certain guests grew uninhibited, and traded their garments for enveloping air, one of the nude swimmers fondly, esoterically sporting with Ratsby:

> "He might have been compared to a summer's day, particularly the last
> hours of one..." (John Cheever, "The Swimmer," 1964)

Midnight bonfires were lit to, "turn on, tune in, drop out," with greater ease against a sea of blue fading gray, a band on the open terrace, with its alternating lights capturing the mood of the alternated lives, within a radiant glare, of the shaming culture of politicized America; the whole LGBT transition having been a mass hysteria, as in the tulipomania of the 1600s in Holland, but they refusing to be shamed, or shaming their new ways, for, in paraphrasing Lincoln, as I would not be mocked, so I would not mock; their nightmare, the DSM-5 one day deceitfully redefining LGBT as a mental illness, upon relegating progressive thought back to old Freudianisms, as in, "Why we should reprove Adam and Eve for never confronting mental illness." But that went against the grain of such a nest of affluent liberalism galore.

So how was that overpaid upper-level executive, or Wall Street trader, recruited for the new job? How did the salary negotiation go with HR? Perhaps something like this: "The job is at four million, are you interested?" "Well, I was thinking more around... eight." "So maybe we can pay... five." "Well, I'm thinking seven, my absolute rock bottom." "Six?" "Seven?" "Split the difference?" "Ok." "Welcome aboard for 6.5." "Done," shaking hands, thinking, *sounds OK to me; what a deserved life it is, at last.*

There were also those combining pitiful greed with political incorrectness, both from the right and left. "Most of what I'm wearing comes from sweatshops or slave labor countries and there's nothing anyone can do about it," rattled off the corporate presidential type, to his press baron boss, maybe the air itself. "Perhaps we should produce a white slavery story about a white slaver who gets kidnapped by Saudis."

"I have aversions to shirts from sweatshops, but not my Mike sneakers," said a ruling class type press baron to her president, both invited to add glamour to a freely cavorting, local and metropolitan, mix of celebrities. Later in a moment of drunken levity, if not buffoonery, he goosed the host; a stretch by the practical joking neighbor, from a War Heroes Hill Swiss chalet style mansion, with sweeping views of the Long Island Sound, in obsessively ambitious, suburban Xanadu, Bestport, Connecticut, enchanted East of Eden; Ratsby hilariously replying, in his deep, German accent, "Just like the old days, old sport. Paracelsus' dictum was, '*Alterius non sit qui suus esse potest,*' meaning, 'Let no man belong to another who can belong to himself.'" It was Blessedport, keen hub of keeping up with the Joneses at their best.

Then the fete met the daylight, with only a few stragglers remaining, the preternatural pair reminded of that time they absconded from their Eden at a similar hour, thinking it would be grand to have a dawn swim to wash away the night. By a quirk of fate, they submerged in the water at the small beach just as cigarette boats were rounding the last shoal and channel buoy, so that if the boats were not visible upon each diving under, for about ten seconds, they were already upon them, near shore, once they surfaced. Engulfed by gassy fumes from the motors they gagged and choked, coughing loud enough to give them away to the boats. Once on the sand the pair tried sneaking into the reeds but were detained by the boat crews. Ratsby, the chief at his side, now came down to the beach, to speak in German to the captain of the boats, who demanded to know, who the two trespassers of their rendezvous were. Ratsby spoke up for them, referring to them as old sports, over and over, until he won his listeners' hearts to their side. As the moles left, they witnessed bales of white brick deftly being unloaded by muscled crews, obeying the chief's instructions for their transfer to the onsite warehouses, camouflaged as greenhouses. Ratsby and a *Deutsche* skipper, whose name was Kramer, were discussing the next scheduled drop of cocaine.

"I fear my little beach is getting more and more visitors lately; these two are illegal aliens and will keep their mouths shut, about our secret business; or they will have *La Migra* to contend with, understand?" The dual dupes sullenly nodded, quietly praying, observing as a major caper occurred before their eyes.

"*Herr Kommandant,* our friends in the CIA, FBI, DEA are all cautioning us, to wrap up the operation."

"We need a last drop, with three times the normal delivery, as a final goodbye, to this lazy Longsnore."

"I worry we are pushing our luck, but I will have everything prepared for next week, at the same time."

And before they knew it, the week flew by, and trembling twins wondered what would happen to them. But nothing happened, because by then the Great Ratsby would disappear for the umpteenth time in his covert life. A body soon found off Port Jefferson, NY was identified as his despite its near devourment. A week to the day of their last meeting, Kramer delivered the augmented merchandise, without a hitch. In a celebratory mood, Kramer dismissed his crew, remaining with Ratsby for a bottle of champagne, after which he wanted to go for a swim offshore, where the Long Island Sound stream started. Ratsby humored his drunk companion, indulging his high spirits, climbing aboard his motorboat and powering fifteen minutes into the ocean, arriving at a fateful spot, miles from the mainland, then being surrounded by a vast churn of bluefish, in a feeding frenzy of bunker fish, with the ocean frothing, as far as the eye could see, interrupted here and there, by venturesome seagulls diving down for some scraps. Kramer, for whatever insane, drunken or drugged out reason, thought it would be a good idea to go for a swim with the friendly fishes; not realizing that at that instant, the up to thirty pound bluefish were in swarm mode, where nothing in their way would be left alive; the result being that before Kramer could come up for air, from his deep dive off the boat, he was dead, mangled, and not a pretty sight at that. After a single breaching, like Moby Dick, Kramer disappeared into a swirl of predators, never to be seen again; an apt end, considering his specializing in faster ways to dispose of the bodies already disposed of, the volume of ashes being so vast, it could not be processed; then a fade out of the scene, destiny expired.

A shocked Ratsby waited half an hour at the agitated spot in case Kramer by some miracle survived. In that time, he began to see how this accident or suicide would be his way out of the current episode with a new identity, provided by unfortunate Kramer, who had recruited his former *kommandant* to NATO. As much as Ratsby hated resuming silly spy games, he felt his soul incapable of resisting, so to protect himself, regardless of what was right or wrong, he wore a cutthroat coat against judgement's elements. What can be said of a man who will do anything to survive, or get ahead, even exploiting his old allies, brothers, partners if it means preserving his own existence? Such really is the fall of man that he would sacrifice all he holds dearest and closest for the sake of his own continuance against death, destruction and calamity. Of such stuff was their latest friend, Ratsby (*SS* Colonel Otto Waldemar Grawitz), made. As it must have been for Columbus, no one caring when he returned from a life-changing expedition or passage, it was certainly so for Ratsby, coming back from his earth-shattering voyage of self-discovery. Adopting a dual moniker, the new Kramer operated as the NATO shadow he always was, without them ever seeing there was a different person now portraying Kramer, and so on to the sketchy, dark horizon. But knowing nothing of Ratsby's past, and considering there was no future, only his absence remained to focus upon, and that is what they did, inventing one story after the next about what happened to him. As for the chief, dressed in cowboy duds and false beard, weirdly they never caught on it was their own creator, keeping tabs on them, as he was wont to do from time to time, when it pleased his curious will.

Behind the scenes, Ratsby made sure the body recovered off Port Jeff was identified as himself, first by taking his own boat closer to shore, then into the opening of the Saugamuck River, just past Spendricks Point, and ditching it and swimming ashore to the river side of his immense property, shielded by some thick woods. There was an old splintered dock there and he came ashore just a little upriver of it where the footpath led back to his stables and mansion. As it was still quite early there was no one astir to see him enter, shower, dress, pack, run out a side door, back toward Spendricks Point, on the same footpath through the woods; following the river up for about one mile, heading toward the Fairy Ln. E. access to the railroad bridge trodden by Lilly, in her mad escape; similarly taking the next train to Grand Central, no one having seen him that morning, nor ever again, in his aspect as the Great Ratsby, dead or alive. Sometime around nine in the morning, a passing sailor noticed the rudderless boat drifting out with the tide, and called for police, who promptly responded, dragging the river for an unaccounted for Bestport entrepreneur. Three days later, the body turned up, and by then Ratsby had paid off everyone involved, once again resuming a nefarious life, of missions and favors for the NATO, CIA, FBI, DEA good guys.

After Ratsby's death the magic seemed sucked out of Longsnore, and it took all their composure for the confused, recovering partiers to promenade through the park, wondering if he could be hiding in one of the many work sheds, garages, log cabins, rooming houses for the workers, so spread out was the grand property. There was also a smelly saltwater marsh at the long egress, and they often asked if he could stay out there alone, as the escaped convict does in Dickens' *Great Expectations*. But never seeing him again they were satisfied he was gone for good. As autumn arrived Longsnore's vast lawns turned drab brown, and their once verdant playground became gloomy, with piles of hoary leaves, turbid gray skies. What had been a locale so well dressed and provided for was now a wasted landscape of its lush origin.

They tried having children, but it was impossible to conceive, given their organ alterations. Distracting themselves from melancholy, avoiding any boozing a while, they had road trips in the environs, visiting rarefied Whale University, just up the highway, in New Haven; dropping in at Isidora's Crystal House Museum of the Sisterhood of Grace, to offer their respects to Geronimo's Ghost (G's G), in the womb, in an ancient, cracked, red clay tribal urn, decorated with earth-colored symbols, faded by time and too much handling; as well as the Whale Art Gallery, to view Van Goon's *Night Bistro*, whose questionable provenance, having been acquired by the museum, after being confiscated from a Russian family by the Soviet Union, under duress and dubious circumstances, seemed to hint that, what is wrong intrinsically shall never succeed, since the start of time. But if museums returned what was ill-acquired, they would have nothing, so what was the efficacy in that, as things would be buried and forgotten if not for them?

When the winter came, our finicky team was daunted with splitting wood for the stove, which was too much for them, so by February, they were in the south of France, enjoying the life of sunny, European leisure. By then Willi was compiling notes for a book about a character without a past, present, future, and new adventures would ensue for the magical mavens, amidst the libertine, old-world intelligentsia. On the French Riviera, they finally met their match, in that Lilly's short infatuation with a French rock star led to unintended consequences, as per her suicide attempt, after she and her lover were confronted by Willi; and Willi, similarly distracted by trysts he undertook, at tennis matches, beaches, bungalows, evening dinners, meant the sides were well matched; only his indiscretions had not led to folly attempts at suicide as hers had; as for the frog rock star she hightailed it to her next show before anything heavy. But it was off to a Swiss sanitarium, in the alpine town of Damnos, for the confused starlet, where the treatment for her depression with anxiety, was long periods in high-altitude, open air, bundled up on a couch. Lilly enjoyed the tranquil hours, hating to be interrupted by anyone, even more so by Willi, or a doctor, as was now occurring much to her discomfort and rising anger at all men, but particularly these:

"While the sun shines the sky swirls above me, clouds torment, now a conceited son of radiant Helios."

"Darling, since our pilgrimage to the Magic Mountain a learned doctor believes I should be admitted:"

> A harmful truth is better than a useful lie.
> (Thomas Mann, *The Magic Mountain*, 1924)

Before them was a long braided Native American, dressed in full alpine gear, with boots, crampons and feathered cap, and skin as dark as tree bark against the Alps, neither of them recognizing Dr. Waterson:

"My professional opinion is, you shall both benefit from an extended stay in these invigorating heights, far from distractions of a modern society, corporate obligations, and especially hounding by the press."

There was no resistance from either, as inside each understood they had burned the candle at both ends. In the end what mattered to their maker was that he stays in touch, premeditating they were fine even if surreptitious means were employed; at least he would be sure they had a rest, before going back to their responsibilities, which they inevitably had to do; their future individual and joint victories still waiting. In a blind spell of filial love, they were never able to identify the masterful headshrinker before them.

And what would the doings of a madcap, financially restructured, year bear at the conclusion of a civil war? Perhaps nothing, but they relate to a time when things were less complicated; our, in love, couple could sit back, smell the roses of their triumph for a moment before resuming their high-pressure studio existences again. In their final trek around Ratsby's empty fiefdom, they held hands, as when they first dated, recognizing that sweet times at Longsnore, redolent of summer blossoms, were over. Little did they imagine the immense changes they would each undergo in the following fifteen years: namely, the recovery from their excessive, European entanglements; again more high life success leading to Lilly's disappearance and child kidnappings; further convalescence and a huge coup with *48 Hours to Mecca*; desperate verbal dissolution, marital separation, attempts to kill each other; and an officially sanctioned persecution, resulting in their lashing out against civil society; not a great record, or one to be proud of.

The FBI's Ten Most Wanted Fugitives must have been guilty, as before they knew it, the captured crew was flown to Guantánamo for detention, imprisonment, in a classified denouement of unlawful actions:

> Character gives us qualities, but it is in our actions – what we do – that we
> are happy or the reverse. (Aristotle, *Poetics*, 335 BC)

Aristotle meant character in a noble sense, as an allegory of moral qualities, and it was never truer said, than about our stalwart protagonists in search of deliverance, as each would soon endure a trial by fire; despite being felonious enemies of the state they were still human beings with the finest of sensibilities. It was clear that after any First or Second Amendment challenge, a fourth estate would always be there to present the wrap-up to the public interest, as that which is done for the right reasons never succumbs.

On *Cucker Snarlson Darknight* Texas Senator Ted Snooze, bamboozled *Cubanazo,* was rambling on in his nasally drawl: "If they had only conspired in the insurrection of Congress, it might have worked."

On *Panderson Scooper 180 Degrees* House speaker Nancy Bologna, staunch defender of liberal rights, even if infringing upon those of others: "I pray the government's vendetta will be swift and merciless."

As Liberty's fame was certain infamy to many, those claiming free speech also actively suppressed her, so news channels had nary a hint of them, as under the conventions of their rendition, the government was under no obligation to provide information regarding possible terrorists captured on the battlefield. Despite the media obsession with exposing things to light, having the body kept the soul without flight. It was a random, defensive quirk in our psyches, which gave comfort in blaming someone, anyone, for our ills when things went against us. Suitable scapegoats to betray could always be found near at hand. The justice system went against them, in a secret trial in Gitmo, Cuba. Lilly and her mother finally had their long-awaited reunion, but it was not the kind of *fete* they imagined it would be, both hearing they were at the prison, yet never seeing each other. So, each called out to her blood at Muslim prayer times, achieving poetic justice, while divine intervention was pending, for almighty God alone is a fair judge:

> How devout men are made by suffering! In prosperity the thought of God
> or saint never enters their heads. (Erasmus, "The Shipwreck," 1523)

The *Guantánamo Elegies* would come only later, after tremendous, silent soul searching in lonely cells, poems of serious reflection, usually laments for the dead, here they were of themselves presumed gone. They were interrogated by the CIA, FBI, DEA, NATO good guys; also, the Fixer, alias the Yellow Kid, was there unofficially. Only one stale item was released from a top-secret list for the press: *The United States reiterates its lease of Naval Station Guantánamo Bay is legal, nonnegotiable, and indefinite.* For our heroes *La Migra* finally caught up with them with questions of their immigration status, as they had been under surveillance since their first appearances on the Adam and Eve spectaculars, only there was never enough evidence to prosecute them for illegal entry, as all their documents seemed authentic and scrupulously detailed, and when cross checked, were OK. Unfortunately for DCF, the entire affair was out of their jurisdiction, but they removed all the children, so at the minimum DCF would care for them while this thing worked itself out, one way or another. Maybe the hidden message was that immigrants should take care what they wished for, before coming here blindly, and getting caught up in the arcane points and obsessions pulling at the civic body. They could also get shot to death, before they knew it, for nothing at all, something which perhaps happened where they came from, but without this hateful randomness connoting much more than mental illness, usually the criminal planning of the deed done.

Wars were consistently fought, by generations of citizens who had nothing to do with their old causes, origins, and early strife, those being factors the older generations experienced, in trapping the younger to fight for them. Recalling old liaisons as haunted wars, each running to a heart-breaking conclusion, once in federal custody certain couples within the platoon became nostalgic, if not for one another, then themselves. The material mates were worried they would never see each other again, after trying to kill each other only in recent memory, and were hopeless, if that was what was to be. Willi and Isidora had to be considered as much/ little as Lilly and Sayer, both relationships born more out of opportunism, on each of four parts, than anything else. Of course, Willi's prodigious philandering and Lilly's occasional dalliances were not as important, in the final tally, only mild to imprudent flirtations in moments of ego weakness. This could also be said for Sayer and Isidora's excesses, from time to time, no shame given to them. Then there were the celibate creatures, such as G's G, P, the *jinn*, wondering how they kept it together; the black preacher, Holocaust survivor, seeming anomalies, needing appraisal as an interracial couple; and the doctor, Colonel, Ottoline, who if they thought in such terms, went outside the group for amours. Of course, there may have been other crushes and infatuations, even unrequited loves, holding court among the squad of unlucky prisoners, so emotional wails at prayer, reached into their very cores.

Upon pulling off the caper, they calmly gathered their tools of the trade, got into their vans, and in their usual, cool fashion drove out of the underground parking lot, heading to the warehouse for fast changes of clothes; then were dropped off at the airport for their flights home, to wait for a knock at their doors, which came soon enough, given the doctor's clues, purposely, left behind, in his futile resistance to the way of the world. It was never known, if he was after acclaim for their victory, leaving traces by which to be extolled, or careless, or both. And he was so proud of this work, declaring it amongst his greatest procedures. When the others heard it was because of his inattention, that they were apprehended, it did not upset them in the least, as they recognized they would be sacrificed, to a cannibalizing Constitution. Besides, the Saudi clown prince was crowing to the press, that he had saved American democracy from regime change by traitors, so they understood, his treacherous dealings were also behind their capture, for he had waited years to pounce on them, hovering patiently, until the moment of his fierce pay back.

The Colonel, especially, felt the stab in the back of his former patron, having done identically to him. Then based upon forced confessions, trumped-up charges, their military court martial occurred behind closed doors. Some of the defendants' testimonies indicated clear coercion, as they appeared staged to a jury member; and self-critical in ways that seemed prepared, as often witnessed in Soviet show trials; for this was tyranny of thought, severe politicized repression, worse than any Soviet Gulag, where exile east to Siberia was a start, then whom to approve to your personal/ public space. Totalitarianism here was enforced through a secret, hooded tribunal, without pity driven public sentiment and opinion. But some, demonstrating defiance at their captors, however, legal/ illegal, the military's enforcements were, stated their true beliefs, despite beatings, water boarding, sexual torment, practiced by a righteous CIA. If some seemed fatalistic it was because they had reached the end of the line of naked human depravity. A curious reporter, who got caught up in the business, was also whisked away to the Guantánamo Bay detention camp, operated by the Joint Task Force Guantánamo, of the Southern Command, Department of Defense, deemed outside U.S. legal jurisdiction; "for the most part," going by Geneva Conventions:

> "But I'm not guilty," said K. "there's been a mistake. How is it even
> possible for someone to be guilty? We're all human beings here, one like

the other." "That is true" said the priest "but that is how the guilty speak."
(Franz Kafka, *The Trial*, 1925)

The Fixer, alias the Yellow Kid: "And so the next day, I showed up at the side entrance to the National Archives, having come in on the early bird shuttle, asking security guards if there was any special news I should be covering, noticing the building was not opening on time, and there were Federal Protective Service and metro police active, now that you mention it. One of the guards offered to get me a scoop, if I would only wait, while he proceeded to inquire. But I was duped, as the next thing I knew, several U.S. Park Police were at my sides, and I was immediately escorted to a waiting command post van, full of FBI agents. 'What are you snooping around for? Are you aware of, or part of, any crimes that have occurred? We know you were called by one of the masterminds, and so you know, U.S. Marshals have been rounding up all your loyal acquaintances, from Moshe and Samir's Washington D.C. Cleaning, on warrants for conspiracy to counterfeit the most holy of national icons, sedition and treason against the United States.' The Colonel's insiders at the bureau would be of negligible help this time around, as being on the right side of history often landed good-doers of their ages in concentration camps, even in a twist of ironic fate, former camp *kommandants*. At the brig, I tried bluffing I knew nothing, as my guilt by association would be hard to prove, 'so please let me go,' to which they said, 'Not a chance...' So I was brought here, as were each one of us, individually on a white U.S. Navy Gulfstream private jet guarded by Marine MPs, which seemed overkill, and I had appeared at the National Archives, with an invitation, which was suspicious at first, until I convinced them I was only a reporter, not a promoter in any way, thereupon, being short of able bodied men or women for their jury, I was drafted to the duty. But before I was empaneled to such, I told the prosecutor I was not a joiner and would never vote along with others for a defendant's guilty verdict, even if presented with the most convincing evidence, I am no judge. At the same time, I told a defense attorney, that if a defendant was in the docket, it must be because they were guilty, and as such, I would not vote to acquit in any way. When the lawyers asked in their follow-ups, if my first or second reply should be admitted, I said, 'Yes.' Now I'm on the jury."

Willi: "If it was not for Christianity, we would still be eating each other, apropos of which the Americas were cannibal central in Columbus' time, transmutation, narcissism run amok, metamorphosis outdone. Canada has always been a sort of poor cousin to the United States, so whatever they do does not really matter, but the whole LGBT transition has never been a mass hysteria there, as the witch burnings here. *Transgret*, or transgender regret, the dismay after transitioning, an intent at reversal, was the tragedy of transgenderism, as also any similarities between transgenders and anorexics at willful, self-determined body transformation, and links between transgenderism and Autism Spectrum, as per propaganda. But truly, how many transgender individuals later regret the change? The queer man or woman reveals the great human being in changing my life, as queers are bent on bucking systems, and I embrace that life."

Lilly: "Amazing, the number of adherents willingly sacrificed by extremists, in the name of Islam. The global climate change movement is a new form of colonialism, forcing developing countries, still in the throes of their own historical early stage of industrial and economic catch up, to conform and adhere to First World living standards, but with Third World capabilities. It should be a costly political game, but especially for poor, weaker players. At least here, Sayer will not be allowed to goose everyone at will. But I shall never renounce the lifestyles my mate and I, or anyone else amongst us, may have chosen; once I was no longer the terrorist, trying to destroy, I became conscious of my inner impulse to thrive."

Dr. Henry Waterson: "I don't care about reparations, declarations, apologies. I want this country to be given back to my people. I confess, at school, I did some bad things to our young tribal members that I cannot forget, yet I decry my rape, by invisible hands of college coeds, and compare my humiliation to that of my tribesman, G's G, held in spectral bondage, a bottle imp, for decades, demanding freedom as well as vindication. And to my children, keep faithful to your dreams of making this a greater country; remember, your father was only a man, not the perfect avatar, you convinced yourselves he should be."

John B. Sayer, in his guise as Corporate Executive Supreme, fulfilled thin-lipped, conservative roots: "Diversity indoctrination was social humiliation. Cultural competence as *auto-da-fe*, was an admission of guilt, a self-confession of deeply held, even unconscious, bias, almost a sin or heretical belief, before the final moment of immolation. For communities of color, their group hatred of whites was elemental and undeniable. How can our hyper liberal leaders beat Islamist terrorism, when they don't even call it what it is? Feminists demonstrating for religious tolerance, demanding equal rights for Islam, possibly more freedoms than for other religions, because Christianity was a fatal cause of the Western tradition, despised now by all good progressives, leftists, activists, bringing inequalities to the forefront, making sure that Muslims were welcome in the office, despite the clown prince just returning from his room, where the Grand Duke John C. waited; why did so many atheists go out of their way, to defend Islam?"

Isidora made the following heartfelt speech: "'Woman is the nigger of the world,' the maternal slave. The Constitution was written during a time of bible literalism, when women served as vessels for royal, aristocratic and family alliances, and slavery was condoned as a right of Christians granted redemption, over heathens denied theirs; showing a parallelism between reproductive freedom and slavery, because the only other beings subject to such treatment, over their copulative ambitions, were beasts of burden; then slaves over which men held absolute mastery, and women in a triad of bad behavior, remorselessly controlling their destinies. Women without reproductive rights would be the new slaves of America, in a crass confederacy of backward, literalist readings of a limited Constitution, written by and for another age, when women were secondary. Perhaps the whole document with all its amendments should, 'go to the place where you belong from now on – the dustbin of history!' and this liberation army should have gotten rid of that antiquated sheepskin when we had our chance. Furthermore, that scoundrel, Thomas Jefferson, was no feminist, considering his out of wedlock family with his captive, black slave, as if he couldn't find socially prominent white women he could paw, prey upon, in his alcoholic, lustful rages, and ironically is now represented more by his black descendants at large, than the shamed white ones:"

> The only freedom which deserves the name, is that of pursuing our own
> good in our own way, so long as we do not attempt to deprive others of
> theirs, or impede their efforts to obtain it.
> (John Stuart Mill, *On Liberty*, 1859)

The Rev. Hannibal P. (Pearly) Gates, spurned by his old Carthaginian Black Baptist Church, asked: "To nig, or not to nig, that is the question: because the word, its use, maintains our old sense of bondage by an alien species, not men, who, introducing this epithet, as also shackles, branding, overseas transports, fettered our self-esteem and worth, not only as to generations past and present, but those further still to come; and the irony of borrowing the dehumanizing, demeaning term of derision, which maybe, out of a primal use for self-defense or self-deprecating gag, evolved into a bantering thing, at times humorous, at others scolding, angry, but also rallying, respectful, even affectionate, endearing; each use (abuse) of the word in our ears like the putting on of yokes of servitude round our own willing necks. Reparations are retribution, but they must be summarily enforced after a conflict, while the sacrifices and costs are freshly seared in a victor's mind, and before time erodes compelling pressures for answerable revenge:"

> A heavy account lies against us as a civil society for oppressions committed
> against people who did not injure us, and that if the particular case
> of many individuals were fairly stated, it would appear that there was
> considerable due to them. (John Woolman, Quaker, 1769)

Patricia (P) Diddy, children's soldier of fortune: "In the hierarchy of social victimization feminists take second place to civil rights advocates. Everything takes second place to civil rights advocacy. Liberals and progressives were all in favor of racial integration and ethnic inclusiveness, only never in their own neighborhoods when they were put in play. Race preferences and bias were two sides of the same coin. Free range could be a euphemism for home schooling, as in free-range, home-schooled children. Free range children were also little waifs abandoned by their parents, wandering the barrenness of a perverse counterculture upbringing. Then the sting of unqualified rejection flushed my face with new emotion, that of not fitting in, even if I were perfect for the job, the unmitigated denial of some basic, elemental right to progress on equal terms with everyone else. It was not long after, I was summarily walked out of the office, in a humiliating and inglorious end to a proud career, realizing, that was the end of that."

Ms. Yael Abraham: "In the van going to the job that night, my sleeves rolled up, the Colonel espied my tattooed number, and asked to inspect my arm closer, seeing immediately it was 169062, almost having an apoplexy, right there and then; and he would not stop staring at me for the longest period, leading to a profound change, not only in our relationship, but also that with Ottoline, my newly found half-sister. For to my knowledge, I was a foundling rescued by Spanish nuns, but really banished from Spain, part of a late war, fascist ethnic diaspora. As Jews were not defined a minority, we were asked if we wanted equal representation, along with other minorities, or to simply lord it over them? Yes, we emphasized. As the Charters of Freedom were written by slaveholders, they were flawed in their origins, and those whose origin is misguided, shall never be corrected. As Thomas Jefferson was the misogynistic abuser of women placed in his tutelage as the slave master, his Declaration was a hypocritical pile of manure.

*SS* Colonel Otto Waldemar Grawitz, who led the initial, primary and only, assault in the civil war, said: "The definition of war crime is a movable feast, depending upon who does it, and especially who wins the war. To the victor not only belongs the spoils, but also a primacy of defining the moment in history. Why is it only a few people who lead all others to war, if allowed to? when you behave like a scoundrel you get scourged. Anyone claiming racial purity should understand that their own heritage is also some movable feast, perhaps wishful thinking, subjected to dilutions by past indiscretions. Usually, it takes a racist to label another the same. Just as the very sanctimonious are often the most prurient, so those on highest alert for racism (ready to take offense) are usually rampant racists themselves; the first to level such accusations, obsessed by color grades; then let it be me owning it who throws down the gauntlet:"

> Culture, which is born of life, ends up killing it.
> (Andre Gide, *The Immoralist,* 1902)

Ottoline, the Soviet Gulag refugee joining the group because she was tired of the country's drift, spoke: "True diversity should be measured by variance of opinion, not by physical differences, as if superficial features accounted for identity. Identity gets nurtured by education more than gender, ethnicity or race. It's intellectual chauvinism, if not fascism, for political interest groups to suppress or boycott new ideas that are contrary to theirs, as with a Democratic Congressional Black Caucus, and Tea Bagger patriots. America did the right thing in voting for a black president, trying ultimately to atone for its own, cruel, mistaken and corrupt past; but the country was, nonetheless, still exposed to what was fully renounced among committed activists, its endemic, inescapable racism; this internally wired, latent tendency, the evil instinct of a mean dog still requiring a sound thrashing, in order to be rooted out, suppressed, then ultimately eliminated, in populations. How would all such blame and anger end, only in our despair?"

Their final judgement fell upon them like an avalanche of lies, constructed from the truth, but distorted: "Your signed confessions, with the CCTV footage, and the testimony of the security guards present that night provide us with more than enough evidence to keep you here for good; this court finds you guilty, as charged, and sentences you to time concurrent, with the lease of the base from the Republic of Cuba. This outcome provides equal treatment to all parties involved, as there are rightists and leftists between you, all tried with the same disregard for the individual reasons, for perpetrating your acts in common. As a final admonishment, we only hope you suffer greatly for your inglorious crimes, but more, for the ways certain ones amongst you have decided to conduct their lives. Yours is not gender equality, it is a gender delusion. You are a man," motioning to Lilly. "You do not have a womb, so you are male; it is not gender equality, because you don't equal a woman," and other hurtful slander. "You are a woman," motioning to Willi. "You do not have a penis, so you are female; it is not gender equality, because you don't equal a man," with other ad hominem attacks. The choicest diatribe was for Waterson, for being responsible for the "scientific quackery" which created them, and then for P Diddy over her "very open gender confusion." The press lords got their earful from the court, over playing both sides for the sake of revenues. The preacher and Holocaust survivor did not escape reproach, for stoking horrid, jingoist, anti-immigrant sentiments. The Colonel, not surprisingly, got breaks from unseen NATO pals, but was reprimanded for the rogue undertaking of his traitorous action against the United States, his erstwhile spymaster. Not even Ottoline was left out of the court's wrath, for ignoring a journalistic obligation to remain impartial in the heat of the moment and report, not participate. These cruel, uncalled for, verbal harangues again convinced them that all great enterprises founded on evil principles cannot but fail, in terms of Guantánamo. They were also aware that that which begins badly can never end well, in terms of themselves, their sentences under this Court of Star Chamber, and any further chances for appeal in such a totalitarian nation, the worst abomination since creation. But was it too late for their salvation?

The scuttlebutt had it that the most legendary prisoner ever held at Gitmo, was Whale graduate, Nathan Hale, from Coventry, Connecticut, who was discovered behind enemy lines, on an intelligence mission, in midtown Manhattan. From the accounts of many eyewitnesses, summarily sentenced, demonstrating the greatest dignity on his way to the gallows, his composed actions in the face of death made him the university mascot, and national symbol of liberty from oppression. There would even be a stoic statue of him, cast in immortal bronze, erected on the Mold Campus. With limited fraternizing of the inmates, Gitmo knew only afterward that their hero, Hale, was secretly hanged at dawn, Sept. 22, quoted saying: "I only regret that I have but one life to lose for my country;" giving great solace to Whalies ever since, that in death, as in life, Hale embodied the service values that were the best of the school, and America. His death struck such a chord within the tight prison community, that every flag at Gitmo was lowered to half-staff in a strange enemy homage to the bravery and true nobility demonstrated by Hale in death:

> But let judgement run down as waters, and righteousness as a mighty
> stream. (Amos 5:24, KJV)

A mighty stream had carried everyone in its path, to the present off-limits shores, surely shark infested, with each of them recalling, the bits and pieces of their lives, when there was still sense enough for all to dream the rubrics of free men, with futures. For our prima donnas, their remembrances of moments of release that summer in Bestport, CT, walking in Fitzgerald's footsteps, if only for a season, would be reason enough to continue surviving in this hell hole of a U.S. black ops site, given they were declared disappeared. Ironically, hardly aware there were tourists sunning at luxury resorts, a few miles distant, they often imagined strolling along the beach at Longsnore, each long day fading into another, holding hands silently as the sun rose over the Long Island Sound. Those were their days of loving, as brief but everlasting, as a waking revery, that seemed more real than life in sleep, but was barely reconfigured by day. Morning reveille was a wake-up call to a daily nightmare of Army MPs in all facets of their lives, and when things got too much to bear, they could always go back to that special time and place, where they first captured the essence of passions beyond themselves, riding on the coattails of heaven's stars.

## 22. Transfiguration

> Me miserable! Which way shall I fly Infinite wrath and infinite despair?
> Which way I fly is Hell, myself am Hell...
> (John Milton, *Paradise Lost*, 1667)

So, it was time for the wrap-up. I felt bitterly betrayed by life, to be a guest at Guantánamo, when I did not have anything to do, with whatever it is they thought I did. It was one thing to be a prisoner if there was slim hope of getting out, but my stay here looked terminal; I would have done anything to facilitate an exit; presuming I already had, going along, despite higher principles, with a kangaroo court, to leap over justice; not signed up for this, as my editor egged me on for scoops, Willi lured me to D.C. scenes. Mine would be a denouement of despair, with the final objective, to get Slay Magazine the story before Pimple.com did; even if lying in the fetal position, I still knew I had responsibilities to my profession. There was a part of me that also wanted to return to Bestport, CT in all its summer glory, for I had soon become a resident of said town, after my early forays to John B. Sayer's, for his July 4th live fireworks extravaganzas; and upon my shadowy interview with the Great Ratsby that wild August when all he did was rattle off statistics about the 1987 stock market crash, my initial pilgrimage to the stunning country club Longsnore, observing directly his spectacular layout, in such a modish village of social distinction. What got me was the egress through the marsh, turning right onto Compost Rd. S., past the War Heroes statue, heading toward Compost Beach, making a right, following the marsh back again to the impressionistic boat marina, full of sunlight gleaming off the salt stung water, where berths are parts of inheritances; finally, around the beach, past those 1777 cannons between boulder jetties, surrounded by parked sailboats, wires clanking in the wind, and beach goers, summer or winter. I was mesmerized by the town. So, I was looking forward to returning there ASAP. But I was fated, as far as I could fathom, to a negligible chance of walking out of here alive; was I ever meant to be an award whining journalist anyway? So much for my sinking career. But I had to leave a summary of the action and how it relates to me as narrator, and a need to compile a book of living legends ten critical years after the millennium. Because things were supposed to have changed by then, at the turn of that great thousand years, which really extends, with every day we awake, to another thousand-year span, commencing at every sunrise. People's understanding and acceptance of alternative expressions should have improved by then, but to no surprise had not, and perhaps a new period of hardening appraisals and outcomes was commencing. So as this internment demonstrated, any hope which our creator should have granted to us, was stalled. As a kid, I always rooted for the underdog; I wanted the Viet Cong to win. It was the same when I read *Paradise Lost*; I was on Satan's side. I was now rooting for my abducted platoon, as underdog champs:

> Until the day when God shall deign to reveal the future to man, all human
> wisdom is summed up in these two words, - Wait and hope.
> (Alexandre Dumas, *The Count of Monte Cristo*, 1844)

One day a junior U.S. Navy attorney came to visit me, dressed in a starched, white uniform, in line with his reputation as a Whale and Hoarvard educated force-feeder, first mentioning the obvious in my case:

> The difference between treason and patriotism is only a matter of dates.
> (Dumas, *The Count of Monte Cristo*)

"You did not show up at the National Archives until after the crime was committed, so you could never have been an accessory; why, it's so obvious I'm surprised no one else has bothered to notice. It should never have been done, this rendition of yours. And this leaves the government in an awkward position.

We are required to release you, humbly needing your cooperation, collusion, acceptance, of a situation, or just plain promising us not to say a word about your illegal captivity in this tropical, penal paradise."

My elegy appears with the others from Guantánamo, because I languished there for two months before I was released, after promising not to reveal any of the murky dealings of our government's black ops. So I was transported back individually on a white U.S. Navy Gulfstream private jet, again guarded by Marine MPs, which seemed overkill, to a quiet tarmac of Dover Air Force Base, with no glaring lights, as close to the National Archives, where my nightmare had begun, as the military thought was feasible, continuing to Bestport, then a mad dash to New Haven, for unlimited Pepe's, Libby's, Mamoun's. And as I pledged to disclose nary a word as the condition for being set free from Guantánamo, well, it's near Christmas, and I have been writing furiously to get it done; mainly so I can be liberated from the forced penance of reporting, which has become all-consuming, to the exclusion of all worldly activities; while ironically it will still be difficult, to unbind myself of a life's fulfillment, to chronicle while I could, and depart my own pages, saying goodbye to these characters no longer in search of an author, for I would proudly claim them as mine. I thought this was going to be my story, but suddenly these personages, in living animation, have taken it over, becoming mythic when metamorphosed to the focused, exuberant ways of literary personae. Regardless, I have put my soul into this opus and have nothing more to give:

"How did I escape? With difficulty. How did I plan this moment?
With pleasure." (Dumas, *The Count of Monte Cristo*)

I must be some sort of internal chatterbox, because I could not keep from churning these words pouring out of me, and if my tale is a caricature, or cartoon, that's OK, as we're a culture of excess that will not stop for a moment, an extremist society in transformation. I wanted it to be a heroic, suspense, political farce: this is a work of the imagination, of unleashed subconscious, perhaps time for journalism to take a back seat to real writing. If I had nothing to say until a bit older, I needed to politely observe before speaking to not sound out of turn, as Hermes' winged sandals and helmet were at arm's length from me. This began when I was eight, on a visit to the Prado Museum, in Madrid, viewing Hieronymus Bosch's *The Garden of Earthly Delights* in dreamy wonder which stays with me to this day, perhaps a harbinger of our shared ends as curious students predestined to read the myths, so I would one day write my own; my aim to make them as real as can be, so readers see, "a description of physical phenomenon," as I do. How will I ever know if I am ranting, raving, uttering, kvetching? Who will tell me to my face? For as a poet and person, I cared about mankind without necessarily being kind to all men, an abysmal failure, I understand. A lot has happened since my last attempts at self-reflection, accountability, despite once calling this overspun *oeuvre*, light romance. If I've teased the telling, up till now, I shall try to be more expeditious in proceeding. Still, you may ask yourself why such a baby boomer is so obsessed with the millennium, considering he antedates it by almost fifty years. I say it is for that very reason, that I was born to see the cusp of one era transitioning to the next, bringing the past to the discussion, for since no one knows the future, all we have is the past to guide us, on a blind quest through the ages still to come. This is my quest for immortality, to create something that will outlast me, perhaps even be relevant to those of the future, as Caesar Augustus vainly decreed by deification, and William Faulkner stated with such distinction in his Nobel Prize speech, for the eternal reflects, "The palm at the end of the mind..."

As I have always been keen to pen a wild and crazy caper, I only humbly hope I am succeeding, even if there is perhaps, a bit too much science fiction getting in the way, because where does sci-fi end and fantasy start? And if pure invention is my goal flights of fancy are doomed to fail; they are too far from reality. Maybe my plot had too much levity, in its initial, comedic form, but I thought I started devising a tragedy, of our origins and growth onto the continents of earth, and then banishment from the garden; the only way of dealing with such tragic circumstances, being to mock them in derision and amusement or at least, the eccentric individuals who made them happen. The Roman satires of Petronius, Juvenal, were the echoes in their speeches, and mine, for abusing abusers was always fair game, in all recorded history. The left erroneously believed mockery and comedy would do the trick, but so far, the eloquent firebrand leader was missing. Would hyperbole have worked against Hitler when a bullet was needed? Or cartoons of a bullet-riddled Frenchman, with the caption, "They have guns. Screw them. We have champagne." Clearly, this would be everyone's swan song, each demanding to be heard, begging that I provide them with their venues to vent; tired of listening to then parroting my rhetoric, thinking it was about time for their versions to come into light. If my take seemed allegorical, well it was, and thanks for the complement. Of course, protagonists have broader meanings than themselves. Otherwise, mine would never be a saga of valiant aspirations, worthy of its recitation. To be an epic poet I must learn to sing as did *the Iliad's* sightless Homer, cosmic mind, all seeing eye, and blind John Milton dictating his *Paradise Lost* to his two daughter amanuenses. I wanted to capture the inside history of an age, so that those succeeding would know what truly happened; additionally, was the need for self-expression, only now there were huge differences, in intent, creation and execution, some people writing books, others spewing off on Fritter. This effort was never about ego or prideful glory but the challenge of putting an idea to order, for all time. I knew that even if I wanted to be closer to others, I could not get near them, for my own, short temper, so with each passing day I felt more distant from the flow of people, society, the economy, unable to find enthusiasm to partake of any scheme, to fit into any one's company. It was either I was incapable, couldn't or wouldn't. Were those traits reactions to my confinement, or in me?

But getting back to not honoring such conditions of secrecy, that is another reason for my fake name, so the U.S. government doesn't know who or where I am, considering I claim no protection from them by means of sanitized Amendments I & II to the Constitution, to send the thugs to get me back to Cuba; or a bunch of crazy, armed psychopaths, of either extreme, don't go to my house in the middle of the night to kill me. Because if there's a sucker born every minute, assassins are born every second. Such a deep alias was more in the tradition of pseudonyms employed by the already anonymous Moll Flanders and Continental Op, so no one would ever penetrate their utter defenses. Challenging my guise as Author Supreme, over my *nom de plume*, I always quipped, that at least it was not a *nom de guerre*. Then I am forced to explain that sadly, this alias keeps the hellhounds off me, helping me avoid dissipation, rather, distractions to the text itself, if anyone ever bothers to read this book. But what does it matter? This is me; my expose has never exceeded the limits of self-promotion; an expression of a dream of what once was, seemed or could have been. My pseudonym was also due to all my recent anti-voting rhetoric, as the news is constantly buzzing, with polls about what everybody thinks. Well, this book is about what I think. Please do not be overly worried or excited, it is not being written by a National Socialist (Nazi) or socialist of any kind for that matter, thank you very much, or sorry to disappoint. I am not extremist. I bear no remorse for any of my writings, or screeds, as they may be referred to, whether the intent with which they are written is what accusers label as, according to the cheap phrase, pornographic: "written for the purpose of exploiting obscenity." I wanted to have my ageless melody played for itself, with no confusion about who sang it or why; it was not for the sake of vanity, notoriety, someone to blame. The work is simply out there, on its own; I didn't need the hassles of somebody not liking it and threatening me; and perhaps the main reason for anonymity is if this endeavor bombs, no one will know who I am. This is a similar sentiment for my reason to not vote; in case my candidate loses I won't have to suffer shame, as being incognito is my safety net for failure. And I invented different creative pseudonyms to distance myself, avoid sure chagrin that would come from the crumbling of a guise as Famous Author, when or if failure of my attempt was realized. It's been a Herculean labor akin to those of the monks at Lindisfarne, rescuing culture, the Western tradition, in their spare time, as more than voices in the dark, ephemeral, online outliers streaming the World Wide Web. Vladimir Nabokov reported that *Lolita* was so real he was once presumed to be the middle-aged narrator, the lustful, mild mannered and murderous

Humbert Humbert, and he struggled to disabuse a rude reader of his hatred. I want everyone to know I lived fully, as T. (Tiddly) Awdry Winks, author extraordinaire, poet chronicler for the ages, historian of the seen and unseen; imprisoned along with my autonomous creations in the tragedy of the platoon, the missing or absent, Hannibal's forever eight-year-old brother; with further distress, realizing three of the illegally incarcerated at Gitmo were my flesh and blood. But please do not confuse me with the author.

So many writers, actors, artists, musicians, had pen names included in the famous quotes throughout; it was impossible to really know who was who, or what was what, and the farfetched feats each claimed. As historians use excerpts and references to give evidence to their arguments, so I have used them here, to buttress mine, assisting, certifying, validating my outside thinking, combining this epoch with theirs. Proven thoughts provided direction, by recalling what other much greater authors said about the state of things before they were forgotten. It was not about what they said, but how they said it, in the metered music of expert minstrels; besides, it was surely erudite to cite those whose facility for transcendental expression, far surpassed mine; who were masters at their trade, not mere, part-time trippers and askers:

> Trippers and askers surround me,
> People I meet, the effect upon me of my early life or the ward and city I
> live in, or the nation,
> The latest dates, discoveries, inventions, societies, authors old and new,
> My dinner, dress, associates, looks, compliments, dues,
> The real or fancied indifference of some man or woman I love,
> The sickness of one of my folks or of myself, or ill-doing or loss or lack of
> money, or depressions or exaltations,
> Battles, the horrors of fratricidal war, the fever of doubtful news,
> the fitful events;
> These come to me days and nights and go from me again,
> But they are not the Me myself.
> (Walt Whitman, *Leaves of Grass*, "Song of Myself," 1892)

Another reason for original sources was to share with readers what influenced me, for a time or season, excerpts buzzing in my head while I fabricated my own account, as they were surely part of it all along. Additionally, ideas of famous writers served the purpose of bringing the pause of reflection to the party, perhaps to the piece itself, a moment when great notions outside the narrative were free to remark on it, perhaps inspiring me to stay on the right track despite doubts and keep to my equivocal manner, and to demonstrate to newspeak cynics that words proclaimed a thousand years ago still have relevance today. I considered suppressing the more traditional (old fashioned) literary custom of addressing mankind as male, as if it were all such; also, all personal pronouns in grammar, due to a potential for falling in the fatal trap of distinctions; and replacing them with a distinct standard pronoun and acronym: "sp;" then decided against this, as being beyond controversial, cumbersome, awkward and antithetical to poetics:

> [By-ends] "...had always the Luck to jump in my judgment with the
> present Way of the Times, whatever it was..." (John Bunyan, *The Pilgrim's
> Progress from This World, to That Which Is to Come*, 1678)

I was always slated for some great achievement, at least many had thought so, but being indifferent to a career, I failed in everything. My expectations were the same as everybody else's, only heightened by a sense of doom. People always expected a lot from me. But we all do as much as we can, and when we can't do it anymore, it's no one's fault. After five years my psychologist said I had paranoia, but I could have told him that myself to start, and saved us both from a lot of trouble, for all the hard work we did.

The shameless sloganeering and pathetic pandering of the press was infuriating; my random anger over the order of things deep seated; I could not seem to shake it off or find the control needed to get ahead. There was no peace. My counselor cautioned against my digressions in blaming the now caged couple. Why they chose me to participate in this farce, I will never really know. But later it came out that they wanted their tale told sympathetically, by someone who would not judge them too harshly, and keep the lid on the macabre ideation of having their funeral ashes molded into frisbees and flung into the ocean. Besides, I had plenty of skeletons in my family's closet, that made me the perfect tool for their secrecy. I was made in Andean heights, a Hermes given to sudden flights; I acknowledge humans are destroying the planet, and it worries me (not at all). OK, so I admit I'm a bigoted and a racist degenerate, but how far off from cold misanthropy? Anytime you feel like educating me, I will tell you to go f*** yourself. I see hell. Otherwise, how could I have written of my characters with such urgency and righteousness? As I was not to the manor born to be a mover and shaker of men, and worldly events, I decided I would at least observe and in my own fashion describe what I saw; and if it seems I am taking too long to spin this yarn, I can always suggest a CliffsNotes version in the future; in the final, dramatic tally there were creeps masquerading as comics, to the misfortune of the truly comedic, so I assumed a comic identity. Even in youth, despite my cynical, defiant attitude, I managed to have enough moral sense to know that I could not afford to be identified as a Nazi. My father fixed it with his U.S. Army pals, so I got invited to West Point; I declined, for not wanting to become a war criminal, or felon, as war itself was a crime. I love America; I love the chaos and brashness of vulgarians more than the soulless, dispassionate order espoused by dreamy social advocates. Dialectically, the only figure I ever tolerated posing in front of a flag was George C. Scott, as Patton. I would never have put up with a cocky T.R., and his braggadocio. Those willing to die for their country are free to do so, and those preferring life are likewise indulged in their belief. Society's obligatory respect for war veterans provides a lot of bluster for patriotic wrap the flag round themselves, types looking to grab headlines in quests for cultural approbation. Nevertheless, why should we all blindly and slavishly idolize those who have fought our wars? It's a sacred duty, say many who have served and done so. But is it? should it be? There is no draft, so no one must serve in today's armed forces anymore; it's only out of a self-imposed, old fashioned, personal duty toward our country, and a supposed, sacred military past, that patriotic youths do so at all. Stop saying they serve for my sake, it's a lie. They do it for their own sakes, because they want to. No one cares either way, if they sacrifice themselves, not even Uncle Sam, so why am I feeling guilty on their accounts, who want to fight our enemies and risk their lives and health doing so? For myself I see no problem in coexisting with our enemies; activists want to change this world, intellectuals to rail against it, artists to express it.

Released from Gitmo on Thanksgiving, I returned to a world angry at rulers and leaders. Word spread of Nathan Hale's September extrajudicial execution. This country felt abused by the out of control lie, elsewhere labeled patriotism, but really jingoism, hubris, in the extreme, like the Roman Empire before its ordained fall; bragging to all, it was the greatest place on earth, drawing people to its sacred shores, because of its respect for freedom to express yourself, as you want, and liberty from oppression; Hale's clandestine, sordid death taken as a patriotic loss by the nation, and a personal affront by an alma mater, where he was revered. Many of the more politically active students wasted no time in organizing angry comrades to action. When I visited our alma mater in the grateful capacity of released POW I observed firsthand, the preparations for defending against the full-scale assaults they foresaw, based on adopting the sanitized Bill of Rights, as *modus operandi* of a romantically inspired and named, Hale's Civil War. As the Colonel once astutely stated, giving up these freedoms will never curtail our faculties of thought and expression, but your chances of getting gunned down by a sociopathic, rageful murderer, are much improved. But perhaps the Colonel erred, as to his latter assertion, because this Ivy League school was being threatened by trolls and militants, accusing it of secessionist antipathies against the republic. But even vulnerable populations, when cornered, rise to bite like rabid rats; and when justice is sidelined, a society of concerned individuals should serve it cold; I supported upheavals for their anarchic qualities. In the final siege battle of its kind in the history of the United States, Whale University's defense of the barricades of Liberty was akin to the revolutions of 1848, with students protecting their final freedoms: humanistic choices corresponding to life goals of innate hope and artistic expression in a stable society:

> Let the ruling classes tremble at a Communistic revolution... proletarians have nothing to lose but their chains. They have a world to win.

> Workingmen of all countries unite!
> (Karl Marx and Friedrich Engels, *The Communist Manifesto*, 1848)

In that same visit, after inspecting the university's underground tunnel system's latest war footings, as a friendly observer, I came across Isidora and Sayer's sorry, lizard faced cronies, on the Crossed Campus, smoke ridden from the impromptu bonfires, burning overturned vehicles, having now succeeded where they failed before in pushing both out of the way to gain control of Warren Bros. Inc. In Hale's name, I requested they provide all assistance they could to our Whale schoolmates, held at Guantánamo, Cuba, they at first dismissing any hint of their betrayal, then taking responsibility for such dastardly behavior. I addressed Donny Craft, descendant of statesmen, Town Crier, ready wannabe, and Junior Camper, the best backslapper of them all, along with a hired muscle guest, Gary Meiser of greediest stomping fame: "Fancy meeting you boys, during such times. I thought you might be less interested in the latest ideas, though I know you studied them at school, between Econ 110, and Sulks and Moans, then forgot them. In memory of Nathan Hale, our stoic school sacrifice, surely there is something you gentlemen can do."

Said Donny: "Tiddlywinks, don't confuse us, with this rabble taking over the school. And who do they think they are, upending everything from the way we have it? No, we're here as alumni fellows of the Whale Corporation, to assess the continuation of Isidora Green's trusteeship under such dark and sordid circumstances. She and John Sayer seem to have fallen off the face of the earth, but surely not Gitmo. We managed to keep the company afloat making money, now we'll do similarly for our rioting school."

Now Town Crier: "Normally I would be in favor of self-expression and political rights, but this seems a bit beyond what I'm comfortable with. I'm interested in being the center of attention, and this behavior is detrimental to my sense of self-importance. Liberals lack leaders, so I have decided to take on a self-proclaimed mantle of the movement, toward a future run at the presidency. However, barricades in the streets are much further than I am willing to go, and this is all detrimental to my hedge fund interests."

Then Camper: "And if you are asking us to get involved with inappropriate bankrolling of illegal, or in the least way underground, activities, on behalf of anyone, you have the wrong party." Now with a big Cheshire Cat grin: "But, old buddy, anything else we can do for you, let us know and we will be glad to help. We are nominating Donny as senior trustee, considering the university has not heard from Isidora since Labor Day. But you don't believe she's mixed up in any of this Bill of Rights business, do you?"

As for me, I could only think, *here today, gone tomorrow,* as they walked through the ramparts to what would be the last meeting of the Whale Corporation, until external threats were neutralized, barricades were removed, and classes began once again. Yet to receive the *Elegies,* I had little news about Isidora; and in the few remaining weeks of the year, I wanted to stir up as much trouble, mayhem, on behalf of the captured platoon, as possible, without being so obvious about it, that I would be sent back to Gitmo. "If you don't like working here, you can just leave." Those were the famous last words of nasty bosses, that great American flourish, in the tradition of, "take it or leave it," the invisible hand, and all that rot. I remembered the time my superiors singled me out, for a *fait accompli*, of firing the entire international advertising department, all their trusted and long tenured subordinates, whom they themselves were too cowardly to let go. And because I was young and wanted to please the owners I did as I was told, firing ten workers, souls I did not really know, who had wives, husbands, children, parents to support, so that giving them the ax goodbye, I estimated, would probably bring misfortune to more than thirty people, perhaps involving suicides. And I hated my bosses for their cravenness, and for having sloughed off an unpleasant duty, on one so new as myself, and hated capitalism because it shirked off the responsibility for bad acts on an anonymous entity. But struggling to progress, I had no choice but to comply with the wishes of the silver spoon crowd upstairs in their quiet carpeted offices. But now I would make it up to myself, and any poor souls I disturbed along the way, by helping the platoon get out safely from Gitmo.

Remembering that my *camera obscura* allowed the perfect amount of light through its pinhole aperture to create the essence of the form, against a darkened screen, illusory in its two dimensionality, I thought it would be nifty to filter out all the irrelevant cacophony in my ears, dizzying perspectives in my sight. As in Plato's allegory of the cave, we live in the world of shadows, confusing our minds from the true nature of things or their forms, that lie just beyond perception, in the world of thought or abstract ideas. And it was in these esoteric heights, that truth, justice, the good, were recognized, idealized, leading the way forward out of darkness, beginning the rational Western tradition, as an alternative, to superstition, the *deus ex machina* of faith-based salvation, or good deeds (good from God), as the means to heaven, and a world view of subscribing blindly to precedents of ancient spells, miracles and ancestor worship:

> Those who wish to seek out the cause of miracles and to understand the
> things of nature as philosophers, and not to stare at them in astonishment
> like fools, are soon considered heretical and impious, and proclaimed
> as such by those whom the mob adores as the interpreters of nature and
> the gods. For these men know that, once ignorance is put aside, that
> wonderment would be taken away, which is the only means by which their
> authority is preserved. (Baruch de Spinoza, *Ethics*, 1674)

For Spinoza, God was not a patriarchal, anthropomorphized myth, as He had been held to be since time immemorial, and which was the version holding back women and minorities, but rather, as with the Big Bang idea of modern eras, an infinite substance, force, of unlimited attributes, eternal and self-causing:

> Einstein's answer to a New York rabbi clears things up a bit. The rabbi
> cabled him in 1929 to ask him if he believed in God. Einstein replied,
> "I believe in Spinoza's God, who reveals himself in the orderly harmony of
> what exists, not in a God who concerns himself with the fates and actions
> of human beings." (Lawrence Klepp, *The Weekly Standard*, "Spinoza's
> God," January 23, 2012)

Spinoza was the first thinker to separate man's free will completely from God's causality or influence, setting man on his own course of humanistic destiny, fostered from the Renaissance, a heretical idea at a time when not admitting God, into every facet of one's life, was deemed atheism. His skillful critique of religion, and the bible, caused him social ostracism, ill health and early death, and placed him in the company of future iconoclastic thinkers, who perhaps distinguished God, from an overarching religion:

> Religion is the sigh of the oppressed creature, the heart of a heartless
> world, and the soul of soulless conditions. It is the opium of the people.
> (Karl Marx, *Contribution to the Critique of Hegel's Philosophy of Right*,
> 1843 – 44)

I would take Spinoza one better, however, start where he did, with the bible. At Whale my comparative religion professor stressed that scripture is not literature, history, philosophy, theology, etc., but the true word of God known through revelation, a unique category all to itself, but still a printed bound volume. So, my first bone of contention would be that the bible was only a tittle, written by men who happened to be saints, but still men. I went back to the moment I was enlisted, into such a wondrous undertaking. Willi promised I was to witness the greatest of regime changes in the wicked history of the West. Such a modification would still only be concessionary, to the true changes that would come by improvements of the bible, the fundamental guide of the Western tradition. As important as this manual was to man's spiritual and civil discourses, it was time to lay it aside; to include it in the library among other classics; as part of the great ideas of the world, it would always hold its place, but never again as the only book. I next went head on, against the concept of Jesus' divinity, because Jesus Christ was only a man, as you or I are, not a god; that was only a man-made myth. Lastly, I made it clear that a gun is a sure means to death or hell. But is abortion mentioned, either in the bible, or in the Constitution of the United States? Because it seemed to be the one case where the original intent by its Signers, was nowhere to be found; could it be even then they knew better than to get mixed up in women's business, as some today forget?

Christmas Eve witnessed my fascination with the Gutenberg Bible, at Whale University, at the Society of Grace's Crystal House Museum for the Ages. Flashback: U.S. land grab, Naval Station Guantánamo Bay, for which there exists only a warped treaty, of a despotic, scientifically aggressive, Protestant, no nonsense nation, over a chronically inbred empire at the end of its tethers, for which transubstantiation was certainly in the, if you believe it, you will see it, realm of magic, as with most observant Catholics. The gospels, now the most published revelations in the world, were ironically keeping this world inert. Archaeologists unearthed two 300-year-old skeletons of a woman and child, underneath Whelps Hall, Whale Chapel's curator of the historic Mold Campus announced. How would our future archaeologists identify the current crop of transgender skeletons? Perhaps genetics would solve the issues of identity. Now rumor flew that Nathan Hale was a trans man/ woman, and as a student, Whale tried outing him; frankly, how Whale University could have anything to do with black ops at Gitmo, given a humongous funding by the U.S. government and allies, for nuclear, chemical, biological, research, is beyond me.

Christmas morning passed in a blur, but I was headed toward my destiny, in midtown Manhattan, at St. Patrick's Cathedral's holiday Mass, my final stop in a black magic crusade of the pagan winter solstice. My object was to desperately heckle, abuse, the homily by the Bishop of New York, so that I should be pontificating on Jesus Christ, our Lord and Savior, being only a man, the bible, the Holiest of Books, only a book, and a firearm, a means of defense, a sure way to Hell, at the same time, the true *episcopus* would be sermonizing the opposite. Strangely, I began feeling a sharp itch on my wrists and ankles, as if my skin was bursting. Now the time had come for me to denounce the old teachings, sterile doctrines holding us back. As I stood up to speak the itch became unbearable, with no amount of scratching done to assuage it. So rather than continue to stand in my pew, in the last possible row of the immense stone structure, I sat back down, and listened to the devout wisdom of a eunuch holy father, nails to my skin. He made it sound as if the church had always been there for the poor and the downtrodden, when really religion was invented by the aristocratic classes, to keep the population at bay. That was why in France the clergy was the First Estate, before the nobles and commoners. And it was because life was a vale of tears that the people in this cathedral, including me, made believe God, Jesus, the bible, the Torah, the Qur'an, were as real as faith allowed, to survive the coming dark days. The more I absorbed the words of our divine natures, basking in Jesus' love, despite no parochial affiliation, the more I exuded radiant, holy stigmata on my extremities. As the Mass glowed, in sublime goodness, I had no sense of wounds, suddenly, being stricken, by four holes bored clean through my joints; I will show them to you, for the asking. It hurt, but not as much as I expected, given the transfiguration occurring to me, for I distantly saw myself bleed in rivers, onto the marble floor of the cathedral, four lesions providing a new lesson:

"But Francis said nothing of this to the Brothers, but hid his hands, and he could not put the soles of his feet to the earth any more... and then they understood that he bore the image and likeness of our Lord Jesus Christ the Crucified..." (Johannes Jorgensen, *St. Francis of Assisi*, 1955)

And the lesson is don't promise any more than you can deliver, whether as a child, parent, grandparent, or the writer of this story. If I used stigmata to make a point, that I had doubts about my doubts, so be it. It was kept quite hushed up by the local parish, as they did not want any specious publicity about a modern-day miracle occurring to an out-of-town pilgrim, during their Christmas service. Within a few days the divine spots upon my appendages were healed, but their scars, physical and psychic, remained. Could they have been psychosomatic expressions of some repressed Freudian urges, or perhaps Jungian symbols? But I never promised anyone I was an atheist, or even an agnostic, in fact, maybe the opposite. Regarding omniscience, my first-person narrator questions God, but also believes in Him, presenting in certain chapters, sublime scribbles from a fitful state, my stigmata only occurring, because I believed. So, there you have it, after all the searching and questioning, over destiny and fortune in history, at the turn of the millennium, it was still about the wonder of a life, that forever held its own magic and love.

One of the gravest faults or shortcomings of the Internet was the error of superficial knowledge, where someone saw a summary paragraph on a subject, and the next thing they were an expert, with as much insight as a meticulously trained specialist. This was the lame layman at work, sadly a majority online. There were platitudes, pious remarks from the peanut gallery, as those flaunting virtue usually have the most to hide. I had a dream of surviving on a lifeboat, and casting my enemies overboard, one by one. As an off the record follow-up aside, on the whereabouts of the Grand Duke John C., of the Knights of Freemisogyny, he was last observed serving his term as an oriental courtesan, in one of the Saudi clown prince's harems, as recompense for the loss of their alchemist, that is, if they have not yet boiled him in oil, claiming indispensable gold in the unlimited use of his organs. For there were rumors flying out of deepest Saudi, of dark, sinister plots undertaken against foreigners and their subjects alike. He was that fatal exponent, bastard Scottish child, of the Enlightenment, forever bound to the Saudi prince's harem. Certain countries, such as the Kingdom of Saudi Arabia, absolute monarchy with nomadic desert roots, had gone from feudalism directly to modern capitalism. As such, their development leapfrogged other intermediate stages of politics; however, such a weakness of not having experienced democracy, meant that they were not ready for the modern age, and the egalitarian concepts which had been foisted upon them, rather than developing naturally. Human rights and justice were Western notions, alien to theirs.

The problem with guns was you could never predict when someone would use them for an evil reason. Sorry to say, gun control never kept anyone from killing anyone else, so gun control did not work, and as they kept making guns nonstop, absence of any restraint meant there were good reasons to have one. Weapons were dastardly, yet in sum, reflected the perverse culminating ingenuity, and cunning, of man. Within the realm of death and destruction, firearms held special distinction of historic evil; but perhaps it was not only, easy access to guns, as in the U.S., that caused fatal aggression; because any implement would do, in undertaking man's innate craving to kill, as evidenced by the latest, Swedish school sword massacre. Granted, when the weapon of choice is a Glock semiautomatic pistol, the number of victims increases exponentially, as in the Norwegian island killing some years ago. But interestingly, these two cases from the most progressive and programmed of European countries belie the presumption that it is only an American phenomenon. Mental illness, derangement and psychosis unleash what is criminally growling within. The instinct to attack and receive pleasure in eliminating other human beings crosses cultures, populations, societies, just as the passions of love, and an urge to procreate, are given to us all.

Here is the grim reality: when I acquire a gun it will not be to defend myself but rather, to kill someone. Taking up arms was a mortal sin, meaning you were planning to kill someone. The stand your ground law was a defense of cowards, but despairingly, could answers lie in more guns, not less? let's go back. The racist, misogynist, anti-abortion, states' rights descendants of the traitors of 1861 were now the gun toting KKK, Po' Boys, Oath Sleepers, cutting deadly swaths through the heart of an evangelical nation. It was a provable assumption, that most of the remaining slaveholder blood in the country, devolved to white men with guns, Republican Party, NRA ranks, in the underdeveloped south, Midwest, Northwest. The virtues exemplified by good guys, with guns, will never outweigh the evils done by bad guys, with guns. Considering recent carnage, though irrefutably grim to behold, with harm done usually one way, only bold souls would bravely, if not foolishly, stand up to a murderous blight upon our lives of merit:

> I have always had more dread of a pen, a bottle of ink, and a sheet of paper
> than of a sword or pistol. (Dumas, *The Count of Monte Cristo*) *

Maybe we need to shun those who keep and bear Arms instead of applauding their Second Amendment privileges. Perhaps, a persecution of gun aficionados, for their anti-social stances, was a big possibility. Do any of us anticipate that he will end up with the short end of the stick with the rest palmed by allies? Little did Thomas Jefferson know that one of his ancient, redheaded Briton ancestors was immolated in a pyre of sacrificial cleansing, not for her own crimes, for she was unblemished still, but for those of a coward, who paid money to have her kidnapped from a neighboring tribe, as the alternate to serve in his stead; bound up within an immense effigy of a man, made of dried wicker, with spacious limbs and torso, along with other human beings, as well as livestock, pigs, goats, sheep, cows, who had earned the wrath of their fellows; blamed conspiratorially for collective crimes, with common curses transferred to them, set fire to, in an atonement of evil sins upon the community; so Jefferson was lucky to be here:

> Others [Druids] have figures of vast size, the limbs of which formed of
> osiers they fill with living men, which being set on fire, the men perish
> enveloped in the flames. They consider that the oblation of such as have
> been taken in theft, or in robbery, or any other offense, is more acceptable
> to the immortal gods; but when a supply of that class is wanting, they have
> recourse to the oblation of even the innocent. (C. Julius Caesar, *Caesar's
> Gallic War*, 58 BC, translated by W. A. McDevitte, W. S. Bohn)

A gun happy heartland, rural minority, was in a civil war with an unarmed coastal elite, urban majority. Identity politics was a precursor to racist politics, even though presented as polar, ideological opposites, for each system sought to look, label, classify, and divide, according to type, order, and ranking. Each side's critique of the other's extremist vanguard was spot on, for each was ugly, contemptible and vile, the weaker party always accusing of excessive partisanship while the stronger portrayed bipartisanship. The calming effects of older people prevented younger ones from spinning off the face of this earth, in their enthusiasm. One party can't govern, the other one won't, the losing party deserving to lose, due to its inept mismanagement. Such is crony democracy, political rallies just shy of mob anarchy, personal partisans at their worst. The inept left and spiteful right, what else remains to hate? Let's kill them all:

> He had, I think, a Slough of Despond in his mind, a Slough that he
> carry'd every where with him... (Bunyan, *The Pilgrim's Progress*)

Politicians always claimed what they were doing was for future generations; that was a lie because they were really doing it for themselves. They ask for us all to sacrifice for the crimes of a few, as excessive altruism of libs vs. the spiraling cynicism of cons. People who ride motorcycles shouldn't throw stones. As I would not be sanctioned, I would never sanction others; besides, sanctions are tantamount to war.

Because not everybody agrees with the United States, and what if they sanctimoniously sanctioned us? Growing up during the Vietnam war, I observed firsthand the utterly mendacious nature of our leaders and government, because everything politicians do is dismal, nothing good, which is exactly why I do not vote. The biggest influence of the Vietnam war was my complete antagonism toward authority, as I didn't believe anybody, or anything, in positions of authority, and would not comprehend that they had anything pertinent to contribute. A modern, spiritual agenda was now weirdly part of the old, Scottish Knights of Freemisogyny, promoting fake fellowship. The left enjoyed relativism, while the right held to absolutism, the good-doers vs. the do-nothings. I am not a Republican, nor a Democrat, I am simply American. Having primal nut allergies, I'm allergic to Democrats/ Republicans; two sides of the same, corrupt coin, that's why I hate both. Andrew Carnegie had one thing right: books, who has them, who reads them, who needs them. This would be the best philanthropy. These days of cancel culture people (politicians, leaders, presidents) accuse others of what they unconsciously fear about themselves. This is the hypocrisy of leadership. I have been apolitical since I was six years old, and American television ran the John F. Kennedy state funeral until I had almost memorized its sad pomp and glory of backward boots and all. Was it related to the Diem assassination, an eye for an eye? tit for tat? JFK, that animal, was he possibly assassinated in revenge for sex with mafia dames or girls? More likely, in revenge for the Bay of Pigs. Two, four, six, eight, who do we assassinate? An Irish American sex addict, OK? The Western tradition seemed reduced to Spanish greed, British bullying, French intrigue, Dutch wiles (the Dutch now on the verge of extinction), how could I not side with natives, when these rascals invaded?

When politicians screwed up, which they inevitably did, I was happy to say I never go for any of them. After casting fruitless ballots, I decided to never vote for anyone born with a silver spoon in his mouth, almost suffocating before his first breath; the single man worthy of my ballot being the one refusing to run, out of integrity; speaking of which, it should be required that journalists never be allowed to elect, if only to avoid becoming invested, co-opted, ruined for selling out their souls in the follies that follow. I decided never to nominate, when all the ballots I cast turned into errors, each side getting odious and arrogant once in power. In polling I donated more of myself than in love making I gave of my passion. I would not decide for someone to rule me, rejecting being ruled, the more you screamed in my ear, the less I listened. How could we pick, when the government never told the truth, and kept so much hidden from its own citizens? Without real data and information, choice was no better than cheers at a football game, in the passion of the moment. We are no better than fumbling, blind men, when expected to poll. I was much too cynical to be a patriot or ever endorse. Because historians see time and world events as one big period of repeated mistakes, and misdirection, while only poets are willing to point a way to the rescue. Perhaps some paranoia was healthy for historians and poets, causing them suspicion, unlocking mysteries from the past while seeking truth. What are you, animal, vegetable or mineral? I thought the Roman Circus was many years ago. We voted against what we did not like as much as for what we did.

> Rules for voting between the poles
> 1. Don't vote for billionaires
> 2. Socialists or communists
> 3. Inheritors
> 4. Self-made men/ women
> 5. Religious Right
> 6. Civil rights activists
> 7. Veterans
> 8. Antiwar activists

History demands an accounting of evil hypocrisies, foisted upon mortals by preponderous personages.

The Hypocritical Oath (Ode to Righteousness)

To do our best to be:

Billionaire visionaries touting environmentally rich products, espousing as a social duty the sacrifice of many to save our planet, sharing priceless, musky insight while withholding overstuffed bank accounts.

Newsmen headlining politically correct morality plays, filling in the blanks with didactic scenarios, set to educate young, yearning masses, sharing innuendo, very cunning, dainty bits, but not accurate bites.

Politicos leaning whichever way the wind blows, kissing babies, declaiming partisanship defeated, and promising miracles for a vote, providing the least required for a photo op, yet not enough to save them.

Popes beatifying saints, even unto these modern times, using Saint Peter's keys to open pearly gates to the deserving, also in securing Vatican vaults, but not from fallen cassocked night creeps on the prowl.

Evangelicals in a Puritan limbo, revealing hacked up truths, even back to Caesars, unveiling blemishes on the bodies of those on midnight rambles with insane Nero, dolled up for groping citizens on the sly.

Activists holding everyone accountable, demanding reparations, explaining away their bigotry, racism, as innocent bias, not institutional, as with Caucasian, inherited privilege, thus preempting all apologies.

Philanthropist progressives peddling influence as their duty, cheering for Everyman, desperate in his ignorance, for improvements he deserves as a human being, because it's really all about progressing up.

Militarists secure in their last refuge, boldly rejecting encroaching enemies, urging all to join the sacred fight to preserve institutions, and a suspect, corrupt way of life, never sending their own to wicked war.

Good-doers not tiring of setting an example to the rest, running on and on, about what's right and noble, and our enlightened duty in the interest of the most possible innocents, if someone loaded foots the bill.

Counselors ecstatic on alternative views, enabling self-love, unraveling fragile mysteries of millennia, through dualist dances, frenzied and ironic, perhaps revealing their own disfunction as cryptic shrinks.

*Medicins* steeped in the lurid madness of life's subtle elixir, probing and poking offered flesh and spirit, to no end, in the ritual called science for lack of better understanding, a cold shoulder to God as needed.

Myself hooked on abstract contemplation of the stars beyond, desiring desperately to hold universality, poems, songs and stories, within my soul, and never let them go, letting people here and now slide by.

It is I who bring life to the book I read, not the other way around, awakening it from a slumber, turning pages one by one until its final thought is in me, perhaps appreciating my opening its covers, extending its priceless wonder when shared, as if it had its own bigger life beyond its author, the reader, me, itself. Right now, unless the correct established percentages of minorities read this book I will be accused of a racist plot. Then again, if I wrote a book that catered to racial subdivisions wouldn't I be equally racist? Such is the quandary of affirmative action. Better yet, to write it for me, despite what anyone says, for I have already sacrificed any overly ornate, flowery, descriptive language, for that of a realist's critique; not for its own sake, but that of the plot and character development; ready choice for the historian/ poet, during a time when phone/ camera/ video has engendered an era of self-righteous tattletale vigilantism.

I know strangers find my fascination with human sacrifice and anthropophagy to be morbid, grotesque, but for clarity, at least I was up front about it, as that which originates in duplicity can never be heeded. Sacrifice ruined the playing field, taking advantage of man's cruelty to other human beings, for the sake of bloodthirsty deity or idol. But it was evil men running the show, who were the bloodthirsty tyrants. The Aztecs sacrificed up to 80,400 victims at the dedication of their great *Templo Mayor*, to honor their gods of war *Huitzilopochtli,* and rain *Tlaloc*: the result being a loss of legitimacy for a waning dynasty. Loyalties to dated handbooks had caused the downfalls of several cultures, serving as an admonition to the United States, if anyone would bother to notice, as in instances of Jews and the Torah, Christians and the bible, and Muslims and the Qur'an. In these cases, the obdurate, blind obedience to such texts, caused closed minded thinking, and expressions contrary to updated intellectual development. Perhaps the Charters of Freedom should be included in this list in which slavish obedience leads to adherence to out of date ideas, for following innately prejudiced beliefs of the 1700s, flawed Age of Enlightenment. Literalism of the KJV and U.S. Constitution, arguably beneficial for having provided moral principles, stalwartness and obedience to early settlers, were what now held this country back in a new millennium of modernity, with a final sprint to the beckoning stars. As an anarchist, but not a nihilist, I see a future on the tumbled present, rising alongside an *aurora borealis*, guiding to new beginnings after a blackout. As the distant, slowly waning stars are to us, so our own, vital, ever blazing sun might be to another sky gazer, equally casual, across this universe, our worth, relevance, but a mere speck in his distracted eye.

During the Mexican Revolution, the *corrido* derived largely from the romance, and in its most popular form, consisted of a salutation to the audience, the prologue to the story, the story itself, the moral, and farewell from the singer, lamenting injustice, as unless there is truth that which follows cannot be good. Well, Christmas is gone, and New Year's awaits; I have just gotten a rough parcel smuggled over, with the *Guantánamo Elegies,* in which each character hints at what it meant to them, an existential retailing of a persona's action; the *ineluctable modality of the visible* behind infernal concentration camp wires. As they had no First Amendment rights, or Second Amendment claims with which to protect them, they cautiously scribed their individual contributions, sneaking them out with the camp laundry to the main base, then through the hands of friendly, anonymous, trans/ queer loyalists defying armed forces hatred. Willi made sure I got them, despite losing respect for me, that I had to vote along with the others for a defendant's guilt, presented with the most overwhelming evidence, as everybody's high judge. Maybe, it was incongruous for me to celebrate freedom, while the platoon still languished in a black hole, but I was delivered to Bestport, CT, used as a getaway by famous artists, writers, actors since the late 1800s; and if Greenitch had big money, Bestport had a lot, but was more fun; a wrap-up of my tale had come. I want readers to know, I will never rest until I have secured the downed platoon's liberty from Gitmo. Well, there you have it, the culmination of a dream for self-expression, wishing I could do it over again, but glad not to relive events for one page longer than it would take to rewrite the past, even to a poetic mind of man, reaching far back to our origins, our earliest thought. Though Aristotle defined a twenty-four-hour period to encompass tragedy, I would hardly be bound by his dictums; one of the few cases in which I go against my betters and apologize. I (attempted) (succeeded) to bridge two millennia into a volume, perhaps another following. For now, I would keep alert, trusting, "human wisdom is summed up in these two words, - Wait and hope," taking time saying what I wanted, and how I wanted to say it:

> Then I saw in my dream, That Christian was as in a muse a while.
> (Bunyan, *The Pilgrim's Progress*)

\*Footnote

Well said. (Author)

## 23. Guantánamo Elegies

## Willi

Everything can be taken from a man but one thing: the last of the human freedoms – to choose one's attitude in any given set of circumstances, to choose one's own way.
(Victor E. Frankl, *Man's Search for Meaning*, 1946 [Austrian psychiatrist, philosopher, humanitarian, Holocaust survivor, 1905 – 1997])

After crisply uniformed MPs came for the Yellow Kid one day, we never saw him again, but thought he had been released, as he had only been brought here because of a technicality, a last phone call I made to him on D-Day, thinking, *he didn't deserve that, did he*? Ottoline got a message to each of us, that we should put down our personal, meaningful, jarring thoughts, as epistles delivered to the liberated Fixer; I replied I would pull in a last favor with *El Comandante,* to utilize antagonized, queer, gender bending minority guards, workers, throughout the prison and naval base, to get the *Guantánamo Elegies* to him. Having no First Amendment, or Second Amendment with which to protect it, we cautiously scribed our individual contributions, sneaking them out with the prison laundry to the main base, in the swift hands of anonymous, transgender/ intersex loyalists defying armed forces bigotry. I made sure he got them, despite losing respect for him, for joining with others in a unanimous vote to convict his co-defendants.

Renditioned

As each essential day erodes to dust,
I curse my birth, the earth, the universe,
As also God, who causes all to us.
And brings me pain and hate, enough to burst,
Scream at the sky, while in my cell alone,
Jump up and down, my knees cut to the bone.
I know exactly why we're here, but still,
Don't want to swallow any bitter pill.

How could the forces of society
Not recognize the saints before their eyes,
Abducted here by sneaky FBI?
The warrant's claim, an empty travesty.
The jackass military made the leap,
And here we're kept, half dead, without a peep.

Geneva Conventions

There's no escape in memories for now,
As my reality is very sad,
At best, a *Pilgrim's Progress* of a slough,
That gets inside my angry brain so bad.
How could an enemy have sunk this low,
To use restraints upon such carefree foe,
When all I wanted was to give him grief?
Perhaps to kill him in his sleep, relief.

"And but for all the army-navy hate,
I'd stand a chance to have another date,
With justice, in a court of law," I cried.
*Detainment for no cause, I won't abide.*
I'll never care about their rules, if I
Am not allowed to live beyond this lie.

Constitutional Convention

The hour had finally come to shape our view,
Of what the future held in store for us.
Perhaps an inkling of a dance for two,
Heard while the music changed, without a fuss,
To something great, kept far above our fates,
A resonance of fine ideals of life,
Where all can grow, and thrive, with darling mates,
Without the fear to bring on sudden flights.

So, let's agree to come together, have
A go at humming bars anew, in time
To renegotiate the stunted rhyme,
And reinterpret social contracts, half
A day ahead of conflicts, as our worth
Depended on a new, light phrase of mirth.

First and Last

They said, I'm born to lead. It's been that way
For my entire life; forever first
To come or go, it must be destiny.
I know there'll be a time we'll play, then stray,
Or bound across the universe, well versed
In chasing truth, to source the best in me.
I would not dare to come or go, without
Assurance of a day when we could doubt.

To follow prompts upon the stage of life,
To take direction for a place to be,
Without the latest, endless string of strife,
Exhibiting the truest shade of me,
Accepting punishment, I'd realize
It's meant to be, while I'm (at least) alive.

*Si, tenian cojones los españoles, hombres sin honor y mujeres sin pudor. En esos tiempos tan antiguos, todos recien nacidos, el deseo supero a nuestra bondad, porque en el Nuevo Mundo todo valio un Peru, como dicen poetas, quienes vinieron después de las conquistas y el desafio moral causado por ellas...* If Adam was the earth and Eve the sky, we deserved better from bad behavior than rough imprisonment in a rotten, tropical garden of America, known as a number, with inmate sprawl causing animal brawls.

# 24. Guantánamo Elegies

## Lilly

...the best of all possible worlds...
(Gottfried Leibniz, *Theodicee* [*Essais de Theodicee sur la bonte de Dieu, la liberte de l'homme et l'origine du mal*], 1710)

But how could such horrible things exist in secret? Wasn't God, or anybody, watching over this world? Critics out there ridiculed my pasted-on smile, as false and studied, and said I must have spent many a long hour training myself how to achieve such a tight, toothy grimace of dissimulation upon command; Narcissus' story may have derived from an ancient Greek superstition that it was unlucky, even fatal, to see one's own reflection. That is why Willi pressed so hard for a soul mate, to avoid self-glory. Even if this would be no casual affair, blossoming into our stoic *doppelganger* love, things were far from rosy, as during one moment of strife my creepy husband intentionally misgendered me following my historic participation in the transnational Transgender Universe Competition, which I won hands down. Being orphaned ourselves, we recalled that Vivaldi filled the souls of orphaned convent chamber performers, with sublime musicianship. If the time of our creation coincided with a Jewish Rosh Hashanah, fall of man, original sin, we were not to blame for charges brought against us by a critical creator, for our bad behavior; my inclination within a New World order, to become, "A Saint abroad, and a Devil at home."

Road to Paradise (Hollywood salute to Bing Crosby, Bob Hope, Dorothy Lamour)

In another imaginary, prehistoric scene of competition over land, natural resources and of course, women, concocted by Thorstein Veblen, the theft of young females, to improve a gene pool, was an accepted fact of life for ancients and descendants.

The raw experience of North African Muslims (to France and Europe inspiring "*le grand remplacement*," "the great replacement" theory, the self-pitying ideology of racial comeuppance from humiliated vestigial racists to help explain to themselves

the browning of France/ Europe/ America), brothers to the stateless Palestinians of wandering fame, translated to my solitary ramblings, with a madness upon me that night, when for whatever reason I escaped into the *cerros*, pretending not to know

where my children were; because I kidnapped them myself in ultimate perversion, full of self-aggrandizing horror, tumult, self-hatred, which in the end, went against the best of all possible worlds to my own demise, bitter defeat amongst the crowd.

I never returned the black Stone, stolen from the *Kaaba,* at Mecca, later our most prized possession, displayed prominently, proudly, above the mantle of our grand California ranch, Pinkton; which also hung, from Longsnore times, the drawing of

me naked, in a huge champagne goblet, I wanted to insert for the cover of a grand novel of our summer escapades Willi had completed, *The Ludicrous and Hammed.* I know I was susceptible to evil influences, but perhaps I was also a dark menace,

myself, adding to my own, as well as my husband's, strife. And since I do not see him all that often, in this concentration camp of misbegotten dreams of liberty and trust, please let him know that despite all his craziness I miss him so badly it hurts.

My greatest crime was tricking that old Egyptian, aristocratic sybarite, into paying me excessive rewards, keeping him on the hook as TJ, while masking I was a boy. In those days, carnal seekers went to great lengths, to satisfy their lusts, while still

insisting they were straight. That whole series of events started the direct chain of causality, to my being here now at this time, this place, far from any actualizations of our beings, as timeless essences beyond direction or destruction from any other.

For all my adventures with Willi I never imagined this would be our common fate, to have our futures erased by an overreaching government hell bent on keeping up the past at present, in an overarching imprisonment of destinies, souls and bodies.

And even when he tried to kill me, I never took it seriously, as it was never in his blood, but the MPs' blood is dry and rancid, like the rusty jungle dirt of our corral, and we're no more than penned up fatted calves, with memories of lives outside.

What was so important, for my ego's sake, was that I would match Willi's itty-bitty, witty verse, as well as having undertaken an entire cinematic reality, presenting transgenders as mythic heroes, rather than two dimensional cartoons, and since I had given up so much for him, I really needed to best him at this.

Trade-Offs

Our hearts knew love, cohabiting, in chase
Of fame and fortune fast, despite your case,
Philandering from left to right, and in
Between commercial breaks, that's what the *jinn*
Shared more than once with me, to goad my shame.
And yet, despite behavior much to blame,
I've let it slide, roll off my back, it stings.
I'll swallow poisoned pride to hide your flings.

Once more to dreams of wealth: *from lives so poor,*
*We trained for movie studio stardom; such*
*Success, we had, now here we're* Limbo *bound.*
No paradise for us, until we've found
The last remaining, sacred truths, so much
Ado about our naked selves, our cores.

Tragically, I never carried out my newfound resolve to get to work right away on the brand-new script, following the thread to rescue my mother, the only woman in my life, still imprisoned in Guantánamo; entitled *48 Horas a Guantánamo,* perhaps based on our prior feature's success, with Willi as coauthor, and starring in the Hispanic hero role, as the local Cuban agent who gives his life to get my mother out. Indeed, such fluidity between the real and the imagined worlds would become a hallmark of our work. If assimilation was a traditional premise of immigration, dangerously, now the object would seem to be continued, aggressive differentiation, considering, these grotesque incarcerations we were subjected to. If Adam was the earth and Eve the sky, we deserved better from bad behavior than rough imprisonment in a rotten, tropical garden of America, known as a number, with inmate sprawl causing animal brawls.

# 25. Guantánamo Elegies

## Dr. Henry Waterson

O vast Rondure, swimming in space,
Cover'd all over with visible power and beauty,
Alternate light and day and the teeming, spiritual darkness,
Unspeakable high processions of sun and moon and countless stars above,
Below, the manifold grass and waters, animals, mountains, trees,
With inscrutable purpose, some hidden, prophetic intention,
Now first it seems my thought begins to span thee.
Down from the gardens of Asia descending, radiating,
Adam and Eve appear, then their myriad progeny after them,
Wandering, yearning, curious, with restless explorations,
With questionings, baffled, formless, feverish, with never-happy hearts,
With that sad incessant refrain, *Wherefore unsatisfied Soul?* and *Whither
O mocking life?*
Ah who shall soothe these feverish children?
Who justify these restless explorations?
Who speak the secret of impassive earth?
Who bind it to us? what is this separate Nature so unnatural?
What is this earth to our affections? (unloving earth, without a throb to
answer ours,
Cold earth, the place of graves.)
(Walt Whitman, *Leaves of Grass*, "Passage to India," 1891 - 92)

Being the causal agent was never harder, considering I felt the ravages of age as much as anybody else. Then Ratsby and I needed to hightail it to greener pastures, Ratsby pretending to be defunct, while I got to *Swisherland* to treat a cracked-up couple, Bestport having run its course with us or we with Bestport, and no matter how culturally appealing, comfortable, quiet, a paradise, we could not stay there forever. Our Longsnore rum runner's bay, and warehouses as greenhouses, were finally busted by Coast Guard, DEA, state, local police in mid-autumn, but we were long gone by then. After convincing spent stars to check into a sanitarium at the Magic Mountain, Davos, they were so at home and happy, I had to keep them from staying there forever, even though the ennui ailing them was chronic, and would always last. Fully dressed as the Chief, they somehow, never recognized my brownness against the white Alps, nor braided hair, which as with most Indians was never cut, as my spirit was in it. *Le Grand Remplacement* was the replacement of one race by another, really, the re-browning of this world, in the reclamation of what was once theirs, a joyous act for my aboriginal brothers, but if actual possession was nine-tenths of the law, we had to possess. As with the Columbian Exchange, there would appear to have also been a Pacific Exchange, but no corresponding, Viking Exchange. Scientists presume that possible contacts between Polynesians and coastal groups in South America at about 1200 AD, produced genetic crosses, similarities, and the adoption by Polynesians of an American crop, the sweet potato. Whoever held the land called it by their own name; what ancient maps and history conveniently labeled, *Mundus novus*, was simply our place; my origin story comes from the chaos that was the world before the Great Spirit; then a peaceful time existed, for more than ten millennia, when native peoples ruled mountain, stream and plain; before this harm to us, requiring vindication. Our first retribution spread syphilis, "Syphilis: a night with Venus, a lifetime with Mercury." This disease was first called Syphilis after an eponymous traitor, heroine in Girolamo Fracastoro, *Syphilis sive morbus gallicus* [Syphilis or The French Disease],

1530. The next vengeance introduced killer tobacco; a final revenge brought tribal casinos to America.

Recall concurrent subjugations of Siberia, Asia, Polynesia, India, as well as North Africa, Arabia, primal cultures celebrating inclusion of multi genders, everywhere across the world, recognizing ancient, ideally tolerant ways defining our heritage.

Perhaps my absolute immersions into the mysteries of life and creation were but a rebellious streak against the powers that be, an internal reversion to delved primal beginnings, as endings to sacred songs of love, hope, renewal and promised joys.

Exposures to *Apache* witchcraft, Neoplatonist alchemy, polished by a Whale M.D. were the means to instill breathing life into my subjects dear, trans mutating them in their outward forms, achieving elemental beings, of absolute good-doer design.

Now adept at inclusivity of the latest social impulses in my vital mixtures, further finding dug-up philosophers' stone, to complete distinct distillations of identities once alienated from us, children challenged the order, before casually running out.

I knew to step back and let them have their say, as above all else, everyone needed their sovereignty; because expanding one's mind involved much more than stating you loved mankind; it meant following your inner desires to the ends of the earth.

So, I was cast adrift by them, rather than they from me, the difference being that in this way, they claimed I was badly behaved, not them. Later the surprise vagaries of life brought us together again when they were mature enough to listen to others.

But I had existed being let down, my creations paying no attention to me at all, as children set course, charting separate ways, leaving parents drowning in turbulent wakes. Then I reasserted my right, as founder, but surreptitiously, so no one knew.

Now my balance returns, combining cunning with experience, as prophets know more by being ancient than being omnipotent; retreating was the best of magnets to draw in those who previously disdained one's approach as anathema to them.

What lies in my future? I don't know, save preserving a vague hope, for the sun to rise each day, the moon to follow her phases, the seasons to know their places, and the end of time to have mercy on us, as God again seems sleepy, and out of touch.

If I was born of mortal thoughts of men, so be it, however, I outlasted them all, by my words, keeping my visit permanent in mythologies and man's ancient dreams; my youthful vigor a bit dissipated, I can still carry on with the best at hellraising,

as occurred with the horny sisters from Whale, when I was a teen. From that time on, I was a rising flame of desire and wanton lust, and I regret some of the hurtful activities I am guilty of, toward my reservation and college minority communities.

Whether it was false spirituality or stupid practicality I stayed true to the teachings of my people. Later I realized that many wanted to believe in me, but were afraid, due to assuming others with the same dilemma, would mock their naivete, resolve.

# 26. Guantánamo Elegies

## John B. Sayer

...Examples of all Ages shew us that Mankind in general desire Power
only to do Harm, and when they obtain it, use it for no other Purpose...
(Henry Fielding, *The History of Tom Jones, a Foundling*, 1749)

It was the biggest deal, when we were kids, to make our own spending money doing odd jobs, such as paper routes, lawn mowing, leaf raking, weeding, retail, restaurant work, despite the family being filthy rich. It was our way of acknowledging the great pecuniary promise in the sky, that there was certainly room for more. In addition, our Christian Scientist and Puritan upbringings prompted us to give back; not too much, but enough, to church charities, raffles, socials, to get us into heaven, keep us out of hell; preceding Chautauqua meetings, homespun kitchen table philosophies, everything important in my life I learned in kindergarten. It was curious that such a nice lady like my mother could nurture such a pack of scoundrel children like us. At a young age I adopted my Superman shirt, of later subway train fame; following an early, religious zealotry, preferring New England style, biblical/ faith inspired, Christian given names, I baptized my daughters Penitence (dubbed, Annoyance), Chastity (Uppity), and my sons Riches and Increase; doing our progenitors proud, as exponents of wild animal spirits driving corporate profits, extolling the family's myth of the self-made man. Gee, we had such fun as kids, playing Allah, *picking the most innocent (dumb) person around, and convincing him of his big reward for playing the game as the person hiding underneath the blanket obeying the commands of the mightiest god, Allah: Me to my younger brother: "In acknowledgement of all your good fortune, Allah commands you to give up something personal of yours, in return, so Allah insists that you take off an item you are wearing..." and before you know it, after a few holy demands from Allah my brother was buck naked, whereupon we pulled off the blanket, exposing him to whatever visitors happened to be over, for their entertainment. Give us your deviants, your downtrodden. I wouldn't hurt a fly, unless it was open, and if you were not watching, I might suddenly, goose you, then turn red laughing; these goosing proclivities of mine being the latent result of a pedophilic incident that occurred, not just in my presence, but to me, one summer twilight eve on 42nd Street, near Bryant Park, forever altering my sense of predator and prey, and how I could get away with anything. It was so surprising to my adolescent mind and sensibilities, but at the same time, not a shock. Goosing perverts were everywhere, was the conclusion. And my assailant was off, into the shadows, disappearing into the steam rising from grimy pavements of a sweltering night...* These are confusing memories of abuse that may have occurred to me when I was twelve, visiting New York. Prior to that, in California on another occasion *a strange person once came up to me: "Little boy, would you like some candy?" with leering grin and stupid, mocking voice. "Do you want some candy, little boy? Do you want to go to Bolinas, Stinson Beach?"* Then the scourge of arms upon the country and its citizens. *Vignette of Dodge City or Tombstone: visitors surrendering guns with marshals to get into town. But my forebears did not relinquish theirs.* I would always subscribe to guns, as per *diktat*, with the infamy of hunting a living creature with anything more than a stone to claim the test of nature. Frugality was our thin-lipped name, as the cheaper you were, the richer you got, even if already loaded, *skinflint, tight ass. Cheapskates cared less about being down one hundred thousand in the market, than ponying up a hundred for lunch.* There's a sucker born every minute, seems to hand it over for nothing; he who behaves like a scoundrel, meaning not in favor of idealism, gets scourged, and if you were a stooge for the invisible hand, you were not an idealist. Finally, the great replacement theory was really, the browning of America, a panic for WASPs. Despite bents of pusillanimous partisanship, most of us are regular people. *That's a lie, as really, we are all divided into extremist fringes despising each other.* My entire life I was trained to believe that we Puritans were the colonizers then founders of this nation, destined by almighty God for greatness, to come into a naked, empty place and transform it to our will.

Little did we imagine it would be pulled out from under us, by marauders flooding in from everywhere.

The Reverend confronting me in my office left me petrified, with a recognition of myself, and those of distant lineage... and then I knew, despite the man before me being black, *it must be true: I was linked to African Americans*, I thought, with the

strange discomfort: *could there be more?* "Why, Odds bodkins," I declared, prior to standing, and giving the reverend a bear hug, calling him my long-lost biblical brother. He was very useful in rounding up all the fringe elements necessary for a

multi racial Committee for Public Safety, to deal with the very issues of universal inclusion, and I appreciated his participation and counsel; together we should have been able to keep these unwanted meddlers, from the most southern climes, at bay.

My shock at realizing I was of a distant, appendant descent from a southern incest plantation over multi generations was as if I had discovered that I might be related to Satan himself, but I managed to accept such, with a stalwart pride in my WASP

whiteness. I could not control the past, any more than my lineage of rapacity and theft, or the many shady things my forebears did in the name of free enterprise and austerity. Being a hatchet man for nasty Wall Street boys and corporate boards of

directors gave official sanction for my willingness to engage in nefarious activities to get the job done, such as drug sniffing dogs, and pacification of warring unions, as was once done with native tribes across this vast continent, leading the studio to

new heights of profit and deviousness. My Army career, special forces training by the CIA, taught me to apologize afterwards, rather than ask permission prior to, as the pinnacle of getting away with murder, for all the apple pie reasons, of course.

Then a succession of Hollywood cocktail and pot parties, along with seducing all available, sexy starlets who dared cross my path, led to my abuse of extraordinary corporate powers, to acquire anything I wanted, and well, you know what I mean.

Playing second fiddle was never really the problem, if I was compensated with the best of them, and I always was, so I shouldn't complain; my feminist chief was the best boss, there was no use thinking I would get one over on her, as I tried before.

What can I say, except that lucre got the best of me, because everything in excess is bad for the soul, if I have one. The chair let bygones be bygones, when I joined forces with her to eviscerate the first two Amendments to the Bill of Rights of the

U.S. Constitution, the very reason we find ourselves in this army stockade/ navy brig of a dastardly, surrealist dystopia, with no rights at all. I'm no practitioner of fake philanthropy to wash away my worldly sins, however, I would gladly donate

my entire soul to the devil, to be released of fake imprisonment in this tropical hell hole. How could the country I gladly celebrate every Fourth of July, my birthday, have renditioned me to such a fate, with tourists sunning at nearby luxury resorts?

## 27. Guantánamo Elegies

### Isidora Green

> And at the end of the first thousand years the good souls and also the evil souls both come to draw lots and choose their second life, and they may take any which they please. The soul of a man may pass into the life of a beast, or from the beast return again into the man. But the soul which has never seen the truth will not pass into the human form. For a man must have intelligence of universals, and be able to proceed from the many particulars of sense to one conception of reason;--this is the recollection of those things which our soul once saw while following God--when regardless of that which we now call being she raised her head up towards the true being. And therefore the mind of the philosopher alone has wings; and this is just, for he is always, according to the measure of his abilities, clinging in recollection to those things in which God abides, and in beholding which He is what He is. And he who employs aright these memories is ever being initiated into perfect mysteries and alone becomes truly perfect. But, as he forgets earthly interests and is rapt in the divine, the vulgar deem him mad, and rebuke him; they do not see that he is inspired. (Plato, *Phaedrus*, 370 BC)

I am an adept, a practitioner, whose spontaneous birth in a lotus flower must have resulted, from a prior *bardo* state, in Limbo, observing the forms while awaiting my turn at reincarnation then transcendence. I evolved far beyond my family's limited concepts, of salvation earned through faith alone, without any attention to the soul. My spirituality was of the ages, also the here and now, as would suit my practical, empirical bents. Prior to this life I recall being witness to the clearest stated universals surrounding me, showing the paths to choose in my difficult moments of despair and panic. A knowledge of perfected ideas contributed to an impulse to reach for the stars, in everything I did. I prepared well for my recent birth, only to find myself trapped here, in this hellhole of monstrous, human, moral and political abuse. I admit, I was an instigator in this plot against our way of life, but it was about time for someone to act. Our mistake was not heeding the Colonel's original advice, to lead a unit to loot and get rid of the U.S. Constitution, Bill of Rights and all amendments, along with the Declaration of Independence; relics of a bygone, antiquated, horrid age of women held in bondage, anachronisms replete with false and deadly Jeffersonian beliefs of unending, social confrontation, political extremism, revolt; for once and for all. I am resentful those sanctimonious prigs, from the Whale Corporation, abandoned me in Guantánamo, just when I needed them, aghast at the true money greed at Whale, its love of lucre. As one of the most committed educational trustees and philanthropists I am as a blind woman who sees. I understand Save the Kids executives making $500,000 a year are nothing, compared to a widespread feathering of nests, yet still a travesty of fairness for modernized mendicant orders, spreading the existence of good deeds; because most executives are mental insects, afraid to engage political differences rationally, either from lack of education, absence of intellectual confidence, or just plain, stupidity. I'll never again contribute to any cause unless I am in control. When I said the Sisters of Fervent Grace's motto shall henceforth be *liberte, dualite, fraternite*, I, Lady, meant it. The original objective of my sisterhood was to get back at the fellows for their exclusive places, and such. But it became much more so, when I saw the effects it had on my sisters, who were no longer anonymous waifs, but important individuals to others, as well as themselves. And though not fathomed by P at the time such a Gypsy marker later tied her directly to me, coincidentally descended similarly, from dispersed *Roma*, most distant of relations, through traces more binding, lustrous, than the ancient wealth of their mountainous, *Punjabi* place of origin, ascribing demonic violin skills to Gypsy blood: *a most beautiful rendition of the* Mendelssohn Violin Concerto...

That must have gratified some pushy side or nature of me that also appealed to the leftist fringes. I will tell you what it is about the left, that is only satisfied by the blood lust against a real, or imagined enemy, that side of us that takes much from

one, to give to another freely, no permission asked; heeding Lenin's *The State and Revolution,* in aiming to dismantle the overbearing apparatus of the state on all our lives; playing music written by a Jew without permission from Nazi overlords, as

"For Mind, for Culture and for Whale!" is still in my mind, like the good old days at liberal W; open to contrary thought, in good form, a *noblesse oblige* politeness, but certainly with antipathy, and even distaste. But how could I ever reconcile the

need to free my soul, to dividing up property confiscated by the state for others to use? Why, wasn't that what we did to tall *Guinea* blacks, proud Native red men? Did we not withhold everything from them, then leave them shivering in the cold?

The difference was how one took, socialist redistribution a crime, but seizing of a Negro bondsman, Indian lands, sanctified by scripture, as well as universal usage, as per my ancestors; but after greed, rapine and extensive pillage were assimilated

into the Western tradition, they had to be balanced by a giving side, which created the great works of the Renaissance and Modern Age, alms to the poor, pockets of gold, silver loot stashed in hoards, before banks and international currency norms.

Beneficence, meaning the good-doer doing his thing, was the quintessence of old Christianity, before becoming an excuse for capitalist excesses such as child labor, which could never be defended, even for those supplicating their way into heaven.

Philanthropy had run its course for me; buying an absolving ticket to the hereafter was not in a slim ledger of penitent obligations anymore; seeing how my ancestors managed to whiten dark spots with the sweet balm of giving, though in small bits.

Still, it was better than nothing, considering the depths of sordidness involved in our generational slave dealing; that could never be atoned for, no matter how hard we tried; nevertheless, I have done my best to be an outstanding corporate citizen,

in bringing on board as many of the desperate and downtrodden as I dared to; with pressure on me to do so, from my Jewish Director, Human Resources, who was a godsend, for without her, I would have never realized what a real bigot I had been.

My last regrets are for Geronimo, for who will care for him while we are missing? He is like a snake that subsists on mere hope, warmth and moisture in the air. But frolicsome co-eds, like us, meant no one any harm; gaiety and mirth, as with most

things in life, got too complicated, beyond anyone's, anything's or God's, control; I knew enough to go back, to the mystical rejuvenating insights of my sisterhood, after recurring sunsets reminded softly, that the far horizon was as close as home.

# 28. Guantánamo Elegies

## Rev. Hannibal P. (Pearly) Gates

> *PIETRO.* – Hark! they sing. [*A song.*] See, he comes. Now shall you hear
> the extremity of a malcontent. He is free as air; he blows over every man...
>
> *MENDOZA.* Who cannot feign friendship can ne'er produce the effects
> of hatred...
>
> *MALEVOLE.* [*Aside.*] O world most vile, when thy loose vanities,
> Taught by this fool, do make the fool seem wise!
> (John Marston, *The Malcontent*, 1604)

I know I am a malcontent, as *MALEVOLE*, full of gripes and vitriol, everybody says so, and how could it be otherwise? I was weaned by the sisters on *liberté, egalité, fraternité*, to be the perfect pickaninny progressive. It was not until my midnight trespass at Whale's imposing Green Memorial Library, that I came to the full realization of the error in my ways; seeing that in America there was no such thing as a black race, but really a mixed-up bag of tricks from everywhere on the planet; and inclusion of all had led to a loss of identity through miscegenation, incest, disease and faulty decent to our current sad state. If you want to express leadership, and need me to contribute to a common cause, then treat me with the same respect you demand from me; but how can I follow you when you only inspire fear and loathing?

> My confronting John B. Sayer in his office left him petrified, with a recognition of himself and those of distant lineage, and then he knew, despite the man before him being black, *it must be true: he was linked to African Americans*, he thought, with
>
> the strangest discomfort: *could there be more?* "Why, Odds bodkins," he uttered, prior to standing, and giving me a bear hug, and calling me his long-lost biblical brother. I was very useful in rounding up all the fringe elements necessary for the
>
> multi racial Committee for Public Safety, to deal with the very issues of universal inclusiveness, and he appreciated my participation, counsel; united we might have been able to keep these unwanted meddlers, from the most southern climes, at bay.
>
> How ironic that I, striving for acceptance and inclusion from society, yet pitifully obsessed with keeping our Latin American, Asian, Euro enemies at the gates, and not an inch closer, was the same xenophobe staring me in the face from the mirror.

I was blowing off steam, taking "the great replacement" theory, the self-pitying ideology of freak racial comeuppance by humiliated vestigial racists, to help explain to myself the browning of black America, whether rightly or wrongly only history would tell, as there were true sour grapes in the term, as if self-applied by those being replaced. Let us not forget, however, that the roots of global racism lie in white Europe, due to its superior, immoral, scientific, technological, military strengths; and never forget that it was white power that freed the slaves, but only after being guilt-ridden, forced to by popular demand. Was not the Golden Rule, do onto others as they have done onto you, with memory and vengeance? If they are frigging disrespectful, disrespect them back double. This was the paradigm of the new, nastier, "in your white face," protest movement. Affirmative action is a type of war reparation, significant in its rubbing salt in the wounds of those humbled and defeated; never accomplishing long term corrections for past bad behavior, increasing the animosities of the prior combatants. Just look at what happened in Germany after the Great War. Enforced reparations ruined the German economy, led to severe societal frustrations, and resulted in the extremist solution of Nazism, with its attendant, evil continental results, and global holocaust. There could be similar reactions against those who preached affirmative action. The sad legacy of Africa is that Africans willingly sold their own people to white slavers, for hundreds of years. If African Americans are so hell bent on changing the vestige identity of slave times, i.e., the names of schools, buildings, bases, state flags, the national currency, etc., they should be wary of taking African personal names, as they may be the names of kings, great historical personages, kingdoms, and geographical regions, and so on; and invariably, most, if not all, African kings and influential men (and women of note) were slave owners and traders, and African ports, places and locations had to do with the slave trade. Why would you honor Shaka Zulu over George Washington, for instance? Both were important slave owners and traders, as well as fierce and victorious warriors, and the fathers of nations; one was black, the other white. Which is more deserving of acclaim than the other? Either both should be in the panoply of revered heroes or neither; maybe dreaming *of a certain Shaka Washington without.*

Thinking of his future

*When hated DCF took away my little brother we never saw him again. How many times had something like that happened to my race, the capturing, dragging forth, in fetters and coffles, the selling off to cruel strangers, in all suffering wrenching,*

*separation from loved ones forever? You know what my response was? you know what I did? I had my own child to love, nurture, protect and raise up in my image, Shaka Washington Gates, so that my lineage, of doubt and blame, would continue,*

*unto another generation, persisting in my efforts to humanize the planet. He is to the future, what I was, thirty-five years ago, abounding in faith, hope, expectation, and I pray he never falls, to become the disappointed idealist his father later was.*

*His name would represent the past spilling into the future, as a waving banner or flag drawing the ex-slave to battle, as his mother is black, yet fair skinned, adding again, to further dilution of the black blood I have been so adamant to preserve.*

*But whatever* Negritude *I lose, I gain with my connections to myself, my past and future lineages, the true, biblical scheme of propagating the spinning sphere itself; please remember that within my cynicism is a spirit awed, by difficult tasks ahead.*

*Of course, respect for my country's flag would never be possible, after this brutal interlude. Would it hopefully be a temporary confinement, until the powers that be got hold of their senses, or eternal entombment, as open ended as Guantánamo's*

*lease? And what would be the reparations cost for this rendition stunt? limitless... In the end, it was about fulfilling a duty to oneself, even before God; if that makes me a humanist, then so be it. And if my private life comes as a shock to those who*

*believed I was more dissolute, I truly apologize you were misled, to begin with; for I am only a man with the same hunger and needs as you; trying to do what's right, before my own fears catch up with me, dragging me down again, whence I came.*

# 29. Guantánamo Elegies

## Patricia (P) Diddy

> I prefer a Church which is bruised, hurting and dirty because it has been out on the streets, rather than a Church which is unhealthy from being confined and from clinging to its own security.
>
> More than by fear of going astray, my hope is that we will be moved by the fear of remaining shut up within structures which give us a false sense of security, within rules which make us harsh judges, within habits which make us feel safe, while at our door people are starving.
> (Pope Francis, *Evangelii Gaudium [The Joy of the Gospel]*, Apostolic Exhortation, 11/26/2013)

The Sunday gatherings at Sayer's riverside mansion in Nam, almost turned me into a Nazi, but I opted out, for more sophisticated spheres of thought and conduct, considering my gender bending asexuality. I would also not fit into any neat racial category, as I was Pan racial, product of the *mélange,* in which a pot of races had been shaken, not stirred, to a new consistency of a coming, multiethnic New World. I returned with PTSD, and when reacquainted with Lady, on my application to Whale College, felt lucky. And though not fathomed by me at the time a Gypsy marker later tied her directly to me, coincidentally descended similarly, from dispersed *Roma,* most distant of relations, through traces more binding and lustrous, than the ancient wealth of their mountainous, *Punjabi* place of origin, and this was my dream.

> *Isidora was my aunt, and we were coming down from snowy mountains in a Gypsy caravan of sixty wagons, forever trekking, and 600 years since leaving our home in distant* Punjab, *enough time to have reached the fertile lands of Mesopotamia,*
>
> *confluence of the Tigris and Euphrates, of early lore, and the valley of the Garden. All was suddenly verdant and fragrant, with perfume of flowers in our midst, and we decided to pitch our tents by the water for the next thirty days stay, as was the*
>
> *custom of our people, before moving on again, ever westward. When night was at its darkest, we were marauded by Ottomans out to capture women for the harems. So, my aunt and I were transported to Cairo and sold in a slave market, to a dark,*
>
> *Scottish sea captain, who, taking my aunt, as his ill-gotten wife, turned me over to a* Grandee, *with whom I sailed to New Spain; whereupon, off northerly shores, our ship foundered, wrecked by a hurricane, and I escaped into a forested Appalachia.*

"When you call me that, SMILE!" I would always be a gung-ho grunt, ready to do service for the right cause, despite the inevitable excesses that would be committed; an assassination meter executing those deserving it, but sometimes, as with the innocent school professor giving his speech in Vietnam, prone to catastrophic errors. "Believe me, I know when I'm bluffing, and by the time it happens it's too late." In later days of my contrition, trying to help kids, I demonstrated; of such fateful steps are our destinies crafted that a young female protester, beaten up on a certain day, had not even planned to attend a rally, but rather went there out of boredom, because she had nothing else to do. From such serendipitous and commonplace events are demigods and heroes made, cast and sold to a public starved for good deeds, transforming the everyday to a poetic reality, in our self-made images, with the many guises we played.

When a poor white trash girl like me, way back in Whale days, retorted to Waterson, that Geronimo's Ghost was the first male accepted into the Sisterhood, what I meant was that he was better at fulfilling society's expectations of maleness, than me; he was simply, more manly. Because by then I had suffered my entire enlistment in the Marine Corps with bound breasts, and a fake crotch, which I later found out was, unusually, distended, and realized it was hard to keep up the ruse forever. So, for the last ten years I have lived in this gender *bardo*, waiting for rebirth in my sex, after having pretended in another. The trouble is I never had good, loving examples in my parents, as they were always stoned. Now, I know I am not one to crow about past, personal friendships or relationships, but since I have been down here, I have developed a most inexplicable crush on the *ayudante companero*; I see it makes no sense, love is blind, as they say, or Eros a sniper in the dark, pinpointing fatal arrows at me. *El ac* may be a notorious cross dresser, but as a West Point graduate, and former officer, he is just the man I would have married, had I wanted; so we are both giving ourselves a late blooming romance, in this military prison, keeping to the disciplined schedule and monitoring, but still finding ways to tryst; besides, I find him to be such a calming presence, and as we did serve together that night in Bestport, kidnapping the Freemisogynist fools, I know I can trust him. Where it leads to, I haven't the foggiest, but first we must get out of here.

Idolizing the Fabulous and Flighty

Of course, reverence for my country's flag would always be possible, even after a brutal interlude. Would it hopefully be a temporary confinement, until the powers that be got hold of their senses, or eternal entombment, as open ended as the lease

for Guantánamo? But reparation was never high on a list of Melungeon demands, for this rendition stunt, in its injustice upon a sad, former U.S. Marine, limitless… I realized there was no single gene in me, that could claim abuse over the others,

so, in the end, which one of my races would dominate to become the victim? And as multi-seeded beings, didn't we see the pointlessness of such an exercise? I will declaim my final laments, for Japanese Americans interned during WWII, which

brings me back to Nam, as does everything announced or intimated: to ultimately discourse on my affirmed love and admiration, idolizing the fabulous and flighty, whom I first laid eyes upon as the New Age Family, which is worth the dedication

of divine temples to, similarly siblings; but the brother and sister connection to be defined in the figurative, circumstantial sense, in no way incest, and undeserving of the social censure it would one day inspire; daring to go all the way, so please,

anything I can do for them, officially or not, I pray to God they know I am on their side; pending green card applicants can never feel secure in their greenery, so I've tried to assist them whenever I could, simply because I am attracted to them, as a

pair of preternatural entities made for change. I only hope the Fixer/ Yellow Kid makes them the protagonists of a novel we all heard he was writing in here. I am certain they would bring Life, Liberty, Happiness to all chapters focusing on them.

As for the rest of us, I only hope God hears our prayers, because if He doesn't, no one else will. We were in a similar predicament to the Grand Duke John C., of Freemisogynist fame, forgotten by the busy world spinning merrily along its orbit.

# 30. Guantánamo Elegies

## Ms. Yael Abraham

> I shall never get you put together entirely,
> Pieced, glued, and properly jointed.
> Mule-bray, pig-grunt and bawdy cackles
> Proceed from your great lips.
> It's worse than a barnyard. (Sylvia Plath, "The Colossus," 1960)

When we finally met it was clear I never knew you, believed it was really you, for even if passing years eased absence, nothing will ever change my having longed for you, in prior time of separation; but after finding you, knowing who you were, wishing I had never come from you, I gazed long and hard in the mirror, comparing our resemblance, as if returning to the past; for I went from being a changeling to a foundling, born April 20, 1944 ("...the same day as the *Fuhrer*, an auspicious omen"), and, raised as a Jew Holocaust survivor victim, I always suspected a Nazi heart; by the time I got to Whale University, I began experimenting with going both ways in my alternative sexuality, as hetero/ lesbian, as well as psyche, as Jew/ Nazi; confronting Sephardic encapsulation of a criminal Nazi core, as my dual nature; recent research showing Hitler's relatives had Sephardic, North African or Berber DNA markers, so he was a crypto-Jew, by his own definition, surely a disconcerting, provocative self-loathing proposition. So perhaps part of me was correct all along, despite being wrong overall, for *Schadenfreude*; (German: lit. 'harm-joy'), a pleasure derived from the misfortune of others. Harm existed only in the memories of those who experienced it. Without the faculties of mind and body, there was no concept or actuality of God. There were so many reasons for Judaism to have inspired Christianity. The antecedent cautioned against transgression of laws and punished, while the successor found forgiveness and gave eternal life; Catholics are taught to care for others, Protestants for themselves, which being true, Christian charity? Whale provided more encounters with the all-American phenomenon, the preppie admitted as a legacy. I was intrigued by the way certain WASPs utilized surnames for a first, as well as a last, name, such as stodgy Cotton Mather, Sinclair Lewis, Cole Porter, Prescott Bush, Thornton Wilder, McGeorge Bundy, Kingman Brewster, as if they were more important for that, Whale U. being a long way from a *Kibbutz*; the irony of my new number, while bearing an old imprinted, inked id, led to my tattoo ratio, measuring the nastiness/ worthiness of Gitmo's goons, the more ink to nastiness, as I am discriminatory of tattoos.

Annual Report

My earliest recollection, really, is the doll from Auschwitz. It's true, he must have been the Archer of Auschwitz. In the van, on the way to the Archives, he stared at my arm and stated for all to hear, "You are my long-lost daughter, taken from me

by morally corrupt, Spanish nuns, at the war's end." There was no time for me, or anyone, to react before being called to action, since then kept incommunicado, for the past two months, jumbling up days, seeming as one, crossing off each sunrise.

Being alone, all I have are memories of loss and hopeful redemption, but I seem to be confusing religions, for my adoptive family were like angels, and I salute them for the proper upbringing they gave me and will always be grateful for their love.

Plagued by asthma and chronic bronchitis, my growth was stunted by such severe infant malnutrition, that I was years behind in stature and weight. But I wanted to make meaningful contributions to my race, and a Western tradition that saved me.

Arriving at Whale College, in the historic, initial women's class, in fall of 1969, I ranked highly in the dining hall flashcard grading, due to more advanced maturity, despite being small and malnourished; then I was tapped for the Sisterhood, upon

protesting the lack of Hebrew blood in the ranks to its founder, to which she said, "Welcome sister." As I also had recollections of my faceless mother, I found the Sisterhood of Grace the perfect antidote for loneliness and wonder at my origins.

So, when Ottoline requested help for compiling the *Guantánamo Elegies,* I did not think twice about risking my life for my sister or the rest of the team. So much for those who accuse Jews of only being in it for themselves, at the expense of others.

Any resentment I may or may not have felt toward her, any unconscious jealousy, was primal in its cast, behind any later personality development we all undergo, as time passes and maturity takes hold on the glands, as well as our sense, for peace.

Advancing as the corporate *kapo* demonstrated that I had true mastery, over all my innate mechanisms for survival, and did what I had to, to triumph. Once president of my alumni sisters, I was part of a Jewish ethos of success and status, within the

community. The power offered by HR was so overwhelming, it was irresistible to my deepest need of controlling others. But I had a mandate to fulfill as the Queen of Quotas, so exercise it I did, to the best of my ability, transforming Lady's place,

which must have gratified some pushy side or nature of me that also appealed to a rightist fringe. I will tell you what it is about the right, that is only satisfied by the blood lust against a real, or imagined enemy, the side of us that takes much before

asking, wants to annihilate for a wise ass retort, or punch out anyone telling them what to do, as badly behaved adolescents ridiculing, humiliating, all those weaker than themselves; and it was all the most harmful fun, as the beaten never dared to

retaliate, or follow, Hitler's *Mein Kampf* dictum, that terror must meet terror, force meet force, for the struggle to triumph, and whoever was not tough enough to help himself, perished. Looking objectively at my duality, Zionism gave me support in

having an ethnic identity used against external enemies, Israel, for the first time in its history, ready to have force meet force, Jews having become as mean, as Nazis. Perhaps my outward form, and inner core, were not as oppositional as it appeared.

But what I want the world to know about me, in case I don't come back, is that my fate was much too strong for me. I was always reacting to perils, even challenges, much beyond my control, never in charge of my own destiny. Perhaps surviving,

as I've done, shows fortitude is cut of random wishes and desires, always hoping for more; I was pulled by powers from above, while settling for the easiest way in or out. So, was it true what they said about Ottoline's aunt's head being mounted?

# 31. Guantánamo Elegies

## *SS* Colonel Otto Waldemar Grawitz

> But what will not Ambition and Revenge
> Descend to? who aspires must down as low
> As high he soar'd, obnoxious first or last
> To basest things. Revenge, at first thought sweet,
> Bitter ere long back on it self recoils;
> Let it; I reck not, so it light well aim'd,
> Since higher I fall short, on him who next
> Provokes my envie, this new Favorite
> Of Heav'n, this Man of Clay, Son of despite,
> Whom us the more to spite his Maker rais'd
> From dust: spite then with spite is best repaid.
> (John Milton, *Paradise Lost*, 1667)

I murdered thousands in my time, and went on as if nothing happened, giving more consideration to the extermination of an insect, spider, bumble bee, WASP, than I had for any of those in the final solution; but when I lost my child the world as I understood it had ended, over a single child mind you. I hid out in the New World, until invited back to the Old, where I really belonged, as the fall of Satan happened there, where convoluted ideas of sacrificing those dearest to us in favor of vengeful gods, still dictated. Recent research showed Hitler's relatives had Sephardic, North African or Berber DNA markers, so he was a crypto-Jew, by his own definition, surely a disconcerting, provocative self-loathing proposition; keeping our blood pure was more innate for my wife and me than for him, in *Schadenfreude*; (German: lit. 'harm-joy') a pleasure derived, from the misfortune, of others. Life existed only for its expectations, by those experiencing it. Without faculties of mind, memory, there was no concept or actuality of time; and if the time of our creation coincided with the Jewish Rosh Hashanah, fall of man, original sin, we were not to blame for extremes brought about by a critical creator, allowing bad behavior against Jews. My brutal suppression of the camp revolt at Sobibor demonstrated my essence was evil, my entire life a staged set of various vendettas of villainy, with sin and death connected. Christ's gift was freely given, man having the choice to accept it or not. When the game turned around, bullies cried even harder than babies, and got the hell beaten out of them justifiably, and perhaps I was the big bad bully so described. Perhaps Maimonides was wrong, with respect to, "acquit a thousand guilty persons than to put a single innocent one to death." Perhaps the truly guilty cannot be spared, despite any mistakes along the way. As a culture obsessed with your important sense of rights, you should thank Thomas Jefferson, the third president, for the aggressive tone of politics in the country. This is what he idealized, a permanent state of tension and political animosity bordering on seditious violence, backed up by a Second Amendment; however, these concerns now seemed far from me. The damage had already been done and I was tired. As I am getting on in years, I think it prudent to purchase a plot at that cemetery I remember, from my own Bestport glory days, as the old sport: the Assumption Cemetery on Beans Farms Road, heading to the beaches, where I will hopefully find peace for my weary bones after this renditioned imprisonment, for the ghosts of my wicked past make it hard to sleep at night, seeming to presage my nearing demise. But before I forget I would like to say a final word, about that summer of my wild and crazy Longsnore parties and love-ins, for a brief time overshadowing our perfect pair; but I was forced to exit stage left, due to fear of discovery and punishment, so I am forever grateful for the support I received from Willi. He wrote a timeless book about me, or shall I say, a former persona, *The Great Ratsby*, which may be a bit of a fabrication, however he did have a flourish for writing poetic prose, even if pompous as a poet.

Running off to the south of France was their best stunt yet, as it removed the studio's pressure off them; the Chief and I hightailing it to greener pastures, the Chief to *Swisherland*, while I resumed a spy's life.

Then it was back to the clandestine trade I was so good at, helping to spin NATO's web of deceit in the First, Second, Third worlds, praying for a Fourth to escape to, where I would not be responsible for my indiscretions, for I did feel their weight.

Perhaps a sardonic example of the mysteries of retribution working against us was our motoring out of the camp that fateful pre-dawn day, not getting ten kms from Auschwitz when my sweet, blond wife was left faceless by Russian sharpshooters.

Being a fascist had taken everything, punishing innocents for my blind loyalty. If I was talented at overthrowing countries, and buttressing vile regimes, how was it that, as with Attila, "There, where I have passed, the grass will never grow again?"

But I was good at being the *Flagellum Dei,* Scourge of God, even if it cost me the exiling of my second child's mother to the Soviet Gulag, for the only sin, really, of having loved me, an enemy agent and murderer of her sister, mounted on my wall.

I will never tell anyone about that murder, for it was the most heinous of all, but I did spare her face, as she requested. I also fully saved the Gypsy violinist, but not the Jew wood carrier. Why, I will never know, but because I could do as I wanted.

Perhaps omnipotence was too much for those of us, who were given command of troops, powers over those condemned, it going to our heads, odiously incongruous that my greatest worry one day at the camp was getting chicken, as an aphrodisiac,

for my sultry wife, while at that same time overseeing the wholesale liquidation of several depreciated racial subsets. What did it ultimately mean, about my specific fall from grace, that I could be more distracted by love's follies, than mass crimes?

Now my balance returns, combining cunning with experience, as the devil knows more by being ancient than being *dem Teufel*. Retreating was the best of magnets to draw closer those who previously disdained one's approach as poison to them.

And regaining my Soviet operative's liberty was the high point of my life, for my dear Ottoline's sake; doing something for someone else was an elixir and tonic for removing me from myself, while the world regained inner strength upon renewal.

Having finally found my lost first daughter I don't even know what to call her, but her number 169062; my baby Alexandra, Aley, so noble, such a joy to her parents, yet already gone into the sands of time, replaced by this Jewish American Princess

(JAP), whom I hardly understand or know; maybe also part of a vengeance against me, by whom or what I'll never guess; except perhaps God, whom I fear the most, since I promised to turn my life over to Him, if she was ever returned to me again.

Whether it was false pride or stupid honor, I always remained true to the teachings of the party, as that is what I was taught. Later I learned to accept those who were different, but by then it was surely too late to change, any of the evil already done.

# 32. Guantánamo Elegies

## Ottoline

[WITCH]
Careful the things you say
Children will listen
Careful the things you do
Children will see
And learn

Guide them along the way
Children will glisten
Children will look to you
For which way to turn
To learn what to be
Careful before you say
"Listen to me."
Children will listen (Stephen Sondheim, *Into the Woods*, 1987)

After crisply uniformed MPs came for the Yellow Kid one day, we never saw him again, but thought he had been released, as he had only been brought here because of a technicality, a frame-up over a phone call, thinking, *he didn't deserve that, did he*? I spread a message through the camp *Bratva* boys that we should put down our personal, meaningful, jarring thoughts, as epistles delivered to the liberated Fixer; Willi said he would pull in a last favor with *El Comandante,* to utilize disaffected Hispanic, black, Arab guards, workers, throughout the prison and naval base, to get the *Guantánamo Elegies* to him. With no writing implements, paper or ink, other than what Dr. Waterson slipped in, we cautiously scribbled our individual contributions, sneaking them out so they would see the light of day (our most intimate, clear, maybe last musings disclosed to a penalizing world), even if we would not, and made sure he got them, despite losing respect for him, for selling out to the Gitmo commander to secure his selfish liberation.

As editor of Slay Magazine, and the novel he was crafting, I was privy to a rough draft he started here and was hopefully completing outside. I already expressed to its author that his style was long winded, convoluted, obstruse, leaving more questions unanswered than solved. With thirty-three chapters in all, he was having a great deal of difficulty finishing the last one, pondering upon, stuck on, the number 33. I saw his obsession with 33, as a symbol of his messiah complex, a need to save this world from itself. I suggested, maybe he was holding on too closely to his characters, like Luigi Pirandello, and had to set them free. He should never confuse his personality with those of his creations, no matter how logical it might seem for his self-analysis. They had their destinies, and he had his, no sense in mixing them up; but this existential dilemma, of personages and their author, should not distract from the more esoteric problems of the work, such as sentences leading upwards into the sky, within paragraphs bringing one down, off the clouds; the whole volume revolving round axes of love/ forgiveness versus hate/ revenge. Furthermore, I had been part of the Fixer/ Yellow Kid's story for so long, I was resentful after living in his shadow, and wanted my own time to explain the thing as I saw it, separately from his interpretation; even to mock his assumption of the *nom de plume* T. Awdry Winks, an easy way to avoid responsibility for the controversial things he says, getting out of Dodge before he's challenged to. Was my interest in Lilly's mother's entombment in Guantánamo, due to my mother's long exile to the Gulag Archipelago? Did my certain lover boy, Brighton Beach henchman, believe that his ancestor, General Zaroff, was the hero of, "The Most Dangerous Game?" Do characters possess souls? will this book ever be published?

Yes, I became fascinated with the idea of imprisonment, vicariously reliving my own desperation, each time I thought of Lilly and her missing mother. Whose business is it, if Zaroff is savvy, if he is loyal? Denying the characters' lives is a ploy most would shun, denying the book's publication a wrong done.

Final Edit

My mother was rescued by the Colonel, to whom I send a tribute, in case we never see each other again, as I feel this is his last campaign. Someone once said no one gets out alive, the good ones drop like flies, and if such refers to him, who knows?

And I have a half-sister, who looks to be his spitting image, hating the sight of me. How shall I reconcile my innocence with her riled animosity? What fault have I if one sibling had her father's eye, while the other wished in vain, to be seen by him.

Absent mothers being one of the ghosts we hold in common, I should think she'd have some empathy for me. After all, we shared the same monster of a father, the Archer of Auschwitz, not a sympathetic fellow, unless one gets to know him, over

time. But still, the only father we can claim as our own, despite his grave failings; considering our lineage, I would be prone to forgive those who trespass against us; if children will listen imagine what they will say about our intransigence and hate.

I can only rely on what I've seen, or read, about our common experience, but there is more than enough conclusive evidence to realize, there is only so much we can ever do to alter destiny, whether ours or someone else's, or if not, it's in our genes.

Knowing the Fixer/ Yellow Kid was my half-brother would never excuse schlocky writing, of which he would be far guiltier without my controlling impulse. Green eyes or not, I never called him by his name, thinking of him always as my brother

or star reporter, with no chit chat, nothing more. I knew he always had my back; I owed him a wrap-up worthy of his trust. It was I who shortened his chapters to a tolerable length, fixing quotes, references, acknowledgements, presenting newer

themes of transformation, alongside ancient myths of metamorphosis, juxtaposing border jumping with historic conquests, mass population movements, across space and time, and spreading the word against fascism, totalitarianism and extremism.

All the lyric poetic distractions were his doing, and I take no responsibility for the sometimes-sappy prose, or stilted verse, as his reveries and impulses were beyond anyone's control, and even magical Fitzgerald was a better prose author, than poet.

This huge task of editing him to respectability, has taken it out of me, considering the limited time I had to finish. After focusing on the main manuscript, I came up with the idea for the *Guantánamo Elegies,* missives to an indifferent, outer world.

If you happen to receive these messages, from locked up souls, please don't ignore them, but add them as final chapters to your original work, as they will help you to bring fulfillment to your perpetual personae, and readers, reflecting vibrant cores.

# 33. Guantánamo Elegies

## T. Awdry Winks

> In my beginning is my end... In my end is my beginning.
> (T.S. Eliot, "East Coker," 1940)

That poet must have been in tune, early on, with Eastern notions of reincarnation and endless existence, with nary an indication of succumbing to our common mortality, as he transfigured into a spirit for the ages. I needed to wrap it up, prior to inevitable, bodily comeuppance, cognitive decline, physical decay, as the millennium was the cusp of unfulfilled promises, unrelinquished baggage, deflated beginnings, society as confused, as Edgar Cayce's transmigrated souls were dissociated, upon entering a new body. There is no justice, only vengeance, empty space remaining from those departed; life's so hard, it's not surprising so many people try to kill themselves, mocking in others what they fear in themselves. I am sick and tired of cowards, criminals, seedy politicians, hiding behind deep-seated Constitutional rights. With many great books written by bad people, while few bad books by great people, the first category would have, the *Little Red Book, Mein Kampf, The State and Revolution*, the *oeuvre* of the Marquis De Sade, and other crazy perverts of history; while the second category would not include any I can think of, save weaponized internet partisan free speech, striking blindly, with unintended mass consequences. Free speech seemed to be getting people in trouble these days, when everyone shot off their mouth with no hesitation, issuing threats or counter threats leading to possible violence until stopped in their tracks. The truth was that after the big one, things went back to normal, with so many regrets surfacing, in due time, each side preaching, touting, to no end, telling the other what to do. Will there be no end to this? After a disastrous election Abraham Lincoln wailed, "It hurts too much to laugh, but I'm too old to cry." We condemned had no choice but delving deeply into our notions, which would never be held captive: *the 1960s as the 1920s in terms of creativity, the 1970s as the 1930s for incipient repressions, the 1980s the beginning of an antiquarian resurgence, to today's libertarian mania, for free speech and gun rights.* As the universe was constantly improving conservatives were out of luck, progressives driving changes here to stay, recalling that we first got up, from all fours, and walked upright in baby steps to start, then colossal strides, before sinking into new depths, of a silence all-consuming in its empty shriek. And the stars used their glowing light to inform, that though eons in arriving, even they were not eternal bodies, allowing there is good and evil, but man himself is not good or evil. Whitman claimed, that after years of competing for, "the usual rewards," a "perturbation" led to his quizzical cameo in *Leaves of Grass*, a new poet's fascination with prognostication, metaphysical reasoning, thus transmitted through the ages. And if man's first millennium began with Adam and Eve their gist will survive successive ones forever. Adrift upon murky seas of infinite possibilities, with no ready notion of forgiving land in sight, the Pillars of Hercules defined the edge of the known world, beyond which lay the mystery of the abyss, dreaded CHAOS! lurking menacingly, at three in the morning in the corners of my room, before my very eyes... *It was a brilliant clear unassuming day whose patient silence was at a far distance suddenly pierced by two sharp claps in the atmosphere and rolling endless rumbling across the land then brown pulpy rains arrived on shattered poisoned winds with bestial inhuman howls and purple lights across multi-scarred horizons without end reminding mortals MAD had been inconsequential blather to those who mattered.*

> This is not drivel but to remind you of the early, exploratory words of our journey, encompassing forever the inner summation of mere being, in this cosmic ordering, prying outer panels to the vivid triptych of our souls: of Eden, lust and reckoning.

> The time had finally come, for the disinterested inquisitor to put his tome out there for judgement, with its sketchy concepts, of original sin, concupiscence, leading to

an instant fall at birth, and the vale of tears, an uphill battle, from then until death.

It was not a very optimistic solution to the parable of life as we now explain it, but faith being all he had to offer, considering the Dark Ages of limited understanding, he was more edgy for his folio's reception than the hundred souls he'd immolated.

Nevertheless, his brethren applauded their monastic superior, for masterful views revealed only to him by God, his allegorical figures personifying the highest and lowest morals in all, vying for pleasure, choice, in a grand experiment of the ages.

Far from a *Mundus antiquus*, which had first drawn us together, before dispersing Everyman to the winds of time, across newly found continents, extending to future freedoms, claimed liberties, iconoclastic creeds, we were reborn at last, in earnest.

So, I did not vote, as I did not like either party enough to endorse them, while not hating either enough to cast for the other. I am tired of elevating those above their merits, consequently above ours, to rule us, by electing them to it, and would only

vote for those who are not running, as texting became a fractured forum of deceit; but I shall never compromise myself, I'll have no truck with philosophy that farts, and have as little as possible to do, with regimes stifling choices for roles to play.

It's enough for me to love my personages, without considering reciprocal feelings, having named them from nothing, conceding only to weak guilt in apologizing for inappropriate words sent, but doomed and a wretch for what I've so loosely let fly.

As omniscient narrator to do-nothing divas, I deserved better than imprisonment in a rotten, tropical garden of America, now a number, proving our greatest fear to be real, not illusory, leaving us alone, disconsolate, at 3 AM, pondering elusive 33,

in a contemporary dialogue of actualized paranoia, Manifest Destiny foisted upon my dreams, as that uncircumcised "Me myself" of pagan influence, pointless pivot round himself, before opening his *Magnum opus* of good-doer thoughts and deeds.

Even if photographs had no breath, nor life, selfies made everyone into stars, for a fleeting meme moment, clicking this: *being enslaved by* Mapuches, *only to find* El Dorado *as a sacrificing cannibal, signaling Henry Hudson, making it home again,*

with enduring, dreadful, rowdy routines of impatiently practicing musketry on the native population; thus, emboldened, at last mutinied to the state our country is in, the Divided Flakes of America, 50 identities united by a Laffer curve of tax utility.

But there was still love, to grasp, keep, perhaps enticing desires, figments, flames, as with *Phaedrus*, because love, truth and justice are Platonic forms of perfection, impossible to achieve in our mortal guises and encumbrances, as reckless drifters.

And if Eros exuded immortality, I learned to offer love's libations, rather than buy brusque brutality, soaring alongside Hermes in ancient woods, to get a message to the waiting world, anticipating hearing of, believing in, the greatness still to come.

# Epilogue

I guess there is not much more to tell, only, I have already described the thing in as numerous ways as I could, so you would see it from as many eyes as possible, hopefully capturing the *zeitgeist* of the epoch along the way. I tried to spin a tawdry tale, as full of life itself, as our lives were, only more so, and if I am not mistaken, everyone was given the chance to vent their spleen. Now for the true denouement, as I am the unfettered wordsmith of this volume, and not the bossed personality of my own composition. As a creator endeavors to soar, fancying Icarus had reason, I had also been the hidden hero of my own story, as the active narrator stumbling forward blindly, sometimes stepping back to consider his results, for writers carefully affirm what they compose, while public speakers let fly, with whatever is needed. In the end it was about doing what one could to get noticed, penning a satire of epic reach and mythic dimensions, encompassing both comedy and tragedy: comedy for the follies of misspent lives, tragedy for numerous failures that could not be averted. I had too many memories needing sharing, and as the young have none, I must have this completed before Alzheimer's sets in, and my mind turns into mush; no ghost writers need apply, as they are hacks unless real ghosts. If enfeebled I shall try recalling I had played T. Awdry Winks, because his identity was mine to follow/ lead on errant wanderings of the soul, lunacy skipping the forgiving, minding preoccupied psyches, who bide their time with aliases, pretexts.

*At the Millennium: Paradise Crossed* was meant to advance ideas of transition, into our working gears. If the book did not grab you, please dismiss it, but at your peril or loss, for being unprepared for future shock. Go ahead, dictate your personal chronicle at destiny's gut-wrenching lead. That's my challenge if you dare see how tough we can all get, with only pen in hand. Who needs guns to make their point? To those who say, the passages of quotes got in the way of the telling, I say, peruse them again; then get another work to read, perhaps devoid of any acknowledgements, along with all the wit, in your hurry to miss out on the latest, most forward-looking thought: mine. I appeal to history before poetry or literary taste, so please let me document sources and references. At least I have no qualms, in showing I have never been that original, still under the tutelage of my betters, until I may join them if ever called upon; a final hope being that the author selections were never tedious, but at least entertaining and instructive, in any case, evidence that other minds out there, from past or present, agreed with me, and I with them.

My early visit to the *Museo del Prado*, before that wonder of wonders, *The Garden of Earthly Delights*, was the first time I was bowled over by the aesthetic power of a work of art. Maybe this hyper-surreal screed of mine, was but the labile rambling, excess gibber, blather, prattle, of the author. Hopefully, it was comedic, clever, amusing, even though no specific personage is a comedian, fool or clown, *per se*; and wasn't about political affiliation, orientation or belief, but more about getting a rise out of two sides joined in mutually assured destruction. This was the birth of a new world order and sorrows following, for we found meaning in our days, by anticipating the simple pleasures they would bring, avoiding the dreaded CHAOS! of three AM alone in bed, wondering if fate would sort out 33, so we would be OK.

Released from Gitmo on Thanksgiving, I returned to a world angry at America and the West; Christmas is gone, and New Year's awaits; I have just gotten a rough parcel smuggled over, with the *Guantánamo Elegies*, in which each character hints at what it meant to them, in an existential retailing of a persona's action; the *ineluctable modality of the visible* behind mean concentration camp wires, I was saved from. Such was Everyman's ascent, to the new millennium I was fortunate enough to welcome; a voice in the dark, indistinct, unobserved, yet hawk-eyed chronicler of a period not so much a date, as a force; and in time, evolving higher, to the "Me myself," who now wishes to those remaining seekers a fond farewell:

> These come to me days and nights and go from me again,
> But they are not the Me myself.

# Genealogies/ Chronologies/ Locales

Prologue

## The Garden of Earthly Delights

> Creation's third day, gray tints and a hollow core of monochrome to fill and color, now freed at last in our celestial reaches, to approximate the secret spheres within, prying outer panels to the vivid triptych of our souls: of Eden, lust and reckoning, the *Museo del Prado*, Madrid, Spain.

## 1. The Mystery of the Stars

2002 – A time as quizzical, fine, as any, however, imbued with the new millennium's cleansing promise: Los Angeles, CA, the Garden of Earthly Delights, new urbanity of infinite dreams, hopes, possibilities; delusions, desires, grand designs run aground, as well, so that just being there was the trip of a lifetime.

## 2. *Mundus novus*

1967? - L'il Lay L'or Ence, Willamina Hernan, the exact dates and locations unknown, due to poverty. They found the meaning of their days, in each successive episode of endurance for their hard existence. Questions: were they divinely made, of thought or word? perhaps His cast-off dreams? born fractious infants of one millennium, *enfants terrible* of the next, not of known, assumed, invented genealogies, their innumerable, anonymous and imagined descendants destined as the generations that flourished, to repopulate lands gone fallow, stale, with revitalized seeds of tomorrows merging to awaking daylight. The genealogy of the spirit of those times was imbued in such descendants as would claim a birthright.

## 3. *Mundus antiquus*

1985 - L'il Lay L'or Ence and Willamina Hernan arrive in the United States of America, a renaissance.

## 4. The Modern Prometheus

1957 - Henry Waterson, M.D., Mescalero Apache country, exact date and location unknown (Native Americans do not measure space, or time, with trivial references to owning them, as does narcissistic, Western man) (Whale Class of 1979, Medicine 1981), Native, no, Original American Medicine Man Supreme, agent of tremendous global social change and upheaval; also, Willy and Lilly's adoptive father; of mixed Original American, Polynesian extraction, skin the color of tennis court clay, straight black hair; descended from powerful *Apache* medicine men, illustrious chiefs.

1970 – Mid March, wanton gang rape of a quiet, studious, sensitive, Indian brave, by a beauteous bevy of over-wealthy, over-impressionistic, oversexed, eastern college girls.

1986 – Our heroes meet, undergoing final reassignment, a process as reckless, as it was irrevocable, glazed in the glowing patina of supreme self-realization, progress, trendiness; despite having no accompanying certificates defining them as millennials through rebirth, Los Angeles, CA.

1988 – Coming-out party for Lilly Lawrence and Willi Hernan, where they were presented to steady Isidora Green, and met kookie, West Point educated, John B. Sayer, before expulsion from the Garden of Eden.

## 5. Immigration (Super) Man

1600 - Deacon J. Bigger Sayer, East Anglia, England, with a sanctimonious, severe, but unpretentious disposition.

1618 – Cloud, Connecticut River Valley, in what became Windsor, Connecticut, *Pequot* princess, lowly, red unbeliever, visited by Humility, the deacon's demure wife; such forgiveness, the only Christian charity Cloud ever knew.

1633 – Sayer's forefathers on these shores, mixing with native peoples.

1813 – Connecticut becomes the first state to pass a child labor law, requiring schooling for child workers. 1822 - Singleton Sayer (SS) purchases 100 slaves, on his way to Texas.

1944 - John B. Sayer MPPM, Windsor, CT (The U.S. Military Academy at West Point Class of 1966, U.S. Army War College, 1979, Whale School of Management, 1981), descended from Sayers persisting in Connecticut for some thirteen generations following Deacon Bigger and his original land grab, secret benefactor to, participant in, nefarious underground groups.

1990 – September - Superman was gone, flying up endless stairs through crowded station, out the revolving door and into the Indian summer twilight, rushing off to his appointment or rendezvous, as were perhaps any number of other successful, corporate comic book heroes on the town that night, New York, NY, suburban Xanadu, Bestport, Connecticut, enchanted East of Eden.

## 6. Geronimo's Ghost

1590s – Rumors of a Gypsy marker tied directly to dispersed *Roma*, most distant of relations, two generations pre-Origin.

1654 – Origin, Grey Green's great great-great-great grandfather, founder of the slave business. 1684 - Grey Green's great great-great grandfather, founding of the slave business.

1714 - Grey Green's great-great grandfather. 1744 - Grey Green's great grandfather.

1774 – Hyde Green, Grey Green's grandfather, the Green-Eyed Monster.

1795 – Greens leave Scotland because of abolitionist sentiment, bound for Jamestown, Virginia. 1804 – Grey Green's father, Bingham.

1822 - Singleton Sayer (SS) purchases 100 slaves, on his way to Texas. 1834 - Gray Green, New York State.

1864 – Children of Gray Green. 1888 – Daughters' weddings.

1890 – Grandchildren.

1904 – Whale University endowment. 1912 - Death of Gray Green.

1916 - Great grandchildren.

1942 – Great-great grandchildren.

1951 – Great-great granddaughter, Isidora Green, MPPM, New York, NY (Whale Class of 1973, Management 1976), polished, articulate heiress to one of America's great fortunes, the Founding Matriarch, and active Sissy, of the Sisterhood of Grace (Sisters of Fervent Grace, Society of Grace), a secret society at Whale University, in New Haven, CT.

1969 – October 10 - First Tap Day for the Sisterhood of Grace, a quiet affair for its founding members.

1970 – Mid-March, hallucinating heavily, the sisters brought their prized heirloom, Geronimo's Ghost, unwitting guest, to new, upscale digs, the society's wondrous, gleaming Museum for the Ages. The next Tap Night, in April, would begin the tradition of G's G coming out of his cell to perform.

1990 - It had certainly been a good year so far, and it was only mid-April, "*`Le roi est mort, vive le roi!*"

a celebratory lunch for the entire board at the 21 Club's reserved secret dining room, and as good fortune had it, it was also Tap Night, New York, NY, New Haven, CT.

## 7. New Meth City

1785 – Patriarch Singleton Sayer, nicknamed SS. 1810 – SS Sayer, the Colonel's father.

1822 – SS arrives in Texas, having purchased 100 slaves in Jamestown.

1835 - Colonel Lucius B. Sayer.

1845 - An eligible *senorita* from one of the most notable, wealthy families in the state of *Nuevo Leon*, Elvira Nubes y de los Gatos, a very beautiful, dusky *mestizo*, as her mother was a fiery, full blooded *Comanche* princess, captured in a raid by her Mexican rancher father.

1865 – Illegitimacy begins (Colonel 30) (short generations, every 15 years).

1880 – Illegitimacy, second generation.

1895 – Illegitimacy, third generation.

1897 – Advanced syphilis, decline in reproduction. 1905 - Colonel Lucius B. Sayer, R.I.P.

1913 - Grandfather Hannibal P. Gates, La Florencia, TX (Pueblo Sayer). 1915 - Elvira Sayer, R.I.P.

1926 - Picking up and leaving without even a firm destination, or the realization they had joined the Great Migration, in search of new horizons, dignity and redemption.

1943 - Rev. Hannibal P. (Pearly) Gates' father.

1973 - Rev. Hannibal P. (Pearly) Gates, M.Div., New Haven, CT, James Hillhouse High School, 1991 (Whale Class of 1995, Divinity 1998), enlightened, modern, as he acted and appeared, was a bitter product of this pernicious trade; descended from African kings on the wrong side of tribal wars, who were subsequently sold into bondage, as their fate, by the victors.

2001 - Once all the introductory formalities were over, Preacher Pearly got to the heart of the matter, looking Sayer right in the eyes, boldly declaring they could be kin, New Haven, CT, New York, NY.

## 8. Gung-ho

1590s – Stories of a Gypsy marker tied directly to dispersed *Roma*, most distant of relations.

1954 - Patricia (P) Diddy, Ph.D., J.D., Ledmont, CT (Whale Class of 1979, Sociology 1986, Law 1989), they were Melungeon, proudly sharing jumbled Jewish, Middle Eastern, African, Caucasian, Native American roots, active Sissy of the Sisterhood of Grace.

1971 – 1974 – Private, U.S. Marine Corps, Vietnam conflict (but never declared war), expert shooter.

1990 – 2000 – Social Worker, Connecticut Department of Children and Families (DCF), Child Protection, New Haven, CT.

2001- Founder-president and thus far sole member of international humanitarian group, *Les Enfants Sans Frontičres*; Greenitch had swank, Ledmont none.

## 9. *Dan de Riber* or Splendor on the Gold Coast

1400s - With such attitudes, was it any wonder it was so easy for white traders, scheming though they were, to acquire already seized, enslaved Africans for the Atlantic Trade? Tragically, as the lineages of New World slave descendants were cruelly obliterated by time, as well as the bad faith of the multi raced captors, withholding their families from them, resulting in helplessness, isolation, Hannibal preserved the memory of his several generations of Texan kin, through the Colonel.

1661 – The first entry of the sordid journal, by a British missionary then sermonizing on the Gold Coast, under the chartered auspices of the Royal Africa Company, and the royal authority of the Golden Stool.

2004 – United Nations Headquarters, New York, NY, New Haven, CT.

## 10. The Corporate *Kapo* and The Archer of Auschwitz

1915 - *Schutzstaffel* (*SS*) Colonel Otto Waldemar Grawitz, Konigsberg, East Prussia (*SS-Junkerschulen*, 1938), descended from indigenous barbarians, pagans, Old Prussians, escaped Nazi war criminal.

1944 - April 20 ("Born on the same day as the *Fuhrer*, an auspicious omen.") - Ms. Yael Abraham (Grawitz), Ph.D., Auschwitz Concentration Camp, Poland (Whale Class of 1973, Psychology 1980), of unknown descent (father an escaped Nazi war criminal, blond, faceless mother), adopted war refugee, Holocaust survivor, bearing a jagged tattoo on her outer, left forearm, an inmate's number 169062, which she could not remember getting, active Sissy, first Jewish Sisterhood of Grace Alumni President.

2004 – Sanctuary, CA, United Nations Headquarters, New York, NY.

## 11. *Camera Obscura*

1956 – The Hungarian Revolution, Grawitz meets a captivating Red Army officer and spy, whose older sister, red headed Rus', beautiful Slav princess, he murdered in the war, who is later exiled to the Gulag, and subsequently rescued by the Colonel, in *48 Hours to Mecca*.

1956 – Ottoline (Grawitz), Novgorod, Russia (Lomonosov Moscow State University Class of 1978), father an escaped Nazi war criminal, mother the Ukrainian (extracted from the *kulak* class) younger sister of the murdered red headed Rus', beautiful Slav princess.

1957 - T. (Tiddly) Awdry Winks, aka the Yellow Kid/ Fixer (Grawitz), *Providencia de las Nubes* (stone-built urban center concealed in the clouds, *Cordillera de los Andes*), Provincia de Cautín, Chile (Whale Class of 1979), father an escaped Nazi war criminal, mother a *Mapuche* princess, with literary leanings.

2004, 2010 - Bestport.

## 12. Womb of The Stars

Recap:

1986 – The proto heroic protagonists meet in paradise, Los Angeles, CA, the Garden of Earthly Delights.

1988 – 2000 – *Our struggles to get ahead.*

1989 – *We were married in a Roman Catholic church by a rogue priest, with imam and mullah attending for my sake, though their presence itched my scars.*

1997 – *Children appeared (after finding the right formulas), with steady frequency.*

1998 – *We acquired Pinkton, our Mt. Olympus, for a song.*

2002 - 03 – There had been news flashes of periodic paramilitary faceoffs in the night, but nothing ever possibly connected, even as the faintest of rumors, to harems, captives, morning milking rituals.

2003 - *48 Hours to Mecca*, leading the leading lady's greatest comeback, filmed on location, released early 2004.

2004 – Ms. Yael Abraham's directive, to get out of Dodge, head for beach and sand at the eccentric and ill-behaved duo's ocean side bungalow in Baja California.

## 13. *Sieg Heil*

2004 - Wild animal spirits poolside, at *bon vivant* (ill-behaved) Lone Ranger John B. Sayer's Baja California oceanside *hacienda,* down the pink, sandy beach from her and Willi's own hideout.

### 14. No Harm in Harems, or Harem in Harm's Way

2004 - Lilly was back, having coffee on the hot terrace, a shade chagrined for her absence from her spouse for two nights straight, a bit the worse for wear, hell raising, hands, face, hair reeking of spent gunpowder. Ocean side bungalow in Baja Cal., Famefield County, CT, New York, NY.

### 15. *48 Hours to Mecca*

2004 - Willi connected with his superstar spouse's super-stare, on blazing patio, after an absence of two nights in a row, an unprecedented liberty presumed within their marriage, so far. Beachside Bungalow Studio, Baja Cal., Saudi Arabia, Israel, Hollywood, CA, New York, NY.

### 16. The Sky is Falling

1346 – Caffa (now Feodosija, Ukraine) was besieged by the Mongols, in the first use of biological warfare, hurling bubonic plague infected corpses over its ramparts, so they rained down on doomed inhabitants, spreading one of the worst pestilences on record.

2004 - Baja California, Sanctuary, CA, Houston, TX.

### 17. *Auto-da-fe* (Renunciation of the Heretics)

9 AD - United Germanic tribes annihilated three Roman Legions at the Battle of the Teutoburg Forest, *Germania*, Roman Gaul, devastating to its national prestige, as Rome was now held off at the Rhine River.

1492 - Among those doomed to be sacrificed for apostasy were two sisters, one blond, the other red headed, during the Inquisition, in a backward-looking, late Medieval/ early Renaissance Seville, Spain, ironically the same year a *Mundus novus* was about to be discovered, launching the Age of Discovery.

2004 - Baja California, Sanctuary, CA, Damnos, Switzerland.

### 18. BFP (Black Female Preferred) or Color Wheel

1191 – Richard the Lionheart massacres 2,700+ bound Musulman prisoners in cold blood, Acre, the Levant, Holy Land, present day Israel.

1521 – Aztecs sacrifice and cannibalize sixty-two evangelical brothers in *Tenochtitlan, Mexico.*

1721 – One Negro Winch Hadi & her son Hani sold at Whale's to slave dealer Origin Green, Glasgow, Scotland.

1802 – John C. Calgoun, effete, snobby southerner with his own darkie valet, joined the Whale Class of 1804.

1992 - Hannibal's first political protest, New Haven, CT. To 2006 - New Haven, CT, Sanctuary, CA, L.A.

### 19. BTC (Bear Trap Capital) or Pecuniary Promise

782 - Charlemagne's Blood Court of Verden, Lower Saxony, Germany, where 4,500 Saxon rebels are executed.

1687 – Elihu Whale as president of Fort St. George, colonialist thief-in-chief, Madras, India.

1890 - Wounded Knee Massacre, near Wounded Knee Creek, Lakota Pine Ridge Indian Reservation. To 2009 - New York, NY, L.A., Sanctuary, CA.

## 20. Civil War

1783 - Christmas Eve, witty Thomas Jefferson had dinner and cups with a stiff George Washington.

To 2010 – At Isidora's summer beach home on the Buyreem Shore in Greenitch, CT, Washington D.C., Marine Corps Brig, Quantico, Virginia, where they were kept incommunicado.

## 21. In Fitzgerald's Footsteps

1995 – August to January 1996 - Spending an orgiastic summer in Bestport at its baddest, and soothing best, the fabled duo, in their youth, as the Beautiful and Damned.

1996 - February – The French Riviera, September – The Magic Mountain.

To 2010 - September 22 - Guantánamo, Cuba (Anachronism of 1776 – Nathan Hale, June 6, 1755, Coventry, Connecticut, Yale Class of 1773, patriot, soldier, executed in Manhattan as a spy).

## 22. Transfiguration

58 BC - Little did Thomas Jefferson know that one of his ancient, redheaded Briton ancestors was immolated in a pyre of sacrificial cleansing, not for her own crimes, for she was unblemished still, but for those of a coward.

2010 – September through November - I felt bitterly betrayed by life, to be a guest at Guantánamo; released from Gitmo on Thanksgiving, I returned to a world angry at rulers and leaders; midtown Manhattan, at St. Patrick's Cathedral's holiday Mass; Bestport, used as a getaway by famous artists, writers, actors, since the late 1800s; and if Greenitch had big money, Bestport had a lot, but was more fun.

## 23 – 33. Guantónamo Elegies

2008 - *Shaka Washington Gates, his name would represent the past spilling into the future.*

2010 – September through December, Guantánamo, in which each character hints at what it meant to them, an existential retailing of a persona's action. Indeed, such fluidity between the real and the imagined worlds would become a hallmark of our work.

## Epilogue

2010 – Christmas is gone, and New Year's awaits; I have just gotten a rough parcel smuggled over, with the *Guantánamo Elegies*, Bestport.

# Quotes/References

## Epigraph

The palm at the end of the mind,
Beyond the last thought, rises
In the bronze decor... (Wallace Stevens, "Of Mere Being," 1954)

## Prologue

### The Garden of Earthly Delights

(Hieronymus Bosch, Dutch/Netherlandish, *The Garden of Earthly Delights*, c. 1480-1505)

### a. *Ante Mundum*

—For he spake and it was done; he commanded, and it stood fast. (Psalm 33:9, King James Version [KJV], Early Modern English translation of the Christian Bible for the Church of England, 1604-1611)

### b. *Initium*

The divine intelligence, being nurtured upon mind and pure knowledge, and the intelligence of every soul which is capable of receiving the food proper to it, rejoices at beholding reality, and once more gazing upon truth, is replenished and made glad, until the revolution of the worlds brings her round again to the same place. In the revolution she beholds justice, and temperance, and knowledge absolute, not in the form of generation or of relation, which men call existence, but knowledge absolute in existence absolute; and beholding the other true existences in like manner, and feasting upon them, she passes down into the interior of the heavens and returns home... (Plato, *Phaedrus*, 370 BC)

...paradise lost... (John Milton, *Paradise Lost*, 1667)

### c. *El Dorado*

*El Dorado* [The mythical Colombian Golden King, covered with gold dust, in his hidden city, obsessed over by Spanish *conquistadores* in the 16th and 17th centuries, to modern treasure seekers today]

The pink palm being empty, in other words, to their vision, they had begun, from far back, to put things into it, things of their own, and of all sorts, and of many ugly, and of more and more expensive, sorts; to fill it substantially, that is, with gold, the gold that they have ended by heaping up there to an amount so oddly out of proportion to the scale of nature and of space. (Henry James, "The Sense of Newport," 1906)

*Paparazzo* [a character's name before becoming the generic term for a celebrity-hounding photographer] (Federico Fellini, *La Dolce Vita*, 1960)

The wolf also shall dwell with the lamb, and the leopard shall lie down with the kid; and the calf and the young lion and the fatling together; and a little child shall lead them. (Isaiah 11:6, KJV)

## d. *Aurora Borealis*

I hope for nothing. I fear nothing. I am free. (Epitaph on the grave of Nikos Kazantzakis, 1883 – 1957, in Heraklion)

*Magnum Opus* [An alchemical term for the process of working with the *prima materia* to create the philosopher's stone]

I was not; I have been; I am not; I do not mind.
[*Non fui, fui, non sum, non curo.*] (Inscribed on memorials of Epicurus' devotees, on gravestones of the Roman Empire.)

## 1. The Mystery of the Stars

Lo! thy dread empire, CHAOS! is restored;
Light dies before thy uncreating word:
Thy hand, great anarch! lets the curtain fall;
And universal darkness buries all.
(Alexander Pope, "The Dunciad," 1733 – 1734)

**Messenger**
[605] Your wife has disappeared, taken up into the folds of the unseen air; she is hidden in
heaven, and as she left the hallowed cave where we were keeping her safe [sōzein], she said
this: "Miserable Phrygians, and all the Achaeans! On my account you were dying by the banks
of Skamandros, [610] through Hera's contrivance, for you thought that Paris had Helen when
he didn't. But I, since I have stayed my appointed time, and having kept to [sōzein] my
destiny, will now depart into the sky, my father; but the unhappy daughter of Tyndareus,
[615] guilty [aitia] in no way, has borne evil [kakai] rumors without reason."

*Catching sight of Helen*
Welcome, daughter of Leda, were you here after all? I was just announcing your departure up
to the hidden starry realms, not knowing that you had a winged body. I will not let you mock
us like this again, [620] for you gave your fill of ordeals [ponos plural] to

your husband and his
allies in Ilion. (Euripides, translation by E. P. Coleridge Revised by the
Helen Heroization team [Hélčne Emeriaud, Claudia Filos, Janet M.
Ozsolak, Sarah Scott, Jack Vaughan], *Helen*, 412 BC)

Eliza Doolittle (George Bernard Shaw, *Pygmalion*, 1913)

I've seen your picture
Your name in lights above it
This is your big debut
It's like a dream come true
So won't you smile for the camera?
I know they're gonna love it
Peg

I like your pin shot
I keep it with your letter
Done up in blueprint blue
It sure looks good on you
And when you smile for the camera
I know I'll love you better

Peg
Will come back to you
Peg
Will come back to you
Then the shutter falls (shutter falls)
You see it all in 3-D
(Foreign movie)
It's your favorite foreign movie (Steely Dan, *Aja*, "Peg", 1977)

Gulag Archipelago (Alexander Solzhenitsyn, *The Gulag Archipelago*, 1973)

We have to distrust each other. It is our only defence against betrayal.
(Tennessee Williams, *Camino Real*, 1953)

"There were two in paradise and the choice was offered to them:
happiness without freedom or freedom without happiness... They, fools
that they were, chose freedom – naturally, for centuries afterward they
longed for fetters..." (Yevgeny Zamyatin, *We*, "Record Eleven," 1920/ 21)

A foreign substance is introduced into our precious bodily fluids, without
the knowledge of the individual, certainly without any choice. That's the way
your hard-core Commie works. (Stanley Kubrick, *Dr, Strangelove*, 1964)

Something is rotten in the state of Denmark... (William Shakespeare [the
bard of Avon], *The Tragedy of Hamlet, Prince of Denmark*, Act 1, Scene IV,
1599-1601)

The dose makes the poison. (Paracelsus, Swiss physician, alchemist, philosopher of the Renaissance, 1493-1541)

...the kindness of strangers...
(Tennessee Williams, *A Streetcar named Desire*, Scene 11, 1947)

Therefore all things whatsoever ye would that men should do to you, do ye even so to them: for this is the law and the prophets. [The Golden Rule] (Matthew 7:12, KJV)

...the intoxication of sweet revenge
(--"sweeter than honey" Homer called it)...
(Friedrich Nietzsche, *On the Genealogy of Morals: A Polemical Tract*, 1877)

Therefore, when Hermaphroditus sees that the limpid waters, into which he had descended as a man, have made him but half a male, and that his limbs are softened in them, holding up his hands, he says, but now no longer with the voice of a male, "O, both father [Hermes] and mother [Aphrodite], grant this favor to your son, who has the name of you both, that whoever enters these streams a man, may go out thence but half a man, and that he may suddenly become effeminate in the waters when touched." Both parents, moved, give their assent to the words of their two-shaped son, and taint the fountain with drugs of ambiguous quality. (Ovid, 43BC – 17/ 18AD, *The Metamorphoses*, Book 4, "Hermaphroditus," Project Gutenberg)

...the fulfillment of our manifest destiny to overspread the continent allotted by Providence for the development or our yearly multiplying millions. (John O'Sullivan, *The Democratic Review*, July – August 1845)

Preamble

Under all is the land. Upon its wise utilization and widely allocated ownership depend the survival and growth of free institutions and of our civilization. (Code of Ethics and Standards of Practice of the NATIONAL ASSOCIATION OF REALTORS, Effective 2012)

...bottle imps... (Robert Louis Stevenson, "The Bottle Imp," 1891)

...the most dangerous game...
(Richard Connell, "The Most Dangerous Game," 1924)

*Medea* (Euripides, *Medea*, 431 BC)

You ought to be in pictures
You're wonderful to see
You ought to be in pictures
Oh, what a hit you would be...

You ought to dress in fashion
And ride in motor cars

You ought to be in pictures
My star of stars
(Dana Suesse, Edward Heyman, "You Oughta be in Pictures," 1934)

The wolf and the lamb shall feed together, and the lion shall eat straw like the bullock: and dust shall be the serpent's meat. They shall not hurt nor destroy in all my holy mountain, saith the LORD. (Isaiah 65:25, KJV)

INELUCTABLE MODALITY OF THE VISIBLE: AT LEAST THAT IF NO MORE, through my eyes. (James Joyce, *Ulysses*, 1925)

## 2. *Mundus novus*

Concerning the Islands Recently Discovered in the Indian Sea

As soon as I reached that sea, I seized by force several Indians on the first island, in order that they might learn from us, and in like manner tell us about those things in these lands of which they themselves had knowledge; and the plan succeeded, for in a short time we understood them and they us, sometimes by gestures and signs, sometimes by words; and it was a great advantage to us. They are coming with me now, yet always believing that I descended from heaven, although they have been living with us for a long time, and are living with us to-day.

Lisbon, the day before the Ides of March. [Christopher Columbus, Letter on The First Voyage announcing his discoveries, 1493] (Samuel Eliot Morison, *Admiral of the Ocean Sea: A Life of Christopher Columbus*, 1942)

Frankenstein (James Whale, *Frankenstein* [film], 1931)

Pygmalion (Ovid, 43BC – 17/ 18AD, *The Metamorphoses*, Book 10, "Pygmalion," Project Gutenberg)

"[T[he famous Fountain of Youth, if I am rightly informed...in the southern part of the Floridian peninsula, not far from Lake Macaco. Its source is overshadowed by several gigantic magnolias, which, though numberless centuries old, have been kept as fresh as violets by the virtues of this wonderful water." (Nathaniel Hawthorne, "Dr. Heidegger's Experiment," 1837)

*...le grand remplacement* [the great replacement]...
(Renaud Camus, *Le Grand Remplacement*, 2011)

...characters in search of an author...
(Luigi Pirandello, *Six Characters in Search of an Author,* 1921)

Holly came from Miami, F.L.A.
Hitch-hiked her way across the U.S.A.
Plucked her eyebrows on the way
Shaved her legs and then he was a she

She says, "Hey, babe
Take a walk on the wild side"
Said, "Hey, honey
Take a walk on the wild side"
(Lou Reed, "Walk on the Wild Side," 1973)

Admiral of the Ocean Sea (Morison, *Admiral of the Ocean Sea*)

...and it is lawful to call it a new world, because none of these countries were known to our ancestors and to all who hear about them they will be entirely new... more populous than our Europe, or Asia, or Africa...
(Amerigo Vespucci, Mundus novus Letter, 1503)

Lawrence of Arabia (David Lean, *Lawrence of Arabia*, 1962)

## 3. *Mundus antiquus*

### a. *Una Guerrilla Perpetua*

FAUSTUS. Had I as many souls as there be stars, I'd give them all for Mephistophilis.
(Christopher Marlowe, *The Tragicall History of D. Faustus*, 1604)

*Dios te salve, María.*
*Llena eres de gracia:*
*El Señor es contigo.*
*Bendita tu eres entre todas las mujeres.*
*Y bendito es el fruto de tu vientre: Jesús.* (*Ave María*)

*Perdona nuestras ofensas,*
*como también nosotros perdonamos a los que nos ofenden.*
*No nos dejes caer en tentación y libéranos del mal.*
*Amen.* (*Padre Nuestro*)

*droog* [friend], *ptitsa* [chick, woman]
(Anthony Burgess, *A Clockwork Orange*, 1962)

...revenge is a dish best served cold...
(Expression, originated in the 1800s, from French)

*Das Kapital* (Karl Marx, *Das Kapital*, 1867)

*Little Red Book* (Chairman Mao Tse Tung, *Little Red Book*, 1964)

I have always imagined that Paradise will be a kind of library.
(Jorge Luis Borges, 1899 – 1986)

Now, voyager, sail thou forth, to seek and find.
(Walt Whitman, *Leaves of Grass*, "The Untold Want," 1891 - 92)

"Do you know why people migrate there? Do you know? Because there is no work here. There is no work," replied Ana Pat. Mejia, 39, who had tried to make the trip with her kids, and her neighbor's son, but was deported back to *Mexico*. "Of course, I am going, again. I must have a house. I do not have a place to live. If I want to, or not, if the *gringos* like it, or not, I am coming." (Recalled by the author, U.S. media, 21st century)

## b. A Perpetual *Jihad*

MEPH. Hell hath no limits, nor is circumscrib'd

In one self place; for where we are is hell,

And where hell is there must we ever be...
(Christopher Marlowe, *The Tragicall History of D. Faustus*, 1604)

*Iblis* (In Islam, the personal name of the Devil)

Our Lord! Perfect our light for us and forgive us our sins, for verily You have power over all things. (Quranic prayer)

My country is not longer only in Africa; we are now part of Europe, too. It is therefore natural for us to abandon our former ways and to adopt a new system adapted to our social conditions.
(H.H. Isma'il Pasha, Khedive of Egypt and Sudan, 1863 - 1879)

Verily, the dwellers of the Paradise, that Day, will be busy in joyful things. They and their wives will be in pleasant shade, reclining on thrones. They will have therein fruits (of all kinds) and all that they ask for. (It will be said to them): Salamun (peace be on you), a Word from the Lord (Allah), Most Merciful. (*Holy Quran*, 36: 55-58)

[America is] the great Satan, the wounded snake.
(Ayatollah Khomeini, 11/5/1979)

## 4. The Modern Prometheus

After days and nights of incredible labour and fatigue, I succeeded in discovering the cause of generation and life; nay, more, I became myself capable of bestowing animation upon lifeless matter.
(Mary W. Shelley, *Frankenstein Or, The Modern Prometheus*, 1818)

Standing Bear later wrote that red flannel underwear caused "actual torture." He remembered the red flannel underwear as "the worst thing about life at Carlisle." (Luther Standing Bear, Oglala Lakota, d. 1939)

Let us go then, you and I,
When the evening is spread out against the sky
Like a patient etherized upon a table...
(T. S. Eliot, "The Love Song of J. Alfred Prufrock," 1911)

High matter thou injoinst me, O prime of men,
Sad task and hard, for how shall I relate
To human sense th' invisible exploits
Of warring Spirits; how without remorse
The ruin of so many glorious once
And perfect while they stood; how last unfold
The secrets of another world, perhaps
Not lawful to reveal? yet for thy good
This is dispenc't, and what surmounts the reach
Of human sense, I shall delineate so,
By lik'ning spiritual to corporal forms,
As may express them best, though what if Earth
Be but the shadow of Heav'n, and things therein
Each t' other like, more then on earth is thought?
(John Milton, *Paradise Lost*, 1667)

"What we've got here is failure to communicate..."
(Stuart Rosenberg, *Cool Hand Luke*, 1967)

...fathers and sons...
(Ivan Turgenev, *Fathers and Sons*, 1862)

Nay but, O man, who art thou that repliest against God? Shall the thing
formed say to him that formed it, Why hast thou made me thus?
(Romans 9:20, KJV)

...invisible hand [self-regulating market forces].
(Adam Smith, *The Theory of Moral Sentiments*, 1759)

Mary wants to be a superwoman
But is that really in her head
But I just want to live each day to love her
for what she is...
Mary wants to be another movie star
But is that really in her mind
And all the things she wants to be
She needs to leave behind...
(Stevie Wonder, *Music of my Mind*, "Superwoman (Where Were You
when I needed You)," 1972)

Animal spirits
(John Maynard Keynes, *The General Theory of Employment*, 1936)

...reefer madness...
(Louis J. Gasnier, *Reefer Madness*, 1936)

To boldly go where no man has gone before...
(Gene Roddenberry, *Star Trek*, 1966)

"Clearly 'inconvenient questions' persist, regarding the recognition of same-sex marriage. For example, must the states permit or recognize a marriage between an aunt and niece? Aunt and nephew? Brother/brother? Father and child? May minors marry? Must marriage be limited to only two people? What about a transgender spouse? Is such a union same-gender or male-female? All such unions undeniably, equally, committed to love, and caring for one another."
(Recalled by the author, U.S. media, 21st century)

Tearful reunion in the USA
Day by day those memories fade away
Some babies grow in a peculiar way
It changed, it grew, and everybody knew
Semi-mojo
Who's this kinky so-and-so?
Papa go

Oh - no hesitation
No tears and no hearts breakin'
No remorse
Oh - congratulations
This is your Haitian Divorce
(Steely Dan, *The Royal Scam*, "Haitian Divorce," 1976)

Some years later, Zeus and Hera were arguing about who got more pleasure from sex: men or women. To settle the argument, they called for Tiresias, who had lived as both. Tiresias took the side of Zeus, saying that women's pleasure was greater, and Hera, in her fury, turned him blind.
(Euripides, *The Bacchae*, 405 BC)

...Dorian Gray... (Oscar Wilde, *The Picture of Dorian Gray*, 1890)

...and as Steele/ Toucht with a Loadstone, dost new motions feele?
(John Donne, "To Mr. Tilman After He Had Taken Orders," 1572)

...Utopias.
(Thomas More, *Utopia*, 1516)

...Tweedledum and Tweedledee...
(Lewis Carroll, *Through the Looking-Glass, and What Alice Found There*, 1871)

I, like the arch fiend, bore a hell within me.
(Shelley, *Frankenstein*)

**5. Immigration (Super) Man**

...if they can get here, they have God's right to come...
For the whole world is the patrimony of the whole world...
(Herman Melville, *Redburn*, 1849)

*The Pilgrim's Progress* (John Bunyan, *The Pilgrim's Progress from This World, to That Which Is to Come*, 1678)

Within these late years, there hath, by God's visitation, reigned a wonderful plague, the utter destruction, devastation, and depopulation of that whole territory, so as there is not left any that do claim or challenge any kind of interest therein. We, in our judgment, are persuaded and satisfied, that the appointed time is come in which Almighty God, in his great goodness and bounty towards us, and our people, hath thought fit and determined, that those large and goodly territories, deserted as it were by their natural inhabitants, should be possessed and enjoyed by such of our subjects. (King James I, Charter of New England, 1620)

But when thou doest alms, let not thy left hand know what thy right hand doeth: (Matthew 6:3, KJV)

Why does the Gospel so command,
"Hide thy good deeds from thy left hand,"?
Because, according to the story,
the left hand signifies vainglory,
which comes from false hypocrisy.
The right hand stands for charity,
which does good, seeking to conceal it,
instead of boasting to reveal it,
so no one knows of it but He
whose name is God and Charity,
for God is Charity...
(Chretien de Troyes, *Perceval; or, the Story of the Grail*, circa 1181)

*Everyman* (Anonymous, *Everyman [The Summoning of Everyman]*, fifteenth century, English morality play)

Take example, all ye that this do hear or see,
How they that I loved best do forsake me,
Except my Good Deeds that bideth truly. 870 (Anonymous, *Everyman*)

Guests, like fish, begin to smell after three days.
(Benjamin Franklin, *Poor Richard's Almanac*, 1732)

...but every Tree is become an Indian for the terrified Inhabitants.
(Colonel Henry Bousquet, letter to General Amherst, 1763, Pontiac's Rebellion [justifying supplying infected blankets, and handkerchiefs to savages a new type of biological warfare, as a final solution])

Once you have but got the Track of those Ravenous howling Wolves, then pursue them vigorously; Turn not back till they are consumed… Beat them small as the Dust before the Wind. (The Reverend Cotton Mather, 1663-1728, New England Puritan clergyman, intellectual, and early champion of "a Collegiate School," later renamed Whale College)

…in every joke a lie has its hidden function…
(Yevgeny Zamyatin, *We*, 1920/ 1921)

He was certainly a card! (Ring Lardner, "Haircut," 1925)

East of Eden (Genesis 4:16 KJV; later quoted, in the common search for human as well as celestial equity, by John Steinbeck, *East of Eden*, 1952)

I don't care if it rains or freezes
Long as I got my plastic Jesus
Riding on the dashboard of my car.
(Eddie Marrs, Stuart Rosenberg, *Cool Hand Luke*, 1967)

I wish I was in the land of cotton,
Old times they are not forgotten;
Look away! Look away! Look away! Dixie Land.
In Dixie Land where I was born,
Early on one frosty mornin,
Look away! Look away! Look away! Dixie Land.
(Daniel Decatur Emmett, "Dixie," 1859)

Wheel about and turn about and do just so,
Ev'ry time I wheel about I jump Jim Crow. (Thomas D. Rice, 1828)

Wa-woo-woohoo, wa-woo woohoo! Wa-woo-woohoo, wa-woo woohoo!
(Rebel Yell of the Confederacy, 1861-1865)

Strike a blow for liberty. (Harry S. Truman, 1930's, referring to joining fellow senators for shots of bourbon at the "doghouse")

And thus, with Christianity on the quarter-deck, and paganism on the forecastle, the Irrawaddy ploughed the sea. (Melville, *Redburn*)

"I want his credentials." (Meredith Willson, *The Music Man*, 1950)

O'er the Land of the free and the home of the brave?
(Francis Scott Key, "The Star-Spangled Banner," 1814)

There I was at the immigration scene
Shining and feeling clean, could it be a sin?
I got stopped by the immigration man
He said he doesn't know if he can let me in

Let me in, immigration man
Can I cross your line and pray?

I can stay another day, won't you let me in, immigration man?
I won't toe your line today, I can't see it anyway

There he was with his immigration face
Giving me a paper chase but the sun was coming
'Cos all at once he looked into my space
And stamped a number all over my face and he sent me running
(Graham Nash, "Immigration Man," 1972)

**In the history of the trans-Atlantic slave trade (1525-1866), 12.5 million Africans were shipped to the New World.** Of them, 10.7 million survived the dreaded Middle Passage, disembarking in North America, the Caribbean and South America. Only about 388,000 were transported directly from Africa to North America, as David Eltis, David Richardson and their colleagues have definitively established in the Trans-Atlantic Slave Trade Database.

2020 worldwide Jewish population of 14.7 million, remaining well below, the pre-war 16.6 million in 1939.
(Marcy Oster/ JTA, *The Jerusalem Post*, April 21, 2020)

U.S. federal statute, 8 U.S. Code § 1227 stipulates the "classes of deportable aliens" who may be removed from the country by the attorney general.

## 6. Geronimo's Ghost

The ownership of women begins in the lower barbarian stages of culture, apparently with the seizure of female captives. The original reason for the seizure and appropriation of women seems to have been their usefulness as trophies. (Thorstein Veblen, *The Theory of the Leisure Class*, 1899)

...the dismal science...
(Thomas Carlyle, "Occasional Discourse on the Negro Question," 1849)

But nothing is so hard for those who abound in riches,
as to conceive how others can be in want.
(Jonathan Swift, 1713)

Indeed, of late, some eateries have become harder to get into than an Ivy League college.
(Daisy Carrington, for CNN, "9 restaurants that are hard to get into [and tips to make it easier]," 3/15/2017)

...the idea of a Millennium when women were to reign supreme in the world.
(Isak Dinesen, *Out of Africa*, 1937)

### Caligula's Garden of Delights, Unearthed and Restored

In an evocative eyewitness account, the philosopher Philo, who visited

the estate in A.D. 40 on behalf of the Jews of Alexandria, and his fellow emissaries had to trail behind Caligula as he inspected the sumptuous residences "examining the men's rooms and the women's rooms ... and giving orders to make them more costly." The emperor, wrote Philo, "ordered the windows to be filled up with transparent stones resembling white crystal that do not hinder the light, but which keep out the wind and the heat of the sun."
(Franz Lidz, *The New York Times*, 1/12, 2021)

*'Le roi est mort, vive le roi!*
(Declared upon the accession to the French throne of Charles VII, after the death of his father, Charles VI, in 1422)

I can hire one-half of the working class to kill the other half.
(Attributed to Jay Gould, robber baron, 1891)

Servant of the Delphian Apollo
Go to the Castallian Spring
Wash in its silvery eddies,
And return cleansed to the temple.
Guard your lips from offence
To those who ask for oracles.
Let the God's answer come
Pure from all private fault.
(Priests to the Oracle of Delphi, classical antiquity)

coffle
(Line, from Arab *kafila*, for caravan)

*Le secret des grandes fortunes sans cause apparente est un crime oublié, parce qu'il a été proprement fait.* [The secret of grand fortunes without apparent cause is a crime forgotten, for it was properly done.]
(Honoré de Balzac, *Le Père Goriot*, 1835)

To be SOLD on the first Monday in October, a large number of Negroe Slaves, likewise sundry Household Goods, Stocks of Cattle, etc.
– Thomas Eldridge (*Virginia Gazette*, September 1751)

Innocents Abroad (Mark Twain, *The Innocents Abroad*, 1869)

...speculative, esoteric creeds of Christendom impute the [a] First Cause, Universal Intelligence, World Soul, ...Spiritual Aspect... (Veblen, *Theory*)

Narcissus (Ovid, 43BC – 17/ 18AD, *The Metamorphoses*, Book 3, Fables 6, 7, "Narcissus," Project Gutenberg)

Oh, let us strive that ever we
May let these words our watch cry be,
Where'er upon life's sea we sail:

"For God, for Country and for Yale!"
(H.S. Durand, "Bright College Years," [Yale University traditional song, etched in stone in a visible spot on the Old Campus], [Yale Class of] 1881)

THIRD CITIZEN. "...and though we willingly consented to his banishment, yet it was against our will."
(William Shakespeare, *Coriolanus*, 4.6.148, 1609(?))

Kiss my aura...Dora...
Ooh - it's real angora
Would you all like some more-a?
Right here on the floor-a?
An' how 'bout you, Fauna?
Do you wanna?
(Frank Zappa, *Overnight Sensation*, "Dinah-Moe Humm," 1973)

## 7. New Meth City

The whisper that my master was my father, may or may not be true;... [slaveholders] administer to their own lusts, and make a gratification of their wicked desires profitable as well as pleasurable;...it is nevertheless plain that a very different-looking class of people are springing up at the South, and are now held in slavery, from those originally brought to this country from Africa;...for thousands are ushered into the world, annually, who, like myself, owe their existence to white fathers, and those fathers most frequently their own masters...

To describe the wealth of Colonel Lloyd would be almost equal to describing the riches of Job. He kept from ten to fifteen house-servants. He was said to own a thousand slaves, and I think this estimate quite within the truth. Colonel Lloyd owned so many that he did not know them when he saw them; nor did all the slaves of the out-farms know him.
(Frederick Douglass, *Narrative of the Life of Frederick Douglass*, 1845)

*La luna... Mirala. Es tu espejo.*
(Jorge Luis Borges, "La moneda de hierro," 1976)

*...toda la vida es sueño.*
(Calderon de la Barca, *La Vida es Sueño*, 1636)

*"Regional refugee crises in Latin America demand humanitarian responses by the United States, never a show of force..."*
(Recalled by the author, U.S. media, 21st century)

*...liberte, egalite, fraternite* (Slogan, Revolutionary France, 1790s)

The past is never dead. It's not even past.
(William Faulkner, *Requiem for a Nun*, 1951)

Bad men need nothing more to compass their ends, than that good men should look on and do nothing. (John Stuart Mill, Inaugural Address Delivered to the University of St. Andrews, 2/1/1867)

*Liebeslieder* (Johannes Brahms, Liebeslieder Waltzes, 1868)

HAMLET. A little more than kin, and less than kind.
(William Shakespeare, *The Tragical History of Hamlet, Prince of Denmark*, 1600)

But there are times when the little cloud spreads, until it obscures the sky. And those times I look around at my fellow men and I am reminded of some likeness of the beast-people, and I feel as though the animal is surging up in them. And I know they are neither wholly animal nor holy man, but an unstable combination of both.
(H.G. Wells, *The Island of Dr. Moreau*, 1896)

**NO DOGS NEGROS MEXICANS or COLORED SERVED IN REAR.**
(Jim Crow Signs, Internet, U.S. media, 21st century)

Red and yellow, black and white,
They are precious in His sight,
Jesus loves the little children of the world.
(C. H. Woolston, 1856 – 1927, 39 hymnals, "571. Jesus Loves the Little Children")

I have been a stranger in a strange land. (Exodus 2:22, KJV)

"We will destroy the enemy at the gates of Stalingrad."
(William Craig, *Enemy at the Gates: The Battle for Stalingrad*, 1973)

I didn't say that the Jews are inferior. I didn't even maintain they are a race. I merely saw that the mixture of different cultures didn't work... Germany will regard the Jewish question as solved only after the very last Jew has left the greater German living space... Europe will have its Jewish question solved only after the very last Jew has left the continent.
(Alfred Rosenberg, Nazi ideologue, and philosopher, 1/12/1946, quoted in Gustave M. Gilbert's, "Nuremberg Diary," 1947)

Odds bodkins (God's body, a mild oath in surprise, traditional English)

The Committee for Public Safety (A committee of the National Convention which undertook the violent Reign of Terror in the French Revolution, 1793-4)

## 8. Gung-ho

From the Halls of Montezuma
To the Shores of Tripoli;
We fight our country's battles
In the air, on land and sea;

First to fight for right and freedom
And to keep our honor clean;
We are proud to claim the title
of United States Marine.
(U.S. Marine Corps Hymn)

...*Ice Storm*... (Ang Lee, *The Ice Storm*, 1997)

...junkie... (William S. Burroughs, *Junkie*, 1953)

The proof of the pudding is in the eating...
(Miguel de Cervantes, El ingenioso hidalgo don Quixote de la Mancha, 1605)

...the good, the bad and the ugly...
(Sergio Leone, *The Good, the Bad and the Ugly*, 1966)

*Dracula* (Bram Stoker, *Dracula* 1897)

**Blackpowder/ Black Powder (pick one and be consistent)** – Use this
term in settings from the dawn of firearms in 9th century China to the
1880s; antique or vintage-style firearms would use blackpowder after that.
(Benjamin Sobieck, *The Writer's Guide to Weapons*, 2015)

Power tends to corrupt, and absolute power corrupts absolutely...
(Lord Acton, 1887)

*Pudd'nhead Wilson*
(Mark Twain, *Pudd'nhead Wilson*, 1894)

"'Why, they are cannibals!' said Toby on one occasion when I eulogized
the tribe. 'Granted,' I replied, 'but a more humane, gentlemanly and
amiable set of epicures do not probably exist in the Pacific.'"
(Herman Melville, *Typee: A Peep at Polynesian Life*, 1846)

The Phoenix Program: a set of programs that sought to attack and destroy
the political infrastructure of the Viet Cong. (CIA Archives)

We don't want to fight, but by Jingo if we do,
We 've got the ships, we 've got the men, we 've got the money too.
(English doggerel song popular during Russo-Turkish War, 1877-78)

And then, in the sniperscope, Bond saw the head of Trigger – the purity
of the profile, the golden bell of hair, - all laid out along the stock of the
Kalashnikov!...
"Trigger was a woman."
"So what? KGB has got plenty of women agents – and women gunners.
I'm not in the least surprised."
(Ian Fleming, "The Living Daylights," 1962)

To call it a program of murder is nonsense ... They were of more value to
us alive than dead, and therefore, the object was to get them alive... Our

training emphasizes the desirability of obtaining these target individuals alive and of using intelligent and lawful methods of interrogation to obtain the truth of what they know about other aspects of the VCI ... [U.S. personnel] are specifically not authorized to engage in assassinations or other violations of the rules of land warfare.
(William Colby, CIA Director, 1973-1976, CIA Archives)

Judge not, that ye be not judged. (Matthew 7:1, KJV)

...terminate with extreme prejudice...
(Francis Ford Coppola, *Apocalypse Now*, 1979)

When thou goest out to battle against thine enemies, and seest horses, and chariots, and a people more than thou... the officers shall say, What man is there that is fearful and fainthearted? Let him go and return unto his house, lest his brethren's heart faint as well as his heart.
(Deuteronomy 20:1, KJV)

...apocalypse now. (Coppola, *Apocalypse Now*)

The Rome Statute of the International Criminal Court (ICC) [of which, the United States is not a member], where war crimes can be prosecuted... follows the definition set out by the 1949 Geneva Conventions, which were ratified by 196 states.

This definition includes acts of:
- willful killing
- torture or inhuman treatment
- willfully causing great suffering or serious injury
- extensive destruction and appropriation of property which is not justified by military necessity
- compelling a prisoner of war to serve in the forces of a hostile state
- willfully depriving a prisoner of war of the rights of fair and regular trial
- unlawful deportation or transfer or unlawful confinement
- taking of hostages

However, the Rome Statute also includes an extensive list of further specific violations, such as intentionally directing attacks against civilian populations, using child soldiers, forced pregnancy and intentionally directing attacks against hospitals. (James Morris, Yahoo UK, 3/25/2022)

## 9. *Dan de Riber* or **Splendor on the Gold Coast**

"Exterminate all the brutes!" (Joseph Conrad, *Heart of Darkness*, 1899)

There is not the slightest doubt in my mind that they prefer human flesh to any other. During all the time I lived among cannibal races I never came across a single case of their eating any kind of flesh raw; they invariably either boil, roast or smoke it... The preference of different tribes for various parts of the human body is interesting. Some cut long steaks from the flesh of the thighs, legs or arms; others prefer the hands and feet; and though the great majority do not eat the head, I have come across more than one tribe which prefers this to any other part. Almost all use some part of the intestines on account of the fat they contain. (Sidney Langford Hinde, former captain of the Congo Free State Force, *The Fall of the Congo Arabs*, 1897)

So much trouble in the world
So much trouble in the world

Bless my eyes this morning
Jah sun is on the rise once again
The way earthly things are going
Anything can happen

You see men sailing on their ego trips
Blast off on their spaceships
Million miles from reality
No care for you, no care for me

So much trouble in the world
So much trouble in the world
(Bob Marley, *Survival*, "So Much Trouble in the World," 1979)

"There are many tribes of men in the forest... that are cannibals, who eat human flesh. These are the fiercest of all. They are always fighting, and they eat many of the prisoners they capture, for they prefer eating to selling them..."

"Do you know by what name those cannibal tribes are called?" I asked.

"I know the names of two of them," he replied. "One is called Fan, the other Osheba." (Paul Du Chaillu, *King Mombo*, 1930)

No more internal power struggle
We come together to overcome the little trouble
Soon we'll find out who is the real revolutionary
'Cause I don't want my people to be contrary

And brother you're right, you're right,
You're right, you're right, you're so right
We'll have to fight (We gon' fight)
We gonna fight (We gon' fight)
We'll have to fight (We gon' fight)
Fighting for our rights

Mash it up in-a (Zimbabwe)
Natty trash it in-a (Zimbabwe)
Africans a-liberate Zimbabwe (Zimbabwe)

I'n'I a-liberate Zimbabwe
(Marley, *Survival*, "Zimbabwe")

*Scores of Civilians Beheaded by Insurgents in Northern Mozambique, Witness Says.* (Recalled by the author, U.S. media, 21st century)

For whatsoever things were written aforetime were written for our learning, that we through patience and comfort of the scriptures might have hope. (Romans 15:4, KJV)

The captains of the steamers have often assured me that whenever they try to buy goats from the natives, slaves are demanded in exchange; the natives often come aboard with tusks of ivory with the intention of buying a slave, complaining *that meat is now scarce in their neighbourhood.* (Hinde, *The Fall*)

Whilst at Birkenau I have seen Grese making selections with Dr Mengele of people to be sent to the gas chamber. On these parades Grese herself chose the people to be killed in this way.

In one selection about August 1944, there were between 2,000 and 3,000 selected. At this selection Grese and Mengele were responsible for selecting those for the gas chamber.

People chosen would sometimes sneak away from the line and hide themselves under their beds. Grese would go and find them, beat them until they collapsed and then drag them back into line again.

I have seen everything I describe. It was general knowledge in this camp that persons selected in this way went to the gas chamber.
(Victor Smart, "Irma Grese, Excerpts from the Belsen Trial and Biography," 2008)

He was capable of being so kind to the children, to have them become fond of him, to bring them sugar, to think of small details in their daily lives, and to do things we would genuinely admire ... And then, next to that, ... the crematoria smoke, and these children, tomorrow or in a half-hour, he is going to send them there. Well, that is where the anomaly lay. (A former Auschwitz prisoner doctor)

Only the Jew knew that by an able and persistent use of propaganda heaven itself can be presented to the people as if it were hell and, vice versa, the most miserable kind of life can be presented as if it were paradise. The Jew knew this and acted accordingly. But the German, or rather his Government, did not have the slightest suspicion of it. During the War the heaviest of penalties had to be paid for that ignorance. (Adolf Hitler, *Mein Kampf*, 1925)

A group of Nazis surrounded an elderly Berlin Jew and demanded of him, 'Tell us, Jew, who caused the war?'

The little Jew was no fool. 'The Jews,' he said, then added, 'and the bicycle riders.'
The Nazis were puzzled. 'Why the bicycle riders?' 'Why the Jews?' answered the little old man.
(Nathan Ausubel, *A Treasury of Jewish Folklore*, 1980)

In a hierarchy, every employee tends to rise to his level of incompetence...
In time, every post tends to be occupied by an employee who is incompetent to carry out its duties.
(Peter and Hull, *The Peter Principle*, 1969)

"One can most easily tell a Jew by his nose. The Jewish nose is bent at its point. It looks like the number six. We call it the 'Jewish six.' Many Gentiles also have bent noses. But their noses bend upwards, not downwards. Such a nose is a hook nose or an eagle nose. It is not at all like a Jewish nose." (Julius Streicher, Nazi propagandist, in a children's story)

## 10. The Corporate *Kapo* and The Archer of Auschwitz

### What were the prisoners supposed to do when the whistle went?

Fall in fives, and it was my duty to see that they did so. Dr. Mengele then came and made the selection. As I was responsible for the camp, my duties were to know how many people were leaving and I had to count them, and I kept the figures in a strength book.

After the selection took place they were sent into "B" Camp, ...which I thought was the gas chamber. (Victor Smart, "Irma Grese, Excerpts from the Belsen Trial and Biography," 2008)

There but for the grace of God goes John Bradford.
(John Bradford, English reformer, martyr, 1555)

Vengeance is mine; I will repay, saith the Lord. (Romans 12:19, KJV)

In 2008, we tried to get readers to rid their inboxes of this kind of garbage. We described a list of red flags — we called them Key Characteristics of Bogusness — that were clear tip-offs that a chain email wasn't legitimate. Among them: an anonymous author; excessive exclamation points, capital letters and misspellings; entreaties that "This is NOT a hoax!"; and links to sourcing that does not support or completely contradicts the claims being made. Those all still hold true, but fake stories — as in, completely made-up "news" — has grown more sophisticated, often presented on a site designed to look (sort of) like a legitimate news organization. Still, we find it's easy to figure out what's real and what's imaginary if you're armed with some critical thinking and fact-checking tools of the trade.
(Eugene Kiely and Lori Robertson, FactCheck.org, "How to Spot Fake News," 11/18/2016)

War is merely the continuation of policy by other means.
(Carl Philipp Gottfried [Gottlieb] von Clausewitz, *Vom Kriege*, 1832)

*The Communist Manifesto*
(Karl Marx and Friedrich Engels, *The Communist Manifesto*, 1848)

When diplomacy ends, War begins. (Adolf Hitler, *Mein Kampf*, 1925)

When they asked me, couldn't you give money out of the United Jewish
Appeal funds for the rescue of Jews in Europe, I said, 'NO!' and I say
again 'NO'... one should resist this wave which pushes the Zionist
activities to secondary importance. (Yitzhak Gruenbaum, January 1943)

...the fall of Japan... (William Craig, *The Fall of Japan*, 1967)

...skipped the light fantastic out of town...
(Tennessee Williams, *The Glass Menagerie*, 1944)

Corporations are people, my friend... Everything corporations earn
ultimately goes to people. (Mitt Romney, U.S. politician, venture capitalist
[heir to wealth, privilege], 8/11/2011)

"The smell was awful — things like that, you do not want to talk about it.
Because the pain and memory of suffering comes back to you. You cannot
deal with it." (Eva Gryka Kohan, Local Survivor)

This way for the gas, ladies and gentlemen...
(Tadeusz Borowski, *This Way for the Gas, Ladies and Gentlemen*, 1946)

"They said separate: children, men, women, and the older people. Me and
my sister were separated with the young ones. I had my little sister in my
arms, and one of the SS came over and picked up my little sister and gave
her to my stepmother. He pushed me to the other side."
(Bella Benozio Ouziel, Local Survivor)

"The finished products (i.e., tattooed skin detached from corpses) were
turned over to Koch's wife, who had them fashioned into lampshades and
other ornamental household articles..."
(A witness at the Nuremberg Trials, 1945-46)

"It is more interesting that Frau Koch had a lady's handbag made out of
the same material. She was just as proud of it as a South Sea island woman
would have been about her cannibal trophies..."
(Stefan Heymann, Sidelights on the Koch Affair)

Birthday of the *Fuhrer*: April 20, 1889

*Funkel, funkel, kleiner Stern,*
*Wie ich mich frage, was du bist!*
*Über der Welt so hoch,*
*Wie ein Diamant am Himmel.* (Lullaby)

"She was beautiful, my little sister. You cannot imagine how beautiful she was. They mustn't have looked at her. If they had, they would never have killed her. They couldn't have." (Charlotte Delbo, Local Survivor)

Violin Concerto in D major
(Pyotr Ilyich Tchaikovsky, Violin Concerto in D major, 1878)

In Auschwitz she wore a pistol and in Belsen she went about with a riding whip. She was one of the few SS women who had a permit to carry arms. I cannot say whether she was wearing a pistol at the time of this incident. (Smart, "Irma Grese, Excerpts")

There was one person who would rub the...a little piece of dirty alcohol on your arm, and the other one had the...had the needle with the inkwell, and he would do the numbering. So my number is 65,316.
(Miso [Mike] Vogel, survivor)

Just before I turned 6, my family was deported to Auschwitz from the Theresienstadt ghetto. My arm was tattooed with the number 169061. There, I was separated from my sister and mother and put into a barracks with older boys – many seemed to be twins. (Rene Guttmann)

In comments ahead of the D-Day commemorations, Russian Foreign Ministry spokesperson Maria Zakharova took a swipe at the ceremony, saying: "The Normandy landings were not a game-changer for the outcome of WWII and the Great Patriotic War. The outcome was determined by the Red Army's victories -- mainly, in Stalingrad and Kursk. For three years, the UK and then the US dragged out opening the Second Front." (Nathan Hodge, CNN, June 7, 2019)

## 11. *Camera Obscura*

All things are a flowing,
Sage Heracleitus says;
But a tawdry cheapness
Shall outlast our days. (Ezra Pound, "Hugh Selwyn Mauberley," 1920)

*Notes from Underground*
(Fyodor Dostoevsky, *Notes from Underground*, 1864)

Speak softly and carry a big stick.
(T.R., U.S. President Theodore Roosevelt, in a speech, 1903)

I'm the punk with the stutter.
(The Who, *Quadrophenia*, "The Punk and the Godfather," 1973)

I got four heads inside my mind
Four rooms I'd like to lie in
Four selves I want to find

And I don't know which one is me
(The Who, *Quadrophenia*, "Four Faces")

"I stick my neck out for nobody." (Michael Curtiz, *Casablanca*, 1942)

Now, I want you to remember that no bastard ever won a war by dying for
his country—he won it by making the other poor, dumb bastard die for
his country. (Franklin J. Schaffner, *Patton*, 1970)

Let me tell you about the very rich. They are different from you and me.
(F. Scott Fitzgerald, "The Rich Boy," 1926)

...and the soul which has seen most of truth shall come to the birth as a
philosopher, or artist, or some musical and loving nature...
(Plato, *Phaedrus*, 370 BC)

"Bohemian Rhapsody"
(Freddie Mercury, Queen, "Bohemian Rhapsody," 1975)

...conspicuous leisure, consumption...
(Thorstein Veblen, *The Theory of the Leisure Class*, 1899)

I don't believe that the hundreds of executions I was responsible for prevented
even a single murder," he explained. "The Death penalty solves nothing.
(Albert Pierrepoint, Britain's official hangman between 1941 and 1956)

From each according to his ability, to each according to his needs!
(Karl Marx, "Critique of the Gotha Program," 1875)

Slough, Delectable Mountains (John Bunyan, *The Pilgrim's Progress from
This World, to That Which Is to Come*, 1678)

Little-Enders, Big-Enders (Jonathan Swift, *Gulliver's Travels, or Travels
into Several Remote Nations of the World. In Four Parts. By Lemuel
Gulliver, First a Surgeon, and then a Captain of Several Ships*, 1726)

You can sail on a ship by yourself,
 Take a nap or a nip by yourself.
You can get into debt on your own.
There are lots of things that you can do alone.
But it takes two to tango, two to tango ... etc.
(Al Hoffman and Dick Manning, "Takes Two to Tango," 1952)

Life, Liberty and the pursuit of Happiness
(Thomas Jefferson, United States Declaration of Independence, 1776)

...[that] a man of good social standing, should descend to the level of a lot
of common scribblers who irritated him and made him angry.
(Leo Tolstoy, *Anna Karenina*, 1874 – 1876)

*Roman Holiday*, (William Wyler, *Roman Holiday*, 1953)

What's Fame? a fancied life in others' breath.
A thing beyond us, even before our death.
(Alexander Pope, "An Essay on Man," 1733 – 1734)

...a description of the people, the manners,
the amusements, the ways of Mansfield Park...
(Jane Austen, *Mansfield Park*, 1814)

*Homo sum, humani nihil a me alienum puto.*
[I am a human being, I consider nothing that is human alien to me.]
(Terence, *Heauton Timorumenos [The Self-Tormentor]*, 163 BC)

## 12. Womb of The Stars

Ma Ma, Where's my Pa? (Republican slogan ridiculing Democrat Grover Cleveland and his possible love child, Presidential Campaign, 1884)

Miss Lonelyhearts (Nathanael West, *Miss Lonelyhearts*, 1933)

...expulsion from the Garden of Eden
(Masaccio, *The Expulsion from the Garden of Eden*, c. 1425)

...Great Ratsby...
(F. Scott Fitzgerald, *The Great Gatsby*, 1925)

They did attack our herds: you could have seen a woman pull a calf to pieces as it bellowed alive in her bare hands!
(Euripides, *The Bacchae*, 405 BC)

Feminazi... (Pejorative term for feminists popularized by conservative radio talk show host, ideologue, commentator, Rush Limbaugh, 1991)

*"We were right there watching him, and there's nothing you can do," he said. "His blood was streaming out, like crazy. He shook a little bit and stopped moving."* (Recalled by the author, U.S. media, 21st century)

*We live in a society where homosexuals lecture us on morals, transvestites lecture us on human biology, abortion doctors lecture us on human rights, and socialists lecture, on economics.* (Recalled, U.S. media)

...Main Street...
(Sinclair Lewis, *Main Street*, 1920)

Guy de Maupassant, who started triumphant ("I can screw street whores now and say to them 'I've got the pox.' They are afraid and I just laugh"), died 15 years later in an asylum howling like a dog and planting twigs as baby Maupassants in the garden. (Sarah Dunant, "Syphilis, sex and fear: How the French disease conquered the world," May 17, 2013)

But the meek shall inherit the earth; and shall delight themselves in the abundance of peace. (Psalms 37:11, KJV)

"I'll make him an offer he can't refuse."
(Mario Puzo, *The Godfather*, 1969)

Gone to the White House, ha ha ha!
(Democrats' post-election retort, Presidential Campaign, 1884)

A woman must have money and a room of her own if she is to write fiction.
(Virginia Woolf, *A Room of One's Own*, 1929)

Yale Daily News
Tap Night rages
PHOEBE KIMMELMAN & NICOLE NG APR 11, 2014

Students dining in Commons on Thursday witnessed a male student dressed as a pregnant woman pretending to give birth on a Commons table with the help of a fake midwife.

On Thursday, campus was invaded by students dressed as pink dinosaurs, astronauts and Aladdin with his monkey sidekick, Abu as members of the junior class sought to fulfill their induction requirements for Yale s secret societies. Commonly known as Tap Night, the event is one of Yale's oldest traditions and serves as the culmination of society tap week, which began on April 3.

"I was asked to be a famous fictional character," said a student outside Saybrook College dressed as a Super Mario character, who asked to remain anonymous. "When [Tap Night's] done just for fun, it's really great."

Many juniors were asked to keep their schedules free for the afternoon to participate in the festivities.

In the early afternoon, one junior girl donned a floor-length red cape and black mask outside the Women's Center, reciting Latin.

"I'm reciting Latin," that s all I'll say, she said.

Many students in festive attire, busy with their induction activities, declined to comment. Among these were men wearing black capes, veils and masks, a Teenage Mutant Ninja Turtle and various Disney princesses.

A female student dressed as the Little Mermaid holding a dining hall fork stood on Chapel Street and smiled at bystanders.

"I am not allowed to speak," she mouthed.

Further down on Chapel Street, a junior pretending to be Belle from Beauty and the Beast passionately sang songs from the Disney film's soundtrack. Outside the Apple Store on Broadway, two students dressed as Harry Potter and Dobby asked pedestrians for socks.

Meanwhile, on Cross Campus, two juniors dressed as Princess Leia and C-3PO from the Star Wars series stood near the Women's Table, gesturing with their hands.

"We're pretending to use the force to ward off you passersby," the male stud...

Don't sit under the apple tree with anyone else but me
(The Andrews Sisters, "Don't Sit Under the Apple Tree [with Anyone Else but Me]," 1944)

Violin Concerto in E minor
(Felix Mendelssohn, Violin Concerto in E minor, 1844)

He read it for the same reason an animal tears at a wounded foot: to hurt the pain. (West, *Miss Lonelyhearts*)

Margaret Mead (Margaret Mead, *Male and Female*, 1949)

Do not trust the horse, Trojans. Whatever it is, I fear the Greeks even when they bring gifts. (Virgil, *Aeneid*, Book 2, 19 BC)

She replied that she would bring in an account of the expenses of it in two or three shapes, and like a bill of fare, I should choose as I pleased; and I desired her to do so.

The next day she brought it, and the copy of her three bills was as follows:—

1. For three months' lodging in her house, including
    my diet, at 10s. a week . . . . . . . . . . . 6£, 0s., 0d.

2. For a nurse for the month, and use of childbed
    linen . . . . . . . . . . . . . . . . . . . . 1£, 10s., 0d.

3. For a minister to christen the child, and to the
    godfathers and clerk . . . . . . . . . . . . 1£, 10s., 0d.

4. For a supper at the christening if I had five friends
    at it . . . . . . . . . . . . . . . . . . . . . . . . . . . . . . . . . . 1£, 0s., 0d.

    For her fees as a midwife, and the taking off the
    trouble of the parish . . . . . . . . . . . . . . . . . 3£, 3s., 0d.

    To her maid servant attending . . . . . . . . 0£, 10s., 0d.
    --------------
    13£, 13s., 0d.

This was the first bill; the second was the same terms:—

1. For three months' lodging and diet, etc., at 20s.
   per week . . . . . . . . . . . . . . . . . 13£, 0s., 0d.

2. For a nurse for the month, and the use of linen
   and lace . . . . . . . . . . . . . . . . . 2£, 10s., 0d.

3. For the minister to christen the child, etc., as
   above . . . . . . . . . . . . . . . . . . . 2£, 0s., 0d.

4. For supper and for sweetmeats . . 3£, 3s., 0d.

   For her fees as above . . . . . . . . . . . 5£, 5s., 0d.

   For a servant-maid . . . . . . . . . . . . 1£, 0s., 0d.
   --------------
   26£, 18s., 0d.

This was the second-rate bill; the third, she said, was for a degree higher,
and when the father or friends appeared:—

1. For three months' lodging and diet, having two
   rooms and a garret for a servant . . . . . . 30£, 0s., 0d.,

2. For a nurse for the month, and the finest suit
   of childbed linen . . . . . . . . . . . . . . . 4£, 4s., 0d.

3. For the minister to christen the child, etc. 2£, 10s., 0d.

4. For a supper, the gentlemen to send in the
   wine . . . . . . . . . . . . . . . . . . . 6£, 0s., 0d.

   For my fees, etc. . . . . . . . . 10£, 10s., 0d.

   The maid, besides their own maid,
   only . . . . . . . . . . . . . . . . . 0£, 10s., 0d.
   --------------
   53£, 14s., 0d.

I looked upon all three bills, and smiled, and told her I did not see but
that she was very reasonable in her demands, all things considered, and for
that I did not doubt but her accommodations were good.

### The Fortunes and Misfortunes
### of the Famous Moll Flanders, &c.

by Daniel Defoe

# WRITTEN IN THE YEAR 1683

## 13. *Sieg Heil*

Patriotism is the last refuge of a scoundrel.
(James Boswell, *The Life of Samuel Johnson, LL.D.*, 1791)

Heaven has no rage like love to hatred turned,
Nor hell a fury like a woman scorned.
(William Congreve, *The Mourning Bride,* 1697)

...cousins...
(Francois Truffaut, *Fahrenheit 451,* 1966 [film], based on Ray Bradbury, *Fahrenheit 451,* 1953)

Remember the Maine! To hell with Spain!
(Rallying cry for the Spanish-American War, as a follow-up to...)

Please remain. You furnish the pictures and I'll furnish the war.
(William Randolph Hearst, 1898)

Oh, give me a home where the buffalo roam,
Where the deer and antelope play,
Where never is heard a discouraging word
And the sky is not clouded all day.
(Dr. Brewster M. Higley, "Home on the Range," 1871-73)

*Die Walkure*
(Richard Wagner, *Die Walkure,* 1870)

Margaritaville
(Jimmy Buffett, *Changes in Latitudes, Changes in Attitudes,* "Margaritaville," 1977)

If anyone reproaches me and asks why I did not resort to the regular courts of justice, then all I can say is this: In this hour I was responsible for the fate of the German people, and thereby I became the supreme judge of the German people.
(Adolf Hitler, justifying The Night of the Long Knives, 1934)

*Viva la patria, mate un judío...* [pre-WWII Argentine fascist street chant]
(From the author's interviews with Argentine *cognoscenti*)

Buffalo Bill's
defunct...
how do you like your blue-eyed boy
Mister Death
(E. E. Cummings, "[Buffalo Bill's]," 1920)

Duty, Honor, Country
(U.S. Army General Douglas MacArthur, farewell address to the cadets of the U.S. Military Academy at West Point, May 12, 1962)

Beware the Jabberwock, my son!
  The jaws that bite, the claws that catch!
Beware the Jubjub bird, and shun
  The frumious Bandersnatch!
(Lewis Carroll, "Jabberwocky," 1871)

Specifically, the plan protects the tax-exempt status of any organization that "believes, speaks or acts... in accordance with the belief, that marriage is or should be recognized as a union of one man and one woman, sexual relations are properly reserved for such a marriage, male and female and their equivalents refer to an individual's immutable biological sex as objectively determined by anatomy, physiology, or genetics at or before birth, and that human life begins at conception and merits protection at all stages..." (Sophia Tesfaye, *Salon*, February 3, 2017)

There shall be no solution to this race problem until you, yourselves, strike the blow for liberty. (Marcus Garvey, major inspiration for the back-to-Africa movement, 1920s?)

Who the (Expletive) made you dumb (Expletive) crackers think I give a squat (Expletive) about your opinions... You exhibit nigga behavior, I'm a call you a nigga. You acting crackerish, I'm a call you a cracker. (Vinita Hegwood, Texas high school English teacher, November 2014)

Africa for the Africans... at home and abroad! (Garvey)

Profits are the mother's milk of stocks. [A wall Street adage]
(Lawrence Kudlow, U.S. economic advisor, business author, television personality, October 31, 2003)

I was once out strolling one very hot summer's day
When I thought I'd lay myself down to rest
In a big [tall] field of [Mexican] grass
I laid there in the sun and felt it caressing my face

As I fell asleep and dreamed
I dreamed I was in a Hollywood movie
And that I was the star of the movie
This really blew my mind
(Eric Burdon and War, "Spill the Wine," 1970)

Political power grows out of the barrel of a gun.
(Mao Tse-tung, Chinese Communist Party speech, 1938)

*Un político pobre es un pobre político.* [A poor politician is a poor politician.]
(Carlos Hank Gonzalez, "El Profesor," Mexican politician, businessman, kleptocrat, 1970s)

With Luger in hand (Steely Dan, "With a Gun," 1974)

**14. No Harm in Harems, or Harem in Harm's Way**

**The Fortunes and Misfortunes of the Famous Moll Flanders, &c.**

Who was Born in Newgate, and during a Life of continu'd Variety for Threescore Years, besides her Childhood, was Twelve Year a Whore, five times a Wife (whereof once to her own Brother), Twelve Year a Thief, Eight Year a Transported Felon in Virginia, at last grew Rich, liv'd Honest, and dies a Penitent. Written from her own Memorandums . . .

by Daniel Defoe, 1722

Tomboy: Tomrig, Rampscuttle (Alexander Smith, *Moll Cutpurse*, 1714)

Be compassionate, for everyone you meet is fighting a great battle.
(Philo of Alexandria, c. 25 BCE – c. 50 CE)

The good is that which all things desire.
(Aristotle, *Nicomachean Ethics*, 350 BCE, [later quoted in a common search for celestial, as well as human, perfection, God's order, earthly divinities] Thomas Aquinas, *Summa Theologica*, 1265 – 1273)

This is no simple reform. It really is a revolution. Sex and race because they are easy and visible differences have been the primary ways of organizing human beings into superior and inferior groups and into the cheap labour in which this system still depends. We are talking about a society in which there will be no roles other than those chosen or those earned. We are really talking about humanism... The first wave was about women gaining a legal identity, and it took 150 years. The second wave of feminism is about social equality. We've come a long way, but it's only been 25 years... Women used to say, 'I am not a feminist, but...' Now they say, 'I am a feminist, but...' Some of us are becoming the men we wanted to marry.
(Gloria Steinem, feminist, and journalist, since 1969, founder of *Ms.* Magazine, 1972)

...poverty, chastity, obedience...
(Benedict of Nursia, Rule of Saint Benedict, sixth century)

He still bent his efforts upon the locomotive figure for the belfry, but only as a partial type of an ulterior creature, a sort of elephantine helot, adapted to further, in a degree scarcely to be imagined, the universal conveniences and glories of humanity; supplying nothing less than a supplement to the Six Days' Work; stocking the earth with a new serf, more useful than the ox, swifter than the dolphin, stronger than the lion, more cunning than the ape, for industry an ant, more fiery than serpents, and yet, in patience, another ass. All excellences of all God-made creatures which served man were here to receive advancement, and then to be combined in one. Talus was to have been the all-accomplished helot's name. Talus, iron slave to Bannadonna, and, through him, to man.
(Herman Melville, "The Bell-Tower," 1856)

Here, it might well be thought that, were these last conjectures as to the foundling's secrets not erroneous, then must he have been hopelessly infected with the craziest chimeras of his age; far outgoing Albert Magus and Cornelius Agrippa... A practical materialist, what Bannadonna had aimed at was to have been reached, not by logic, not by crucible, not by conjuration, not by altars, but by plain vise-bench and hammer. In short, to solve nature, to steal into her, to intrigue beyond her, to procure someone else to bind her to his hand -- these, one and all, had not been his objects, but, asking no favors from any element or any being, of himself to rival her, outstrip her, and rule her. He stooped to conquer. With him, common sense was theurgy; machinery, miracle; Prometheus, the heroic name for machinist; man, the true God.
(Melville, "Tower")

Nevertheless, in his initial step, so far as the experimental automaton for the belfry was concerned, he allowed fancy some little play, or, perhaps, what seemed his fancifulness was but his utilitarian ambition collaterally extended. In figure, the creature for the belfry should not be likened after the human pattern, nor any animal one, nor after the ideals, however wild, of ancient fable, but equally in aspect as in organism be an original production -- the more terrible to behold, the better.
(Melville, "Tower")

*DSM-IV* (The DSM-IV constitutes the fourth edition of the Diagnostic and Statistical Manual of Mental Disorders (DSM) created by the American Psychiatry Association also known as the APA, 1994)

"Did you know Santa Fe is the dyke capital of the United States?"
(Truman Capote, *Answered Prayers*, 1975)

PEGEEN. Aye. Wouldn't it be a bitter thing for a girl to go marrying the like of Shaneen, and he a middling kind of a scarecrow, with no savagery or fine words in him at all?
(John M. Synge, *The Playboy of the Western World*, 1907)

God helps those who help themselves.
(Algernon Sydney, *Discourses Concerning Government*, 1698)

All hope abandon ye who enter here.
(Dante Alighieri, *Divine Comedy*, "Inferno," 1306-1321)

What next befell me then and there
I know not well—I never knew—
First came the loss of light, and air,
And then of darkness too:
I had no thought, no feeling—none—
Among the stones I stood a stone,
And was, scarce conscious what I wist,

As shrubless crags within the mist;
For all was blank, and bleak, and grey;
It was not night—it was not day;
It was not even the dungeon-light,
So hateful to my heavy sight,
But vacancy absorbing space,
And fixedness—without a place;
There were no stars, no earth, no time,
No check, no change, no good, no crime
But silence, and a stirless breath
Which neither was of life nor death;
A sea of stagnant idleness,
Blind, boundless, mute, and motionless!
(Lord Byron [George Gordon], "The Prisoner of Chillon," 1816)

Old soldiers never die; they just fade away. (U.S. Army General Douglas MacArthur, farewell address to the U.S. Congress, April 19, 1951)

## 15. *48 Hours to Mecca*

[Scheherazade] possessed courage, wit, and penetration. She had read much, and had so admirable a memory, that she never forgot anything she had read. She had successfully applied herself to philosophy, medicine, history, and the liberal arts; and her poetry excelled the compositions of the best writers of her time. Besides this, she was a perfect beauty, and all her accomplishments were crowned by solid virtue.

"My story is of such marvel that if it were written with a needle on the corner of an eye, it would yet serve as a lesson to those who seek wisdom." (Anonymous, *The Arabian Nights: One Thousand and One Nights*, The Islamic Golden Age, 8th to 14th centuries)

Continental Op (Dashiell Hammett, *The Continental Op 36 Short Stories*, beginning 1923)

Yassuh. Boss. Whatevuh you sez. (Attributed to Al Jolson, white [Jewish] musician, who portrayed Negroes in blackface, in the 1920s)

Summertime/ And the livin' is easy/ Fish are jumpin'/ And the cotton is high (George [and Ira] Gershwin, *Porgy and Bess*, 1935)

Men are born and remain free and equal in rights. Social distinctions may be founded only upon the general good. (Largely composed by the Marquis de Lafayette, assisted by [revolutionary] Thomas Jefferson, *The Declaration of the Rights of Man and of the Citizen*, 1789)

How strange and eventful has been the brief history of this marvelous city, San Francisco... But it has been through its season of heaven-defying crime, violence, and blood, from which it was rescued and handed back to soberness, morality, and good government, by that peculiar invention of Anglo-Saxon Republican America, the solemn awe-inspiring Vigilance Committee of the most grave and responsible citizens, the last resort of the thinking and the good, taken to only when vice, fraud, and ruffianism have entrenched themselves behind the forms of law, suffrage, and ballot, and there is no hope but in organized force, whose action must be instant and thorough, or its state will be worse than before. (Richard Henry Dana, *Two Years Before the Mast*, 1840, 1869)

I cannot forecast to you the action of Russia. It is a riddle, wrapped in a mystery, inside an enigma; (Winston Churchill, Radio Broadcast, 1939)

Mary, Mary, quite contrary... (English nursery rhyme of uncertain origins)

Though nothing can bring back the hour
Of splendour in the grass, of glory in the flower;
We will grieve not, rather find
Strength in what remains behind;
(William Wordsworth, "Ode: Intimations of Immortality from Recollections of Early Childhood," 1807)

In those days we did not trust anyone who had not been in the war. (Ernest Hemmingway, *A Movable Feast*, 1964)

You only live twice:
Once when you are born
And once when you look death in
the face.

After BASHO
Japanese poet, 1643-94
(Ian Fleming, *You Only Live Twice*, 1964)

Stellify
stellify ( st l fa )
vb, -fies, -fying or -fied
(Astronomy) to change or be changed into a star
[from Latin stella a star] (*The Free Dictionary*)

Wizard of Oz (L. Frank Baum, *The Wizard of Oz*, 1900)

Iron Curtain (Winston Churchill, Speech, Fulton, MO, 1946)

Matt Helm and Mrs. Peel (1960s spy spoof characters)

"We experimented with the makeup," makeup artist Troy Surratt said. "We did a much stronger brow and a bold lip for a French sort of feel. The way I shaded her eyebrows with the pencil, I created an uplifting effect. Then, I finished with a shimmering, silky-beige shadow on her lids and went with no mascara at all. Sort of a reaction against all the

fake lashes we've been seeing on the red carpet."
(www.justjared.com, 2/11/2015)

And remember Ibrahim and Ismail raised the foundations of the House
(With this prayer): "Our Lord! Accept (this service) from us: For Thou
art the All-Hearing, the All-knowing."
(*Quran*, Al-Baqarah [2], Ayah 127)

The Black stone descended from paradise, and it was whiter than milk,
then it was blacked by these sins of the children of Adam. (Tirmidhi)

Behold! We gave the site, to Ibrahim, of the (Sacred) House, (saying):
"Associate not anything (in worship) with Me; and sanctify My House for
those who compass it round, or stand up, or bow, or prostrate themselves
(therein in prayer)." (*Quran*, Surah Al-Hajj [22], Ayah 26)

I have only created Jinns and Men that they may serve Me. No Sustenance
do I require of them, nor do I require that they should feed Me. For Allah
is He Who gives (all) Sustenance, Lord of Power, Steadfast forever).
(*Quran*, 51:56-58)

By time, indeed, mankind is in loss, Except for those who have believed
and done righteous deeds and advised each other to truth and advised
each other to patience. (*Quran*, 103: 1-3)

*The Ugly American*
(William Lederer & Eugene Burdick, *The Ugly American*, 1958)

When a character is born, he acquires at once such an independence, even
of his own author, that he can be imagined by everybody even in many
other situations where the author never dreamed of placing him; and
so he acquires for himself a meaning which the author never thought of
giving him. (Luigi Pirandello, *Six Characters in Search of an Author*, 1921)

*Curtain: Poirot's Last Case*
(Agatha Christie, *Curtain: Poirot's Last Case*, 1975)

...little grey cells of the brain...
(Agatha Christie, *The Murder of Roger Ackroyd*, 1926)

## 16. The Sky is Falling

[A myth is] ...a description of physical phenomenon in imagery borrowed
from human life...
(James G. Frazer, *The Golden Bough*, 1922)

Every believer is a priest and ... every seeking child of God is given directly
wisdom, guidance, power.
(Charles Edward Jefferson, Congregational clergyman, 1860-1937)

Let all the 'free-will' in the world do all it can with all its strength; it will never give rise to a single instance of ability to avoid being hardened if God does not give the Spirit, or of meriting mercy if it is left to its own strength." (Martin Luther, *On the Bondage of the Will*, 1525)

...came in from the cold.
(John le Carre, *The Spy Who Came in from the Cold*, 1963)

By free choice in this place we mean a power of the human will by which a man can apply himself to the things which lead to eternal salvation, or turn away from them.
(Desiderius Erasmus, quoted in Matthew Barrett, "The Bondage and Liberation of the Will," 2017)

Did you ever hear of Chicken Little, how she disturbed a whole neighborhood by her foolish alarm?
(*The Remarkable story of Chicken Little*, Degen, Estes & Co., Boston, circa 1865-1871)

Back across the ocean floor
The four of us were ripe for more
Paradise was nice but then
you can't stay there forever
(John Sebastian, "The Four of Us," 1972)

Syphilis: a night with Venus, a lifetime with Mercury.
(A popular saying, since 1497)

Like Saturn, the Revolution devours its children.
(Jacques Mallet du Pan, political journalist, and propagandist, 1793)

Then came Chicken Little. Fox Lox caught hold of her, and eat her all up, and then finished his supper with the rest, - and all this from the foolish fright of Chicken Little. (*The Remarkable story of Chicken Little*)

A person may cause evil to others not only by his actions but by his inaction, and in either case he is justly accountable to them for the injury... It is not because men's desires are strong that they act ill; it is because their consciences are weak. (John Stuart Mill, *On Liberty*, 1859)

The law of heroes and good-doers cannot be eluded.
(Walt Whitman, *Leaves of Grass*, "To Think of Time," 1900)

I think that climate change is one of the biggest issues that we're going to have to think about and look at in the future. These huge storms and tsunamis that are happening all over the world, everyone's kind of saying, like, oh, like, these huge disasters are happening all the time. And it's just because of a lot of the things that we've done.
(Recalled by the author, U.S. media, 21st century)

Happiness is a warm gun.
(Lennon-McCartney, "Happiness Is a Warm Gun," 1968)

According to the general in charge of Russia's NATO-facing Western Military District, Russia's new definition of war is never declared, and never ends. What is more, it can achieve its aims without using armed force at all. (Keir Giles, "Why Russia has been ramping up hostile action," CNN Opinion, 10/07/2016)

You don't make poor people rich by making rich people poor.
(Leon Cooperman, Wall Street investor, hedge fund manager, 2019)

All right, Mr. DeMille, I'm ready for my close-up.
(Billy Wilder, *Sunset Boulevard*, 1950).

The dying Tartars, stunned and stupefied by the immensity of the disaster brought about by the disease, and realizing that they had no hope of escape, lost interest in the siege. But they ordered corpses to be placed in catapults and lobbed into the city in the hope that the intolerable stench would kill everyone inside. What seemed like mountains of dead were thrown into the city, and the Christians could not hide or flee or escape from them, although they dumped as many of the bodies as they could in the sea. And soon the rotting corpses tainted the air and poisoned the water supply, and the stench was so overwhelming that hardly one in several thousand was in a position to flee the remains of the Tartar army. Moreover one infected man could carry the poison to others, and infect people and places with the disease by look alone. No one knew, or could discover, a means of defense.
(Narrative of Gabriele De' Mussi, 1348 or 1349)

Abamboo, I love you. I offer the best of the food I have to you. Be good to me. Do not let sickness come to me, Abamboo. Kill my enemies, those who wish me evil by witchcraft.
(Paul Du Chaillu, *King Mombo*, 1930)

SGANARELLE [aside]. Phew! Could I have been wrong after all? Can I have become a doctor without knowing it?
(Moliere, *Le Medecin malgre lui [The Reluctant Doctor]*, 1749)

...territorial imperative...
(Robert Ardrey, *The Territorial Imperative*, 1966)

I believe that man will not merely endure: he will prevail. He is immortal, not because he alone among creatures has an inexhaustible voice, but because he has a soul, a spirit capable of compassion and sacrifice and endurance. The poet's, the writer's, duty is to write about these things.
(William Faulkner, Nobel Prize speech, 1950)

## 17. *Auto-da-fe* (Renunciation of the Heretics)

*Auto-da-fe* (Act of faith, Portuguese)

If today you can take a thing like evolution and make it a crime to teach it in the public school, tomorrow you can make it a crime to teach it in the private schools, and the next year you can make it a crime to teach it to the hustings or in the church. At the next session you may ban books and the newspapers. Soon you may set Catholic against Protestant and Protestant against Protestant, and try to foist your own religion upon the minds of men. If you can do one you can do the other. Ignorance and fanaticism is ever busy and needs feeding. Always it is feeding and gloating for more. Today it is the public-school teachers, tomorrow the private. The next day the preachers and the lectures, the magazines, the books, the newspapers. After a while, your honor, it is the setting of man against man and creed against creed until with flying banners and beating drums we are marching backward to the glorious ages of the sixteenth century when bigots lighted fagots to burn the men who dared to bring any intelligence and enlightenment and culture to the human mind. (Clarence Darrow, *The Essential Words and Writings of Clarence Darrow*, 2007)

Your suns and worlds are not within my ken,
I merely watch the plaguey state of men.
The little god of earth remains the same queer sprite
As on the first day, or in primal light.
(Goethe, *Faust*, Part One, 1808)

My mother was of the sky/ My father was of the earth
But I am of the universe/ And you know what it's worth
(Lennon-McCartney, "Yer Blues," 1968)

One pill makes you larger
And one pill makes you small
And the ones that mother gives you
Don't do anything at all
(Jefferson Airplane, "White Rabbit," 1967)

Here rise to life again, dead poetry!
Let it, O holy Muses, for I am yours,
And here Calliope, strike a higher key,
Accompanying my song with that sweet air
which made the wretched Magpies feel a blow
that turned all hope of pardon to despair
(Dante Alighieri, *Divine Comedy*, "Inferno," 1306-1321)

If all mankind minus one, were of one opinion, and only one person were of the contrary opinion, mankind would be no more justified in silencing that one person, than he, if he had the power, would be justified in silencing mankind. (John Stuart Mill, *On Liberty*, 1859)

Metadata is what allows an actual enumerated understanding, a precise record of all the private activities in all of our lives. It shows our associations, our political affiliations and our actual activities.
(Edward Snowden [banished NSA whistleblower, accused spy, political fugitive], 2014)

If mankind had always been logical and wise, history would not be a long chronicle of folly and crime.
(James G. Frazer, *The Golden Bough*, 1922)

They say you're judged by the strength of your enemies.
(Marc Forster, *Quantum of Solace*, 2008)

The principal ingredient of our people is the Nordic race (55%). That is not to say that half our people are pure Nordics. All of the aforementioned races appear in mixtures in all parts of our fatherland. The circumstance, however, that the great part of our people is of Nordic descent justifies us taking a Nordic standpoint when evaluating our character and spirit, bodily structure, and physical beauty.
(Harwood L. Childs [translator], "The Nazi Primer," 1938)

Besides, critics continued, Augustus seemed to have superseded the worship of the gods when he wanted to have himself venerated in temples, with god-like images, by priests and ministers... After an appropriate funeral, Augustus was declared a god and decreed a temple.
(Tacitus, *The Annals of Imperial Rome*, c. 117)

Man is the measure of all things. (Protagoras, c. 490 – c. 420 BC)

...*conversos* (*marranos*)... (converts [swine], medieval Spanish)

O my God, I am sorry for my sins because I have offended you. I know I should love you above all things. Help me to do penance, to do better, and to avoid anything that might lead me to sin. Amen.
(Roman Catholic Act of Contrition)

The peace of the Lord be with you always.
And also with you.
(Roman Catholic Worship Refrain)

**Iago:**
O, beware, my lord, of jealousy;
It is the green-ey'd monster, which doth mock
The meat it feeds on.
(William Shakespeare, *Othello*, 1603)

## 18. BFP (Black Female Preferred) or Color Wheel

It is not circumstantial liberty conceded only to us that we want... It is the absolute acceptance of the principle that no man, whether born red,

black or white, can be the property of another.
(Toussaint Louverture, 1743-1803, Haiti's most important revolutionary leader, a former slave)

I will not be used as a tool for their purposes. I am not a token, mammy, or little brown bobble head. I am not owned by Lack, Griffin, or MSNBC.
(Melissa Harris-Perry, academic, political commentator, cultural activist, 2016)

...is ugly both in meaning and aesthetics and deserves the same treatment as the stained-glass window...
(Sean O'Brien, *Information Society Project*, Yale Law School)

I take higher ground. I hold that in the present state of civilization, where two races of different origin, and distinguished by color, and other physical differences, as well as intellectual, are brought together, the relation now existing in the slaveholding States between the two, is, instead of an evil, a good, a positive good... I hold then, that there never has yet existed a wealthy and civilized society in which one portion of the community did not, in point of fact, live on the labor of the other.
(John C. Calhoun, American statesman, southern slavery apologist, 1837)

Amazing grace! How sweet the sound
That saved a wretch like me!
I once was lost, but now am found;
Was blind, but now I see.
(John Newton, "Amazing Grace," 1779)

"Privileged Skull and Bones members mocked the assault on Abner Louima [NYPD brutality victim] by crying out repeatedly, 'Take that plunger out of my ass!'" [Ron Rosenbaum, '68] wrote. "Skull and Bones members hurled obscene sexual insults at initiates as they were forced to kneel and kiss a skull at the feet of the initiators."
(Allison Phinney, *Yale Daily News*, "Skull and Bones video airs on ABC," April 25, 2001)

*Lux et Veritas* (Yale University motto)

The dog barking at you from behind his master's fence acts for a motive indistinguishable from that of his master when the fence was built.
(Robert Ardrey, *The Territorial Imperative*, 1966)

...elephants can remember...
(Agatha Christie, *Elephants Can Remember*, 1972)

The first thing we do, let's kill all the lawyers.
(William Shakespeare, *Henry VI*, 1592)

*Steal This Book*
(Abbie Hoffman, *Steal This Book*, 1971)

Then after they had danced the papas laid them down on their backs on some narrow stones of sacrifice and, cutting open their chests, drew out their palpitating hearts which they offered to the idols before them. Then they kicked the bodies down the steps, and the Indian butchers who were waiting below cut off their arms and legs and flayed their faces, which they afterwards prepared like glove leather, with their beards on, and kept for their drunken festivals. Then they ate their flesh with a sauce of peppers and tomatoes. They sacrificed all our men in this way, eating their legs and arms, offering their hearts and blood to their idols as I have said, and throwing their trunks and entrails to the lions and tigers and serpents and snakes that they kept in the wild-beast houses I have described in an earlier chapter. (Bernal Díaz del Castillo, *The Conquest of New Spain*, 1567)

Birds do it, bees do it
Even educated fleas do it
Let's do it, let's fall in love
(Cole Porter, "Let's Do It, Let's Fall in Love," 1928)

Then the king of England, seeing all the delays interposed by the Sultan to the execution of the treaty, acted perfidiously as regards his Musulman prisoners... In the afternoon of Tuesday, 27 Rajab, [August 20] about four o'clock, he came out on horseback with all the Frankish army, knights, footmen... ordered all the Musulman prisoners, whose martyrdom God had decreed for this day, to be brought before him. They numbered more than three thousand and were all bound with ropes. The Franks then flung themselves upon them all at once and massacred them with sword and lance in cold blood. (Beha-ed-Din, quoted in Thomas Andrew Archer, *The Crusade of Richard I*, 1189 – 92, 1889)

Peace is not the absence of conflict, but the ability to cope with it. (Mahatma Gandhi, 1869-1948, Indian anti-colonial, nonviolent resistance martyr)

...Stephen King's alien anus parasite. (Stephen King, *Dreamcatcher*, 2001)

[CINDERELLA]
Mother cannot guide you.
Now you're on your own.
Only me beside you.
Still, you're not alone.
No one is alone, truly.
No one is alone.

Sometimes people leave you
halfway through the wood.
Others may deceive you.
You decide what's good.
You decide alone.
But no one is alone. (Stephen Sondheim, *Into the Woods*, 1987)

...the skin of her teeth...
(Thornton Wilder, *The Skin of Our Teeth*, 1942)

## 19. BTC (Bear Trap Capital) or Pecuniary Promise

The only thing which is of lasting benefit to a man is that which he does for himself. Money which comes to him without effort on his part is seldom a benefit and often a curse.
(John D. Rockefeller, *Random Reminiscences of Men and Events,* 1909)

The impression was gaining ground with me that it was a good thing to let the money be my slave and not make myself a slave to money.
(John D. Rockefeller, *John D. Rockefeller on Making Money: Advice and Words of Wisdom on Building and Sharing Wealth*, 2015)

I am bound to be rich–bound to be rich– bound to be rich!
(Ron Chernow, *Titan: The Life of John D Rockefeller Sr.*, 1998)

My internship at Room 5600 was a long time ago... great memories, working at the Rockefeller Family brain trust... Imagine a young man from the Bronx sitting down having lunch in the 5600, break room with John D Rockefeller III... a true gentleman... Also Mrs. Peggy Rockefeller was special and a classy lady. FYI, when my father passed away the office reached out to me and offered their support... flowers and the use of a car and a driver... Priceless!
(Anonymous, New York City businessman, recollection, 2016)

...madness of crowds'... market bubble... tulipomania...
(Charles Mackay, *Extraordinary Popular Delusions and the Madness of Crowds,* 1841)

CBC Radio · Posted: Apr 21, 2017
Author and film historian Noah Isenberg.

Even before Casablanca's premiere in 1942, the Warner Brothers studio was well-known for its efforts to bring the rise of fascism in Europe to the attention of the American public.

In 1939, the studio produced Confessions of a Nazi Spy, one of the first openly anti-Nazi films made in Hollywood.

"They were accused by the very vocal nativist, isolationist faction in Congress of being premature 'anti-fascists,'" Isenberg says.

"I think it was in 1938 ... that Groucho Marx made the claim that Warner Bros. is 'the only studio with any guts' in Hollywood."

Isenberg sees clear echoes of the isolationism that prevailed in the late 1930s and early 1940s in the current U.S. political climate.

"We're dealing with a moment in time that I think really calls to mind this period when we were being called upon … by a film like Casablanca to think about what it is that we can do to help the cause."

In tropical climes there are certain times of day
When all the citizens retire
To tear their clothes off and perspire
It's one of those rules that the greatest fools obey
Because the sun is much too sultry
And one must avoid its ultra violet ray

Papalaka papalaka papalaka boo
Papalaka papalaka papalaka boo
Digariga digariga digariga doo
Digariga digariga digariga doo

The native grieve when the white men leave their huts,
Because they're obviously definitely nuts!

Mad dogs and Englishmen
Go out in the midday sun
The Japanese don't care to.
The Chinese wouldn't dare to,
Hindoos and Argentines sleep firmly from twelve to one
But Englishmen detest a siesta.
(Noel Coward, "Mad Dogs and Englishmen," 1931)

*Damnatio ad metalla* (Condemnation to the mines, a cruel punishment meted out to practicing Christians, during the Roman Empire)

…Yahoos? (Jonathan Swift, *Gulliver's Travels, or Travels into Several Remote Nations of the World. In Four Parts. By Lemuel Gulliver, First a Surgeon, and then a Captain of Several Ships,* 1726)

The theory that most of the sudden declines or particular sharp breaks are the results of some plunger's operations probably was invented as an easy way of supplying reasons to those speculators who, being nothing but blind gamblers, will believe anything that is told them rather than do a little thinking. The raid excuse for losses that unfortunate speculators so often receive from brokers and financial gossipers is really an inverted tip. The difference lies in this: A bear tip is distinct, positive advice to sell short. But the inverted tip that is, the explanation that does not explain serves merely to keep you from wisely selling short. The natural tendency when a stock breaks badly is to sell it. There is a reason an unknown reason but a good reason; therefore get out. But it is not wise to get out when the break is the result of a raid by an operator, because the moment he stops the price must rebound. Inverted tips!
(Edwin Lefèvre, *Reminiscences of a Stock Operator,* 1923)

My apple trees will never get across
And eat the cones under his pines, I tell him.
He only says, 'Good fences make good neighbors.'
(Robert Frost, "Mending Wall," 1914)

Madame Defarge (Charles Dickens, *A Tale of Two Cities*, 1859)

I can still see the butchered women and children lying heaped and
scattered all along the crooked gulch as plain as when I saw them with
eyes still young. And I can see that something else died there in the bloody
mud, and was buried in the blizzard. A people's dream died there. It was a
beautiful dream . . . the nation's hope is broken and scattered.
(John G. Neihardt, *Black Elk Speaks,* 1932) [Wounded Knee Massacre]

When the king heard of this disaster he decided not to delay, but made
haste to gather an army, and marched into Saxony. There he called to
his presence the chiefs of the Saxons, and inquired who had induced the
people to rebel. They all declared that Widukind was the author of the
treason, but said that they could not produce him because after the deed
was done he had fled to the Northmen. But the others who had carried
out his will and committed the crime they delivered up to the king to the
number of four thousand and five hundred; and by the king's command
they were all beheaded [decollati] in one day upon the river Aller in the
place called Verden [Ferdun]. When he had wreaked vengeance after this
fashion, the king withdrew to the town of Diedenhofen [Thionville]...
(*Annales qui dicuntur Einhardi [Annals of Einhard]*, 815, James Harvey
Robinson, *Readings in European History, Volume I: From the Breaking Up
of the Roman Empire to the Protestant Revolt*, 1904)

To them who by patient continuance in well doing seek for glory and
honour and immortality, eternal life: (Romans, 2:7, KJV)

I would rather earn 1% off a 100 people's efforts than 100%
of my own efforts.
(Rockefeller, *John D. Rockefeller on Making Money*)

They see nothing wrong in the rule that to the victor
belongs the spoils of victory.
(William Marcy, senator from New York, 1832) [American western
frontier traditional expression]

Up for grabs. (American colloquialism, 1945)

The personal character and career of one man are so intimately connected
with the great scheme of the years 1719 and 1720, that a history of the
Mississippi madness can have no fitter introduction than a sketch of the
life of its great author John Law. Historians are divided in opinion as to
whether they should designate him a knave or a madman.
(Mackay, *Extraordinary Popular Delusions*)

The history of all hitherto existing society is the history of class struggles.
(Karl Marx and Friedrich Engels, *The Communist Manifesto*, 1848)

You can't have your cake and eat it (too).
(Popular English idiomatic proverb)

GCT (Grand Central Terminal)

Justice at this first stage is good will among those approximately equal in power to come to terms with each other, to "come to an agreement" again with each other by compensation—and in relation to those less powerful, to compel them to arrive at some settlement among themselves. —
(Friedrich Nietzsche, *On the Genealogy of Morality: A Polemic*, 1887)

It may be true that blood is thicker than water, but money is thicker than blood. (Mexican drug lord, Apocryphal, twentieth century)

## 20. Civil War

...they do for their gods every detestable thing that Jehovah hates, even burning their sons and their daughters in the fire to their gods.
(Deuteronomy 12:31, KJV)

There stands in their midst a bronze statue of Kronos [Baal Hammon], its hands extended over a bronze brazier, the flames of which engulf the child. When the flames fall upon the body, the limbs contract and the open mouth seems almost to be laughing until the contracted body slips quietly into the brazier. Thus it is that the 'grin' is known as 'sardonic laughter,' since they die laughing. (Greek historian Cleitarchus, 400 BC)

There was in their city a bronze image of Cronus extending its hands, palms up and sloping toward the ground, so that each of the children when placed thereon rolled down and fell into a sort of gaping pit filled with fire. (Greek historian Diodorus Siculus, 1st century BC)

We were told that the flesh of young children, as a very dainty bit, was also set before him sometimes by way of a relish.
(Bernal Diaz del Castillo, *The Conquest of New Spain,* 1567)

...eating human meat, just like we take cows from the butcher's shops, and they have in all towns thick wooden jail-houses, like cages, and in them they put many Indian men, women and boys to fatten, and being fattened they sacrificed and ate them.
(Diaz del Castillo, *The Conquest*, 1567)

the tree of liberty must be refreshed from time to time with the blood of patriots & tyrants. it is it's natural manure.
[Thomas Jefferson, letter to William Stephens Smith, Nov. 13, 1787, Re Shay's Rebellion in Mass.] (Dan Evon, *Snopes*, "Did Thomas Jefferson Say the Tree of Liberty Must Be Refreshed 'With the Blood of Patriots and

Tyrants?'" 9/11/2019)

...infertile general's... (John K. Armory M.D., *Fertility and Sterility*, Volume 81, Issue 3, "George Washington's infertility: why was the father of our country never a father?" March 2004)

Mr. Revolution (Evon, *Snopes*, "Did Thomas Jefferson Say?")

[Jefferson] cannot live but in a revolution, and all events in Europe are only considered by him in the relation they bear to the probability of a revolution to be produced by them. [British dinner partner of Jefferson's] (Evon, *Snopes*, "Did Thomas Jefferson Say?")

Yankee Doodle went to town
A-riding on a pony
Stuck a feather in his cap
And called it macaroni
("Yankee Doodle," traditional American folksong, 1770's)

...*la Terreur* [the Terror, the Reign of Terror] (16,594 official death sentences, plus 12,000 executed without trial, September 5, 1793, to July 27, 1794)

de Tocqueville
(Alexis de Tocqueville, *De la democratie en Amerique*, 1835)

He perfected the terror by substituting permanent war
for permanent revolution [on Napoleon].
(Karl Marx and Friedrich Engels, *The Holy Family,* 1844)

While the State exists, there can be no freedom.
When there is freedom there will be no State.

A revolution is certainly the most authoritarian thing that is possible. Revolution is the act whereby one part of the population imposes its will upon the other part by means of rifles, bayonets, and cannons, i.e. extremely authoritarian means.
(Vladimir Lenin, *The State and Revolution*, 1917)

I am gliding down the stream of life, and wish, as is natural, that my remaining days may be undisturbed and tranquil; and, conscious of my integrity, I would willingly hope, that nothing would occur tending to give me anxiety; but should anything present itself in this or any other publication, I shall never undertake the painful task of recrimination, nor do I know that I should even enter upon my justification.
(*Infoplease*, "The True George Washington: Enemies: The Press," Updated September 23, 2019)

Nor could such a judge be a king who wished men he had sentenced to

cruel death to be boiled and roasted in his presence; or one who

commanded his officials to send him the heads of adversaries (actual or potential) whom he had ordered killed. He was cruel, all right...
(B. Netanyahu, *The Origins of The Inquisition in Fifteenth Century Spain*, 1995)

...just off the boat... a sucker born per minute... buy the Brooklyn Bridge?
(American colloquialisms for naivete)

Demoralize the enemy from within by surprise, terror, sabotage, assassination. This is the war of the future. (Adolf Hitler, 1934)

It was because Adolf Hitler and his party faced so much criticism and resistance among the press that I became particularly interested, in joining their movement. (Ardent Nazi party member, Friedrich Jorns)

Linda Coombs, a Wampanoag tribal leader and activist, said she's glad attention is being paid to what's largely a forgotten chapter of history.

"People are unaware that the Great Dying happened," she said. "At school, you're pounded with the story of 50 Pilgrims dying during their first winter. But during the Great Dying, about 50,000 Wampanoags died, as well as who knows how many other tribal people to the north in what's now Maine. It's kind of nice to see those numbers lined up side by side."
(William Cole, The Associated Press, June 10, 2021)

And if thy right eye offend thee, pluck it out, and cast it from thee: for it is profitable for thee that one of thy members should perish, and not that thy whole body should be cast into hell.

And if thy right hand offend thee, cut it off, and cast it from thee: for it is profitable for thee that one of thy members should perish, and not that thy whole body should be cast into hell. (Matthew 5:29-30, KJV)

I John Brown am now quite certain that the crimes of this guilty, land: will never be purged away; but with Blood. I had as I now think: vainly flattered myself that without very much bloodshed; it might be done. (John Brown's Last Prophesy, Charles Town, Virginia, December 2, 1859)

"But in Wyoming the law has been letting our cattle-thieves go for two years... The courts, or rather the juries, into whose hands we have put the law, are not dealing the law... They cannot hold a cattle-thief. And so when your ordinary citizen sees this, and sees that he has placed justice in a dead hand, he must take justice back into his own hands where it was once at the beginning of all things."
(Owen Wister, *The Virginian*, 1902)

So lofty an end hardly consorts with so low a beginning.
(James G. Frazer, *The Golden Bough*, 1922)

Mine eyes have seen the glory of the coming of the Lord

He is trampling out the vintage where the grapes of wrath are stored,
He has loosed the fateful lightening of His terrible swift sword
His truth is marching on.

Glory! Glory! Hallelujah!
Glory! Glory! Hallelujah!
Glory! Glory! Hallelujah!
His truth is marching on.
(Julia Ward Howe, "Battle Hymn of the Republic," 1861)

Leviathan (Thomas Hobbes, *Leviathan or the Matter, Forme and Power of a Commonwealth Ecclesiasticall and Civil*, 1651)

... spread garlands of flowers over the iron chains which weigh men down, snuffing out in them the feeling of that original liberty... and make them love their slavery by turning them into what are called civilized people. (Jean Jacques Rousseau, *Oeuvres de J.J. Rousseau: Avec Des Notes Historiques, Volume 9*, 1763)

*This is the way the world ends*
*This is the way the world ends*
*This is the way the world ends*
*Not with a bang but a whimper.* (T.S. Eliot, "The Hollow Men," 1925)

*History of the Peloponnesian War*
(Thucydides, *History of the Peloponnesian War*, late fifth century BC)

The shot heard round the world. (A phrase that refers to the opening shot of the battles of Lexington and Concord on April 19, 1775)

Amendment I: Congress shall make no law respecting an establishment of religion, or prohibiting the free exercise thereof; or abridging the freedom of speech, or of the press, or the right of the people peaceably to assemble, and to petition the Government for a redress of grievances.

Amendment II: A well regulated Militia, being necessary to the security of a free State, the right of the people to keep and bear Arms, shall not be infringed. (Amendments to the U.S. Constitution in the Bill of Rights, proposed September 25, 1789)

## 21. In Fitzgerald's Footsteps

[A documentary film of the Fitzgeralds' wild summer in Westport, CT stimulated the author's own recollections.] (Robert Steven Williams, *Gatsby in Connecticut: The Untold Story*, 2020)

I lived at West Egg - the least fashionable of the two...

...it was a factual imitation of some Hotel de Ville in Normandy, with a tower on one side, spanking new under a thin bead of raw ivy, and a marble swimming pool, and more than forty acres of lawn and garden.

My own house was an eyesore, but it was a small eyesore...
(F. Scott Fitzgerald, *The Great Gatsby,* 1925)

He and his bride, Zelda Sayre, a mere 19, had decamped New York City after their planned honeymoon was cut short when they were asked to leave the Biltmore. According to Fitzgerald biographer Andrew Turnbull, the management suggested that they move on because, "the continuing hilarity of their presence [was] considered prejudicial to good order and restful nights" for the other guests of the hotel. (Patrice Fitzgerald, Neighbor, Patch, "F. Scott Fitzgerald Slept Here," 1/28/2010)

And I've seen him [Richards] twice at CVS. I will refrain from making any snarky remarks about what he was doing in a "drug store."
(Dan Woog, *06880 Where Westport meets the world,* "Keith Richards' Local 'Life,'" December 21, 2010)

...the Beautiful and Damned...
(F. Scott Fitzgerald, *The Beautiful and Damned,* 1922)

"...and in the eyes of the middle-class exaggeration passes for beauty."
(Stendhal, *The Charterhouse of Parma,* 1839)

*The Ludicrous and Hammed*
(Willi Herman, *The Ludicrous and Hammed,* 1997)

Nothing is difficult in the eyes of a lover.
(Marcus Tullius Cicero, 106 – 43 BC)

They did both look as though they had just stepped out of the sun, their youth was striking. Everyone wanted to meet him.
(Dorothy Parker, of F. Scott and Zelda Fitzgerald, 1920)

He stretched out his arms toward the dark water in a curious way, and, far as I was from him, I could have sworn he was trembling. Involuntarily I glanced seaward – and distinguished nothing except a single green light, minute and far away, that might have been the end of a dock.
(Fitzgerald, *The Great Gatsby*)

"I own I never greatly liked him. I thought he wanted that Generosity of Spirit, which is the sure Foundation of all that is great and noble in Human Nature. I saw a Selfishness in him long ago which I despised; but it is lately, very lately, that I have found him capable of the basest and blackest Designs; for, indeed, I have at last found out, that he hath taken an Advantage of the Openness of my own Temper..."
(Henry Fielding, *The History of Tom Jones, a Foundling,* 1749)

...the sun also rises. (Ernest Hemingway, *The Sun Also Rises,* 1926)

...April is over, April is over. There are all kinds of love in the world, but never the same love twice. (F. Scott Fitzgerald, "The Sensible Thing," 1924)

Stover at Whale...
(Owen Johnson, *Stover at Yale*, 1912)

Lucy and Ricky Ricardo
(Lucille Ball and Desi Arnaz, *I Love Lucy*, 1951-57)

He might have been compared to a summer's day,
particularly the last hours of one...
(John Cheever, "The Swimmer," 1964)

Turn on, tune in, drop out.
(Dr. Timothy Leary, Harvard harbinger of the new millennium,
popularized counterculture-era phrase, 1966)

As I would not be a slave, so I would not be a master.
(Abraham Lincoln, August 1, 1858)

*Alterius non sit qui suus esse potest*
[Let no man belong to another who can belong to himself]
(Paracelcus, c. 1493 – 1541)

...Moby Dick... (Herman Melville, *Moby Dick; or, The Whale*, 1851)

*Great Expectations* (Charles Dickens, *Great Expectations,* 1861)

*Night Bistro* (Van Goon, Dutch Post-Impressionist, *Night Bistro*, 1888)

A harmful truth is better than a useful lie.
(Thomas Mann, *The Magic Mountain,* 1924)

Character gives us qualities, but it is in our actions – what we do – that we
are happy or the reverse. (Aristotle, *Poetics*, 335 BC)

How devout men are made by suffering! In prosperity the thought of God
or saint never enters their heads. (Erasmus, "The Shipwreck," 1523)

...the way of the world. (William Congreve, *The Way of the World*, 1700)

We do plan to, for the most part, treat them in a manner that is reasonably
consistent with the Geneva Conventions.
(Donald Rumsfeld, U.S. Secretary of Defense, 2002)

"But I'm not guilty," said K. "there's been a mistake. How is it even
possible for someone to be guilty? We're all human beings here, one like
the other." "That is true" said the priest "but that is how the guilty speak."
(Franz Kafka, *The Trial,* 1925)

Woman is the nigger of the world
(John Lennon, "Woman is the Nigger of the World," 1972)

Go to the place where you belong from now on – the dustbin of history!
[re Mensheviks, Congress of Soviets] (Leon Trotsky, 1917)

The only freedom which deserves the name, is that of pursuing our own good in our own way, so long as we do not attempt to deprive others of theirs, or impede their efforts to obtain it.
(John Stuart Mill, *On Liberty*, 1859)

To be, or not to be, that is the question:
(William Shakespeare. *Hamlet*, 1599-1601)

A heavy account lies against us as a civil society for oppressions committed against people who did not injure us, and that if the particular case of many individuals were fairly stated, it would appear that there was considerable due to them. (John Woolman, Quaker, 1769)

Culture, which is born of life, ends up killing it.
(Andre Gide, *The Immoralist*, 1902)

I only regret that I have but one life to lose for my country.
(Nathan Hale, September 22, 1776)

But let judgement run down as waters, and righteousness as a mighty stream. (Amos 5:24, KJV)

## 22. Transfiguration

Me miserable! Which way shall I fly
Infinite wrath and infinite despair?
Which way I fly is Hell, myself am
Hell... (John Milton, *Paradise Lost*, 4, 75, 1667)

Until the day when God shall deign to reveal the future to man, all human wisdom is summed up in these two words,-Wait and hope.
(Alexandre Dumas, *The Count of Monte Cristo*, 1844)

The difference between treason and patriotism is only a matter of dates.
(Dumas, *The Count of Monte Cristo*)

"How did I escape? With difficulty. How did I plan this moment? With pleasure." (Dumas, *The Count of Monte Cristo*)

They have guns. Screw them. We have champagne.
(*Charlie Hebdo*, Cover, 11/17/2015)

*the Iliad's*... (Homer, *the Iliad*, c.8th century BC)

...there's a sucker born every minute...
(Attributed to P. T. Barnum, American showman, 1810-1891)

The reputation of "Ulysses" in the literary world, however, warranted my taking such time as was necessary to enable me to satisfy myself as to the intent with which the book was written, for, of course, in any case where a book is claimed to be obscene it must first be determined, whether the intent with which it was written was what is called,

according to the usual phrase, pornographic, — that is, written for the purpose of exploiting obscenity.
(John M. Woolsey, United States District Judge, December 6, 1933)

*Lolita* (Vladimir Nabokov, *Lolita*, 1955)

Trippers and askers surround me,
People I meet, the effect upon me of my early life or the ward and city I live in, or the nation,
The latest dates, discoveries, inventions, societies, authors old and new, My dinner, dress, associates, looks, compliments, dues,
The real or fancied indifference of some man or woman I love,
The sickness of one of my folks or of myself, or ill-doing or loss or lack of money, or depressions or exaltations,
Battles, the horrors of fratricidal war, the fever of doubtful news, the fitful events;
These come to me days and nights and go from me again, But they are not the Me myself.
(Walt Whitman, *Leaves of Grass*, "Song of Myself," 1892)

[By-ends] "...had always the Luck to jump in my judgment with the present
Way of the Times, whatever it was..."
(John Bunyan, *The Pilgrim's Progress from This World, to That Which Is to Come*, 1678)

Let the ruling classes tremble at a Communistic revolution. The proletarians have nothing to lose but their chains. They have a world to win.

Workingmen of all countries unite!
(Karl Marx and Friedrich Engels, *The Communist Manifesto*, 1848)

Cheshire Cat (Lewis Carroll, *Alice's Adventures in Wonderland*, 1865)

Those who wish to seek out the cause of miracles and to understand the things of nature as philosophers, and not to stare at them in astonishment like fools, are soon considered heretical and impious, and proclaimed as such by those whom the mob adores as the interpreters of nature and the gods. For these men know that, once ignorance is put aside, that wonderment would be taken away, which is the only means by which their authority is preserved. (Baruch de Spinoza, *Ethics*, 1674)

Einstein's answer to a New York rabbi clears things up a bit. The rabbi cabled him in 1929 to ask him if he believed in God. Einstein replied, "I believe in Spinoza's God, who reveals himself in the orderly harmony of what exists, not in a God who concerns himself with the fates and actions of human beings." (Lawrence Klepp, *The Weekly Standard*, "Spinoza's God," January 23, 2012)

Religion is the sigh of the oppressed creature, the heart of a heartless world, and the soul of soulless conditions. It is the opium of the people. (Karl Marx, *Contribution to the Critique of Hegel's Philosophy of Right*, 1843 – 44)

"But Francis said nothing of this to the Brothers, but hid his hands, and he could not put the soles of his feet to the earth any more... and then they understood that he bore the image and likeness of our Lord Jesus Christ the Crucified..." (Johannes Jorgensen, *St. Francis of Assisi*, 1955)

I have always had more dread of a pen, a bottle of ink, and a sheet of paper than of a sword or pistol. (Dumas, *The Count of Monte Cristo*)

Others [Druids] have figures of vast size, the limbs of which formed of osiers they fill with living men, which being set on fire, the men perish enveloped in the flames. They consider that the oblation of such as have been taken in theft, or in robbery, or any other offense, is more acceptable to the immortal gods; but when a supply of that class is wanting, they have recourse to the oblation of even the innocent. (C. Julius Caesar, *Caesar's Gallic War*, 58 BC, translated by W. A. McDevitte, W. S. Bohn)

He had, I think, a Slough of Despond in his mind, a Slough that he carry'd every where with him... (Bunyan, *The Pilgrim's Progress*)

...anthropophagy... (The eating of human flesh by human beings.)

Then I saw in my dream, That Christian was as in a muse a while. (Bunyan, *The Pilgrim's Progress*)

## 23 – 33. Guantónamo Elegies

### Willi

Everything can be taken from a man but one thing: the last of the human freedoms – to choose one's attitude in any given set of circumstances, to choose one's own way.
(Victor E. Frankl, *Man's Search for Meaning*, 1946 [Austrian psychiatrist, philosopher, humanitarian, Holocaust survivor, 1905 – 1997])

### Lilly

...the best of all possible worlds...
(Gottfried Leibniz, *Theodicee [Essais de Theodicee sur la bonte de Dieu, la liberte de l'homme et l'origine du mal]*, 1710)

A Saint abroad, and a Devil at home.
(John Bunyan, *The Pilgrim's Progress from This World, to That Which Is to Come*, 1678)

**Dr. Henry Waterson**

> O vast Rondure, swimming in space,
> Cover'd all over with visible power and beauty,
> Alternate light and day and the teeming, spiritual darkness,
> Unspeakable high processions of sun and moon and countless stars above,
> Below, the manifold grass and waters, animals, mountains, trees,
> With inscrutable purpose, some hidden, prophetic intention,
> Now first it seems my thought begins to span thee.
> Down from the gardens of Asia descending, radiating,
> Adam and Eve appear, then their myriad progeny after them,
> Wandering, yearning, curious, with restless explorations,
> With questionings, baffled, formless, feverish, with never-happy hearts,
> With that sad incessant refrain, *Wherefore unsatisfied Soul?* and *Whither O mocking life?*
> Ah who shall soothe these feverish children?
> Who justify these restless explorations?
> Who speak the secret of impassive earth?
> Who bind it to us? what is this separate Nature so unnatural?
> What is this earth to our affections? (unloving earth, without a throb to answer ours,
> Cold earth, the place of graves.)
> (Walt Whitman, *Leaves of Grass*, "Passage to India," 1891 - 92)

> ...cracked-up...
> (F. Scott Fitzgerald, "The Crack-Up," 1936)

> ...Syphilis...
> (Girolamo Fracastoro, *Syphilis sive morbus gallicus [Syphilis or The French Disease]*, 1530)

**John B. Sayer**

> ...Examples of all Ages shew us that Mankind in general desire Power only to do Harm, and when they obtain it, use it for no other Purpose...
> (Henry Fielding, *The History of Tom Jones, a Foundling*, 1749)

**Isidora Green**

> And at the end of the first thousand years the good souls and also the evil souls both come to draw lots and choose their second life, and they may take any which they please. The soul of a man may pass into the life of a beast, or from the beast return again into the man. But the soul which has never seen the truth will not pass into the human form. For a man must have intelligence of universals, and be able to proceed from the many particulars of sense to one conception of reason;--this is the recollection of those things which our soul once saw while following God--when

> regardless of that which we now call being she raised her head up towards

the true being. And therefore the mind of the philosopher alone has wings; and this is just, for he is always, according to the measure of his abilities, clinging in recollection to those things in which God abides, and in beholding which He is what He is. And he who employs aright these memories is ever being initiated into perfect mysteries and alone becomes truly perfect. But, as he forgets earthly interests and is rapt in the divine, the vulgar deem him mad, and rebuke him; they do not see that he is inspired. (Plato, *Phaedrus*, 370 BC)

...*bardo*...
(*Bardo Thodol [Tibetan Book of the Dead]*, 8th century AD)

## Rev. Hannibal P. (Pearly) Gates

*PIETRO.* – Hark! they sing. [*A song.*] See, he comes. Now shall you hear the extremity of a malcontent. He is free as air; he blows over every man...

*MENDOZA.* Who cannot feign friendship can ne'er produce the effects of hatred...

*MALEVOLE.* [*Aside.*] O world most vile, when thy loose vanities, aught by this fool, do make the fool seem wise!
(John Marston, *The Malcontent*, 1604)

...fear and loathing...
(Hunter S. Thompson, *Fear and Loathing in Las Vegas: A Savage Journey to the Heart of the American Dream*, 1971)

## Patricia (P) Diddy

I prefer a Church which is bruised, hurting and dirty because it has been out on the streets, rather than a Church which is unhealthy from being confined and from clinging to its own security.

More than by fear of going astray, my hope is that we will be moved by the fear of remaining shut up within structures which give us a false sense of security, within rules which make us harsh judges, within habits which make us feel safe, while at our door people are starving.
(Pope Francis, *Evangelii Gaudium [The Joy of the Gospel]*, Apostolic Exhortation, 11/26/2013)

...shaken, not stirred... (Ian Fleming, *Diamonds are Forever*, 1956)

When you call me that, SMILE! (Owen Wister, *The Virginian*, 1902)

## *SS* Colonel Otto Waldemar Grawitz

But what will not Ambition and Revenge
Descend to? who aspires must down as low

As high he soard, obnoxious first or last
To basest things. Revenge, at first thought sweet,
Bitter ere long back on it self recoils;
Let it; I reck not, so it light well aim'd,
Since higher I fall short, on him who next
Provokes my envie, this new Favorite
Of Heav'n, this Man of Clay, Son of despite,
Whom us the more to spite his Maker rais'd
From dust: spite then with spite is best repaid.
(John Milton, *Paradise Lost*, 1667)

It is better and more satisfactory to acquit a thousand guilty persons than to
put a single innocent one to death.
(Maimonides, Sephardic Jewish rabbi, physician, philosopher, 1135 – 1204)

*The Great Ratsby*
(Willi Herman, *The Great Ratsby*, 1999)

There, where I have passed, the grass will never grow again.
(Attila the Hun, c. 406 – 453 AD, *Flagellum Dei [Scourge of God]*)


**Ms. Yael Abraham**

I shall never get you put together entirely,
Pieced, glued, and properly jointed.
Mule-bray, pig-grunt and bawdy cackles
Proceed from your great lips.
It's worse than a barnyard.
(Sylvia Plath, "The Colossus," 1960)


**Ottoline**

[WITCH]
Careful the things you say
Children will listen
Careful the things you do
Children will see
And learn

Guide them along the way
Children will glisten
Children will look to you
For which way to turn
To learn what to be
Careful before you say
"Listen to me."
Children will listen
(Stephen Sondheim, *Into the Woods*, 1987)

**T. Awdry Winks**

In my beginning is my end... In my end is my beginning.
(T.S. Eliot, "East Coker," 1940)

Edgar Cayce
(American clairvoyant, healer, Biblicist, 1877 – 1945)

It hurts too much to laugh, but I'm too old to cry.
(Abraham Lincoln, after a disastrous election)

...the usual rewards... perturbation...
(Walt Whitman, *Leaves of Grass*, 1891 - 92)

...Laffer curve...
[the optimization of the relationship between tax rates and tax revenues]
(Arthur Laffer, American economist, 1974)

*Phaedrus*
(Plato, *Phaedrus*, 370 BC)


**Epilogue**

...future shock...
(Alvin Toffler, *Future Shock*, 1970)

# IMAGES

1. Hieronymus Bosch, Dutch/ Netherlandish, *The Garden of Earthly Delights*, The exterior, c. 1480-1505, Museo del Prado, Madrid, Spain.

2. Bosch, *The Garden*, The interior.

3. Lukas Cranach the Elder, *Adam and Eve in Paradise*, Detail Tree of Knowledge, 1530, Gemäldegalerie Alte Meister, Dresden, Germany.

4. *El Dorado*, Museo del Oro, Bogotá, Colombia.

5. John Collier, *The Last Voyage of Henry Hudson*, 1881, Tate Britain, London, England.

6. *Aurora Borealis*, Aurora Borealis aka Northern Lights captured February 2020 in the Lofoten Islands, Northern Norway. {OC} (2400x3000): r/EarthPorn (reddit.com)

7. Walt Whitman Stamp, PZAndrews, https://www.pinterest.com/pin/520658406899325244/

8. Carlisle Indian School, Carlisle Indian Industrial School Presentation | Juniata County Historical Society

9. The Humanity of General Amherst, Amherst and Smallpox (umass.edu)

10. Jay Gould, American History USA

11. Slave Auction, https://en.wikipedia.org/wiki/File:Slave_Auction_Ad.jpg

12. Isis wall painting in the tomb of Seti I, https://en.wikipedia.org/wiki/Isis

13. Geronimo, Geronimo - Wikipedia

14. Frederick Douglas, portrait, Frederick Douglass - Wikipedia

15. Cannibal Feast - Fiji, Early Accounts of Cannibalism (cultofweird.com)

16. Crematorium Majdanek, Crematoria in Majdanek death camp. (Post-Liberation). - Collections Search - United States Holocaust Memorial Museum (ushmm.org)

17. Left to right: Dr. Josef Mengele, Rudof Hoss, Josef Kramer, right, AP.

18. *Herr* Hitler, The Berghof of Adolf Hitler at the Obersalzberg near Berchtesgaden: Photo d'actualité - Getty Images

19. Auschwitz Children, Reuters.

20. Masaccio, *The Expulsion from the Garden of Eden*, c. 1425, Santa Maria del Carmine, Florence, Italy.

21. Jean Metzinger, *La dance, Bacchante*, 1906, *Kroller-Muller Museum*, Otterlo, The Netherlands.

22. *Moll Flanders*, UK edition frontispiece, 1722, https://en.wikipedia.org/wiki/Moll_Flanders

23. Chief Eunuch of the Ottoman Sultan Abdul Hamid II at the Imperial Palace, https://www.ancient- origins.net/history-ancient-traditions/famous-and-powerful-eunuchs-ancient-world-006268

24. Don Pedro Lagos Marchant (1832-1884), a Chilean Infantry commander, Pedro Lagos - Wikipedia

25. *Miss Lonelyhearts*, first UK edition cover, 1949, Miss Lonelyhearts - Wikipedia

26. Luther and Erasmus, https://servantsofgrace.org/erasmus-luther-romans-free-will-debate/

27. *Plague*, https://www.history.com/news/6-devastating-plagues

28. *Habit des Medecins*, Homöopathie in der Covid-19 Pandemie | magic soul ∞ Tools for Change (magic-soul.de)

29. John Verelst, *Elihu Yale with Members of his Family and an Enslaved Child*, ca. 1719, Yale Center for British Art, New Haven, CT.

30. Jean-Leon Gerome, *The Tulip Folly*, 1882, Walters Art Museum, Baltimore, MD.

31. James Worsdale, *Elihu Yale with his Servant*, before 1721, Yale University Art Gallery, New Haven, CT.

32. *Hernan Cortes*, File: Weiditz Trachtenbuch 077 Hernan Cortés.jpg - Wikipedia

33. Wounded Knee Massacre, Aftermath of the Wounded Knee Massacre, South Dakota. 1890 News Photo - Getty Images

34. Bill of Rights of the U.S. Constitution, https://en.wikipedia.org/wiki/File:Bill_of_Rights_Pg1of1_AC.jpg

35. *The Beautiful and Damned*, cover, 1922, https://www.biblio.com/book/beautiful-damned-fitzgerald-f-scott/d/432675743

36. Zelda Fitzgerald, *The Beautiful and Damned*, cover sketch, 1921, https://creazilla.com/nodes/6856616-zelda-fitzgerald-the-beautiful-and-damned-cover-sketch-illustration

37. Van Gogh, *Night Café*, 1888, Yale University Art Gallery, New Haven, CT.

38. Berghotel Sanatorium Schatzalp, Davos, Switzerland, The Magic Mountain - Wikipedia

39. *Barricade bei der Universität am 26ten Mai 1848 in Wien*, https://repository.library.brown.edu/studio/item/bdr:225996/

40. Celtic Human Sacrifice Wicker Man, Halloween: The Great Cover-up (logosresourcepages.org)

41. Beatus of Liebana, *Adam and Eve*, c. 950, Escorial Beatus, Spain.